The Legend of Eve

dREAMWORDS Publishing, LLC
Publishers since 2018
New York 12207

dREAMWORDS is a registered trademark of DreamWords Publishing, LLC.
Copyright 2018 by Anonymous
All rights reserved.

Library of Congress Cataloging in Publication Data
Anonymous.
The Legends of Eve: Book of Fire (A Warrior's Past #2) / Anonymous.
—First edition.
ISBN (paperback): 978-1-7327884-4-2.

Summary: "Two siblings must deal with their troubled pasts while preparing
for the devastating Shadow Army that will destroy the world.
But when they meet, they realize their greatest threat isn't the Army.
It's themselves."—
Provided by publisher.

dREAMWORDS books may be purchased for business or promotional use. For
information on bulk purchases, please contact the dREAMWORDS Publishing Pre-
mium Sales Department by email at FGB@DreamWordsPublishing.com.

First Edition—2019/ Cover design and illustrations by @RyKyArt

Printed in the United States of America and sold internationally

To the dreamers—
never stop dreaming
&
To the ones who are scared to dream—
believe in yourself, even if no one else does

Before you begin this journey, we encourage you to take the quiz (www.thelegendsofeve.com/quiz) to find out which element you were born to control. The quiz results give you the chance to have your own character be a part of the world of Gaia. Our first winner is pictured here! May the element provide you hope when you need it most.

THE ELEMENTIAL SCHOOLS

GROUNDSTONE the School of Earth

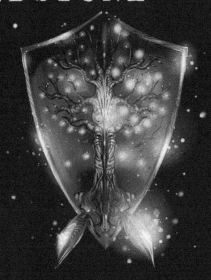

FUJITA the School of Wind and Wisdom

SERENI the School of Water

HARAHN'DE THE SCHOOL OF FIRE

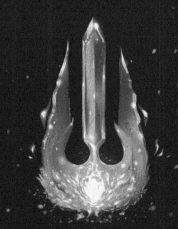

Welcome to GroundStone.
We hope you enjoy your stay.

THE GIFT

THE VILLAGERS STILL HADN'T RECEIVED their princess, but unfortunately they were *blessed* with more than enough high-energy, rowdy princes. Three of them to be exact. And many eclipses had passed since the Queen dared to try again. That was because the last two attempts had resulted in misfortune, misery, and miscarriages. But worst of all, with a heart torn to pieces, she believed that wanting a princess had been a terrible mistake.

The Queen's home had sunk into a hole of depression despite standing atop a sandy hill overlooking the village. The normally brown bark that formed the foundation had turned gray, some of its windows boarded with strings of ivy, leaves missing from its roof, and thorns spreading unchecked over the walkways. Once a welcoming space, where all the kids would play, the shrine was now dilapidated and drained of its life.

A few years later, something unexpected had happened, she was pregnant again, except this time she was expecting twins.

One of the village's elders had ran faster than anyone could have expected, screaming down the hill and alerted as many people as she could.

"There will be two! There will be two! A prince and a... princess!"

The news was heard, and the entire village had emerged from their straw huts and sand domes. Nobody could contain their excitement, for they had waited just as long as the Queen for a princess. Hidden in the creased pages of their most ancient books were legends that mentioned the nurturing powers of a girl that could not be found in a boy. The birth of a princess would bring a better harvest and an end to the drought that had appeared out of nowhere.

All the villagers wished for an answer that could explain the different weather—for it was strange that a beautiful summer's morning could turn into the harshest winter's night on the same day.

But a princess was to finally be born, the whole village came together at the temple to discuss the potential names for the new prince and princess.

"Amyr!" shouted many people.

"But what of the princess?" shouted the ladies wrapped completely in a white cloth.

They were the healers, the ones who pressed their palms to the Queen's stomach and told her the splendid news. They lived alone in the inner sand domes, practicing rituals to bring about a better harvest than the last.

There was a frenzy to know more about the princess.

"What did she feel like? Will she be a healer or a warrior?"

"She will be as great and as beautiful as our Queen," the elder told the eager villagers, after drawing a relic in the sand. "She is exactly what we had been waiting for. The Queen will finally be the happy leader we remembered her to be. Oh, Divine, it is time, it is time!"

"But what if... *it* were to happen again," said a male by the high-snapping fire, "she has been through enough. Was it wise to try again?"

The villagers exchanged worried looks.

"Oh, Sual, that is nothing to worry about, the princess is as healthy as Gaia and as strong as the sun."

"To the Divine, I pray that you are right," Sual said, scratching his beard. "I remember many eclipses ago, when *I* was a child hearing her cries..."

As months followed, excitement had increased throughout the land. The village created vibrant veils of the most beautiful flowers they could find. The drought had made it very difficult, but they traveled far and wide to make sure the new prince and princess slept in a bed of nature's finest.

But over in the Queen's shrine, in the dark and boarded up home, the Queen was rocking back and forth on her branch, praying to every Divine that had ever existed in story.

The King emerged with a glazed look that spoke of his worry, not for the children, but of his wife that had seemed to have withered away.

She was consumed with fear. The joy that was supposed to be attached to birth had turned to dread. The day was coming. While the Village rejoiced and celebrated and partied until the morning, the Queen wept, unable to sleep.

By the following morning, everyone in the village had surrounded the shrine. They wore white veils and lush vines wrapped around their necks and limbs, symbolizing their connection to nature.

As the healers entered the shrine, the first screams were heard. And many had followed.

Then, just when the shrieks were sounding horrific, they stopped and a pleasant cry was heard that changed everything.

The village erupted in an uproar.

"It is... the prince!" a voice shouted from inside.

"Our prince!" The village howled, lifting their staffs before slamming them into the sand.

The village awaited for the next set of screams.

Seconds passed.

Then minutes...

Then an hour...

And once the silence had reached its third hour, that was when they heard a strained voice say: "It *was*... the princess."

Gasps spread throughout the crowd, immediately followed by hiccups of tears and sobs. The healers had no report as to what happened to their princess, but they commented on how black the Queen's eyes were, as if it was like looking into a well with a void of nothing on the other end. This time there was no emotion from her, neither sadness nor anger.

The villagers wanted answers but none were found. Before they could find the cause, the princess was buried in the garden, and her flower remained an object of curiosity for a while.

After a few days of silence, the villagers came together again to discuss their future with a King who was always gone hunting and a Queen who remained as an uninhabited shell. There were talks of a mutiny, of new leadership, not for any reason other than survival. They loved their King and Queen, they truly did, but there was no guidance, no plan for their future. The drought had become worse, crops were more difficult to harvest, and the King had to venture miles away to find the first sign of fresh meat.

It was then when the talks had become most serious, a most curious bundle of leaves and ivy was found at the Queen's door. It was as if this was the village's last chance to save the Queen, their village. No one dared touch it until the King had arrived from the hunt. Never had they seen a gift wrapped with such care, as if every vine was hand-stitched.

The King lifted it in his hand. "Who gave us this gift?" he said to a subdued crowd. Murmurs and whispers hissed their way through the village like snakes. The King looked around once more before summoning his Queen.

Several moments passed before she came to the entrance. There was a slow clunk followed by a shuffle from cloth being dragged through sand. In her hand she held her staff carved from the strongest oak in all of Gaia. This type of wood could only be held by the most powerful warriors. One would never guess, but there was a time when she could take on an entire village with one swing. But some said she was still just as lethal.

"What is this?" she said with a strained voice. It seemed to have taken all of her energy.

"A gift... from the village."

And when they pulled the golden leaves to the side, the anticipation grew with each layer revealed.

"What could it be?" she said as her frail fingers peeled off one last leaf.

Their eyes widened, almost as wide as their smiles. A tear fell from the Queen's eyes, forming into a stream that poured down into the gift in her arms. In that moment when the tears splashed, a shriek resonated from within.

The village gasped.

"What do we name her?" the Queen said, her brown eyes glowing.

"She is a gift from the village... from the Divine..." the King said as he painted two brown bars on the baby's cheeks, mirroring his own face paint. The clay absorbed into her skin as if they became birthmarks. "Her name is... S'rae."

Though hundreds of miles apart, S'rae and Vayp woke up at the very same moment. They gasped as if they shared the same dream and stared ahead as if looking directly at one another.

Somehow... and someway their eyes narrowed in unison.

"I will find you!" they growled through clenched teeth.

1

VAYP SAW S'RAE WISP AWAY into dust as if she was a ghost, her glittering silver image was the only color in the gloom that filled this hollow valley. Though he didn't believe in the afterlife, a part of him wished she was a ghost—dead, like she deserved. But the hairs that stood up on his arms let him know that it wasn't his imagination. He knew what was happening. It had been about three days since the Mechas and Gabrael fought at the Valley of Gaia when S'rae first appeared in his mind—the visions and dreams of her since then had become more clear. That could only mean one thing. After years of training at Opella under his father, the King Si'ard, Vayp knew every tracking spell, after all; S'rae was trying to track him down by linking their spirits, and to his surprise, it was somehow working.

He didn't know how. She was never around when they practiced. It was a family secret only passed down from father to son. His lip curled with disgust thinking about someone like her using an ability that was only meant for *his* family. The disrespect. She was not one of them. Not anymore, at least.

She was once considered family. When she was adopted, they called her a gift from the Divine, their favorite child, Opella and mommy's little princess. *I was their real child, though.*

Vayp never understood why there was such a difference be-tween a prince and princess, but the legends must have been true. Once Opella had found their princess the droughts ebbed away, crops were harvested, and they no longer needed to travel beyond the sand dunes for fresh meat.

But she was no longer the Princess of Opella, he refused to have her name be attached to his. She was a murderer, and if his family had known that she was the one who killed Ah'nyx, his Sol, they would have exiled her. Or worse. Sols were sacred, a connection that flowed thicker than blood. They were the animal that a human linked their mind, body, and soul to. It was said to be impossible for one to die before its owner, but his did. He always had a feeling that he knew who was the culprit... and it was only when he arrived to this valley when he had found out the truth.

A ripple of black lightning flashed overhead, somehow illumi-nating the dark valley. He took a long breath, going over the plans he'd memorized in the days he'd been stuck here. Han'sael, his only friend, was seen floating inside a container, tubes attached to his body. The two shadows who had abducted Han'sael were no-where to be seen, though.

Vayp clenched his fists at the thought of Han'sael. It was Vayp's fault that they captured him. He was the one who led the shadows to the Valley of Gaia. The one who put everyone in danger. The traitor. The villain in their story... but maybe now he could be the hero. *Maybe.* Though his plan had almost no chance of working, he was willing to risk his life to save Han'sael. *You're all I have now.*

Vayp took a few steps toward a cliff. He was still cautious about where to step; the first few days were no different than being blind, but after days trapped in the darkness, his eyes adjusted and he was finally able to see shapes and images. But no matter how much he tried to study his surroundings, he still had no idea where he could be. He saw mountains far off in the distance that looked like dark grey triangles against a black canvas. Everything was some shade of black or grey... except the shadows, they were made from something so void of light that they somehow appeared as silhouettes.

These shadow men would strike fear in even the greatest warrior. Yet... it was very odd for Vayp to admit this, but they no longer scared him. It was tough to fear something that kept him alive. He didn't know why they hadn't killed him yet, and he never dared to ask.

Another flash of lightning illuminated two figures in the distance. It was... *them*. But what were they doing? And what was up with the lightning? He'd only just received the rest of his senses as if he had become accustomed to the darkness. One with it. But there had been nothing but silence since he'd been here. And now, the silence in the dark valley was broken by a distant crackling and pitter-patter, as if a rainstorm had appeared.

Suddenly, a cold white light forced its way through the mountains and flooded the valley. Almost like it was day.

But it *definitely* wasn't.

Vayp peered ahead at what looked like several silhouettes bubbling to the surface.

He became aware of a steady *thud, thud, thud*—like the sound of a heavy heartbeat. Throbbing. Pulsating. Getting closer.

This can't be good. He wondered if this was the same scare that he had seen when he first arrived, when he gave the shadow the Book and Eye of Eve. When a large shadowy hand, the size of a mountain, erected from the ground before fading away into the night. Something terrible was definitely in the works; and in that moment, he realized that his plan to save Han'sael and right his wrongs had suddenly seemed irrelevant.

He staggered to the edge of the cliff and peeked over the precipice.

And then he jumped back and rubbed his eyes. Hard.

There was no way he had seen what he'd seen. And there was no way the *thuds* were what he heard.

He leaned over again, getting a better look.

He wished his eyes were wrong. Beneath him were hundreds... no... maybe thousands of shadowed figures. They were stumbling around as if they were infants learning how to walk. Or were they the dead remembering how?

Suddenly the superstition of the afterlife didn't seem so stupid to Vayp.

He shook his head and felt his heart pound against his chest. *Was this all my fault? That can't be*—he gulped—*I hope it's not... the Shadow Army.*

Oh... but it is, a cold voice sent a chill through his brain, appearing as a thought. *Without you, none of this would have been possible. He will be very grateful.*

He? Vayp thought only for a moment about the only *he* he could be referring to. The only *he* who struck fear in all, even Gabrael, the God of Fire, and King of Gods. The *he* whose only equal was said to be Eve. The *he* who is the reason time is stuck in an infinite circle, because it is he who always wins The Last Great War, obliterating all life before the Divine One creates the Big Bang to reset time. There is only one *he* he could be... he must be Geddon, the God of Darkness.

This is the end, Vayp thought as he turned to glance at Han'sael, who had bubbles floating up from his masked face and tubes connected to his torso, arms, and legs.

It is not yet the end, the cold voice returned. *But the end will be soon. This is all a part of the plan. One that you are still a part of.*

Plan for what?

For Geddon to be reborn, of course. And this is why I choose to keep you alive.

What do I have to do with this?

You are as vital of a piece as any. If all goes as planned, which my déjà vu says it will, then you will help bring Geddon to life.

How do you know?

I have my ways. And I have seen your fate. I know what needed to be done… and I know what will be done. After we rejoin with our master, we will then have their greatest weapon in our possession. Not even Gabrael and his Guardian Raaz'a will be able to stop it.

Their master? Rejoin? And what is their greatest weapon? *I thought I did enough? You have the Book, you have the Eye. I did everything you wanted.*

I would advise you to remember who you are talking to. Yes, indeed, you have done everything we have wanted. But I have yet to give you what you wanted. The reason you have joined us. The reason you did anything and everything. I always keep my word. You wanted Ah'nyx back, and I have promised to return him to you.

Vayp's heart stopped. He thought about Ah'nyx; Vayp saw his brown fur and different colored eyes staring into his. It briefly sucked the gloom out of his situation and brought him back to a time when life was good, perfect. When he felt a purpose, a life worth living. *What do I have to do to get him back?*

If you thought what you did at the Valley of Gaia was bad, I am afraid that you are in for much worse.

Worse? Vayp thought about how he was already the villain in their story. The idea of it getting much worse than that seemed impossible, but then again, he was no stranger to unfortunate fates.

What if I told you that to create a life… you must take one.

Vayp froze. What was he getting at?

I have seen your fate. You are perfect for our destiny because you will do anything to get Ah'nyx back, is that correct?

Vayp thought deeply for a moment, his eyes shifting toward Han'sael before quickly looking away, and sighed. *I will do anything.* Which he would, but the idea of being involved in another terrible plot made his stomach twist.

What if I told you that I saw your future. I saw Ah'nyx back in your arms… and all that you had to do to get him back was… take a life. What would you say to that?

10

I would ask who.

Splendid. Great answer, indeed. I won't tell you who... I will show you. The shadow materialized in front of Vayp. Black steam flowed off the silhouette of his lean figure. *Close your eyes. But be careful, ones who see their future become obsessed with their fate. I have seen it ruin even the strongest of minds. You cannot change what has been done. Are you ready?*

I think so.

You either are or are not.

I am ready.

The shadow's cold hand touched Vayp's forehead and images blazed through his mind in bursts. He saw Opella, his home, the village that raised him. He saw Ah'nyx, happily twirling around, chasing his tail. Then Ah'nyx's cold body in the middle of the village. A funeral that brought everyone together one last time before the bombs rained down from the Mechas, obliterating everything in sight. Vayp saw the shadow lunge its blade toward him, scarring his cheek with an incurable substance. He saw GroundStone, its grand golden walls glittering in the sun and yellow mountains and pyramids seen in the distance. He saw new students with their Sols, which still made his gut churn, and then the many arena challenges, where professors raised his arms as he won match after match; the arenas were the only thing he liked about his time there. He saw the airship take him away to the Valley of Gaia. The courtyard, in front of a volcano-like spire, where the top students from Fujita, the School of Wind and Wisdom, Sereni, the School of Water, and GroundStone, the School of Earth and Rock, stood. He saw Gabrael and the Book of Eve, which made him briefly think about Destrou, the Boy Who Never Lived, who the book was written about. Then a Mecha came and destroyed the Spire, Han'sael was taken by the shadows, and Retro'ku, the son of Gabrael, entered the Chamber of Eve and completed the challenge, a red orb was blazing in his hand. This was the same orb that was still ignited inside one of the sockets on the Book of Eve. He then saw fire. Lots of it, as if he was transported into what some of the scriptures said an underworld would look like. Except it wasn't an afterlife… it was… it was GroundStone? Or what was left of it. Its unbreakable walls were somehow destroyed, and every last bit of its sprawling trees and wildlife were ablaze. Vayp looked around and saw that Ground-Stone was completely destroyed. But something else had caught his eye. What was that? Right before the fire, he had seen something flash through the sky that looked like… no, they were extinct, that would be impossible. And before he could think about what he had seen, he thought about who he hadn't seen yet… as if she was erased from his memories… from his past, present, and future.

Just as he thought about *her*… she appeared in front of him. She had changed. She no longer carried the same crinkle in her smiling eyes, like he remembered. She seemed worn, like a warrior returning from war, yet fierce, as if also ready for battle. Vayp saw himself, and in his hand was a metal staff, its blade shimmering in the night. Vayp and S'rae glared at one another, their narrowed eyes showed no love, they blazed with anger. Vayp felt something tug at his chest, but he couldn't describe why, as if seeing them like this made him uncomfortable? Guilty, maybe? Before he could register what was happening, he saw himself dash forward, screaming as he pulled the blade back and his eyes widened as he watched himself stab straight through S'rae's chest. He saw her lifeless corpse next to random chunks of metal. Then, as a sunrise glowed over what was left of GroundStone, everything faded to white. Vayp then saw a bundle of green fabric on a shiny floor emerge before his eyes. A familiar scent reached his nose, urging him to see what was inside. When he peeled the last layer open, his heart dropped. It was… Vayp's eyes watered and his heart sank… it was… Ah'nyx… It was really him! Ah'nyx smiled at Vayp with the widest one he had ever seen, and it felt so real that he reached out to grab Ah'nyx. But instead of holding his Sol, his hands made contact with a cold frame that sent a chill through his body. He knew then that he had touched the shadow.

It was then when the visions escalated quickly, blurring by as if he was watching his life pass by in a rocket. He couldn't see what happened, the images blended together so quickly they distorted into a stream of murky water that rushed through his mind, with an occasional face popping up. He tried to let go of the shadow but he couldn't, as if his body had molded into the shadow's. Then suddenly there was darkness, a complete, pitch black void darker than anything he could have ever imagined. A shrieking, horrific scream reverberated through the valley. It was then when the entire valley shook with such a force that the shadow had jumped back in awe, releasing Vayp. The ground ripped open for miles as a deep hum overwhelmed the sounds of rocks crumbling. And as the hum grew louder, a black shroud covered the valley; it became so dark that, for the first time, the shadow was invisible.

The power. This is incredible! You have a great destiny ahead of you indeed. I have never felt such a power from a human before. We will indeed make a great team! There may be more uses for you, after all. It seems Va'han was right, it was in our fates to meet.

Vayp was a sweaty mess, trying to absorb everything that he saw before his thoughts disappeared, like remembering a dream after first waking up.

So tell me, what is this great future that you saw? What is it that you will do to get your precious Ah'nyx back?

Vayp's eyes kept darting from one side to the next so quickly that he felt nauseous. Then they stopped and widened, he remembered what he must do. No, not what he must do… but what he will do. *I will.* He thought once more about the series of events. *I will… kill S'rae.*

S'RAE LOOSENED THE GRIP on her bow as the arrow that had formed in her other hand dispersed into swirling steam. Her bow and arrow were quite different than the ones GroundStone, the School of Earth and Rock, were normally used to. For one, her bow was created from wind and spiraled so quickly it became solid. For another, in the empty silence of her room, her arrow had appeared out of thin air without so much of a whisper. And GroundStone being the home of the Guardians of Gaia, when they unsheathed their weapon, it was done so with the thought to protect, the value that most defined them, but S'rae had a very different intention, it was to kill... her brother.

Though Vayp's silvery image had dissipated away, still she wished she was quick enough to shoot an arrow through him before it faded. Again. These visions of him had been getting more clear ever since Gabrael first tasked her with finding his location. It was difficult. Actually, it was more like impossible. She had never been taught how to track, the little information she could remember was from the times she'd hide herself while Vayp practiced. She was good at controlling Earth in many different ways, but she was great at hiding. She would hide as a statue, mold into the straw or stone walls, into the sandy ground, there were no limits to the depths she'd go to learn things she wasn't supposed to. Maybe it was her love of learning that pushed her on this constant pursuit for knowledge, it was why she was a great fit for Fujita, the School of Wind and Wisdom, after all. But maybe... just maybe she wanted to learn everything to overcompensate for the one thing she lacked. Of all the things she was great at, there was one thing that she longed to be good at more than anything. It was the one thing that she was the worst at while everyone else made it look so easy: getting a Sol.

S'rae stood up straighter, shaking off the visions of her many failed Sol attempts, and walked toward the open window. One hand still held her bow, the other reached out in the darkness for her amulet, which was on the window ledge. *Why'd I fix this stupid thing? I should have just thrown it away...* She whispered *"ya'raea"* as dozens of lights flickered overhead for a moment before glowing bright, her ceiling now appeared as a starry night's sky. She examined the amulet carefully, her fingers grazed over the carving of a lotus on one side, and on the other, the letters V.A.S. reflected the light from the stars in her room. Except these stars were constantly moving about, some appearing as shooting ones when they zipped by overhead. That was because they were not stars at all, they were unique fireflies with the specific purpose to provide light.

Unlike Fujita and their technologically-advanced society, GroundStone didn't have the luxury of infinite electricity. In fact, during Srae's brief stay here, she had realized that GroundStone didn't have any luxuries at all.

They do not need material things when they have each other and nature, that was what the Guardian had told her. Though they didn't have much and was considered the poorest of the four kingdoms, Srae couldn't help but appreciate the abundance of nature that surrounded her that she could never find at Fujita.

She stared out the window and saw GroundStone's tall, golden walls in the distance. Scattered throughout the area and alongside the walls were massive statues of various animals she had only previously seen in books. The night was making the transition to morning, so there was an almost hypnotic bluish purple that made the trees and stone temples glisten. Birds of different sizes flew across the sky as waves of silhouettes. It was so... beautiful. She felt like she was finally… where she belonged, finally a place where she could call home again. Oh how she missed using that word. *Home*.

Her new room now had the exact opposite feel than the one she had at Fujita. Instead of a shiny marble floor, there was sand and dirt and stone. Instead of the ivory four poster bed with silk curtains, she now had what looked like an elongated tree stump with vines and flowers growing out the sides and extending to the ceiling, a veil of nature that seemed to have a mind of its own. And instead of a sophisticated communication system that would instantly transport a holographic message to another student, she had a messenger animal. It wasn't quite a Sol, but it was the closest she ever had to one, so she had no complaints. And of her many options, she actually chose a squirrel. Yes, a squirrel. Sure, it wasn't as cool as a lion or a fox or a panther or a… well, pretty much every other option, but B'se, which was short for his real name 'Best Squirrel Ever,' was hers and she didn't care what anyone else had to say about it. B'se was going to be her messenger until she finally got her own Sol, which was going to be soon, they said.

Before she pushed the glass window open, she noticed her faint reflection. A skinny girl frowned at her, her brown eyes narrowed under her frizzy brunette hair. She saw the brown bars painted under her eyes, the tribal marks of Opella, her home. The only other person left who wore the same markings was her brother, Vayp. The traitor. *We are the last of them. Of us.*

S'rae tried to recall the vision she had of Vayp, maybe there was some clue that could give away their whereabouts, but all she remembered was darkness and an odd, repetitive thud. A thud that seemed to get louder as if it were right outside. Or maybe they were just in her head?

Immediately, she opened the window and felt a cool breeze pass by her, ruffling her brown robe, hearing it swish softly in the wind. *I wanna know what's going on out there. Where can you be? I will find you. I promise.*

She stared outside, her eyes darting from the temples to the pyramids as if expecting to see something out of the ordinary. But had she been a Fujita student who was born and raised there, she would have found many of these things at GroundStone quite unusual. For starters, hanging by a branch, directly to her left and no farther than an arm's length away, there was a monkey that had just scratched its butt before sniffing its finger, only to squeal with disgust and fall backward into the vines of her third story window. To her surprise, large rhinos and elephants were found walking through some of the wide streets, seeming as though their purpose was to protect the villages before sunrise. Their thundering stomps rumbled the ground as they passed. Maybe those were the thuds she had heard? Maybe. But there was something so oddly distant about the thuds that she couldn't explain, as if they were far away but still in her mind.

She looked out through her window once more. There was something so peaceful and precious about watching animals fill the streets before the sun rose and humans packed the area with their traffic and the commotion that came with it. Although GroundStone was the poorest kingdom, it was the most populated, the home for any and all who wished to find one. But as far as S'rae could see through the darkness, there wasn't a human in sight, just dozens of different animals performing very different tasks. Giraffes were moving here and there, creating tall, beautiful archways made of vines, leaves, and broken branches, the path leading straight to the center of GroundStone. On the other end, to the west, she saw gorillas and various primates tie bundles of flowers together, and sloths carefully mash berries in a barrel.

Why were these animals acting so differently? They had never been up this early performing random tasks, what could be going on? Then suddenly it dawned on her, the elephants and rhinos were flattening the roads, the chimps and gorillas were collecting flowers, sloths preparing food, and giraffes helped with decorations—how could she forget? She had spent the past few weeks focusing primarily on tracking Vayp, and making friends with Fujak and Lynn, that she had forgotten that tomorrow was only the greatest day of the year: Orientation Day! This was the first official day of the new school year, where students from all over the world would come together and take part in a festival of introductions, cultures, but, most importantly, fun.

She felt a smile appear on her face, the only other times she wore a smile this wide were right before she dove behind a rock when she'd hear Retro'ku's voice appear around a corner. No matter how much she tried to mimic the cool way Lynn would compose herself around him, Srae would always end up saying something so foolish that she'd pretend to faint just to avoid the awkwardness altogether. Yes, she knew that made the moment even more awkward, but at least her eyes were closed, so she didn't have to see the cringe on their faces. She couldn't help it, his soft voice would make her skin tingle. And eye contact? Forget about it. She had to practice and prepare a sentence before she'd say it to him, because the moment their eyes met, she'd freeze and forget what she had to say. And whenever she froze, she'd always ask him, "Do you know where B'se, my squirrel, is?" Even if he had been in her hands the whole time.

But anyways, tomorrow was the most important day, not just for the fun events, but because she could now enroll as a student, which meant... which meant... she could now finally get her Sol! Of all the many dreams she's had had, this may had been her most prized one. There were very few things that she'd had wanted more than a Sol. That was when she knew she was too preoccupied with finding Vayp, when he consumed her mind more than her getting a Sol.

Then she shook her head as she heard them again. The thuds. She listened closely to the silence in the room, then poked her head out the window. Nothing. She felt an uneasy tug at her stomach that made her feel like something was wrong… terribly wrong, but she couldn't quite put her finger on it. *These noises… where are they coming from?*

S'rae then shook herself mentally. Was she being stupid? Maybe these were just signs that she should go to sleep and prepare for the big day tomorrow. The first day of her new life. As it happened, she saw the sun start to rise over the horizon. It was the most beautiful sunrise she had ever seen. She saw a family of felines cast silhouettes against the sun as they prowled across the wall. And the silence now faded as birds began to sing their morning songs.

Guess it was too late to think about getting some more sleep now; so she decided to take advantage of this breathtaking sight… but that was until the *thuds* got louder. Too loud. Like a jackhammer inside her head. At once, her eardrums felt like they were bleeding and about to explode as a vice grip squeezed her head tighter. She closed her eyes, trying her hardest not to scream. And her eyes would have remained shut if it weren't for trying to find out the source of where this ear-splitting, shrieking scream came from. It was the loudest noise she had heard yet as if someone screamed at the top of their lungs inside her ear. And as her eardrums vibrated, a droning hum overwhelmed the scream.

S'rae opened her eyes again. At least she thought she thought she did. S'rae's breathing got heavier. Her eyes were open yet all she saw was darkness, a complete void of light darker than anything she had ever seen. She lost all cool, and screamed at the top of her lungs, yet she heard nothing. And before she could process what had happened, it was over. Just like that, the darkness and the scream and the droning hum all faded away and she saw the bright sunrise emerge from the gloom and heard the birds chirping once more.

What does all of this mean?

S'rae strolled back to her bed and sat down on it, rubbing her palms over her ears. They no longer throbbed, but that wasn't what bothered her; she had something else entirely on her mind. She knew with all certainty that the only *thing* capable of turning a morning's sunrise into night were those of the Shadow. The people who were once meant to control Fire, but had defected. It was this duality with the elements that had made the elemental quizzes become most strict. This duality that prohibited students from being accepted into Harahn'de, the School of Fire. And it was the reason why Fujita had made sure that harsh punishments would happen to anyone who would defy their system of balance. No one was allowed to practice more than one element... yet... yet here she was... at GroundStone, the School of Earth and Rock, ready to train under a second element.

It was this duality that concerned her. What would happen if Fujita's authorities found out that she was here to practice Earth? What would they do? She knew she wasn't supposed to, but Gabrael... their destiny... the Book of Eve needed a top student from each element to retrieve the Elemental Orb from the challenge. That was why they were here in the first place, Vayp had brought them here, and it was Vayp who was supposed to unlock it. But plans had changed. He was now with *them*, and he was most likely the source behind the night that had appeared out of nowhere. S'rae rubbed her palms against her ears once more. *Gabrael doesn't think I have what it takes to get the Earth orb... But if he thought Vayp was good enough for the challenge... then why doesn't he think I am? Vayp isn't better than me. I'll show him why.*

The beauty about GroundStone being the most open of the schools and kingdoms was that she was able to take as many courses as she wanted—unlike Fujita and Sereni, there was no set curriculum; so she had decided on the courses that would best prepare her for the challenge ahead. Unfortunately… the only person she had to keep this a secret from was Fujak, her once enemy but now a good friend. Well, they started out as good friends then became enemies and now were working on rebuilding their friendship again. It was going well, she thought so at least, they had great conversations and long walks while exploring this new school before classes started. He was a good listener and she had found out many things about him that she would have never known, like he actually had a sense of humor. It was weird just thinking about Fujak making her laugh, she had grown so used to him being the reason people laughed at her. But she liked that their friendship was growing by the day and knew that if he knew that she planned to practice the Earth element, it could fracture whatever progress they've made.

Though they were friends, he was still a student of Fujita, the School of Wind and Wisdom, the creators of all laws of the land. He wasn't just any student, he was their prodigy, their ideal student, and also happened to be the son of its Headmaster, Yosh'i. And right when she thought of all the things he'd say about her decision, her door flew open with a BANG and there *he* was, sweat-soaked and wide-eyed, with a sharp spear in his hand that swirled in waves of wind. Like S'rae, he no longer wore their silver robes from Fujita, instead he was draped in brown.

"What's wrong?" Fujak shouted, scanning the room as his staff now formed into a bow with an arrow strung back. "What happened?"

S'rae was too caught off guard to reply, her jaw still dropped. She didn't know if she was ready to tell him what she saw, he was too logical to believe it anyways. It was all just in her head, he'd say, just like the Fujita Professors had always told her whenever she had questions about unexplainable events. "Err—"

"Screaming," Fujak said, breathing deeply. "Was that you screaming?" Within a second, a breeze passed by S'rae, her hair dancing in the wind, and she saw Fujak at the open window, arrow pointing at nothing in particular. "Were you attacked? Where'd they go?"

A part of her didn't know how to feel. Yes, Fujak completely intruded in on her privacy... but she couldn't help but smile then chuckle. "I'm fine," S'rae said. "But thanks for checking on me."

"Are you sure?" Fujak came to her. "You're quite good at keeping things to yourself... so are you sure you're okay?" S'rae saw the concern in his eyes, they were indeed genuine. It made her smile waver slightly, just thinking about how he'd handle the news of her practicing another element.

"Yes, I'm fine, really," S'rae said, pulling the loose ends of her robe closer before tying them up with a vine. "It means a lot that you came... when you thought I was in trouble. Thank you." S'rae's eyes met his. "Thank you again, I appreciate it."

Instantly, Fujak's bow and arrow disappeared, and he let out a comforting sigh, then sat down on the bed beside her. "Don't scare me like that."

"You're the one who scared me," S'rae chuckled, pushing Fujak's shoulder.

"I'm sorry." Fujak put his head down. "I shouldn't have overreacted."

"That wasn't an overreaction, dummy... that was you being a friend. And that's what friends do."

Fujak smiled at S'rae, but for a moment it flinched slightly. "Yeah, we're friends, that's what friends do." He paused for a moment, as if collecting his thoughts. "You know... I know this is a lot to handle with everything that's going on... with... you know... what happened, and who did it. And I know Gabrael is putting a lot of pressure on you, so... if you ever needed someone, like a friend, just to talk to, you know how to find me."

S'rae stared out the window at the inky purple-blue sky. She thought about what he was offering and it made her feel warm inside. As far as she knew, everyone else was dealing with their own issues: Lynn, the student from Sereni, the School of Water, had left her sisters, they had a bond tighter than any siblings she had seen, they were the Sereni Sisters, after all; Gabrael and Raaz'a were caught up on damage control and trying to make their stay at GroundStone as welcoming as possible; Retro'ku was always closed-off and training every second he could get, he had this strong desire to make sure he was ready for the battle that he knew was coming; and Fujak, well, Fujak went from the cool, popular student with a bright future ahead of him, to giving it up all for… well, S'rae didn't really know exactly why he did, but she believed it was so he could find his own name, create his own path and destiny, not the ones predetermined for him. The truth was that they all had their struggles to go through, so Fujak's willingness to accept S'rae's and be there for her… suddenly made things feel… okay.

"Well…" Fujak said, his fingers twirling around in his hands. "Well… since everything's okay… I guess… I guess I'll go now." Fujak hesitated for a second before standing up. "Glad that you're okay."

"Wait," S'rae said, grabbing Fujak's hand. It wasn't until this moment when she realized just how lonely she had been all this time. She never wanted to look like she was weak, but having the comfort of someone around who actually cared about the struggles she was going through, made her feel like a real person. Like her life actually mattered and she wasn't just being used to do this and do that. She felt like a fifteen-year-old girl who wanted to live life, no longer wanting her life to be dictated by her emotions or other people's plans. She just didn't know how to feel; she felt trapped in a destiny that was not her own, with the stakes too high to even consider being free…*just trapped*. She didn't know what to say or do, but she knew that she didn't want to be alone tonight, not after what happened. "Can you…" S'rae said, looking away, slightly embarrassed. "Can you… maybe just stay here, just for tonight, I don't want to be—"

"Of course," Fujak replied, a subtle smirk playing at his lips. "I thought you'd never ask."

"Me neither."

As S'rae and Fujak laid on opposite ends of the bed, the veil of vines and flowers that extended to the ceiling wrapped around them like a shell. Though Fujak moved quite a bit in his sleep, and found himself momentarily cuddling next to S'rae, and her mind was preoccupied with the sadness of Vayp, the worry of the dark night that had appeared, and the glee of what tomorrow may bring, she knew that sleep would be impossible, yet still she didn't mind. It was actually the best rest she had had for as long as she could remember. And she needed it. Tomorrow wasn't just any important day… it was going to be her best day ever, she was sure of it… for it was the day when her dream would come true. And she would finally find her Sol.

3

BY THE TIME S'RAE WOKE UP and hopped out of bed, her room was completely different than it had been just the night before. The floor, once sandy, was now spotless, revealing a stone floor with intricate patterns carved into it that she hadn't noticed before. And even the sun seemed to be shining brighter than usual, its rays shone through the window, channeling down onto a table that whistled with a peculiar sound. A sound she was all too familiar with from her days at Fujita.

She walked over to the table and noticed three slices of crescent-shaped goatbread, a bowl of fresh berries ranging from green to purple to red, and levitated in the air, whistling a sweet song, were spiralling streams of sand that spelled out: "*Hope you slept well.*"

If S'rae could see herself right now, she'd know that her cheeks were as red as the monkey's butt from last night.

Though it must've been in her head, the food tasted even better than it normally did. As if a kind gesture somehow made the berries sweeter. And as she finished breakfast and went to take a shower before starting the day, she couldn't help but think of a way to thank Fujak. A simple 'thank you' seemed so boring and not sufficient enough to express her gratitude. Maybe she would return the favor? Yes, that was it! She would prepare a dinner for him—except there was one problem, she had absolutely no idea how to cook, bake, or anything else food-related for that matter. Unless he liked a sand sandwich, she was out of luck.

She pressed her hand up against a wooden door that looked more like the entrance into a tree. Another blatant difference between Fujita and GroundStone were the showers. She didn't know which one she liked more, so she appreciated both in their own way. At Fujita, the showers were highly pressurized with wind, allowing her to tamper with how hard or soft the water would hit her. She enjoyed the way the water blasted her skin like tiny knives and would swirl around her like a wonderful twister-filled sauna. It was glorious. But here, at GroundStone, it was entirely different. She walked into the room and was suddenly transported into what looked like a rainforest, and for all she knew, it was one, she wouldn't be able to tell the difference.

She felt the soft rocks at her feet as she made her way to the end, where a hole in the ceiling gave way to gorgeous sun rays that striped through the leaves overhead. When she looked around, she saw green leaves, moss, and jagged walls that resembled a waterfall without the water. But once she said the words *"shal'lal,"* a movement was heard overhead, like the sound of a gate opening, followed by the rushing of water, then moments later she gasped as water fell from above. It was practically her own personal waterfall.

And it was glorious, indeed. Something she hoped the people here never took for granted.

GroundStone's philosophy was to connect man with nature, not just to let them know that they could co-exist, but to show them that they are one with it. One cohesive entity sharing the planet together. All beings were a part of nature, so it was GroundStone's goal to remind students and citizens that they were all equally connected with Gaia and its lifeforce. And as the warm water caressed her body in soothing waves, she couldn't help but appreciate feeling this close to nature. It made her feel... complete.

Then a *creak* was heard overheard. *Maybe nature was a little too close*. When she looked up, the same monkey from last night was hanging from a branch, staring at S'rae, except he wasn't alone, he brought friends.

"Umm..." S'rae said, covering herself. "I know you're animals and all, but... can I get some privacy?"

SPLASH! The monkeys fell into the little pond at the bottom of the waterfall.

"Guess not," S'rae said as the monkeys moved closer to her, slowly. She stepped back, grabbing her towel before wrapping it around her body. "This is cool and all, it really is, but I have to go now." She squealed as more splashed in front of her, then she let out another startled scream as she looked up and saw dozens in her shower, filling up almost every rock-lined crevice. "Okay... okay... I know you animals are working extra— Ahh—" she squealed again when water splashed into her face. She didn't know if she should feel nervous or scared or creeped out. Maybe all three. "I know you're working extra hard for today, it's the big day, but umm... I'm old enough to know how to take my own shower, thank you very much." Still, they inched their way toward her. "Well, anyways—err... goodbye!" She pressed her back against the door, slipped out, and slammed it shut. "Looks like no more showers for me! Back to Smelly, Stinky S'rae it is!" she giggled. And when she turned around to face her room, halfway between throwing the towel on the ground, her eyes widened, the widest they had EVER BEEN! Because as she stood there in a towel that barely covered herself, and her wet hair stuck to the sides of her face, and after just saying one of the most embarrassing things ever, she *would* see Fujak and... Retro'ku!

She let out a silent "*Eek!*" and quickly went to hide, but her towel had been stuck inside the door. She wanted nothing more than to faint and sleep this entire month away. Maybe by the time she woke up from the coma, they'd forget any of this happened.

"Umm… sorry," Fujak apologized, covering his eyes and looking away as S'rae tried to unhinge the towel from the door. "I heard screaming again and—"

"And we wanted to make sure you were okay, Miss S'rae," Retro'ku said in his silky smooth voice with an accent that rolled off his tongue. His dark brown skin glistened in the sun, the shadows contouring around every muscle on his arms, and his gaze remained fixed on S'rae, as if this was a perfectly normal situation.

He would be wearing a sleeveless shirt right now. Mmmm… okay, stop, S'rae, and focus. No… not on him, on the situation. No… stop looking at his mmmm… muscles. Okay, I give up. S'rae wished the "mmms" were only in her head, but judging by the way Retro'ku smirked, she may have accidentally let them slip out.

Fujak narrowed his eyes and glared at Retro'ku with a sideways glance. "Yes," Fujak said, "as *I* was saying, we wanted to make sure you're okay."

"I am," S'rae said, frantically tugging at her towel and trying her best to cover herself. "Err… I'm… I'm doing just—" She yanked harder. "—just fine. I just need to—" She pulled on the towel with all her strength until she heard a tear. "Welp, I'm just going to need you two to leave… Like right now. *Please.*"

"As you wish, Miss S'rae," Retro'ku said. He turned around and left, taking the heat along with him.

Fujak sighed as he saw S'rae's cheeks flush red. "Well, sorry, it's just that with everything that's going on… and with Vayp out there and all… we need to be careful. That's all."

"I know," S'rae said, taking a deep breath to recover herself once Retro'ku left. "Y-yes… we need to be. But um… I just wanted to say thank you for everything you did for me today."

"You're welcome, it's what friends do, right?" Fujak said, the way his eyes dropped it seemed as if he wanted to say more. "Just remember, if you ever need to talk, I'm here for you."

"Thank you... but I meant thank you for what you did this morning."

"Oh, the message? I didn't want to wake you up, it's the least I could do."

"Yeah, and thanks for the breakfast, too! It was delicious!"

"Breakfast? I didn't... wait, you had breakfast?" Fujak turned toward the door, S'rae noticed his fists clench. He shook his head then said, "Well, I hope it was good then." His voice lost some of the cheerfulness it previously had. "We have a long day ahead of us. It should be fun." A half-smile drifted across his face before he left the room.

If he didn't send her breakfast... then who did? The last thing she wanted to do was assume... but maybe... just maybe it could have been... no, don't be stupid, S'rae. It *obviously* wasn't *him*. But then who?

By the time S'rae arrived downstairs, Gabrael, Raaz'a, Lynn, Fujak, and Retro'ku were all seated around a lavish stone table. They remained in conversation and none looked up as she entered. There were little chimps carrying plates and bowls to and from the table, some containing various fruits and berries. Gabrael grunted, his eyes were focused and furious as he spoke to Raaz'a. Fujak was at the other end of the table not paying attention to the fact that his fork and knife had missed its target: a long, freshly-toasted loaf of goatbread. He looked annoyed and sour, staring at Lynn and Retro'ku talking.

"Hi," S'rae said, sitting down next to Fujak, whose knife had carved a line into the table.

The sulky look on Fujak's face had vanished almost instantly. "Oh, hi!" He pulled away his fork and knife, awkwardly placing it onto his plate. "So... today's the big day, huh?"

Fujak had only assumed that S'rae was excited just to get her Sol, which there were no rules against, but had he known S'rae's real plan to become an Earthie, a GroundStone student, she knew he would not be as happy. But Fujak was her friend now, she didn't want to hide the truth any longer. "Err… yeah, about that… I have something that I want to tell you. I—"

"That can wait, S'rae." She heard a deep voice that sent a chill through her body despite carrying enough heat to melt the skin off her bones. She turned her attention toward Gabrael, the God of Fire, King of Gods, and Headmaster of Harahn'de. His brown face glistened in the sunlight. His beard no longer had the same stubble, instead it was growing as if to show he had much more on his mind than hygiene. His black cloak and robe swished about as he approached S'rae. "I am glad that you could make it, because we have most pressing matters that we must address before today's festivities."

S'rae had a feeling that she knew why there was a hint of alarm behind his voice, it must have had to do with the void of darkness she had seen last night. Of course he would know about it. "I understand," she said.

Fujak and Lynn glanced at one another with a most curious look on their faces, as if they were the only ones who didn't know what was going on.

"Retro'ku," Gabrael said, turning to his son, who had still been stuffing his face with bread, berries, and everything else he could find. "I understand you work best and the train the hardest when you are alone… but, we need you. I need you."

"Whut, farthuh?" Retro'ku said, talking with his mouth full before taking a deep gulp. "Tell me."

"These three students are the greatest from their schools. Their destiny is far beyond anything we could ever imagine… and I believe they are ready to know our secrets."

"But fathe—"

"It is time, my son… And if you ever were to become a King, you must first understand how to teach. A true leader is not defined by how powerful you are, but how powerful you make others around you."

Retro'ku appeared defeated. His natural smile had faded and the stars in his eyes seemed to as well. "But father... I must be ready. You do not understand. You did not see what I saw. I must be ready."

"I can only fathom the destiny that lies ahead for you, but there comes a time when the best way to learn is to teach."

Retro'ku took a deep breath as if not wanting to argue. "As you wish, father." His soft voice and his smile returned. "If this is in the stars, then it has already been decided."

"Indeed, it has." Gabrael nodded then turned his focus to S'rae, Lynn, and Fujak. "Death will come. And we must be ready."

The air had been sucked from the room. What was supposed to be her greatest day could not have started off any worse.

"It will be my pleasure, master," Raaz'a said, his silvery hairs poking out from under his black hood, "to watch over Retro'ku while he trains them."

"Excuse me?" Fujak had a bit of fury to his tone. "Train who? Us? For what, exactly?"

"I understand your frustration, Fujak," Gabrael said before turning his focus to Raaz'a. "As for you, Raaz'a, I have a more useful way to utilize your gifts." Gabrael then returned his attention back to Fujak. "I indeed understand why Fujak, of the Fuj family, would object to this. I am not here to persuade, because you have your beliefs, and the last I wish to do is have someone question their faith during this time of need. But you will not attempt to persuade me, the King of Gods, do we understand ourselves?" S'rae saw Fujak take a deep gulp as sweat trailed down his face. "I have waited over three thousand years. I had told Fujita as well as Sereni that locking up our walls would not stop a Shadow Army from existing, but rather, it would very well stop them from being defeated. And now... now I am afraid a Shadow Army has risen. And what

31

they are most afraid of… is now down to three." Gabrael looked at Raaz'a and Retro'ku with such defeated eyes that it seemed as if he was ready to say his last goodbye.

S'rae felt the table shake as Fujak's eyes widened. Lynn gasped and turned her head toward S'rae and Fujak as if hoping for an answer.

"What do we do?" Lynn said. "If this is true… shouldn't we tell everyone? I need to tell my sisters!"

"It is most unfortunate for me to tell you this," Gabrael said. "But this information must remain only between us. The last thing we need right now is chaos. The only reason I am telling you all this is not because you are the destined ones… but because—" he glanced at Retro'ku, who begrudgingly nodded his head. "—we need more students of Fire."

"Absolutely not!" Fujak spoke up. S'rae was taken aback by Fujak's tone.

"*What* did I tell you?" Gabrael's eyes burned into Fujak's.

"I mean no disrespect, King of Gods." Fujak bowed his head for a moment before raising it up, a fire indeed burned in his eyes when he spoke. "You are risking our lives by wishing to train us. The world has rules and laws for a reason, it is what has kept peace for millennia. Fujita will *not* take this lightly."

"Fujita will have no way in knowing. GroundStone is the safest, most protected place in all of Gaia for a reason."

"That's what they said about Harahn'de, too," Fujak said, and S'rae saw what little content mood Gabrael may had had completely vanish away.

S'rae felt a piercing cold sweep the room. Prickles of goosebumps flared from her toes to fingers, and she watched as her breath danced in the wind. Even the sun's light faded from a crisp yellow to a muted gray. And when Gabrael opened his mouth, S'rae felt every word as if they had dug themselves into her. "I have done *far* worse things than punish—"

"Father," Retro'ku said, quickly standing between Gabrael and Fujak. "I assure you he meant no disrespect, for what he said is true. Harahn'de *was* said to be the safest place in all of Gaia, yet it fell. How sure can we be that we are safe here?"

The room normalized. S'rae felt the warm air wrap around her as the sun once again brightened the room.

"Son... we are not safe anywhere. There are only three of us... against an army. GroundStone can only buy us time... but it is us who must defeat them... and I am afraid that we may not be enough." Gabrael looked at Fujak. "Which is why we need more, and it is why Retro'ku *will* train you. If anything, all you would need to learn is how to master this." Gabrael stuck his hand out, his loose robe flapping about. At once, the hilt from his belt shot into his palm, erupting into a fiery blaze. He waved the flaming sword around. "You see... it is fire... and fire alone that can kill the Shadows. You are a logical boy, Fujak, why would you not want to be prepared *when* they attack? Because it is not a matter of if, only *when*."

A very tense silence followed those words. Raaz'a, who was looking extremely nervous, fidgeted with his cloak and said, "The Shadows will be upon us. They will strike and I am afraid Gabrael is right, we will be no match for them. Maybe—" Raaz'a cleared his throat. "—just maybe, we could ask assistance from Vy'ken? He would be most helpful during these times."

"Vy'ken is to *not* be told of this," Gabrael growled.

"Why, Master? You, of all people, know how valuable he would be."

"Indeed. And I, of all people, know how damaged his mind is. The Shadows will find a way to corrupt him, as they already had, and we cannot risk it. You should know this."

Raaz'a put his head down and looked away when Gabrael shot him a look, as if Raaz'a knew to never speak of it again.

Fujak's pale face, slanted silvery eyes, and slick black hair with silver streaks, glowed a tinge of gold as the fire scorched brighter. "I have a bad feeling about this, but… what other alternative do we have?" When Gabrael said nothing, Fujak sighed and tapped a finger on the table. "Then we must make sure Fujita does *not* find out about this… or we will have two deaths to worry about."

"So… when does it start?" Lynn said, and S'rae was glad that she had asked exactly what was on her mind.

"Today," Raaz'a said, energy back in his voice. "My Divine, we have no time to waste!"

As excited as S'rae was to learn how to control Fire… especially from Retro'ku… one look at the worry in Fujak's eyes and she couldn't help but feel unsure. Fujak genuinely seemed concerned as if he knew what Fujita was capable of more than Gabrael did. Were their lives now in even more danger? Surely since Fujita was logical, they'd understand why their law of balancing nature wasn't as important as defeating a Shadow Army, right? She could only hope.

With a *poof* of smoke, Gabrael and Raaz'a had vanished and the tenseness in the air seemed to have left the room with them.

"So, when would you like to start?" Lynn asked Retro'ku with a smile.

The smile on Retro'ku's face vanished all too quickly. "*I* would *not* like to start. Discuss that with my father." He stood up and headed toward the door. "*I* have training to do. I mean no disrespect, but you all will just get in my way. I have a war to prepare for. An end to stop. I will *not* fail this time." His shadow leapt up from the ground and stood beside him, its steamy black fingers gripped Retro'ku's shoulder. And in one BANG, Retro'ku rocketed toward the heavens, leaving behind a red aura that mixed in with the black smoke that blasted through the sky.

Will not fail this time? What'd he mean by that?

"Well…" Lynn said, brushing off crumbs from her clothes. For being such a beautiful and proper girl, she sure was a messy eater.

She flipped her blonde hair and twisted it into a bun atop her head. "I don't know about you, but I can*not* wait to change for the parties today! I'm tired of looking homeless." Lynn looked at S'rae and Fujak, who said nothing. "Oh, come on, put a little life in you two, don't be so boring."

"We were just told that we're all probably going to die," Fujak said blankly.

"I'm sorry, but do you want me to change your diaper, too?"

"What?"

"I'm not used to you being such a baby. Everyone's going to die eventually, there are worse things than death, you know?"

"Oh yeah? Like what?" Fujak lifted an eyebrow.

"Like being seen in public with this hideous thing on." Lynn slapped her thighs.

Fujak shook his head and S'rae chuckled. Lynn pulled her arms in and started to shuffle underneath her brown robe, as if ready to—

"Are you undressing in front of us?" Fujak said, alarmed.

"*Hah*, you wish!" Lynn winked at Fujak… and something inside S'rae suddenly felt different, but she didn't know why or what, it felt like a tight squeeze of her stomach. She shook it off and watched Lynn as she twirled around. One spin, two spin, three spins, after each spin, S'rae saw the color leach out from her brown robes until Lynn stopped, and in front of S'rae stood the most beautiful girl in all of GroundStone, maybe even Gaia. Like, wow! Lynn's brown robe had transformed into an elegant white gown with blue sparkles that grazed the ground, as if she was walking on glittering water. It matched her piercing blue eyes perfectly.

Yupp, S'rae once again accepted that she'd be considered the ugly frog when they walked together. She liked it when they both looked homeless together, it made her feel less like the unpretty one, but now people would definitely think S'rae was Lynn's servant. A part of her would rather not be seen in Lynn's presence, not like this, at least, S'rae was already thinking about being ignored as everyone gave Lynn all the attention.

"What do you think?" Lynn said, twirling around once more. The word elegant wasn't a strong enough word to describe her "It even has pockets!" Lynn jumped in the air with her hands deep into her dress. Okay, maybe there was a better word than elegant, but S'rae had a brief vision of her trying to do a similar twirl, she saw herself crashing into the wall and being tied up and lost in the fabric. Far from cute. *How does she make it look so… effortless?* "Sooo…. What do you think?" Lynn said once more, smiling wide and twisting her hips, hands still deep in her pockets.

Fujak briefly looked at S'rae before answering. "Err… you look… great. D-don't you think, S'rae?"

They were about to meet hundreds… maybe thousands of new people. This was her chance to have the best first impression possible for students and professors. If she were to start a new life at GroundStone, might as well make the most out of it. Luckily, there was no one better to help S'rae out than Lynn. "You look absolutely breathtakingly perfect… and I want you to teach me!"

* * *

"How does she look?" Lynn asked Fujak as S'rae walked out from behind a veil of vines and flowers.

S'rae emerged wearing a green dress that fit her like a glove. She noticed Fujak's jaw drop as he mouthed "wow" to himself.

"I mean… she looks… she looks like she's ready for the day," Fujak said.

"That's it? Just ready for the day? Looks like she's ready to slay the day and make it her peasant, that's what," Lynn said. "Boys' opinions never matter anyways, that's lesson number one!"

The confidence Lynn had in S'rae meant the world. For someone as flawlessly perfect as Lynn to say things like that just felt… well, it felt… amazing.

"So, now that you look like the Queen of Gaia," Lynn said, "what are you going to do for the talent show?"

S'rae's smile wavered. "Umm… no one told me *anything* about a talent show?"

"Well," Fujak said. "It's not really a talent *show* it's just a section to show off your talent to passersby."

"Oh great…" S'rae grimaced. "I hope these people like to watch me sleep then."

"Oh, come on!" Lynn said, throwing her hands up. "There must be *something* you're great at."

"There are *many* things she's great at," Fujak said, and S'rae felt her cheeks flush. "I'm sure she'll think of something."

"T-thank you," S'rae said politely. After many years of being picked on and bullied, it still hadn't set in completely that Fujak was being nice to her. It was weird because it wasn't like he was nice, he was *very* nice. Like very very nice!

4

"SOOO... DO YOU KNOW WHERE RETRO'KU IS?" S'rae asked as she twisted her hips once more while looking at the mirror that was somehow held up by two branches. She pulled on the tight fabric of her green dress and flattened out whatever wrinkles may had been left.

"This is your third time asking me... in like thirty seconds," Lynn said as she was fixing her own white gown in the mirror opposite of S'rae. "Why do you keep askin— wait... I get it!"

"Get what?" S'rae said, still focused on her reflection. She never knew that she could enjoy a reflection this much, the girl staring back at her was no longer someone who made her quickly look away. This new girl had her hair tied into a bun with a loose strand that dangled in front of a face that now glowed a rich bronze.

"Oh S'rae... it's happening!" Lynn turned around and met S'rae's eyes in the mirror. "It's so happening!" Lynn's lips, redder than usual, smiled wide.

"Nope... it's certainly *not* happening... whatever it is that you think is happening... well, it's not!"

"Mmhmm... it most definitely is." Lynn grabbed S'rae's shoulders and twisted her around so they were face-to-face. Lynn had done a great job with S'rae's makeup, but an exceptional job on her own face. Just when S'rae thought Lynn couldn't look any more perfect, she had to prove her wrong. "You… you want him to see you in this, badly, don't you?" Lynn twisted her head and grinned.

"No… nope… not at all… that's definitely *not* what's happening!" S'rae took one more glance at her reflection then winked. "I don't know what you're talking about. I just want to see if he's okay, that's all."

"Mmhmm… right… you're not too good at this whole lying stuff. Listen, there is *absolutely* nothing wrong with wanting to be seen when you look your best. You look fabulous. Show it! Show the world! Don't ever let people make you feel bad for feeling good about yourself! Look at me!" Lynn twirled around once more, the blue sparkles at the bottom of her dress appeared as majestic waves of water. "I couldn't wait to get out of those clothes. This isn't an everyday thing for you, so enjoy it!"

S'rae's face scrunched up at that comment and Lynn took notice.

"I'm sorry, I didn't mean it like that. It's just that… well, I would hate to be seen in public with the stuff they make us wear."

"Maybe S'rae's just more confident than you." S'rae heard a voice from behind as the door opened. S'rae's eyes widened nervously, as if not wanting to be seen as vain, and snapped her fingers. At once, the mirrors turned into sand and flowed back onto the floor. The branches that supported the mirrors fell to the ground just as Fujak appeared with his hands behind his back.

S'rae noticed Lynn pouting, as though being told that someone was more confident than her was the worst thing that could be said, but it made S'rae's reddened cheeks glow brighter.

"One for you." Fujak pulled a hand forward and gave Lynn a vibrant red rose, her frown quickly turned to a smile. "And one for you." He turned to S'rae.

S'rae's eyes widened as Fujak handed her a purply-blue lilac that resonated with a pulsating glow. "These are my favorite!"

"I know," Fujak said. And both Lynn and S'rae perked up at that comment, staring at one another with a shocking curiosity.

"How would you know?" S'rae and Lynn asked at the same time.

"Umm… yeah, *okay*! I need to figure something out. *Now!*" Lynn said in a matter of fact way. "What's *this*? What's going on over here?" And when both S'rae and Fujak said nothing, Lynn pressed on. "*This*! Like… I don't get how you two were ever enemies! I mean… he knew your favorite flower? Really? Even at the Valley when he *tried* to hate you, he still said some good things about you."

"He said good things about me?" S'rae was taken aback and slowly turned toward Fujak, whose cheeks became flush. "Like what?"

"Oh quite a bit…" Lynn said, "like—"

"That's not important." Fujak went to leave.

But with one flick of S'rae's wrist, the door slammed shut. She was too curious, and if there was one thing she learned about herself, it was how crazy she'd get if something was left festering in her mind for too long. She needed to know *now*!

"Whoa, S'rae, look at you!" Lynn clapped, as though she was a proud parent. "Taking control! I like, I like! So… what happened between you two? Why'd you two hate each other?"

"I don't really know," S'rae lied. She thought back to a time when she and Fujak were friends, and he had brought her to the top of their private terrace that overlooked the entire sky as the sun set. It was a magical moment. "Well… we just kinda fell off, I guess."

"Fell off? Hmm… sounds like a breakup," Lynn said as she made herself comfortable on a chair, crossing her legs, and smiling wide, as if gossip talk was her favorite thing ever. "Please, go on, sooo… were you two… like dating?"

"Ew! No!" S'rae said, then quickly looked at Fujak. "I mean not ew like it's Fujak, but just that I didn't date boys."

"So… you date girls then?" Lynn uncrossed her legs and perked her lips with curiosity.

"NO!"

"Hmm… well I think if you were to give it a try, you'd see what you've been missing out on." Lynn winked.

S'rae froze at that comment, not knowing how to address it, so instead she continued on as if nothing had been said: "Well, since we are friends now… I guess it's fine to talk about it." S'rae looked at Fujak, who raised an eyebrow. "Well… Fujak wanted to kiss me and I didn't want to… and I guess that's how it happened."

"Excuse me!" Fujak's eyebrows raised higher. "Is that what *you* think happened?" he laughed. "Honestly?"

"Err… I thought so—"

"Well, hate to be the bearer of bad news, but that's as far from the truth as possible," Fujak said. "Yes, you hurt me. Yes, my family didn't like the idea of someone like you, no offense, but an Earthie, getting close to and hurting a Fuj, so they decided to expel you." S'rae's eyes lit up at that word. "I pleaded with them not to; so they told me that you could remain only as long as I stopped being friends with you. The Fuj name is the most prestigious in all of Gaia, they never wanted it to be disrespected again. And if they saw us ever being friends, you were gone; so I became your enemy, even if that meant not becoming the top student. But it wasn't because of you not wanting to kiss me that hurt, I was scared and pressured by my friends to ask. It was what you said afterwards that hurt. A lot."

"You… were my enemy so I could stay in school?"

"Yes." Fujak scrunched his nose.

"But… I never said anything after that night to hurt you."

"It's not what you said to me… you know what, nevermind," Fujak said, making his way to the door. "It's in the past… it's not important anymore."

"Oh but it is," Lynn said, her eyes wide as if excited to get to the juicy parts. "We're almost there, come on! Just say it already!"

As Fujak opened the door to leave, a burst of wind passed by him. S'rae was in between him and the door.

"It's important to me," S'rae said. She wanted to know what he thought happened between them. Her time at Fujita was a miserable five years of being bullied by everyone and anyone, and she had always put the blame on Fujak for that. She needed to know the truth. "What do you think I said about you?"

"Let's just say… you're not the only one who can channel soundwaves. But it doesn't matter anymore… we're friends, right?" Fujak said, and S'rae could hear the pain in his voice as if it wasn't all right. "Good luck today."

And just like that, Fujak left the room and took the air with him. Not only did he know her secret of stealing whispers by channeling soundwaves… but he could do it as well? Her jaw dropped. What was it that she may had said? It felt like forever ago and if there was one thing she knew that she excelled at, it was being able to forget and block out the worst moments of her life, not remember them.

But before S'rae or Lynn could say anything else, there was a loud horn followed by drums that made the entire room shake and its contents rattle. They looked at one another with wide eyes and palms to their faces—this could only mean one thing… Orientation Day had just begun!

S'rae scrambled to her feet after putting on her shoes, so happy she felt everything in her tingle with excitement. She pulled Lynn by the hand across crowds of people dressed in white and gold robes and made it into an open terrace, the smell of fresh flowers and incense filled the air. A shimmering gold road glowed from the entrance to the temple in the center of GroundStone. And far off in the distance, she saw GroundStone's golden gates, stretching to the sky, roar open. Hundreds of doves swooped in through the crack and fluttered and soared overhead, looking like a majestic snow storm that filled the sky. And once the gate fully opened, the drums and horns sounded louder, this time carrying a rhythmic tune.

"Yay! It's the Ramal sand village!" an excited boy clapped, pulling on his mom's robe. "They're here! I love when they come!"

And S'rae soon understood why. A large mass, looking like a tidal wave of sand, came thundering through the gates. S'rae would have tensed up in fear if it weren't for the crowds on both sides of the street cheering.

Men and women dressed in a caramel-colored robes were riding the massive waves on top of shields and what may had been turtle shells. They performed amazing twists and flips all while traveling up and down the waves that roared by.

S'rae coughed as a burst of sand shot into her mouth, which had been stuck wide open.

"This is so amazing!" Lynn said, twisting around to look at the waves make their way to the temple. "Why does surfing sand look so much more fun than water? I definitely want to try that!"

Lynn may had said more but it was tough to hear her over the enthusiastic crowd.

"Ooo… ooo… the Eazima Tribe!"

"Ooo! The Asada Clan! They have the most gorgeous zebra lions!"

"Oh… my… divine! The Liamur Village! Those lemurs are the cutest things ever! I want to squeeze them to death! I so wish I had one! *Oww*! I'm sorry, okay?" the girl said, looking down at a pink panda that had kicked her shin and balled its fist up, shaking it.

S'rae couldn't help but laugh at how excited the kids were when each village passed through the gates. She and Lynn both stared on with widened eyes as the various tribes strolled and danced and mystified their way through GroundStone. She saw some ride their fusions of lions and panthers and wolves; others strolled by on mammoth elephants twice the size of the largest elephant she had seen; some rode on rhino camels and sand sharks. Then there was a tribe that made Lynn shake her hips as the chimps and monkeys played the drums while the men and women, who were dressed in green with bangles and bells hanging from their hips and arms, danced about, swirls of sand spiraled around them. S'rae loved seeing the diverse cultures that were represented in the GroundStone district; they all had their unique Earth specialty and animals and they each looked so differently, too, ranging from fair to dark skin, straight to curly hair, bald to massive afros. Orientation Day was just everything she had hoped it'd be. She easily understood why this was considered their favorite day. Seeing a parade where animals and humans from different villages joined together to show off their cultures was an experience she'd never forget.

Tap. Tap. Tap.

S'rae looked down and saw an adorable squirrel with a roll of parchment attached to his back. "Thanks, B'se!"

She pulled off the piece of paper, and read:

GROUNDSTONE, SCHOOL OF EARTH AND
ROCK, INITIATION CEREMONY

All first years must report to the Mu'tadi Temple after the parade ends. It is located here. (The words on the paper dissolved and formed into a map. An X marked where S'rae was and a line of sand traveled through GroundStone landing on a star as the words Mu'tadi Temple appeared.) *You are to be here no later than the third bell or we shall begin the ceremony without you. After this ceremony concludes, you will rejoin the day's festivities no longer as visitors of GroundStone, but students! There will be games, a chance to show your talents, and, of course, we finish off with GroundStone's favorite: the grand arena to crown a new champion!*

The ceremony is an event of three parts. For to become a Ground-Stone student you must connect to nature and the spirit of Gaia through your Mind, Body, and Soul.

The first section will be for your mind as we find the perfect quill for you.

The second section will be for your body as we find the perfect home for you.

And the last one will be for your soul as we find the perfect Sol for you.

Please be reminded that if you are a first year student from a GroundStone district, who has already linked up with their Sol, you are still required to support and encourage your peers through this process. As you know, it is an emotional experience, a rebirth some would say, so they will need all the support they can get.

And finally, remember that here at GroundStone we take pride in helping you find yourself, who you are truly meant to be. And by the time you leave us, we want you to know that you are unique, you are special, and that you matter just as much as anyone else. You and only you will be the best you that Gaia has ever seen. It is our job to guide you down your best path, but it is you who must take control of your destiny. Find yourself and you will change the world.

Remember those words whenever you feel all hope is lost. Have faith and faith will have you.

Please remember to dress accordingly.

Leonna, Professor of Healing and Herbs

"Wow," Lynn said, "so you're actually doing this! It's really going to happen!"

"Yeah," S'rae said, looking over her shoulder. "Just don't tell Fujak about it."

"Don't tell Fujak about what?" Fujak appeared from the crowd. He looked strikingly handsome, wearing white pants and a white cloth that wrapped around his body all the way up and around his mouth. His piercing, silvery eyes were looking prettier than ever. *Okay, how about you don't use the word pretty when thinking about his eyes, S'rae? Okay, thanks.*

"Umm," S'rae said, looking at Lynn who looked back in awe, both appeared to be at a loss for words.

"Just tell him," Lynn said, "he's just going to find out one way or another."

Fujak raised an eyebrow, redirecting his focus to S'rae. "Tell me… what exactly?"

"Well, today's the day I get my Sol…"

"And?"

"And…" Just as S'rae was going to tell him, she felt her insides scrunch together uncomfortably. It felt like she was being watched. By who? Her eyes scanned the crowds, looking pass Lynn and Fujak and the large hippos that stomped by… and she saw someone staring in her direction… or was it directly at her? The longer she stared at the cloaked person, the more her stomach twisted. Then finally, by the time the largest hippo yet walked by, the person was no longer there. Was this all in her head?

"Well…" Fujak said. "And… you were saying?"

S'rae shook off the paranoia and wanted to curl up into a ball before telling Fujak the truth. "And… it is… also the day..." S'rae hated how awkward she gets when she's nervous. Without realizing it, she had twisted her head and body so much that she was looking at Fujak upside-down. Before she could speak again, the bells sounded. *Saved by the bell!* "Sorry, gotta go get my Sol! Talk to you later, meet you at the party when the ceremony is done!" S'rae ran as fast as she could away from Fujak and Lynn, toward the building that was marked the Mu'tadi Temple on her map.

"Everyone! Everyone! Stand around! My name is Professor Leonna and I will be your guide throughout this ceremony. I would like you all to feast your eyes on the magic of GroundStone and all of its glory!" Professor Leonna shouted to a crowd of students inside the temple. She wore a brown robe with a hood over her head, barely concealing her bright blue hair.

For a temple for new students, it was dark and ancient. A few old women were standing in a corner, drawing relics in the sand. One of them lifted her hand as dust swirled around and wrapped around the dozens of pillars that had surrounded the students. It wasn't until S'rae trailed the sand with her eyes that she noticed the pillars were actually tree stumps and the ceiling seemed to be made entirely out of the trees' snowy white leaves.

As S'rae surveyed her surroundings even more, she couldn't help but feel out of place, not just because she was the only one wearing a skin-tight dress with her hair and makeup done while the other students wore brown robes, but she felt like she had just walked into a nursery. The first-year students, though ten years old, looked like they might as well had been five. *They literally look like babies.* And to make her feel even more like an awkward giant, a little man in a dark brown robe, who was limping on one side, walked toward the students with a staff clunking against the ground. All the students seemed to give the man his attention; they nodded at him, and the man raised his staff, saying, "The mind has a mind of its own, you cannot force it, but you can give it tools to guide it down any path you choose. The right path, I would hope."

"Why yes, absolutely," Professor Leonna said. "Just as I had stated in the paper I sent out to each of you, this is the first section. The one for the mind." She clapped her hands excitedly, but after a few moments of being the only one clapping, she quickly stopped. "It usually gets a better reaction than that, I swear." She lifted her hand and somehow pulled a staff out of her sleeve that was twice the size of her arm. She slammed it to the ground and the entire temple rattled, debris fell from overhead.

The students had suddenly gone completely still and silent.

After the debris finally settled, Leonna spoke once more.

"GroundStone will be your new home. Some will spend five years here and then move on to different pastures, others may remain here and help GroundStone flourish by providing our kingdom with whatever skill you mastered. While a student here, this is where you will make most of your friends. Look around, some of these students to your left and right may become your best friends. Enjoy the time you share. Enjoy the memories you will create. Trust me, these will be the best years of your life. Make the most out of your time with your friends while you can, because once you are no longer a student, and life happens, you'll find yourself with absolutely no friends and three kids, including a husband, who might as well be considered the son I never had—oh you useless, delicious man candy—and a Sol. And when you finally think you found new friends, you realize they only liked you because they wanted to be around your dog. *Hmmph*!" Professor Leonna huffed and puffed before slamming her staff again.

S'rae looked at the kids, who looked confused as if they had absolutely no idea what she was talking about.

Then one of the students whispered to another: "Umm… so, if she teaches healing, who heals our healing professor?"

"Yeah, she needs a hug."

"Excuse me," S'rae said to break up the awkward silence, "but… what exactly are we supposed to do during this mind section?"

Everyone was looking at her. The old man limped and clunked his way toward her. His eyes scanned her green dress before making eye contact. "Are you a student? You're a bit… old to be here."

"Y-yes," S'rae said nervously, hoping to not start off on the wrong foot. "I want to become an Elemental… a—a Master of Earth."

"Ah, we have an ambitious one, I see." This time his eyes drifted away from hers and landed on her face paint just below them. "Ah, hmm… I've seen that mark before. Hmm… what tribe did you come from?"

"I came from Opella, sir," S'rae replied.

At once his eyes widened and he took a step back, almost falling over. "Oh my, my apologies... err—"

"My name is S'rae."

"Yes, S'rae. Well, carry on then. I wish you the best during your trials!" For having a limp, he seemed to have hurried away too quickly.

Why was he being nice all of a sudden? What about Opella made him change his tune? Even Professor Leonna now gave S'rae more attention.

She walked up to S'rae and handed her a staff. "I would like for you to do the honors."

"What would you like for me to do?"

"Well, slam it of course, but... I want you to whisper these words before you do." She leaned in close to S'rae's ear, and said: "*Hik'ma.*"

S'rae repeated the words as the staff embedded itself into the ground. At first nothing happened, then she heard movement overhead. The white leaves of the trees that made up the ceiling began to shuffle around, as if there was a draft, but there was no such breeze. The longer S'rae stared at the white leaves, the more they moved... as if they were alive. And it wasn't until the first leaf hopped off the branch, when she realized... they were alive, but they were not leaves. The branches were filled with hundreds of tiny birds that took the shape of leaves.

And before S'rae could speak, every single bird had swooped in and circled around the students, its feathers shedding from their wings, appearing like a beautiful winter's snowfall. S'rae couldn't help but savor the moment, snow was one of the things she appreciated the most about Fujita, but she had never seen a sight like this before. This was nature's art at its finest.

"Now students, hands out students please," Leonna said, placing her palm up as if to guide the students. "The feather that lands in your hand is the one that nature had intended for you. You and only you were meant to retrieve this feather. This is destiny's first way to connect you to nature."

S'rae and the students stuck their palms out as hundreds of crystal white feathers drifted through the air, landing all around them, on their heads, shoulders, and feet.

"I caught one! I really caught one!" a girl said as the feather glowed in her hand before doubling its size.

"How wonderful!" Leonna clapped. "One down, only a few dozen to go!"

As minutes passed, student after student jumped around with excitement, celebrating their very own quill. And although she was one of the last to catch one, a feather had finally made its way down onto S'rae's hand. It felt as soft as a feather should, except when it resonated, she felt a burning sensation in her palm.

"*Nazif!*" Leonna said as she waved her staff around. At once the students were stuck in a twister of white feathers that circled its way up to the ceiling, re-attaching themselves to the birds that were now back on the trees, taking the shape of leaves. "Congratulations! The first step is now complete! Now, I ask you all to take out the paper I sent you and observe the next location on the map."

When S'rae unrolled her piece of paper, she saw an 'X' that showed her at Mu'tida Temple, and then she followed a line that went so far east that it stretched to the other side of the paper. She flipped the paper around and the line trailed so far that she once again had to flip the page. Then finally, the stream of sand had zipped across miles of GroundStone to finally land on a spot called Al'jism Plateau.

"I will see you all there in a minute."

"Wait!" Almost all the students said in unison.

Then a girl almost a foot shorter than S'rae spoke up. "That's like an hour away, how do expect us to get there in a minute?"

"I don't expect you to get there in a minute, I said I will see you in a minute, but I expect you to get there much sooner than that."

The students all looked around, as if hoping someone had an answer.

"This is your first school lesson that we teach at GroundStone, even before you become an official student, it is called the Sandsportation Spell. Cool name, huh? I came up with it myself. Well, I suppose with the help of Di'Tukia, of course. *Very* little help, but don't tell her I said anything." Leonna dug her staff into the sand at her feet and drew a relic. "You see, on your map, right next to the name of the building, there is a symbol. Each building has one. That is to let you know which design to draw into the ground before you cast your Sandsportation Spell. If everything works out perfectly, you will be sucked into the ground and just a few seconds later, you will appear at the front of the building. You must be *very* careful, though! The symbol must be as accurate as possible, so it is important to not be nervous and have a clear mind, or you may find yourself accidentally in the Sol stables, covered in poop. Don't ask me how I know... it was a long night, okay!"

The students stared at one another blankly.

"Okay, since you all do not have your own staff yet, you must use your quill to draw the relic. See the symbol on the paper? Perfect. Yes, draw it just like you see it! Great job! Good. Good. Excellent. Umm... absolutely terrible. Do you want to have a bad time? Because that's how you have a bad time." Leonna pointed at a sloppy relic drawn into ground, as if done so by a very shaky hand. "Everyone, look at him, this is exactly what you shouldn't do. Do you see how the line curved instead of straightened out? Those are the little details that will be the difference between making it to class on time and getting dry humped by a swarm of mating monkeys. Believe me, it's not fun!" S'rae noticed the poor boy curl up as he fixed his relic. "Do it like this. Yes! Okay, much better! Nice improvement! Okay, everyone looks ready! Now that your relic is drawn, whisper *"almua'salat"* and see you all in a minute!"

S'rae watched Professor Leonna get sucked into the ground, and a few seconds later, she was no more, just a swirling patch of sand that came to a stop.

S'rae whispered the words and felt a vice grip clamp around her ankles, pulling her into the ground. It felt weird, like dry water engulfed her body. She closed her eyes just as the ground reached her head and after feeling a whirling sensation that made her want to throw up, she opened her eyes and was atop a plateau that gave her the most beautiful view of the GroundStone region. She saw the tall golden walls that surrounded them like a valley, but also noticed how peaceful the center of GroundStone looked from faraway. The pyramids and temples and towers and trees carried an interesting juxtaposition, the idea of being a city surrounded by nature... or better yet, nature engulfed in a city.

"Glad to see you all made it... at least I think we all made it." She surveyed the area, pointing her finger at students and mouthing words to herself. "Great, we're all here, that's a first!"

S'rae looked over and noticed the tiny girl shaking. Was she cold? Scared? Nervous? S'rae remembered what it was like when she first attended Fujita and didn't know anyone... she remembered how good it felt to have someone introduce themselves to her and ease the nerves of being a new student with no friends. That person had a name... it was Fujak. S'rae couldn't help but think what she may had said that was the reason their friendship was broken. A part of her was mad at herself for ruining a great friendship; maybe her five years at Fujita wouldn't have been so miserable, but then again, if she didn't go through that, where would she be right now? *I suppose everything does happen for a reason.*

"Hmm... where is she," Leonna asked, apparently talking to herself. "She's never late, she should be here any second now." And just as Leonna said that, a cloaked figure appeared next to her out of thin air... as if it were a ghost.

"Sorry for the delay." A cheerful voice was heard from the figure. Much more cheerful than S'rae had assumed. "My name is Professor Di'Tukia, nice to meet all of you, I am the Professor of Transportation Spells... and the creator of..." She glanced over at Leonna. "—the Sandsportation Spell."

"Oh don't go and bring that up already! We went over this already, I thought of it and you helped make it, I get credit for it!"

"As long as I'm alive you will never get credit for it!"

"Well, I think I have an idea how to solve this issue then," Leonna said.

The two ladies stared at one another for a few long moments, until finally someone said something. "Tea tonight at my place?" Di'Tukia said, giving Leonna a hug.

"Of course, I'll bring Hazelnut to keep Samaniel company!"

"Oh, great! Looking forward to it!" Di'Tukia said. "Anyways, my what a lovely class we have here! As many of you will know, this is the second part of the ceremony: the Body. This is what tethers you to not just to GroundStone but also to the world of Gaia itself. However, unlike the Mind part, you have three choices here: Sand, Ground, or Stone."

"Which one you think you'll get?" A boy whispered to S'rae. "I'm from the Ramal Sand Tribes, so I hope I get sand!"

"Er... " S'rae said, "I actually have no idea what I'll get, I honestly didn't even know there were options."

"You didn't know there were options? What thc? You know... for being such an old lady, you really don't know a lot about this Earth stuff."

"Old lady?" S'rae wanted to turn this little twerp into a balloon and watch him soar away, but she held her composure. Tried to, at least. "*Hah.* Surely you really don't think I'm that old, do you? Right?"

"Well, you're not *old* old. You're probably just a little older than my grandma, do you need a cane, too?"

Yupp, this little punk will get what he deserves. Oh great... S'rae picking fights with little kids, what a great legacy to leave as a destined one. What'd the Great S'rae do? Oh, she picked fights with kids who hadn't even hit puberty yet, you know, serious, life-saving stuff. There is Gabrael, the King of Gods. Raaz'a, the Guardian of Fire. Retro'ku, the Prince of Gods. Then there is the Great S'rae, the Fighter of Babies. Classy.

And while S'rae thought of her new arch nemesis being a ten-year-old boy who was half the size of her, there was a great scraping of stone and the next moment, S'rae found herself being lifted higher into the air. The plateau began to levitate. She had a terrible feeling about this trial.

"So," Professor Di'Tukia spoke, "although you have options, you do not actually get to choose which route to take, it chooses you. And it is something that we like to call the Trust Fall."

The twerp grinned at S'rae. Probably because he had noticed how nervous and sweaty she became at the thought of the name. What exactly did she mean by trust *fall*?

"So, do we have any volunteers who wish to go first?" Di'Tukia asked.

"Ow!" S'rae lifted her hands to her mouth as something almost crushed her toes. When she looked down, she saw a rock near her feet. She then looked to the side and saw the twerp chuckling. *Oh... I can't wait to—*

"Thank you for volunteering, S'rae is it?" Professor Leonna said. "Starting off both challenges, you're already off to a great start here, I see! Usually no one wants to volunteer for this, especially once they see what happens, but you're very brave! Foolish, but brave!"

Oh great! S'rae was brought to the center of the plateau where the students and both professors circled around her. Professor Di'Tukia had clamped S'rae's feet down to the ground using some type of stone contraption, so tight she couldn't even wiggle her toes.

"I assure you this is perfectly safe," Di'Tukia said. "All you must do is trust that you will fall exactly where you are destined to. Whichever path you are meant to take: Sand, Ground, or Stone, it will choose you. Have faith and faith will have you."

There was silence. S'rae stared all around her, feeling like they were watching her at her deathbed. The looks on their faces said it all, they felt bad for her, as if they knew more than she did about what to expect. She took a deep breath as Di'Tukia muttered a few words before taking several steps backward.

It was beginning… S'rae felt it. But what was it that she felt exactly? *OH! Why are the students upside down?* Why was there pressure on her toes digging into the stone clamps? And why was there blood rushing to her head, with her hair on end? The world had flipped upside down and she was staring down at an endless sky with the deep abyss of space waiting for her.

This is not happening right now! The only thing she was thankful for right now was that her dress was skin-tight, not flowing over her head. S'rae had one thought about falling deep into space and she couldn't help but scream. But before the scream could escape her mouth, the clamps released her feet and she fell toward the bottomless sky. It was a terrible free-falling feeling that seemed as if it would last forever until she made it into space and died of strangulation. Is this how her life would end? She fell deeper through the sky. She clutched her chest and screamed at the top of her lungs, horrified. It felt as if the plateau had become the ceiling and she was falling farther and farther away from it. This was it… she was about to break the plane and fall off the planet completely. She saw stars closer than she had ever seen them before. The air was thin, too thin, so thin she struggled to manipulate it to help her out. And just as she felt herself breaking the planet's atmosphere, ready to enter space, gravity had shifted. Instead of falling into outer space, she was now falling back down to Gaia.

This made her scream louder. She screamed as she picked up speed, shooting through the sky like an arrow. From here, she saw Gaia like she never thought possible, it looked so small. She saw Fujita to the north, the great wall wrapping around its borders. She saw the desert to the east of GroundStone. In the center, between Fujita and GroundStone, surrounded by a mass of water, she saw thick clouds that protected the Shrine of Elements from outside eyes. That was essentially the capital of Gaia, where the Gods and Elementials would convene. She saw Sereni far to the West and was shocked to see that the series of islands that made up their district were perfectly symmetrical and looked like a masterpiece designed by the Divine himself. She saw beyond the central continent to the regions of the Kingdoms not governed by the Shrine of Elements and its rules. And when she turned to the infinite body of water that was to the west of the continent, all she saw was… nothing… just a layer of misty white, as if nothing existed over there. But how was that possible? She then remembered Gabrael saying something about the Forgotten Continent. Could that be it? Hidden from all? Forgotten?

She then stopped focusing on the beauty and mystery of Gaia and instead thought about how her death was moments away. What could she do? What was she supposed to trust? What was supposed to happen? How could anything survive a fall at this speed. Even if something were to save her, the impact alone would kill her. But what scared S'rae the most was that what was waiting for her at the plateau was not a solid surface, it was even worse. There was just a black hole that looked like an endless abyss. Was that where she was supposed to fall through? She didn't know, but she had to trust her instincts, maybe that was why it was given the name Trust Fall?

As she fell into the hole, vines burst out from the walls as though trying to catch her, but they didn't, she still ripped through them, with no sign of slowing down. The deeper into the hole she got, the bigger the vines were, until they became leaves four times the size of her. They hit her skin like soft pillows. Thud. Thud. Thud. Each leaf she hit felt more comfortable until she finally landed on a bed of leaves that felt like feathers on her back.

She let out a sigh of relief. *I made it. I'm alive!*

And when she rolled off the bed onto the solid ground, she splashed right through the stone and stumbled forward, regaining her balance. Her eyes widened. But how? She was back atop the plateau with the students clapping and cheering and running toward her to hug her. Even the little twerp boy was excited to see her. Maybe he wasn't so bad after all. And when S'rae looked down, she noticed a vine wrapped around her brown robes. Wait... brown robes? What happened to her skin tight dress that Retro'ku was supposed to see her in? Where'd it go?

"Congratulations, S'rae," Di'Tukia said, "you have passed the next trial. This is your body. These are your clothes. And your rope is a vine, meaning you are of the Ground family. On your vine is a seed. This seed, when planted in your student village, will grow into your tree. And inside your tree is where you will live. This is the home that nature has designed for you. In time, your tree will grow big and wide and join the network in the sky, connecting your tree house with theirs. Patience! It will happen soon enough! Like a seed, you must nurture it first and it will grow."

Professor Di'Tukia shook S'rae's hand one last time, and Leonna led her to the outskirts of the plateau where she watched dozens of students partake in the Trust Fall. It looked so odd from this perspective, as if they had jumped on the world's best trampoline that launched them into space, only for them to fall down into a hole, and stumble out of thin air; some would bounce into stone that molded and bent like a trampoline; and others would *splat* into sand that absorbed them into the ground, as if they had landed into a puddle. After nearly an hour later, all the students had survived.

S'rae noticed that the twerp was sad, his eyes were welled up and no longer had that fiery energy to him. Although S'rae had put him on her arch nemesis list, she couldn't help but feel sorry for a kid who was already sad on his first day, a day that was supposed to be his best day ever.

"What's wrong?" S'rae said to him.

"N-n-nothing." He sniffled and wiped the snot on his brown robes.

S'rae looked down and noticed that he wore the same belt that she had, a green vine, not the one that swirled with sand, like the one he was expecting. "It's okay that you got into ground... it was meant to be for a reason."

"But... but... I really wanted to tell my dad that I did it... that I didn't let him down... that I'm not a failure."

"He won't think you're a failure because the planet chose a different path for you. Think about it like this... you were great for Sand, but you're perfect for Ground. I can already imagine all the great things you'd do here at this school, I can already see you becoming a top student!"

"Really?" His eyes lit up at those words.

"Yes, really! Imagine how proud your dad will be once you show him you've made it to the top of the list, which will definitely happen! I see it in you! I really do!" She was being genuinely honest at this point, the fact that it hit him this hard means he had passion. And passion and work ethic are two of the intangibles that all the most successful people she knew had. It was why she admired Fujak so much, even when she hated him. *Fujak... he's so going to hate me.* A part of her realized that she saw Fujak in this twerp, which was how she knew he'd become great. "What's your name?"

"You can call me Yash."

"Well, Yash, you know... you aren't so bad for a little twerp."

"And you aren't so bad for the oldest grandma at GroundStone," he chuckled. His warm smile that appeared made S'rae smile.

S'rae couldn't help but laugh. "I guess I deserved that."

"Well! Looks like everyone is finished!" Professor Di'Tukia

said. "My time with you all is done for now. I hope you enjoy the rest of the ceremony with Leonna. And maybe I will see some of you in my class! Sandsportations with Di'Tukia, look it up! Take care."

And just like that, she walked into an invisible door in thin air and didn't come out the other side, she was somewhere else completely, and the inquisitive mind of S'rae went wild with a million questions, officially wanting to know more. *I'm definitely taking a class with her!*

"Students! Congratulations! Two down and only one more to go!" Professor Leonna said. "Mind, Body, and now... the Soul! I am sure some of you may know exactly what this next part will entail... since some of you may already have one."

S'rae's eyes lit up. This was the part she had been waiting for for years. This was the moment when she'd finally have her own Sol. She did an awkward, excited shuffle dance in place and did not care how pathetic she looked, this was her moment!

5

S'RAE AND THE OTHER FUTURE GROUNDSTONE STU-
DENTS rode down from the plateau on the backs of flying
beasts. S'rae was still trying to wrap her head around how some
of these animals were flying without wings; panthers and lions and
gazelles were galloping and sprinting across the sky as if they were
on solid ground. Much like what she had done at Harahn'de, when
she changed the principles of air to allow her to swim toward the
sky, maybe these animals had found a way to alter air to become
solid like solid earth? Yet another thing that S'rae now wanted to
figure out.

She held on tighter to the mane of her lion as she jostled about
when they landed. She pet its mane once more, feeling its rough fur
through the cracks of fingers, before he ran and dove through the
soil, as if it was a pond of water. A part of her wished that maybe
he would have been her Sol, but she brushed that idea away. She
knew her Sol was waiting for her. And this was the chance for them
to finally meet. Her eyes watered just thinking about connecting to
her animal. *My own Sol! I can't wait to finally meet you!*

S'rae heard commotion and saw Leonna fall off of her gorgeous
winged horse, rolling down its wing. Unlike the tumbling Leonna,

this animal was graceful and elegant and glowed a bright white light that looked like it was designed to be the Sol of the Divine One.

"Always a fun time!" Leonna said, twisting to her feet and brushing the dirt off her clothes. "Very well, do we have everyone? Great! Stay close, for now we must enter the underground tunnels of GroundStone! This is my *favorite* part of the tour."

As the students huddled up together, the ground rumbled and separated into a large circle. Slowly they descended into the ground as if it were an elevator. "Sorry about how brown and grey everything looked up there," Leonna said as she closed her eyes and placed her palms together, a soft hum resonating from her chest. "Ever since the droughts, and our water restriction, GroundStone just isn't as green as it once was."

"I love how it looks here," S'rae said, appreciating the nature that surrounded her.

"Oh, you love it, do you?" Leonna smiled. "Well, you haven't seen nothing yet! It was once truly the most beautiful sight ever, outside of the Valley of Gaia, of course! Because nothing can match that beauty!"

S'rae felt the muscles in her face droop. She thought about the disaster that she had seen at the Valley of Gaia. It was already a deserted wasteland when she had first arrived, contrary to the lush valley she expected, but now... now it was a metallic graveyard, filled with hundreds of destroyed Mechas. S'rae kept her mouth shut, she knew Gabrael didn't want her to talk about her time there, but she also didn't want anyone else to have a ruined fantasy of how the Valley was supposed to look.

S'rae then thought about Eve. The Valley was once her home... but she left... why? She thought about how she had found the Eye of Eve inside of a stone in the ground and how that was the clue that led them here... to GroundStone. And how Gabrael believed with all certainty that Eve was here, but where could she be?

"The Valley was home to Eve and Gabrael," S'rae said, "*of course* it'd be beautiful!"

S'rae heard a wave of gasps.

The platform stopped at once. S'rae stumbled and braced herself, grabbing on to the closest boy near her.

"Do *not*... mention... that man's name *ever* again," Leonna said, a darkness in her tone that S'rae was not expecting. "We do *not* speak of people like him here. They do not deserve our breath."

S'rae knew it'd be dumb to ask, but she had to, if there was one thing she had learned about Gabrael it was that he was not nearly as bad as the rumors claimed he'd be. "Why do you think he's bad?"

"Why do I *think* he's bad?" Leonna's mouth barely moved. "I do not *think* he's bad. I know he is. If you knew what I *know*... you'd know. But I do not wish to tell you what I *know*... for I do not wish for you to have trouble sleeping, which is why we *do not* talk about such people here. I am appalled they even let him inside our walls. There are some wounds that time should not be allowed to heal." Leonna shook her head, removing the grimace, then smiled as they descended once more.

The ground rattled as their platform landed. The space was so big and dark that S'rae didn't know if it had an end. The stone walls had ancient relics carved into them, the ceiling was too high to make out, and the only source of light were from the fireflies scattered about, looking like they were traveling through a galaxy.

A plump, black-haired man in brown and green robes stood there. He had a very confused face and S'rae's first thought was that he was drunk.

"Escort us to the houses then the Valley of Dreams, please, Sir Coars," Leonna said.

"Alrigh' everybody, gather roun' gather roun' this is just like every other day," Coars said. "Well, 'cept this is the first day before your last day of becomin' a first year, for your first day. Or somethin' like that. Sounds 'bout righ'!" He clapped and dozens of stone boulders appeared from the ground, forming a long, connecting line. "Righ' this way, kids."

Before S'rae sat down, she couldn't help but notice that this thing looked like a giant snake made of rocks.

"Don't you worry now, little girl," Coars said. "He don't bite!"

S'rae heard a grumble, coming from the dark tunnel a few feet ahead of her.

"Oh shush, you! Already complainin' already and you haven't even done nothin' yet! You miserable little—"

"Okay," Leonna said, "everyone is strapped in and ready to go."

"Ready are we?" Coars said. "Great, let's get this goin', I'm missin' out on the parties in the aboves, you know how much I love the Ka'hul Tribe's drinks, Leonna!" Coars licked his lips and clapped his hands, and they were off.

They slithered their way through miles of tunnels.

"How long is this?" the tiny girl asked, who was sitting inside the boulder just ahead of S'rae's. Each student had their own one, that was how enormous this *thing* was.

"Oh, this little guy is just a baby, too! Aren't you?" Coars said, but once another grumble was heard ahead, he replied with: "Oh *blah blah blah*! Get your ego in check, little one, you're just a little baby compared to the real Nyxio!"

"Err…" the girl said. "I meant how long is this trip, the tunnel looks infinite."

"Oh, right, I knew that's what you meant. Well, there are hundreds, maybe thousands o' miles o' tunnels under GroundStone, so many tunnels that not even I know all of 'em, and I practically live in 'em. I could spend the rest of my miserable life travelin' down every dang ol' tunnel an' I'd never be able to explore 'em all. Some are new. Some are old. Some are seen. But some… some are hidden. And those… now those are where the real treasures lie!"

The grin showed his crooked teeth and made S'rae wonder just what he had seen in some of these hidden tunnels; but even more curious, how did he find things that were hidden?

They sped through a section of tiled stone floors, much different than the raw tunnels they had been in earlier. S'rae could hear the drone of hundreds of voices up ahead—they finally made it back—but Leonna stood up and pointed to the right.

"Everyone, look there! In a few moments you will see older students training for whatever it is they like training for these days. You have Rock Bowl, or something like that, there is Wave Racing, Speed Skating, and of course, GroundStone's very own favorite: Boulder Dash!"

"Oh… em… dee!" S'rae heard the tiny girl's voice echo off the walls. "I can't wait to play Boulder Dash!"

"Hah!" a boy said. "You're a girl, you won't really play, you'll be just stuck healing the ones who can actually play."

S'rae could see how that one comment drained the life out of her. S'rae leaned into the girl's boulder and whispered: "What's Boulder Dash anyways?"

"What's Boulder Dash?" she was taken aback, appearing almost disgusted. "What's Boulder Dash? Umm… only the greatest sport ever? What's air? What's a school? I know this is GroundStone and all, but have you literally been living under a rock?"

"Jeez, just a simple question," S'rae said.

"A disrespectful one! I don't even want to explain it. Look!" she said, pointing at an open underground arena, where robed students were seen rolling boulders that doubled, tripled, and quadrupled in size before smashing into a pillar. Some pillars fell, others did not. By the way some clapped and cheered and others pouted and stomped, she could tell that knocking down the large pillar was the objective. There were other students who zipped through the open space, leaving behind a trail of sand as they skated across the ground. Then there were waves erecting from the ground as students ran on top of them. "Those kids are runners! That's what I want to be when I make the team!"

"Are they playing Boulder Dash?" S'rae asked, pointing at the ones who ran on top of the waves of dirt and gravel and sand.

"No, they're just practicing for it! But look at how good they are! Do you see the arch of that one wave! You know how tough that is to do? *Whoa*! Would you look at that? *Look*! You need at least a strong, angled kick start on your good foot to get that type of air! So amazing!"

"Sounds like you know a lot about this," S'rae said.

"I love watching and studying the games, my brothers would play it all the time."

"Do you ever play?"

"Not anymore," the girl said, putting her head down once again.

"Why?"

"Because." She looked at the boy who had made that comment. "All they wanted me to do was heal. They wouldn't let me run."

"Hah!" the boy laughed. "Told you! Girls are healers, let the boys *actually* play!"

"You know," S'rae said, "my village told me the same thing about our games. Do you know what I did?"

"What?" the boy said.

"I beat them so badly that they never wanted to play again. And they never did."

The boy's eyes widened as he went silent and sat back down.

The girl smiled.

"What's your name?" S'rae asked.

"Emi."

"That's a beautiful name. Well mine is S'rae. And here's a lesson that I learned from a friend: boy's opinions *never* matter! If you wanted to be a runner, just do it. I have faith in you."

S'rae appreciated the crinkle in her smiling eyes, and for some reason, it briefly reminded her of Elu, the way Destrou would describe her. She quickly shoved the thought away, it would only anger her, thinking about how Vayp had taken the Book of Eve from them. And she refused to let Vayp ruin this important day.

"Wow!" Emi gasped. "What's that?" She pointed at a shiny door that must've been about twelve feet high. It was golden with the most beautiful intricate carvings S'rae had ever seen.

She only had one guess as to what was behind that door. She had seen a similar one at Fujita and another at Harahn'de, right before Retro'ku went in to retrieve the fiery elemental orb. This door was the reason she was becoming a GroundStone student, the reason she would train and practice and prepare herself for the greatest challenge of her life… because that door was no doubt the Chamber of Eve, it awaited her when she proved to Gabrael that she was ready.

As they passed the door, a blinding light came over them and S'rae saw that they were all now outside, staring at hundreds of sprawling trees to the left, and to the right, there were just as many enormous mounds of dirt that looked more like magnified anthills.

"Thank you," Leonna said, shaking Coars hands. "I hope you enjoy all your beverages! Looking forward to seeing you at Smitty's before the arena match!"

"You betcha!" Coars smiled. "I'll leave some extra for you, don't you worry!" He hopped onto the hundred foot long rock snake that slithered back into the tunnel.

"So here we are! To the left, if you received Ground, you will plant your seed at the Forest of Life. To the right, if you received Sand, your new mound awaits you in the Range of Might. And, of course, if you received Stone, your home is underground in the mines: the Chasm of Guardians. Although each House is separate, they all connect underground, like where you saw the students training." Leonna then pointed to the trees. "Your houses will eventually grow above, and your branches will link you to your own community, but your roots will keep you connected to the other students. It will provide you access to the student rooms and tunnels below. And the same for you." Leonna pointed at the mounds. "Much like an anthill, you will find that your community is intricate and connected, but the deeper you go, you will also find yourself with access to the common rooms below." She now pointed to the ground. "And the mighty protectors of Stone, it is because of you the tunnels exist and it is because of you the students will always feel most safe. They say that if war were to ever happen, underground is the safest place of all. I look forward to seeing the great things that each one of you are capable of."

After S'rae and the other students planted their seed, created their mound, and dug their hole, they walked through the Forest of Life into an open valley that spanned as far as S'rae could see.

"This, students… is the Valley of Dreams," Leonna said. "It is where your dreams will come true, for which the name became possible. It is every Earthies dream to find *the one*. This is where I found my precious little Hazelnut, I will never forget the moment our eyes met." S'rae noticed Leonna get teary-eyed just thinking about it. "*Aww*… my little cutey, Nutmeg."

"I too remember that day quite vividly." S'rae heard a voice from behind. When she turned around, she saw a beautiful brunette girl with sapphire blue eyes, dressed in brown robes with vines embroidered into the fabric. She saw a girl who couldn't possibly have remembered *that* day quite vividly, for she looked much younger than Leonna, and carried a youthful glow that couldn't have been much more than that of a twenty year old.

"Oh!" Leonna gasped, startled. "Olivia, you are always known to make quite an entrance, I couldn't even sense your arrival, and I was actually trying this time."

"I guess it's a gift I picked up over the years." Olivia smiled.

S'rae noticed a cloaked person to her side in a dark robe with fur under its hood and down its collar; he stood there barely moving and not saying a word. She couldn't see any of his features, but for some reason, she felt something twist in her stomach as if… as if…

wait, was that the same cloaked person who was staring at her before? S'rae had the deepest curiosity to know who this person was now. And she definitely wanted to know why his presence made her feel most uncomfortable, tying her insides into a knot. Something wasn't right about him but she couldn't put her finger on it, she could only feel it. *Always go with your gut instincts now, S'rae. Don't be so naive anymore.*

Before she could think much about her discomfort, Olivia pushed her arms to the sides of her body and took a deep breath. "Your Sol awaits each one of you," Professor Olivia said. "I have seen many Sols pass through these walls, and I can tell almost instantly which person they belong to. It is not because a person has a long neck that they would get a giraffe, for a Sol's compatibility transcends pass the physical. The connection dives into the realm of the spiritual.

"Whether you believe in an afterlife or not, we are all connected to nature, and we are all a part of this Circle of Life. We at GroundStone do not simply treat nature as one of us just because it is the good thing to do, we do so because nature one day could very well be one of us. When you die, you become a part of Gaia's lifeforce. And Gaia can then choose how to use you once more. Maybe you are reborn as a bug... or a lion. And if you were reborn as a lion, you could find yourself searching endlessly for a human that you once had a connection to in a past life. Maybe your Sol was a lover, maybe a friend, maybe a mother, or a brother. We do not know the *why* a Sol was destined to connect with you, we only know the *when*. And that is why you are all here with us today. In a few moments this valley will be filled with hundreds of animals. Some who have traveled a mile or two to get here... while others have traveled the world. Your Sol may have traveled farther than you could ever imagine, simply because something in its heart told it that it will find you here and now... and that your lives will be complete because of it.

"It came here for *you*! And this is why they say the connection one has with its Sol is the greatest one life could ever create. It is a beautiful tradition that Earthies still cling on to. It is our close link to nature and Gaia that helps us keep this ritual alive... and it will live on through you. With no further more to say... you have awakened your Mind... you have been given your Body... it is now time... to embrace your Soul."

The cloaked boy walked up to Olivia. "The rain looks like it may be coming in sooner than expected, I hope we have time for everyone."

"We will make time," Olivia said, "this is their moment."

She then pulled an instrument from her robe. It was a crystalline flute of some sort, maybe an ocarina, that shimmered as she placed it to her lips.

Who would have thought that the most beautiful, crisp tunes could come from such a small instrument. The sounds were so hypnotically pure that the high notes sent chills through S'rae's body. She noticed they had the same affect on others, judging by the way they'd shiver. The song played throughout the entire area, so loud that it seemed to be echoing off of nothing at all.

And then after a few moments, the drums came. Or were they drums? There was a rhythmic pounding that made the ground shake.

Gasps were heard. And when S'rae searched to find out why, she released a gasp of her own.

Off in the distance, appearing as a line of silhouettes on the horizon, were hundreds of dots making their way toward the students.

As they came closer, S'rae saw that some were as tall as a giraffe while others were as small as a rodent. These were... these were... *their* Sols.

S'rae's eyes began to water and her sniffles were interrupted by the dozen other ones all around. This truly was an emotional experience. It hadn't even started yet but S'rae saw tears streaming down the students' faces. If she could see her own, she'd know her face would look no different.

It was actually happening… one of those animals… one of them… was going to be her Sol. She was so happy that she didn't even care to think about the type of animal, she would take anything.

The rolling thunder of the stomps stopped at once. About a hundred yards in front of the line of students, there was a line of the most beautiful animals S'rae had ever seen. There were blue panthers, a zebra with red stripes, snakes, elephants, and on top of their tusks were monkeys, chimps and various species of birds, some black, some more colorful than a rainbow.

If S'rae could read their minds, she had a feeling that the animals were just as nervous as the students were, for there were way more animals than there were students, which meant some of these animals would be left without an owner. That thought alone made an extra tear drop from S'rae's eyes.

S'rae saw the cloaked boy say something to Olivia, so she quickly twirled her fingers around to channel the soundwaves.

"I do not like this, Olivia," the boy said, his voice hoarse. "There are more animals than usual. A lot more."

"Indeed," Olivia said. "And what do you think of this?"

"I… I think… that something may be terribly wrong."

"And you think this why? Did they say something?"

"No… but I do not think they came here to join us, I think they came because they were running away from something. Something must be going on beyond these walls for this many animals to relocate from their homes."

"Maybe they no longer have homes."

"That is what I'm afraid of."

Olivia then turned to the students. S'rae quickly looked away as if not wanting to give the slightest idea that she had eavesdropped on their conversation. "Children." Olivia's voice carried the grace and power of a God. "Your Sol… awaits you." She played one last tune on her ocarina before placing it back into her robe.

And then… it happened. The first animal made its move. S'rae felt her body tense up as a wave of gasps breezed by.

It was an adorable, little lemur, eyes wide and *very* cute, and its ears were almost the size of its body. He crawled through the open field, and it was almost instantaneous—the students knew exactly who this Sol was meant for, because, though the lemur was fifty feet away, one of the girls had dropped to her knees and cried.

It walked up to her, placing its hand underneath her chin and lifted her head up. S'rae could have sworn that she had seen fireworks erupt behind her eyes. They widened with an excitement that she had never seen before. They gazed into one another's eyes for what felt like a minute before it leapt into her arms.

"Congratulations," Olivia said, smiling wide. "We have ourselves our first Sol!"

All students clapped and cheered for her, and she still couldn't contain her excitement, crying into her arms as she held her Sol. It was *her* Sol! And now this made S'rae even more anxious to see which one would be hers.

The ceremony carried on for a few more minutes; a panther, a lioness, a winged horse, an elephant rhino, and even an iguana had made its way to their owner. The one that shocked S'rae the most was the tiny insect that buzzed through the sky, landing on a girl's shoulder. She was the smallest girl of the bunch and she cried once she realized the insect was her Sol. But these tears didn't seem of joy, she had seemed most disappointed.

"Why… why did I have to get this small bug?" she cried. "I know I'm small, I don't need to be reminded of it!"

Olivia approached her. "You must understand… that the connection between Sol and owner does indeed transcend beyond the physical. The connection you share is deeper than that. Much like yourself, your Sol thinks she is tiny and inadequate compared to the others, but what neither of you know yet… is who you will grow into. For this bug… it will go through many, many transformations, much like yourself. And by the end, she will know that who she is now did not define who she will grow to become. And that is something greater than you could ever imagine."

S'rae smiled at Olivia. The way her words rolled off her tongue, the way the tiny girl was now beaming wide at her bug, and the way Olivia walked away with her head high, S'rae saw someone who was indeed much more powerful than what meets the eye. She knew there was more to Olivia than being just the Sol Professor, for the way she carried herself made S'rae believe that Olivia was even more important than Gabrael himself, but she couldn't put her finger on the why. *Who… are you?* She gazed at Olivia with amazement.

And as the minutes went by, more and more students had found their Sols, S'rae grew even more excited, knowing that hers will be coming up any second now. She congratulated Yash on his shimmering black raven; Emi had received a beautiful black panther; one student, named Plumita, had a gorgeous wolf who had black and white fur leap onto her and smother her; but even more interesting than the insect and a rainbow-colored gorilla, was a snake that slithered its way into the arms of a student named Madison.

S'rae found it most interesting because she had imagined herself running away very fast, even if it was her Sol, but Madison had shown no such fear, only love, lots of it. Speaking of her Sol… S'rae looked around and saw that the rain was coming, and she had hoped that her Sol would come before they were caught in a downpour.

A few more Sols had found their owners, and S'rae looked around once more as the rain began to pour down. She felt a tear roll down her face, thankful that it blended in with the rain… because as she surveyed the open valley, she realized that… she was the only one remaining.

S'rae held a tight grip onto her brown robe to stop her legs from shaking, but still they trembled. She tried her best not to look at the students, who were staring at her, she didn't want them to see the fear in her eyes. Was it fear? Or was it something far worse.

The rain started to pour harder. Her heart stopped as she noticed one of the animals jump off the tusk of an elephant. She wiped her teary eyes, excited that it had finally happened. She couldn't explain the excitement that pulsed through her body... until... the animal walked away from her, as if to seek shelter from the rain. And as it walked away, the other animals soon followed. Within moments, S'rae was found alone in an empty field, feeling even more empty inside.

The rain poured harder.

Her legs were shaking and she tried her hardest not to burst out and sob, but it was tough... oh it was so tough.

Finally, she felt a hand touch her shoulder. It belonged to Olivia. "I'm sorry... but we must go... and finish the ceremony now."

"No..." S'rae felt tears pour from her eyes. "Please... I know... I kno-know he's c-coming. Maybe he's just... maybe he's just... just lost." She hiccuped as the occasional sob made it difficult to speak. "Please, I beg you... just give him a few more minutes... I know he'll come. I just know it."

Olivia's eyes drooped as she looked into S'rae's. "You're right... maybe." Her lip flinched as if it was impossible for her to smile while seeing S'rae like this.

So wait they did.

One minute passed.

Two.

Then ten.

And S'rae remained still in the downpour... all alone. Then she felt Olivia's hand on her shoulder once more. "I'm sorry."

And it all happened too quickly. S'rae's body crashed to the ground as a puddle splashed into her face. She sobbed uncontrollably, slamming her fists into the ground. "WHY! WHY ME!?" Her tears poured harder than the rain. "WHY DON'T THEY WANT ME!? WHY! WHAT'S WRONG WITH ME? PLEASE DIVINE! I WANT TO KNOW! WHY DO YOU HATE ME?"

Aside from the severe pitter-patter of rain, nothing else was heard. The students remained silent and still as S'rae curled into a ball, never wanting to be seen again.

"I am most sorry," Olivia said. "I can only imagine the pain you feel right now."

"You can't imagine this pain!" S'rae said, feeling like her heart and world was crushed by the hand of a Divine. "NO ONE CAN!" She wanted to stop crying, she truly did, but the more she thought about stopping, the more it hurt when she thought about the *why*. The why she was crying in the first place. "Why don't they love me?"

Olivia placed her hand on S'rae's back. "So, this has happened before?"

S'rae didn't know how to respond, she didn't want Olivia to know how pathetic she was, but now everyone did, so what was there to hide? "Like a million times… and it hurts more after each one."

"Hmm…" Olivia said, standing up with her fingers to her chin as if in deep thought. "I think I may have an answer."

S'rae froze and her eyes widened.

"I think… I may know why."

S'rae said nothing, she only twisted her muddy face toward the sky to make eye contact with Olivia.

"I think… the reason you haven't found your Sol yet… may be because your Sol is waiting for you."

"Waiting… for *me*?"

"You cannot tell *anyone* about this." Olivia went onto her hands and knees to speak directly to S'rae. "Sols are a connection of the spiritual. You are a very special case. Which leads me to believe that your Sol may be just as special."

Still, S'rae was too numb to say a word, she only listened.

"I want you to meet me at my temple, I will put the marker on your map. Meet me… but do not tell *anyone* that you're coming to see me."

"Why?" S'rae finally had the strength to say a word.

"Because…" Olivia said, her voice losing its cheer and turned most serious, "even the rumor of *this* animal being your Sol… could get you killed."

6

S'RAE WALKED WITH HER HEAD DOWN toward the center of GroundStone, looking away whenever there was a kid laughing and playing with their new Sol. But when she accidentally saw a wolf pup leap into a girl's arms, a wave of jealousy chilled her to the bone. Or… was it anger that she felt? One thing that she knew for sure was how there was no more joy at GroundStone. And now a different feeling weighed her down. Guilt. It tore her up from the inside as she thought about the only other person who could relate to the emptiness she felt. She suddenly realized just how terrible and lonely his five years here must had been. Because no matter where she looked, everything was a reminder that they did not belong—couldn't walk two feet without seeing a Sol. She promised herself not to feel bad for *him*. The enemy. The traitor. But still, she had to wipe the tears that had fell without warning. *I know it hurts, a lot, but it's still not an excuse to do what he did! Don't do it! Don't feel bad for him or forgive him! Don't be weak! Don't fall for people's tricks and lies anymore. No… not anymore!*

S'rae finally found the strength to draw herself up proudly… until a force collided into her back, sending her to the ground.

"So… where is he?" An excited Lynn had practically mounted

S'rae. "This is amazing! Like what? A Sol? Sure! Sign me up! So what is he? A dog? A… a… umm… what are those things with a—" She snapped her fingers and rolled her eyes as if trying with all her heart to remember. "—a, oh yeah! Let me guess, a sloth! We *all* know how slow you are to get dressed in the morning! Wait, please don't tell me it's *another* squirrel, it's not, is it? Tell me! Come on! Better be something cool! But *please* not another squirrel, I *know* he's been eating my food!"

S'rae tried to speak, but she felt tears building up before a word came out. Being silent was the only thing that would stop her from crying, so silent she was.

"Come on!" Lynn helped S'rae up. She took one good look at S'rae's mud-smeared face, hair, and clothes, and probably noticed the bags under her eyes from all the crying, and at once, Lynn looked the saddest S'rae had ever seen her. Her hands creeped up to her face to cover her mouth. "Oh no… I'm sorry… I'm so sorry."

"No, it's fine. It's okay, I'm fi—" S'rae stopped, realizing that she was crying yet again. "It's okay. I'll find one soon. I know I will. Th—*hic*—the professor said she'd—*hic*—she'd help me. I'll find one. Don't worry about me. I'm fine."

Lynn's lips twisted and scrunched up, her eyes still looking like she was at a funeral, and maybe that was exactly what she was looking at: the death of a once happy person, S'rae thought. "Right," Lynn said softly. "Okay… well… I hope you do find the one."

"What's going on over here, Adalia?" S'rae's ears perked up at that name, she hadn't heard it since she left the Valley of Gaia. And when S'rae turned around, her jaw dropped. Again, she saw exactly who she did *not* want to see right now. There was Fujak and Retro'ku just standing there, both looking handsome in their own way, but, clinging onto their shoulders, smiling and laughing, were Kaul, a tan boy with long black hair, and two others, who she didn't know the names of. One was a tan girl, who had always grinned at S'rae as if she wanted to eat her, and the other was a pretty boy… or a handsome girl, she didn't know what gender the person was, and never wanted to ask. They were dressed in the same brown robes she last remembered them wearing, because they were the Ground-Stone trio who were sent to the Valley of Gaia with Vayp—the ones who bullied her, the reason why S'rae had narrowed her eyes.

S'rae was already upset about not getting a Sol. Then on top of that, she had tried so hard to get Retro'ku to see her when she was done up in a gorgeous skin-tight dress, but nope, now… of course he *would* finally see her when she was covered in mud with swelled-up eyes. And to make it all worse, these three were here, probably ready to make her time even worse.

"I know, weird huh?" Lynn whispered to S'rae. "I saw them playing around so I decided to re-introduce myself. They're actually very nice and fun to be around! Don't worry, the Fujitas aren't here to spread nasty rumors about you before they meet you!"

"Hi," the girl said, reaching her hand forward to S'rae, "Adalia said a lot of amazing things about you! My name is Carm'illa, but you can call me Milla, like *me yuh*, nice to meet yuh!"

Meet? S'rae was so out of it that she had to remind herself that Raaz'a had given them Archon's blood to make them forget about their time at the Valley of Gaia. "Err… nice to meet you, too," S'rae said blankly, completely caught off guard.

"You know," Milla said, "You're a lot prettier than Adalia said you'd be, just my type." She winked at S'rae, and S'rae noticed how Lynn glared at them, as if upset that someone was finally getting more attention than her.

S'rae felt herself recovering, slowly. She let out the best smile she could and introduced herself to Kaul and the other person, whose name was Brick.

"So…" Lynn said, twisting her hips around. "Who's ready to get this party started? There will be dancing… there will be games… and yes, there *will* be food—yupp, definitely can't forget about the food, and yes more *dancing*!" Lynn shimmied her hips. "So…

who's ready?"

"I am curious to see what your talents are," Retro'ku said to S'rae. And S'rae's eyes went wide as she scanned the area, looking for the best thing to jump and hide behind.

"Umm... m-my t-talents?" S'rae said nervously.

"Yes, Miss S'rae, there is a talent show, they said, and I would love to see what you will do. I will show how I train."

"Of course you *would*." S'rae heard Fujak say under his breath. "Showoff."

"Oh, right, well, I've been putting *a lot* of thought into it," S'rae lied. "You know... there are just so many things I'm good at that, *pfft*... t-that it's just so tough for me to choose, you know? Well, I know... I know what you're thinking... look at this girl covered in mud who can't even get a *Sol*, what could she possibly be good at?" Lynn gave S'rae a sharp, sudden look as if urging her to stop talking. "Well, I'm not as pathetic as everyone may think... be-cause... I—" S'rae tried her hardest to think of something she may be good at. She felt sweat soak into her shoes. "Well... I happen to be good at—*Ahem*! Oh yeah, of course!" S'rae clicked her fingers and waved her head as if to convince everyone that a thought had suddenly appeared... but it did not. "I will... be... doing... you know..."

Tap. Tap. Tap.

OMD! Saved by the squirrel! Thank you, Divine, maybe you don't hate my completely.

"Sorry, squirrel time!" S'rae reached down and grabbed the paper off B'se's back, and read—hoping, praying, wishing for good news:

GROUNDSTONE, SCHOOL OF EARTH AND ROCK, CORE CLASSES

It has been brought to our attention that you have yet to com-plete your orientation ceremony. Though you have successfully completed the Mind and Body, we see that the Soul part remains incomplete, thus you are no longer able to attend our more complicated courses that you had scheduled. Our deepest apologies!

However, we have had many students who needed to wait several months before completing the Soul section, so do not feel alone. When you do complete the ceremony, you will be eligible to attend the courses you selected next year.

Until then, here are our introductory courses you can choose from:

INTRODUCTION TO SOLS: A Guide to Understanding

HISTORY OF THE FOUR KINGDOMS and GROUNDSTONE

EARTH-SHAPING FOR BEGINNERS

and

THE LAWS OF THE LAND

We are looking forward to helping you down the path to find yourself. For you will become the best you that Gaia will ever see.

Best of luck on your journey,
GROUNDSTONE CORE

So much for hoping for good news. S'rae found the paper crumbled inside her clenched fist that was shaking uncontrollably. A rage had burned inside of her, unaware of how to control it. Could this day get any worse?

"Is everything okay," Fujak said, gently placing his hand on S'rae's hip. The touch was soft and comforting, but Fujak suddenly pulled away as if feeling the rage that trembled within her.

She tucked the paper into her robe, and knew that the moment she opened her mouth, tears would pour from her face, but yet she had to speak because she did not want to be the downer while everyone was happy, wanting to enjoy the festival. So she took a deep breath, stared at the ground for a few moments, then said, in an unnaturally composed voice: "Who's ready to have fun? Time to party, right?" It took everything in her to pretend to be happy. Her smile was usually her best disguise to hide her sorrow, but even today... right now, she just couldn't. Her life was going downhill, too fast... she needed something... anything... to let her know that life didn't hate her.

"Well," Lynn said, apparently not trying to smile as wide as she normally would. "Let's have us a great ol' time!"

As the group skipped and joked and laughed their way toward the festival, S'rae followed them just a few steps behind. No one would notice her this way, which she didn't know if that was a good or bad thing yet.

Then Fujak slowed down and broke away from the group. "I'm sorry... I know how much you've been wanting a Sol," Fujak said, not making eye contact. "I've never seen someone so happy about anything like the way you are when you talk about Sols. I believe your passion will prevail. The Divine One works in mysterious ways, you'll find the one. You deserve it, more than anyone I know."

"Thank you," S'rae said, feeling slightly better. And since now that she had no way in taking the courses needed to prepare for the challenge, she figured it was a good time to tell Fujak the truth. "There's no point in taking the challenge anymore."

"Why?" Fujak raised an eyebrow.

"No way I'll be ready." S'rae paused, composing herself. "I wanted to become a GroundStone student to ready myself for it... but I can only take the courses for dummies since I don't have a Sol." S'rae was expecting anger... or disappointment at least from Fujak, but neither came.

Fujak patted her shoulder. "Everything happens for a reason... there is a reason for this, I know it." Fujak's body shivered intensely for a brief moment as he looked at his hands. "Did you feel that?

Déjà vu. This is *still* a part of our destiny… I believe it. And I know you'll… we'll be ready when the time comes."

S'rae knew exactly what he was talking about. The moment he touched her shoulder, she received a wave of memories as if she had experienced this moment before, but yet feeling it for the very first time. It was difficult to explain, but she too looked at her hands and said: "I hope you're right… because I need some good news. I *need* it."

"Need good news do ya?" Milla said as she turned around. "Well, I have something that you'd like to hear."

"What's that?" S'rae said.

"Well, there was a boy who was in your exact situation. He couldn't take any courses because he didn't have a Sol… weird… what was his name? Hey, Kaul, what was that loner kid's name? You know the weird one who'd always be in the Sol's den?"

"That creepy hot boy?" Brick said.

"Uhh, nope! Don't think we're talking about the same kid then," Milla said.

"Uhh, yup! We're *definitely* talking about the same kid," Kaul said, "because he was definitely creepy and he was *definitely* hot." He bit the corner of his lip.

"Um… *ew*! Because… well, if he's what you two consider a hot boy, then that *definitely* explains why I like girls."

S'rae saw Lynn gaze at Milla the same way Han'sael would stare at food. She quickly shook her head to not bring up memories of him, again she didn't want to ruin her day any more, as if that was possible.

"Well," Milla said, "he didn't have a Sol but he still found a way to take advanced courses."

"How?" S'rae's eyes lit up.

"The arena tournament at the end of the festival. The winner of it gets to take any class they wish. He wasn't just the winner of it, though… he was *the* winner of it!"

"Yeah, the kid won every arena match GroundStone had," Kaul said. "Hmm… maybe that's what made him so hot? All I know is you're lucky he's not around or you *definitely* wouldn't have a chance to win!"

S'rae's body tingled with anger at that comment, not only because of what he said, but because of who he was talking about. The only boy they could be talking about was Vayp, whose name apparently had been wiped from their memory. It was bad enough that Gabrael didn't think she was on the same level as Vayp, but now these kids, who knew nothing about her, thought so too? Counting her out already? "I bet you I'd beat him." S'rae growled.

The trio all looked at each other, they stared at one another long and hard for a few moments. Their lips flinched a little before finally bursting out with laughter.

"I tried so hard to hold it in!"

"Me too!"

"Oh my! That was a great laugh!"

S'rae grimaced.

"No offense, girl," Milla said, "but what are you even good at? Like, do you have a specialty?"

"I do!" S'rae lied, but she used this time to think of something. She thought back to her days when she was all alone at Opella and had made statues that she considered her toy family. She'd roleplay and create little adventures with them. "I can make statues."

"And… who can't do that? It's quite common here," Kaul said. "Listen, I'm not trying to be a jerk, but these are skilled people at the arena, you need to make sure you're ready, or you can get seriously hurt."

"Well…" S'rae said, "I'm going to try for it—"

"Wait." Fujak held his hand out toward S'rae. "Please don't." He then grabbed S'rae by the arm and pulled her to the side. "Don't do this—"

"You think I'm not good enough either, huh?" S'rae said.

Fujak pulled back and raised an eyebrow as if confused. "What? *No*, not at all. Actually, the opposite. I think you could definitely win this, and I'm worried about who would find out if you did win. News like this would travel fast, and if it reached Fujita... I'm scared to know what they'd do to you to send a message to others... to show them not to defy the laws of the land."

"You and your laws of the land!" Though S'rae was happy to hear that Fujak had faith in her abilities, she hated that Fujak may had been right. What would happen if Fujita found out someone, well, not just someone, but their top student, was caught practicing two elements? What message would they send? S'rae thought only for a moment before it made her eyes widen: death. S'rae's eyes dropped.

"Yeah," Fujak said. "Yes... that's *exactly* what I'm afraid of," Fujak said as if he had read S'rae's mind just from one look. "Promise me you won't enter it, please!"

"Fujita laws aren't always right you know?" S'rae crossed her arms, frustrated.

"They are fair and just and right, they are what kept peace for millennia."

"Fair and just and right are relative... this is *not* fair."

"But it's the right thing to do... just trust me. Please."

S'rae pouted. "Fine!"

"He *would* be doing this shirtless," Fujak said to S'rae as they made their way slowly down the golden road, passing by the performers showing their talents.

And of course S'rae would still be staring at Retro'ku and not pay attention to where she was walking. BANG! She fell to the floor, rubbing her head as she hit a sign that said: "Pay Attention To Your Surroundings: Crowded Area." Oh, the irony.

Fujak helped her up, but still S'rae had her eyes locked in on Retro'ku as a swarm of girls circled around him, swooning and gasping and cheering while he and his shadow put on a show. They fought at speeds so fast that it was tough to pay attention to all the movements they made, she only saw certain flashes of kicks and punches as if they fought under a strobe light.

"You know… he's not as modest as you think he is," Fujak said, glaring at Retro'ku with a curled lip.

"I happen to think he's… er… confident," S'rae said, not wanting to say what she really thought about him and his *mmmm… muscles*. "And he has every reason to be… he's been training for like three thousand years."

"No one needs to train that much," Fujak said as they made their way to an open area on the street. "I think he's just cocky."

"Apparently he does need to train that much… for some reason. I guess he knows something we don't. And I think… Well… I think you're just jealous." S'rae made a look at Fujak, expecting a reaction out of him, but instead his face remained flat.

"I think… you're right." Fujak went to his section, where he took his shirt off as well. He clapped his hands together as a ball of wind entrapped him inside. At once, he levitated into the air, as if he became weightless, and began to perform a choreographed performance to the beautiful music that the wind whistled. He was twisting and flipping and twirling through the air. The large crowd that had surrounded Retro'ku began to split up and make their way toward Fujak.

Great… not sure how I can top these two. At least Lynn isn't here. But S'rae had thought too soon. Dancing to the harmonies that Fujak's wind had created, Lynn was seen dancing elegantly in her dress that splashed like hypnotic waves whenever she kicked her leg up. And as she danced and swirled, spurts of water followed her hands, flowing through the air in sparkling blues. It was… absolutely beautiful to watch.

"Ooo!" The crowd gasped as more and more people came to watch Lynn, Fujak, and Retro'ku. S'rae was shoved farther away from the performances, so far that she could only hear the music, the ooo's and ahh's, and the gentle splashes of water mixed in with the roars of flames.

Well… I guess it's good that no one will pay attention to me now.

S'rae spent the next few minutes making sculptures of different animals from some foxes with wide ears to big horned sheep to an adorable, tiny sand cat, to a cottontail camel and many others. Each one had its own story, faces that she remembered when she was a child at Opella. And right when she had wanted to stop, she thought of another animal to sculpt. Then another. And another. Before long, she was staring at about two dozen animals. They held memories… ones as great as they were terrible. For these animals weren't just any ones… they were her *almost* Sols. S'rae teared up just looking at them again. *Why couldn't just one of you be mine?*

Seeing as no one showed up or even cared about her sculptures, she decided to sit far away from them, so that no one thought of her as the talentless girl who couldn't draw a crowd. She still heard the gasps and clapping from the other three's audience that had since multiplied. And here S'rae was… the loser that she was expecting to be.

Not a single person cared about the work she spent what felt like hours on. Just as she lifted her hand to make her statues crumble to sand, an older couple strolled on by, dragging their canes along the dirt. They observed each sculpture. And they finally stopped at one. Wow! It made her stomach twist with excitement that someone actually cared about her art. She had to listen in on their conversation. They must have loved the attention to detail, or the way it looked like there was a story inside their eyes. She spent so long on their eyes!

"These look boring, maybe they should be dancing or fighting or flipping around."

"Yeah… talent ain't what it used to be like no more. I like art that means something."

The couple turned around and waved and smiled at S'rae. S'rae didn't smile or wave back.

"Poor girl… at least she tried, I suppose."

S'rae felt like today couldn't get much worse, the dagger in her heart just dug a little deeper. And just when she went to snap her fingers to turn her work into dust, a cloaked person had appeared in front of the statues. Where did he come from? He remained motionless as if he had been there the whole time… but surely he wasn't just a second ago.

Great… I should have destroyed them when I had the chance. More embarrassment.

The cloaked figure continued to stare at each sculpture, touching their faces and staring into their eyes.

S'rae, who was still sitting far away, stared up at the sky, watching the glow of an occasional flame flying overhead, and pictured some of Retro'ku's fighting moves. She was itching to find the courage to approach him, maybe to start their training since she now couldn't become a GroundStone student. S'rae saw herself in black robes, and imagined the sensation of hearing an audience clap and applaud for her as she burst into flames, soaring through the sky, fighting at lightning fast speeds, as Retro'ku stared at her with a glowing smile. "This is my greatest student." She imagined him saying.

S'rae snapped out of her fantasy and did not realize that she had slept walk—for she found herself directly in front of her statues, and when she looked up to her left, she let out a startled scream.

"It's okay," the cloaked person said, looking down at her, "I brought you here because I'm most curious about your statues."

"Er…" S'rae stood up, feeling very uncomfortable, like she had when she saw that— "wait, are you the one who's with Olivia?"

"I am, but I do not wish to talk about me, I wish to understand your art more."

"My art?" S'rae pulled back. "Why?"

"You see this." His finger grazed along the face of a fox. "The precision is most fascinating. It looks… so real. But that is not what impresses me the most." He then pushed his head closer toward the foxes eyes. "Their eyes… I love the attention to detail… it looks as if there is a story inside them. You've captured this moment… one which most people could sculpt their entire lives and never replicate as precisely as these. This is flawless. You've captured a special moment. A special moment when they are most happy."

"Well… it was a special moment," S'rae said.

"Was?"

"These are my *almost* Sols…"

"Almost Sols, hmm…" the cloaked man said, "well, these are masterpieces indeed… I would consider them perfect, and you are a very talented student with a more gifted eye for details." He touched the face of a sand cat. "Almost Sols, aye? Ahh yes… makes sense. You were the one left in the rain, no?"

"Yupp… that's me." S'rae cringed. *I guess that's how I'm always going to be remembered.*

"What an interesting… coincidence." The way he said that made S'rae's stomach churn uncomfortably. "What *did* Olivia tell you?"

"Nothing," S'rae lied, remembering what Olivia said about keeping it a secret. Suddenly she felt the danger that she spoke of. Maybe even he was not supposed to know about their secret.

"Right. Of course she said *nothing*." The cloaked person examined a few more statues, silently. The noises around them had changed. The singing and clapping had stopped. So too did the sounds of fighting and the roars of flames. But she could hear screams, and the sound of people running. S'rae stood up, alarmed, and felt a sharpened arrow form at her fingertips, but the cloaked man, who placed his hand on S'rae's shoulder, said, "No reason to be alarmed. They are excited that—"

"Get your hand off her." S'rae heard a deep, powerful voice

laced with so much hatred she had no idea who it belonged to. When she turned around, she was shocked to see Retro'ku there, pointing a blazing sword at the cloaked man's back.

"I assure you… I do not want any problems," the cloaked man said.

"I assure you… there will be problems if you still have your hand on her before I finish this sente—" The cloaked man released S'rae. "Smart move."

S'rae was shocked to see this side of Retro'ku, she had only known him as the silent soft-spoken one, where did this Retro'ku come from? And as she gazed into his eyes that faded from red back to a soft brown, she saw the old Retro'ku reappear.

"It's starting!" Lynn came screaming by, almost tackling S'rae. Lynn, Fujak, and the GroundStone trio came at the perfect time, S'rae had felt a tenseness in the air that made breathing difficult. There was a power radiating from the two of them, Retro'ku and the cloaked man, that felt life-threatening; she felt herself collapse to the ground as if they had somehow affected gravity. And even after the others came, still, the two did not break eye contact. "It's starting! Let's get great seats!" Lynn said once more, grinning wide. "Watching boys beat each other? Sign me up! Take that, patriarchy!"

"What's going on over here?" Fujak said with a straight face, looking at Retro'ku and the cloaked man. "Do we have any problems?"

"There are no issues here," the cloaked man said, pulling his robe in closer.

"Good," Fujak said, "carry on then. Hope you enjoy the arena tournament." And as the cloaked man walked away, Fujak whispered to Retro'ku and S'rae. "I don't trust him. Something about him feels off."

Retro'ku's eyes stayed fixed on the man until he was out of sight.

"Well, let's see what the fuss is all about," Fujak said. "The arena it is!"

The students hurried out to the center of GroundStone, S'rae at Lynn's heels.

From the torches of the fires burning on the paths, S'rae could see more students running toward the gigantic stone stadium: the Grand Colosseum. Roars of laughter and drunken yells were gathering toward them; then came the rolling thunder of drums and horns, which made the ground shake.

"Quick!" Milla said, "If we want seats together, we need to get there *now!*"

A crowd of Earthies, tightly packed and moving together, was slowly squeezing their way through an entrance. The stairs into the stadium was the most green S'rae had seen since being here. There was thick grass with colorful flowers blooming on the sides, despite the gold and brown that existed everywhere else. They scrambled upward with the rest of the students, which slowly parted ways into the seats to their left and right. They kept following Milla until they reached a row in the center that had more than enough spots for them. Their seats were long stone slabs, but as S'rae sat down, the stone molded into soft sand that cushioned her butt. She never would have thought that stone seats would be the most comfortable ones she had ever sat on.

S'rae watched as thousands of Earthies were filling up the colosseum, which rose in levels surrounding the long oval desert below, where the challenge would be held. A bright gold light radiated from the building as if it still reflected the light from the setting sun. It made everything inside appear as day, though S'rae could somehow see the stars flicker in the sky. This stadium was so massive that she wondered if everyone in Gaia could fit inside.

When S'rae looked up, she saw a balcony that looked as if it were meant for Gods... and well... that was because it was. Gabrael and Raaz'a sat down to the left of an empty throne. To the right of the throne were two more empty seats. Five seats… yet Gabrael and Raaz'a were alone? S'rae had trouble understanding why that may be the case, then she remembered the rage in Leonna's voice when she spoke about Gabrael. If the rest of GroundStone felt the same way about Gabrael as Leonna did, then maybe it was safe for no one to be seen associating with the enemy. S'rae could only imagine the chaos that could ensue.

And as the stadium filled up, the drums sounded once more and a booming voice made the seats rattle. "Welcome to the Ground-Stone Arena!" A voice was felt, not heard. It practically vibrated like bass from the stone seats. "This marks the end of our Orientation Day! And as expected, we will bring you excitement, we will bring you fun, but most importantly, we will be bring you a NEW CHAMPION!" The crowd roared as the entire stadium trembled. Thousands of Earthies stomped their feet as S'rae cupped her mouth from the nausea of the shaking. She observed the line of students for Retro'ku, wondering if she could sit next to him, but it seemed as if it would be impossible to move in this tightly packed space. At least she was happy that Lynn, who was biting her nails with excitement, was to her left, and Fujak, who scanned the crowd with paranoid, narrowed eyes, was to her right.

"AS WE ALL SHOULD KNOW," the voice boomed, "THIS IS A LAST MAN STANDING DUEL. OUR GREAT CHALLENGERS WILL ALL FACE OFF AGAINST ONE ANOTHER AND THE LAST ONE WHO IS NOT KNOCKED OUT OR TAKEN OUT WINS!"

The crowd erupted into a roar, followed by more quaking stomps.

"GREAT. GREAT. GREAT! AS THE DOORS OPEN, OUR COMPETITORS WILL BE REVEALED AND THAT IS WHEN THE MATCH WILL BEGIN!"

"Are you excited?" Fujak nudged S'rae's shoulder.

"Don't talk to me during this." S'rae crossed her arms and

pulled her hood over her head. "I'm still mad at you!"

"I understand," Fujak said, looking down. "Well—"

Fujak bumped into S'rae as the ground rumbled with the most force yet, feeling like Gaia was about to split into two. Fujak turned to see the source of the explosion and that was when the gates started to open.

"NOTHING WILL STOP THE ARENA FROM STARTING!" The gates opened and hundreds of students, dressed in brown robes, ran onto the field. "LET THE GAME BEGIN!"

* * *

Fujak saw dozens of students pour out from the many tunnels that circled below. At once, boulders large and small were slung across the arena, the stray ones that missed their target and launched at the crowd of spectators were turned into waves of sand that sprayed them. It seemed to make the crowd roar louder, as if they enjoyed being blasted by sand.

"This looks like a lot for anyone to handle," Fujak said to S'rae, who only grunted at him. Apparently she wasn't joking about the whole not talking part.

Think of something funny to say. Come on… and make it so funny that she'd laugh, and then I could say how I thought you weren't going to talk to me. Then she would say that laughing isn't talking, which she'd be right, but then I would say "but now you're talking to me." Then she'd push my shoulder. And then… well… then I win. That's all I'd really want, really. Just her doing her playful shove. I feel like I crossed the line touching her hip. WHY would you reach for her hip? Shoulder! Next time just the shoulder! Jeez! Maybe I overthink too much, maybe she didn't even notice that I touched her hip on accident. Was it an accident? Am I overthinking? No, this isn't overthinking, is it? But… how can I get her to talk to me? Oh yeah, a funny joke. Hmm… let's see… nope, won't work. That won't work. That definitely won't work. Ah… maybe this one.

"Er…" Fujak coughed. "Want to hear a joke about Fujita? I'm

still thinking about it."

S'rae said nothing, which made Fujak awkwardly press his palms together. *Guess it wasn't that funny. Actually, no... it was such a terrible joke—if I didn't laugh at it when I thought about it, why would she? Smooth move, Fujak.*

"Did you get it?" Fujak said softly. "Because Fujitas think all the time... and I was still... err... thinking about it?"

S'rae still said nothing, she just remained leaned forward with her fists deep into her hood, as if resting her cheeks on them, and observed the fight intensely.

Maybe Fujak would have better luck commentating on the fight, yeah, that would work! He watched below as already half the competitors had been eliminated in just a few minutes. He paid attention to one, who had been launching dozens of boulders at other students. The moment one made contact, it would wrap around the person and sandwich them to the ground, eliminating them at once. It seemed like it was an effective strategy that most were using, but none better than him.

"He's doing it all wrong," Fujak said, glancing sideways at S'rae, "if you show your strongest hand too soon, you become the target. The trick is to appear weak, and save your strongest hand when the enemy thinks you have nothing left. This person just unnecessarily put a target on his back. If he went to Fujita, like us, he would have known efficient strategies to victory." *Yeah, that compliment should get at least a comment from S'rae, right?*

Nope, she remained still and silent, probably focusing on the same boy that Fujak was.

"See," Fujak said, pointing at the boy, who was now surrounded by dozens of Earthies, "What'd I tell you? *Presence of Mind During Battle 101*, simple strategies." Fujak shook his head. "I think he would be your biggest competition, but at least you're definitely smarter than him. Well, any person at Fujita would be smarter than him."

S'rae grunted

"I'm only joking!" Fujak brushed his hand through his hair. "Well, kinda joking."

Okay, I'm making progress. Got something out of her. I hope she doesn't stay mad at me forever. She can't blame me, she's smart enough to know that I mean well. She is the smartest person I know, after all, just don't ever tell her that! I just don't want to see what Fujita would do to her… she doesn't deserve it.

"OH MY!" The commentator's voice boomed. "WHAT A TURN OF EVENTS! IT SEEMS AS IF THE REST OF THEM HAD DECIDED TO TAKE ON THIS ONE BOY. CAN ONE DEFEAT THE TWENTY THAT ARE REMAINING? PLACE YOUR BETS!"

Fujak watched as the boy created a large shield that was deflecting the rocks and boulders that other students were throwing at him. The shield was crumbling after each strike, until finally it shattered into rubble and was no more.

"Just like I said," Fujak rolled his shoulders up proudly, "he would have had a chance if he listened to me."

Just then, as the boy was defenseless and the other boys created new rocks in their palms for the final strike, the lone boy placed his palms together and leapt into the air. The balls were launched, but before they reached their target, they slowed to a stop and fell to the ground.

"WOW!! AMAZING!! DID YOU SEE WHAT JUST HAPPENED! HE SLOWED THE BALLS AND DID NOT EVEN NEED A SHIELD! AMAZING! WHOA! WHAT'S HAPPENING TO THE BALLS? LOOK!"

Fujak narrowed his eyes as he focused on the balls bubble up and mold into people.

"AMAZING!! HE CREATED AN ARMY OF SAND CLONES! TRULY IMPRESSIVE! IS THIS LEGAL? YES? NO? OH, IT IS! APPARENTLY IT HAS NEVER BEEN DONE BEFORE SO

THERE IS NO RULE AGAINST THIS, YET, AT LEAST!"

The stone clones all created their own rocks and boulders in their hands, and then launched them at the boys who stood there motionless, in shock.

"WOW! HE DID IT!! HE ACTUALLY DID IT! I HOPE SOME OF YOU PLACED YOUR BETS! HE ELIMINATED THE COMPETITION! AMAZING!! I WOULD LOVE TO SEE HIM FACE OUR PREVIOUS CHAMPION, THAT WOULD BE AN AMAZING DUEL INDEED!"

"Wow!" Fujak jumped up along with the other students, who clapped and cheered for the victor. "I'm actually impressed! A deserved win, definitely!" Fujak turned to S'rae, who was still sitting in place. Was she so upset with not joining the arena that she wouldn't even show any emotion? Fujak began to feel sorry for her, but it was for the best. Hopefully she'd get over it.

"SHOW YOURSELF, CHAMPION! YOU ARE NOW THE CHAMPION OF GROUNDSTONE. YOU ARE GRANTED ACCESS TO ANY AND ALL CLASSES WITHIN OUR WALLS! SHOW YOURSELF!"

As the cloaked person removed the hood, so too did his clones. And as the clones removed their hoods, they crumbled into dust.

Fujak leaned in to get a better look. "Hey, S'rae." His eyes narrowed. "I think..." He looked harder. "Wow... I think the champion is actually... a girl!" Fujak turned toward S'rae... at least where he thought she would be sitting, but instead of S'rae... there was just a... a pile of dust and sand.

"CONGRATULATIONS, S'RAE!! OUR NEW CHAMPION!!"

Fujak's eyes widened. He felt a wave of panic rush through him. In his hand he held a bow that swirled in waves of wind. He stood up quickly, his eyes darting from side-to-side in a frenzy, scanning the crowd that roared as sharp arrows formed at his fingertips.

He slung an arrow back and pointed it. *This is NOT good.*

* * *

S'rae stood there, light blinding, her palms shaking, and everything around her seemed to go mute. She didn't know if that was because she was scared out of her mind… or if she had already lost it. Fujak would hate her, but worse, this tournament was meant for boys mainly, not a girl. She could already imagine the treatment she'd get, the brooding glares, the envy, the same way Fujita had treated her whenever she won a competition. They hated it… and hated her even more because of it. But… she honestly did not care anymore. She didn't care about anything, she didn't even care if her clone statues were against the rules or not… all she wanted to do now was whatever the heck she wanted. Nothing was going her way, so why not control over what little she had left in her life. Not the failures beyond her control… but this tournament… this moment… the proving to Gabrael, Fujak, and the GroundStone trio that she was good enough to win it—this was all worth it, even if it meant getting in trouble, or worse.

S'rae tore her eyes away from the blinding lights and looked over her shoulder to see mobs of angry people storming at her. She saw the way they were screaming with their fists held high. She was ready to take the punishment. *I just don't care anymore.*

And here they came, they practically tackled her, she felt hands all around her as she was hoisted onto their shoulders… and then… thrown into the air? What was happening?

As her senses finally started to settle in, she realized that the roars were there… but so too was the clapping and cheering? Wait… they actually liked that she won? That she cheated the system? That she snuck in using her own way? They didn't care… and they still celebrated? It felt… AMAZING!

"CONGRATULATIONS TO S'RAE, THE CHAMPION OF GROUNDSTONE! GROUND! STONE! GROUND! STONE!"

The crowd chanted "Ground! Stone!" as they kept launching her into the air.

She saw Lynn, the GroundStone trio, and Retro'ku, who was smiling wide, this alone made it all worth it. As she looked up at the top booth, Gabrael and Raaz'a were nowhere to be seen... but neither was Fujak. Where could he be? Was he really this upset that he'd walk out the moment she won?

"You were amazing!" Lynn said as S'rae was thrown into the air once more. "I told them that you could win it! I told them!"

"That was very impressive," Kaul said, "but... I still don't think you'd be able to beat the previous champion."

"WHAT?!" Lynn shouted. "You're crazy! Did you not see her destroy the competition and slap patriarchy in the face!" She laughed devilishly. "Oh, it was so glorious! I would love to see it again!"

"Kaul is right," Milla said, "she was impressive, but I really don't think she's on his level yet, but I must say... I would do ANYTHING to see them two face off. It would truly be the greatest matchup GroundStone has ever seen!"

S'rae didn't let their doubt affect her, she knew where she stood with Vayp... yes, they were equals at Opella, but neither of them had really put all their effort in when they faced one another, it was sort of an unspoken agreement. *I bet if I tried my hardest, he'd go down!*

"Where's Fujak?" S'rae shouted after no longer being thrown in the air. Instead, she found herself on the shoulders of a giant man, who might as well had been a gorilla. Maybe it was.

"I don't know," Lynn said, "we came straight down here to try to get to you first before they swarmed you!"

"I hope he doesn't hate me," S'rae said. "I hope he forgiv—"

S'rae stopped talking at once. Somehow... between the roars, the claps, the cheers, and the stomps, S'rae heard a peculiar noise that she had heard hundreds of times before... at Fujita: the tightening of an arrow... before—*SWOOSH!*—S'rae heard the sound that was without question the release of an arrow. And when her eyes widened, tracking down the source, she saw that it was… heading straight for her heart.

With no time to react, the wind had already acted before she had the chance to process what was happening—she was about to die! Her body twisted with the help of the wind that pushed her up and twirled her around as she watched the arrow rip through her robes and head straight toward—her eyes widened even more—the arrow was a moment away from striking down a poor boy in the crowd. She knew exactly who it was; he held his black raven in his hands as he screamed. It was Yash.

S'rae, while twirling in air, twisted her fingers and pushed her palm to the air. A wind current chased the arrow, shooting it straight to the sky, before hitting Yash. The moment the arrow's silvery streak made contact with a cloud, the sky erupted with a SONIC BOOM that made the planet shake.

BANG! BANG! BANG! Horns and drums ripped through the arena.

"THIS IS AN EMERGENCY! EVERYONE EVACUATE THE STADIUM!" The voice rattled S'rae's eardrums. "EVERYONE EVACUATE THE STADIUM! TRANSPORT TO THE GUARD-IAN'S TEMPLE! I REPEAT TRANSPORT TO THE GUARD-IAN'S TEMPLE!"

"Come with me," Milla said, grabbing Lynn's hand. She drew a relic in the sand, and at once hundreds of stone monuments erected, looking like a miniature mountain range.

"Here," Kaul said in a panic, sweat glistened his forehead. He grabbed S'rae and showed her how to draw the relic. "This is the protection Sandsportation Spell, it will take you underground to our Safe Space. Do it. NOW!"

S'rae's hands were still shaking… what was happening? What just happened? Was that… a murder attempt… on her? And… who did it? She thought about the sound wind made, she thought about the arrow targeting her heart, and the first name that came to her mind was—NO, it couldn't be him! It couldn't... not Fujak. Not her friend, he wouldn't, right? She didn't know, all she knew was that he warned her for a reason, but maybe he warned her so he wouldn't have to do the deed? Maybe?

Just then, she heard his voice. "S'rae!"

S'rae looked up, eyes wide. She suddenly spotted Fujak, a long bow in his hand, and he started shouting her name once more.

"Leave! NOW!" Kaul said as he drew the relic in the sand. A spike shot up around him before getting sucked into the ground.

S'rae's hand was shaking too much. She... messed up. Maybe she should have listened to Fujak, after all.

"S'RAE!" S'rae turned and saw Fujak staring straight at her. He then dashed toward her.

S'rae didn't know what to do... should she ask him... ask him if he did it... or should she run and go with her gut instincts? Fujak was closing in on her, quickly. She had to make a decision.

"I'm sorry." S'rae cried as she quickly drew the relic in the sand.

Tears were flowing down her eyes as Fujak came within arm's reach of her. And a second later, she was gone. Safe... for now.

* * *

It felt as if S'rae was sucked to the other end of planet of Gaia. This trip was nothing like the one that brought her to the plateau. Instead, she felt a burning sensation that started at her toes and traveled up through her nose. She found herself coughing and choking on nothing at all. She tried to keep her eyes open but she feared going blind from the pebbles that grazed by her skin. It felt like one moment she was on solid ground... and then the next her head was being crushed by the weight of her own body. And now... it felt like every part of her body was getting punched by a gorilla. And when she curled up into a ball, trying to absorb the pain, she found herself in a dark room.

She fell, knees forward, onto the cold stone floor and felt her legs buckle.

Injured and shocked, covered in mud, she stumbled to her feet, holding onto a shelf for support. A shelf? Where was she exactly? There was no one else around and the musky smell that burned her nose let her know that it was definitely a place she had never been to before. All she could tell was that this was some type of room for a professor, with shelves filled with books and cobwebs. Maybe a deceased professor? Nothing in here said that this room had ever been used.

A claw that may had come from an eagle, fangs inside a jar, and tusks from an elephant were spread around. Heads of different animals were mounted on the walls, various knives, swords, and arrows lay against the wall. And worse, she was unable to see a door that could let her out of this room. Did people come here to die?

She desperately patted around the darkness for some type of handle. Nose still burning from the moldy smell of the room, she covered her mouth and nose with one hand while searching with the other. She finally found a door and moved silently through it… until… she heard voices. They were distant and muffled, but she found a corner to hide and circled her fingers around to listen.

"How many times do I have to tell you, I said NO, I will *never* tell you where she is!"

"But you have sworn to protect her."

"Yes, and that is *exactly* what I am doing! Why do you think she left the Valley of Gaia? Because she was unsafe… because she knew death awaited her there… because you. Are! Evil!"

"She was *not* afraid of me."

"*Hah*! Is that what you wish to believe? Eve was afraid for her life, that's why she left… and after what you did, you monster, I understand why. And now you want me to just tell you where she is? I am no fool."

"Forgive me, master, but may I speak?"

"Certainly."

"I understand your concern, Olivia, but Gabrael and I are here to protect her. A Shadow Army has been created and we have every reason to believe that it's destination is here... for her... for Eve. Now, we respect that you wish to fulfill your duties as her protector, but how can you protect her when she dies by their hands? And the last thing we want is an Eve controlled by them. Have you ever heard of The Eve of Darkness?"

"Of course I have... and that's why I wish to keep her away from the likes of you! I told you once, twice, a dozen times, I will *never* tell someone like you where she is! You are a monster! It has been three thousand long years... do not act like I forgot what you did to *him*! Never mind... what you did to *them*!"

"My wish was never for him to try."

"LIES! Do not spread your lies to me! He told me... he told me he wasn't ready. He told me that he kept telling you that he wasn't ready... yet still... still you pushed him. You are the reason we are in this mess... and you deserve whatever it is that is coming your way."

A long moment passed. S'rae could hear footsteps followed by the sounds of a cape dragging across the floor. "I understand your pain... I have felt your pain for just as long. But it is not I who will suffer... it is us. Do not let our past cloud your judgment. Eve is in danger. You are sworn to protect her. So I hope you reconsider."

"Then you will be hoping for three thousand more years. This is my destiny, to protect her. Now go! Leave!"

"I am sorry."

"Do not apologize to me. Apologize to *him*. And maybe then you will be given the chance to apologize to *her*."

S'rae heard the sound of a door opening then slamming shut. Silence had swept the room until—

"You can come out now, whoever you are." The female's voice said. "I know you are here. You are safe with me, do not worry."

S'rae looked quickly around and spotted exactly who she

thought she would: Olivia.

"Oh... it is you." Olivia smiled. "I told you to come see me, but I did not mean this soon."

"I'm sorry... it was an accident," S'rae said.

"Ah... not when it comes to this. I do not believe in such coincidences. I believe you are exactly where you were destined to be. And with that being said, I believe destiny brought you here for me to tell you the answer that you seek."

S'rae felt her heartbeat escalate, was she going to tell her about how to get a Sol?

"You see... S'rae, is it?" When S'rae nodded, Olivia continued. "None of this happens by chance. You are a girl who cannot find her Sol... who happened to go on a quest to the Valley of Gaia... who happened to come to GroundStone... then stumble into my classroom... by accident? Oh no. This is no accident." Olivia walked into the center of the room. It was a circular open area with pillars that shot up to the sky. Statues of many different animals were in between the columns. They were beautifully elegant... yet hauntingly mysterious. Olivia drew a relic into the ground as the circle in the center hissed. White smoke poured out from underneath.

The ground rumbled as the circle spun quickly. Before S'rae knew it, the ground twisted downward, revealing a spiraling staircase that seemed to head straight down into the core of Gaia.

"Follow me, S'rae," Olivia said as she waved her hand to her chest. At once, the ground at S'rae's feet moved toward Olivia in a flash, and S'rae was there staring down into the deep abyss of a hole. "Remember... do not tell *anyone* what I am about to show you... do we make ourselves clear?"

S'rae nodded then gulped.

Olivia spoke while they walked, her hand grazing many statues of beasts S'rae had never seen before. "You see... the animals that exist today... are the ones that have survived. Some have survived natural extinction... others... have survived slaughter. Do you know which animal was slaughtered to extinction?"

"N-no." S'rae felt sweat bubble up into her robes.

"Do you know why an animal would be slaughtered… into extinction?"

"F-fear?"

"Ah… you are a smart one." Olivia nodded as her hand grazed by a statue of a phoenix. "The fear of there being something more powerful is why one would wish to kill innocent animals. Why yes… this animal was indeed powerful beyond words… but nature does not use power in the same way that humans do. It was this reason why the animal was able to live in harmony, protecting Eve and Gaia as the apex beast of the planet.

"But… then that was until they found out that humans were able to connect with this animal. Only a select few born every few millennia possess the power… the ability… the special something about them that would allow them to harness this beast as their own Sol. They became the true Guardians of Gaia, the Protectors of Eve. Until… fear."

Olivia placed her palm onto a door. Black smoke poured out from the crack… then it changed to red, blue, purple, green, then gold… until finally the door opened.

"S'rae… I believe the reason you have not found your Sol yet… is because you are special," Olivia said as the smoke cleared and the statue of a great beast revealed itself. S'rae had seen this beast only once before in her *Myths and Legends* class. This beast wasn't just any beast—"S'rae… I believe that your Sol is waiting for you. And that your Sol… is… a dragon."

Before S'rae could say a word, Olivia hushed her. Olivia's eyes widened as she looked up at the hole of the stairs.

"I do not believe we are alone…" Olivia said, "again… do not tell anyone about this."

"I won't." S'rae felt her knees tremble. For someone as powerful as Olivia to appear scared, it made S'rae cower from the inside.

Her hands were now shaking and she held them to brace herself. "Olivia, I have a question."

"Yes?" Olivia spoke softly as the statue of the snake-like dragon with wide wings faded back into the darkness.

They walked their way up, Olivia seeming careful to watch her step as the spiraling stairs underfoot turned to sand before wisping away.

"Are you really here to protect Eve?" S'rae asked, looking down at the vanishing stairs.

"Yes." Her voice now softer.

"How do you know where she is?"

"Because… I'm the one who helped hide her."

"Well… how do you know she's still alive?"

"Because… I would be dead if she wasn't. We are linked… it's the reason I was able to live the past three thousand years."

"Wow… that's a long time… you don't look a day over… fifty?" S'rae shook her head at such a stupid comment. And of course, the beautiful Professor Olivia, who did not look a day over twenty, would raise her eyebrow at S'rae. "Err… I mean… you look great for your age."

"Which is… fifty?" Olivia shook her head with a pleasant smirk. They made their way to the top as the spiral staircase sealed back up to the floor, as if it was never there. "Here." Olivia gave S'rae an emblem. "This will allow you to take my courses… I want to work with you and have as much time with you as possible."

"Why are you doing this?"

"Because… as you heard Gabrael and Raaz'a speak… danger is coming… the end is near… and I believe that by you and I meeting like *this*… it is the planet's way to tell me that it is ready… and that it will fight back. I believe you may be one of the Guardians of Gaia, a Protector of Eve. And I will help you find your dragon."

S'rae's eyes lit up at that statement. *My dragon?* She didn't want to believe it until it actually happened, she was tired of getting her hopes up, but something about this felt so real. Olivia was a master of Sols for a reason, after all.

"Do you think—" S'rae spoke.

"Shhh…" Olivia lifted her hand.

S'rae remained still. She didn't even breathe.

"I believe… wait… no… hmm… someone is after us… but… it's not me?" Olivia looked at S'rae, her eyebrows narrowed most curiously. "Why… would *they* be after you?"

"Who are *they*?" S'rae felt her stomach drop. "Who is after me?"

"Unless…" Olivia gasped, but then it happened all too soon. Her eyes widened as they both heard the *SWOOSH*! S'rae's heart dropped, knowing exactly what that meant: death.

Olivia placed her hand on S'rae's chest.

And everything went black. S'rae seemed to be spinning very fast—the screaming in her ears was deafening—she tried to open her eyes but wind smacked her face as if she were stuck inside a tornado. And then it ended just as quickly as it had begun.

She was dizzy and now even more confused… as she looked… at herself? She was no longer staring at Olivia, but she was staring at herself… from Olivia's location… had they swapped bodies? It didn't make sense… what happened?

And when she about to ask… she saw herself cough up blood. And then she saw herself say, "The… Sol…"

"The Sol?" S'rae said, fear tightening her chest as she watched the blood trail down her lips.

"Adari." And just like that, S'rae saw the life drain from her eyes. When she collapsed to the ground, S'rae saw an arrow that swirled in waves of wind was lodged into her back. The body that she thought was her own had suddenly morphed back into Olivia's. She had somehow switched their places all within the blink of an eye? How? But why?

S'rae then screamed at the top of her lungs as tears poured down her face. Olivia was… dead. Just like that. What happened? Who did this? What did Olivia mean by the Sol… Adari? Is Adari the name of a Sol? And now how would she find her Sol? Her dragon? Olivia couldn't die… she couldn't die right now.

S'rae cried into Olivia's body until another *SWOOSH* was heard. When S'rae looked up, Fujak stood there with a bow in his hand and arrow slung back. He was sweat-soaked and his eyes were wide and crazy-looking.

"Put it down." S'rae cried to Fujak. "Please… just… put… it down…"

"It's not what you think," Fujak said with his arrow still pointed at her.

BANG! Fujak fell to the ground as mud wrapped around his body and mouth before hardening into metal. Two Guardians, wrapped completely in metal armor, entered the room. They took one look at S'rae, crying over the body of the dead professor, and said, "TAKE THE MURDERER TO ALSI'JIN!"

Its voice scared S'rae into silence, but she had to speak once she saw them pick up Fujak's body and cast a relic in the sand, as if transporting him to wherever this Alsi'jin place was. "Wait! Where is he going?" S'rae screamed.

"Alsi'jin, where he deserves."

"And what's that?" S'rae said, tears still pouring from her eyes.

"The place where murderers go to die."

"But… you can't do that. He… he gets a fair trial."

"This was the fair trial… he was caught red-handed. He's not your friend anymore. Do not mourn those who wished to see you dead. He will get what's coming to him, once they get information out of him." The Guardian grinned.

S'rae's eyes blackened. She knew what that really meant, getting information. The prison system for murderers was not kind, she studied this extensively at Fujita. S'rae didn't know how to feel, her whole life had just been flipped upside-down.

Was Fujak getting what he deserved? Was he the murderer? S'rae wished she knew the answer.

What she did know… was that there was a murder. She found out that dragons may still exist… but not only that… one may be her Sol. And the only other person who knew about this secret was now dead. But what was worse, Olivia held a much greater secret within her: the whereabouts of Eve. Now how will they find her?

And as Fujak was absorbed into the sand, and S'rae was a crying mess, searching her mind for any answers to make sense of this, she looked up and saw a crow that was so black, it was darker than the night.

It screeched as it leapt into the air, then dove into a shadow that rippled like a puddle of ink.

S'rae's eyes were wide, filled with fright.

Is this our destiny? Is this how our lives end?

It was in this moment… when S'rae realized their lives would never be the same after today.

7

DARKNESS.
It surrounded Destrou inside the Box, seeping into his brain until he and the darkness became one.

But he wasn't alone. Somewhere in the darkness, he could hear the breathing of another. It were those breaths alone that kept him somewhat sane. Each one contained much more than oxygen, they were filled with hope. Hope that they'd somehow survive this... together.

Destrou's heart would race each time there was a void of silence. He hated it. He needed to hear something, anything. The white noise of *him* breathing let Destrou know that his world hadn't crumbled completely. It did crumble, though. He didn't know how long he was in there, the minutes had blended into days, but it felt like yesterday when he had lost his love, Elu.

He learned a hard lesson: that time with someone can be taken away in one instant. That he should spend each moment with someone as if it was his last. And that was why he couldn't stop his hands from shaking whenever the thought of a life without Ranmau crossed his mind. Much like Elu, it could happen at any moment. Death wasn't rare in the Box, survival was.

I am Destrou, he is Ranmau, her name was Elu, he thought over and over again. It kept his brain from shutting down, a sharp pulse to keep his heart beating. But more than repeating their names to never forget them, he repeated them because of the sharp coil of pain wrapped around his chest. *I will find out who really killed you... and I will kill him.*

It was obvious to Destrou that blaming Ranmau was *their* plan to separate them. To weaken the brothers, strengthening their chances to win the tournament. The tournament that was issued by the Supreme General, who was the leader of the Crystal Soldiers and rumors said he was even more powerful than the King. The Supreme General told the Guardians of each Village to find the strongest fighter from each village to join the Crystal Soldiers. This was their one chance to escape, alive. Yes, the boys would do anything for freedom. But there was no way Ranmau would do what they accused him of. He knew how much Destrou loved spending time with Elu.

What he would do to be given the chance to stare into her eyes again. To hear her laugh. To see the life pulse through her body as her adrenaline kicked in... nothing ever seemed to scare her. But then he remembered the way her eyes widened with fear when the liquid ice tower barrelled down on them. He remembered praying to the Divine One for the strength to protect her. But now as he sat in the darkness with a deep cold wrapping around him like a blanket, he felt a stabbing pain in his chest for not being there when she needed him the most. *If only...*

Try as he could, Destrou couldn't remember the exact shade of blue that sparkled from Elu's eyes. He couldn't recollect the tinge of brown that shone through her blonde hair. The way hues of blue, purple and green from the aurora borealis danced together in the sky. That was her dream... to see its beauty. Destrou was happy that he experienced the aurora with her. But thinking of the colors and dreams did not change the fact that they had all eventually dissolved into nothingness. Each moment he spent in the darkness, the dreams turned to nightmares and colors faded to black. Darkness was all that he saw. And what he had become.

The pain that came from thinking about Elu felt like a claw digging into him, threatening to bleed him out from the inside.

Somewhere outside the Box, a knock was heard, then laughter rang out. The Villagers enjoyed this punishment. They knew the damage that could be done, many soldiers have lost their lives to the Box. But still, the Villagers found humor in their pain. Their laughs were sharp, like the tip of a sword digging its way deeper into Destrou's side.

He pressed his hands to his ears, or at least thought he did. He couldn't feel a thing, not a pulse nor heat, and the pounding and laughing became louder, like a stampede of hyenas charging straight at him.

"I am Destrou, he is Ranmau, her name was Elu," he whispered through chapped lips.

Destrou finally understood why he'd hear screams from within the Box. They would scream for days, until their throats tightened. They cried out random names as if they never wanted to forget who their friends were. But were they ever friends if they were forgotten so easily? Life moved on as they never existed; their stories never to be told.

But for Destrou, he only had three names to remember; the only time it was fortunate to have so few loved ones.

It was love that made Destrou enter the Box. Yes, he didn't want Ranmau to be alone during his worst, but the real reason why he joined pained him almost as much as seeing Elu's corpse: If it weren't for Destrou, Ranmau would be living the life he was destined for. He would be gone, forever, enjoying the freedom he had always wanted.

But Ranmau gave up his dreams the moment he chose to plummet down the Wall to save Destrou.

The Wall that surrounded the Village was said to be impossible to climb. Not only was it hundreds of miles long, but it was probably just as tall as it was wide. If he could see past the clouds, he'd know. Despite its intimidation, Destrou knew that Ranmau had thought of escape, just like every villager had at one point in their lives. But Ranmau was not like everyone else. If anyone in the entire Kingdom could do it, it was him and him alone.

As foolish as it seemed, Destrou had once imagined escaping. He leapt over the Wall, but his mind was unable to produce what life would look like beyond it. He just fell into an empty abyss, similar to the one he was in now.

Now. Speaking of *now*, what would happen? Their lives had changed right before they had entered the Box. Ranmau's arm had been broken, which meant things would never be the same. Destrou had grown so used to the role as the protected that he had never considered being the protector. Was that even possible? To protect Ranmau the same way Ranmau protected him? Destrou was not special, not like Ranmau. It was something that he was always reminded of every other week during the challenges. Destrou would try with every ounce of his being to win, but Ranmau made victory look easy, as if he had expended more energy eating than he did in the challenges.

If Destrou wasn't able to protect Elu, who was loved... how could he protect Ranmau, who was hated?

Death had once scared Destrou, but with each second that passed in here, it was not his death that he feared, it was Ranmau's. The pain of losing someone he loved was crippling. Something he never wanted to experience again.

Still, he knew he had to survive the Box. *They* had to.

But surviving was not as simple as he had hoped. Each breath felt like an Archon's claw sunk deeper into his brain. He didn't want to know if Ranmau was going through the same internal battle. Most likely he was, but thinking about him in pain made the claws dig more.

And so he curled up into a ball, forcing himself to dream of Elu singing and dancing with Eve. He needed to grasp onto happy thoughts to survive.

I am Destrou, he is Ranmau, her name was Elu.
I will find out who really killed you...
And I will kill him.

* * *

Vayp had stopped reading and found himself wiping his teary eyes, without knowing why he had even been crying in the first place. Maybe it was because he had already related to Destrou when he was the loner with no friends... but now he saw himself in Destrou on a deeper level. Like Destrou, he too lost someone he cared about... by the hands of someone he cared about. And he too will kill the person responsible for that death. But then why was he crying? He didn't know the answer. *I know who killed you, Ah'nyx... and I will kill her... I will get you back.*

It looks like you may not have enough time to do so, a chilling voice entered Vayp's mind.

"What do you mean?" Vayp said, slamming the book shut, the flaming red orb on the cover blazed. It glowed bright, highlighting the capsule that Han'sael was floating inside, the very container that Vayp had been sitting against while he read.

Ndege has some splendid news for us... well... good for us, bad for you. A black crow, as dark as the shadows, rested atop the shadow's shoulder. It lifted its head and fluttered its wings as the shadow pet it. Vayp saw black particles splash from its wings as if it was made of ink. *The good news is that we will no longer have to worry about countering their tracking spell.*

"Why?" Vayp said, though he felt a pang of dread as to what the bad news would be.

Because... we will be going to them. They say that the great GroundStone's walls are unbreakable... oh how lovely it will be to see it fall. When Vayp said nothing, the shadow tilted its head. *Our plan has been made simpler... for it appears that... GroundStone has Eve.*

Vayp's eyes widened. What they planned to do with her he had no idea, but a part of him didn't even want to know.

Oh... but surely you'd like to know, no? It will be a glorious event, indeed. The Eve of Darkness has powers beyond measures... it defies all rules of time and space, and it is the one thing more powerful than the Divine One himself. It is Time's greatest weapon.

Vayp looked up at Han'sael, who was still floating inside, and he wondered why they'd need Han'sael if Eve was all they were looking for, but then he questioned if any of this even mattered anymore. If they were sure to win, sure to defeat GroundStone, to overwhelm Gabrael and Raaz'a, to capture Eve, just as they had done each time Time reset itself, then why... just why did any of this matter? If their fate was settled, why keep him and Han'sael here?

Because... I told you... I keep my promises. The shadow looked to his side and glanced at the other shadow. *I am a man of my word. And this is why you must keep reading, we do not have much time. For once the Shadow Army and the Mas'ahk are ready... we attack.*

Mas'ahk? Vayp remembered hearing of a Mas'ahk from one of the stories his father would share... but surely it was not the same one in the myths... because—Vayp's eyes widened—

Oh the Mas'ahk is very real, indeed. You see... it is created not just from any dead souls.... but its power comes from the dead whose murdered souls still haunt them. And it so happens... we have picked the perfect location for such a resurrection. The Mas'ahk from your father's stories will be nothing compared to this one. GroundStone WILL fall.

Just as Vayp was trying to process the danger Gaia was in, the ground trembled with such a force that Vayp felt his brain rattle against his skull.

Ah... he will be ready soon. And then it happened; a hand as dark as the night and as large as a temple burst through the ground, boulders the size of houses shot into the air. *Oh how wonderful he will be!* The shadow held his head high, as if already soaking in the victory. *GroundStone… the Guardians of Gaia… the Protectors of Nature… I will never understand why they pride themselves on being unbreakable… on having an impenetrable defense. Relying on defense only prolongs the inevitable, but death will still come. Why give their people a sense of hope. Hope that they could survive, even though they will not. Here is something to learn, young Earthie: defense will never win a fight, a battle, or a war. If you truly want to unlock your power… embrace the killer instincts I see within you. Embrace it. And victory will always be yours.*

Vayp watched nervously as both shadows drew nearer and nearer, examining Han'sael, bubbles floating from his mask. The shadow paused and pressed its arm cleanly through the solid glass. Vayp's stomach twisted as he saw the shadow lift Han'sael's chin up.

The shadow turned toward Vayp and saw what must've been a look of pure dread on Vayp's face. *Why do you look so scared?*

"What… what are you going to do to him?" Vayp said.

He is a part of a separate promise… which is why you must keep reading… that book. He pointed at the Book of Eve, the orb still blazing in the darkness. *Go on. You do not have much time.*

"But what about…" Vayp gulped, afraid to ask this question, "… the bad news?"

Ah… the bad news. Well… it seems as if you are not the only one interested in killing S'rae. She will be dying soon… let's just hope that it is by your hands… or you will find yourself without either of them in your life. How unfortunate.

Muttering darkly, Vayp backed up, knocking into Han'sael's container. Someone else was trying to kill S'rae… why? An emotion burned within him… but he couldn't understand exactly what he felt. Was he mad that someone else would kill her before him… or just mad that someone was trying to kill her? He wished he knew the answer… or maybe it was better if he didn't know. It'd make his deed that much easier. *Don't feel bad for her. She did this to me… she's the reason for this. I will get you back, Ah'nyx. I will make her pay for this.*

Ah yes… the killer instincts… the true sign of strength. But… Time is not on your side… you know what you must do. And just like that, the shadows vanished, taking the sense of dread with them.

Vayp was now left alone with Han'sael, thinking about what the future may hold. Clutching his robe to his face, Vayp's eyes darted around. The book was lying to his side, an eternal flame ignited inside the orb; a burning question made Vayp reach out and grab it. There was only one other person who could relate to Vayp's situation. He slammed the book open and flipped through the pages until he found blank ones, then went back a few pages until he saw words. Vayp punched his fists on the ground out of frustration. It was impossible to skip ahead to find out what Destrou would do in his situation, for the words only appeared after he finished reading the previous sentence. *Do you kill Ranmau, Destrou? I need to know! What happens between you two… the brothers? Is this how Ranmau's story ends…*

Vayp's eyes scanned the empty page as he watched the words "You okay, Ranmau?" burn onto it.

8

"**Y**OU OKAY, RANMAU?" Destrou said, steadily reaching out to Ranmau in the darkness, who was only an arm's reach away. The Box didn't afford the luxury of space, but Destrou didn't mind.

"Ranmau... you okay?" he asked again, expecting at least a grunt to conserve energy.

There was no response.

Destrou nudged Ranmau and felt his body as cold as ice. The shove rolled him over to his side.

A putrid scent burned Destrou's eyes and nostrils. He recognized this smell, how could he forget it? It was of decay, like the rotten meat he had been forced to eat. It was of... death.

Thud! Ranmau's body crashed into the wall of the Box as if he were a frozen statue. His eyes were wide open, unblinking and white. His mouth was barely open, unbreathing and silent. He was lifeless, just like... Elu.

Ranmau... is dea—

Destrou woke up in a frantic hurry. His palms were sweaty while his lungs attempted to burst out of his ribs with each deep inhale. He scanned the room, wondering if he was reintroduced to reality. He grabbed onto the fur sheet on top of his bed and dug his fingers in between its fluffy strands. His fingertips grazed over the soft fabric in circular motions; disorientation weighed down his face as if he was expecting a different texture. The sense of touch let him know that he was no longer dreaming; the confusion subsided and he became relaxed as he examined the room. Ranmau was sound asleep on his bed. *It was just a dream.*

The feeling of alleviation was great yet horrifying. There was a dichotomy waging an emotional war. He tried to be happy that it was just a dream and Ranmau was still alive, but he was overwhelmed with the feeling of helplessness that came with it.

He woke up with his greatest fear lodged into his mind as a reality. That thought crippled him. He felt weak and his insecurities rekindled a memory he had tried desperately to forget. One that had been locked away for years: Death was inevitable, it will happen. He tried to clear his mind to not relive it, but it was too late. The nightmare had already begun.

* * *

"What are you doing over here near the Edge?" Ranmau said, patting Destrou's head. Ranmau joined, sitting next to Destrou at the Edge, overlooking the Forest of Ness, its darkness looking like a black canvas with gray spindly branches. The brothers were almost shoulder to shoulder, Ranmau was only a few inches taller. Their feet dangled over the cliff as if dancing to the wind that surged by. "You shouldn't be out here alone, you know this, Destrou. I don't trust the Village. Come on, let's go back and train. Our first challenge is coming up soon—we need to be ready! We will win this, I know we will. Why? Because we're kinda too awesome. And by kinda too awesome... I mean way too awesome. And by way too awesome... I mean—"

"I get it!" Destrou laughed. "You really think we have a chance? I'd be happy if we can win at least once. That's all I need. Imagine how great that'd be with extra food... and warmth! Mmmm!"

His mouth dripped with hunger as he jumped around excitedly. "I promise to get you some food when I win!"

Ranmau laughed, pushing Destrou. "No way! You won't even win in your dreams, your mind knows better than to lie to you like that! But I promise you that I'll get you some extra food when *I* win—at least once." Ranmau smiled, peering over the Edge. "And one day, I'll also be a Crystal Soldier, meet the Supreme General, and fight to make this world a better place! None of these problems will exist anymore! I will change it all, I promise."

"I believe it. And you'd make the best Crystal Soldier ever!" Destrou replied. He stood up then pointed at the Forest. "I wonder what's out there. Is the world big or small? I can't even see the end of the Forest." He pressed his fingers together, creating a circle with each hand, and placed them to his eyes. He squinted as if it made him see farther. It did not.

"I think it's probably really huge. One day, we both will be able to find out what's out there. That's a promise that I will definitely keep! There's a world out there, Destrou, I want us to see it."

"That'd be great, but as long as I'm with you I don't really care where I am." Destrou smiled, lowering himself to kneel over the Edge.

The Edge appeared to be less refined. It seemed as if the Snake, a contraption the Villagers used to collect food from the cliff, had not been used as frequently. The wall that fell underfoot wasn't as deep into the Forest nor as smooth.

They both stared into the darkness, unable to see the bottom.

"Okay, I'm ready to go back now," Destrou said as he stopped drawing circles in the snow and stood up. His gaze remained on a fixed point inside the Forest. "But... I have a question... have you ever wondered what—never mind."

"No, go on. What were you going to ask? There's no bad question that you can ask me." Ranmau smiled.

"I don't know... it's just that... do you ever think what death is like? Like what actually happens to us and where we'd go?"

"Are you thinking about this because the Commander hasn't came back since he went in?"

"No... I mean, yes. I mean, that is kind of where I thought about it, but have you ever thought about what would happen to *us*? Like really thought about it? Would I ever be able to see you again? I don't know what I would do if we couldn't be together anymore."

Ranmau pressed his hand onto Destrou's shoulder. Destrou's face leaned against his chest. He had a careful touch, but was stern enough to guide Destrou's view in the direction that he wanted. With one delicate twist, they faced the Forest of Ness, straight ahead. He leaned Destrou forward, looking down at the Forest emitting its darkness. "What do you see, Destrou?"

"What do you mean?"

"What do you see?"

"Nothing... darkness?"

"Now close your eyes." Ranmau gently placed his hands over Destrou's eyes, shutting them. "Now what do you see?"

"I don't know? More nothing... and more darkness."

"Well, when you think of death... think of that nothing and darkness. Nothing and darkness forever. And that... that is death."

Destrou's eyes created a glaze. Streams of ice flowed down his face with no sign of them stopping.

"What's wrong?" Ranmau said, a rare inflection of worry in his voice.

Destrou's head jerked each time he attempted to open his mouth. He shielded his emotions within his thin white shirt, completely burying his face inside it.

He finally mustered up the strength to say: "I... don't... want... to... be... without you." He clamped his mouth shut with his shaking hands. "I... don't... want... to... die..."

Ranmau placed his hand on Destrou's head, caressing him with a slow and steady touch. "Destrou, you should know one thing:

when we become great, we will never die, because our story will live forever. You shouldn't be scared of death, I think there is something worse."

"What's worse than death?"

"Being forgotten," Ranmau said sternly, as if it was a fact, not an opinion. "There is nothing worse than being forgotten. I would rather die and be remembered than live to be forgotten. I want stories to be told about us the way that the Commander told us stories about the Supreme General. I want our lives to mean something. So, that way you won't have to worry about dying, because we will live on forever. This doesn't have to be our life—we can change our destinies. And if you're the first to go, I'm going to tell your story for as long as I live."

* * *

"I... don't... want... to... die," Destrou said softly, attempting to control his severe shivers.

Wait… judging by the cold that pierced his body like knives, he knew exactly where he was now: the Box. All of that was just a dream… or dreams? A dream within a dream within a dream. How cruel. He was no longer in the comfort of his own room. There was no bed, warmth, or joy—only the Box. His mind had reached the point of no return and was no longer able to differentiate between his dreams, nightmares, or reality. Just like the terrible nightmare he had when Elu turned into one of *them*. Impossible. He vaguely remembered something about the Guardian confirming that something bad had happened to Elu, but that must have been a bad dream, too. He no longer knew what was his imagination and what was real.

When he fully awakened, he tried to hold onto the freeing feeling of the dream, but within a moment it drifted away, leaving him sadder and lonelier than ever. The grim truth was that any nightmare would be more satisfying than this reality of starving inside a barrier of ice, the Box, awaiting his likely demise. His greatest fear was relived each time he woke up, wondering if the last time he was with his brother... would be the last time he was with his brother.

In the Village and in life, it was only until the next day when one knew that it was their last day with their friend. No one could truly know when that last day would be. He woke up with the fear that every yesterday was his last day with Ranmau. And that he would never know until it was too late.

Unable to see his hand in front of his face, Destrou struggled to lift it, reaching out toward Ranmau. His body ached, sending sharp, stabbing pains from his fingers to toes. He inched his hand near him. His body wished for him to stop, but he needed to know. His frigid fingers cracked as he extended them outward. He groaned, pressing his hand against Ranmau's chest. It was still.

Though he was too numb and couldn't feel his own body, somehow he felt his heart pound against his chest. His worry overwhelmed him and his nightmares became a reality.

Please... alive... be... alive... please.

Destrou was barely able to think out loud; even the ease of thinking became difficult. Transferring thoughts into words proved to be impossible, like talking through lips sewn together.

His heart sank. Death was upon him, sucking the air out of his lungs. It finally dawned on him as his breathing became heavier: There was no pulse or beat to Ranmau's heart. And though it was Ranmau's heart that stopped, something within Destrou did as well. It must have been true what they said: when two hearts beat as one, when one stopped beating, the other followed.

Destrou's heart slowed down. His eyes sealed shut, his head leaned backward, pressing against the solid ice. He felt his body shutting down and knew his brain must have been next. His life flashed before his eyes in distorted images; it was his time to say goodbye.

Then a soft whisper resonated inside of Destrou's ear, but it was waived off as another mind trick.

The faint whisper was heard again. But in that moment, Destrou's heart had already stopped beating.

Seconds had passed, and there was still no beat. His cold body turned colder. His eyes gracefully shut.

The two brothers sat there as frozen statues representing hope. Hope for a better life where love could outlast hate and where freedom wasn't a luxury stripped from many and given to few. Could this be the purpose of life… to live, freeze, and die in this Village blocked off from all life—blocked off from the Kingdom? Could this be the end of their story?

It was. They tried, they fought, they failed. And now they'd be forgotten... just like the others. Life would continue as if they had never existed. Their bodies would be buried, if the Village was kind, but more than likely they'd be used to satiate the hungers that ran rampant.

Then a shuffle was heard, a soft movement from within the Box that stated otherwise, that their purpose was much greater. That their story would not end. Not now, at least.

"I... don't... want... to... die—" Ranmau said with a strained whisper, reaching deaf ears. "—either,"

Ranmau reached his hand out in short bursts, grabbing Destrou's fallen hand.

In that moment when their hands united, waves of life surged through Destrou's body. His eyelids flared open with a gasp.

Ranmau?

9

ITH... INK... TO... DAY. I THINK... TO... DAY... TODAY... IS... THE... LAST... DAY.

Destrou's shivers made processing thoughts extremely difficult. He knew that joining Ranmau was a dangerous risk, but he also knew that the warmth of his body would help him not freeze to death. He refused to allow Ranmau to go through this punishment alone. After all, Ranmau was sent into the Box because of him. If he never came back to save him from the Leader and his hoard of boys, then he would be free. Freedom... there was nothing that Ranmau wanted more than that, at least that was what Destrou had always thought. But he had his glimpse of freedom and chose to come back. That one action meant the world to Destrou. Though he only had about two months to live before he would fight Ranmau in the tournament, two months until Ranmau killed him and reclaimed his freedom by joining the Crystal Soldiers, Destrou felt like he would die happy knowing that at least he was loved.

Loved... he felt loved before... she had a name... what was her name? Being stuck in the Box for a week nearly melted his brain into a slush of distorted memories. There was a vision of crinkling, smiling blue eyes, a white cloth wrapped around her forehead, nose, and mouth. *Your name what is? Can't forget...*

He kept his body close to Ranmau's, feeling the slow pulses of his heart. Throughout this week of hell, he felt Ranmau's heartbeat vibrate so slowly that he nudged him to make sure that he was still alive. But this was their last day, he had to make it.

No words were exchanged the entire time. Destrou took no offense, because he knew that Ranmau needed time for himself to reflect on the situation.

Freedom... he had... it. No more now...

Destrou held back a whimper to not awaken Ranmau.

Arm... broken... Wall... now... imposs... to... climb. Protect Ranmau...

A loud shuffle was heard overhead followed by a *creak* that shook his insides. The ice slab began to slide.

Destrou slowly poked Ranmau to let him know it was time. It was actually time. Did they really survive the Box? Destrou attempted to stand up, but there was an unbelievable blinding light that peered through the opening, forcing him back down as he covered his eyes. It felt like he was being reborn, as if this was his first time seeing light. But maybe this was the beginning of a new life, he knew that things would be different the second they left the Box. How different exactly he had no idea, but his heart skipped a beat just thinking about it.

Ranmau stood up with his eyes closed, holding his injured arm. "Prisoners for a week... and now I imagine this is what they want us to accept as freedom," he said underneath his breath, barely loud enough for Destrou to hear him.

Destrou glanced at Ranmau who appeared in a way that no one had ever viewed him: defeated and distraught. Physically, Ranmau looked weak, but Destrou knew that the real damage was done to his mind. It was tough to watch. Ranmau was always the confident, unbreakable hero; but for the first time, Destrou looked at Ranmau as a victim who needed help.

The two of them hunched over the Box and collapsed to the ground, their legs gave out from underneath them. At once, it felt like a thousand knives poked at his cramped muscles. As they struggled to stand, using each other for support, the Village preyed on them with narrowed eyes. In that moment, any slither of hope that the Village had changed while they were gone vanished.

The brothers were broken physically and mentally. They reached the lowest point that they could ever reach and and Destrou knew they had a decision to make: either view it as a crux that buried them deeper or as a tool that lifted them to a point higher than they ever thought possible.

Destrou lifted Ranmau's good arm over his shoulder and they limped toward their igloo. Their home, which was once viewed as a last resort to escape misery, had never looked so welcoming.

As they made their way through a gauntlet of boys pounding stone clubs against their palms, Destrou turned his attention to Ranmau. His silver hair drooped messily over his sunken face. His grey eyes no longer had stars in them, the glittering fire that always told Destrou that things would be okay. Without thinking, Destrou pushed his forehead into Ranmau's cheek and whispered, "I will protect you. You were there for me when you were at your best; so I will be there for you when you are at your worst." It took everything in him to force back the tears.

Destrou knew it was a foolish, impossible task, but more than that, he knew that Ranmau was no longer able to protect the both of them. His soul was broken, Destrou saw it in his eyes that drooped as if they were drained of life. Destrou knew their roles were now reversed. The Village was wild, any day could be their last, so Destrou did not have time to think about his decision. It was made. There was no other option: the protected needed to become the protector. *I can do this.*

Destrou was numb outside, but inside he was a wrecking ball, wondering how he will be able to achieve any of this: winning a challenge, getting extra food, and protecting Ranmau in his current state. It was in that moment when he realized just how amazing Ranmau was.

It was not until the burden was placed on his shoulders when he truly understood the adversity that Ranmau went through to provide comfort and security for the both of them. As if he thought it was impossible to love Ranmau anymore than he had, he couldn't help but smile once more at Ranmau with a glowing respect.

Destrou gave one final look at the boys surrounding him. He did not expect the Village to be happy to see them survive the Box, but he was not expecting this. The glaring looks, the life-threatening air that circled around them. It was as if everything about their lives changed yet somehow remained the same.

The Leader stood at the entrance to their room with an unforgettable grin, squeezing his calloused palm with his fingertips. His long black hair was tied back into a bun and his white fur pauldrons seemed larger than before, making him appear more intimidating than Destrou remembered. The Giant stood on the other side of the entrance, smiling creepily through his long grizzled hair that drooped over his face, revealing his missing teeth—reminding the brothers that there was unfinished business.

The worst had indeed yet to come. The world as Destrou knew it had been flipped upside down. The past crumbled to pieces the moment the Box sealed shut.

Their new life began the moment the light shone through the opening of the Box. Destrou knew the Village wouldn't wait for them to recover, they were vultures ready to pick apart corpses. So, that night it would begin. It needed to. Destrou would have to train to become the person he had always looked up to. It sounded impossible just thinking about it. Ranmau was the untouchable, the great, Destrou was always just the sidekick.

But thinking like that wouldn't help the situation, he had to just suck it up and prepare for the unknown, but he couldn't do anything until after he rested, so he carefully helped Ranmau onto his block of ice called a bed before limping to his side of the igloo.

As the night crept in and the purple sky faded to black, Destrou still couldn't sleep. Being so exhausted as he was, he thought this would be the easiest part, but it wasn't. He was already off to a terrible start. At first, he blamed it on the foul odor that kept seeping through the window with each breeze, but in the back of his mind he knew that something else kept him up. His mind couldn't let go of one haunting question and his sleep suffered because of it.

As more hours passed, Destrou found himself sitting on top of his igloo, gazing out at nothing in particular. Thoughts of what will happen to them tomorrow briefly crossed his mind, but there was still something more pressing that troubled him, but he couldn't put his finger on it, like a snowflake being swept away by the wind. He then focused on the Wall, the icy barricade that stretched throughout the entire Village and reached somewhere beyond the clouds. A part of him hoped that it would provide an answer, but all it did was remind him just how terrible his life was.

When another wave of this putrid stench hit Destrou's nostrils, he finally decided to find its source. He slid down the igloo and noticed a string of rope, with rotten food dangling from it, surrounding his window. The putrid smell of decayed food coupled with feces and urine made their igloo an unbearable place. Destrou rattled the rope, but firm knots held it together tightly. It seemed like the Village wasted no time to welcome the brothers back.

Ranmau didn't mind the scent... but he seemed to not care about anything anymore. He hadn't moved in hours, and just stared up at the ceiling. It seemed as if neither of them were going to get some sleep tonight.

"I can't get that stupid thing off," Destrou said through the window with a nasally voice, clamping his nostrils with his fingers.

Ranamu said nothing.

"Is this how it's going to be?" Destrou asked, entering the igloo, hopping into his bed.

Ranmau still said nothing.

"I just want to say thank you for coming back for me. I'm... sorry that... your arm—"

"You would have done the same for me, right?" Ranmau replied, unblinking.

"Of course. And I will do the same for you. That's what brothers should do."

"Yeah," Ranmau said coldly.

Destrou narrowed his eyes. Something felt off about Ranmau, but Destrou couldn't figure out exactly what. He knew Ranmau enough to know that this wasn't about the Box, something else was on his mind.

Ranmau didn't move—not even a flinch when the cold night's wind blew his hair onto his face; finally, he blinked, and just as Destrou was about to say something, Ranmau's eyes began to glaze.

Destrou placed his head down, his dark dreads falling to hide his face. A stream of ice trickled down his brown skin underneath. He couldn't stand to look at his brother like this. Ranmau had never looked so defeated—so vulnerable.

"I will protect you, brother," Destrou said sharply. "You can trust me. I won't let them hurt you."

"You can't even protect yourself... how are you going to protect the both of us?" Ranmau said, turning his face away from Destrou, rubbing his eyes.

"I won't tell you how, I'll show you." There was something within Destrou that made his body come alive. He wanted to prove everyone wrong, especially Ranmau.

Minutes passed, and Destrou knew he should have focused on getting rest, but despite his exhaustion, sleep remained out of reach. Something was still locked away in his mind that needed to escape; it had been clawing at him since the moment he saw Elu's frozen body. Elu... Elu! That was her name! Then suddenly, without warning, the thing that troubled him most was finally starting to surface. He thought about the lies that the Village and the Leader had spread. But, there was something oddly genuine about the Leader's anger when he accused Ranmau of killing his sister, an emotion of sorrow that was too unlike him, as if... as if... he was actually telling the truth. But there was no way it was true, Ranmau wouldn't do that, he knew Elu was Destrou's friend. His only friend. Then Destrou felt terrible, thinking about the moment Ranmau's arm was broken in half; he was wrongfully punished for something... he didn't do. He wouldn't do, right?

For several hours, Destrou remained motionless, staring through his window, wondering why he felt as empty as the starless night before him. The Box had damaged his mind, but his memories slowly recovered. Maybe it was for the better because when the question appeared in his thoughts, it crushed him harder than the Guardian ever could. He realized that what was missing wasn't a what, at all, but a who: Elu... and the truth about her murderer. He couldn't fight back the question anymore.

He tried to open his mouth but something flickered behind his eyes. He looked away and rubbed them.

He then turned back to Ranmau, his mouth wide open, his lips trembling, as if afraid of the answer that he may hear. "Did you—" Something caught Destrou's throat. *Why is this so hard?* He took a deep breath before trying again. "Before we went into the box... the Leader said something that I... that I just... don't believe. I don't like to believe everything that I hear... especially if it's coming out of his mouth; but... but then the Guardian said it—" he tried to finish his thought but he was arrested mid-sob.

Ranmau turned away from Destrou, revealing his back. "We don't have to talk about this now. We should just get some sleep. We need it."

"I don't think you understand... I can't go to sleep. I just can't. I've been trying, like really trying, but... it's the only thing on my mind. I—I try to shut my eyes but… it keeps me awake. I just… I just need to know something," Destrou said, sniffling into his shirt.

"I know what you're going to ask," Ranmau said bluntly.

"You do?"

Ranmau made a glance at Destrou before turning away. Destrou had never seen his eyes so glassy before.

"If you do… then… what's the answer?" Destrou hiccuped.

Ranmau said nothing.

"It was a lie, right? You wouldn't do that to Elu… she was my friend—my only friend. You knew that. You wouldn't do that to Elu… to me, right?"

Silence.

Ranmau laid on his bed pretending to be asleep—as if for his own benefit. As if he knew that his greatest fear would turn into a reality if he answered Destrou's question. That would break him; Destrou wasn't strong enough to hear the truth. His heart was too big; unfortunately the biggest hearts were also the most fragile.

Destrou reached over Ranmau's bed, pulling Ranmau closer. "Please." Destrou sniffled. Their noses nearly touched, Destrou looked into his brother's grey eyes and in their reflection, he noticed his once brown eyes were now bloodshot around his dilated pupils. "I need to know… I need to get these thoughts out of my head—please! Please! I need to sleep!"

Ranmau took a deep breath and squirmed about before wincing, as if he had the urge to put his arms around Destrou. As if he wanted to tell him that everything will be okay. But the way a tear fell from his eye, he knew. He knew that life would never be the same if… no, *when* the truth was uncovered.

"It wasn't… a lie," Ranmau said softly.

Destrou had never known the full power of words before, the way they could suck the life out of a person and make the whole sky feel like it was falling, but now he did. After a few long moments of silence, Destrou eyes wandered around, collecting his thoughts. He must've heard incorrectly. The Box had disoriented him, after all.

"What?" Destrou said, staring at Ranmau as if he told him that everything good in the world perished. "What wasn't a lie?"

"About Elu."

Destrou slouched back, crashing into his bed.

"No. I don't get it," Destrou whimpered. "Not Elu... not you. I don't think we're thinking of the same question, no, it's *not* the same question then. That's *not* what happened. I don't think we're talking about the same thing, we're not! We can't be."

Destrou struggled to sit down on his bed. He tried to balance his quivering hands on his knees. His body trembled in a way that he had never experienced before. It was as if he was told that his brother killed his best friend—his only friend, his love.

"You wouldn't do something like that to me though. I—I know it's a lie." Destrou heard the irritation in his own voice. "I know it is."

After nothing was said, Destrou sank into his bed and regarded Ranmau with a stare as hateful as the eyes of the Leader.

He shook his head so many times his neck hurt. His fingers dug into the fur of his bed with all the strength that he had, staring toward the ground but at nothing in particular. His teeth clenched to the brink of shattering. His body was engulfed with a rage that he didn't know how to control.

"Tell me that you didn't mean to," Destrou growled, his eyelids sealed together holding back the pressure behind his eyes.

Ranmau said nothing.

"You're sorry, right?" he screamed, slamming his fists onto the ice. He heard a crack that might have been his bones, yet he didn't flinch. He felt no pain.

Ranmau remained still as if Destrou had been talking only to himself.

"Don't you care at all?" Destrou screamed so loud that he didn't care if he woke up the Guardians. "*Anything*? Does any part of you care about anyone other than yourself? They were right—*you* are the enemy." Emotions poured from his face. "I'm talking to you! Elu was an amazing person, the most amazing person who meant the world to me—and you don't even care. She went through too much and had too much left to do. She was going to travel the world and do so much. Much more than you ever would, you krillen!"

"We don't know what she would have done," Ranmau said softly, with no emotion behind his voice. "She died. It happened. It's over. This is what happens in life, in the Village. There's nothing we can do about it now. It's in the past. Can I go to sleep now?"

"Can you go to sleep now?" Destrou shouted, practically tearing the dreads off his head. "Are you serious? Stop trying to make it seem like everything is okay. Everything isn't okay and it will never be okay. You don't even care about how it makes *ME* feel."

"It's unfortunate that it happened," Ranmau said, glancing over at Destrou, who still had his fingers in between his thick, dark strands. "I don't wish death for anyone, but she was at the wrong place at the wrong time. Nothing personal. At least she doesn't have to suffer anymore—I probably did her a favor. Death happens... no one can escape it. Not you. Not me. Not her. Not anyone. You have to accept that death is just a part of life. It's in the past—get over it."

Destrou fell to his knees and threw up, gagging as he coughed and spat out whatever was left in his empty stomach. His whole body shook with such force that it seemed like the vomiting would never end.

"You!" Destrou snarled at Ranmau, "Y-you, you don't deserve... you don't deserve anything! You are a monster and now it makes sense why everyone hates you. Did you want to make an enemy out of me, too? Well, you win again... like you always do. Because I hate you! I hate you and I wish—"

Destrou wanted to stop his hateful thoughts but they kept spewing out. He wanted to shut off his brain, but words kept launching out of his mouth, piercing through Ranmau like daggers dipped in despair. His eyes stung with each word he yelled out. And out of frustration, he grabbed a stray bone near his bed and threw it at Ranmau.

The bone ricocheted off of Ranmau's broken arm, falling to the ground.

"Ow!" Ranmau screamed, clenching his elbow. Agony was on his face. "Did you really have to do that? Go to sleep already. We don't need to do this. We just went through too much."

"It's already in the past—get over it," Destrou growled.

He forced himself to get into bed, curling into a ball away from Ranmau.

Ranmau did the same, his body turned away from Destrou.

Ranmau was silent except for the occasional sniffle. It was as if he knew that anything that was said could not be unsaid and his words would do more harm than good at this point.

A burning hatred engulfed every one of Destrou's emotions. A thought drifted through his mind that he needed to suppress—it scared him that his mind would even think of such a thing.

What's wrong with me?

The thought appeared again—this time more vividly. It settled down, infesting the forefront of his mind.

He envisioned that dreadful day: walking outside of his igloo, spotting the white shroud that contoured over a human body. He walked toward it with bated breath. When he reached the body, it was much larger than he expected. His eyelids sealed shut as he pulled the shroud off, revealing the corpse. When he opened his eyes, it was no longer Elu lying there lifelessly—it was Ranmau.

A smile broke the gloom in his face.

"If only you two could just swap places," Destrou said, rubbing his eyes. He made sure to say it loud enough so Ranmau could hear him. "I didn't think that I could miss someone this much, but I miss you, Elu…. I miss you so, so much. I wish I could be where you are… or you could be here… or we could be anywhere together. I just wish that I had the chance to tell you that I miss you and I am glad that you existed during my time here."

Elu's smile haunted him, pressing against the back of his mind, leaking out from behind his eyes.

His vision of Ranmau had forever been tainted. In one moment, his whole world changed; his view on life… his purpose of life… his desire for life… he felt everything drift away. If he could have found a way to shut down his emotions that didn't resort to death, he wouldn't have hesitated. The monster slowly began to reveal itself again. He saw a massive Archon prowl through his mind, dragging a long sword, ready to end Destrou with one swing.

That night, Destrou laid staring at the vast night's sky, wondering if he'd ever sleep again. Every time he closed his eyes, the haunting image of Ranmau murdering Elu, her blackened eyes filled with horror, plagued his mind. In his dreams or not, he could swear he kept hearing the contagious laughter of Elu followed by her screaming cry for help.

Destrou knew that he would never forget hearing her voice and laughter; he accepted that sleep now became an impossible dream. He hoped that he could fall asleep by waiting for the fatigue that came after the tears, but the tiredness never came… only more sorrow.

He decided that there was too much on his mind and the only way to get some rest was if his body was no longer physically able to stay awake.

His body was beyond the point of no repair. He needed sleep, but couldn't get any. He wanted to forgive Ranmau, but couldn't find it in him. He desired to protect him, but his body was unequipped to handle the role. He wanted to be the very best version of himself, but he felt that he was the lowest he had ever been.

"I know what I need to do. I either become my best or I don't… there's no more trying," he said, slamming his fists on the ground.

"Our lives will be in danger. I know it. They will try to hurt us…
and, most likely, even worse. I know it. If I don't step up… who
will? Ranmau can't even protect himself now never mind protect
the both of us. What happens when I get bullied and need help? And
worse… what happens if he gets bullied and needs help? I don't
think I can help him…. I don't even think I want to help him—not
after what he did. Maybe I should just let them ki— no! What am I
doing? Who am I becoming? What am I supposed to do? As much
as I hate you… you were there for me when I needed you. I don't
know…. I don't know if I want to be there for you when you need
me anymore. I don't think I have it in me. I don't know what to do,
but no matter what I can't do nothing."

Failure was no longer an option. His new life started that night;
he needed to forget who he was in the past and nurture who he will
become in the future.

No more excuses. I need to just do it!

And with that, he dashed off into the night toward the Crater, not
just to train but to run as far away from the day as he could.

10

T HE NIGHT WAS DARK, but any obstacles emerged as darker shadows and he was able to make his way quickly through the Village. He leapt over the railing into the Crater, jolting toward the center of it the moment he landed on his feet. He stopped in front of the large ice spike in the middle and examined the poles embedded into the ground. His near-death experience when the Giant had his life in his palms flashed before his eyes—yet another nostalgic moment when Ranmau saved his life that drifted through his memories.

"I don't want to help you... but I need to. Will this hate ever go away?" Destrou said to himself. "I need to keep reminding myself that Ranmau saved me too many times to let him down when he needs me the most. I just wish this was easy, to forgive."

Destrou noticed small silhouettes flashing here and there along the barrier of the Crater, moving about, stopping and turning, before jumping down into the Crater.

The voices came closer, forcing Destrou to hide behind the spike. He buried himself in snow, tucking his cloak over his knees and feet, appearing as a large mound of snow.

"You sure you saw him come here?" a whisper floated through

the darkness, catching Destrou's ears. The silhouettes carried an undercurrent of danger.

"Yeah, I definitely saw him come over here," another voice whispered.

Destrou stood behind the spike just a couple of feet from the two boys. He could feel their uneasy presence. *Are they looking for me? What do they want with me?*

"Well, it'd be very stupid of you to bring me to this place where nothing is happening when I could be sleeping," the boy said with a deep, unpleasant tone.

Destrou recognized the voice. He heard that voice too many times during his most painful moments. That commanding tone could only be the Leader's.

The Leader walked to the spike, a foot or two from Destrou, and dug his hands into the thick snow, spreading it around to reveal a murky object in the ground.

What are they looking for? Destrou thought, peering through a tiny opening.

The Leader stopped shuffling and waved his hand, luring the boy closer.

The dark-haired boy hesitated, leaning forward with a stumble.

"You don't want to end up like Faily and them now do you?" the Leader asked, grabbing the boy's head, slamming it to the ground.

The boy was lucky enough to press his palms against the thin layer of snow, preventing his face from smashing into the solid ice.

"No... no, I don't. I'm sorry," the boy shivered. "It won't happen again."

"It better not," the Leader said. "If it does... you'll end up down there instead of them. This is what happens when you fail me. I'm sure you don't want that to happen, right?"

"No, I promise to not let you down again," he said, whimpering.

Destrou's face grew pale. His breaths became difficult to swallow, knowing that worse would happen if he were caught. Ranmau was sound asleep and he was too exhausted to outrun either one of them. His heart pumped faster.

"They haven't had anything to eat," the Leader said. "They'll be too weak to defend us tomorrow. I know Ranmau won't be able to do much, but we still can't go easy on him, okay? Loyalty is important. I need to make sure that everyone knows what to do and doesn't screw up like you did tonight, okay? Tomorrow... the brothers will pay. It's going to be great."

"Yeah... it's going to be great. This is what you've been waiting for," he replied.

"No," the Leader growled, "this is what *we*... the entire Village... have been waiting for. They've been taking food from all of us, not me. This is what we all want."

"Yes, I'm sorry. *We*. I—I meant *we*, I swear. This is what *we've* been waiting for. We can't wait to see them fall."

A minute passed, then five. Several more. Destrou squirmed on his heels, wondering how long it'd take for the Leader and the boy to leave. He sat there, perfectly patient and still, staring into the darkness.

Shimmers of an odd light reflected off of the spike; it cast a shadow of blurred colors on the ground, as if he stood next to an aurora borealis. He sat motionless, squinting, trying to figure out what was happening on the other side. There was a movement of some kind. The sound of scraping followed by shavings floating to the ground. A large mass grew in his throat. *What's going on?*

The scraping ended. The footsteps of the two were heard faintly in the distance as they exited the Crater. Destrou waited a few moments before revealing his hiding location. One minute passed, then two. It was better to be safe than sorry. He crawled around the large spike, hoping to uncover their plan, but everything seemed untouched as if no one was ever there.

I know they did something, but what?

He bent down onto his knees and shuffled the snow around.

Beneath the snow the ice was as clear as crystal. His eyes lit up in disbelief. A shiver jolted through his body as he saw a pale face appear underneath the ice, staring into his eyes as if he were still alive.

Destrou jumped back, landing on his rear. He took small, quick breaths through his nose. Was that someone he recognized? He almost looked familiar but there were too many boys in the Village and he wasn't close to any of them.

Perspiration drenched his hands, his clothes, his hair, everything. A fear he had never known filled him to the point of worry: he and Ranmau were next. Their deaths may come sooner than the tournament—unless he prevented it.

He may not have known what the Leader's plan was, but he knew that he needed to stop it.

Despite his body having no desire to be pushed, Destrou wasted no time to continue his training. The next day was not certain nor was it guaranteed. But that night, all he could think about was stopping whatever it was that was going to happen.

While the Village rested, he pushed his mind and body to the brink of exhaustion. With bruised knuckles, he embedded deep imprints into the solid ice. With calloused palms, he moved boulders that were twice his size.

After an hour or so, a wrenching feeling forced him to stop immediately—his stomach tossed and turned. The Leader's words rang in his ears, he was absolutely right. They hadn't eaten in what felt like weeks; they were too weak. Their bodies lacked the energy to perform simple duties, never mind fight off the Leader and his followers. He knew what they needed but food in the Village was scarce; there was no way to randomly make it appear—or was there?

Another memory came to mind, hearing the laughter of Elu as they left the Guardian's lair. *Food.* He turned to look at the tip of the NoGo, seen just over the cusp of the Crater's barrier.

I know it's crazy, but I have nothing to lose and everything to gain.

The final traces of starvation crept up on him, and he made up his mind. Elu showed him how to get food, now he needed to obtain it on his own. *If I get the food for you, I feed you for tonight, but if I teach you how to get it, I feed you for a lifetime, even if it ends tomorrow,* Destrou remembered Elu's voice. He missed the way she would make light of the worst situations. Right now, she'd be smiling because she'd have an answer, she always did.

Thank you, Elu. You're looking out for me even when you're not around.

Less than an hour later, he found himself behind the Guardian's lair, shuffling his hands around the snow, looking for the tunnel.

She made it look so easy, he thought, struggling to find the way in.

Destrou was smart—he was confident enough to know that. But nothing about the snow tunnels made sense to him. Was it *how* Elu shuffled her hands or was there a trick she didn't teach him?

Trying with all of his will to avoid it, his mind kept wandering back to the memories of Elu every time he closed his eyes or thought. Normally when his imagination was filled with negativity, his brain would fill it with positive images. Laughter. Life. Love. Instead, it replayed Elu, screaming for help before turning into a frozen shell. He needed to empty his mind to go through with his plan—to go through with life.

Destrou stood up, hoping that the answer would come to him.

"Rub your hands together," whispered through his mind. He heard Elu's voice as if it was the soft wind that grazed the back of his neck. He turned around quickly, but nothing was there—no one.

He didn't understand it; his mind was overwhelmed trying to cope with the sheer impossibility of his situation. Surviving tomorrow. Breaking into the Guardian's lair. Stealing food. How could he do it? He wasn't Elu... he wasn't Ranmau... he was just Destrou.

I refuse to be just Destrou.

He rubbed his hands together, mimicking the same circular motion Elu would do and placed his palms where he remembered the hole to be; the snow melted instantly, revealing the tunnel. He smiled. He wasn't *just* Destrou. The new Destrou made things happen and didn't need help. The new Destrou was the help.

He never imagined himself sneaking into the Guardian's room by himself. But there he was, inhaling the foul odors, reminding him that this task was as unpleasant as it was dangerous.

He worked his way around the corner of the spiraling staircase, staring at the food door straight ahead. Their snores were just as awful as he remembered them: ear-splitting and pungent.

He arched down into a crawl, inching his way toward the open doorway. Despite the light being dim, he was able to make out minor changes to the door. It looked differently. There was something over the door but he couldn't make out the exact details.

He knew where he needed to go but something came over him. Instead of avoiding danger, he crawled directly toward it, turning into the Guardian's room. The air immediately warranted a cough as it reached Destrou's nostrils. There was a putrid smell that made his eyes water. He wondered if the Guardians had ever taken a bath.

I don't know why you made such a big deal out of the liquid ice machine. It's not like you ever used it. Destrou thought about the time the Guardians punished him for destroying the liquid ice tower, which was the Village's only source of a shower. After it broke, that was when they announced that Ranmau would fight Destrou to the death to become a Crystal Soldier and gain freedom. And for the first time… it occurred to him… *I could kill Ranmau now… I could get freedom?* A deep snore interrupted his dark thoughts. A part of him was glad that it did.

Observing Elu had its benefits as he mastered her crawl, gliding through the Guardian's room, hardly making a sound. There were slight interruptions in the Guardian's snores but other than that the path was clear.

The light that reflected off of the ground gave him a clear destination. Shimmering off of a paper on the wall, he saw a painting with five circles on it and slowly made his way there. The snores grew unbearably loud, forcing him to press his palms against his ears. The bed was at least twice the length of Destrou's body. And it was covered by the white fur skin of a large beast, its head and claws still attached. Though he had seen the Guardian many times, he was still in disbelief at the sheer size of him.

As Destrou reached the end of the bed, the Guardian's hand fell down, inches away from his face. He slowed his breathing down. Even just the slightest breeze caused the Guardian's hand to twitch. Instead of turning back around, Destrou was determined to look at the painting. He learned to trust Elu's judgments and stories, she had once mentioned a story about there once being four elements in this world and how they were used to trap the Archons inside of the Forest of Ness, but that seemed impossible! The Guardians only told stories about the three elements, but this was something that he needed to see for himself.

How could there have been four elements?

At the end of the bed, he hunched up to his knees, pulling his face closer to the painting. He saw it. There was a picture of four circles around a larger fifth circle. The fifth circle in the center had a large tree in the middle with many trees surrounding it. Inside each of the four circles there were different emblems, each with their own faded color. It was dark and too far away to make out the details. *What does any of this mean, though?*

The room rumbled as the Guardian's hand turn over the bed, followed by his body crashing to the ground. Destrou's whole body shook with the quake.

The Guardian stood up, facing the entrance and made his way toward the corridor. Destrou immediately slid underneath his bed. The slight noise caused the Guardian to turn around with a snarl.

Nothing was there.

The Guardian made his way into the Commander's room, waking him up with one loud smack.

"Ow," the Commander shouted, "Wot are yah doin'? Wot was that for?"

"I'm hungry," the Guardian said. "Just letting you know that you can eat now, too. If you want."

"I thought yah'd never ask," the Commander replied.

Destrou squinted his eyes in pain and held his ears as he heard the shriek of ice scraping against ice.

A loud crash boomed that sounded like a solid object slammed on the ground.

"Mer," the Guardian said, "let's see them try to get through this. Mmm... our secret stash of Sensu. Gotta love it!" Their laughter echoed into the room, trembling the ground beneath him.

They must've sealed the door shut. For several seconds, he felt like the world had frozen in place. A thick silence was followed by a rumble of the food door closing, and it turned into a quake as the Guardians made their way back into their rooms. The tremors were more powerful the closer they came to the room, chattering Destrou's teeth.

The faint smell of citrus rejuvenated him for a moment until it was accompanied by the scent of mold from the Guardian's feet, inches away from his face.

I failed... I can't get through that door. His body wanted to be filled with terror, thinking about what the consequences might be, but his mind was intrigued by the fresh scent. Sensu?

There was something about this food that smelled differently— it was unlike anything that he had before. It had such a strong scent that it eventually overwhelmed the Guardian's feet. Destrou's head rose into the air, his nostrils flared open with deep sniffs. Just the smell alone gave him life. He hunkered low, struggling to quiet his heaving chest.

"Mmmm," the Guardian moaned, "the Sensu meat always does the trick."

Sensu meat? He had never heard of it before, why was it a secret?

Crumbs sprinkled to the ground. Normally he would have been disgusted at the idea of eating food off of their floor, but he was too curious and hungry to resist them. He reached for a crumb, squeezing it with his fingers, bringing it closer to his mouth. It had a gooey texture that clinged to his fingers as he tried to space them apart. Saliva dripped for his mouth, pressing his finger between his lips, sucking on it.

Destrou felt his face heat up—he was caught off guard because he'd expected at least a little disgust. *Wow, that was... amazing!*

He locked his fingers again as he peered down the doorway that led into the corridor, as if expecting the Commander to enter at any moment.

The bed above him shook like it was about to crumble. The rumble was soon followed by loud, thunderous snores. And just like that, the Guardian was out cold. Destrou wished he could fall asleep as easily. It must be nice to not have a single care in the world.

Then soon after, the same rumble came from the Commander's room.

Destrou poked his head out from underneath the bed and temptation took over. He knew better than to steal the remaining food resting on the platform near the Guardian's bed, but his craving overcame his judgment. Destrou was rejuvenated in a way that he couldn't explain. The small taste of the crumbs was enough to fill his body with energy. He wanted more of it. No, he needed it.

Destrou stood up and grabbed the food.

He won't notice just a little bit missing, would he? He pinched the food. *Okay, maybe a little bit more.* He pulled off a bigger piece. The texture was soft, ripping easily at his fingertips.

Moments passed, and before he knew it, he licked his fingers clean and there was no more food left for the Guardian.

Oops!

The addiction was too strong to resist. Destrou didn't know which he felt more strongly at that moment: joy at being full of energy or anger for eating all of it. Despite being a small amount, the food made him feel better than ever.

A few minutes later, Destrou escaped from the building, laughing out loud as he sprinted through the snow. He went silent, as if someone interrupted him, remembering the last time he laughed after escaping the NoGo. He sighed, wishing that Elu was here to share this experience with him again. "I miss you too much," he said.

I just want to see you again.

Destrou sat back against the wall, panting with his palms on his cheeks. He searched his mind for a solution. He knew that he didn't want to go back to his igloo—he refused to be around Ranmau. The sense of home he had with him had disappeared.

In that moment, he thought of the tunnels and a place to escape to: the Tree. So to the Tree he went. It was the place to escape to, after all.

His feet wandered until he stumbled across the familiar spot. He rubbed his hands together, revealing the secret tunnel.

He shuffled the snow to the side and crawled into it. He knew that his imagination was playing a cruel joke on him, hearing Elu's jokes bounce off the walls. The skin of his fingers grazed the smooth sculptures engraved into the walls as he walked down the spiral staircase. He observed the leaves, branches, and vines of ice that circled around him—the masterpieces that Elu helped create. A shiver crawled up his spine. Even though it wasn't his first time there, it still amazed him as if it was his first impression. But it never shined as bright as it did when Elu was around.

"This is the place that I go to find myself... to understand life," he said, vaguely remembering Elu's words.

He reached the hole in the wall, leading toward the Forest of Ness and climbed in. He crawled through the darkness until it expanded, allowing him to stand. It was then when his jaw dropped and a gasp of air escaped his lungs. His stomach sank and eyes grew. There was someone sitting over the ledge.

"Elu?" he said, his voice trembled to a whimper. He blinked his eyes, wishing that his mind wasn't playing a trick on him.

He didn't want to look. He didn't want to ask how. He didn't because he knew that this must have been his cruel imagination running wild again. He didn't because Elu died—he saw her pale, beautiful face drained of all its life. He didn't because the last night he saw her, he saw something that may have been a dream... no, it definitely was a dream, one of the many that blended together with his reality while he was stuck in the Box. Because in his dream... he saw... he saw an... Archon standing over a cliff. He didn't know what was true anymore, but surely that wasn't, Archons were extinct, gone after the First Great War hundreds of years ago. But yet Destrou stood motionless, gazing blankly at the silhouette that was sitting at the edge, hot tears made his eyes sting.

"Destrou?" a soft whisper made its way to his ears.

That voice... it was real... but how? *Elu... You're... you're alive?*

* * *

"What! Elu? How?" Vayp said, pulling back, slamming his palms on the book. A part of him wanted to be happy for Destrou, but he was more filled with jealousy than anything else. If only Ah'nyx could appear just as easily. But could that have been Elu?

Suddenly, Vayp was hit with the brief sight of Ah'nyx in the future, from his vision. He peeled open the green fabric... and saw *him*. It felt so real. It actually happened... or will happen... as long as he finished his deed.

"But someone else wants to kill you first," Vayp said, then he glanced up at Han'sael. "Someone wants to kill her, Han'sael." Vayp knew he wouldn't get a response back, but it only felt fair to let him know since they were all good friends. They *were* good friends. He felt his face drop as he thought about the power beyond those words.

"We *were* good friends."

Vayp had went five long years without a friend… and the connection he had made with S'rae and Han'sael was the first sign that he had a chance to be normal and happy, because for the first time since Ah'nyx, that was exactly how he felt. Like he had a chance to no longer be damaged.

"NO! STOP!" Vayp pursed his lips. "She did this! She's the reason all of this happened!" Again, he looked up at Han'sael as if to have him understand. How would Han'sael feel about Vayp killing S'rae? Would he understand? Would he no longer be his only friend? These thoughts troubled him more than he would like. "I'm sorry if you'll end up hating me, Han'sael… but there is something that I have to do. Something that I will do." Vayp's hand trailed down the glass as he reached out for Han'sael. "But I will get you out of this… somehow… I will. I promise!"

It wasn't until now that Vayp's vision had actually dawned on him. The *how* he killed S'rae. They had battled. They were fighting… something that they promised to never do again. It was the promise that they had made sure to keep ever since they had their first and last battle in front of their entire village. It was a battle to find out who was the Champion of Opella.

* * *

"We *so* got this, Vayp!" a much shorter S'rae said as she squatted down. The ground rumbled as dozens of boys circled them. Beyond the boys, sand domes, straw huts, and mountains were seen in the distance. "Let's show them why it's a mistake to mess with the S'rayp duo!"

"S'rayp duo?" Vayp laughed. "That's a *terrible* name for us!" He playfully pushed S'rae as he too squatted down and the ground rumbled harder. "I like Vay'rae more!"

"Vay'rae… hmm…." S'rae pressed her fingers to her chin. "I *love* it! Good thing you're the smart one out of us!"

Vayp smiled wide, a glow beaming from within. He had always been called the dumb one in the village, but the only one who would ever let him know that he was smart, amazing, great and special beyond words was S'rae. Any chance she got, she would throw a compliment his way. And that was what he loved about her. Well, one of the things.

"I don't know why they think they actually have a chance this time," Vayp smiled at S'rae. "This one's the most important of 'em all! A champion's getting crowned! No way our streak is ending today!"

"Our streak will never end! As long as we're together, we will never be stopped, right?" S'rae smiled back.

"Right!" Vayp made the first move as a boy jumped in with a flying kick. He placed his palm to the ground as a hand made of sand burst from the ground before wrapping around the boy and throwing him back at the crowd.

Then S'rae followed with a move of her own as two boys struck at her. Instantly, two statues of her appeared as she heard their fists break when they punched her clones.

Vayp couldn't help but laugh at the statues S'rae had created. She had always found the fun in fighting, and because of that, the arena, which was once Vayp's most hated event, quickly became his favorite. It wasn't until the first one S'rae had joined, when girls were finally allowed to pair up with a boy, when Vayp saw that the arenas weren't as terrible as he had thought. She made them entertaining. And Vayp loved that she made something so filled with anger and hatred built on the backs of a thirst for victory… into something that felt more like playing than fighting. Because of her, she turned his worst nightmare into his most favorite hobby. There was laughing, not swearing. Smiling, not crying. Instead of creating statues with intimidating poses, to strike fear in her opponents, S'rae's statues had always been something goofy, like sticking her tongue out, her yawning, or Vayp's favorite, one of her *very* awkward dance moves. Whatever the pose was, no matter how ridiculous it looked, they had worked perfectly, resulting in healer's needing to mend broken bones as they punched or kicked solid stone with full force.

Though Vayp and S'rae had won each duo arena challenge since that first one, this one was different... because it wasn't a duo challenge, yet still they worked together as if it was.

"Watch out!" S'rae shouted to Vayp as a boulder was thrown at him.

Vayp turned and placed his palms forward as the boulder slowed to a halt in midair. When he shot his palms away, the boulder burst into halves, then quarters, then dozens before he launched them at the crowd.

"Wow!" S'rae said as she cartwheeled away from a boulder. "You really are the greatest one here! Yeah, that's right, I have the coolest brother *ever!*"

Vayp froze for a split second; she said that word again: *brother*. It wasn't like he hated being called her brother... it was just that... well, never mind, this was a battle, there was no time for thinking.

Vayp said nothing to that comment and he noticed the way S'rae's smile had flinched briefly.

And after a few minutes of standing back-to-back, dodging and deflecting boulders, while launching many of their own in response, Vayp and S'rae realized... that they were the last two left.

For a few long moments their backs pressed against one another, feeling their deep breaths inhale and exhale.

"What... er... what happens now?" S'rae asked over her shoulder.

"I… don't know," Vayp said over his.

"Do we… well… are we supposed to fight each other now?"

"I guess… we didn't think this one through."

"Do I have to like *hit* you, hit you. Or can I just *hit* you, like this." S'rae lightly threw her elbow back into Vayp's ribs.

Vayp laughed as he flinched at the contact. "Maybe not as soft as that."

"Well?" a voice boomed ahead. A great man with fur pauldrons and a lion's head as a crown walked forward. He was their father, the King Si'ard. "A champion must be crowned."

"So… do… like… *I* make the first move?" S'rae said, and it pained Vayp to hear her voice crack. This was clearly something she wanted no part of… and neither did he.

"Umm… sure," Vayp said, "but don't go easy on me, okay? I actually am curious to know who's better. You always say I am… but I always think you are."

"Really?" S'rae squealed. Vayp felt her jump up, most likely pressing her palms to her cheeks as she had always done when she got really excited. It was one of Vayp's favorites. "You really think so?"

"Of course, I never won arenas before we became a team," Vayp said before putting his head down.

"Well… that's because we kinda make an *amazing* team, if I say so myself! Maybe by ourselves we are equally great… but together… we are *unstoppable!*"

"Unstoppable!" Vayp grinned. "I like it!"

"I *love* it!" S'rae squealed. "The Vay'rae duo. Always and forever!"

"Always and forever!"

And then it happened, they turned around and engaged in an exciting battle that was followed by ooh's and ahh's. Whenever a move was made that had almost always worked on the village's boys, it was always countered. When S'rae created a stone statue,

Vayp had already absorbed into the ground, before launching up through it with a flying uppercut, only to be met with a stone S'rae who had smacked her butt at him. Whenever Vayp had launched a perfectly timed boulder, S'rae had pushed off of it and jumped high into the air. And when Vayp thought this was the perfect chance to land a solid blow by launching a boulder at her, before it made contact, it turned into many versions of a kicking S'rae that she had twisted in air, before throwing them back at him.

"I can't even land a strike... and I'm actually trying to now!" Vayp said, diving away.

"Same!" S'rae grinned. "This is more fun than I thought! Let's see who gets the first strike in!"

Their defense was exceptional, it wasn't until they had dueled one another when they realized that their greatest strength had always been avoidance and never being hit. Earthies had always prized themselves on being defenders, the Protectors of Gaia, but no child had seemed to excel at defense better than these two.

Strike after strike. Dodge and defend. No punch or kick was landed... until *BANG*!

The two had just leapt over a boulder and punched one another across the jaw at the same time.

They fell to the ground, almost on top of each other, and held their faces.

"Ow!" S'rae still held her jaw. "So *that's* what it feels like to be punched by you! Yikes! I feel bad for those kids!"

"Speak for yourself!" Vayp held his own jaw, trying to stretch his mouth. "Jeez, you hurt!"

"Umm... Vayp... can—" S'rae said softly. "Never mind."

"What? You can always speak to me," Vayp whispered.

"I... I just... it didn't... I don't," S'rae, who was normally someone who couldn't stop talking, was at a loss for words, and Vayp understood why.

"I don't want to either," Vayp said.

"Don't want to what?"

"I never want to fight you again."

"*Phew*! I'm glad you think so too! It just didn't feel right. I never want to hurt you ever again."

"Never!"

"Let's make a promise!" S'rae said excitedly. "Let's *never* fight each other again."

"Promise!" A stone hand appeared from the ground next to S'rae.

She laughed as she shook it. "You're such a weirdo. I love it!"

"So... who wins?" Vayp said. "Dad needs a champion."

S'rae twisted her head to look at Vayp... he saw that her eyes were more glazed than usual. "You do... you're his *real* family," she smiled. But Vayp saw beyond the smile, to the eyes that watered up. He saw the pain behind that statement.

"Are you sure?" Vayp said, feeling his own eyes watering.

"I am sure." S'rae wiped her eyes and smiled wide. "You deserve it. More than anyone I know!"

"Well... let's never find out who the stronger one is. From now on... it's the Vay'rae duo. Always and forever."

"Always and forever." S'rae's eyes watered.

* * *

"Always and forever." Vayp rubbed his eyes. "Always and... forever..." He looked up to the sky, seeing nothing but darkness all around him, and felt a tear roll down his cheek.

11

THE NEXT FEW DAYS AFTER OLIVIA'S DEATH had really taken a toll on GroundStone. All classes were cancelled, and GroundStone had found itself covered in gloom as if the sun had stopped shining as well. Though the mourning period would last a week, students could not wait for the classes to finally begin. They wanted, no, they *needed* something to distract themselves. GroundStone, normally a bustling city, where humans and wildlife alike were seen everywhere, was now depressing and deserted. Not even the birds would sing in the morning. The animals had stopped working and the faculty took their time off to pray to their Divine. Retro'ku, Gabrael, and Raaz'a were rarely seen, as if they had more pressing matters to deal with, and Lynn was always out with the GroundStone trio; so S'rae had been left alone, which may have been for the best.

Though Olivia's death had hit her hard, something else bothered her even more than that. Fujak, the person who she had spent the past few weeks rekindling their friendship, the one who seemed most close to her... was the one who... tried to murder her? But why? All because she had practiced two elements? Was that the reason? Who else could it have been? Fujak was the one seen with a bow in his hands during both shootings. But why didn't he shoot her when he had the chance again, it just didn't make sense? And now, he was locked away in Alsi'jin, home of the most horrific stories in GroundStone. Did he deserve to be there? She wished she knew the answer.

And what did Olivia mean when she mentioned the Sol named Adari? S'rae had too many questions.

Not everything was completely terrible though, the funeral was one of the most beautiful things she had seen. Everyone was dressed in white, and hundreds of white doves had been released, their stray feathers creating a gorgeous snowfall, and now it looked as if GroundStone had been covered in several feet of snow. And rather than burying Olivia into a plant in a burial garden, Gabrael had fought tirelessly with the elders to seal her body. So there she remained in the center of GroundStone as an object of prayer… and Fujak… well, he became the most hated.

It was impossible to walk more than a few feet without hearing a nasty comment that mentioned the name Fujak. Something about that made S'rae's stomach wrench tighter; they hated him before they even knew for sure if he did it. She supposed that was the Fujita in her speaking, always looking for justice through just laws and a fair trial. It was their code. *But don't be so naive anymore, S'rae.*

The only silver lining about any of this was that it seemed like Retro'ku had been in a nicer mood, as if he was trying to break S'rae out of her misery.

"Miss S'rae, would you like to train now?" Retro'ku said, entering her room without knocking.

S'rae's eyes went wide as she heard the door open. She didn't even so much turn to see him, she only mumbled and stuttered before finally speaking. "Hi, yes… thank you, I'd love to."

Slowly, she turned around, scanning the room, as if searching for the best escape route. She needed to leave *now*. How was she supposed to continue the conversation before the… oh no… too late. This was *exactly* why she wanted to leave, before *this* very awkward silence began, when she had no idea what to say next, and Retro'ku would stare at her as if expecting her to say something… so… she said what any sane person would say.

"Do you know where B—"

"Where B'se is?" Retro'ku smirked.

"Mmhmm…" she sighed nervously.

"Why yes, as always, he is right there… in your hands."

And oh… what do you know… B'se was exactly where he always was whenever she asked this stupid question. She pet B'se nervously, trying her hardest not to do her creepy wide smile, but she knew she was failing. Right about now would be the perfect time to turn into a statue, she thought.

Thankfully, footsteps were heard approaching the door. "Ready to train?" Lynn walked in, looking as beautiful as ever. She was dressed in black clothes with a scarf that wrapped around her neck, looking like she was training to become a ninja. And when she noticed S'rae's raised eyebrows, she said, "Hey, I'm taking this *very* seriously! Come on, this is fire we're talking about! No one has practiced this in *three thousand* years! I can't wait!" She made cute, funny noises with her mouth, most likely trying to imitate fire, as she pushed her palms out in different directions. "Pshh… psshh… pshhh. *Boom*! Let's go!"

S'rae felt happy when Lynn finally showed up, maybe today would be good for S'rae, a nice breath of fresh air after being alone in her room for the past few days.

When they walked out, S'rae quickly appreciated how majestic the 'snow' was. It made the normally brown and golden temples and streets look like a winter palace. She loved the way the giant statues of animals, that looked more like sculpted mountains stretching beyond the clouds, were now dusted in white. She even enjoyed the fresh smell of flowers and the *crunches* her feet made as they trekked their way through a white forest, before arriving at a secluded hill.

S'rae's mouth dropped at once. No, it wasn't because of the gorgeous view from this hilltop. No… it wasn't even because the beautiful white doves she saw swooping around them overhead. But of course, she would be staring at the now shirtless Retro'ku, who was stretching.

"You need to stop being so weird around him," Lynn whispered to her.

"What? I'm *not* being weird," she said as she wiped the drool from her mouth.

"If you want to have a chance with him, just pretend that you're not like every other girl who swoons over him. You need to be different."

"Who's saying I even want a chance?" And when Lynn tilted and shook her head, S'rae continued. "Okay, well, that's easy for you to say, you like girls, and maybe Han'sael, but I don't even think Retro'ku likes girls."

Lynn's eyes had widened at the mention of Han'sael's name, but she didn't say anything about it. "So… you think he likes boys?" Lynn raised an eyebrow.

"*No*! I mean not *no* like it's a bad thing if he *did* like boys, I just think he doesn't like anything else other than training."

"Well, he sounds boring to me," Lynn whispered, looking over her shoulder at Retro'ku. "Now… Milla… she's someone I have my eye on." Then S'rae noticed Lynn's face grow sour at once.

"Oh, really!" S'rae gasped. "I'm surprised you haven't gotten her yet, she likes girls doesn't she?"

"Yeah…" Lynn perked her lips and gave S'rae a nasty look. "I just think… well, I think she likes someone else, which is bugging me because I don't see what she could possibly like about her."

"Oh, who does she like?"

"You." Lynn kept a straight face as if what she said wasn't the least bit disrespectful.

"Oh… umm… me?" Lynn pouted and turned away from S'rae. "Well, can I ask a dumb question?"

"Better than anyone I know." S'rae heard the tude in Lynn's voice.

S'rae was taken aback. "Umm… hmm… so… do you not like me or something now because you think she may like me, even if I don't like her back?"

"Maybe." Lynn began stretching.

"And… you don't think that may be a little bit absurd?"

"Nope." Lynn showed off her flexibility, performing a full split while making her head touch her knee. "Not at all."

Great. This was exactly what S'rae wanted. She had the idea of starting the school year off with two good friends, getting her Sol, and taking new courses to prepare herself for the Earth challenge… and so far, absolutely none of that went her way, except for taking courses, at least she found a way by winning the arena tournament.

But there was no more Fujak. Lynn was apparently upset with her and not afraid to show it. And… worst of all, no Sol.

Well, at least she had training with Retro'ku to look forward, some slither of hope that her time at GroundStone wouldn't be a complete wreck.

"The magic of fire," Retro'ku said, walking toward the girls, "is that if you were born to control Fire… you would know."

"How?" S'rae and Lynn asked at once.

"Because…" Retro'ku pulled out a hilt from his robe, "the fire that burns within you would be enough to ignite this hilt."

He threw the hilt at Lynn, and S'rae had to jump back, because the moment Lynn had caught the hilt, a blazing fire had erupted from it, scorching twenty feet high.

S'rae noticed Retro'ku's eyes grow the widest she had seen them.

"My Divine," he mouthed to himself, the fire painting his dark skin gold. "The fire *truly* burns within you! I have never seen such an exhibit from a new student… I must tell Gabrael at once! We have ourselves our first pupil of Fire!" He smiled as his eyes scanned Lynn from head-to-toe, and S'rae immediately felt a hot wave of jealousy pass through her. "But more than a pupil, we have found a truly gifted one!"

Lynn smiled wide as Retro'ku took the hilt from her hands. The flame dispersed as black smoke danced in the wind.

"And now, it is your turn." Retro'ku grabbed S'rae's wrist, a chill shocked through her body at his touch. He opened her palm, and placed the hilt on it.

Silence was heard, except for the occasional wind rustling the snowy feathers.

Nothing happened… not even a flicker.

Seriously? S'rae felt a hot rage burn within her. *Can* anything *go my way now, please?*

"Hmm… no worries, Miss S'rae… this is quite common. Fire can be taught, I shall work with you." And as S'rae put her head down, Retro'ku placed his finger under her chin, lifting it up. Their eyes met, and for that brief second, all of her worries seemed to disappear. "You are special, Miss S'rae, I have faith that the Fire burns in you as well, it may just take time to unleash it. Have faith… and faith will have you."

S'rae tried her best to keep the smile on her face, but the damage was done. Lynn was perfect, of course, and S'rae was a failure, once again. And as Lynn and Retro'ku were practicing fighting with blazing swords, S'rae was left alone, trying to make her hilt ignite.

Retro'ku had told her that she needed to think of a moment that she feared the most. She needed to hold on to that fear, accept it, and overcome it to unleash the fire within. He made it sound so easy, but it was tough to think about what she feared most. She thought about the Shadow Army, but nothing happened. Not even a spark when she thought about not getting a Sol. And even when she thought about failing out of school, still nothing.

Of course! A light sparked in her head. She remembered when she channeled the massive tornado from the sky back at the Valley of Gaia… it was the fear of the Mechas that helped her… and oh yeah, the fear of losing her family.

And then it happened… a little spark ignited at the hilt.

"Look! Look!" S'rae said, happily waving around her flaming… candle. "I got a flame! I knew I could do it!"

"It is a… start," Retro'ku said, observing the flame that was no bigger than his fingernail, "but I am afraid this may not even harm an insect, never mind a Shadow Army. Keep practicing, some progress has been made!"

Retro'ku left to train with Lynn again. And for the next hour or so, S'rae was stuck with her candle of a sword, watching Lynn practice cool moves. She truly was a quick learner. She learned how to make a flame combust on her fingertip, how to make fire burst from the soles of her feet, allowing her to levitate off the ground, and of course, she learned how to create a ball of fire within the palms of her hands. Retro'ku had her shoot fireballs at him as he dodged each one. They were laughing, smiling, and having a great ol' time… while S'rae was still there with her pathetic candle sword.

Days would pass and still S'rae was stuck with only her candle flame and failed attempts. Lynn, on the other hand, was able to levitate off the ground so much that she was practicing sword fighting with Retro'ku without her feet ever touching the ground.

NOT FAIR!

It was true that S'rae maybe wasn't meant for Fire, but that didn't mean it didn't hurt to see Lynn excel at it. And now Lynn was getting all of this extra quality time with Retro'ku and she didn't even like him! S'rae wished she could trade places, so she kept going through all of the fears she'd ever known. None of them seemed to work well.

When they left the cliff that night, after hours of training, S'rae found B'se waiting for her in her room. She didn't know if she should be happy or sad to see a piece of paper on his back, she'd grown quite used to bad news by now. She pulled it off B'se's back and read.

GROUNDSTONE, SCHOOL OF EARTH AND
ROCK, BEGINS!

Congratulations, student! Tomorrow is the official start of the school year! We apologize for the delay and appreciate your patience. Olivia was more than a beloved person, she was the greatest Sol professor the world has ever seen. To replace such an amazing person would be impossible, so we had to qualify a list of exceptional candidates for this new position. We believe we are happy with our decision and would like to announce our newest Professor of Sols: Belem'nos.

Though he does not have a Sol of his own, his knowledge of Sols rivals Olivia herself, and we know that she is smiling down on us right now for our decision. There is no greater person to continue her legacy than a man whose unique passion for animals and Sols was what awarded him the position of being Olivia's very own assistant. That prestigious position gave him the experience and knowledge to become a true master in the field.

Please, students, give your new Professor a warm welcome, for he is dealing with the loss as hard as anyone we know.

We look forward to seeing the great you all will become!

May this GroundStone year bring you great fortune and blessings.

Have faith and faith will have you.

Leonna, Professor of Healing and Herbs

S'rae woke up early the next morning and was too anxious to go back to sleep. She got up and put *her* brown robe on and tied *her* green vine around her waist. These were *hers*; Ground chose *her*. They were her Body, she wondered how long it'd take her tree to grow, because that will be *her* new home. It made her suddenly feel like she was worthy, that she mattered. She searched everywhere for her quill, until B'se came strolling in with it attached to his back. "Thank you!" This was her Mind. The only thing missing was her Soul, which she held onto the hope that it may be waiting for her, but more than likely only more disappointment awaited. She checked to make sure she had everything she needed, looked at her courses on the wall, then opened up her map. There were many numbers counting down at different locations. One spot said the word *LUNCH* and another said *SANDSPORTATION SPELLS WITH DI'TUKIA*. S'rae smiled then bit her tongue and narrowed her eyes as she traced the symbol with her finger. She wanted to make sure she got it just right this time, no more mistakes!

And when she drew the relic onto the ground, her feet started to sink. She saw the contents in her room spin around rapidly as she sunk quicker into the sand—she closed her eyes ready for the severe pulling moment, when it felt like gravity magnified—and when she was yanked through the ground... she opened her eyes.

"Yay!!" a boy screamed as he stormed by S'rae on top of a bull. She quickly jumped to the side directly in the path of a gazelle that leapt over her right before they collided. A stampede of students and animals came from all different directions. Underfoot, cats and dogs and even a raccoon scurried about between her legs. And overhead, birds of every color swooped by chirping and singing away. There was a great commotion of stomps, conversations, and just overall chaos. As far as she could see in this vast, open temple, there were hundreds of students dressed in brown traveling every which way to make it to their first class on time.

It was getting so loud that S'rae couldn't even think as she opened up her map to make sure she was at the right location. There she was on the map… right on top of the *SANDSPORTATION SPELLS*… but surely they weren't going to have to class in this crowded area. And just as the noise reached its loudest, it all went silent once a boy screamed, "OH EM DEEEE!! LOOK!!"

At once, the crowd of students and animals stopped bumping into one another. The silence appeared too quickly, as if someone had flipped a switch. And when S'rae lifted her head from her map, she saw that a circle of animals, boys, and girls surrounded her, all staring directly at her. S'rae's eyes went wide as she slowly put her head back down and tried to pretend to read the map again.

"IT'S HER!" a girl screamed. "THE CHAMPION!"

Then just as quickly as it came, the silence turned back into an uproar.

"Teach me how you did that!"

"I've never seen a girl win before! Now I want to try!"

"Girls kicked butt! Can you sign my Sol's butt?"

"Where did you learn to do that!?"

"You're the coolest Earthie *ever*!"

A million questions were thrown at her and she suddenly realized how her village must have felt when she'd barrage them with questions of her own. But unlike them being annoyed… this felt… well… it felt amazing. She felt important, despite feeling like a failure at everything else.

"Please… please… our Champion cannot be late for class," a woman appeared, wearing a black robe with the hood covering her eyes and a cape with blue stitching in the shape of roses. "I am most happy you decided to take a course with me, I know you will not be disappointed!"

S'rae had recognized that voice, it belonged to Professor Di'Tukia, the Professor of Sandsportation Spells. "I'm sorry… I'm having trouble finding the room."

"That is because you looked everywhere… but *up*."

And when S'rae lifted her head, her jaw dropped. She saw dozens of students standing and sitting on top of the ceiling.

"Oh don't you worry," Di'Tukia smiled, "you'll get used to it. Just here... hold on to this." Di'Tukia put a vine inside S'rae's hands and muttered some words. At once, S'rae's feet kicked out from underneath her as she slid down the vine and landed on the... ceiling? Or was it the floor? "Welcome to my class!"

S'rae looked up and saw many sad faces looking down at her as they waved and walked away.

"You're a Champion now," Di'Tukia smiled, "you'll have to get used to this extra attention. For now, please, find a place to sit."

The first few rows were already packed with students, some pushing and shoving one another around, some trying to squeeze an extra friend in. The seats were long stone slabs facing a giant staircase that had its steps painted to look like she was staring into a wooded tunnel with a light at the end.

Amazed, S'rae walked up to the stairs and felt its rough texture. She looked up to see where they led and saw a wooden door.

"That is my office," Di'Tukia said. "Or... well, at least one way to get to my office." Di'Tukia walked over to S'rae, placing her hand on her shoulder. "Would you believe me, class... if I told you that it is impossible to open that door?" Di'Tukia smiled. S'rae had seen what she was capable of. After watching her walk through an invisible door while at the plateau, S'rae was officially sold on taking her class. When the students shook their heads, Di'Tukia continued. "You see, it is impossible to *open* that door... but some doors... are not meant to be *opened*. This locked door isn't meant to close you out... it is meant to open the door in your *mind* to find better, different ways to enter." Di'Tukia walked over to a desk that looked like a tree stump with vines and sat on it. "I must say... the mind is quite a powerful thing. You could spend the rest of your life exploring it, and it would be equivalent to never leaving this room after wanting to explore Gaia. You see... the mind has ways to make you believe something isn't... what it actually is. For example…" Di'Tukia lifted her hand and the tree stump of a desk had changed from a dark brown and mossy green to a golden brown, and the vines became stripes, and what once looked like handles, were now—S'rae gulped—fangs. The desk was not a desk at all… it was a saber tooth tiger. "This is my lovely Samaniel… and don't worry, kids, he's an angel, he wouldn't hurt a fly." BANG! Samaniel's paw had crushed a beetle before licking it up. "Er… well, that's awkward. You see, well… we're… uh… we're still working out the kinks for our new meat-free diet… have to be prepared for the droughts!"

S'rae slowly stepped backward from this massive beast.

Another boy tried to run away, but Di'Tukia grabbed him and began pushing him toward Samaniel. "Samaniel will be here almost every class, so you students must get used to him. Pet him… go… there you go… just like that. See, that wasn't so bad was it? He's a sweetheart!"

The poor boy screamed as he ran to the back of the classroom.

"Now… where was I?" Di'Tukia looked up for a moment. "Ah yes! The mind! So, as I was saying, the mind has many ways to make you believe that you are looking at something that you are not. Take this as another example." Di'Tukia placed her foot on the staircase. "Lovely stairs, no? S'rae… please… I would like for you to walk toward the light." She pointed at the painted stairs and the light at the end of the tunnel. "There! Down this tunnel."

"Er…" S'rae stepped forward.

"Go on… don't be afraid. Just believe that you can walk through the stairs… and just do it."

"Um… okay, I guess." S'rae was weary because she had been used to these types of games at Fujita, when students would trick her into doing things that were obviously not going to work. So she thought about walking through the stairs, but nothing happened, the stairs were solid and she simply walked up three steps before making her way back down.

"Ah okay, now class, pay attention," Di'Tukia said, placing her hand up to silence the giggles the class made. "Now, S'rae... I simply want you to walk up the steps again... that is all."

S'rae looked at the class, who appeared as shocked and confused as she was. "Okay..." But the moment she went to step on the stairs, her foot had fell through and she found herself tripping and falling face first onto a wooden path, where twigs and branches formed a deep, dark tunnel. When S'rae turned around, all she saw was a black wall.

Where am I?

S'rae was silent, staring ahead at the only source of light. The twigs crunched at her soles as she pressed forward. Then other noises accompanied the crunches... they were songs... beautiful ones that birds would sing. And when she drew nearer and nearer to what seemed like a cliff, her eyes widened and jaw dropped.

"Beautiful, isn't it?" S'rae gasped with fright, feeling her stomach sink as someone touched her shoulder. It was Di'Tukia. *Phew!* "I like to come here from time to time... just to appreciate it."

And there was a lot to appreciate. They seemed to be standing on the branch of a tree that was a mile high, overlooking a massive crystal blue ring that circled around them. This was no ordinary ring, though... for it was a waterfall that surrounded them. An endless wall of water, flowing eternally.

"Where... are we?" S'rae's jaw felt like it was locked open.

"You wouldn't believe me if I told you," Di'Tukia said, grabbing hold of S'rae's hand. Then a blinding light overcame all her senses, and once the light faded, S'rae found herself back inside Di'Tukia's room, staring at the tunnel painted on the stairs.

"So... are you just going to stand there the whole time?" a boy said to S'rae.

"Just stand here?" S'rae's eyes widened as she turned to Di'Tukia.

"I told you... the mind... is a powerful thing." Di'Tukia turned to the class. "The first day is always the quickest, so I cannot keep you away from your next class for long! Please look at your maps and make your way there, I am *not* responsible for tardiness! Just remember! There are many secrets here at GroundStone. MANY. I say this because curious minds will always remain curious, so I will not tell you to not explore GroundStone, but all I will say is… to be careful where your curious mind takes you. For there are some things at GroundStone that are left hidden for good reason. Good-bye class! See you next time!"

When S'rae arrived in front of the giant stone doors labeled DANGERS of GAIA. Defend all, but trust none, she felt an uneasy pulse shock through her body. The doors were so big even an elephant could have walked through them. The stone walls were lit with many carefully-placed fireflies, creating glowing tribal designs that made this dark tunnel even more spooky. Somewhere a sound was made, like a rat running across sand, and then a loud grumble came from the doors.

The doors rumbled before transforming into a stone face that said in a very deep voice, "You are late."

"I'm sorry," S'rae said, taking one more look at the map. There she was, standing on top of **HOW TO CHEAT DEATH**: *Advanced Courses on Surviving the Dangers of Gaia*. "Hmm… Dangers of Gaia… this must be the right place."

"Why should *I* allow you in?" the door grumbled. "For being late would have already gotten you killed, dear. You have already failed the class."

"Failed? But it's just the first day!"

"In life… when you are in the jungle… and a wild Wa'hash devours you and your family in one gulp… do you think… it will decide differently, just because you told it… *it's just the first day?*"

S'rae gulped. "N-no, sir."

"Precisely. This class is meant for people who take surviving seriously, and it is clear you do not." The face swirled around before molding back into the doors.

S'rae had to think of something. If the Earth Challenge would be anything like the Fire one, then she knew she'd need to prepare herself against whatever monster awaited her. When in doubt... the sympathy card had always worked. She worked up her best sad face and said, "Please... I *need* to know how to defend myself!"

"Why?" The face appeared once more. "Why... would you *need* to know how to defend yourself?"

"Because..." S'rae was stuck stuttering... until she thought of the arena. "Because... I am the Champion of GroundStone... and... someone tried to kill me... and... and I see on your door, it says *trust none* and I-I need to learn what that means, because... well, because the person who tried to kill me... was my best friend. And..." Although S'rae had only been acting at first, now she felt genuine hot tears build up behind her eyes just thinking about her next comment. "—and... before that... the person who I trusted the most... betrayed me."

"And who... *who* was this person... that you trusted the most?"

S'rae took a deep breath to stop the tears from falling. She wanted to seem sad yet strong, not fragile and weak. "He was... my brother."

"Ahh... you too... have been deceived by a loved one." The stone face had turned to sand, in fact, the whole door became a wave of sand that splashed to the ground, revealing a vast room with only a handful of students and a large man with a very stern face. He lifted his silvery hand... wait, silvery hand? S'rae's eyes narrowed and noticed that his hand was metallic. Her eyes then widened as she thought about Earth's duality: Metal. *When your Soul is not meant for Earth, your body will harden into Metal*, she remembered Gabrael's words. Then why... how... was this man a Professor at GroundStone? This already spooky setting had suddenly felt life-threatening. "Please, come in." His voice boomed across the room. "You are allowed in... because you are already one step ahead of the class. For you have already learned our first lesson: to *trust none.*"

His eyes lingered for a moment on S'rae's brown robes, which she had clutched to prevent her hands from shaking, and then onto her eyes, but not just her eyes, right below them. At once, his eyes blackened as he took a step back. He appeared shocked... or confused... or... afraid? S'rae couldn't tell. Why would he—then she remembered what was beneath her eyes: her face paint, the marker of her tribe, of her home: Opella. *Why does Opella make people treat her differently? Is it because... they know what happened?*

The man's mouth quivered for a few moments before speaking once more. "Please, have a seat."

Unlike her previous class, this room had more than enough seats. The room was big enough to fit hundreds... yet there were only about a dozen students in attendance. She quickly found a seat in the back. It was unlike her to not sit in the front row, but something about this professor made her uneasy.

"My name is Professor Fa'laz," his voice boomed as he tucked his arms behind the back of his black cape and robe. "As I stated previously, those of you who chose this course did so because you have a fear for the uncertainty. You know that one day a great battle may be thrust upon you... and you wish to be ready. And that is great, but the first lesson you must learn... is do not trust anyone or anything... that is not your Sol." A growl was heard, then a large black panther emerged from the shadows, taking some of it with him. But S'rae noticed right away that their relationship was quite different, no affection was shown. This could not have been his Sol.

But it was. "I know what some of you must be thinking," Fa'laz said, "why does it look like he doesn't even know me? How many of you know what truly happens when a Sol dies?"

S'rae's eyes widened. She felt a vision creep up into her mind that she quickly had to block out. No... now was not the time to think about a Sol dying, she was an expert at sealing off terrible memories for a reason, it allowed her to function.

When nothing was said, Fa'laz continued, "While it is true that a Sol cannot die before its owner… what the Shrine of Elements refuses to teach people… is that your Sol does in fact die… many times throughout life… sometimes it can die and be revived without you ever knowing. Mer… I say screw the politics of babying you all with roses and flowers… and here's the darn truth about the death. This… *this* is what happens when your Sol dies too many times." Fa'laz pointed at the panther, who prowled back into the shadows, not once acknowledging Fa'laz. And S'rae saw the pain in his eyes, it was the exact eyes she remembered seeing when she looked at Vayp—*no STOP! Do not think about this right now!*

"What happens when a Sol dies," Fa'laz said, walking to his stone desk, where a great axe and shield rested on top, "is you lose a little piece of your Soul each time. Each time a Sol dies and gets revived, a piece of it gets lost in the universe. And after so many battles… with your best friend protecting you every darn time—" S'rae saw a tear drop from his eye. "—Well… after so many deaths… he eventually forgets you ever existed." S'rae could have sworn she heard a suppressed sob from a man built like a rhino. "And each time you think you got your best friend back… you realize he only sees you as the person who brought him food, not the person you shared a lifetime of adventures with."

S'rae found herself wiping the tears from her face, and noticed other students doing the same. This was not the type of environment she was expecting from the *Dangers of Gaia* class. She took the class wanting to find out ways to defeat a Shadow Army and unbeatable beasts, not cry about one's life partner forgetting they ever existed. She saw a damaged man, one who must have been dealing with far greater issues than S'rae ever had, and still… she wondered about his hand. How did a Professor at GroundStone defect to Metal and still have a job?

"So… let's begin with the first test," Fa'laz said, and at once

S'rae's heart jumped. She gasped. So did the students around her. A test on the first day? What would she have to do? Defend herself against him... or worse—S'rae swallowed—against the panther? "This test only has one question."

S'rae heard a collective sigh pass through the room. *Phew!* S'rae wiped the sweat off her forehead.

"My question is this... how many of you would sacrifice yourself to protect everyone in this room... though you do not know one another?"

S'rae saw all the students twist and turn in their seats as if to finally pay attention to the other students, as if this wasn't a question but more of a statement of what could very well happen. But nothing was said.

"You all have failed the first test." Fa'laz turned away.

"But!"

"Wait!"

"Failed already?"

"Let me explain!" Fa'laz stomped his feet and the entire room rattled, dust fell from the ceiling, creating a misty glow. "Here at GroundStone... we are PROTECTORS! It is what we were born to do! By the end of our lessons, I hope all of you will be able to answer the question... and then, I will go back and change your grades." Fa'laz turned back to face them and let out a gentle smile. "This day was just simply introductions... but tomorrow... be prepared for beasts that will make your skin crawl so much that you will be beggin' to the Shrine to get you out of this class. But too late, you are here now... and it means you are here for good."

S'rae swallowed. This was more like the class she was expecting, but now a part of her wished it could go back to the tear-jerking part of it and less of the *I'm about to die* one.

"And before you all leave here, I want one last closing word: There could be a time when you are surrounded by a thousand hungry wolves... yet still... you... and you alone... would be your greatest enemy there. You will find that the greatest enemy you may need to protect yourself from… is yourself. Be careful… be aware… and *trust none*."

Fa'laz waved his arm as a burst of sand sent the students flying out through the open door. And as they fumbled to collect themselves, the sand shifted underneath them, molding into the stone doors.

And just like that… S'rae realized that she may have regretted signing up for this class.

What was next? S'rae opened the map and saw numbers ticking down on a dot that said *SOL MASTERY* with OLIVIA BELEM'NOS. Seeing Olivia's name simply crossed off the map made S'rae's stomach churn. She wanted to ball up the map and throw it away, but what good would that do? So instead she balled up her anger and observed the ticking numbers. She didn't have much time between classes, so she quickly drew the relic into the sand and felt the ground rip her through the earth. *Please don't be a terrible class.*

12

S'RAE GASPED ONCE SHE OPENED HER EYES. About a dozen gazelles galloped by her, followed by a dozen more lions and panthers sprinting by, then some elephants and rhinos clunked and stomped after them. At first S'rae had thought that the gazelles were in danger of being eaten, but as her eyes trailed them and their streaks of dust, she saw that all the animals were playing with one another.

Where is the class? S'rae looked around and saw that she was the only student standing inside an oval-shaped desert surrounded by grand golden walls and seats that could entertain thousands. Then it occurred to her as her chest tightened; when she closed her eyes, it was as if she could hear the *SWOOSH* right before the arrow was launched again… because she was here again… the arena… the place where someone had tried to murder her.

BANG! S'rae's shoulders locked up and her heart jumped as two rhinos had collided head first into one another.

S'rae's breathing was heavier and she tried her best to calm herself down. There were many animals around, it should have been an easy task, she loved them, but still, she imagined the arrow, a moment away from ripping through her chest, shoot by her, and then she saw Fujak running after her. She clenched her palms to stop them from shaking, but she felt her whole body tremble with fright.

If she could see her eyes, she knew they'd be blackened and dilated. Why was she the only one here? Was this... was this another trap? She looked around again, observing the animals play fighting with one another. Their happiness was enough to bring a smile to S'rae's face. Maybe she was overreacting. Yeah, that was it. But that still didn't explain why there were no students here.

Might as well make the most out of it, she thought. All alone with dozens of different beautiful, adorable, cute animals? No complaints here!

And as she walked by chimps, winged horses, giraffes, and many different kinds of felines and canines, she froze in place as she saw one that stood out from the rest. There was only one that made her eyes glaze and her lips quiver. There... playing by itself... was a... a lone wolf pup. Not just any wolf, but one with soft brown fur and looked... very familiar. S'rae felt her stomach twist as she walked slowly toward the wolf. It was happily digging little holes in the sand, and when S'rae drew nearer, it lifted its head up and S'rae had almost cried on the spot.

"Your eyes," S'rae cupped her mouth with her shaking hands. "Your... eyes!" S'rae fell to her knees, her hands still shaking as she tried desperately to shake the vision that appeared in her mind, but it was impossible, for this wolf pup was nearly identical to... Ah'nyx.

Just thinking about the name made S'rae collapse harder, her face sobbed into the sand as the pup sniffed her hair. "I don't get it... I don't get it... is it *you*? Is it actually you?" She lifted her head and stared into the pup's eyes again, one was blue and the other white... just like Ah'nyx. But how?

She tried her hardest to block Ah'nyx out, but it felt impossible, like forgetting how to breathe. It would break her... thinking about it always did. Was this a cruel joke from the Divine? The

Divine's way to punish her even more, showing her proof of her biggest mistake?

"Why are you doing this to me?" S'rae cried into her palms. "Why?" When she closed her eyes, she saw a brief vision of Ah'nyx in the darkness and she let out a shriek that startled everything, she heard the way hooves stomped on the ground and animals squealed and huffed and puffed.

S'rae remained curled into a ball for a few more moments, until she felt something nudge her back, feet, arms, and stomach. When she opened her eyes, she saw all the animals circle around her, as if to console her, and when she looked at her knees, there the wolf pup was, cuddled into a ball of his own, pressing against S'rae's stomach.

Is he… is he… my Sol? S'rae felt her heart warm up as she pet the wolf pup's fur, it was smooth like silk.

S'rae suddenly smiled wide as the reality of the moment dawned on her: she had an adorable wolf pup cuddled in her lap… and dozens of animals circled her as if smiling along at the moment. *Maybe… maybe he's my Sol?*

Then whispers were heard. A rhino's ears flipped about as if she heard them too. When S'rae circled her fingers, she targeted where the whispers were coming from.

"Are you sure it's her? She should be dead, it couldn't be. Listen… no, you aren't listening, there is no way anyone could survive that attack. Trust me. She'd be dead."

And as the voice faded away, the animals parted to the side and S'rae's chest tightened as she saw a cloaked figure stand before her.

It was *him*… The only person whose presence could make her feel uncomfortable, but he was alone. Was he the voice she heard? But if he was, who was he talking to? And were they talking about her—the one who should be dead?

"So you're the reason they're all bundled up here," the cloaked man said. "I didn't expect a student to be here, I sent out messages saying classes were cancelled today."

S'rae narrowed her eyes at him. "I didn't get any message." *Sounds like a trap. Don't be so naive anymore, S'rae.*

"Did your Sol send—oh... it's you, the one in the rain."

"Yes, that's me, the one in the rain." S'rae's eyes narrowed even more.

"Or should I say, the exceptional artist, that better?" S'rae said nothing, her lip curled. "But... it looks like you found yourself a new friend." He pointed at the wolf pup on her lap.

"Yupp, he's my new pet."

"Oh really? Why is *he* always the favorite when I find someone with the animals?"

"Nope, he's just my favorite. That's all... just mine."

"Right... you and that other boy's. Well, does *he* have a name?"

"Mysol. His name is Mysol."

He laughed. "Mysol... like *my* Sol? At least you didn't name *him* Onix."

S'rae felt a cold knife travel from her chest to her stomach at the mention of that name. "Wh... how.... Why... where did you get that name from?"

"That's the name the boy gave *him*. He'd rarely ever be in class, he'd spent most of his time here or in the Sol dens, with *him*... and that's what he'd call *him*."

S'rae felt her heart sink to her stomach. At once, she felt absolutely terrible—for there was only one person that boy would be. She turned to rub her eyes as she thought of the pain Vayp must have went through being here, and seeing this pup as a daily reminder of what he had lost. *Don't... don't do it, S'rae. Do not feel bad for the enemy. The traitor. Don't do it! Stop thinking about it. Breathe... slowly. Concentrate. Stop... don't let it break you, again. Don't think about them. Don't.*

"Well..." S'rae said, doing her best to compose herself, "his name is Mysol... because that's his name. Ain't that right, Mysol?"

She puckered her lips as the wolf pup licked her face.

"Well, I think *she* likes you," the cloaked man said.

"She?" S'rae flipped Mysol over onto her back to look at her... yupp, she was *definitely* a she. "Er... how'd you know?"

"Well, aside from the obvious, male wolves typically have broader faces and blockier muzzles, but hers is slender and perfect... isn't that right... Mysol?" Mysol barked loudly and wagged her tail. "I think she's happy."

"That makes the both of us." S'rae smiled, digging her face into Mysol's belly.

"Makes the three of us." He smiled. "She's a different one... she grows much slower than the rest, but with a proper owner and a great diet, she'll be right up to speed in no time. I think you'd be perfect for her."

At once, S'rae lifted her head and narrowed her eyes, again. *He's being nice.* Her lips curled. *Too nice. Remember what Fa'laz said, trust none.* She wanted to ask him why he was being nice, because now there was always something wrong when someone was too nice. The last two people who were this nice to her deceived her. She was betrayed by her brother... and her best friend tried to kill her. What was next? She did her best to push away the sinking feeling in her stomach.

"You don't have to look at me like that," he said, "I come in peace, you know."

Don't be so naive anymore, S'rae. You fell for this trap twice already. "That's exactly what a liar would say."

"Umm... I really don't think that's what a liar would say."

"Mmhmm..."

"Mmmm... no." He shook his head. "Nope, pretty sure they wouldn't."

"Well, looks like you learn something new every day."

He crossed his arms. "Is this the impression you want to give your new Professor of Sols?"

S'rae's eyes widened at that comment. *It's him? Of course it'd be him. Who else would Belem'nos be?*

"You'd think you want to be on my good side, you know?" Belem'nos said. "I am allowing you to take my class even though you don't have a Sol."

"Not true," S'rae said, reaching into her robe and pulling out the emblem Olivia gave her, and raised it high to the sky as if it were a trophy.

"Most interesting indeed," Belem'nos said, his eyes drooped a little, as if briefly remembering Olivia. "You wouldn't be able to take the course without it... so why you? Why'd she give this to you?"

S'rae remembered what Olivia had said, *do not tell anyone.* A part of her knew she shouldn't trust him, so she didn't. "She liked my... personality." S'rae smiled.

"Hmm... it may have been a good day for you then. Did you have breakfast that day?"

S'rae's eyes narrowed harder. But... she hated the fact that he may have been right, she hadn't had a single thing to eat all day. *Yupp, I hate you!*

"You can call me, Bele," he said, reaching his hand down to help her up. "S'rae, is it?"

She disregarded his help and stood up on her own, puffing her chest out. "Hi, Bele, yes, S'rae it is, the, *ahem,* Champion of GroundStone." She puffed her chest out more, to let him know just who he was talking to.

"Right... and one of the visitors of the Valley of Gaia, no? Quite a special one, I see."

S'rae tried her hardest not to blush. She twisted her lips a little before saying, "Why yes... I suppose I *am.*"

"Tell me a little about the Valley of Gaia... how was it? Was it... as beautiful as the stories claimed?"

"It was," she lied. He didn't need to know about anything that was going on.

His face scrunched up. "Are you good at many things, S'rae?"

"Why... yes... I suppose I *am*."

"But... lying isn't one of them, huh?"

She pulled her chin back to her neck. "Excuse me? And how would you know I'm lying?"

"Let's just say that *everyone* is a liar, but some happen to be better than others... and you happen to be the worst I've ever seen."

She gasped, but said nothing.

"So," Bele said, "you are lying. Why?"

"No!"

"Hmm... lying about lying... oh how the plot thickens." He gave a smug face that was so punchable that S'rae had balled up her fists without even knowing. "Aw, that's adorable. I see your clenched fists. You remind me of a lion."

S'rae's face glowed. *That's right! Fierce like a lion, don't get on my bad side!*

And as if he had read her thoughts, he said, "Oh no, I'm so very sorry, not the lion you're thinking of... I meant to say a lion baby... and by lion baby... I really mean lying baby."

"I am *not* a baby!" S'rae pouted.

"Sounds like something a baby would say," Bele did yet another punchable smirk. "How old are you anyways?"

"Err... fifteen," S'rae said, and when Bele smirked, she continued, "fifteen... point nine, practically sixteen."

"Did you really just say *point nine*?"

"Mhmm..."

He chuckled. "Well, tell me about your time at the Valley of Gaia." S'rae shook her head. "Well, fine... how about your time at Fujita? I've read so many great stories about their technological advancements!" His eyes became wide with energy. He went on and on about ballistic coefficients, Fujita working on space travel, their rocket thrusters that may now be able to orbit Gaia, and on and on and on about the research of Professor Ki. He was such a dork and S'rae hated that she liked that about him. "Please tell me you at least took a course with Professor Ki!"

"He was actually my favorite professor... and *I*," S'rae let out a smug smile of her own, "was his favorite student."

"They must have fed you well over there," he chuckled.

"Hah! Hah! You think you're so funny!" S'rae hated that he got a little chuckle out of her. "Well, maybe I'd tell you about the Valley of Gaia and Fujita if you were nice to me and I actually liked you."

"The next wave is coming."

"Umm... and what's that supposed to mean?" S'rae said.

"Well... the next wave is coming. It's a saying from my old village, it helped us have a carefree, positive outlook on life. You see, life is like the ocean, it moves in waves: You feel lifted, but then right after, you crash to your lowest point. But why feel sad... when you know that right after, you'll be picked up again.... Because... the next wave is coming. So, you hate me now, but you'll like me later." He smiled.

"Well, I'm pretty sure this ocean doesn't have waves... it's more like a still lake... that dried up."

"Oh," Bele laughed, and somehow that was more annoying. He was supposed to feel offended, not humored. "Well, fine, Miss Still Lake S'rae, how about this, you don't have to like me, but if you teach me what you learned, I will teach you what I learned."

"That won't be necessary."

"Why?"

"Lost interest."

"In the class... or the professor?"

"You're a professor, I'm sure you'll figure that one out."

"Oh," he chuckled, "good one! Your personality, I think I know *exactly* why your Sol hasn't found you yet."

"And why's that?"

"Oh… let's just say that if I was your Sol, I'd take my time too."

"Oh!" S'rae scoffed. "Is that so?"

"Yeah, and by *take my time*, I mean a whole life*time*."

"Sounds like a long time."

"Wouldn't be long enough."

"Well… tell me then… how could a Sol professor, who doesn't have a Sol, help me out? And since you're so much older than me, looks like your Sol is doing a great job avoiding your lovely personality, too, Grandpa." *Good one, S'rae, you should thank Yash for that line later*. She no longer cared about being liked by this jerk, who probably thought he was the greatest thing on Gaia since waterfall showers.

"Hah! Well, I'm nineteen… point one."

"Sad… I guess some people don't age well," S'rae smirked. "I bet your father looks younger than you."

And then something happened, S'rae couldn't explain it, but the power she felt made her shrink as if gravity had magnified and was pulling her deep into Gaia. S'rae couldn't even lift her hands, but when she lifted her eyes, she saw the pain in his, it suddenly occurred to her that he may have lost his family as well.

"I'm… sorry," S'rae said softly. "I-I shouldn't have said that… I… I lost my family too."

Then the pulling feeling faded away, she no longer felt her spine crack and tighten. She saw him look up as a tear formed. "No worries… the next wave is coming, that's what I try to tell myself."

S'rae now felt absolutely terrible. She puffed for a moment, then stared at the ground, mad at herself for being so weak. "The Valley of Gaia… it was not beautiful. It seemed drained of all its life, the School of Fire had no students, and… all we did was read from a book."

Bele smiled. "I am sure there were many books there… some that the world must no longer teach from."

"Well… yeah, I did see some." S'rae closed her eyes to remember. "There was... one about... the Eve of Darkness? Another... I think... it was called... the Prophecies of Va'han." S'rae heard a gasp and opened her eyes. Bele looked on with wide eyes as if she was the professor teaching him life's greatest mysteries. She felt kind of important... she liked this feeling. "And oh yeah... there was one about..." The life immediately got sucked from her body. Her eyes widened as she let out a gasp of her own.

"What's wrong?" Bele came to her. His soft hands wrapped around her shoulders.

"It's just that... Olivia's last words... I thought she was talking about a Sol... named Adari. But now... now I remember a book at the Valley... it was called the Sol'adari Pact." S'rae's eyes met Bele's blackened eyes. "Do you know what that is?"

Bele took a deep breath and looked away for a moment. S'rae could see his hand shake as he pressed it to his lips. "Here is the deal, S'rae... you tell me all that you know... and I will help you find a Sol."

"No..." S'rae shook her head. "I don't want anymore disappointment. I'm done with that heartbreak."

"Then... then... I'll show you why not having a Sol can be more rewarding than having one."

Now *that* comment made S'rae's eyes light up. "I don't believe it."

"Then... let me show you." Bele walked up to S'rae and placed his fingers to her temples, she couldn't have stopped him if she tried. Her whole body had seized up. "I want you to think about an animal, any animal." She felt her head squeeze tighter. "Now... close your eyes. Do you see it? Yes... perfect... now whisper these words *ruw'hi*."

S'rae felt like she was in a state of bliss. She didn't feel anything... yet she felt *everything*. The soft wind that brushed her skin felt like feathers massaging her. The birds chirping suddenly sounded like songs... with words... telling her how beautiful life was. It was as if the songs they'd sing had been songs all along. Even the soil at her feet felt like it was pumping life into her, as if she was a tree a part of Gaia's lifeforce. She couldn't explain what was happening… but she never wanted it to end.

Then finally, Bele's words sang to her again. *Whisper these words… ruw'hi.*

So *ruw'hi* she said. And immediately the world spun so fast that she saw stars swirl into rings of light. Night turned to day then night then day all within the blink of an eye. A seed fell, roots sprouted from it, a stump and branches grew wide and tall, then it withered away… before completing the process all over again.

And finally, *open your eyes* reached her mind as a thought, but it wasn't her own voice… it was… Bele's?

And when she opened her eyes, she saw GroundStone like never before. It looked MASSIVE… like a hundred times the size it normally was. But… so did this leaf. The leaf was almost the size of her. And when she reached out to grab it, she saw tiny little hands with even tinier claws. She placed them to her face… she had seen similar hands like these before… they almost looked like… B'se's!

OH EM BLAZING DEE! AM I A SQUIRREL RIGHT NOW?

I have no idea WHY you would choose a squirrel, but yes… that is exactly what you are right now. What do you see?

Umm… first of all, ONLY cool people would choose a squirrel. And second of all, HOW am I squirrel right now?

Because you are not linked to a Sol… with a lot of help from a very gifted person… which is me… you have the freedom to link into other animals. It's one of the few perks you have. If you hold your end of the bargain, I will show you many more that you've been missing out on.

S'rae ran up a tree as insects and bark and twigs blurred by her. She leapt to a branch then another then another, and then tried her biggest leap yet. She soared what felt like a mile through the sky as she missed her branch, but clawed onto another, which used her momentum to catapult her back into the air.

DEAL! THIS IS SO AMAZING!!

She then found herself dashing through the streets of Ground-Stone, only to skid to a stop to nibble on a nut she saw. *Mmm… it actually tastes amazing as a squirrel!* It truly was an amazing experience to see life through the eyes of an animal. She felt her heartbeat vibrate against her chest and she was on such a high alert that any motion would cause her head to twitch. She saw so many little details that she had never seen before: the texture on the leaves and stone, the little grooves in foot prints, and even the insides of trees as she found cracks to run into. There were so many little cracks that it suddenly dawned on her just what Coars and Professor Di'Tukia had mentioned, there must have been a million hidden spots, and now her curious mind wanted to find them all.

One peculiar spot, at the base of a temple, hidden by moss and vines, really caught S'rae's attention, because it looked like it had the same phoenix symbol that was on the emblem Olivia gave to her. But before she could check it out, a massive hoof was about to squash her.

She ran away and sprinted deeper into the woods. Excitement pulsed through her bloodstream until she heard a SNAP! When she quickly turned to hear the source, she saw a lone cloaked figure standing there, barely hidden in the shadows. Her already fast heartbeat escalated to a jackhammer, making her body shake.

What… who was that?

Who was what?

Just… a person… a person was there staring at me.

You sure he was staring at you? You're a squirrel right now.

Oh believe me, I KNOW I'm a squirrel right now, but I don't know…

She shrugged it off and ran deeper into the forest, feeling the fresh soil crunch underneath her claws and when she took a turn to head back to GroundStone, she stopped dead in her tracks.

Umm… I see that person again. There… in the distance was a cloaked silhouette. *Ummm… am I being followed right now?* Though it was a voice in her head, she heard the way it trembled. She didn't want to show it, but she started to feel terrified.

Hmm… we can end this then, S'rae, if you aren't okay with it.

No… no, it's fine. This is too amazing to stop!

She dashed up more trees, deciding to take the high road, leaping from branch to branch, then slid and practically swung and flipped down a stringy leaf, only to land perfectly on her feet. *Yeah, I'm kinda great at being a squirrel!* And when she looked up, she squealed. *Ahh!! This isn't funny! It's that person again!! This isn't funny at all.* The silhouette remained motionless, in the distance.

What does he look like?

I'm not trying to find out. She dashed away from the cloaked figure and immediately heard *THUD THUD THUD THUD*, getting louder and louder as if something massive had closed in on her. She turned around, breathing heavily, but nothing was there. Her eyes scanned the woods, feeling like her stomach was ready to implode from the pressure. *I don't like this… I'm scared. I think… he was chasing me.*

When she turned around, she let out her biggest shriek yet. She stared directly into a masked man, who was lying down on its body as if to look at S'rae at eye-level.

What's wrong? S'rae, tell me, what's wrong?

S'rae screamed as she ran away, but it was too late, she heard a SWOOSH, then collapsed to the ground, feeling her body trapped into the soil. And when she looked at her squirming body, she saw that an arrow was lodged into her side, swirling in waves of wind.

She was lifted in the air. She saw the cloaked figure's brown robes before being placed in front of its face. It was a horrific mask that looked like it belonged to a once living person that was now faceless.

I'm scared. S'rae screamed. *I'm really scared! Help!*

What's wrong? What do you see?

But she was too frightened to say anything else. She felt her soul get ripped from her body and she was left as a frightened shell, incapable of doing anything, not even breathe.

The masked person grabbed S'rae's tiny neck. And with his free hand, he drew a line across his neck slowly. Then SNAP!

S'rae felt her neck break and at once she fell to her hands and knees, crying into the sand that made up the foundation of the colosseum. She was back in her own body.

"Tell me… what happened?" Bele held S'rae in his arms… or tried to, but she was freaking out, clawing and kicking and punching at nothing at all, trying to free herself as she screamed at the top of her lungs. "You're safe… you're safe with me, I promise, what's wrong? What happened?"

"I…" S'rae cried before she could get a word out, but though she was still trembling, something about being wrapped in Bele's arms felt like she was the safest she had ever been. "I… was killed."

"Like… hunted?" Bele's eyes were wide.

"No…" Her lips trembled. "Like… murdered."

Bele looked into S'rae's eyes, and she couldn't explain how she felt… but the way fire burned in his eyes let her know that she was with someone who cared about her safety. He was a Professor at GroundStone, the School of Earth and Rock, after all, protecting was in their nature; but this… this felt like she was in the safest place she could be right now. And she didn't know how she felt about that. She knew she shouldn't trust him… trust none… but she felt so safe.

Bele pulled her back in and caressed her back and head with soft touches that sent chills through her spine. He was treating her like the baby he called her out for being, but it was exactly what she needed right now as she curled up into his chest and cried. There was a warmth about him that resonated within her, as if it reached out and soothed her heart, letting her know that everything was going to be okay.

"It's okay, S'rae… it's okay…" Bele squeezed her tighter. "The next wave is coming."

"But it's not…" The most disturbing thought suddenly crossed her mind. "I think… they got the wrong person. The killer… is still out there."

13

FUJAK

FUJAK CLASPED THE METAL CHAINS between his hands, at least that was what they felt like. Even though he could not see in this darkness, his sense of touch gave him some vision. The chains must have been from some kind of metal, just like everything else around him, because they'd *clang* whenever he slammed his hands against the wall. He had been locked in here for what felt like weeks, though it may have only been a few days. His mind, the one thing students of Fujita were best known for, felt like it was diminishing, rotting away by the second. His thoughts were sluggish, which may have been the result of the sour drink they had given him during the questioning.

Who sent you to kill the Champion? Why did you murder the Professor of Sols? The more he thought about the questions and the bitter taste in his mouth, the less he could remember what actually happened that day.

"I would never try to kill S'rae!" Fujak slammed his hands against the wall again, the clang echoed in the darkness. "I wouldn't! I wouldn't… right?"

Why would I try to kill S'rae? He tried to recall that day, but the images were distorted.

"I did not kill anyone!" Fujak screamed once more.

"Oh, would you *please* shut up already!" He heard a voice shout from beyond the wall.

Fujak wiped his eyes and brought his ear closer to the wall, feeling the cold metal chill his cheek. "Someone's here?"

"Oh no… you're just talking to an imaginary person… who wants you to just shut up already. So listen to this beautifully elegant voice inside your head and keep your babying to yourself. Please… and thank you. Sincerely, the pleasant voice inside your head."

Fujak's lip curled. "Sorry that I was disrupting the fun time you were having over there."

"Yes, let me enjoy my party in peace, thank you!" Fujak heard more mumbling behind the wall, but he had no way in channeling soundwaves to hear what may have been said.

He had tried many times already. This Alsi'jin place… it seemed like a metal fortress, where the cold metal numbed his limbs and seeped into his skin.

"Well," Fujak cleared his throat. "At least I won't be missing you when I leave."

A burst of laughter practically made the wall shake. "Oh my! You may be as pathetic as you are stupid! When *I* leave!" The voice laughed harder. "Oh… when *I* leave! He said *when I leave*!" The voice laughed for about a minute more, slapping sounds like palms against thighs were heard as well. "Oh wow! That was great, at least you're good for laughs, so for that, I will say thank you for being the annoying baby across the wall. But I'm not sure if you're funny or insane, because you're in Alsi'jin… there is *no* leaving Alsi'jin, there is *only* dying."

Fujak cleared his throat again, or tried to, he ended up choking before a word came out.

"Yes… you'd be lucky if they strangled you to death," the voice said. "… but this warden guy… he will have a lot more fun dragging

188

it out. Trust me... you'll be begging for a quick way out of Alsi'jin once he gets started with his *fun*."

"Nothing bad has happened yet... just feel a little groggy, but they're giving me a fair chance... a fair trial. I *will* be leaving once I prove my innocence."

"Oh... I see they've been giving you a little sip of their juice, huh? Losing your mind yet? It won't be long til you forget who you are and why you're even in here. And then it won't be long til they convinced you that you did a dozen other crimes you were never a part of. There is *nothing* fair about this system. You're screwed, little baby."

"Not true," Fujak said loudly. "Laws are what made peace happen for millennia. They are just and fair... and if you don't believe in the system, maybe you deserve to be here."

"Looks like the system is doing you very well, huh? Different beliefs... but yet here we are... in the same place."

"I've already told you, unlike you, I won't be here for long. I will be free once I prove my innocence."

"Right... that's what everyone who lived and died in that room before you said also—that they were innocent... and look where they ended up."

"Well, I am *actually* innocent."

"And so was I... and *them*."

"Right." Fujak held back a slight laugh.

"What? You think you're the only *innocent* person who got stuck in here? You really are as stupid as you sound. *Oh how just and great these laws are... we are perfect... we make no mistakes... we have fair trials... and only lock away and kill the very, very, very bad people of the world*! Is that what you honestly think happens?"

Fujak froze for a moment, soaking in the question. Could it be true... that other innocent people were locked away for life? "I don't believe you. Without the laws, chaos would break free. The laws of the land were designed to give free trials and justice to those—"

"Can you PLEASE shut up about justice and fairness right now!" Fujak may have been hearing things, but it sounded like the person behind the wall may have been crying. Fujak heard the pain in the voice, so he remained quiet. "Until you hear the stories of those who died before you... do not talk about things you don't know about. Got it? You can spend all day reading about the stupid laws from the stupid books, but until you see what they actually do to people... like you *right now*... then you'll finally know what really happens to us."

Fujak felt terrible, a tight feeling in his stomach. Normally, he would have regurgitated all the information he learned for the debates at Fujita, but right now, he either did not have the energy... or did not know what to think. For the first time... he had experienced doubt.

"So... does the little baby have anything to say?" the voice said.

"Yes," Fujak said, "if you think you're innocent... what did they lock you up for?"

There was nothing but silence for a few long seconds.

"Just what I thought," Fujak said. "Real criminals get locked up, innocent ones will be given their fair trial."

"You wouldn't believe me even if I told you... no one does."

"Well, it looks like we have plenty of time. Entertain me."

"I don't need to talk about it with someone like you... only for you to just throw it into my face."

"If you're innocent, what is there to hide?"

"Pride... There are some things more important, you know." The way the voice cracked sent a chill down Fujak's spine.

Fujak took a deep breath, placing his hands against the cold metal, and said softly, "I'm sorry for whatever it is that happened to you... but when you do want to let it out to someone... I have time. Everyone's voice deserves to be heard, that is what makes the system fair. And I'll listen."

"T-thank you."

"You're welcome."

And after a few moments of silence, the voice said, "So… who is this girl… S'rae?"

"Oh… a girl they thought I tried to kill."

"And why would they think that?"

"Because… I—" Fujak didn't know if he should admit that he was from Fujita, it seemed like this person had just started to open up to him, and that would surely ruin it. Fujitas were the reason this system was created, after all. "I was found at both locations… when the murder attempts happened."

"Hmm… you sound guilty to me."

"But I'm not."

"Sounds like a tough one to prove."

"I would *never* try to kill her. She's the last person I'd try to kill."

"Oh… that's a big statement! Go on… what do you mean by that?"

"Nothing."

"Oh no you don't! You cannot say something like 'she's the last person I'd try to kill,' and leave me out to dry like I'm some kind of wet noodle! Details! Like you said, we have time!"

Fujak felt his face drop just thinking about someone trying to kill S'rae. "She was my first true friend."

"Was? What happened?"

"Well… we're friends again."

"Well, that didn't answer my question, did it? What happened? She *was* your first true friend?"

"Er… well, she was the first person who accepted me for me. She didn't like me because of who I was… or the family I was a part of… she liked me because I was me. And around her… I wasn't afraid to be anyone else but myself. She made me feel comfortable in my skin. You know… you can't see me right now… but

I wasn't always like this… there was a time when I was pretty much the ugliest kid in the school. I was short, pathetic—"

"So, you're one of those ego boys who thinks they're attractive, huh? I'm surprised they found a cell big enough for your head. But hey, at least you didn't lose the *pathetic* part, though. You still seem to have that going for you."

Fujak couldn't help but chuckle. "I suppose. But… in a place where people expect the most out of you… she just wanted me to be me, and it meant the world. Finally, someone who I could just be me around and not feel like an out of shape, ugly, pathetic loser." Fujak clenched his fists just thinking about a time when he was made fun of by everyone.

"A little harsh on yourself, no?"

"I was… and she was the only one who made me feel like it was okay. As if the old me was good enough. As if I mattered. Like I didn't need to live up to the name. I could just be me."

"Then what happened? She sounds like she's a great person."

"I wanted her to make friends, so I took her up to our family's terrace. And that was exactly what happened. After, the girls swarmed her and wanted to know what it was like… but then—" Fujak felt his throat clog up and eyes glaze just thinking about it. "—then they started to make fun of me… as they always did. But S'rae was my first true friend… she'd stick up for me, right?" He felt a tear roll down his cheek. "What she said hurt… it hurt a lot. I thought being me was finally good enough for someone… that I didn't need to live up to a big name, that I could just be myself. But I was wrong… and it hurt… a lot." Fujak wiped the tears from his eyes. "But… we're friends now, and that's what matters."

"Yeah," the voice said softly, "that's what matters." A few moments of silence passed. "It sounds like… um… it sounds like there is something still there."

"I-I don't know. Everything happens for a reason. If I didn't go through that, I wouldn't be the person I am today."

"And… are you happy with who you are today?"

Fujak paused for a moment. "I think so." But he didn't know the answer for sure.

"It sounds like to me… that you were never able to be the person that you wanted to be. And who was that, exactly?"

Fujak's eyes glazed over. It wasn't just his answer that got him emotional… it was the question. Not a single person had ever asked who he wanted to become—it was always expected. He was Fujak, the heir of Fujita, the son of the Headmaster, he was destined to be a Headmaster… that was his life. But was it the life he wanted? No. "I don't know anymore."

"Well, that's very sad to hear."

"It's never too late. I'd like to think that this journey is about finding who I am really supposed to be. And once I leave here… I think that's exactly what I'm going to do."

"Well," the voice was now softer, "I'm sorry… but this is Alsi'jin… you may never get the chance."

As the hours and days passed, Fujak found himself in a conflicted mood. On one hand, he was upset that he was still in this prison, though knowing he was innocent, but on the other, he found himself thankful for this opportunity to just sit down and talk to another person about life, goals, dreams, opinions, different cultures, and any other topic that would randomly come up. Fujak graduated almost at the top of his class at the most competitive school, filled with the brightest minds in all of Gaia… yet… here he was learning so much that was never taught in schools. It made him realize just how little he knew about the world outside of what was told in the books. A part of him… *no… that would be crazy, right?* A part of him was actually content that destiny led him here?

"Do you ever feel like… that things just happen for a reason… even the bad?" Fujak asked.

"Are you saying that because you're happy you have the absolute best person to talk to beyond the wall?"

"Well, I guess," he chuckled, "yes."

"I used to think like that… but then nothing good has happened since coming here."

"What about this?"

"Okay… I'll admit, a part of me is happy that I called you out for being a pathetic baby, because talking to you… is different." Fujak could hear the sounds of feet hitting metal as if the person was pacing their room. "But it's also kind of sad when I think about it."

"Why?"

"Because…" Fujak heard a suppressed sob. Was that crying? "Because… a part of me feels like may-maybe we could have been good friends if we met at a different time, under different circumstances. And what I don't like about this… is because whenever someone dies here… it just happens. But you… you're a friend… and now—"

"Nothing will happen to me," Fujak said. "I will be proven innocent… and when I get out of here, I will make sure to amend laws and get you and others out of here as well. I will come back for you."

"I wish you were right… I really do… but the only way to leave here is by a coffin. And… I like you… I just don't want to see that happen."

"Well… if anything does happen, I at least want to know your name, friend," Fujak said. "My name is… Fujak." He did it… he realized the mistake he made right when it left his lips. Someone who passionately hated the system, and understood the laws better than most Fujitas Fujak knew, would definitely know where the name Fujak came from.

"Fujak… Fuj… ak?" Fujak heard a gasp. "Are you a—"

"Yes."

Moments of silence passed. Fujak was expecting something

harsh, but instead he heard: "So… that means… what you're saying is… you may *actually* be able to free us?"

Fujak's eyes glazed. "I will do everything in my power to try to right the wrongs of the system. I believe in it, but nothing is perfect, so thank you for making me realize this."

"Wow! I… I actually… believe you."

Tears fell down Fujak's eyes, but they were of joy. It felt like he had finally found his purpose. This… this was who he was meant to be. "Everything happens for a reason. And I believe good things will come from this bad situation."

"I hope so."

"So… what is your name?"

"You can call me Reyna."

Fujak pulled back, almost hitting his head on the cold metal. "Er… Reyna, huh? That's quite a feminine name, no?"

"Umm… yes? Usually girls' names are feminine, so there's that!"

"Wait!" Fujak's eyes widened. "You're… a… girl?"

"Err… last time I checked I was, yupp."

Fujak stood up and paced around the room. None of this made sense… why would a girl be locked up… *here*? Fujak wanted… no… he needed an answer. "I need to know… why… why are you here? *Here*, where they send killers and terrible people? And where'd everyone else go? Why is there only the two of us?"

"You mean the three of us," another voice was heard behind the wall on the opposite side of the room from Reyna.

"WHAT?" Both Reyna and Fujak gasped at once.

"How long have you been here?" Reyna shouted. "When did you get here? Were you here before me? And what the… what have you been doing this whole time?"

"Just someone trying to get some sleep," the voice said. "I've been here for… oh, I don't know… days, weeks, months, they all sort of just blend together."

"Well," Fujak said, "now you know pretty much everything about us."

"Indeed... and both of you sound like good people, good friends, even. It's a shame to see you two up in here, especially since one of you will die before you even get to see the other."

That thought sent a spear through Fujak's chest. Would he die before getting to see or free Reyna? Or worse... would she die while they were here? "And what about you... are you a good person?"

"Me?" the voice said weakly. "I don't know if I am good or bad. I'd like to think that what I did was good, but many would view it as bad."

Fujak gulped a difficult breath, feeling it hit a solid wall in his throat. "Like what did you do?"

"Oh... I kill people," the voice said quite calmly.

Both Fujak and Reyna gasped.

"But... I kill bad people only. People who deserve it. And I couldn't help but question... why would someone want to kill that girl, S'rae? She seems like a good person, at least based on everything you said about her. I don't approve of killing good people. So why, why would someone want her dead? Maybe she's evil and you don't know?"

"No! Not S'rae... she can be a bit of a jerk sometimes, yes, but her heart means well."

"Interesting," the voice said. "And what about you, Reyna, what brought you here?"

Fujak's eyes lit up, his curious mind ran through a dozen different scenarios, but none of them made sense why a girl who seemingly wouldn't hurt anyone would be in here. Unless. Fujak's eyes widened even more.

"The Shinshei Law," both Reyna and Fujak said at the same time. And Fujak's heart dropped.

"The Warden found a way to get me in here for something else I didn't do, because he couldn't prove that I was guilty of breaking

196

the Shinshei law. But I know… I know the Shinshei Law is the real reason I'm here."

The Shinshei Law were the Sacred Laws of the Land. The ones that would result in death when found guilty. Then Fujak's eyes lit up as he recalled the day of S'rae's attempted murder. She had practiced another element—that could definitely be the reason why someone would want to kill her. But which Shinshei was Reyna accused of?

After a long silence, Reyna continued, "I was accused of turning a GroundStone professor into Metal."

Metal. Fujak took a step back, hand to his lips. If this was true, she was more powerful and dangerous than anyone here. This whole fortress was metal… why would they lock her up here? Unless that was the point. If she could break out of the unbreakable fortress, it'd prove the Warden right that she was guilty. Smart… kind of.

"So… did you?" Fujak said. "Did you break a Shinshei Law?"

The long pause before Reyna's response made Fujak's stomach twist. "I don't know," she said. Fujak heard her slam her palms against the wall. "Please… please don't hate me, Fujak. I'm not a bad person, I swear."

Saying that someone who could control Metal wasn't bad was like saying a Shadow was good. And judging by the Shadow Army that was preparing to destroy the world of Gaia, Fujak knew how crazy that sounded. He didn't know what to say, so he said nothing.

The slams on the other side of the wall grew louder. "I knew I shouldn't have said anything. I *KNEW IT*!"

Fujak felt a pang of regret tighten his chest. He learned to not cast judgment too quickly: Justice will never be served as long as the other's voice was silenced. That was what Professor Ki had taught him. "So… what did the warden get you for instead?"

The banging on the wall stopped at once. "No one believes me… so there's no point in talking about it." Fujak heard the sniffles after her words, the ones that carried a weight of sorrow that could bring even the strongest person down.

"Tell me," Fujak said softly, "I promise to listen."

There it was again. The sniffles. It must have taken everything in her to talk about this, and Fujak understood exactly why. He too had difficulty talking about troubled pasts.

"After… I was free… the Warden… he went crazy. He lost more than just the trial. And I felt sorry for him. I went to apologize to him after what happened. And when I visited him… he locked the door. With us inside." Fujak heard Reyna's voice crack and stutter right then. "He… he locked the door… and…" Fujak heard her crying beyond the wall, unable to finish a sentence. "I can't… I'm sorry. You wouldn't believe me anyways, no one does."

"What happened?" Fujak felt his stomach sink as if he had already came to his own haunting conclusion.

"He didn't let me out until he got what he wanted… and after, I didn't know what to do. I kept it inside for as long as I could… until family asked why I was so miserable, though I was free. And then finally… I found the courage. I told them, my family, I told the council, I even told the GroundStone faculty… and not a single person believed me… because I was the 'Metal Girl'. And they said that I was afraid of him catching me for something else… and that I wanted him to be locked up so he wouldn't get me. And they were right… I was afraid of him. And this was why. They said he was a good man. The Warden is the most fair and just and good man in all of Gaia, and that is why he was given the title, the Keeper of Justice. But I know the monster he really is. They threw me into Alsi'jin under the law of lying under oath to undermine an authority. He got what he wanted… I'm here in Alsi'jin for something I didn't even do. He won." Reyna burst into tears. "And there is nothing I can do about it."

Only until after Reyna had stopped talking did Fujak realize his fists were clenched so tightly that it felt like his veins were about to burst. *The monster he really is.*

198

"I would love for a world when men can suffer the same fates they subject us to," Reyna said.

"Not all men are evil, Reyna."

"There are evil men… and then there are the men who allow the evil ones to exist. Both are just as bad in my eyes."

Fujak said nothing. And before he could say a word, a door banged open somewhere in the darkness. The stomping sounds of metal on metal was followed by a subtle shriek that sounded like a sword dragging across a metal floor.

"And now… it's time again." Fujak heard the quivering in Reyna's voice. "He's ready to punish me… again."

"Reyna… Reyna… Reyna… oh how it has been too long. Much too long, if you ask me." The deep voice was far away, getting nearer and nearer. *Clang. Clang. Clang.* The soul-stirring metal on metal sounds caused Fujak's shoulders to lock up, as if *he* was coming for him. He could only imagine the fear Reyna must have been going through. "You're next up, huh. Let's make the most out of this, shall we?" Fujak heard a belittling laugh that made his clenched fists squeeze tighter. He knew that voice, it was the same one that would keep asking *"Why did you kill the Professor of Sols?"* over and over again as they forced liquid down his mouth.

"It's time," Reyna said softly. For someone who had such a strong personality, the way the warden's presence made her voice shrivel up had Fujak imagining the worst.

Fujak slammed his fists together, wishing there was something he could do about this. But what could he do? He was trapped, helpless. *And then there are the men who allow the evil ones to exist. Both are just as bad in my eyes,* Fujak remembered Reyna's words. He was no better than the Warden if he did nothing.

So something he did.

"Is that the pathetic, ugly warden that I hear coming?" Fujak said loudly. And at once, the *clangs* stopped.

"Stop!" Reyna said softly. "What are you doing? Don't get him mad."

"Why not get him mad? What's this short, stumpy person going to do?" Fujak said even louder.

"Oh… is that so?" Fujak heard a voice in the darkness. Then the *clangs* became louder and fiercer, as if he dug the sword into the ground with each step.

"What are you doing! Stop this, you're crazy!" Reyna said. "You don't have to do this!"

"You're right… I don't have to. I want to."

"Why? Why are you doing this?" Fujak heard the genuine sorrow in Reyna's voice.

"Because… we are not all the same. You can trust me. And… I… believe you."

Fujak heard Reyna fall to the floor and sob.

"I don't know what to say," Reyna said.

"You've said more than enough. You don't deserve this. If this helps you believe that there are still some good people out there, then it worked," Fujak smiled. Then his smile faded as a *BANG* made his room shake.

He felt footsteps get nearer and nearer until he could practically smell the scent of the Warden and his sweaty body odor.

"You think this is a game, do you?" the Warden said. "I've done far worse for less. You think you and your kind are better than us, huh? Your minds are powerful and unbreakable. You meditate so you have a high tolerance to pain. Well, I know just what will make you break… will make you scream, boy. They always break. *Always* scream."

Fujak lifted his head higher, though he felt his insides collapse. "And one day… I will hear you scream, too." He didn't care about the consequences of making that threat, he only wanted to make a promise, a goal to look forward to.

"Oh… you will be a lot of fun… I can already tell. Hearing you scream may be the most satisfying one yet. Oh yes, it will."

Fujak felt cold hands wrap around his neck and pull him through the even colder hallways. As he passed Reyna's room, he heard her whisper, "I'm so, so sorry."

Fujak was thrown into a grey metallic room, where blades, needles, chains, and whips were scattered throughout the floor, some hanging on the walls. He was forced onto a metal table that made his body numb. After a few minutes of being strapped down onto it, it felt like the very knives he saw on the floor were digging into his back, arms, and legs.

The Warden had been gone for what may have been an hour. Smart. This waiting for what was to come was one of the first ways to deteriorate one's mind. But Fujak remained calm. This was the Fujita in him, mind over matter. Focus. Do not show pain. Do not show misery. Do not scream.

The door banged open, the sheer force almost blew out the candles that barely lit the room.

"Fujitas are quite the specimens," the Warden said, walking in with a dagger in his hand. "Because of you, I would not be here, serving justice." He grinned and Fujak felt his lip curl. "They have created a system where I am free to punish even one of their own... with no consequences... imagine that. But what's most interesting about Fujitas... is the way you carry yourselves. As if you are all the greatest things that ever blessed Gaia. But that's where you're wrong." He reached over and grabbed a crystal container. The inky substance inside slushed around as the Warden brought it to Fujak's nose. He recognized the bitter scent immediately. "You see, Archon's Blood is the greatest thing to grace Gaia. It has dozens of uses... and even still, we are finding out new, marvelous ways to use it. It is effective to control populations, but I find its best uses happen to be... well, for punishment."

Fujak pulled his head away as the Warden shoved the jar in his face.

"What's most remarkable about Archon's Blood... is that the

scars it leaves are incurable. A life lesson to live with… forever."
The Warden twisted the dagger and dipped the tip of it inside the
container. The dagger sizzled as the inky substance moved its way
up the blade as if it had a mind of its own. "It's a shame… you have
such a handsome face. You must have truly been one of their greatest. You're the exact type of person I love to break down. The one
who thinks he's smarter, better, and more attractive than everyone
else. Well… look who is calling the shots now."

The Warden inched the blade closer to Fujak's face. "Say goodbye to your pretty little face."

14

BELE HANDED S'RAE A BOWL OF FRESH BERRIES with a side of honey and goatbread.

"Thank you," S'rae said. She was still shaken up after what had happened with the masked person, but Bele had done a great job comforting her. Not only did he bring her to this beautiful room inside the Professor's Palace, but he had been treating her to delicious foods, and lots of it. Yes, he knew exactly how to make her feel better. She lifted from her seat and walked across the room, passing through rows of golden bookshelves, toward the glowing window. She gazed out at the alluring backdrop of GroundStone, noticing how the walls and temples and statues created a maze of some sort, and the moment she bit down on a berry, a dozen fruity flavors splashed into her mouth. She couldn't explain the amazingness that just occurred—it was unlike anything she had ever eaten. From just one berry, she tasted what seemed like a strawberry, blueberry, then even a mango of some sort. Eyes wide, she looked over at Bele, who was smirking, as if waiting to hear what S'rae had to say. "That… now *that* was amazing!"

He bowed. "I'm very glad to hear that. It's a new blend I created. You're actually the first to try it."

She licked her lips as a quick shiver ran up her spine, she felt rejuvenated. "No, but really... what'd you do? How'd you create such deliciousness?"

"Now, now, you of all people should know that there are some secrets we must all keep to ourselves."

S'rae turned her eyes away from a massive gorilla, one of the many hundred foot tall statues, which looked like a baby compared to the tallest ones, and met Bele's gaze. Why would he say that? Did he know S'rae was holding a secret within her? Maybe this was his way to get on S'rae's good side to get what he really wanted.

"I must ask again," Bele said, grabbing an oak staff that was leaning against a table, "did Olivia tell you *anything*?"

She heard the urgency in his voice as he approached, and when he reached her, she noticed beneath his fur-lined cloaked and his silky shirt, were what looked like a series of tattoos on his chiseled chest. *Umm... okay! How about you never again think of his chest as chiseled, S'rae! NEVER! AGAIN!*

She didn't know if she should tell him, Olivia had made it very clear to not tell anyone about their secret. *Even the thought of this Sol being yours could get you killed*, she remembered Olivia's words. But did she mean to keep the secret from Bele as well? It was too big to share and she already had one person trying to kill her, one was more than enough for her, thank you. But all of this, the way he had held her in his arms, the way she felt so safe and comfortable in them, the way she felt so secure in his presence... and of course, she was upset to admit this, but the way his food tasted, yes, the food was *that* good, good enough to make her reconsider her better judgment. *Damn you, you delicious berries.* Somehow she felt like if there was one person to tell this secret to it was him... and only him.

Bele placed his finger under S'rae's chin and lifted. At once, S'rae's eyes widened. Not because a professor had just touched her chin delicately, yes, that was supposed to be creepy, but somehow it wasn't… and that was because of his eyes, they pulled her in: they were gripping, green, and gorgeous. *Okay, gorgeous? Chiseled… and now gorgeous? This is NOT happening right now! Nope! We are definitely putting a stop to these words, S'rae!*

She quickly pulled away from the trance and turned back to the window. She only now realized she was breathing heavily; this wasn't good. She had considered him the creepy cloaked person without ever actually considering what he had looked like up close. A part of her wished she could unsee what she saw and go back to thinking he was grotesque.

"You can trust me," Bele said.

S'rae looked to the floor, disappointed in herself for falling for a hug, pretty eyes, and great food. "Olivia… she thought my Sol could be a… dragon."

"Thank you." She heard footsteps behind her, heading toward the door.

"Wait!" S'rae screamed. She turned around, and within a second, a breeze whipped Bele's robe and S'rae was in front of him, her hand on his chiseled chest. *Chiseled! You said it again! S'rae… you stop this. You stop this now!* She quickly pulled her hand away and brushed it on her clothes, appearing as if she was disgusted. "That's it? *Thank you?* I just mentioned a *dragon* and that's all you're going to say, and now you're just… just going to leave?"

"I already knew," Bele said without the slightest bit of excitement in his voice.

S'rae pulled her chin to her neck. "You already—then why would you ask?"

"Well… now I know you trust me." Bele smirked. "And now… I have work to do."

"Work?" S'rae felt her chest tighten. What did he mean?

"Well… we have a dragon to find, and I happen to have an idea where yours may be." Bele walked by S'rae and headed toward the door. "The next wave is coming."

S'rae was in her room thinking about everything that had just happened. None of it made sense, but at the same time, it did. *The next wave is coming.* This was what Bele meant. Despite all the bad that had been happening to her… maybe… just maybe, there was a good wave waiting for her to pick her right back up. She wanted to believe it.

She found herself drawing random pictures into the sand, most of them different smiley faces, until she heard laughing and screaming outside her room get louder and louder then BANG!

The door flung open and there Lynn was with the GroundStone trio, all clinging and jumping on one another as if they were still having the greatest party ever.

"You're missing out on all the fun!" Lynn said with her head inside a headlock.

"Yeah, where have you been?" Milla said, who had her arms wrapped around Lynn's waist.

"School," S'rae said, waving her hand as a gust of wind blew her drawings away. She didn't feel like ruining their fun with a sad story of how her day really went.

"Oh, yeah, I forgot about that school stuff," Kaul laughed, rubbing his knuckles into Lynn's now messy hair. "My best advice would be to not take it too seriously, enjoy the time while you can!"

"Yeah!" Brick said. "Like the Solermony Ball!"

At once, the trio gasped and stopped.

"Oh my, that's coming up soon, isn't it!" Milla grinned, taking a subtle glance at Kaul and Brick. "Can't we can go this year since we were the top students last year?"

"Pretty sure that's the perk to being privileged," Brick smiled.

"Hah! Privileged and poor, gotta love it," Kaul said.

"Err… what's the Solermony Ball," S'rae said, standing up and brushing the sand off her robe.

"Uhh… only the greatest time of the year!" Brick said.

"Uhh yeah, it's when students' Sols mature," Milla said.

"Mature?" S'rae said.

"You know… when their Sol becomes different," Milla said.

"Different… real *mature* word to use," Brick said. "What she was *trying* to say, is that it's the ceremony for Sols where you get to watch all the plain Sols turn into something *special*!" Brick clapped their hands and placed them to the ground, the room rumbled and shook. "Like take my baby for example, it started out as a normal ostrich thingy, I don't know what it was, that's what *they* called it." Brick flicked her thumb to Kaul to Milla.

"Umm… it *is* an ostrich," Kaul said.

"Well, nope I don't think it *was*."

"I'm telling you we do, and it's an ostrich," Milla said.

"Well, I just don't like the name, okay! How about we call it a… Glory Bird." Brick then turned to S'rae. "That sounds better, right? Don't you think?"

S'rae's eyes widened, this was one argument she wanted nothing to do with. Plus, she started to feel queasy from the rumbling that didn't seem to stop.

The other two simply sighed and covered their faces, as if embarrassed.

Brick shimmied their shoulders. "Anyways, before I was rudely interrupted, my Glory Bird was all plain and brown when I first got it, but after the Solermony Ball, it turned into *this* beautiful Glorious Bird!"

The ground stopped rumbling. And from the spot where Brick had put their hands, the floor swirled around until a head emerged from it. Within seconds, S'rae immediately recognized the beautiful Sol that appeared before her: it was a vibrant bird with a fluffy body made of rainbow colored feathers, and long lanky legs, so long that it had to curve its even longer neck so that its head wouldn't touch the ceiling.

"There you are, baby!" Brick squealed, wrapping their arms around its furry belly. "See, isn't she so much better now? This is what happens! So you go to the Solermony and see all these beautiful Sol transformations, then after, you get the MOST beautiful dance, with the most beautiful theme, and the most beautiful food!"

"Er… I don't think you're using the word *beautiful* right," Milla said.

S'rae couldn't help but chuckle at Milla's comment, but a part of her glowed inside with a bright new energy. This… this was part of the new wave that was coming, and now that S'rae felt like a dragon could be her Sol, she no longer felt jealous about the idea of seeing others happy with their own. She imagined all the different transformations, each one seeming better than the last: a fiery fox, a pitch black, shadowy panther, even the idea of a snake that could turn invisible made S'rae squeal inside.

"I don't even care that she doesn't know how to use *beautiful* right," Lynn said, "beautiful food will be there? Count! Me! In!"

"Hah!" Milla laughed. "Sorry, but this event is sacred, meant only for ones who have Sols."

At once, S'rae knew her face matched Lynn's, scrunched up and frowning.

"But," Milla grinned, "if you're lucky… maybe… just maybe someone would you take as their date." Milla glanced over at S'rae and winked.

Lynn's eyes narrowed and whatever happy mood she was in vanished instantly. She crossed her arms. "Hmmphh… well, I didn't want to go anyways."

"What's wrong, Adalia?" Milla said. "Jealous?"

S'rae saw Lynn's lips curl and nostrils flare, as if her head was ready to explode.

"Let me guess." Lynn's eyes narrowed at S'rae. "You're going to ask *her*, huh? You don't even know anything about her!"

And just as quickly as S'rae felt lifted that someone would find her more desirable than Lynn, she was instantly brought back down to reality.

"Ew, no!" Milla laughed. "Her?" She flicked her finger at S'rae before laughing again. "Oh, honey, she's not in *this league*. I've wanted to go with you since the second you walked in and took my breath away. *She* was just part of the plan."

Great. Used for another plan. S'rae's face went flat.

Lynn broke out into a huge smile. "Well… it just looked like you liked her more than me."

"Of course it did," Milla said, "how else would I be able to get someone like you. Admit it, you wouldn't have liked me if I was obsessing over you."

Lynn puckered her lips and shrugged. "Hmm… so *you* finessed *me*!"

"To get who I want, you better believe it," Milla said, grinning at Lynn.

S'rae couldn't believe what she saw. Not only did Lynn's face redden, but she took a few steps back and twisted her body from side to side while pressing her curled palms to her face. Was she… giddy? Even perfect girls can feel flustered? No way!

"So…" Lynn said, fanning herself, "does that mean I get to go with you to the Solermony Ball?"

"I get to walk in that place with the most beautiful girl in all of Gaia? That sounds like a dream come true to me," Milla said.

Lynn squealed and pushed her shoulders up before dancing around the room. "I am sorry for ever thinking she liked you," she said to S'rae. "I mean no offense, but it just didn't make any sense."

"Oh," S'rae said blankly, her face falling flat. "No… no there is absolutely *nothing* offensive about that."

"Wow!" Brick clapped then slid a few coins into Kaul's hands. "Mission accomplished! I ain't even mad that I lost. Now, *that* was impressive! I don't know how you did it!"

"Oh, never doubt what she's capable of," Kaul grinned, flipping the coins before placing them in his pocket.

"I was a bet, really?" Lynn appeared flattered or frustrated or offended, S'rae couldn't tell.

"Milla said she'd get you to be her date and I honestly didn't think she had a chance," Brick said.

"And I saw this as a great chance to buy me some new gloves before the first BoulderDash game of the season!" Kaul opened up his own map. "Speaking of, first practice is soon, we have to go! Feel free to come check it out if you want, it'll be at the colosseum! We need all the support we can get."

"More like you need to win so you can stop embarrassing our tribe!" Brick chuckled.

Kaul shook his head and said nothing, but S'rae saw the pain in his eyes, the way they scanned the ground, looking at nothing in particular. "Right, well, being poor sure doesn't help. Other teams have actual gear and we're left with worn hand-me-downs. But that's why we practice! We'll win once, finally! Trust!"

And with that, the four of them were absorbed through the ground; Lynn smiled as she flung her arms around Milla's neck, and S'rae was glad to see that she was happy, it meant they could now be friends again.

S'rae decided to check her own map only for her jaw to drop. There, right there—S'rae pointed at the map—there was a count-down in red that showed she was already a few minutes late to her next class. She had no idea that GroundStone had classes this late in the day. Mad at herself, she drew the relic into the sand and found herself being sucked through the ground.

The journey to this classroom was much different than the previous ones. Not only did it take longer than usual, but she found her body squeezing tightly as if a dragon was crushing her with its weight. S'rae felt her body about to implode before she collapsed onto a stone floor, panting from the effort of squirming free from an invisible hold. She sat still, confusion weighing her down even more, listening to the furious thumping of her heart.

But after a few seconds to reorient herself, she suddenly realized where she was. She gulped as she looked down and ahead through the slit of metal bars.

"How nice it is of you to join us, S'rae." S'rae heard a voice beneath her. "You're late… again. Twice in two classes… you must really take surviving seriously, I see."

"I'm sorry, Professor Fa'laz, sir," S'rae said, sweat pouring down her face. Her thumping heart was now frantic. She wondered why out of all classes it had be *his*, again? She'd rather have creepy monkeys in her shower again over this, but then again she was the one who decided to sign up for the Advanced courses. She shook her head, mad at herself. *Too late to change out of it.* "I didn't mean to be late, I swear!"

"Oh, trust… if you meant to be late, you would be in a much worse location than inside a cage in my classroom, I assure you that." A loud rumble underfoot was heard as a stone column rose the Professor up to S'rae's eye level.

S'rae shivered and looked away from him. The way his eyes blackened would have given her nightmares.

He reached his metal hand forward, gripping the steel bar with a *clang*. "This will be your new seat in class, until you've proved yourself ready to take this class seriously. Do we understand?"

"Ye-yes," S'rae said. For someone who always had a gift to successfully plead her innocence with teachers, she was surprised by the effect he had over her. He silenced her fight for justice with just a stone cold gaze.

"Great. That is the wisest decision and thing you've said all class." The ground rumbled again as the column sank the professor out of her sight.

She spent the rest of the class only listening in on what was being discussed, which was unfortunate because he was teaching the students how to take notes with their quills. Much like the mystery behind the map, one roll of parchment was apparently all they needed to take lifetimes' worth of notes.

At first, S'rae found herself regretting that she had even signed up for this course. But by the time the professor finished teaching them about basic shields-from-stray-stones creation spells, she knew she chose the right one. She wanted… no, needed to be ready for the worse—and as she heard the *clangs* of metal from chains beneath her and a slow, growling breath that rumbled the room, she knew that the students were getting their first lesson on how to defend against a powerful beast.

S'rae stood up, pressing her cheeks into the cold metal bars, trying to get a good look at the beast they'd be defending against. No luck.

"You see, students," Professor Fa'laz said, "your shield is strong enough to withstand *almost* any attack that is thrown its way." S'rae heard a loud thud as if a rock fell to the floor. "But *almost* does *not* cut it in battle." S'rae heard a slash then a thud then gasps. "If you relied on the shield to save your life, your family will remember you as the fool who failed. I am not here to breed fools, I am here to prepare you for the dangers that *will* occur in life, in battle, and in war. Shields may protect you, but they will not save you, only your hearts and smarts will."

S'rae heard footsteps then the sound of chain links rustling, then gasps again.

"Do any of you know what beast this is?" Professor Fa'laz said.

S'rae could almost hear the shivers from the students; she felt a breeze pass by her.

"Y-y-ye-ye-ye."

"Say it, boy!" The power in Professor Fa'laz's voice made her cage shake.

"Ye-yes!"

"And?"

"I-it is a… c-ca-can-canavar."

S'rae gasped, falling back into the metal bars behind her. Normally the feeling of cold knives jabbing into her spine would get a reaction out of her, but now… all she could think about was a canavar. Thoughts flashed through her mind that she quickly needed to hide. No… they were coming in too quickly, she had to close the lid of her mind. *Breathe, S'rae… breathe! Don't think about it. Don't think about that night. Don't… don't. Not. That. Night.* Though her legs were still shaking against the bars, she felt calm enough to pay attention to the lesson.

"Ah, yes, a canavar it is," Professor Fa'laz said, "though I would hardly call it that… this is a baby canavar, a canavel, we call them."

"Th-that's a baby? But it's *huge!*"

"Yes, they are quite big, but this little guy is only ten feet fall. Heh, full grown, they can be almost forty feet."

S'rae heard gasps.

"*Forty feet!*" She heard almost all the students scream at once.

"Yes, but their height isn't the scary part," the professor said as S'rae heard more clangs from the chains. "You see these, right here, yupp, stone is infused into their fur. And you see these, look, look at that shine, the claws are infused with metal. These are without question the deadliest creatures around, at least now they are. I say that 'cause many of the most powerful beasts have gone extinct, but these, these have survived, they're still here, and they are the apex predators in Gaia. Good luck trying to defeat one of these in the wild. It'd be impossible."

"Not true," S'rae said, seizing her legs to stop them from shaking.

"What was that, late little girl?" the professor said.

"Not true… it's not true that it'd be impossible to beat one. It happened," S'rae said, breathing heavily to not relive the memory. *Don't think about that night. Don't…*

"Hah!" the professor belted a laugh that tossed her cage from side to side. "You know nothing what you speak of. You're just a girl who had never fought a real battle before. Do not believe what you read in your little books."

"It wasn't in a book… it was in real life."

"Not happening in real life, sorry," he laughed.

"Just because you haven't seen it, doesn't mean it didn't happen."

"Hah! Well, this is quite true, little girl. So, who was this great, imaginary hero that you're speaking of, and why have I never heard of him?"

"Because it wasn't a *him*, it was a *her*… and you're speaking to her."

Her entire cage lifted and rattled and tossed her around as Professor Fa'laz belted out in laughter so hard that the entire room felt like it was going to collapse. "Oh my, you almost had me there! You know, for a second, I was actually looking forward to hearing a story I may have never heard before, but instead, you're just a funny one. I always appreciate a funny one in class, makes it less boring. You may be late, little girl, but at least you're funny… And because I love good laughs, you're free now, but *never* be late again!"

At once, the stone at her feet vanished and she fell to the ground. Her gaze landed on large claws that glowed silver and black. She slowly lifted her head to see a bear-like beast that was covered in stone-like fur.

S'rae gulped.

"Don't worry, had him since he was a baby, and he won't bite because I fed him before class, but you trying to tell me that you beat—" he held back a laugh, "—you defeated one of *these*?"

"Well, it wasn't just me… but yes."

"Oh… and who helped you? The Divine?" His chuckle was followed by others from the students. Great, they probably thought she was a liar.

"It was me and my br—" She stopped herself, she did not want to bring him up ever again. Not only that, the idea of considering him her brother felt like a sword digging into her heart. *Stay strong,*

S'rae. Breathe. "It was me and a village boy."

"BOY!" He belted in laughter again. "You 'spect me to believe that a girl and a boy defeated the most powerful beast in all of Gaia? Something that trained soldiers can't even take down? Oh, you're so lucky class is finished or we'd make a joke out of you all day!"

S'rae's lip snarled, but surprisingly it wasn't because of the idea that the professor and students would consider her a liar and the joke of the class; no, that didn't even bother her. The thought that festered in her mind was something far more powerful. This memory wasn't just any memory, it was quite possibly her second worst one to relive. One would think it was terrible because it involved a canavar... or Vayp... but no, this was a terrible memory to relive because sometimes the most painful moments to be reminded of were once the greatest ones to live.

And because of that she held a straight face as she walked the halls back to her home. She refused to dive into this thought; it'd break her. She knew it would. It had too many times before. But now, she was no longer that weak girl who would cry herself to sleep at Fujita, she needed to be more than that. She needed to be S'rae, the Champion of GroundStone, the Destined One for the Earth Challenge.

She tried her best to clear her mind as she walked through GroundStone, so much that she had completely lost track of where she was going. She found herself at a temple that she had never seen, yet it felt so familiar that she could have sworn she had been here before.

"Why do you look so familiar?" she said to herself as she walked up to its golden walls. She pulled her head up to see the beautiful towers, it seemed like a palace designed for a God. Most likely it was. But how... why did this look familiar? It wasn't a feeling of déjà vu, she was used to that sensation by now, this was entirely different. Then it suddenly dawned on her, the last time she saw this temple it was MUCH larger, and that was because the last time she was here, she was a squirrel.

Just the thought of being a squirrel zipping through streets and trees brought a smile to her face... until she thought of the masked person who had killed her; it felt like a cold blade trailed down her chest as she remembered the way the killer drew a finger across his neck. Why was he after her? And what did the Sol'adari have to do with it?

"What were you trying to tell me?" S'rae said, pulling out the emblem that Olivia had given her. "I need a sign... something... *please*... just tell me why this is happening to me." S'rae felt tears start to build behind her eyes. There was only so much pretending she could do... it was so difficult to convince herself that things were okay. They were not. And she felt the full grunt of it seep out through her eyes.

And as she wiped her eyes and put the emblem back into her pocket, she heard rustling from the bushes. Without thinking, a bow and arrow were already in her hands, pointing straight at whatever was hiding behind there.

Now was not the time to play it safe. *Trust none.*

S'rae remained still and focused; unlike GroundStone Earthies who would summon spells with the ideal of protecting in mind, Fujitas must always be focused and clearheaded. She didn't even blink as the arrow was getting looser in her fingertips, almost ready to kill whatever it was that—

Then suddenly a squirrel jumped out of the bushes, followed soon after by a wolf pup.

"B'se!! It's you!! And... Mysol!!" S'rae squealed as the bow and arrow vanished into waves of wind and the animals jumped on top of her. They all rolled around as B'se scattered across her body from her head to toe and back a few dozen times, while Mysol kept licking her face. "Don't scare me like that, you two! I could have killed you!"

They played around for a few more moments until the emblem

fell out of her pocket and rolled into the bushes. "Look what you two did!" S'rae laughed as she shielded her face from Mysol's licks.

She went on her hands and knees and crawled into the bushes, which seemed much deeper than she had thought. The deeper she went, the darker it became. So dark that she could no longer see what was in front of her, so she used her hands for vision, feeling for the emblem.

Then finally her hand touched a hard surface, her fingers grazed it, feeling a head and fiery wings with her fingers. "Found it, you two!" But when she went to pick it up, it was lodged into the ground. Curious, S'rae crawled in closer and saw that it wasn't an emblem, at all. It was... wait... she recognized this, too. She had seen this mark when she was the squirrel traveling through GroundStone. "I asked for a sign... and I guess she gave me one. I don't believe in coincidences, that's what Olivia would say."

A chilly breeze swept through the bushes and when S'rae heard rustling behind her, she turned around and saw B'se nibbling on the emblem. "You're so amazing, I love you! This is *exactly* why you're the best squirrel ever! Living up to your name, B'se!"

B'se squealed with joy and handed the emblem to S'rae then ran off to play with Mysol. She smiled just hearing them bark and squeal at one another.

S'rae twisted the emblem in her hand from front to back. *No way... this can't be real.* Somehow and some way the two phoenixes were identical in shape and size. *But how? What does this mean?* The curious Fujita in her told her to press the two symbols together. So of course that's what she would do.

She closed her eyes and pressed her palm forward.

It happened immediately: S'rae felt as if her hands had been seized by a tornado and was thrown irresistibly forward. She felt her arms and legs extend as if she had suddenly become a hundred feet tall; if there was ever a feeling of what it'd be like to get sucked in through a blackhole, she was sure this was it. She sped through specks of light that changed colors so frequently she was sure it was probably a rainbowhole, not a black one; her scream was muted as a howl of wind whipped her hair into her face and then—

She fell face first into a pile of mud; the emblem bounced off her head before falling into the mud with a splat.

S'rae wiped her mud-smeared eyes and looked up. There were tunnels all around and when she looked over her shoulder, her eyes widened and she gasped. In front of her was the most beautiful tree she had ever seen. There were specks of green light on it that looked like glowing, pulsating moss. This moss was everywhere, lighting up the many tunnels and the spiral staircase that circled around her.

But where was she?

The more she observed the walls and the vines and flowers that lined them, the more it felt like she had been here before. But much like being at the temple, it wasn't a feeling of déjà vu, this was different; but she couldn't explain why this place seemed so familiar.

There was an odd juxtaposition of opposites, feeling like she was outside in a vast wilderness, yet somehow trapped inside a cave. Wait a second… she remembered a description like that.

Her eyes widened as she turned around once more. The tree, the tunnels, the spiral staircase… *I don't get it. No…*

She ran into one of the tunnels where she saw a circular room with a tree carved into the ground. *No way!* Her heart was thumping against her chest, this time it was filled with excitement.

This… this can't be what I think it is.

She walked up to the wall that circled around her, mesmerized by the life pulsating through in waves of green. Her fingers grazed the wall, feeling the roughness from the vines and leaves that covered it, but when she pushed her hand all the way through, it was slippery smooth in the places where the light resonated.

And when she pushed the leaves and vines to the side, her mouth dropped.

This cannot be real!

She saw shapes and images that looked like the earliest form of hieroglyphics. Could these be—she pressed her quivering hands to her lips—Dream Words... just like in Elu's cave?

Her breathing became heavier as her hands trembled harder. It was tough for her to contain her excitement. She had almost forgotten completely about Destrou, the Boy Who Never Lived, and Elu, and Ranmau, but this... this was the greatest reminder she could have ever asked for. But what was this place? Who created it? And did they... did they know about Destrou? And how?

After clearing all the vines out of the way, leaving a sparkling wall that glowed patches of green, she was given the answer.

There... in the center, carved into the wall... were five words that would forever change her meaning in life: The Boy Who Never Lived.

S'rae fell to the floor. Since no one was around, she had no problem sobbing into her palms. She suddenly felt so small and inadequate... yet at the same time feeling like destiny had a greater purpose for her.

But what... what was her destiny?

She looked at those five words again... and she now understood that they were all somehow connected. A part of a bigger plan. It reminded her why she needed to train for the Earth Challenge. That she had a true purpose in life. And to never forget who the true villain was. There was something much bigger going on that she couldn't put her finger on, but one thing she knew for certain was that Destrou was more than just a story in a book... he was the Boy Who Never Lived... and his story *will* be told.

15

DESTROU STOOD IN DISBELIEF. His senses were too alert. The moment must have been real. Here he was inside the Tree. The fresh air tickled his nose just as it did before. He felt the cold breeze wrap around his legs and torso. He heard the humming sound of silence interrupted by his beating heart. Everything felt real... but... her... this couldn't... it couldn't be real. Because he was here… staring at—

"Elu?" Destrou said again, walking toward the person who must have been Elu, they were the only two who knew about this place.

"Destrou?" the voice said again, except this time Destrou noticed the tone wasn't as soft as Elu's. It was familiar but not the type of familiarity that he hoped for. "It is you!"

"Ascel?" Destrou replied, recognizing the voice. Destrou didn't know much about Ascel, but the few occasions they had met involved Elu. Ascel may had been Elu's only other friend, so it made sense that she would share her place with him.

"How'd you know about this place?" Ascel said, turning around, pulling his hood over his head.

He sat in his one-piece outfit, its animal head used as a hood with short stubbed ears on top. Both of his feet hung over the ledge as he sat at the cliff. In the faint light he looked pale, bleached of all color, wrapped completely in white. He had a crystalline glaze over his eyes—Elu's death must have hit him hard, too.

"The same way that you did... I guess," Destrou said, his tone was soft and his eyes drooped. He briefly recalled the time she first showed him this glacial masterpiece. He remembered the way his mouth dropped and eyes widened at the sight of the intricate sculptures, trees, vines, and leaves all carved perfectly out of ice. She did this, well some of this. She was so amazing, and it hurt thinking about how wide her smile was when she grabbed his hand and hurried him into all the different rooms. Each carried a different vibe, with various sculptures carved into the walls, yet all were the same: perfectly beautiful, like Elu.

Destrou and Ascel remained where they were, unknowing what to do next. The last memory he had of Ascel was of him forcing him into the trial. It wasn't the most pleasant memory. Destrou waited in the center of Village, waiting to hear the punishment that the Guardian would deliver for destroying the liquid ice tower. Though Destrou had a million things on his mind, he said nothing.

Ascel glanced at him for a few more moments then turned back around, looking at the Forest.

Destrou did not know how to respond. There was no greater sign of respect or trust in the Village than freely giving someone their back. Did he trust Destrou? Respect him? Why?

Before Destrou could ask a question, Ascel spoke first: "Did you ever wonder if anything ever lived on top of the trees before?" Ascel asked, pointing straight ahead of him.

"Heh," Destrou smirked. He felt his nerves calm down. "I don't know... but I'm glad to hear that was the first question you asked me. That was mine, too."

"Really?" Ascel smiled. "That's exactly what Elu said."

"I know," he replied, slowly inching his way closer to Ascel. Although Destrou moved in steady movements to not alarm him,

Ascel seemed unphased by the advance. If anything the smile on his face grew, pushing his reddish cheeks up. "That's exactly what she told me too." It felt weird to find something in common with a Villager, but it also felt comforting. Relaxing almost, as if he found someone who was going through a similar range of emotions that he was. He wondered if Ascel was doing a better job at handling the death. Anything would be doing a better job than he was, he thought.

"I don't bite, you know," Ascel said, playfully chomping in the air.

Destrou stepped back quickly, raising his fists in the air. He didn't mean to—it was a reaction that just happened after years of being bullied.

"I can see why he liked you," Ascel chuckled.

Destrou stood there, frozen for a moment. *Why'd he call her a he?* Destrou was under the impression that Ascel was her closest friend. He should've known the secret, the whole Village knew now, didn't they? It surprised him in a way that made his face show a little more color. If Elu didn't even tell Ascel about her secret, then what they shared was more special than he could have ever dreamed. She was a rare, genuine friend, trusting him with her life. She did say that only one other person knew the secret, after all. The Leader, Eli'jah, her brother, the terror of the Village.

"What do you mean... you knew why Elu liked me?" Destrou replied, stunned by the question. As tempting as it was to tell Ascel the truth about their friend, he made a promise to Elu to not tell anyone. Though it seemed as if most of the Village knew already, what kind of a best friend would he be if he didn't keep his promise? But how was it still a secret to him? Had he been dealing with the death away from everyone? Had he been here, at the Tree, this whole time? Did the Leader make a point to keep it a secret? But no, that couldn't be it, because even the Guardian made an announcement that Elu was a girl, didn't he? He did that, right? Or was that his imagination, too? It felt real. It was right before the Guardian broke Ranmau's arm, wasn't it? Destrou was even more confused, he couldn't remember what the chain of events were like now. Few things felt real. None of this made sense.

"I thought it would be scary being next to you, but it actually doesn't feel bad at all," Ascel said.

"Me? Scary?" Destrou chuckled. "I didn't think anyone would ever call me scary."

"No," Ascel said. "I don't mean *YOU* being scary... I mean scary being with you. You know, being seen with you. Like I thought I'd feel paranoid, but it's actually not so bad." Ascel gave a slight shrug of his shoulders. "You make it seem okay, I don't know. I guess I thought that I'd feel like I was going to get killed or something." Ascel paused, maybe realizing that it was the wrong time to talk about death. And that must have been the reason, because when he noticed Destrou look away and rub his eyes, he said, "I'm sorry. I miss him, too. He was my best friend. I... loved—"

"You... loved him?" Destrou turned back around. *When you didn't know he was a girl? You loved him when you thought he was a boy? What does that mean?*

"I don't know, I think so." Ascel looked away. "I was jealous that he'd sneak around with you instead, but I should have joined him instead. We could have all been friends."

"Why are you being nice to me now?" Destrou asked, clenching his hands behind his back. "What's in it for you?"

"What's in it for me? Nothing."

"Then don't be nice to me. I'm bad luck."

"Bad luck?"

"You see what happens when people become friends with me? It's not a good idea."

"Elu dying wasn't your fault... you know that, right?"

"I don't know. If Elu never met me then s—he'd still be alive," Destrou paused. "I just know that I hate *him* now for it."

"Elu?"

"No... Ranmau."

"Really? You shouldn't blame Ranmau either."

"If s—he... if he didn't try to... if he didn't try to..." Destrou tried to finish his sentence but emotion swelled up behind his throat. "Elu would still be alive... if he didn't try to help me."

"That's Elu... that's not you or Ranmau," Ascel said. "That was his decision. Elu woulda did what Elu woulda did. He woulda done that even if you didn't want him to. That's the typa friend he was. He wouldn't want us to know when he's helping even when we knew it."

"So... you knew, huh?" Destrou said. "About Elu getting food?"

"Yeah," Ascel chuckled. "We always made a silly bet wheneva I gambled all of my food away to someone else. He knew when I was starving and had no more food left... and then BAM, outta no-where we would bet food. And I always won. He was so smart that he knew exactly how to lose."

A smile broke out from underneath Destrou's sorrow. "Heh, what wasn't he good at?"

"Nothing. He did it so well, too... without me knowing what he was doing for a long time. I knew that was his way of helping me out without making me feel like a pity krillen or something. Then one day it just hit me... and I couldn't even be mad. I miss him so much. And that's why I think I loved him. He was so nice and great."

"I miss him, too... More than I ever thought I would," Destrou said, pausing to let the sadness in the air pass.

"Did you love him too?" Ascel looked at Destrou with glazed eyes as if trying to read his face for the truth.

"What?" Destrou's eyes widened. How was he supposed to re-spond to a question like that? "I don't know what love is. But when did you two become friends?" he asked, wanting to change the con-versation. He pressed his palms on the floor for support and inched his butt down as his feet dangled over the ledge. The two of them sat side by side, facing the Forest of Ness.

"You wouldn't believe me if I told you," Ascel said, turning his head to the right, not breaking eye contact with Destrou.

"How?"

"Well... because you and Ranmau."

"Really? I don't get it?"

"It was about a year ago... and you and Ranmau kept making it to the end of every challenge. Everyone started to really, really hate you two. Like REALLY hate you two. Like really, really, really hate you two."

"Yeah," Destrou said coldly, "you don't have to keep reminding me."

"Sorry, but what I mean is that a part of me couldn't hate you, because I thought it was... amazing. Plus... Ranmau and his muscles..." Ascel licked his lips before biting the corner of it.

Destrou could have sworn he heard a soft "mmmm" coming from Ascel's closed mouth. He felt embarrassed, but couldn't explain why, all he knew was that he felt his cheeks heat up as his smile widened. "Wow."

"Exactly. Wow. It was just wow-ly amazing how we could all gang up on you two and we would still end up losing. I always wanted to be that great. Like, I always wanted to know what it felt like. I always wanted to be like you two."

"Wow!" Destrou gasped. He struggled to find another word to describe his astonishment, but all he could say was "wow" again. He never would have expected those words to come out of any boy from the Village, besides Elu. Did anyone else feel this way about him... about them, the brothers? "You really think we were amazing? I don't know what to say."

"Yeah! And then..." Ascel said, pausing as his head sank to the ground.

"And then what?"

"There was that day... well... I don't think you'll remember it, but I won't ever forget it."

"Which day?" Destrou said intently, focusing on each word.

"It was that day when you and Ranmau won another challenge and the prize was the cloak that you have now."

"Yeah," Destrou said. "Of course I remember that day. Ranmau gave it to me right after he got it."

"Yeah… do you remember my brother?"

"I didn't know you had a brother… who was he?"

"I have two, but he was the one who wore this before me," Ascel said, standing up, showing Destrou his full outfit. It was a complete one-piece suit that looked like it could have been a bear cub's fur skin with stubbed ears on the hood. It was much too large for him. The sleeves drooped over his hands, practically scraping the ground.

"I—I…" Destrou hesitated for a moment, retracing his memories. Though the images were foggy, a faint vision of a tall, handsome boy wearing the white fur skin like a glove drifted through his mind. "I… Wow, I do think I remember him. I remember it not being so saggy on him, though."

There were so many boys in the Village that it was difficult for Destrou to remember all of them, especially since he didn't have a friendly relationship with any of them. One of the boys could have vanished and he would have never known.

"Yeah, he wore it better than I ever will," Ascel said with a smile, but Destrou heard a sadness in his tone that tugged at his heart. It reminded him of the way he'd talk aloud when thinking about Elu.

"Wasn't he the real Leader… before the Leader challenged him or something?" Destrou asked.

Since the Village had a strict moral code, the loyalty of the boys went to whoever owned the title of the Leader. Once challenged, whoever won assumed the role and gained the respect of all. The Leader built up the resentment toward Ranmau so much that Ranmau was unable to challenge him for the title. It was an unwritten law that the Village would never respect Ranmau enough to become the Leader. Few said that it was the Leader's plan to solidify control out of greed and power, but Destrou knew it was because of fear. After that, no one had dared challenge him—not even the Giant, who few believed had a slight chance to win. But when even the Giant and his enormous frame was afraid to challenge the Leader, that said something.

"Yeah, and nothing was the same after my brother challenged him," Ascel said. "The Leader told him to finish his plan that night. It was a very, very bad plan. Like a very, very, very bad plan, but my brother didn't want to do it. Like… I remember that night because it was the last night that I saw him…. Before he left, he told me that I shouldn't hate you and Ranmau and that we should all stop treating you badly and how we should all just stick together… That the problem was bigger than us… the problem was the Kingdom." Ascel's voice started to break. He continued. "My brother didn't want to hurt you and Ranmau so the Leader called him Faily… because he failed him. Silly, I know, but I never saw him again after that. I didn't know what happened to him or where he went but I wasn't allowed to ask questions. My brother gave me this suit and left. No one knew anything, anyways. It was like he was never my brother… like he never existed. I had so many questions to ask… I had a million that I wanted to ask but I didn't want to be punished. There isn't a day that passes when I don't miss him."

Destrou's heart dropped when he thought about the face that he saw in the ice. 'Faily' was what the Leader called him. That was his brother. He was dead, buried in the ice near the spike inside the Crater… and Ascel had no idea. Destrou then thought about how he'd feel if he lost Ranmau. He thought about how the Leader said they had a plan for the brothers tomorrow, and although he hated Ranmau for what he did to Elu, he felt his insides collapse at the thought of something terrible happening to him. "I'm so sorry…."

"Sorry for what? It's okay! It really is," Ascel said with a quivering smile. "I like to think about it like this: the less I know, the better. I like to imagine him escaping over the Wall or going into the Forest and living a great life. He's so much happier right now and I'm happy for him. Imagine all the great adventures he must have done already! And this suit! This suit, it was his, and it will always remind me that I had a great brother."

"Yeah," Destrou said, trying to hold back his tears as a huge mass formed in his throat. "I wish the best for him, too. I'm sure he's in a better place."

"See, and that's how Elu and I became friends," Ascel said cheerfully. "You are a good person... and my brother knew this. He made me believe, too. He made sure that I didn't trust all of the evil things that the Leader said about you two. They all couldn't have been true. So, I finally decided to ask a question and the closest person near me was Elu."

"What did you ask?"

"Umm..." Ascel said, turning away, his red cheeks appeared rosier.

"What? You can tell me?"

"I don't know... it's embarrassing, I guess."

"You have to tell me now," Destrou said, clenching his arms across his chest.

"Well, I asked him why we always had to gang up on you and Ranmau when we could try to be friends with you instead," Ascel said, covering his face with his droopy sleeves.

"Wait..." Destrou replied with his jaw dropped as if the world that he had been living was a lie. "You wanted to be friends?"

Destrou had lived his entire life being one of the two enemies of the Village. He had dreamed of the day when he would be surrounded by a group of friends cheering him on, but instead the dreams were shattered each time he was surrounded by a group of boys stomping him down. He lived a lonely life. Ranmau grew cold and Elu was his only escape from a dark reality. The idea that others wanted the same thing that he wanted created a flaw in his perception of the Village and its boys. Maybe they weren't all bad. Maybe there was hope. Maybe the problem wasn't them, after all.

"Well, yeah, you two are awesome," Ascel smiled. "And when I asked Elu that… he jumped around screaming. He said that he was happy that he found someone who asked questions and actually thought about life differently. And that's how we became friends."

Destrou gave a subtle smirk, that was exactly how he'd picture Elu handling the news. He didn't know what hit him harder: the surprise that the rage he felt all night was lifted or the shock that there was more to the boys of the Village than he thought. He thought that all of the boys were his enemies who loathed him, but the only two that he got to know changed his view. The only two… Destrou learned a very important lesson: that he shouldn't judge a boy until he got to know them first. He realized that they could have more in common than what was at the surface.

"But please… don't blame this on Ranmau," Ascel said, gently touching Destrou's shoulders. It shocked Destrou to not react to it defensively, instead, it reminded him of Elu. "You have a great brother, too. Elu wouldn't blame him… so you shouldn't either."

"Elu isn't here to blame anyone."

"Believe me… I saw it… it wasn't his fault. I mean, it was but it really wasn't. Ranmau was trying to protect you, he thought you were dead. And he was mad. He was mad because he loves you. If I was as brave as Elu, I would have tried to help, too. And if I died… I wouldn't want you to blame him for my death. I would want you to realize that the problem was bigger than that, like what my brother told me. And that's what Elu would want you to do."

Destrou said nothing.

"I don't even have enough fingers on my hand to count how many times he saved you…. And believe me… he needs you now. The Leader has a very, very bad plan now. Like very, very, very bad plan. Much worse than before."

"I know," Destrou said, standing up. "I heard him talk about it. I think he wants to… you-know-what… us tomorrow."

"No," Ascel said. "I know the Leader and the way that he thinks is very, very bad. He is going to make it so that you'd want him to kill you. Tomorrow will be bad, but he's going to wait for the right time to you-know-what Ranmau. I just hope that when the Leader's ready… you will be too, because Ranmau sure won't be."

"Thank you for helping me," Destrou said, patting him on the back. "If something bad really is going to happen tomorrow, then I need to make sure I'm ready. I'm going to need to get some sleep." Before he turned around, he had to let Ascel know what plagued his mind. "I want to forgive him. I really do, but a part of me wishes that he can switch places with Elu."

"The great Ranmau and Destrou duo. The unbreakable twins. The brothers against the Village. I woulda never thought those words would ever come out of your mouth."

"Me neither," Destrou said softly. "That's what scares me."

"Believe me… he needs you. More now than ever before. Just think about all of the times he was there for you. You'll make the right choice."

"Thinking is the worst thing that I can do right now. I don't know why I feel this way but the more I think about him… the more I want to let the Leader do whatever he wants to him."

Ascel had a genuine look of concern on his face. It seemed as if he cared more about the brothers' relationship than Destrou did. Why? Destrou realized that night that when one door closed, another one opened. It was up to him if he wished to seize the opportunity or not.

His first new day started the moment he was finally able to lay down, close his eyes and silence his thoughts. There were only a few more weeks until the tournament. Their future was as unknown as life beyond the Wall. The brothers' lives were on borrowed time and their time became about surviving the next day, instead of living it.

230

16

THAT NIGHT DESTROU HAD A DREAM that Ranmau hung over the Edge, holding on for his life with his only good hand. The other was broken and wrapped up around his torso. Ascel shouted to Destrou to save him. Destrou looked over at Ranmau, their eyes connected for what seemed like an eternity. He gave Destrou a discouraged look as he stood there not moving a muscle, as if he knew what Destrou was thinking in that moment. His fingers inched further from the Edge, but still Destrou just watched. Ranmau lost all traction, screaming for Destrou to help the entire way down. Destrou did nothing as Ranmau fell to his death, but he woke up right before Ranmau splatted.

Panting and bewildered from the dream, Destrou flipped out of bed and glanced over at Ranmau, who was sweaty and shaky and in very bad shape. As much as Destrou despised him, he was relieved that it was just a dream. For the first few moments after he woke up there was a massive weight of guilt pressing down on his chest. Would he just watch him die? Would he want to feel that guilt forever? He didn't know the answer.

How could he hate someone who looked so vulnerable? Ranmau's arm was broken in half, barely healing; his head shimmered with sweat, his eyes were closed yet twitching, and he trembled in his sleep. Those weren't injuries from the Box—what else was wrong with him?

"How'd you... sleep?" Ranmau asked, shivering and struggling to lift an eye open. He was not himself, at all.

Destrou looked over at him. It bothered him to see Ranmau like this: the one who needed help. He was the savior; the amazing one. The best. Despite being in terrible condition, Ranmau still managed to give his confident smirk. Some things never changed.

How could Ranmau still have a sliver of confidence when everything went wrong? He was a wreck. The broken arm. The Box. The missed chance for freedom. The starvation. And then, the enlarged target on his back being the new prey amidst a crowd of predators.

"I—I slept well," Destrou said. To his astonishment there was no interest in replying back with the same question; that would warrant a conversation. He knew that Ranmau knew that was a lie, that he did not sleep well, but Destrou refused to give him the opportunity to question it. Do not lie and do not ask questions. Those were the rules of the land. The unspoken agreement between them.

Ranmau scrambled to his feet, cradling his injured arm. "Be careful out there," he said. "I know that the Leader will plan something today... so don't do anything foolish and don't treat me any differently, okay? I'm fine."

Ranmau turned his arm over, untying the cloth that was wrapped around his elbow and shoulder. Destrou cringed as he saw a blood-stained, disfigured elbow with a bulge bent in the wrong direction. It was a disgusting sight that even Ranmau couldn't look at for too long. He winced every time he touched the purply, pale skin.

"I keep telling myself that everything is fine..." Ranmau said softly, "but... I don't think I'll ever be able to use this arm again."

Destrou said nothing. What was worse, he felt nothing. Neither sad nor happy.

Ranmau stood up calmly. When the light hit his arm, it was an even deeper purple than Destrou thought. He wondered how a part of the body could look dead while everything else was still alive.

"I know that you hate me right now," Ranmau said, bracing himself as if a stinging sensation shot through his body, "but I need my arm. I won't last a day out there with one arm—you know this. If you can just help me put it back in place then you can go back to hating me, okay?"

Destrou leaned forward and banged his hand against the side of the igloo. "That's the arm that you used to kill Elu... right?"

Any time there was a thought associated with Elu and Ranmau, rage filled his heart. The hatred would trigger visions that flashed through his mind. He wanted to control them, wanted to pry the toxic thoughts out of his head, but it was like wanting to stop the sun from rising. He closed his eyes and took long, deep breaths. The air tingled his nose, calming him with a peculiar freshness. He remembered Ascel's words. He remembered Elu's. They were not the problem.

"Wrap your arm up." Destrou hated the sight of blood. He walked toward Ranmau's bed, grabbing his arm.

Ranmau screamed in pain.

"On the count of three," Destrou said, grabbing Ranmau's wrist and elbow. "One... t—"

Ranmau scrunched his eyes shut as Destrou yanked his arm out of its socket. It wasn't gentle. There was no grace.

A *pop* was heard as Ranmau flopped down on his bed, screaming at the top of his lungs. By the pitch of his voice the pain must have been excruciating. He stuffed his face in his fur sheet, panting deeply into it, gripping his elbow with his palm; his legs kicked out sporadically as he tossed and turned in his bed.

Destrou felt cold—too cold. Absolutely no emotion was shown when he stared at his brother in pain. Just a few days ago, if he saw Ranmau limp he would have attended to him. But now, nothing.

Ranmau's breathing slowed down to a moan. He turned over and glared at Destrou, his thick eyebrows contracted slightly. "I—I thought this would help... but... I still can't feel my arm."

"Still?" Destrou straightened up. His confused face darkened as he surveyed Ranmau. Ranmau looked from his arm to Destrou and back again as if he didn't want Destrou to see him defeated. "Why didn't you say something? You made it seem like everything was fine."

"It's what I do. I *always* try to make it seem like everything's fine," Ranmau said. His words, normally sharp, were sluggish.

"When is it not fine for you? You're the great Ranmau," Destrou said contemptuously.

"Always," Ranmau said softly, rubbing his chin and looking down at the ground.

Destrou said nothing.

"I wanted you to never lose who you were.... I wanted you to stay happy. You were always the happy one. I didn't want to ruin that. I wanted you to always believe that life was good even though it isn't. It never is, never was, and never will be. I didn't want you to turn into me... but I failed. I failed you."

"Then stop pretending like you wanted to be here. You never wanted to be here with me. Admit it! You left me and I knew you would!" Destrou said strongly, his darkest thoughts finally rising to the surface.

"It was *never* about you," Ranmau said at once, taking a deep breath before continuing. "I had it... I had my chance." He glanced outside the window with piercing eyes. "I saw it.... I was able to stare freedom in the face... and it looked better than I could have ever imagined it would. I was on top of the Wall. I did it. I did the impossible."

"No you didn't. You didn't make it up the Wall," Destrou shouted.

"Oh... I didn't?" Ranmau gave a short laugh and shook his

head.

"Yeah… you're just saying that to make me feel bad. It's not going to work anymore. You're not going to turn this around on me."

"What do you think I'm some kind of krillen?" Ranmau said, whose hand tightened around his knee. "I'm Ranmau—of course I made it up the Wall."

"Yeah, right." Destrou said, rolling his eyes. "Well, then what did it look like, oh-so-great Ranmau?"

"I don't care if you believe me or not. I have nothing to prove. I had freedom waiting for me. I saw the sky—it was… it was beautiful beyond the clouds. There were mountains and valleys as far as I could see. There was this… life out there… and it was waiting for me. It was everything that I had ever wanted. I saw the horizon in front of me with nothing and no one stopping me… except you. I couldn't picture having my freedom and leaving you here left to die. I couldn't leave you… not like this."

Destrou paused for a moment. *Is he actually telling the truth?* Somewhere under his rage he felt a ripple of guilt; but then his guilt turned back to anger. "But you did leave!" he yelled. Emotion burst through his eyes. "You did and I *always* knew you wanted to. You never cared about me."

"I always did," Ranmau said, though it sounded like he meant it, his grey eyes were colder than ever. "This isn't life. This isn't life for anyone. There are bad things that happen here that I never want you to experience."

"Stop acting like you care bout me," Destrou shouted, "I hate you."

"I had my wish… I had what I wanted!" Ranmau shouted back, and Destrou went quiet, though his heaving breathing still intensified. "I had it and gave it up for you. You see this?" He said, pulling his disfigured arm out. "This was for you! I could have left you to die. Don't make me regret coming back for you."

"I didn't ask you to come back!" Destrou shouted, rage making his skin tingle. "I was just something holding you back, anyway. I knew how worthless I was—how worthless I used to be… but not anymore. Now you are. Now you're the worthless one."

Ranmau was now shaking his head, his lip curling.

Destrou didn't know how to suppress his emotions. They were all overflowing at once—empathy, sympathy, rage, hate, and love. He did what any distressed boy would have done when they needed to confront their emotions: he ran. He ran as fast as he could with no intentions of looking back.

He wanted to hate his brother. He wanted to hate him to show how much he cared for Elu. He didn't want to feel like their friendship was anything less than genuine—mourning made it feel real. He wanted to hate him because that's how much it hurt him that he left. He wanted to hate himself for no longer being the happy boy. He wanted to watch his brother suffer yet wanted to set him free. He wanted many things, but what he wanted the most was to be alone. *Am I really turning into Ranmau*, he thought, rubbing his stinging eyes. *Am I now the cold one?*

The faster Destrou ran, the faster the images came. And before he knew it, he slid to a stop, reaching the Edge. A part of him wanted to jump—to end all of the misery. Elu wasn't there to stop him this time. He needed her here, telling him that there was more to life, and that after all the bad there was something good waiting for him. But what good remained? She was the good... and now she was gone... because of *him*. How was he supposed to just forget it happened?

He stood there, his feet hanging over the cliff, chunks of ice broke off, falling into the abyss. Even after long moments had passed, no sound was made, as if there was no floor. As if what awaited him was a black hole, a void of nothingness and darkness, just like death. But he needed to ask himself: what good would come from jumping? Both of their lives, his and Ranmau's, would end with this jump. And they would have won. Their story would end, never to be told... along with Elu's.

He felt the monster grow within him again. He felt its claws dig into his mind. *I can't let the monster win.* The Box's effect became more apparent. His mind felt fragile, as if it would break at any moment. But... maybe it already had?

Looking down into the Forest, he thought about the chance he had to flee the Village with Elu. *If only... I just said yes that night... everything would be fine. You'd be alive and we'd be together. Why was I so stupid?* He kicked chunks of ice off of the cliff deep into the Forest. A part of him was surprised at how far they went.

"Am I wrong for acting like this?" His scream echoed a dozen times. "I wish I knew how to deal with all of this. Why can't I stop any of these thoughts? Why can't I control my own body? I just need to be alone... forever."

* * *

Ranmau dragged his feet out of the igloo. Before he left, he caught a glimpse of his reflection in the ice. His face was much skinnier, his cheekbones and jawline were more prominent. The space around his eyes deepened, making his eyes bulge out effortlessly. At the entrance there was a gauntlet of boys surrounding him that created a path straight to the middle of the Village. His arm laid lifelessly limp next to his body. It flopped around with each step as he passed the brooding glares and hisses.

He had a staggered step that hesitated each time he lifted his feet. One of the boy's stuck his foot out in front of Ranmau, tripping him as he crashed to the ground. The pain was unbearable, but he refused to give them the satisfaction of showing it.

He rolled to his side as the boys erupted with laughter, then scrambled to his feet, cradling his arm. Once he got to his feet, the rest of the boys huddled around him. He felt their anger. He saw their eyes narrow. But worse, he looked into their eyes and saw exactly what they were thinking. And it was death.

He needed to follow the guidance that he always gave Destrou. *Never show them weakness*. He had finally realized how difficult it really was.

"Is your arm alright? Let me see," the Leader demanded, seizing his wrist.

Inside, Ranmau fell to pieces—the pain was so excruciating that pressure behind his eyes swelled up. On the outside, he remained calm. Everything was fine. There was no pain. No anything.

The Leader let go, somewhat disappointed in Ranmau's reaction. "Where is the other one? The stronger of the two," he laughed.

Laughter trickled throughout the crowd. It was protocol for the rest of the boys to laugh after he did or it would result in punishments far worse than death.

"I don't know where he went," Ranmau replied, biting the inside of his lip from the pain.

"Hmm... that's a shame. He's going to miss out on all of the fun." The Leader's grin twitched into a smile.

"Lots o' fun," the Giant laughed, stepping into the circle of boys that now surrounded Ranmau. He held a large stone staff in his hand that he pounded against his palm. An ugly snarl made his lip curl up.

But before the Giant had his fun, he was interrupted by the shriek of ice scraping ice. This meant only one thing: the Guardians were awake. Ranmau knew that the Guardians didn't just save him from a bad situation, if anything, their arrival had just made it worse.

The door slid open as two giant mammoths of humans pursed their lips, grunting and groaning their way to the center. The Guardians were tall with waists as wide as an igloo. Their faces were completely covered with white hair, Guardian Ko'dral's beard stretched wide and curled behind his fat cheeks, while Commander Gronk's was long, twisting over his potbelly. They appeared to be more displeased than sleepy. This was never a good sign. That look only meant bad news for the Village, just as Ranmau had expected.

They made their way onto the icy platform as the boys huddled around.

Each boy shoulder bumped Ranmau when they passed as if he was invisible.

"Mer..." the Guardian snarled. His breath reached Ranmau and the other boys in the front. It smelled horrid and thick, as if he had eaten rotten meat for breakfast. "This was the last straw." The Guardian grunted as he slammed his fists together. "One of you krillens came into our room and stole all of my food. If you tell me who the krillen is, only he will be punished. It's nothing a quick throwing off of the Edge wouldn't solve."

"Yah," the Commander said, "if yah steal from us again we gon' take food from all of yah. Yah got that? No mo' food for alluv yah."

The boys in the crowd all looked at one another as murmurs broke out.

"Who was it?"

"Was it you?"

"I think it was him."

"*Him*?"

"What about the twins? No one stole food until they got out."

"Yeah, it has to be them!" The boy shot a very angry look at Ranmau.

Ranmau was unable to hear all of the whispers but based on the seething looks he received, he knew that the situation had become dangerous.

"Now since it was my special food from our Crystal Soldier days, I decided to make this next challenge extra special," the Guardian said, rubbing his fingers through his beard as debris sprinkled onto the ground. "This next challenge will be the most difficult one yet and the winner will get some Sensu meat. This challenge is the last one before the tournament, so whichever of you krillens wins this, very lucky you'll be. I know someone out there who really, really needs it," he said, scanning his eyes through the crowd until they made contact with Ranmau. He then gave a nasty grin. "Good luck winning it, krillen."

Just then, when the Guardian winked, Ranmau knew that he was in danger.

"The challenge is tomorrow. Good luck making it through training," the Guardian said firmly. There was something about his statement that sent a chill down Ranmau's spine. He sensed the uneasiness in the air, it was as noticeable as the gray that over-whelmed the sky. What did they have in store for him?

Ranmau turned around to see a furry boy, Ascel, leaning against an igloo. His eyes shone in the light. Why was he just standing there? Ranmau looked around once more and saw that the Leader and the Giant were gone, swallowed up by the crowd of boys.

"I guess it's time," Ranmau said, walking away from the crowd. *I hope I'm ready.*

* * *

"You ready to train?" a boy said, shoving his palm into Ranmau's chest.

Ranmau refused to respond, instead he noticed the Leader and the Giant emerge from a crowd as they walked into the center of the Crater. Large spikes, like glaciers, circled around the Leader. There were many staffs that poked out from the ground, their main weapons of choice when training.

The Leader looked strong and ready as usual. The Giant wore a band of fur around his forehead, trapping his long brown hair underneath it.

"You ready to train?" the Leader asked Ranmau, clenching a large pole in his hands.

Ranmau smirked. He refused to answer the first time the stupid question was asked, why would anything change?

There was a short silence. Finally, the Giant let his mouth turn up at the corner. "Who you fightin'," he said. "Me want you."

"Now, now," the Leader turned to the Giant, a gentle smile playing at his lips. "Your turn will come soon enough. Let others have a little fun first."

Ranmau glanced around, not looking for anything in particular. He imagined how he'd be able to take them all on if they attacked at once. But unfortunately, each plan that he had mapped out in his head had the same outcome... he knew he'd lose. *If only I could use both hands, the rest would be easy.* He hunched his body in the direction of his broken arm, clenching it with his hand.

"Now, it'd be unfair for the great, the *untouchable* Ranmau to fight only one of you krillens." The Leader grinned. "So... how about three? No... four?" He pointed at a pack of boys nearest Ranmau.

"Let's get him," growled a voice from behind. When Ranmau turned around, he saw a boy pulling his hair to the back of his head. He grabbed a pole out of the ground and leaned against another one. Another boy leaned against the other side of the pole, and when he crossed his arms, his shirt had a tear down his chest, showing the contour of his ribs. These boys were much too small and thin for Ranmau, they were more like a test trial for the Leader to observe Ranmau more than anything else. The Leader was still as predictable as ever, Ranmau thought.

Smart of him, though.

Suddenly, a gust of snow burst by Ranmau. He raised his left hand, tracing the snowy wind with his finger. When he dropped his hand, the spiral hung there for a few moments—he was as ready as he could be.

As the boys inched closer, poles in their hands, Ranmau extended his leg out, spiraling around, and kicked up a tornado of snow, blurring their vision. Ranmau couldn't see them, but they couldn't see him either. But he didn't need sight... he only needed to hear the shuffle their feet made when it slid across the snow and the deep breaths made before they lunged for an attack.

When he heard a crunch in the snow, he knew exactly where they were. He stepped forward, leapt in the air, and kicked his foot into the jaw of the nearest boy. It was only a second's fall and his friend caught him as he slid lifelessly into his arms.

Before Ranmau landed, he continued his turning motion, kicking his other leg out, connecting into the jaw of the boy who had just caught his friend. His eyes immediately rolled into the back of his head as he carried his friend down with him into the snow.

With only one swift move, the two boys laid on the floor unconscious. If Ranmau couldn't use his fists, he had to resort to his legs, which were just as deadly.

The surrounding boys' faces went pale, as if they just now understood that their plan was not going to be as easy as they had expected.

"Yo-you g-go in there and he-help them out," a smaller boy said to a dark-haired one, his shaking finger pointed directly at Ranmau.

Ranmau didn't really know any of them, he never needed to. They were numbers to him, numbers didn't need names or titles. But they all knew his name; he was Ranmau. And it was time to show the Village that his name still meant something.

The dark-haired boy said nothing, only held out his hand. The smaller one walked up to him, placing a sharp shard in his hand.

"Follow me," the dark-haired boy said, leaning in with a single swift move, feet first. They rushed in with a steadfast plan that failed as quickly as it began. Within the cloud of snow there were the sounds of a hammer smashing into two solid objects, followed by the loud thumps of bodies landing on the ground.

And once the snow settled, Ranmau glared at the Leader, who narrowed his eyes at the four unconscious bodies on the ground.

It was clear that beating Ranmau would take much more than a few emaciated boys.

Complete silence settled over the Village. As Ranmau leaned in to get a better look at the boys, the faint, heavy breathing of the

Giant in the distance echoed across the Crater. Ranmau leaned forward as far as he possibly could, hoping to get a glance at his new challenge.

With a sudden thrust, the Leader pushed a boy into an upright position, his face crumpled in confusion.

"You... you want me to go in there?" The boy gulped then looked around. "Who else is coming?"

Questions filled the air as everyone stepped back, as though not wanting to be called.

Then the Leader stepped forward with his arms crossed. "The rest of you," he smiled.

"I wanted a challenge, but this is a bit much," Ranmau said to himself. He felt a shiver of fear, something that he'd never expected to experience. He almost screamed in frustration but he bottled it up.

The Giant had just entered. He stomped toward the Leader, and with every step he took, there was a loud thud. He nudged the Leader with his elbow and the army of boys began their steady walk toward Ranmau.

Dozens of boys soon surrounded Ranmau. He clenched his elbow; protecting his arm became the top priority.

A couple of boys grabbed some whips and ropes from the large spike, others reached for poles. But Ranmau could sense a trembling fear that had come over most of the boys, who circled about with sulking faces, spiraling the ropes and poles in their hands and not saying much at all. Ranmau assumed they were all just as scared as he was. And he was right.

Then it happened, the first move was made. A boy lunged his whip at Ranmau, wrapping it around his injured arm, feeling like hundreds of hornets were trying to stab their way out of his bone.

With all the strength he could muster, he grabbed the whip with his free hand and pulled the boy toward him. Nearby friends held onto the boy and grabbed the rope, pulling with all of their weight.

"We need more," a boy yelled. His fingers were red from the friction. "Help!"

The rope creaked as if it was going to snap at any moment.

While others came to help, one of the boys on the opposite end emerged with a whip.

A sudden *snap* burned Ranmau's skin as it whipped around his wrist tightly, pinning Ranmau down from pulls on both ends. It felt like he was being ripped in half.

Ranmau screamed and pain filled his mouth. The boys stared at him, grinning, as if relishing Ranmau's first defeat. They clapped and cheered with one another, as though the fantasy they'd spent years dreaming about had finally come true.

Though no words were said, their glowing smiles seemed to speak exactly what was on their minds, and even Ranmau's: that the great Ranmau was great no more.

Ranmau struggled to stand up, but the first boy lunged his fist as hard as he could into Ranmau's jaw. The snow around them immediately became tainted with red.

The next boy jumped in the air, kicking his foot out straight ahead into Ranmau's knee. He collapsed instantly.

The next boy stormed ahead and lifted his knee into Ranmau's nose. Blood splattered into his hair, dripping down his face.

Ranmau screamed again and bent his head toward the ground, his arms still extended in the air, as though he was being crucified. He would have fallen to the ground if he could.

Before he could dwell about his situation, many boys ran in, kicking and punching and kneeing and elbowing his entire body.

The punishment continued on for a few moments until the Leader's deep voice echoed throughout the Crater. "Stop!"

The Leader prowled toward Ranmau with crossed arms. An idle smirk rested on his face.

"So, how did life become so great that it blessed me with the chance to see you like this? The great Ranmau finally where he belongs, beneath me, beneath *his* leader." The Leader pressed his hand underneath Ranmau's chin, lifting his bloodied face upward. "You don't look too well. I expected more out of you, to be honest."

A weight settled on Ranmau's chest, like each one of the Leader's words kept piling up. Tension built up inside of him until he couldn't hold it in anymore. He wanted to cry, or scream, or... spit.

So he did just that. His head cocked back before spitting blood into the Leader's face. He grinned, revealing reddish teeth.

The Leader's demeanor changed. He leaned back, calmly wiping his face. He let out a harsh laugh that ended as quickly as it began, then slapped Ranamu across the face. The smack was so hard and fast that Ranmau wasn't even able to flinch in time.

"Finish this krillen," the Leader said to the boys, walking back to his original location.

Ranmau felt the heartbeat in his throat. He stared at the Leader in silence and pressed his lips together, tasting his own blood.

"If they did this to me... what would they do to Destrou if I'm gone? He wouldn't make it," he whispered to himself.

Wind rushed over his forehead, breezing through his silvery strands as he closed his eyes. In his mind he stood on top of the Wall again. He was free. The air was thicker and the sight was beautiful; he appreciated the way the mountains hid behind the clouds. It was calming. He smiled for a few moments before he turned around and jumped off of the Wall.

He opened his eyes. "It can't end like this. We will be free," he said to himself, loud enough so that the others could almost make out his words.

Before the boys could respond, Ranmau jumped up, twisting his body, pulling the ropes closer to him. The boys who held onto the rope helplessly lunged toward him. With one, agile move, both of his feet connected into the boys' chests the moment they came in range. He felt vibrations on his heels as if something broke. There was a crunching sound—the type of sound that'd occur when someone stomped on thin ice.

Moving as fast as he could, Ranmau dodged the onslaught of attacks thrown his way. Whips cracked. Poles thrust. Punches and kicks thrown. He ducked to avoid high strikes, almost falling. Reaching out, he grabbed hold of a boy's twirling whip and pulled it out of his hand. Ranmau knew that he wouldn't be able to hold them all off for long; his strategy was purely defensive. He whipped the rope around, making sure that the boys kept their distance. Whenever someone stepped in range, the whip slapped them across their face, knocking them out.

He stepped back, panting, and took a look around. There were too many. He couldn't fight them all off. Fatigue began to wear him down.

The rope felt heavier. He was losing all of the strength in his only good arm. He pushed aside the swelling panic and set himself to work, dropping the rope. His victory relied on his legs.

Once the rope fell from his hands, the boys pounced, lunging in as fast as they could. Ranmau understood his slim chances, but he fought as hard as he could. He evaded the attacks, move by move, and countered them with kicks of his own. Then he repeated the whole process.

Dodge, move, strike, turn. He needed to make sure that he defended his back at all times.

Dodge, move, strike, turn. The boys fell at an alarming rate. Over and over, one by one, down they went.

It was too exhausting; Ranmau's breaths were heavy, he felt his heart pound at his chest. His other hand joined his limp one, dropping to the ground. His feet could no longer take the abuse. His throbbing arm grew in pain. He couldn't feel his fingers when he needed them to move, but he felt everything when they were in pain. The cruelty.

The unstoppable Ranmau collapsed to the ground, heaving in every breath. He was no longer the invincible one. Boys surrounded him with shackled steps. He was too tired to put up a fight. He had always been in great shape that he had no idea what it felt like to be exhausted.

He hated it, being winded and the feeling of fire burning his lungs after each breath. He hated feeling inadaquate, being useless.

In his darkest moment, as he saw his end draw near, a faint whisper was heard: "I'm sorry, brother."

* * *

"I don't know what to do," Destrou said to himself, pressing his fingers through his dreads. "What can I do? What should I do? What would you do?"

Destrou sat frozen over the Edge, a trembling feeling growing in his stomach. He'd been through a full range of emotions in such a short time frame. It was exhausting. Love, loneliness, sadness, fear, worthlessness, even the tiniest bit of happiness. Was it possible that hate overwhelmed love? The truth dawned on him, no matter how fast or far he ran, he couldn't run from the pain.

The terrible feeling in his gut formed into something much worse, something told him that Ranmau was in trouble.

"He'll be okay by himself. He is Ranmau, after all," Destrou said. "What does it matter, anyway? We only have a few days left to live before the tournament ends... why does any of this matter? Ranmau was right, death is going to happen to everyone. Nothing I can do to stop it. If one of our lives is going to end at the tournament, why not just end it now? Why do we have to drag out the misery? So they can enjoy it more? Maybe it would be better off if the Leader kil— No! Stop! I'm starting to sound cold like Ranmau. Why am I having these thoughts, does he think about these things, too?"

Destrou stood up, glaring down into the darkness of the Forest of Ness. His toes peered over the Edge, barely keeping his balance. He lifted one of his feet in the air, inching it in front of him as if he was taking his final step. "This pain is too much. I can't do it anymore."

This time he was going to do it. He was going to jump. Elu wasn't here to save him.

Before his eyelids sealed shut, Destrou was shocked into silence, noticing a single snowflake, twinkling in the sky, drifting its way down toward him. He froze in place. He had never seen one by itself, usually they came in flurries. He couldn't help giving it all of his attention. It floated around him, grazing by his nose, twisting to the back of his head. He pulled his foot back in, quickly turning around, reaching his hand out. The snowflake gracefully fell onto his palm, melting almost instantly. When he lifted his head, his eyes fixated on the Crater, seen faintly in the distance.

The end to his misery was just a jump away, but the thought of it vanished just as quickly as it appeared. "Ranmau? Are you in trouble?"

17

RANMAU'S FACE BURNED as a boy threw a ball of ice, striking him across the cheek. He had seen the attack coming and may had dodged it if he had a slither of energy left. He fell to his knees, and looked up, appreciating the purples and yellows that filled the sky from the setting sun.

"I think it's time," the Leader said. His eyes scanned Ranmau and his lip curled, as if he was a predator preparing for the kill.

"Bout time," the Giant said, stepping forward and cracking his knuckles.

Ranmau pulled himself up into a kneeling position and wiped the blood from the corners of his mouth. He knew that on a good day the Giant would fall, but today was far from a good day. It was his worst, and the Giant wanted to take full advantage of it.

Ranmau barely had the energy to keep his eyes open. He felt alone. There was not a single friend in the Village, his only friend he had had now wished he was dead. His eyes made contact with Ascel, who quickly looked away. When he turned back around, the Giant was directly in front of him. His face was too scarred and aged for a boy who was only seven years older than him. He held a staff in his hand that was sharpened down to a keen point.

"Make easy. Give up. Kiss my feet," the Giant laughed, pressing his fur-covered feet against Ranmau's red lips.

They were disgusting; Ranmau tasted fungus on the bunions that poked out of the Giant's shoes. He would have vomited if his body had the energy.

"Does this make you feel strong, attacking me when I have nothing left?" Ranmau asked. "You always wanted a challenge—so wait until I'm ready." He needed to try anything to stop this from happening.

The Giant hesitated briefly, looking back at the Leader.

"No!" the Leader shouted. "I mean... no." He lowered his voice. "This is what you have been waiting for. This is your chance to show everyone that you're better than Ranmau."

"This doesn't show anything. He wants you to do this so you're the one who gets hurt by the Guardian."

"Huh?" the Giant said, confused.

"Don't listen to him. Just do it!" The Leader raised his voice, saliva oozing from his mouth.

"Uhkay... uhkay." The Giant shrugged his shoulders then lifted the spike above his head, preparing to strike Ranmau with the sharp end first.

Before the Giant landed his attack, a scream from behind froze him in place, followed by a loud thud. He looked up, his brows furrowed and his eyes darted from side-to-side, as if wondering what to do next. He strained his eyes in the direction of the noise, but he saw nothing but the equally confused faces of the boys.

Then, out of the crowd, Destrou leapt over one of the boys, grabbed the boy's staff in mid air, ripping it out of his hands, and lunged it toward the Giant. The staff spiraled through the air, creating a fluttering sound as it soared from one side of the crowd to the other.

It hit the Giant's arm. The spike flew out of his hands, embedding itself deep into the ice an inch from the Leader's feet.

With effort, Ranmau forced his attention back to the crowd, and he noticed that Destrou was running toward him.

Destrou had a look that Ranmau had never seen before, there was no smile on his face and his eyes narrowed like the Leader's when he'd yell. He looked like... the Leader. No, even worse... he looked like... me, Ranmau thought. The Village had a way of making the worst out of everyone. Ranmau felt his heart sink to his stomach seeing how it was finally changing Destrou.

No... It's happening...

* * *

"I will not let you die, not like this," Destrou said to himself. He wanted to forget the pain, the death and everything else. Right now, he wanted to keep his promise and protect Ranmau.

He punched and kicked his way through boys until he was able to see the Giant standing above Ranmau. The spear no longer in his hand, but it was replaced with a whip wrapped around his palm.

Destrou braced himself, forming a new plan as he ran toward Ranmau. Deep breaths burned on their way down. He jumped over the wall of boys, sliding feet first, stopping a few inches in front of Ranmau's fallen body. A snowy mist exploded in his face.

"You okay?" he asked, glancing down at Ranmau.

"Never been better," Ranmau grinned. The grin seemed genuine, almost as if his remark wasn't sarcastic.

When Destrou looked up, his eyes pierced through the Giant, staring directly into the Leader's, not breaking eye contact.

In front of him was Ranmau, the Giant above him, the Leader behind them and Ascel to his right. Behind Destrou there was an army of injured boys, some standing, but most hunched over or lying face first from his attacks.

The height disadvantage between him and the Leader was evident. But it no longer affected him. Redirecting his focus off of the Leader, he arched his head back and glared at the Giant. Destrou had Ranmau's eyes, blackened and serious.

"How about you fight someone who has two arms?" Destrou said firmly. To his astonishment, the confidence in his voice surprised him. Maybe it was the Sensu meat talking.

The gasps throughout the crowd was followed by a breakout of chatter.

"Hah," the Leader laughed, "don't think that you're great now just because you beat up some krillens. I could do that with my eyes closed—don't be crazy now. Go away, little boy. Your chance will come after we're finished with him."

"I don't know why you're so afraid," Destrou said, pointing his finger at the Giant. "For a big guy, it's funny that you're so scared. Afraid of little Destrou?"

"Scared? You? Never," the Giant snarled. Frustration overwhelmed his face.

"Prove it... krillen."

The recovering boys shot up as if they received a burst of energy. Eyes widened. The murmurs dispersed through the crowd.

"Did he actually call him a krillen?"

"Wow... what is he thinking?"

"Oh boy... Destrou's going to regret that."

"Time to say goodbye to Destrou."

"Call me *krillen*?" the Giant's nostrils flared. His fists clenched as he pounded them onto his chest. "No one calls me... krillen. You gone down!" He kicked Ranmau's side with all the strength that he had, sliding him a few feet across the snow.

"You're going to regret that," Destrou said, glaring at him with seething eyes.

The look was frightening enough to make the Giant take a step back.

The Leader peered at Destrou. "I thought you'd rather wait until the tournament... but if this is how you want to die, then the Giant can help you out."

"Always hiding behind him. Now we know who the real krillen

is," Destrou said.

The Giant held back a chuckle. The crowd of boys gasped once more.

The Leader's face twitched. "Finish this krillen! And make it hurt!" He pulled the sharp spear out of the ice and threw it at the Giant.

The Giant caught it, immediately turning around, and lunged it at Destrou's chest.

Destrou jumped back as much as he needed to. The point barely scraped his body, grazing his shirt.

All at once, he was in the air and grabbed onto the spear. Instead of moving away from the Giant, as the boys expected, Destrou held onto the weapon and swung forward, kicking the Giant in the mouth.

Stepping back, the Giant twisted around and threw them both off balance, sending Destrou flying over his head.

For a moment, Destrou's legs were where his arms should have been—he saw the world as if the sky had fallen from beneath his feet. Before his head collided into the ice, he flipped around landing on his feet.

The Giant collapsed to the ground with a thunderous BANG.

"Get up!" The Leader roared. "Can't you do anything right? Do I always need to do everything?"

The Giant rolled onto his feet and charged at Destrou.

Destrou ducked away from him, stuck his foot out, and tripped the Giant. The Giant fell forward while running and crashed into a crowd of boys, flattening them under his weight.

The Giant stood up with nostrils flaring. "Stop runnin'! Fight, krillen!"

"Okay, let's make this a fight then," the Leader said, throwing a staff toward Destrou. It had a striking resemblance to the one that he used... or tried to use during their first confrontation. The fight when the Giant nearly killed Destrou... until Ranmau came and saved him, as he always did. That thought alone reminded Destrou why he was doing this.

Destrou caught the pole with both hands. Despite being too weak to balance it completely, he had more of a handle on it than he did before.

For a moment, everything seemed frozen in time. Then the strikes were unleashed and he dodged each of the Giant's attacks, countering with strikes of his own, hitting different parts of his body.

The Giant stomped into the ground out of frustration, the spiderwebs of cracked ice underfoot grew after each one. Even the thick ice couldn't handle his strength. But this fight wasn't about strength, it was about speed, and Destrou knew that.

"Stop runnin', krillen," he screamed, showing Destrou his hands again. "Over for you now, boy."

He unwound the whip from his hands, grinning the entire time. Despite the haunting images of the last time the Giant used that weapon, his face purple, struggling to breath as it burned around his neck, Destrou remained unworried.

"Not this time," Destrou told himself.

The Giant cracked the whip, missing Destrou a few times. Gasps filled the air, but no one appeared to be more impressed than Ranmau.

The Giant's face grew red. His veins bulged as he pulled the whip over his head, preparing to strike with all the strength he had.

The whip cracked around Destrou's pole, pulling it out of his hands.

Destrou stepped back, putting all of his weight onto his rear knee, crouching down into a fighting position. He was not scared. He was not intimidated. He was not anything. He felt nothing other than the urge to protect his brother. The urge to defeat everyone in his way. There was no room for failure.

After a few more strikes, the Giant finally made contact, cracking the whip around Destrou's wrist, pulling him in closer as he punched his fist forward.

Another miss.

Destrou knew the damage that the Giant's punch could do, he had seen the way a boy's eyes would roll up, but he also knew that the Giant couldn't hurt what he couldn't touch.

Destrou's strategy worked until the Giant struck at him suddenly, wrapping his arms around Destrou's body and squeezing the life out of him.

Destrou lost his breath for a moment, and on reflex, he wrapped his legs around the Giant's body. The thought of losing again briefly flashed through his mind, but he made sure to bury his doubts quickly. This fight was different. In the back of his head he had always known his unfair advantage would save him, as he always did, but today, there was no such help. He was the help. He was the last defense. The stress of the situation took a toll on him, he felt his heart race, knowing that if he failed right now, this may have been the end of him and his brother.

I don't know how you lived like this, Ranmau... I don't know how you could do this every day. Destrou almost choked up.

He was snapped back into the moment, feeling his bones crack from the Giant's arms tightening around him. The Giant's body was so wide that Destrou barely connected his feet together around it.

With a tight squeeze of his own, Destrou's legs were able to loosen the Giant's grip enough to lunge his forehead into the Giant's jaw.

The Giant momentarily lost consciousness, stumbling with each step. Destrou's stomach lurched as he began to fall, he knew to not press his hand down to brace for impact. He had seen what happened to one of the boys who tried: his arm snapped in two; so he wrapped his arms around the Giant's neck, holding on tight.

Destrou's head ricocheted off the floor. The sounds of ringing accompanied the spiraling images of the boys circling around him.

He didn't know if he was free falling or lying on the ground. To make things worse, the Giant's weight pressed on his chest, making each breath more difficult.

The both of them started to regain consciousness, shaking off their daze. The Giant lifted his body. Destrou still held on, using the remaining strength that he had. The Giant slammed his body back down, crushing Destrou's back against the ice.

A spiderweb of cracks formed underneath Destrou.

The Giant repeated the slams until the cracks burst into a crater.

Destrou's grip loosened, his body trembled with pain, the pain was unbearable.

The Giant lifted his body again, this time Destrou no longer clung on to him, he remained lying inside the crater. The Giant grinned, arching his fist back, preparing for a strike. He lunged all of his weight into the punch. This one aimed to kill.

He missed, burying his fist deep into the ice.

Destrou countered with a headbutt, busting the Giant's lip open. Blood trickled down his mouth onto Destrou's face. This happened twice more.

Destrou grabbed the dangling rope and wrapped it around one of the Giant's hands. After the next miss, Destrou wrapped the rope around the other one. In a craze, the Giant used his tied-up fists again to crash down into Destrou's skull. Destrou squeezed his head in between his arms, headbutting the Giant's jaw again.

Destrou freed his foot out just enough to connect his heel into the Giant's mouth, then wrapped his legs around the Giant's neck and arm.

The Giant groaned, picking up Destrou's body a few feet off the ground then slammed him into the ice.

BANG! The impact was strong enough to make Destrou's eyes cringe, but he still held on. He needed to.

While the boys hooted and hollered, Ranmau laid on the floor with a smirk on his face, as if he knew something the others did not.

The Giant slammed Destrou again, cracking the back of his head on the ice. The way that the ground shook, it seemed like that slam hurt even more than the last. Despite the feeling of needles piercing into his back, Destrou hung on, squeezing his legs tighter.

"Yeah, slam him harder!"

"Break his head open!"

"He's going to regret this! Kill him!"

"Kill the krillen!"

"He's not going to last long!"

Destrou didn't know how much more punishment his body could take. Why did he continue to endure it? *Keep squeezing, just like he taught me.*

The Giant's slams continued, but much like the excited chatter in the air, the slams slowed down after each one.

The Giant lifted Destrou one last time, barely an inch off of the ground before falling back down. For a few seconds, he laid motionless on top of Destrou.

And after a few more moments, the silence was broken by a loud snore. The Giant was knocked out cold.

Destrou's legs had cut all circulation to the Giant's brain, putting him to sleep. It was one of the many techniques that Destrou and Ranmau practiced on one another, never knowing when it'd come in handy. He rolled the Giant off of him, wiping the blood from his face.

He did it. Somehow he defeated someone who was twice his size. If Destrou was to break his eye contact with the Leader, he would have noticed a hint of a smile on Ranmau's face.

"Let's go," Destrou said to Ranmau, glaring at the Leader.

Ranmau pulled himself up, shaking the entire way.

Everything in Destrou's body wanted to attack the Leader, but he knew that he wasn't ready. Though he had defeated the Giant, it was too close of a fight. The Leader had been known to make quick work out of the Giant, so Destrou knew his limits.

Although he was the smallest in the Village, he let the statement be known that he was no longer the krillen to mess around with. Ranmau was not as vulnerable as they thought.

"As much as I don't want to... I will try to keep my promise," Destrou said, guiding Ranmau to their igloo. "I won't let them hurt you."

Ranmau hesitated for a moment, as if in disbelief that these words would ever come out of his mouth: "Thank you... Thank you for protecting me, brother."

Destrou said nothing. His mind was filled with thoughts, making it impossible to speak. He knew that he needed to train twice as hard now. If Ascel was correct, then this was nothing compared to what the Leader had planned. With the challenge being the next day, Destrou knew to expect the worst. It was going to be a long night.

18

ESTROU FOUND HIMSELF AWAKE for the past hour or
so, just staring at Ranmau's bed through barely-opened eyes,
as though pretending he was still asleep. The silence helped him in
many ways. To gather his thoughts was one way. But the silence
also allowed him to space out and not think at all, which seemed to
be most helpful right about now.

"So, today is the day," Ranmau said, lifting his head up.

It was early, right before the sun had the chance to rise over
the Edge. The deep sockets around Destrou's eyes revealed that he
didn't get much sleep. He became obsessed with training—with
his promise. To him, it was obvious that Ranmu needed food. His
body was cold, too cold. He was emaciated, losing almost all of
his muscular definition. But mentally he was weaker. He shivered
when speaking, his words were too sluggish and slow.

"Yeah, it is," Destrou said coldly.

"There is something that I want you to promise me," Ranmau
said, staring at Destrou. There was definitely something wrong with
the way Ranmau's eyes looked. They were glazed… wait, had he
been crying?

"Promise?" Destrou said. "What kind of promise?"

"Today is the challenge."

Destrou raised his eyebrows. "Yeah, we went over that already."

"I don't think we will win this one."

Destrou's eyebrows rose so high that he touched his forehead to make sure they were still there. He had never heard Ranmau talk about defeat before. It was too unlike him. "Okay? And I think we will," he replied confidently. "This is the biggest one yet. Our most important one. Maybe you don't, but I think *I* at least have a chance."

"I don't *think* you have a chance," Ranmau replied. "I *know* you have a chance... And that's why I want you to promise me something." Ranmau spoke as if Destrou had already won the challenge. On any other day in the past, that acknowledgement from Ranmau would have brightened his day and carried over for a lifetime, but not today. Today he simply glared at Ranmau, wondering where he was going with that comment. "If I'm not able to win... then I want you to give up."

"What?" Destrou shouted, starting to feel more angry. "No, not happening... I've been waiting for this moment. I've been training for too long to just give it up."

"I know that this is what you've wanted for a long time... but please... just promise me this. I don't ask for much." Ranmau's eyes met Destrou's.

"What? No way!" Destrou snapped. "What about *needing* the food do you not understand? We need the food. You need it. We can't just give it to the Leader—we won't stand a chance when the tournament comes up. Believe me."

"I'm not worried about the tournament," Ranmau said, and there was no trace of doubt, or anything for that matter, in his voice.

"Well, that's where you're wrong, you need to be worried about it. We only have a few weeks left. One of us will be free and the other dead. Isn't this what you always wanted... freedom? I'd rather have it be one of us than one of them."

"Just don't. The food isn't as important. It's just something called Sensu meat anyways."

"Sensu meat?" Destrou's eyes widened, remembering the night inside of the Guardian's room. "Really?" He hesitated. "In that case we *definitely* need it then!" *This may be able to heal you.*

"What do you mean we *definitely* need it?" Ranmau paused. "How... do you know about Sensu meat?"

Destrou said nothing.

The awkward silence said more than enough for Ranmau.

"Destrou, brother," Ranmau said, looking around as if to check that they couldn't be overheard, "please just promise me that you won't win."

"We will lose the tournament if he gets the Sensu meat... I can't promise you anything."

"Well this is more important!" Ranmau said.

"What's more important? Your jealousy? More than your freedom? More than becoming a Crystal Soldier, something that you always dreamed about since you first heard about them? More than meeting the Supreme General, the one person you always wanted to meet? Why do I want them for you more than you? Why is your pride more important than all of that? Just admit it, you hate the idea of being the worthless twin so much that you don't even want the Village to see me as the better one and you as the weak one," Destrou said, getting to his feet and brushing off his clothes. "Well, they already know you are. Give it up, you're nothing anymore. You don't want them to see me as the winner? If it comes down to me and you again, I won't go easy, just like you never went easy on me."

Destrou had no desire to say all of those hurtful words, but a blinding rage overtook his body. He hadn't figured out how to pacify the anger once it started. His moods were at the mercy of something that he couldn't see or understand, as if his mind had a switch that he had no control over. A monster that he couldn't tame. He felt

261

like a helpless prisoner in his own body, watching the turmoil unfold through eyes that were not his own. The insults were powerful; words had the power to dig deeper than a sword ever could, leaving scars that would never heal.

"Fine," Ranmau said coldly, turning his back to Destrou, taking a few deep breaths. "If that's how you feel, then I hope it does come down to the both of us. And if it does, then either you let me win or—"

"You're terrible, you know that?" Destrou let out a laugh that choked out into a grunt. He pounded his fists together, shaking his head. "You really want to show everyone that you're the best so much that you don't want me to win? You never wanted me to win. It's *always* about you. The great Ranmau always needs to win. I didn't think that I could hate you any more than I do, but I was wrong. Let's just get this over with. Good luck out there, brother."

"Wait," Ranmau shouted, snatching Destrou's arm. "You don't understand." The look of concern on his face was genuine. Destrou had never seen his eyes droop with so much sorrow.

"Don't understand?" Destrou said, yanking his arm away from Ranmau's hold. "No, *you* don't understand. You don't understand that if he wins this competition, your dream is gone. He WILL win the tournament with that food. What don't you understand about that? And I thought that freedom was everything that you wanted for us."

"It's not everyth—"

Destrou stormed out of the room, so fast his heart pounded. He had the sudden urge to scream but he held it back. He no longer wanted to be viewed as frail by anyone, including himself. He was not a krillen. Not anymore.

Why am I filled with all this hatred? I don't know how to stop it, what's wrong with me?

* * *

"Alrigh', krillens," the Guardian said, waving a large slab of Sensu meat, pressed tightly in between his fingers. Juices squeezed out of it, dripping onto the platform. The boys seemed so hungry for food that a few of them pressed their bodies against the platform, leaning forward to catch the drops with their tongues. "Since one of you took it from us, I guess the secret is not so hidden anymore. Here is your gift." He pulled the meat in closer to his face. His nostrils flared open as saliva oozed out of his mouth. "Mmm... do any of you know what makes this so much better than the garbage that we feed you?"

The boys said nothing, they knew better than to answer a question.

"Because this is what we Crystal Soldiers would eat before battle. We would have never settled for the garbage you krillens eat," he laughed.

"Yah," Commander Gronk laughed, "garbage food fuh garbage boys."

"This is a special challenge," the Guardian said, his sunken eyes looked crazed under his wild eyebrows. "It will be the last challenge for one of you before you leave and join the Crystal Soldiers. Only the best can join them, so I want to make sure that I send them the very best. You better not disappoint. Whoever wins this challenge gets all of this." He held the meat overhead, outstretching his arm so that the entire Village could see. "And believe me, this will be more than enough to make sure you win the tournament."

Destrou glanced over at Ranmau, narrowing his eyes at the sight of him.

The challenge was too important for the brothers to be torn apart before it began. Destrou knew this. They needed one another if they wanted any chance to win. *Separating us is exactly what they want.*

"Since this is a special challenge with Crystal Soldier food as the prize and the chance to become one in two weeks, I thought it was only fair that this challenge would be something that us Crystal Soldiers would do. You know, just to see if you boys really are fit to call yourselves one."

Murmurs broke out through the crowd.

"What does that mean?

"Do you think Ranmau can still win?"

"He has never lost."

"What do you think it can be?"

"Silence!" the Guardian shouted, lifting his hand. At once the crowd went silent. "This challenge will push you in ways that you have never been pushed before. You will need to be strong, fast, fit, and smart. Our challenges are never for the strongest or the fastest, they are for the best. The very best. If you don't think you have what it takes, then give up now. Just know that during the trials to become a Crystal Soldier... many lives were lost." He pointed south, toward the Valley. "The challenge will begin there. Ahh... the great memories of being the best. I remember winning like it was yesterday. I'd be shocked if any of you krillens has what it takes. Not everyone can be as great as me." The Guardian grabbed his belly, it hardly jiggled, instead it shook like a boulder. "This is the same trial that we had to go through back in our Crystal days, but of course we weren't as pathetic. We were actually warriors, not useless krillens."

"Hah," the Commander laughed. "Yah, they wouldn't last a secon'. They're lucky they have a chance tuh give up. We didn't. Yah either made it o' yah dead."

The Guardian's voice boomed across the Village as he explained the new challenge, boasting about how it was their way to eliminate the weak from the strong. There were five parts. It would begin with the fifty or so boys stretching across the Valley to retrieve one of the twenty emblems. After that, they would enter the Ruins—the area forbidden by the Guardian and unexplored by the Village. When inside the Ruins, they would remain there until someone claimed the final emblem. Each stage had a limited amount of emblems to advance: they went from twenty to ten to five until there were only two remaining. The Guardian growled, emphasizing that there would only be two left in the final stage. He paused, as if the boys didn't understand the message, repeating himself again. By the inflection of his voice, it seemed like his subtle way of saying that when two entered the final stage only one would live to tell about it.

"And to the sole victor, we will be waiting for you," the Guardian said with a deep snarl that grinned through his teeth.

Destrou and Ranmau gazed at one another from a distance. With no words spoken, they understood that more than ever before, they needed each other. Not just to win, but to survive.

Ranmau and Destrou kept an unblinking gaze on one another. They were surrounded by dozens of boys who filed in a single line, leaning forward, pressing their palms on their knees. They stared straight ahead at the Wall, its shimmer glowing as serenely white as ever, as if it was welcoming them to a brighter future. How could something so beautiful represent an object of terror; there was no such welcome of a bright future, only fear and a greater sense of dread as the boys looked ahead at the nearly hundred foot fall into the Valley.

Destrou heard the way the boys' breaths would hiccup, their voices shake. There was an uneasiness in the air, but the brothers seemed unfazed. They were ready. They knew that they were outnumbered and that the Leader was up to something as usual, but they had a plan. It was simple: stick together at all costs. Since their first challenge, the two of them had made it to the finals each time. But this time was different: Ranmau's arm was broken. Their strength now became their weakness. Their minds were as fragile as their malnourished bodies. And the breezes from the boys breathing down their necks were heavier.

The boys angled inward toward the brothers and glared at them with brooding eyes that unveiled a malicious intent.

The ground beneath them was still. A soft wind carried swirls of snow, disrupting its purity, and wrapped around the boys as they waited. Destrou listened for the horn and focused on the Wall straight ahead, a pounding heart made him aware of how many seconds passed. Each beat was one beat closer to starting.

Any moment now, he thought, wiping his sweaty palms on his pants. His focus was wholly on the Wall. He no longer heard the deep breaths. Or the wind howl. He looked over at the other boys, their mouths moved but no sound escaped. Even the way he twisted his soles into the snow didn't make a sound. *I'm ready*.

Then it happened.

The ground quaked as every boy pressed their foot forward. The horn blared, echoing throughout the Valley. The race began. There was no looking back—speed was the advantage for the first stage.

Destrou shifted his weight, and something immediately found its way beneath his foot. He tripped and pressed his hand forward, sliding it through the thin layer of snow, touching the ice below. He felt the weight of a few boys press onto his back. Hands wandered his body, pulling his hair, grabbing his wrists and feet. It felt like three or four people.

He glanced over his shoulder, spotting a group of boys already on top of Ranmau, pressing their weight on top of him, pinning his face into the snow.

Ranmau screamed in pain as one of them kicked his injured arm multiple times. His feet sprung out sporadically, warding off more attacks, but there were too many boys surrounding him.

Destrou looked ahead in the distance. The other boys had already reached the ledge, dropping down into the Valley. He noticed dozens of boys using ropes to climb down—for had they jumped, the fall would have been fatal.

They were already too far ahead. Destrou needed to react quickly. He pulled his arm, lunging his elbow backwards, and felt a set of hands detach from around his hair. He turned onto his back, kicking both of his feet upward as blood splattered onto his clothes. He stood up quickly, watching their bodies drop to the ground.

He paused for a brief moment. Ranmau was in trouble, but the other boys were already too far ahead. There were only twenty emblems, he needed to go now, there wasn't enough time. He took a deep breath to calm down and remind himself of the plan: stick together at all costs.

Destrou jumped forward, landing his heels into the side of a boy's body, his knee no longer lodged behind Ranmau's neck. Before Destrou landed on the ground, he twisted in the air, shooting his feet out, colliding into the sides of the other boys' faces. The life was sucked out of their eyes almost instantly, as he watched their bodies crash onto the snow.

Destrou lifted Ranmau up. "We need to go... now!"

Ranmau glanced around at the six fallen boys, clenching their bodies in pain. A subtle smile revealed itself behind his smirk.

With no time left to think, their legs already advanced, heading straight for the Wall.

"No!" Destrou screamed, looking around in frustration. He pulled up one of the many ropes that was embedded into the ice at the cliff. Its tattered fibers were jagged and shortened. He observed the rest of the ropes hanging over the ledge. One by one, they were all cut. The other end of the ropes rested in distorted spirals nearly a hundred feet below. The drop was too high for them to jump. There was no other way down—or was there?

"It's over," Ranmau said in disbelief, shaking his head.

"Not if I can help it," Destrou replied, running back where they came from.

"What do you mean?" he asked. "You're going the wrong way."

"Don't ask questions, remember? Follow me."

Destrou sprinted to a stop then turned around, facing the Wall. A memory briefly appeared in his mind. He remembered Elu bringing him to this point. He remembered running. The vision was jaded. All he could recall was the fear he felt surging through his body and the roar from the winds as Elu led him toward the leap of faith. He tried his best to point out exactly where the slide was.

"Trust me. Let's go!" Destrou sprinted ahead, Ranmau followed close by. He reached behind him to grab Ranmau's wrist, but connected with his hand. They picked up their pace. Destrou could feel Ranmau's blood thumping against his fingers. "Jump... now!"

Right before they reached the end of the cliff, they leapt into the air, crashing through the hidden tunnel. Their faces pulled to the back of their heads as they free-fell. They slid down the slope and glided onto the frozen surface of the Valley. Their feet gained no traction as they stumbled. The Valley was frozen solid, a thin dusting of snow on its surface created a cloudy trail as they sprinted through.

Ranmau's eyebrows arched as he looked at Destrou. "How did—"

"They are already climbing the Wall!" Destrou shouted over the wind fluttering in his ears. Through the cracks from his dreads that flurried across his face, he saw small dots move up the Wall.

"A few of them already got an emblem. There are only a few left," Ranmau shouted, looking ahead at boys dropping down the blank white canvas. "It looks like they are about to get the last two now."

Up ahead there was a man-made barricade of the remaining boys. Their arms were locked over one another's at the elbow. It was clear what their purpose was. Destrou and Ranmau had different plans.

Destrou looked at Ranmau, giving him a nod.

Ranmau nodded in return.

They had become so used to excelling in the challenges together that simple gestures translated into elaborate plans.

"Me or you this time?" Destrou shouted.

Ranmau said nothing.

"Me or you?" Destrou shouted louder. The manwall was close and their pace wasn't slowing down. "I need to know!"

They were moments away from colliding into the line of boys. The way their arms clenched around one another, locking each other in place, it seemed impossible to go through—but that was never the plan.

"Me," Ranmau shouted, inches before contact.

Ranmau leapt into the air, twisting his body over the heads of the boys. Their attention momentarily shifted to him spiraling over them as Destrou performed a swift move, feet first, thrusting his body into the ground. He pulled his chest and arms back, stretching his legs, sliding between the legs of three boys.

"Are you serious?" one of the boys shouted, turning around, looking at the back of the brothers' heads. "How do they *always* do this?"

Destrou glanced ahead, feeling the same rush of power that he felt when he defeated the Giant. His heart raced and the distance between him and the Wall faded quickly.

"What's the plan?" Destrou shouted.

Ranmau said nothing. While running, he kicked his shoes into the air, catching them in mid-stride with his good hand.

Despite his injury, Destrou knew to not question Ranmau's actions. If there was another lesson that he learned from his brother, it was that he could never go wrong mimicking greatness.

"What now?" Destrou shouted, holding his shoes in his hands.

Ranmau said nothing. Snow instantly exploded at his heels, picking up a large white cloud. As if their pace wasn't fast enough, Ranmau doubled it.

There were two emblems left. Two boys were about fifty feet high, pressing their bodies against the Wall, outstretching their arms, grazing the emblems with their fingertips.

Destrou's heart raced faster. *Why aren't you slowing down?* he thought to himself as they came within a moment from slamming into the Wall.

Ranmau leapt into the air, slamming his foot into the Wall then the other foot followed. His hand bounced off the Wall, providing additional leverage as he kicked up the Wall again. His arm pushed against the Wall, meeting with his feet, launching himself into the sky. Ranmau glided through the air, reaching the body of the boy who almost had the emblem in his palms. With one quick swoop, he snatched the emblem out of the Wall, free-falling to the ground.

Destrou momentarily lost his breath. *Seriously? I have to do that?* He hesitated. *Looks like fun!* His feet moved faster by the second. He calmed down and focused. He jumped at the Wall and kicked as hard as he could. One step, two steps, three steps, push. He lunged his body weight upward, inching closer to the emblem, but there was a problem: he was too short. He felt the momentum diminish before reaching the emblem. Gravity fought his power, halting him down to a stop. His body descended. In desperation, he reached up with both of his hands and, in one, quick stride, he grabbed the boy's pants, pulling them down, revealing a rear so pale that it must have never seen the light of day; then Destrou reached higher and pulled his body weight up using the boy's shirt.

The additional weight was too much for the boy. His fingers lost all traction. Gravity propelled him downward as Destrou pressed his feet on top of his shoulders, jumping off of him for the extra momentum that he needed. The boy catapulted to the ground. Destrou braced himself against the Wall and grabbed the emblem.

"I did it!" Destrou shouted as his stomach lifted to his heart.

Destrou crashed to the ground, crouching his knees upon impact to absorb some of the damage.

There was the sound of struggling followed by groans. For a moment, he thought that Ranmau was in trouble, but when he turned around, Ranmau stood above numerous boys, who clenched their faces as they twisted and turned and groaned. Ranmau smiled at Destrou. Then his body wavered slightly, stumbling, bringing him to the ground. His body went limp and eyes rolled and wandered to a stop.

Destrou rushed to where he lay, motionless in the snow. "Ranmau? What's wrong?" He called his name again, nudging his body, but there was no response. Destrou pressed his hands, feeling for anything that could be a reason why he collapsed. A puncture. A wound. Anything? When he lifted his shirt, his mouth dropped.

Ranmau's chest and abs were covered with a purplish blue bruise that looked as if his skin wanted to crawl out of his body. He was not well, but how long had this been going on?

He needs that Sensu meat, Destrou thought. "I need to get him it, I think he's dying. Why do you always try to make it seem like everything is okay?" he screamed, his eyes swelled, holding back tears. A lump grew in his throat, pressing his ear against Ranmau's chest.

A few moments ago Ranmau's heart pumped with adrenaline. Now, all Destrou heard was... silence.

* * *

"Wait!" Vayp screamed, slamming his palms on the pages, the words glowing like a dying flame. His stomach sank as he thought about Destrou's reaction to losing his brother: he was mournful, instead of the happy person Vayp was expecting. "Destrou... *he* was the one who killed Elu... isn't that what you wanted to happen? For him to die?" Vayp sat up, turning his head to look at Han'sael floating inside the container. "Ranmau killed Destrou's love, Hanny..."

Vayp pressed his palms against his thighs and squeezed tightly. Destrou wished for Ranmau to die, yet he was heartbroken when he did; Vayp felt his heartbeat escalate as he wondered what would happen when he kills S'rae. *When.* He saw the vision. He saw what had happened and what will.

"Would..."—Vayp choked up, staring at Han'sael as if hoping he'd provide an answer he desperately needed—"... do you think killing S'rae may be a mistake?" And when Han'sael said nothing,

Vayp looked up to the sky, but there was no sky, instead he was staring at a monster that was hundreds of feet tall, yet still only half of its shadowed body had been erected from the ground. "That's the end. That's the Mas'ahk, Hanny." Vayp turned back around to Han'sael, his stomach churned as he saw how helpless Han'sael looked. "Do you even like that I call you that? Sorry, it's the best nickname I could come up with. If you don't like it, I can change it." Vayp turned away, disappointed. He tried any way he could to make the best of the situation. A part of him had always wished someone would care enough about him to give him a nickname, so that was why he decided to call Han'sael "Hanny". Letting his mind wander to random things helped distract him from thinking about how anything could ever defeat this monster. The end was most definitely near, and all Vayp could now think about was the throbbing pain in his chest, telling him that he was the reason. "Did I make a mistake?" He gazed at Han'sael.

This is no mistake, for because of you, the most powerful Geddon will be reborn, the Divine One will be defeated, and the Circle of Time will remain. A thought entered Vayp's mind with a voice so cold it sent shivers through his body.

"But why… why does it have to happen? Why do you want the Circle of Time to happen?" Vayp said aloud, though no one else but Han'sael was around.

We all have our reasons… even you. There will come a time when even you will wish for the Circle to remain. And only then will you be glad that all of this is happening as planned. You will thank me.

Vayp thought for a second about his role in this and how he will be remembered and he immediately found himself wiping his eyes.

Do not cry, little boy. As long as you are the hero for some, you will always be seen as the villain to others. It is not in your stars to decide how others will remember you. A shadow materialized in front of Vayp, black smoke simmered off its body.

He looked Vayp directly in the eyes, and all Vayp saw was an empty darkness, a shell void of all life.

Eventually you will learn a harsh truth: that when you do things for the right reason, people won't be sure that you have done anything at all.

Vayp looked down at the book, seeing the now fuzzy words through blurred eyes.

"This... this is my destiny?"

It is... it is in the stars.

At once, Vayp felt a lightness in his stomach as if he had fallen from the sky.

See... did you feel that? Déjà vu. This moment has indeed happened before. All is going as destiny planned. The shadow lifted his head. *The Mas'ahk is almost ready. You must finish reading the book, you do not have much time. The Shadow Army will be ready soon. Master will be most pleased.*

Within the blink of an eye, the shadow vanished, leaving behind black smoke that drifted away.

But Vayp couldn't read right now, he was not ready to see what happened to Destrou and Ranmau. Right now he only wanted to think about... S'rae.

What happens when she dies? Will everything become better? Vayp crashed to the ground, digging his nails into what felt like rough sand.

The hope of saving Han'sael was all that kept Vayp sane while he was here, the only brightness in a world that had never looked darker. The shock of seeing himself kill S'rae had only gotten worse, and the fear of what lay in the future had started to sink in. That moment... that battle between them, it was coming, he felt as if it was prowling toward him like an Archon, ready to end a life. He had never been this helpless before; it was more than the feeling of entering his first arena match, which being the first without S'rae had caused a serious panic attack, and even more than when he had arrived at GroundStone with no Sol or home. Vayp had difficulty trying to find the good in life… or what was left of it; it felt as if not only his world was ending, but the entirety of Gaia was about to collapse along with it. And it was his fault.

Vayp needed something, anything good on his mind to remove him from this gloom; so he thought about Destrou and Ranmau's past. He thought about their times when they were happy and kind to one another, when they were the best of friends.

Vayp looked up once more, his eyes scanning the giant shadowy frame of the Mas'ahk. It was without question the largest thing he had ever seen, even larger than—Vayp gasped. It happened all too quickly: his eyes widened as tears welled up.

A memory had flashed before his eyes. A moment so sacred that it hurt just thinking about it.

The enormity of the Mas'ahk reminded Vayp of the Vay'rae duo's most secret adventure; the one that forever changed their lives and was never told to a single soul. It was their biggest secret not only because it was too tragic to tell, but because they knew no one would believe them, even if they did.

* * *

"Don't worry about everyone else," a young Vayp said, dressed in a white robe with swirls of golden sand embroidered into it, "we don't need a Sol anyways! We have each other! The Vay'rae duo!"

"Always and forever," a young S'rae said, dressed in the same colors, though she wore a white cloth wrapped around her face.

The two of them ran away from the crowd of young boys and girls, who were clapping and cheering at the arrival of their new Sols. But not the duo, no Sol awaited them, again, so they decided to have fun on their own.

"Let's go to Gaia Rock!" S'rae said, her smiling eyes twinkling.

Vayp smiled back, loving the way S'rae would always thirst for a new adventure together. "Okay, but just make sure we're back before the ceremony ends, they'll kill us if they find out we ditched them again." Vayp looked over his shoulder at the sand domes and straw huts of Opella before chasing after S'rae. The sounds of laughter and celebration slowly faded away.

"*You must support your own,*" S'rae mocked, sounding like a dying old lady with a thick accent. She jumped up a hill, leaping from rock to rock as Vayp followed. "Why do we have to support them, anyways? It's not like they even like us or anything."

"Yeah, Senju is still mad that you broke his hand," Vayp laughed.

"Well, *I* didn't break his hand. He just happened to punch my statue's *very* hard butt." S'rae giggled.

They climbed their way all the way up to the top of Gaia Rock that overlooked the village of Opella. She saw golden mountains off in the distance, and behind her was a long drop into the Abyssal Plateau, a dark, wooded area that used to be the place where they'd hunt for food, but now it was forbidden. *No food awaited, only death*, the Village elders would say to the children at night.

"Do you think monsters really live in their now?" Vayp said, walking up behind S'rae and placed his hand on her shoulder. "Do you think they really ate all our food?"

"I don't know," S'rae said, "but... I do know they're not lying about the whole hunt shortage. Been days and they still haven't come back yet."

Vayp and S'rae laid at the edge of the cliff, feet dangling off the edge as they talked about the stars, life, which Sol will be theirs, but mostly they made jokes about the Opellans down below, who were still dancing, laughing, and partying away.

"Why do you want a squirrel so badly?" Vayp laughed.

"Why *wouldn't I* is a better question!" S'rae stood up quickly, a wide smile on her face as she stomped her feet, just as she'd always do when she got excited. But just as quickly as her excitement came, it had vanished. The gray clouds in the sky swirled about, darkening without a moment's notice. Then the horns blared from below as the Village cast spells to protect their homes with stone domes.

Vayp's eyes widened at once, panic in his voice. "We need to go, *now!*"

S'rae's look of fright made something inside Vayp collapse. But before they could start on their path, the roaring rain and wind swept through the valley. Within a second, they were caught in a storm so severe that Vayp couldn't hear what S'rae had screamed at him.

The storm was the worst one they had ever seen, and right when Vayp went to pull S'rae toward Opella, the rocks crumbled underfoot and they found themselves sliding down a roaring wave of mud and grime.

They hadn't perfected their molding spells yet, so they were completely at the mercy of nature and her fury. The rushing river had pushed them deeper and deeper into the forest, and each time they tried to grab a tree to stop themselves, nature proved too powerful, thrashing them even harder.

Vayp had found it difficult to breathe, water found its way up his nose and down his throat, but still all he could think about was not letting go of the world that was in his hands: S'rae.

"What's that!" S'rae gurgled as water splashed into her face.

And when Vayp looked ahead, his mouth dropped. He quickly tried to think of a spell that could save them in this situation, but all he could create was a stone hand that dissolved into mud as it reached out for them.

Nothing was stopping them… they were heading straight off the plateau with no certainty on what awaited them below.

"Vayp, I love you!" S'rae screamed over the roar of the water, and those words made something inside Vayp come alive. He knew she said those words because she wanted them to be her last… but not today!

And as they were launched off the plateau, and a few hundred feet drop awaited them, Vayp slammed his palms together and threw his hands up. The muddy waterfall slowly hardened into a curving slide that scraped their backs as they tumbled their way deeper into the forest.

"You saved us!" S'rae said as she wiped mud off her eyes before wrapping her arms around Vayp's neck.

He didn't know how to grab her back. He wanted to return the hug, but nerves froze him in place as she dug her face into his chest. He then gently caressed her head. "I'll always protect you, S'rae."

"I know you will." S'rae cried into his chest. "I know."

They spent the next few hours trying to find a way out, but everywhere they looked there was a rushing waterfall of mud.

"Looks like we'll have to wait out the storm," Vayp said as he dug his hands into the mud. The mud bubbled for a few moments before arching over their heads and formed a dome. "This will be our new home. It's not the best, but it should be enough."

"If the home has you in it," S'rae said, a sparkle in her eyes, "then the home will always be enough."

Vayp smiled wide, a sparkle in his eyes that matched S'rae's. "Vay'rae duo."

"Always and forever," S'rae said.

The two of them lay cuddled up next to one another, providing the body heat that was needed. Their clothes were drenched and Vayp could feel S'rae shivering. And each time she trembled a bit harder, Vayp made sure to squeeze her tighter. "You're going to be safe," he said. "I won't let anything happen to you."

"Thank you," S'rae said, leaning her cheek into his shoulder. "Thank you."

The pitter patter of rain and the roars of thrashing mud were once sounds that caused dread for them, were now soothing as they lay in their new home.

"This doesn't feel so scary anymore," Vayp said.

And S'rae turned her head to look Vayp directly into his eyes. "I knew you'd save us."

They stared at one another for quite some time, not saying a single word, as if they were just appreciating the now, *this* moment.

"S'rae..." Vayp said, taking a deep breath. "I—"

BANG!

S'rae screamed as the roof of their dome crumbled into pieces. Rain filled their new home up instantly. And when Vayp looked up, he screamed the loudest he had ever screamed.

He was staring into a yellow eye that was practically the size of him.

"Get out, now!" Vayp screamed as he pushed his palms upward.

A geyser of mud shot up into the eye as a roar erupted in the darkness, so loud the ground shook.

Vayp and S'rae scrambled to get their footing, but when they tried to run away from the beast, the water was pushing them closer to it.

"Is that what I think it is?" S'rae screamed.

"That's *definitely* a canavar!" Vayp screamed back. "We are dead!"

S'rae's eyes went wide at Vayp's comment, and he immediately found himself regretting saying that. He was supposed to be their protector, he was supposed to make her feel safe.

The beast, which looked like a fifty-foot-tall bear with stone fur and claws the size of a hut, had pulled its paws from its face and stared at S'rae and Vayp.

"What do we do?" S'rae said.

Vayp said nothing.

"Vayp... what do we do?"

Vayp still said nothing. What was he supposed to say? This was probably their last moment together, there was only one thing that came to his mind. "S'rae, I love you too."

And S'rae's shoulders locked up, a half smile on her face as if she knew why he said it. That these were to be the last words they'd hear. "I—"

As the canavar lifted its fist and began its descent, ready to flatten Vayp and S'rae, a pack of dire wolves had leapt over them, biting onto the arms and legs of the canavar.

"Dire wolves!" S'rae smiled, a shock of amazement.

"What are they doing? They only protect their pack, not humans!"

"I don't know," S'rae said, stumbling to get footing.

"Let's go!" Vayp grabbed S'rae's arm and pulled her away, at least tried to. She was a lot stronger than he thought, because she remained still, staring ahead at the dire wolves battling against a canavar. Her eyes drooped as if she knew what Vayp had known as well… that it was a losing battle for them.

"We can't do anything about it," Vayp said. "They saved us, let's not let their deaths be in vain."

"But… they saved us. We can't… we can't just let them die."

"We can, S'rae! We can! Or that *thing* will kill all of us."

S'rae's eyes watered up. "I don't want them to die for us."

Vayp froze for a moment, knowing what that comment meant. S'rae was the strongest and bravest person he knew after all. Though unspoken, what Vayp really heard was *I'm not leaving them to die.* And Vayp knew there was no convincing her. He saw the fire in her eyes. Her decision was made.

And just like that, she slammed her palms together as a swirl of mud hardened into a staff with a spear at the tip, and ran ahead toward the canavar.

Vayp thought only for a second about a life without S'rae before doing the same. A sharp spear formed into his hands and he charged forward.

The dire beasts were slung here and there, some breaking their backs against the sides of trees.

Vayp saw S'rae run up a wave of mud that carried her higher toward the canavar's head.

Vayp followed suit and created a wave of mud that spiraled

around its legs. He jabbed the spear into its ankle only to hear a clang as if it was made of metal.

But S'rae didn't strike, she was still running up the wave higher and higher, passing its waist, then torso, until she leapt and landed atop its head.

The canavar went to slap the top of its head but a stone hand had grabbed its wrist. It roared as it turned to face Vayp, who had a clenched fist of his own that was trembling as if it took everything he had, before stomping down at him.

A large dire wolf leapt over Vayp and turned into a giant statue of itself that kept the canavar's foot an inch away from crushing the both of them.

Vayp looked at the dire wolf, tears beginning to fall from his eyes. "But... you're going to die."

The dire wolf nodded as if understanding what Vayp had said.

"But... why—" the dire wolf's long spindly tail had whipped Vayp away before the foot finally crushed its way down.

"NO!!" Vayp screamed, tears flowing from his eyes. He gripped his staff, a fire now burning in his eyes as well. Mud swirled around Vayp in spurts and waves, slowly molding into a hammer that was twice the size of him. "Your death will not be in vain!"

Vayp ran up a wave of mud, watching S'rae flip around atop the canavar's head, avoiding each swipe of its hand. Vayp then jumped off the wave, and as he flew through the air, the wave of mud began to swirl around him, doubling and tripling the size of the hammer until it was the size of a temple. Vayp then screamed as he angled the massive hammer down onto the canavar's head.

S'rae had rode a wave down just before the hammer crumbled on the canavar's skull. It lost its balance, stumbling for a bit.

Vayp had landed next to S'rae. They both looked at one another, nodded, then placed their palms together in a ball. They looked up at this massive beast that was stumbling about as they chanted words together.

The ground shook and rumbled as green light striped through the cracks of their fingers.

"AL'LAH," they screamed as the ground shook even more, trees fell and rocks levitated all around them. "HA!!!" They stretched their palms out toward the canavar as giant stone spikes burst from their palms.

They kept screaming as dozens of spikes launched from their palms. The bigger the spikes, the more they cratered into the ground underfoot.

And finally, after what felt like a minute of screaming, the two stopped and took deep breaths. They had given it their all, channeling a spell that was meant for only an Elemental to master, not two children.

And when they looked up, the beast had fallen and crashed into trees, spikes piercing through every part of its body.

"We... we did it?" S'rae said, hands on her knees as she tried to catch her breath.

"I think... we did," Vayp said in disbelief. "I think we did it!" Excitement came once it hit him what they had done. But then it faded quickly as he looked at the battleground around them.

"They gave up their lives to save us," S'rae said, hugging Vayp from behind. "I will never forget this moment."

"Me neither," Vayp said, pushing his cheek down onto S'rae's forehead. "But we can't tell *anyone* about this, they'll never let us go anywhere together." And when S'rae nodded, Vayp continued, "Plus, you know they wouldn't believe us even if we did. This'll be our secret."

"Our *biggest* secret!" S'rae said, squeezing Vayp tighter.

Then the both of them turned around quickly, fresh spears formed into their hands as they were ready for another attack. Something shuffled behind them.

"What do you think that is?" S'rae said. A faint whimper was heard from the movement.

"I don't know, but it looks too small to harm us," Vayp said as something squirmed, stuck underneath the rubble. "I think it's scared. Don't worry, we won't hurt you."

Vayp walked over and lifted his hand as the rocks levitated into the air before shooting out in separate directions.

"What is it?" S'rae said.

But Vayp couldn't speak... because the moment their eyes met, something overcame him. He saw lifetimes flash before his eyes. He felt joy, love, peace and harmony all at once. He saw laughter and fun and adventures with the loves of his life. But most of all, he saw a life worth living for, one worth dying for. And now it felt as if he had never lived life until this very moment.

S'rae gasped. "What... what do we name it?"

* * *

"His name *was*... Ah'nyx." Vayp fell to his knees and cried, alone in the darkness.

S'RAE HAD NO IDEA HOW LONG SHE WAS TRAPPED in here, this cave that looked identical to Elu's Tree inside the Book of Eve. Except instead of ice, everything around her was lush, green, and full of life. A freshness made her nose tingle and though silence was all around her, she heard some sort of droning hum that made her think it was nature's way of speaking to her.

"I wonder if the Dream Words spell actually works for these?" S'rae said, her fingers caressing the tribal carvings etched into the bark of the walls. S'rae still couldn't process what had happened and how, but right now her curiosity was piqued.

She placed her hand to her chin and scrunched her face. "What was it called?" She squeezed her eyes tighter, and thought carefully about the time Gabrael had read the Book to her. "Was it... *glin'gern klin...* something?" S'rae shook her head and slapped her palms to her thighs; she hated when she had to recall something that was so close to being remembered, yet still evaded her, like water seeping through the cracks, she felt her chance slowly ebbing away.

"That was *very* close." A soft voice was heard from behind S'rae that made her soul momentarily leap from her body.

S'rae squealed and turned around, then gasped. A boy, not much older than her, with brown hair, fair skin, and a hat tipped to the side, stood leaning against the entrance with a wide smile.

Her first instinct was to create a weapon from stone or wind, but neither worked.

"Oh no need, fighting is not allowed here," the boy said, his smile grew wider, which somehow made S'rae feel like everything was okay.

"W-who… are you?" S'rae heard the jitters in her voice.

"Me? My name is Sianu, but *who* are *you*?"

S'rae said nothing; though his presence was calming, she still felt nervous beyond words, her shoes became soaked with sweat.

"It is okay, I do not wish to hurt you," the boy said, "but I must ask… how did you know about the *Ge'hirn klin'gen*?"

A light immediately clicked in her mind, that was exactly what it was called, even the way the letters rolled off his tongue. "Wait… how do you know it?"

"I mean no disrespect, but I believe I was the one who asked you the question first," the boy's wide smile turned into a smirk.

"I… am S'rae."

The boy's eyes widened. "It is you. You have finally come."

S'rae took a step back, knocking her head against the wall. "Sorry, what?" she said as she rubbed the sore spot.

"It is happening just as Va'han told me it would, but—" S'rae noticed how the boy's cheery attitude faded away, "but… where is my… my other visitor?"

My other visitor? S'rae thought for a moment about who this person could be. "Wait. Do you mean Olivia?"

"No, I do not know an Olivia," the boy said, staring at the ground for some time before lifting his head at S'rae. "But I know that destiny works in wondrous ways. You are here just as the Prophet said you would be. And I am afraid that means danger awaits you."

S'rae felt a mass in her throat. "D-danger? What do you mean?"

"Death. Death awaits you."

The way he said it so calmly almost made S'rae not quite grasp what she had heard. "Death?"

"Yes, but that is why you are here. Though you will not escape death, I am to give you something that may help save you when you do die."

"*When...* I die?" S'rae felt heart collapse to her stomach.

"We all die, death is not what you should fear."

"And what should I fear if not death?"

"A life... where you watch *everything* die before your eyes."

Her immediate reaction was to fall and curl into a ball, but shock, or was it fear, froze her in place. A million questions surged through her curious mind, but somehow she only had the courage to ask one: "What is this place?"

"This is one of my greatest creations. A place where time is frozen, or at least chilled." The boy walked across the room. Each time his hand touched a circle on the wall, its glow nearly blinded S'rae. "I was sent to GroundStone because I was trusted with creating a similar room. Except one where time has quite the opposite effect than this."

"Y-you... created this?"

"Mmhmm." Sianu nodded proudfully. "It took quite some time, but it was worth it."

"Er... how long?"

"Well, I suppose that depends on your perception of time. In here, it took a few hundred years, but for you... out there, it was only a second, *maybe* two."

S'rae couldn't wrap her head around that concept, so she didn't try. "Does that mean... I'm trapped in here?"

"Trapped?" Sianu laughed. "Oh no, you are free to leave whenever you wish. Me—" Sianu looked at the ground once more, S'rae could see his smiling eyes waver slightly. "Well... me, *I* am trapped here."

"Why?" S'rae said, a pang of sorrow making her chest tight.

"Well, I am but a memory here, a vision of the real me frozen in time. I am not what I would consider a real human, and I am afraid that the moment I do leave, I will exist no more."

"Why?" She was still in such shock that it felt like "why" was the only word in her vocabulary.

"Because—" S'rae heard his voice crack with emotion. "I am sure the real me would no longer be alive, most likely dying thousands of years ago. So… here I am. And here you are. And I am glad we are to finally meet."

Everything felt so surreal, she had to find out more about this mysterious boy. "How… how did you know about the *glin'henr*… err..." S'rae rolled her eyes, mad at herself for already forgetting the Dream Words spell.

Sianu chuckled. "That is an interesting question. How do I answer such a question? How do I know about something that I created? Hmm… I suppose—"

"Wait, what?" S'rae moved forward, looking around, her footsteps echoing off the walls. As amazing as this place was, and as much as she wished to try out the Dream Words spell, she couldn't quite suppress the feeling that Sianu might have been lying to her. How was it possible that he created a spell so powerful that even Gabrael was in awe of it. A spell that was inside the Book of Eve, which was a story from the beginning of time? Nevertheless, she put her hands on one of the glowing circles, then turned to Sianu and said: "Prove it."

"Is that your way to kindly ask me to show you my gift?" Sianu smiled. "I mean no disrespect, but you will never make friends if that is how you demand things."

S'rae felt her face go red. "Er… I'm sorry." She decided to switch it up, the idea of him being a friend seemed too good to be true. "Does it get lonely here?"

"Oh no, I have the best visitor I could ask for, but there has not been a visit in some time."

S'rae's heart dropped as she twisted the emblem in her hand. "Who was she?"

"The best friend anyone could ever ask for. The person who I wished to name this room after because whenever she was around… time stopped, and all that mattered was appreciating the moment, with her. She gave me life, and a reason to live… to exist… even in this form."

S'rae couldn't help but smile at how excited Sianu was when talking about her. "How'd you two meet?"

"Oh." Sianu's fair cheeks flushed with red as he twisted his foot into the ground. "I suppose it is not the greatest story one could share."

"I'm sure it's amazing!" S'rae said. A part of her understood why Lynn was so nosey for gossip, S'rae wanted nothing more than to hear about this love story.

"Well, it is embarrassing because… when I first met her… she was actually trying to—you know what? I would rather show you instead. It's this story, right here." Sianu playfully grabbed S'rae's wrist and brought her to a section on the wall that swirled with pink and green lights. Normally the idea of a stranger grabbing hold of her would result in them kissing the dirt, but not Sianu… there was something so pure about him. "Now close your eyes, S'rae… yes, like that. Now… it is *very* important, when channeling a water spell, that you be in a complete state of bliss and peace… serenity, we should say. Yes, just like that, good job, S'rae. Now, whisper these words *just* as I say them. *Ge'hirn klin'gen.*"

And once she said those words, she felt her entire body become engulfed in water, yet when she opened her eyes, she was completely dry… and—she rubbed her eyes to make sure they were working—she stared ahead at an absolutely lush and gorgeous terrain that looked like it could be… GroundStone? The temples remained the same, but rather than being surrounded by gold and brown, there were pinks, blues, reds, purples, and colors she had never seen before. *THIS!* This must have been what Leonna was talking about when she said how beautiful GroundStone once was. Flowers sprouted from the vines that circled the temples and columns and posts that lined the sparkling bricked roads.

"It is beautiful, no?" Sianu said, his body slightly transparent.

"Watch out!" S'rae screamed as a giant mammoth stomped down onto him. But before she could react, the mammoth kept stomping ahead, and Sianu was standing there as if nothing had happened.

"We are perfectly fine here," Sianu said, brushing his shirt. "No harm can be done. We are not traveling through time, we are merely vessels traveling through a moment, a dream, a Dream Words."

Sianu pointed at a boy talking to a group of gorillas on the corner, who were selling bananas of all different sizes and colors. "That was me. I had just come from my home with one mission in mind. However, they wanted me to attend school while I was here working on my next creation, but I knew I wasn't going to fit in. I just knew. And do not mind the look, mother said it was best to adapt into the new surroundings."

S'rae took one good look at the boy, who wore socks to his knees, a hat too big for his head, and a shirt held together by ropes across his chest, and wondered how that could have possibly been a good idea to fit in.

At once, the scenery blurred and distorted as a breeze turned the temples, animals, people, and Sols into dust that slowly morphed and twisted and molded into a new environment.

Within seconds, they were inside a lush forest. Though she couldn't smell anything, she imagined the scent of flowers and fresh rainfall.

A boy sat by a fire, but he was not alone. There were dozens of different animals laying around the fire with him.

"And there I was," Sianu said, "trying to find my Solmate, until—"

The boy looked up, twisting around, as if he heard Sianu speaking. He stared into the darkness for a few moments longer then shrugged, but when he turned back around and sat, all the animals had left. The scorching flame had faded to logs that now glowed red. Darkness settled over him.

Then S'rae heard a distinct SWOOSH that made her shoulders lock up and her chest tighten. "Watch out!" she screamed to the boy.

And within a blink of an eye, the boy was no longer sitting, but instead, he was standing with an arrow between his fingers.

"Wait…" S'rae looked over at Sianu, who was smiling, a twinkle in his eyes. "How?" That movement was quicker than anything S'rae had ever seen. It was as if he didn't move, but rather he was standing, when just a moment before he was not. She couldn't explain what she saw.

"I am not sure why you would shoot an arrow at me," the boy said, "but please, next time you choose to, do not startle my friends. I was quite enjoying my time with them."

The arrow dispersed into swirls of smoke, and S'rae heard the rustling of wind and footsteps fade off into the distance.

"Wait… someone tried to kill you… too?" S'rae said to Sianu.

"I suppose you could say they *tried*. But it was such a poor attempt that I could not take it seriously. But… I will give the person credit… because they kept trying each day after that."

S'rae watched dozens of visions of the boy catching arrows and evading death while performing mundane tasks. One time he was cleaning his clothes and ducked as an arrow ripped through his shirt. He simply threw it away and bought a new one as if he didn't even notice the arrow stuck into the wall.

"I… I don't get it," S'rae said, dumbfounded. "Why are you so calm?"

"I was more curious than calm. I would ask myself, why would this person want to kill someone who means them no harm? Who means no one no harm. I never wished ill for anyone, even my father's enemies."

S'rae looked at Sianu with a glowing respect. Someone was trying to kill him, but still he wished to find the good in the situation? Although she could relate to what he was going through, she wished she could have even the slither of his courage to handle it in the same way.

"But why aren't you scared or angry?" S'rae said.

"Why would I be?"

"Er… because they're going to kill you?"

Sianu laughed. "Oh no, no, no, there is a *big* difference between *going* to kill and *trying* to. This killer was simply *trying* to, with absolutely no chance in succeeding," he smiled.

S'rae had swallowed her breath and couldn't help but appreciate his confidence, his calm.

"Watch," Sianu said. "This is my favorite part."

The boy had just caught two arrows, spilling his cups of tea into the soil of the forest. "You know, you do not have to keep doing this. I mean you no harm. I am not a bad person, nor will I ever be. Feel free to introduce yourself to me. My name is Sianu. And yours?"

After a few moments of silence, a voice was heard in the darkness. "I will not speak to your kind."

"Well, you just have."

S'rae heard a deep breath. "Why won't you just die already?"

"I suppose it is not in my stars. Why won't you just stop and enjoy the tea together. I had made the two cups for us."

"For us?"

"Yes, as I am sure you know by now, I was expecting you. Do you like your tea with olive leaves and my favorite, lemon spice?"

"Yes… I mean… no… I mean… I cannot."

"You most certainly *can,* you just choose not to. Here." Sianu waved his hand to his chest and the ground reeled toward him, bringing a masked person from the shadows into the light of the fire.

S'rae froze in place. She felt her heart throb against her chest. This… this person… was wearing the same mask as her killer. S'rae fell back, horrified, her shaking hands pressed to her lips.

"What is wrong?" Sianu said, giving S'rae his hand.

"That person… that person is trying to kill me too."

Sianu's eyes dropped as he lifted her to her feet. "I am most sorry, but I believe this is why it was in the stars for us to meet. And for us to watch *this* vision."

S'rae watched the boy and the killer sit down and talk. Each day that had passed, S'rae noticed that the killer's body had become more relaxed. Instead of the shoulders that locked and fists clenched, the shoulders were relaxed and the palms now rested on the thighs.

It wasn't long until the big question arrived.

"So, now that you know I do not wish for you to be my enemy," the boy said to the killer. "And now that you know I would never wish to harm anyone, do you trust me enough to reveal yourself?"

"I—I do not understand why I am sent to kill you. They had always warned us that the final kill would be the most difficult, but I was not prepared for this."

"Final kill? So, you have killed others?"

"Yes… I am sorry. But… the people I killed were bad, very bad people. There was a purpose behind their deaths, but for you, I do not understand—"

"What do you mean by final kill?"

"You are my one hundredth, and after that, I become free."

"And what do you wish to do with your freedom?"

"I never thought about that."

"Maybe we could enjoy some more tea when you're free," the boy smiled with a chuckle.

"But… you'd be dead… oh," the killer chuckled. "That was

another one of your bad jokes, I see."

"I suppose I would like to think I am getting better at them."

"I suppose…"

S'rae felt a tension in the silence that followed, but surprisingly, not a hostile one.

"So… friend," the boy said, and S'rae saw that the killer's shoulder's locked up, "can I see who you are?"

"Friend?" S'rae could hear the killer's voice crack. "Why… why do you want me to be your friend? I want to kill you."

"You do not *want* to kill me. You were *sent* to kill me. But you won't."

"How do you know I won't? Why do you trust me?"

"Because… you are my friend."

"Do not trust anyone… not even your friends or family."

"Well, then maybe you are more than just a friend, friend. I do not believe in coincidences. I believe this, this moment was in our stars."

The killer let out a few deep breaths, grabbed the mask, and pulled it over the head, and S'rae's eyes widened at once.

S'rae fell back, slamming into the wall inside the Tree; the vision had ended. And she found herself trembling uncontrollably. Her legs shook as she stared at the markings on the wall.

"What is wrong?" Sianu said, placing his hand down for S'rae to grab.

"That person…" S'rae's voice was shaking along with the rest of her body, "that person who tried to kill you… that was… Olivia."

20

WHEN S'RAE STOOD UP, it took her a moment to remember exactly what she had seen—who she had seen. Then the flash of Olivia's blue eyes appeared again. She clutched her shaking palms before Sianu gently placed his hand on her arm.

"It is okay, S'rae," Sianu said. "You are safe here, I promise."

"But… but I won't be safe… not once I leave," S'rae said, her trembling hands now pressed against her chest as she tried her hardest to breathe. "I… I don't know who to trust anymore."

"You need to trust yourself, and have faith. Have faith… and it will have you."

S'rae looked up into Sianu's eyes, they were brown, smiling, and wonderful. They had a calming ability that made her feel like everything was okay, even though deep down she knew that wasn't the case.

"Thank you," S'rae said. "I needed that."

"I am glad that I could help," Sianu said before his eyes narrowed. "Speaking of help." He turned away and pressed his hand on the wall. The entire room glowed a bright white light before fading to blue. Then the room shook as the light burst apart into what looked like beads of water that gravitated toward Sianu's hand. Within seconds, the room became pitch black, except for the circular blue aura on the wall. Sianu put his arm into the wall and began to pull something out. The room shook more fiercely, and S'rae reached out into the darkness and grabbed onto what may have been vines to brace herself from falling.

As Sianu walked toward S'rae, he held a medallion that contained a blue gem that resonated with swirls of water. S'rae was sure it had a mind of its own.

Sianu gently grabbed S'rae's wrist and opened her palm. The moment the medallion touched her skin, visions blurred by so quickly she didn't have time to register a single image. But she couldn't explain what had happened, only that she felt rejuvenated beyond words—just like when she had found the Eye of Eve.

"What is this?" S'rae took a deep breath, the salty scent of fresh waves filled her nostrils.

"This... this is the Eye of Va'han." And when Sianu snapped his fingers, a vine burst from the wall, wrapping around the medallion then around her neck. "It is yours... do not lose it."

Great, she thought, another important relic that she was tasked with not losing, she wondered how long this would last. *I give it a day*.

"Why are you giving this to me?"

"This is what will save you, S'rae," Sianu said as he took a step back and smiled, as if happy that he fulfilled his purpose. "At least I hope it will."

"Yeah, what happens to me? Can you tell me?"

"What has happened will happen. As the Gods have said, we do not have the ability to change what is in our stars, but... as the Boy Who Never Lived has proven, maybe we do."

S'rae gasped at the idea of hearing someone else talk about Destrou. "How do you know him... Destrou?"

"Let's say I knew him a little too well that I got in trouble for it. You are not the only one who needed to tame their curiosity." And as if noticing the perplexed look on S'rae's face, Sianu continued: "But that is something I am forbidden from discussing."

"Can you at least tell me… what happened between you and Olivia?"

"Ah, you know her as Olivia, I knew her as Heron'da. As an angel. As someone who risked everything so we could be together… and I just hope I did not—" A tear fell from Sianu's eyes. "I just hope I had listened to her… that the real me listened to her."

"Why, what did she tell you?"

"You saw what she told me. And she told me that a thousand times more: *do not trust anyone*… not even your friends or family."

"And what do you think you did?"

"I was not meant for my element, not meant for Earth. I knew from the beginning that Water was my calling. Water values family, love, loyalty, and trust. And, unfortunately, I trust all, to a fault."

"Why?"

"Because… I would rather trust and be made a fool than not trust at all."

"Well, I have faith that everything worked out okay for the real you… but what happens now?"

"Well, now we say our goodbye."

"Goodbye?"

"The Eye of Va'han is the magic that kept me existing. Without it, I will no longer be; the room will lose its power, though its tunnels may still have some use for you. You see, its power is unmatched in its own way, rivaling even that of the Eye of Eve. And much like Eve, the Eye of Va'han is needed to be protected at all costs. And this was the way to make sure it would never get into the wrong hands."

"Then why are you giving it to me?"

"Because… it is in your stars to receive it, S'rae. Va'han said that this may save you… so I am glad the day has finally come… and I hope destiny is kind to you, friend. You deserve it."

Without thinking, S'rae had lunged forward and wrapped her arms around Sianu. "You are a breath of fresh air." She felt tears forming. "It was so nice meeting someone so nice and kind and caring and trusting... and I wish... I wish—"

"I know, S'rae... I wish it too."

"What?"

"That we would have made great friends had we lived in the same moment together. But Time works in wondrous ways. Maybe I will see you again in another life, when we are squirrels."

"Squirrels! How did you know I love squirrels?"

"I did not." Sianu squeezed S'rae tighter. "Be safe out there, S'rae. And remember... have faith... and faith will have you. Trust that the world is good. And with good, anything is possible."

"I'll miss you, Sianu," S'rae said, but before she had finished her last word, the room distorted into nothingness and she found herself on her hands and knees inside bushes.

She looked around and saw the phoenix relic on the cover of the tunnel and heard barking just outside, which must have been Mysol. S'rae then thought about what Sianu had said, how hundreds of years inside the room would only be a second outside of it. It was as if she was never gone.

But when she looked down and saw the glowing medallion on her chest, she knew that it had happened, that it wasn't a dream, that Sianu was real... and that—S'rae gulped—that death awaited her. And now Olivia's last words being "Sol'adari" had a whole new meaning to it. What role did she have in this? And then S'rae's heart dropped as the next question appeared: *what role does Bele have?*

S'rae glanced at the medallion in the mirror one last time before tucking it underneath her shirt. The timing could not have been any better as Lynn had just came barging in.

"There you are!" Lynn said, breathing heavily. "You know, for someone who doesn't have a lot of hobbies, you're sure difficult to find."

"Maybe hiding is one of my hobbies," S'rae smirked.

Lynn grinned then leapt at S'rae and squeezed her waist. "You know, I actually missed you! It hasn't been the same without you!"

"It's not like I died," S'rae said, and immediately she saw the life drain from Lynn's face as she pulled away.

"Don't joke around about that!" Lynn said, shaking her head. "But I'm here to get you because we have more training to do. You've been missing out on some pretty cool stuff! Retro'ku taught me…"

And as Lynn went on and on and on about all of the amazing spells she had learned, like vanishing and reappearing and extending her flaming blade out a dozen feet, S'rae couldn't help but feel annoyed that she was still stuck on the first lesson: creating a flaming sword.

"And I can even *fly* now! Yupp, you heard that right! Like actually fly! Pretty fast too!" Lynn's eyes widened as she hopped and skipped and led the way to the colosseum. "How's your sword coming along? You know, we can spend one of these nights finding out your fears! I want someone to train with! Retro'ku is… well, Retro'ku is… let's just say… him going his lightest is still too much."

"I'd *love* for him to go light on me," S'rae smiled.

"What does that mean, S'rae?" S'rae heard a voice from behind that made her eyes widen and feet sweat. "Why would you *love* for me to go light on you?"

"Yeah, S'rae," Lynn grinned. "Why *would* you want that, huh?" If Lynn's cheeks reddened just after saying that comment, S'rae could only imagine how red hers were right now.

"Err…" S'rae turned around and saw Retro'ku. She prayed to all the Divines that had ever existed that he wasn't shirtless, and she was happy to see that it worked out. It would have definitely made this awkward situation even more awkward if he—

Fire then combusted around Retro'ku, engulfing him in a flame that scorched ten feet high. His shirt dematerialized into ash and

S'rae found herself just staring at his rock hard abs.

"I said are you ready?" Retro'ku crossed his arms, a slightly annoyed tone to his voice. "I have asked you about ten times and you failed to respond. Are you okay?"

"What? Huh?" S'rae wiped the drool from her lips and shook her head violently. "Err... yes, I'm ready, sir Retro'ku, sir!" *S'rae... if you do not stop acting like a fool in front of him, I will hurt you!*

They passed through the colosseum's golden gates, crossed the entrance quickly, and were soon striding across the sand toward the center, where three cloaked individuals were standing. She wanted to ask who they were but before she could two of them had *poofed* in front of her as smoke filled the air.

"S'rae, it is nice to see you again," Gabrael said in a soft, welcoming tone. "It has been too long. I hear you have had some difficulties with your training."

"Er..."

"It is okay. I also hear you have stopped trying to track your brother."

"Er..."

"And that is also okay, we do not want to make it easier for them to find us."

S'rae turned to look at Lynn, who looked straight back at her, both wearing the same fear-filled expression.

"What... does that mean?" Lynn said before turning to Gabrael.

"Well, we have reason to believe that we will not be needing to go to them... for they... will be coming to us," Gabrael said, and when he snapped his fingers, the five of them had combusted into a flame and appeared in the center of the arena, standing next to the other cloaked individual.

S'rae grimaced as she immediately recognized the frame.

"Oh, it is you," Fa'laz chuckled, "the Canavar Slayer!" This time his laugh was so loud that S'rae noticed sand fall from some of the columns. "She's a funny one this one, Gabrael."

Gabrael glanced at Fa'laz and narrowed his eyes. "She is a special one… and you will treat her as such."

S'rae smiled at how quickly Fa'laz's grin faded, as if those few words were enough to silence him for the rest of the school year.

"As I promised," Gabrael said, "you help us train to prepare for battle and I will make sure we remove that metal from your hand."

"That is most gracious of you, my King," Fa'laz said genuinely. "I will finally be accepted back home."

"You will," Raaz'a said, who walked up to Fa'laz and grabbed his metal hand. "I am most intrigued by it… who had the gift of doing such a thing?"

"Gift? This… is *not* a gift," Fa'laz growled. "It is a curse."

"Ah yes, a curse," Raaz'a said. "Well, this is something we could speak more about at a different time then."

Fa'laz glanced at Gabrael, who said nothing, then nodded at Raaz'a. "If the King wishes."

"That is not something that concerns me," Gabrael said, raising his hand as his hilt burst into a flame. "Right now, I wish to make sure our pupils are ready for the battles that will occur. And since you are the seasoned veteran of wars, maybe you could use one of your goliaths to help train Lynn here?"

S'rae felt uneasy. Gabrael had completely disregarded her as if she wasn't good enough. *Only Lynn?*

Lynn looked at S'rae and mouthed "You got this!" to S'rae, as if understanding how hurtful that may have been.

S'rae tried to smile, but she knew she was a failure.

"And as for you, S'rae," Gabrael said, "you will work with Raaz'a. He is a master at fear, finding and overcoming it. There is no better person to help catch you up to speed."

Raaz'a and S'rae went to a far corner of the arena, where she practiced trying to create a flaming sword by thinking about everything that scared her, but none seemed to work well. Perhaps it was because she was half-paying attention; she couldn't help but focus on Fa'laz, who was channeling a spell into the sand.

And as S'rae thought about her fear of the Sol'adari, and a flicker ignited from her hilt, the ground rumbled uncontrollably. She turned her attention to Fa'laz as sand began to bubble up toward the sky. Right when she thought it couldn't possibly get any higher, it kept morphing and molding until it was about fifty feet tall.

When Fa'laz clapped his hands, the sand burst and before S'rae's eyes was a massive rock giant, who was made entirely of boulders and had gaps of space where joints would be.

"I-is that what I will be fighting?" Lynn gulped; and suddenly S'rae didn't feel jealous anymore.

"It is," Gabrael said. "I want you to use everything that Retro'ku taught you to defeat it."

"Umm…" Lynn wiped her palms onto her black robes. "I guesso… I'll try my best."

"Try? This is a battle, this is war, there is no *trying*," Fa'laz said. "You try, you die. You fight, you write… your history and theirs."

"He is right," Gabrael said. "And in battle, surprises are expected… BEGIN!"

"What?" Lynn immediately dove out of the way as the giant's boulder fist punched a crater into the ground where Lynn had just stood.

S'rae wished she could help, but as the fight intensified, she realized Lynn didn't need it. Each time the giant went to smash Lynn, she had vanished into smoke and reappeared at a different location on its body, stabbing at it with her flaming sword.

But although she was succeeding defensively, nothing seemed to be affecting the giant's armor.

After a few near misses, Lynn had leapt dozens of feet into the air. A flaming aura burst around her as she chanted words. The more seconds that passed, the higher into the air she floated, until she grabbed her sword with both hands and screamed so loud the arena quaked.

S'rae couldn't believe how quickly Lynn had learned these abilities, because what she saw next made her understand exactly why Lynn was a chosen one.

Lynn, fully ablaze, nearly a hundred feet in the air, had swung her sword down, looking like a river of lava splashing down onto the giant.

And the moment it made contact, it sliced the goliath completely in half before bursting into a million pieces.

"You did it!" S'rae screamed.

Lynn nodded at S'rae and pounded her fist to her heart as she floated to the ground. Her flame faded away and her clothes and hair fell still, no longer dancing crazily. She panted, pressing her palms against her knees.

"Decent," Gabrael said, unimpressed, "but we will need more from you."

"More!" Lynn shouted.

"And less," Gabrael said. "You do not want to use up all of your fire in battle, or you will be useless. Fire is about knowing when to strike and knowing when to conserve your energy."

"Did you not see what I did to it?" Lynn pouted.

"RETRO'KU!" Gabrael roared.

"Yes, father?" Retro'ku *poofed* in front of Gabrael.

"Show her."

"But... only one, father?"

"No." Gabrael looked at Fa'laz. "Can you create fifty?"

Fa'laz choked up for a second and grabbed his throat. "I do not believe I heard that correctly... did you say—"

"Fifty," Gabrael said. "I only asked for fifty because I was afraid that was your limit."

"Fifty, my King... fifty giants is a scary endeavor."

"Scary... for you. *He* is not you. He is my son."

Retro'ku still had a smile on his face while he was stretching.

"Do you think you can handle fifty, son?" Gabrael said.

"Sure," Retro'ku said blankly.

"See, he is not entertained," Gabrael said to Fa'laz. "How about one hundred?"

Retro'ku stopped stretching at once. His normally twinkling eyes turned red and narrowed. His smile vanished and all that remained was a face void of all emotion. A flame burst from his hilt as he curled his lip and slid his feet into a ready position.

"Now... my son is ready," Gabrael smiled.

It wasn't long until Retro'ku was in the center surrounded by a hundred rock giants.

S'rae wasn't even fighting and she couldn't help but feel her heart trying to escape her chest with each pump. Surely this wasn't possible. How could one boy take on all of these?

"BEGIN!" Gabrael shouted.

And just as Gabrael shouted the word, a flame erupted from Retro'ku and red lights had flashed throughout the arena; but Retro'ku hadn't even flexed a muscle. And just like that, his flame faded away and he put his hilt back into his robe.

What happened, S'rae thought. Why wasn't he fighting?

And as Retro'ku walked to Fa'laz and placed his hand on his shoulder, dozens of red lines appeared on the rock giants before they exploded and crumbled to the ground.

Fa'laz appeared dumbfounded, muttering the same incoherent words. But he wasn't the only one, S'rae and Lynn were both standing there with their jaws dropped, in complete disbelief as to what they had just witnessed... or didn't. Because S'rae didn't see Retro'ku even move so much as an inch, yet somehow... he did *that*?

Then suddenly the most pressing question appeared: if Retro'ku was capable of that, why would he need to keep training? Unless, the dangers that awaited them were even more powerful than she had thought. And that single thought was enough to make S'rae fall to her knees. If Retro'ku wasn't ready for the Shadow Army, how would any of them be?

"And what is this big hunk of mess we have going on here?" A voice boomed through the colosseum. S'rae looked up and saw Professor Leonna standing there with a small dog resting on her shoulder. "You all must clean this up, *right now*! We have preparations to do before the big Solermony Ball, which you,"—Professor Leonna looked at Gabrael—"are not invited to."

"He is your King," Raaz'a growled, "show some respect."

"He is *your* King, not mine." Professor Leonna turned away from them and raised her arms at the hundreds of students who were piling into the colosseum. "Now, wait, wait, wait, children! We will not advance until the trash gets cleaned up and evacuates the arena. And oh yeah, we can clean up this mess, too." Professor Leonna then pointed at the crumbled up pieces of rock giants.

S'rae's jaw dropped. Did Leonna just call Raaz'a and Gabrael, the King of Gods, trash?

"Yes, yes, I'm sure they thought this was impressive, my little Nutmeg." Leonna pet her dog. "Oh, I know that's something you'd be able to do with both paws tied behind your back, but you don't need to show off in front of them." The little dog growled and barked.

"I must ask you kindly to show some respect to our King," Fa'laz grabbed Professor Leonna's arm.

She pulled her arm away. "Whoa, w*hoa,* relax there, Metal Man, you're not my type! I like my men like I like my man, smart enough to *never* touch me like that ever again."

"I assure you, I have no interest in big girls," Fa'laz grinned.

"Heh!" Professor Leonna raised an eyebrow and turned to her students. "It's always a man with childbearing hips who says they don't like big girls. Sir, you are a big girl; so please leave the premises before my little Nutmeg makes you." The little dog wagged its tiny tail furiously. But shocking as it was, Fa'laz must have known something that S'rae did not, because he took one good look at the miniature dog and S'rae could have sworn she saw his hands tremble with fright.

And without so much of a word, Fa'laz had strolled away.

"Smartest thing he's ever done, isn't that right?" Leonna rubbed her nose against Nutmeg's.

"S'rae," Gabrael said, emerging from a puff of smoke, "after you are finished, you can continue your training at the cliff with Retro'ku."

"Yes, after this," Professor Leonna said, "she is the Ground-Stone Champion, and we are looking forward to seeing her defend her title at the Sol Fest!"

"Sol Fest?" S'rae said.

"Yes, the wondrous events that precede the Solermony Ball!" Professor Leonna clapped before giving Gabrael a nasty look. And when Gabrael, Raaz'a, and Retro'ku had vanished into a swirl of black smoke, Leonna's lip curled. "I still do not understand why they'd allow the likes of him here. But enough about them, we have MUCH to look forward to!"

When Leonna pushed her hand out and an oak staff appeared in her hand, she twisted it around before slamming it into the sand. The ground rippled for a few moments before the rubble molded into large, arching loops and sweeping, twisting swirls.

S'rae turned around and saw golden stone columns with relics carved into them rumble from the ground. And what once looked like an arena meant for battles and bloodshed, had now resembled a playground.

"There will be four events, but you can only choose one to participate in!" Leonna's voice echoed off the walls. "Over here will be for the ones interested in the arena, like our GroundStone Champion here, S'rae!" The crowd of students gasped when Leonna pointed at her.

"That's really her!"

"I can't believe I'm breathing her air!"

"Do you think now she'll sign my Sol's butt?"

"Yes, yes, children, we have the Champion here with us today," Leonna continued, "but this is not about her, it is about us... and providing our community with the greatest shows on Gaia as first years!" Leonna turned and pointed at the giant swirls and arcs of sand that looked like tangled wires intertwining one another. "Over there we have the Wave Riders! And here, we have our most prized sport: Boulder Dash with their illustrious Wave Runners!" Leonna pointed at the golden columns that had now morphed into goal posts with vines as a net.

"Eek!" S'rae heard a familiar squeal. "I can't wait for Boulder Dash!" And when S'rae scanned the crowd to find the source, she saw exactly who she was expecting: it was Emi, the adorable girl who was so obsessed with Boulder Dash she talked S'rae's ear off about it during the entire rock snake ride. And by her side was her Sol, a beautiful black panther.

S'rae walked up beside Emi and tapped her shoulder. When Emi turned around, her jaw dropped. "Nice to see you again, Emi, your panther is growing up to be quite beautiful."

Emi stood there for a few moments, mouth still wide open, not saying a word. "You... you remembered me?"

"Huh? Of course I remember you."

Then a smile beamed from her face as whispers circled around.

"Wow, Emi knows the GroundStone Champion!"

"I imagine you'll be entering into Boulder Dash, no?" S'rae said.

Emi simply smiled wide and nodded her head multiple times.

"WAIT!" Another familiar voice was belted as a boy stormed to the front of the line with a binder that looked like an ancient, leatherbound book. He was Yash, the boy who thought S'rae was a grandma. His shimmering raven was resting on top of his black turban that looked like the perfect nest. "The fourth event... you didn't say anything about the fourth one! Isn't that for the Card Duels Tournament!" He threw his arms into the air with the book in his hands, smiling wide, as if he was showing off his most prized possession.

"Oh, why yes," Leonna said dully. "Yes, how could I ever forget. Over there, far, far, far in the corner is where you will practice with your cards for their new tournament."

Yash grinned wickedly. "I will warn all of you, mere mortals, I've been waiting my whole life for this day, saving up every gold I could mine just to create the perfect deck to destroy all mortals who wish to perish under its might!" Drool was practically salivating from his lips.

Not a single word was said during the entire time he stomped his way toward the corner.

Emi broke up the silence and said, "You're going to do amazing in the arena again, S'rae! You were so perfect!"

"Err…" S'rae said, rubbing the back of her neck, "I don't think I'll be doing it."

"Excuse me, *GroundStone Champion*," Professor Leonna coughed in a way to make sure that title was heard loud and clear. "You are the Champion, everyone will be expecting you in the arena again!"

"I just don't think I want to again," S'rae said.

"Foolish," Leonna said, "you are the best we've seen, well, practically as good as the boy before you!"

"I just… don't know."

But nobody wanted to hear that she did not want to enter the arena again; nobody wanted to hear that she wasn't ready; not one single person seemed to have noticed the way her hands shook when just thinking about the arena again. That was because the moment she thought about competing again, she saw horrific images of an arrow shooting straight at her, she felt her heart jackhammer into her chest, and then she saw Olivia's cold blue eyes close just before whispering "Sol'adari." But S'rae couldn't get away; she was dragged back toward the arena section whenever she tried to observe the Wave Riders, who were now sitting inside in a stone vertical ring that revolved around them so fast, they practically looked like a blur whenever they blazed by S'rae.

"Yes, it looks fun, it really does," Leonna said, "but many of them have been practicing Wave Riding since they were born. You are a natural in the arena, S'rae! I have faith you'll win again, so you don't worry about that."

But all S'rae wanted to say, without looking like an arrogant jerk, was that she knew she would win, but the possibility of losing wasn't what scared her… it was the fact that everyone thought they had captured the killer, but she knew the person was still out there somewhere, and entering the arena again felt like a mistake waiting to happen.

But S'rae managed to sneak away when Leonna went to stop a fight from breaking out at the card game section. She didn't know what they were fighting about, all she heard was "my deck *this* and my deck *that*."

S'rae watched in awe as students channeled spells into the ground that turned their shoes into rollerballs, stones at the soles of their feet that made them run a hundred times faster than they normally would. She saw the way they'd ride waves of sand before jumping into the air and launching a boulder into the goal posts. Watching the waves take them through the sky brought a smile to her face. It reminded her of some of her best childhood days, when she'd practice creating waves of her own. And then she thought about the time she had battled against the canava—S'rae's eyes widened as forbidden moments began to surface. She felt her hands clench so tightly that her fingernails dug into her skin. She needed to avoid that memory at all costs, it'd break her. It always did.

S'rae closed her eyes. *Breathe, S'rae. Relax. Breathe. It's fine. It was in the past, look ahead to the future. Look ahead.* Her breathing calmed down. And when she opened her eyes, she saw Emi grinning at her.

"You want to try Boulder Dash, don't you?" Emi winked.

S'rae looked over her shoulder and saw Leonna wagging her finger at the boys while little Nutmeg dragged a boy across the dirt and away from the crowd. "I do want to, yes."

"Well, here's the trick about waves." Emi lifted her foot and pointed at her toes. "You want to focus all of your energy into these toes, right *here*, so when you kick the ground, the sand shoots out exactly where you want it to go. But too hard and it'll crumble. And too soft, and it'll break before it reaches its peak. You need to get it *just* right!"

S'rae smiled at Emi and gently pat her head. "Do you remember how I was in the arena?" S'rae said to Emi, and when she nodded, S'rae continued: "Well, that's not the only thing I'm good at." And just like that, S'rae's eyes turned white as the ground rumbled. She channeled all of her energy into her foot that stomped onto the ground as a massive wave shot S'rae into the air. Her hair danced in front of her eyes as she eclipsed the students training below. She watched them all stop what they were doing as they arched their heads and saw her run across the sky on a stream of sand. And when she landed in the stands of the GroundStone colosseum, an eruption of cheering, whistling, and clapping was heard from below.

Leonna's head popped out from one of the stone seats next to S'rae, and soon her after, her whole body emerged.

"S'rae... where in the love of Gaia did you learn to do *that*!" Leonna's voice cracked. "But more importantly... why would you have ever gone to Fujita? You were born for GroundStone. You are exactly where you belong... and I wish to see just how great of an Earthie you can become."

"Thank y—" S'rae's train of thought had been distracted by the most peculiar squirrel sitting in the stands, staring directly at her. She knew it wasn't B'se because she had made him a vest to protect him from arrows; but something felt odd about this one, perhaps because of how still it was, not even its tail moved.

"You are most welcome," Leonna said, hopping around most excitedly in front of S'rae, who kept shifting her head to keep an eye on the squirrel. "Now here is the thing... disregard what I said earlier about you being the GroundStone Champion and how you need to do the arena event." Leonna shook her head. "Oh no, no, no, forget I *ever* said that. You see... what you did right there, I think you could finally end the First Years' Curse!"

"Err... First Years' Curse?" S'rae ducked her head to look through Leonna's armpit.

"You like the name? I came up with it, don't let that Di'Tukia tell you otherwise! But yes, the first years have never won a Boulder Dash game at Sol Fest since... well... forever! BUT, I think with you, I can finally give it to ol' Di'Tukia!" Leonna grinned wickedly as she rubbed her palms together. "Yes, yes, yes, we will *finally* win!"

S'rae wished to be excited, but she was too focused on the squirrel who was now nowhere to be found. Odd.

And after Leonna absorbed the two of them into the ground, they emerged in front of an eager crowd that erupted into a frenzy.

"Can you please teach me!"

"Was that just your toes for that wave, or did you put some sole into it?"

"Yes, yes," Leonna interrupted. "We know our Champion is quite impressive, but please, we must now prepare her for... BOULDER DASH!"

Despite the compliments she had been given, S'rae found herself walking away from the colosseum in a funk that she wished she could explain. She had her head down, thinking only about where she had failed, not succeeded. She didn't know what was worse: that she was a failure at Fire... or that Gabrael had given her false hope. Maybe the fire didn't burn in her eyes. Maybe she was meant only for Earth and Wind, and maybe that was perfectly fine. Gabrael was wrong about her, and it hurt because it heightened the deepest insecurities in herself, telling her that she was never good enough.

Then a different type of sorrow weighed her down: regret. She couldn't help but think, once again, that she had made the wrong decision to attend Fujita. At Fujita, whenever she did well, it was matched with jealousy and hatred. Here, they adored her. And now she was even more frustrated that she could not explain the emptiness she felt. The sinking feeling in her gut that told her despite receiving everything she had ever wanted—love from friends and strangers, being popular and liked—still there was *something* missing.

Then her eyes watered thinking about how the last five years of her life could have been different. Maybe if she had attended GroundStone instead, she and Vayp could have fixed things; maybe none of this would have happe—*No stop! Don't take the blame for this! He's the traitor!*

S'rae put her foot down—quite literally judging by the crater at her feet—and decided to not be completely useless against the Shadow Army. Whether she'd admit it or not, she knew she played some role in the Shadow Army's arrival; so if she wasn't able to help out in battle as a pupil of Fire, then maybe she could find other ways to help. The last thing she wanted was to go back to train with Retro'ku today and for him to think she was a quitter, a loser with nothing to provide for the battle that awaited. So after rummaging through her head for a few minutes, S'rae thought about Fa'laz, how Gabrael considered him a veteran of war. Maybe she could pick his brain about what non-Fire students could do against the shadows.

Though it was completely against her best interest, she shook her head, rubbed her sweaty palms against her robe, and drew his relic into the sand.

When S'rae arrived at the giant stone doors that said *DANGERS of GAIA. Defend all, but trust none*, she felt her palms begin to sweat.

The familiar moldy stench spreading from the tunnel to the room met her nostrils as she pushed against the doors. As expected, they didn't budge. And S'rae's fingers tingled with warmth as she felt around for any type of opening.

And just when she was about to give up and turn around, the door liquified and morphed about before forming into a stone face that grumbled: "I was not expecting two visitors today. We are just finishing now."

The giant doors groaned open as Raaz'a glided by, not even acknowledging her as he passed. Though his face was covered by his hood, he seemed to be annoyed or frustrated, she could tell by his quick pace and heavy breathing.

The door slammed shut as Raaz'a left.

"What's wrong with him?" S'rae said, turning back into the now empty room.

"He inquired about how I received this," said the deep voice of Fa'laz right behind S'rae, making her heart leap. He raised his metallic hand that glistened from the candlelight.

"What did you say?" S'rae tried her hardest to appear calm when she turned to face Fa'laz.

"That it was an accident," Fa'laz said mournfully, "and no more harm should be done to the person. They have went through enough difficult times already." His voice dropped almost to a whisper. His eyes focused on the ground for a few moments before staring at S'rae, who quickly looked away.

Though Professor Fa'laz remained still, the ground rumbled and swept him to the far end of the room without him ever needing to take a step. He sat in his chair, which looked more like a metal throne before the fire, and faced S'rae.

"And why is it that you are here, Canavar Slayer?"

S'rae wanted to lash out at him for mocking her traumatic experience, but that wouldn't help her. Right now, that was exactly what she needed: help... and answers.

"I want to be ready for the Shadow Army," S'rae said, staring at the ground. "And I don't want to be useless."

"Well, I am sorry that I cannot help you out. We all will be useless, except for *them*."

S'rae knew who *them* was, the group she was supposed to be included in but only Lynn was. "Well... what if they aren't enough?"

"What do you think I have this for?" Fa'laz's metal hand *clanged* against a tablet resting on the arm of his chair. "Though my tribe will never accept me back... I hope this letter will reach them." S'rae was almost sure she heard his voice crack before he finished.

"Why won't they accept you?"

Fa'laz said nothing, he only balled up his metal fist before slamming it onto the chair. Dust fell through the cracks of the ceiling as the room rattled.

"That is not your concern, Canavar Slayer."

"I—I'm sorry." S'rae put her head down. "But please... there must be something in your defense books that can help us. Something that maybe I can do to help, even though I'm not Fire."

Fa'laz snapped his fingers and the walls shook for a moment before a book bulleted into his hand. "This book may have what you are looking for... but you will not be happy with what you find."

Fa'laz's voice was so cold, S'rae felt a chill shock down her spine. "Why? What's in it?"

"Powerful spells. So powerful... you are forbidden from channeling them."

"Then why... would you show me?"

"So you can understand... how useless you will be against them."

S'rae felt her lips pucker up; she bit back what she wanted to say and instead said: "The Shinshei Laws?"

Fa'laz nodded and threw the book at S'rae. She was glad that she didn't try to catch it, because the moment it landed next to her feet, it embedded deep into the ground, smoke billowing from the cracks. It must have weighed a ton.

It took all the strength she had to lift the cover and flip through its pages. And as Fa'laz sat there staring longingly at the tablet now in his hand, S'rae quickly read through a few pages. Nothing seemed like it'd help against a Shadow Army. One spell made the caster swap bodies. Another gave the ability to connect to another person's Sol when they did not have a Sol of their own.

"Why would someone do this *Muba'dala* spell?" S'rae looked up at Fa'laz.

It took a while before he answered. He gently placed the tablet on the floor and wiped his eyes before saying, "It is a forbidden protection spell."

"How could connecting to someone else's Sol be a protection spell?"

Fa'laz chuckled. "Oh how pleasant it is to be so naive and innocent. Do not let the world change you, Canavar Slayer."

S'rae shook her head and kept reading. This book had an infinite list of spells no longer allowed on Gaia, but none piqued her interest quite like the last. That was because there was no description; and it was the only one written in a brownish, maroon ink, as if it was written by the blood of Gods. And maybe it was.

"What about this one... the *Kiya'shin*?" S'rae said, placing her finger onto the page.

Before she could lift her head, the book had absorbed into the ground. "That is enough reading for you."

"Why? What is that one about?" S'rae stared at the spot where the book once was. "The book didn't say anything."

"That is because... it should never be mentioned. *Ever* again. Which is why I think we are done here."

"But—"

"We are *done* here." This was the deepest she had ever heard his voice. She knew at once to not ask anymore questions. But now, knowing herself all too well, it will drive her insane if she didn't find out what this *Kiya'shin* was.

She lifted up from her knees and brushed off her robes. "Well, thank you for helping, kind of."

"Just do not mention that spell to anyone. Do I make myself clear?"

S'rae only nodded before running out of the room; the last thing she wanted to do was lie to someone who looked like they enjoyed eating students for breakfast. But the truth was... her heart pulsed with a new energy that told her she may have just found what she was looking for.

By the time she made it to the top of the hill, Retro'ku was seen sitting at the cliff side by side with his shadow. Red lines glowed on his back and arms like hot embers, taking the shape of different tribal patterns.

When a leaf crunched at her foot, the shadow turned around, squealed, then vanished into the ground.

Retro'ku wiped his eyes before turning around and smiled when their eyes met. "Sorry if I kept you waiting long."

"No... it's okay," S'rae said, already feeling her nerves get the best of her. "I just came. Sorry for... err... interrupting your quality time."

"It is okay, S'rae." S'rae couldn't explain it, but she still felt something wiggle in her stomach whenever he said her name. "It was just time with my inuwa."

"Your inu-what?"

Retro'ku chuckled. "I am most sorry, I believe you would just call it my shadow." His smile glowed once again before fading all too quickly.

"What's wrong?" S'rae said, not used to seeing anything but a smile on his face.

"It is just that... no, never mind."

"No, tell me, you can tell me anything."

His smile reappeared. "That is most nice of you, S'rae." He turned back to the gorgeous panoramic view of GroundStone with the pyramids, statues of animals the size of mountains, and the sun that added a gold glow to the already golden setting. Retro'ku sighed before continuing: "It is just that... sometimes when I am with my inuwa... and I just talk out into the wind... it feels like I am with him again."

"With who?"

S'rae noticed Retro'ku gulp and take a deep breath. "With my brother," he said, wiping his nose.

"I'm sorry," S'rae heard the sorrow in her own voice. She wanted to ask what happened to him, but she knew she would not like to have that question asked to her, so she fought off her deep curiosity, which said a lot.

"It is okay," Retro'ku said "There are some things in life that are beyond our control. Death is one of them. And this,"—S'rae now heard his voice carry a weight of conviction—"this is why I train."

"You're so powerful! Why do you need to train so much? Like how can anything beat you!"

"Because I have seen my future. I have seen the deaths that I could have stopped, if only I was stronger. So now, I have trained every day since. I will be ready. I *must* be ready."

"Don't you ever... want to have fun?"

Retro'ku said nothing for a few moments. "I wish I knew what fun was."

Everything inside S'rae told her to SHUT UP and NOT RUIN THIS MOMENT, she felt her hands shake and her knees buckle just thinking about taking this leap of faith. She closed her eyes tightly and said: "Maybeeee... weeeee.... cannnnnnn.... haveeeeeee..... funnnnnnn.... together?" And just like that, without expecting to, she had completely fainted to the ground.

Except... she thought she did.

In the time it took from her to faint and fall to the ground, Retro'ku had already held her in his hands. It was so quick, she didn't even have time to process what had happened, never mind to dare say a word.

"Are you okay, S'rae?" Retro'ku said, his piercing gaze channeling life into her.

"I am now." *No, did you really just say that? S'rae, you are forbidden from saying another word this entire year! Do not say anything about B'se, squirrels, or make any weird noises, okay!*

But the smile on Retro'ku's face made her pang of regret sting a little less. *Okay, S'rae, you get two points for that one. But don't mess this up!*

"So, how can we have fun?" Retro'ku said.

And S'rae felt her face drop. Here she was staring at a handsome boy who had spent every second of his hundreds of years on this planet training alone—well, with his inuwa—to the point that he didn't even know how to have fun. Suddenly, instead of seeing Retro'ku as the untouchable son of a God whose presence alone would make her nervous, she saw him as a boy who deserved more. A person who deserved to live.

"Well… I would say we could go to the Solermony Ball, but that's only for people with Sols."

"Let them have their own fun that day then." Retro'ku smirked. "And let us have ours?"

Wait… what just happened? Was what she thought just happened actually what had just happened? Or was she completely overthinking what just happened? She needed answers.

Did he just… ask me… on a date?

S'rae couldn't help it, but she knew if she saw herself right now, her face would be the same color of a monkey's butt.

Don't mess this up, S'rae. You only have ONE WORD TO SAY. That's it, S'rae! JUST! ONE! WORD! I'm going to kill you if you mess this up.

How could one word feel like it could take one decade to say? "Er... yes."

"Great!" Retro'ku flipped backwards dozens of feet into the air and landed with a flaming sword in his hand. "I am looking forward to it! And now, we must train."

And the smile that had blazed on S'rae's face had just been doused. She had just made the greatest accomplishment in the history of life, and now she had to tell him how useless she would be? That there was no point in them training?

"Er..." S'rae rubbed the back of her neck. "I don't think I have the fire in my eyes."

"You may not be a natural like Lynn, but if my father says you have the fire in your eyes, you do. It will just take longer. You may have some fears hidden, even from yourself."

"But... what if he is wrong?"

"My father is *never* wrong." But then Retro'ku paused for a moment, and S'rae saw tears forming in his eyes. "Well, not about *this*, at least."

S'rae wanted nothing more than to ask him for details, but she knew how much of a mistake that would be. Between what Leonna had said about Gabrael and now this, S'rae was beginning to think that maybe she was the naive, innocent girl. Maybe she was wrong about Gabrael.

She tried to think about anything to switch up the conversation, but before she put much thought into it, her mouth had already rambled on: "Have you ever heard of *Kiya'shin*?"

And right when it left her mouth, she instantly regretted it, thinking back to her inner voice telling herself repeatedly to NOT RUIN THE MOMENT!

And at once, the moment was ruined in the form of an explosion that rattled the planet of Gaia.

Retro'ku had erupted into a flame so bright and tall that the sky darkened upon impact. The once bright blue sky had now turned black with crackles of lightning dancing in the clouds. But worst of all… was Retro'ku's eyes. They were blackened, but where his pupils would be, there were red symbols that blazed with fire.

"NEVER!" Retro'ku's voice seemed to echo inside her skull, rattling her brain. "NEVER mention that in my presence. EVER AGAIN!"

S'rae had wanted to apologize. She wanted to reach out to him, but all within the blink of an eye, Retro'ku had burst through the sky, leaving behind a trail of black and red smoke from the cliff to the horizon.

S'rae fell to her knees and sobbed into her shirt. *I TOLD YOU NOT TO RUIN THE MOMENT!*

"Why can't you just think before you speak!" S'rae screamed aloud. "Why do you ruin everything!?"

"You do not ruin everything." S'rae heard a voice from behind, making her jump to her feet.

When she turned around, she wiped her eyes and shook her head. It was Bele, standing there, tossing a berry into his mouth.

"You know," Bele said, "for someone who excels at nearly everything, you are quite hard on yourself."

S'rae rubbed her eyes even more. "Heh, excels at nearly everything? I think those berries got you drunk."

"Some actually do, maybe you're right." He tossed another berry into his mouth and his shoulders locked up as his head cocked back. "Oh, now *that* was good! Here, have one!"

"I don't want one." After spending time with Sianu and seeing that Olivia was the killer, S'rae knew she couldn't trust anyone. And Bele was at the top of the list. Maybe he could poison her.

"Of course you don't want one." Bele threw a berry at S'rae, who caught it without thinking. "Yeah, you know, most people who don't want one… would have just let it fall."

"I… I don't like wasting food."

"And I don't like sharing food, yet here we are. And there you are, enjoying my delicacy."

S'rae hated that everything in her told her not to eat it, yet still she put it in her mouth as waves of citrus fruit splashed onto her tongue. This time she tasted fruits she couldn't even name, but delicious was an understatement.

And as S'rae licked her lips and moaned, Bele walked up to her. "You won't hear this often from me, or probably ever again... but you were right."

"I'm right a lot, you have to be more specific."

"Oh!" Bele pulled his chin back and grinned. "Want another one?" A berry rolled through his fingers.

"No!" She eyed it for a few moments longer before grabbing it and stuffing it in her mouth. Mistakes could never taste so good. "But right about what?"

"Well, squirrels are quite fun!"

Her eyes lit up. "Wait... was that you?"

Bele smirked. "I wanted to see if you were ready."

"Well, you have a creepy way of doing it."

"Want another one?" But he had already given it to her before she even replied. "Well, I didn't want you to get nervous with me watching you."

"Umm... why would I get nervous?" S'rae wanted to punch his punchable smirk.

"It just happens."

"Maybe to people who don't think you're the creepiest person on Gaia."

"Oh, back to being rude S'rae, I see. Now, what did I do to you?"

"You came here."

Bele chuckled. "Oh, I see. Well, I just wanted to tell you that I know you are ready."

"Ready for what?" S'rae was sure this was an invitation to a trap. She needed to stop being the naive little girl.

"For your dragon."

S'rae practically choked on air. She was so caught up with ev-erything else going on, between learning Earth, trying to train Fire, and preparing for a Shadow Army, she had almost forgotten about this dragon talk. But then Olivia's eyes flashed as a vision, and S'rae couldn't help but think that maybe Olivia was included in one of the people she shouldn't trust.

"Why do you think I'm ready for a dragon?" S'rae said, raising an eyebrow.

"For starters, you're the most impressive student who has ever stepped foot inside GroundStone." S'rae hated that she felt her face peel into a wide smile. She tried her hardest to make her face rest flat. "And... a dragon is said to be left only for the best of the best... and I think I found her."

Okay, S'rae, do NOT fall for his tricks. Do not let him butter you up. No... stop smiling. You stop smiling right now!

But she did not stop smiling. If anything, she made it worse with a giggle and a snort.

She hated that he was putting to rest all of her insecurities, al-most effortlessly. Because right now, she felt strong and powerful and ready to take on a Shadow Army, while just a few minutes ear-lier, she felt inadequate, useless, a dead weight to lug around. She hated that she wanted to not trust him, yet she couldn't shake off the warm feeling in her stomach when his words would reach her ears.

"So," Bele said, "after we go to the Solermony Ball, I will take you to your dragon."

Wait... huh? She even squeezed her fingers into her ears to see if they were working properly. "Er... sorry... we? And Solermony Ball?"

"Yeah, after we. Go. To. The. Solermony. Ball. I will take you to your dragon." And now he went right back to being that jerk with the punchable face, talking to her as if she was a baby.

"Well, sorry to ruin your imaginary plans, but I can't go," S'rae said, crossing her arms.

"But you can... and you will."

"Oh, is that so?"

"Yes, I'm a professor now. I've never been to one. You've never been. It'll be our first."

"Aren't you supposed to ask someone to go with you? Not tell them they are? It doesn't work like that, you know."

"Right... just like you saying 'no' to my berries doesn't work either. Some questions are rhetorical and only asked to be polite."

"And... you chose not to be polite because?"

"Because polite is for later. Right now, I just want to enjoy my berries."

S'rae felt her face go flat. "And what's later?"

"Can't tell you." He threw a berry into the air and caught it with his tongue. "It's a surprise for you."

A surprise? Don't do it, S'rae. Don't trust him! He's being too nice. Don't be naive.

"I'll take you to it right now." Bele stuck his hand out and S'rae stared at it for a few moments. "Do you trust me?"

All S'rae could think about was what role did Bele have in all of this? She didn't want to be a fool and trust someone like him. Everything in her told her not to, but then a different voice said otherwise. Sianu's words began to ring through. S'rae had been logical her entire life, it was what helped her avoid many potentially bad mistakes. But... what if they weren't mistakes that she had avoided? Since her time at Fujita, she had lived life as if it was something fragile, meant to be protected with no risks taken. But around Bele, he made her feel safe yet powerful, not delicate and fragile. What if behind what she thought were mistakes waiting to happen were things greater than she could have ever imagined? Sianu had said that he would rather trust and be made a fool than not trust at all. And he even trusted the very person who had been trying to kill him, who ended up being the greatest gift life could have given him.

What if… what if now was the time to finally see exactly what existed behind the doors she'd normally keep closed.

She hated Bele for many reasons. She hated how easily he could sway her emotions. She hated that his punchable face could also make her skin tingle. She hated the way he thought he could get anything he wanted, and hated even more that it worked each time on her. She hated the idea of someone being the puppetmaster of her emotions, and hated that he knew just what to say to bring a smile to her face when all she wanted to do was be mad. She hated that she tried her hardest to hate him… only to realize she didn't hate him at all.

If this were to be a mistake, then let it be the greatest one she will make. She thought of Sianu as she looked Bele in the eyes, and even thought of him when she slid her hand into Bele's.

She could only hope that what Sianu had said was true: to trust that the world is good, and with good, anything is possible.

"I trust you," S'rae said. And what scared her the most was that she meant it. She prayed to the Divine that this was not a trap. Gaining her trust was a difficult feat, now she only hoped it wouldn't be used as a weapon against her.

21

"WAKE UP!" DESTROU SCREAMED. He shook Ranmau so hard that his body lifted off of the ground. Nothing happened, he had been motionless ever since he collapsed. There was not even a thump in his chest—he was as still as the snow around him.

Running out of options, Destrou questioned what to do. Should he abandon him the way that he was—defenseless and around a gang of predators?

If I stay, then I'm going to lose the challenge. But if I leave and win... I think the Sensu could heal him. It could probably heal everything. And if I don't do anything... we both lose. He needed to make a decision now before he had no options to choose between.

He remembered what happened to the lost boys whose heart stopped due to starvation or other reasons, there was no saving them. It was hopeless, anyway. Sorrow overwhelmed him as liquid ice poured from his eyes and nostrils. The sorrow turned into rage, filling his mind with thoughts of Elu and Ranmau. Rage turned into frustration, striking his forearms onto Ranmau's chest.

One hit, two hits, three hits, his mind blanked out as he let out his frustration the only way that he knew how. He lost track of time and didn't know how to stop. Emotion poured through his eyes, blurring his vision.

"Don't leave me, not like this!" he screamed many times. No matter how much revenge he wanted for Elu's death, he did not want it to end like this. He couldn't feel anger, only fear. The fear that his world crumbled before his eyes and he was not ready to accept it. He needed Ranmau, more than he thought. "Please don't leave me... I need you. You're all I have. I'm sorry!"

Tiring himself out, he flung himself back, sitting against the Wall, pressing his palms against his soaked eyes.

A cough was heard through the crying. Destrou shot up and lunged his body toward Ranmau.

"You're alive?" Destrou screamed, covering his trembling lips. His eyes were glazed over and his pumping chest made it difficult to breathe in between his sobs.

"I'm fine," Ranmau said softly. His eyelids opened hesitantly. He had a momentary gaze of confusion, looking around until his eyes focused on Destrou. He leaned his head back into the snow, taking a deep breath. His chest rose and fell.

"No!" Destrou screamed. "No you aren't! How am I ever going to know you need help when you always say you're fine?"

"It's okay," Ranmau replied, "that wasn't the first time that happened. I'm fine now. It has been getting better." He coughed.

"Better? How long has this been going on?"

Ranmau said nothing.

"Why do you always keep hiding things from me?"

Silence.

"That's it, get up!" Destrou said, surprised at how strong his voice echoed off of the Wall. "We are winning this stupid challenge whether you want to or not. You need the food and we are going to get it. No one will stop me. Not you, not the Leader... no one. It will help you. Believe me, this will make you feel better than ever."

"Heh," Ranmau smirked. "I guess I do have another challenge

to win. I hope you enjoy second place again."

"Yeah, right," Destrou laughed, wiping the tears from his eyes. "You're going down."

Ranmau surprisingly received a burst of energy, rolling onto his feet as if everything was okay.

If this was something that happened before, why would he keep it to himself? Ranmau seemed okay, so maybe he was fine, but the fear still lurked in the back of Destrou's mind—the fear that at the blink of an eye his world could be torn apart. Again.

The horizon expanded for what looked like miles and none of the boys were visible; they had a lot of ground to cover. Luckily, they were rumored to be the fastest in the Village. But unfortunately, the next stage was less about speed and more to do with grit.

* * *

They made it to the entrance of the Ruins. It had large columns made of a mixture between ice and stone with deep engravings that seemed to have been carved by a jagged object.

"I guess we have to go in there," Destrou said, grabbing onto a column. His hand grazed along patches of smooth and rough textures.

"Make sure to stay close," Ranmau said, wincing as he pressed his arm against his chest.

It worried Destrou that Ranmau was so reserved. The sympathy that he felt finally started to break even with his animosity. He felt that he shouldn't still be mad, but, to him, to not be mad would be to forget what he did to Elu.

It's bad enough that I'm starting to forget little things about you, Elu—like how large your smile was or the way your nose moved when you laughed. If I forgive Ranmau for what he did to you, I would be a terrible friend. That wouldn't be right—we were great friends. No. Better than great, you were my best friend. And I'll never forget you.

Ranmau grabbed onto Destrou, breaking his trance. "Destrou?

I've said your name four times already, are you okay?"

"Yeah," Destrou said, shaking his head and stepping into the Ruins. "Let's do this."

The tunnel of ice glowed a bright blue, tainting everything in his vision with a blue filter. His hands, his clothes, the rocks, everything the light touched appeared more blue. The deeper they looked into the tunnel the more the blue faded to black. They wanted to press on quickly but they knew that they needed to walk with caution. With the darkness obscuring the visibility of what was ahead, it created a perfect opportunity for a stealthy ambush.

Destrou knew this. And by the way Ranmau's hand pressed ahead and his eyes shifted from side to side, he knew that Ranmau understood the danger as well.

"The Leader won't make this next stage easy. We need to be careful," Destrou said to Ranmau, pressing his hand on the blue ice. He was mesmerized by its formation and clarity, the way it bubbled and reflected light.

"I don't know how many boys the Leader will keep behind this time, but the more the better—that means less are moving forward," Ranmau smirked. "I hope they brought everyone if they want to actually stop us."

They walked deeper into the Ruins, fascinated by how massive the ice sculptures and buildings appeared. They were made with a hybrid material that had a smooth yet rough surface—something that seemed fused between stone and ice, like the columns. The layout was surprisingly organized with equal distances between the buildings. Different shapes and sizes surrounded them. Some of the buildings had three windows stacked on top of one another and others had two. Despite being perfect in design, they were rugged and old. Time appeared to have won the battle.

Who used to live down here? Why was this place off limits?

Destrou remembered his conversation with Elu about things once living inside of ice.

I wish you could see this... maybe you'd be able to answer all of the questions I have right now.

Destrou walked deeper into the cave, tossing the emblem from palm to palm. There was an eerie hum that resonated in the walls, as if this place was alive. He searched for an alternate route anytime he passed by a ray of light where snowflakes shimmered and danced around weightlessly. And as he inched closer into a black void, his heart raced and chest pumped.

He waited for a moment. He didn't know if the tunnel was getting smaller or if the buildings were getting larger, but the space definitely got tighter and darker. The buildings at the end fused into one another, connecting with the ceiling as if they were one entity, trapping them inside.

The odd white noise that hummed from behind the walls vanished. The Ruins became completely silent—too silent. Destrou hated silence. It forced his mind to drift away, and whenever his thoughts wandered he always heard Elu's voice, triggering emotions that weren't always good.

A faint noise interrupted the stillness, but he couldn't recognize where it came from. It was difficult to see his hands in front of his face never mind the location of sound.

"Did you hear that?" Destrou said, turning around.

Nothing.

He waited a moment, pacing his eyes back and forth. Darkness. When he turned back around, the obscure silhouette that was Ranmau was gone.

"Ranmau?" he whispered softly. He repeated it again, softer. "This isn't funny... where'd you go?"

He heard another noise. A faint shuffle. This time it sounded close by—too close. He placed his fists up near his face, readying himself for anything.

The Leader must've given them orders to ambush us here. It makes sense, there isn't a lot of room for us to move.

He slowed his pace down, tip toeing his way deeper into the cave.

He pressed his fingers against his lips, making sure that he wasn't going crazy. He seemed to have lost all of his senses. It was pitch black, there was complete silence, and his body became numb to the point that he had forgotten his feet were still pressing forward.

Where did he go? Don't tell me he's the scared one now, too. This whole protecting him thing is a lot more work than I thought. How many am I going to have to fight off of him now?

Destrou felt a breeze drift across his neck. Someone was behind him, it was too late. In that instant, he whipped around, and punched his fist into a clenched palm.

"We are good to go now," Ranmau said calmly, releasing Destrou's fist.

"What?" he replied. "What do you mean? Where'd you go?"

"There were six of them... which means we don't have much time. We need to go now."

Before Destrou's question reached his lips a loud thud interrupted him.

There was another thud—this one was louder. And another. And another. The noises sounded too familiar to him. If he wasn't mistaken that was the sound of bodies hitting the floor.

"That was only fou—" before he finished his thought, two more loud shakes vibrated the ground. He paused a moment, trying to process what happened but he couldn't get a clear image in his head. All he saw was darkness. "How did you... wait... huh? I guess you really must be fine." Destrou shrugged. Just when Destrou thought Ranmau couldn't impress him anymore, he was wrong.

"That means we have a clear path," Ranmau said, pressing forward. "But, again, we need to move, *now!*"

Ranmau led the way deeper into the Ruins and down a few rough staircases into an open area. Beyond the space, the floor changed from ice to stone, and the walls reflected a deep white glow, revealing an illuminated pillar in the center. Destrou placed his hand over his eyebrows, squinting so he could see.

Faint sounds of grunts and moans echoed the closer they made it to the center. The grunts stopped and were replaced by soft slapping sounds that softened until they disappeared completely.

"They are close," Destrou whispered. "We still have a chance."

They looked around, wondering where the noise came from. The room was a pure white circle filled with scratch marks and gashes on the walls and floor.

Battles must've happened here.

"There!" Ranmau pointed at a hole in the center of the room. The pillar was moved enough so that a body could fit in it. The hole was dark and mysterious and no wider than the width of their torsos.

"I wonder how deep it is?" Destrou said, pulling off one of his shoes and dropping it into the hole. He leaned his head closer to the opening, pressing his ear to the edge.

He expected to hear a sound. Instead, he heard silence. Seconds passed, and still nothing.

"Welp," Destrou shrugged his shoulders, "this is the only way down and I need to make sure you get that food."

"What are you doing?" Ranmau asked as Destrou stood up and brushed his knees.

"See you down there." Without second-guessing his decision, Destrou jumped into the hole. Ranmau's eyes widened—probably because he was shocked that Destrou wasn't afraid. Destrou had always been afraid of heights and the unknown, but it was now apparent that something was very different about him. And maybe Ranmau was beginning to realize that Destrou was no longer the brother he used to be.

Destrou felt weightless. It was an eerie feeling, pressing his heart against his ribs and his brain against his skull. For a moment, he had the urge to throw up—not the contents in his stomach but his stomach itself. He wrapped his arms around his chest, grabbing his elbows. He wanted to scream with everything that he had but remaining silent was too important. He had no plan for what happened after he landed, and after freefalling for seconds, he began to question if he would even survive.

Wind wrapped faster around his ankles and torso. The air felt different and cooler, something in its texture had changed. He looked down, forcing his eyes open against the pressure of the wind. He saw something shimmer below, but he couldn't tell if it was moving or if it was because of his quick descent. He braced for impact, wondering if these were his final moments. And after sealing his eyes shut, he saw Elu in the darkness.

When his eyes closed he fell in love with the way he remembered her scent, her smile and her laughter. The memories were perfectly beautiful—just as she was and how she would remain forever. If these were to be his final thoughts, then he would have died with a smile.

Destrou plummeted deep into a large body of liquid ice with a *splash*. His feet shot up over his head and his legs and arms shot out to his sides. He was helplessly engulfed by it, twisting and turning with no free will. He didn't know if he was right-side up or upside down. His body sank to the bottom of it as his feet pressed against a rough texture—it felt like stone. Realizing that he couldn't breathe, he quickly pushed off the ground and kicked his way up to the surface.

Soon after, a dark figure shot past him, streaming a million bubbles into his face.

"Ranmau?" he tried to scream but only bubbles, large and small, burst out of his mouth. He was confused and in awe at the same time, but he had no time to think—his lungs were screaming for air.

When he pushed his way up to the surface, he tried to grab onto anything to lift himself above it. Every time he slapped his arms against the liquid ice, it splashed into his face. There was nothing solid to grab. He had never been fully submerged in it before. Up until then, he had no idea that liquid ice could amass up to this point.

His only reaction to stay afloat was to flail his arms, gasping for air in between the water gushing over his face.

"Ranmau?" he screamed. His attention focused on the formation of bubbles rising to the surface, popping into a ripple.

His heart pounded, his lungs burned and his mind raced. He slowed his breathing, needing to calm himself down. Without focus he was doomed—they both were. Something then nudged his body, it was a soft touch that felt more like a bump than a push. When he turned around, he saw a body, face-down, drifting around him. The body was not much bigger than his and it was still. Lifeless.

Can liquid ice kill? Destrou thought, looking around with wide, blackened eyes, trying to remember the exact location where the bubbles came from.

"Ranmau!" he screamed. His voice ricocheted off the darkness. He didn't know how to navigate and his clothes felt like they were ten times heavier as if boulders were shackled to his ankles. Staying afloat seemed impossible but none of that mattered. What mattered most was keeping his promise. "I WILL PROTECT YOU!"

He took one last deep breath before giving in to the sinking feeling. He sank toward the bottom, using his legs and arms for momentum, pushing him farther down. The liquid ice was dark and murky, obscuring his vision. It had a soft, silky texture—he felt it move all over his face. It deafened his ears, muffling any sound that entered. And there was now a stinging sensation behind his eyes and in his chest.

Relax. He calmed his mind, trying to block out the feeling of knives stabbing his lungs.

He closed his eyes. Elu's voice appeared in his mind. He remembered how she told him about her crazy idea that the world could have once been completely covered in liquid ice. Well, it didn't seem so crazy anymore.

If you were right about the tournament, maybe you were right about the liquid ice... What else could you have been right about? None of this makes sense. How is there this much liquid ice? What did they do to get this? Why were they hiding it? He paused, feeling Elu's soft hands press against his own. *Does that mean maybe there really is something different about me and my hands? Could I be... special?*

Bubbles blew from his mouth, shouting at a dark figure in front of him. Was he seeing things? His body trembled with pain. Suffocating was painful but not as severe as the pain of losing his brother. He grabbed the shadowed figure and fought with every last strength that he had to push to the top. The more energy he exerted the more his lungs cried for air. He pushed and pushed, slowly losing consciousness.

It was Ranmau.

A wave smacked his face. He gasped for air, pulling Ranmau up to the surface.

With a calm, deep breath, Ranmau slowly opened his eyes. "Thanks," he grinned. "I can get used to this. I never realized how easy life was being a Destrou. I don't have to do anything."

"Stop scaring me like that. It's not funny at all," Destrou shouted, mad at himself for chuckling.

When he looked around, he saw solid land in the distance. There were ice and rocks all around them, enclosing them inside like a dome of some sort. Icicles, large and small, hung from the ceiling of the cave, covering every inch of the space like an upside down forest.

"Who knows how much time we have... the challenge could already be over," Destrou said, struggling to keep both of them afloat.

Ranmau's eyes widened. "Wait," he coughed, pointing at the floating, lifeless body. "We can't leave him like this."

"What? There's nothing we can do. We need to go now," Destrou said.

"There is always something we can do." Ranmau squeezed Destrou's arm.

Destrou hesitated a bit, glancing at the boy then stared ahead at the patch of land. "Okay. You're right," he said, "but I'm going to need some help."

Destrou swam—or at least tried to—grabbing onto Ranmau's shoulder as he held onto the boy. They had never been submerged in liquid ice so the act of swimming was a new experience, luckily they were survivors and quick learners.

When they reached land, their bodies crashed to the ground. They rolled onto their backs, their chests rose and fell with agony.

Destrou wanted to advance, but his body was in shock. He was in awe that there was this much liquid ice hidden away. He couldn't stop the questions from overflowing his mind. Where did it come from? How did they create it? Who created it? His questions were interrupted by a sound behind him.

"Destrou?" a voice echoed from the shadows.

Destrou jumped up, immediately placing his fists in front of his face.

His vision was blurry but he could recognize that one piece outfit from anywhere.

"Ascel?" he replied. "What are you doing down here?"

"I couldn't leave him here like this," he said, looking at the lifeless body. His eyes watered before he finished his sentence. "Thank you so much for rescuing him. I tried. I really, really did but just couldn't do it."

"You're welcome," Destrou replied. "But to be honest, it was actually Ranmau's idea."

"Ranmau?" Ascel said, gazing into his eyes. "Wow, thank you so much! I tried and tried but gave up and you didn't. That means a lot to me. A whole lot."

"Yeah," Destrou said, placing his head down in between his palms. "But any chance that we had to win this is pretty much gone now."

"No way," Ascel replied with a high-pitched screech. "This place is huge and confusing. You have plenty of time. Most of the boys didn't even know where to go... but I found a faster way."

"Really?"

"Yeah, and since you helped out my brother, I'll definitely help out you two. Watch out, though, this next part is scary. Like really, really scary." Ascel paused, realizing that his brother was still motionless. "D-do you think he's fine?"

"If the Leader can get by it, then we can. I think we'll be fine but thanks for the warning. And about your brother... that's nothing a few whacks can't solve." Destrou clenched his fists together.

"What are you doing?" Ascel asked alertly.

"No worries," he said. "It worked on Ranmau. I know what I'm doing... I think. Maybe... Actually... how about you just look the other way?"

A few thuds later, the boy coughed liquid ice into the air.

"Brother! You're alive," Ascel shouted, jumping onto the boy's body. "I thought I lost you. I already lost Faily, I really don't know what I'd do without you."

The boy struggled to say words, but the thankful glow on his face let them know he was okay.

Destrou glanced at Ranmau. The idea of losing one another flashed through their heads. He could tell by the sparkle in Ranmau's eye. To Destrou, the challenge evolved from a competition for food to one for survival. It was designed for the Crystal Soldiers, after all. He knew that it was only going to get more dangerous. *We need to stay together*. He looked at Ranmau, whose eyes then had the same perplexed look—nothing on his face suggested otherwise. They were on the same page.

Though the Guardian had warned them that people could die,

still Destrou did not expect this level of danger.

"Thank you so much," Ascel said, standing up. "Follow me and I'll show you how to get to the next spot. Like I said... you need to be careful though. I heard some pretty terrible screams from inside. Had to leave, got way too scared." He motioned to his brother who rolled over onto his stomach. "Hey, you. Stay right there. I'll be back for you. My word!"

"Why are you helping us?" Ranmau asked curiously. There was a strong presence to his voice. One that was as robust as the wall that he created, not trusting anyone from the Village.

"You helped us without asking," Ascel replied. "Why not?"

"He's good," Destrou said, patting Ranmau on his back. "He's a good one—they all aren't bad."

"Don't be so quick to trust people," Ranmau whispered into Destrou's ear. "Once your guard is down that is their best time to strike. The true enemy is one who poses as a friend."

"I trust him... trust me on this," Destrou whispered.

"I trust you... it's the Leader I don't trust," he whispered. "Lead the way," Ranmau said to Ascel, narrowing his eyes at him.

"Okay, but I'm telling you—be careful... this next stage doesn't look easy," Ascel said.

"Don't be so quick to trust people," Ranmau whispered again into Destrou's ear.

Ascel led the way through a dark stone tunnel laced with more scratch marks and deep gashes. It looked similar to the previous room—a place where fighting and maybe killing happened. The Guardian wasn't lying: becoming a Crystal Soldier must have been serious... and deadly.

They all stuck close together, holding one another's hands as the tunnel became slippery during its decline into darkness.

"How much food would you bet me that I'd lick the wall?" Ascel said, breaking the awkward silence.

"What the? Nothing?" Ranmau said, alarmed at the question,

glancing ahead at Destrou with a puzzled look.

"Nothing, aye? Okay... okay... How much food would you bet me if I eat two handfuls of snow?"

"Err...?" Destrou said. "Nothing?"

"How much would you—"

"Nothing," Ranmau interrupted him.

"Aw man... this isn't fun," Ascel said. "Well, good thing you didn't bet because I already lost that one before."

"Um... you lost the same bet that you just—never mind," Destrou said. "No wonder you keep losing food, you're not too good at the whole betting thing."

"It's fun," he replied. "There's nothing else to do really, so why not?"

"Because some of us want to eat?" Ranmau said, sighing with a hint of agitation. "Losing isn't fun. Has anyone told you how— hmm, how can I put this nicely? How... dumb you are?" Ranmau made it obvious that making friends with a Villager wasn't a priority.

"Be nice," Destrou said. "He's not *that* dumb."

"Okay, I'll be nice." Ranmau sighed. "You're not dumb... you're just not smart."

"Easy for you to say, boy who wins all of the time. But, thanks to me you may be winning the food so yeah, listen to Destrou, be nice," Ascel replied. "And I may be dumb... but, but, but—" he said waving his finger in the air as if he found a profound discovery. "—I'm not as dumb as I was yesterday... that much I know. I think. Well, yesterday I was pretty smart."

"I don't know how you can deal with this, Destrou," Ranmau said coldly. "This is torture."

"Hey, want to know how I'm special, too?" Ascel said, bouncing up and down.

"No," Ranmau said coldly. "Not at all."

"I happen to be the best at something. Do you know what it is?"

Nothing.

"Do you?"

Nothing.

"Do yah, huh?"

"Oh yeah, and what's that?" Ranmau sighed, clearly agitated.

"Who else do you know is the first person out each time? I know exactly what it takes to lose quickly so I don't have to go through the rest of it. Smart if you ask me. Let's see you try to find someone who is as good at losing as me. Good luck!"

"Can I hit him?" Ranmau looked at Destrou. "It won't hurt... it'd just knock him out."

Destrou chuckled, enjoying himself.

"No, but seriously! I am the best at something. You wanna know?"

"No," Ranmau said blankly.

"Take a guess."

Ranmau said nothing.

"Well, you woulda never guessed it anyways, because I'm the absolute best at tying! Like tying knots and stuff! With rope! Cool, huh?"

"That's exactly what I've always wanted to be the best at," Ranmau said sarcastically.

"You say that now, but you won't say that when I tie you up so tightly you wouldn't be able to move. It even worked perfectly on the Giant! They don't call me the Master of Ropes for no reason."

"No one has *ever* called you that," Ranmau said.

"Well, not yet! But they will be! I'll betcha on that one too! Hey, do you know what I realized?" Ascel asked calmly.

"Wow... I can't deal with this," Ranmau said bluntly. Destrou knew that Ranmau had always preferred silence. "This is the last time I want to hear you speak, okay? So, what did you realize?"

"Jeez... someone needs food. You aren't yourself when you're hungry, you know that?"

Ranmau looked at him in a life-threatening way.

"Okay, okay. I'm sorry, but do you realize that no one is able to see how they look when they're sleeping?"

"Seriously? That was the question? Are we there yet? I don't know how much more of this I can deal with," Ranmau said, as if wondering how anyone could have the patience to listen to him. He sighed, noticing Ascel's widened glare, as though wishing for Ranmau to ask him to continue. "Well, what's your point already?"

"Yes! Well, it's interesting," Ascel said, walking faster, "because if you were able to see how you looked when you were sleeping, then you'd be able to know how ugly and not-perfect you really are, Drooly."

Ascel sprinted ahead, laughing. Destrou joined in, bursting out in laughter, but Ranmau's face was as flat as the Valley.

"That wasn't even funny..." Ranmau said with a smirk that cracked into a smile. "Plus, I know I'm not ugly. And anyone with two working eyes would know it as well."

Ascel jumped out of the tunnel, landing onto solid ground, bracing himself for Ranmau.

To his surprise, nothing happened.

As annoying as he was, it seemed as if his personality started to grow on Ranmau. It was a glimpse of light amidst a dark time. Maybe that was why Elu kept him around.

Destrou stepped ahead and noticed how darkness enveloped the middle of the room. At the very end, there was a cylinder of light that channeled downward at an angle. Inside of it there were three shimmering objects.

"Three of them left," Destrou said with enthusiasm. "We can make it to the next stage. We can do it!"

"Something is wrong here. Where did everyone else go?" Ranmau asked, looking at Ascel.

"Well... that's why I said to be careful."

Across from them, a shadowed object vibrated. Then, in the

distance, they heard a whimper followed by a scream.

"Help... help us!" the voice echoed.

The scream hit Destrou with such force that he stepped back, placing his arm across Ranmau's chest. "What's out there?"

"Whatever it is... it doesn't look too good."

"Please... help us," a deeper voice shrieked in pain.

"We can't wait much longer," Destrou said. "The longer we wait, the less chance we have to win." He sat back on his heels, trying to think. "We can't see what's in front of us, but whatever's out there must be dangerous. What is it?"

"What happened?" Ranmau screamed at the voices.

There was no reply.

Destrou took a few steps forward.

"Wait," Ascel said. Destrou looked ready to force his way in, but Ascel placed a hand on his shoulder and pulled him off to the side. "You're about to cross the line. That's when it starts."

"When what starts?" Destrou said, looking down at a line carved into the ice.

"I don't know what... but that's when the loud noises and the screaming started. There was a lot of it. Too much."

Destrou pressed his hand against his mouth as his eyes wandered about.

"This doesn't look good," Ranmau said. "Started with fifty. Twenty of us moved on. Six stayed behind to stop us. Two of you were back there. There are three medallions left over. Seven are still moving forward—so there must be three stuck in this darkness. It looks like not everyone made it across." He looked at Destrou, his eyes carried a level of concern. "You should move on, I will help the ones who are trapped."

"What?" Destrou replied. "No. That's crazy."

"They will die down here. No one has came back for them yet... and knowing the Leader, no one will."

"Well, then we will do it together. Family always stick together, remember?" Destrou said, reaching his hand out.

Ranmu paused, as if shocked by the bravery he saw in Destrou's eyes.

"Yeah, you're right," Ranmau said softly, clenching his palm into Destrou's hand. "Always."

Destrou looked up, squinting his eyes at shimmers that contrasted against the black canvas. He walked closer toward the darkness. Ascel didn't resist him as he worked off his last remaining shoe, placing it into his hand. Ascel tried to say something, but his eyes were dilated with fear, and when he tried to speak again, Destrou didn't respond, instead he pressed his hand on Ascel's chest, making him take a step back.

"Get away," Destrou said with an urgency.

He moved ahead, creeping at the edge of the light before the darkness overwhelmed the area. He bent down on one knee, grazing his hand over the smooth ice. Slowly he rose up and surveyed the area. The ice. The walls trapping them inside. And the emblems.

"Some people may die," he thought to himself, remembering the Guardian's words.

He looked up and kept his eyes on the shimmers above him. He arched his arm back and released his shoe into the darkness.

The shimmers disappeared all at once in a line from closest to farthest as a series of BANGS thundered throughout the area. Immediately after the shimmers faded, his train of thought was interrupted by continuous screeches that boomed through the area. The ground rumbled with consecutive crashes that sounded more like cutting than collisions.

"Ahhh"

"Ow!"

"Help us!"

"Make it stop!"

"Please help us!"

Destrou's eyes widened as he noticed the dark canvas above

him was replaced with new shimmers.

"Okay," Destrou said. "Ascel was right when he said to be careful." His eyes swept around full circle, making contact with Ranmau. "Because this isn't a challenge—it's a deathtrap."

22

A DEATHTRAP. Destrou could almost see the sharp icicles—or whatever they were—crash into the ground and cut through flesh. Each stage began a new threat, a new way to end a life, and a new elimination, getting more violent the deeper they entered.

"I don't know what will happen once we pass that line," Destrou said, "but I know that we need to stick together and—"

"And not run straight," Ranmau said, his eyes darting from up to down and side-to-side as if analyzing the situation. "It looks like they crash down after you move ahead. If we keep moving in angles, we may be able to dodge where they are going."

"Makes sense," Destrou said.

"Wow... you two are actually going in there? Like really going in there?" Ascel said. "That's even more dangerous than I thought."

"We need to go in there," Destrou said. "We... I need to win this."

"Get ready," Ranmau said, shaking Destrou. The abrupt shakes had always helped them remove any jitters they had.

"Get ready," Destrou replied, shaking him back.

There was enough time for Ranmau to explain the strategy to Destrou—about saving the boys first, and how moving in angles and staying close would help them make it out alive.

"I will protect you," Ranmau said.

Relief flooded Destrou's face. The feeling of brothership finally started to reveal itself in a way that he had almost forgotten.

Destrou remembered the last time Ranmau said those words. *I will protect you*, he said. Any sense of danger that was surrounding him fled the scene. When Ranmau made a promise it was as if his life was attached to every word of it. The strength of those words would instantly make Destrou feel safe and tame any negative thought that ravaged his mind. But he also knew that whenever Ranmau said those words it was because danger lurked in its shadows.

That thought alone sent a chill, like a cold finger down his spine.

"I will protect you, too," Destrou said, nodding at Ranmau.

With stuttered breaths and pained eyes, Ranmau tied his long silvery hair up and fixed his shoes.

Destrou glared ahead at the darkness, mapping out their route. There wasn't going to be any room for error. One small mistake and missing out on the food would be the last of their worries.

"On the count of three," Ranmau said.

Destrou's heart raced.

"One."

His chest pounded.

"Two."

He took a deep breath and closed his eyes. It's now or never. I won't fail you. I promise.

"Three."

His eyes shot open, and he grabbed onto Ranmau's hand as he dashed forward, feeling the cold of the icy floor jolt through his body.

Once again, rolling thunder roared as shards of broken ice splattered past their bodies. Though their vision was obscured by a blanket of darkness, they heard every burst and felt the force of every icicle that shot past them.

The explosions shot fragments into Destrou's bare feet that hurt more than he expected. It wasn't the impact that wounded him—it was the sizzling, a burning sensation that felt like hot oil splashed onto his skin. *If that hurt... what if it actually hits me?*

He had no time to think, though. One pause in their step could be their last.

"Help," a voice yelled. The scream bounced off of the walls numerous times, making it difficult to know exactly where it came from.

"Here," Ranmau shouted, yelling over the thundering roars. The constant crashes were accompanied by the sounds of liquid funneling down a drain.

Ranmau pulled Destrou's hand into a new direction as they ran in a large circle around a dark silhouette on the ground. The circle became smaller as shards of ice surrounded them.

"Now's our chance," Ranmau screamed. "Grab him."

With a swift motion, Destrou dove hands first into the center, wrapping his arms around a cold body that almost made his hands numb. But pulling the body was more difficult than he expected— there was some resistance as if he was glued to the ground. His body peeled off of the ice with a wretched, tearing sound.

The boy screamed as Destrou saw pieces of his flesh still attached to the ice.

Despite his determination to complete the challenge, Destrou squirmed in a way that he wasn't used to. The boy's loose skin flapped against Destrou's body, making his stomach twist. He was born into a Village where the most graphic thing he had seen were accidents that would occur during spear fighting. The boys labored daily and only involved themselves in actions that inflicted pain when they were needed, but they weren't prepared for this. This challenge was designed for Crystal Soldiers and the boys were just... boys. Replaceable, disposable subjects of the Kingdom born into a life of slavery that was masked as labor. They had the freedom to leave whenever they wanted... but they all knew what freedom really meant. The ones who wanted freedom would never be seen again, their stories forgotten. Winning the tournament was their only real chance to see the world outside of the Village.

There was an epidemic that spread throughout the world. A disease that forced one group to feel inferior than the next. The truth was that the separation between the Villages and the Kingdom was not a disease created by the Villagers. It was one created by the Kingdom. The disease infested the boys' minds, making them believe that they were the problem and didn't deserve freedom. Although it may not have been the case, it seemed as if they could feel a noose tighten around their necks whenever they tried to say the word.

Elu's words about war clouded Destrou's mind. The challenge was designed for the survival of the fittest—leaving the weak to be left behind and die by the hands of their own peers. *Elu was right... the Kingdom doesn't care about us. It looks like they'll kill off anyone if they aren't good enough.*

He remembered her words about what the real problem was: the system, not the boys. The same words that Faily, Ascel's brother, would say. Maybe Ranmau knew about that all along? Was that why he wanted to save the boys?

Destrou realized that maybe there was a lot more to Ranmau that he didn't know.

Although the Village had built animosity toward the twins, they all had strict values that opposed the Kingdom's. They had a code. They had their word. The boys needed to stick together. If they didn't, there was no one else to rely on. They couldn't let the Kingdom win more than they already had. That was when the Leader stepped up to the position. He became the Leader and united the starving boys and established an order, protecting them from one another. He wasn't always the bad one. There was a time when the boys needed a strong voice to guide them down a path of unity, to-getherness, brotherhood. He instilled the notion that every life was valuable and every role served its purpose. Unfortunately, when one had been in a position of power for too long, time proved its ability to wither away the same moral fibers that made them whole.

In the eyes of the Kingdom, their lives were worthless. This challenge reflected their values and it was something that no boy could have possibly trained for. This deathtrap was a culling de-signed to kill and execute—how could they have trained for a battle between life or death? They needed help... but why did Ranmau choose to help out the enemy? The question still puzzled Destrou.

"*Now!*" Ranmau shouted.

Destrou tucked his shoulders down, diving over the barrier of ice before it vanished into the ground.

Shards shot down as Destrou, carrying a boy slightly larger than him in his arms, sprinted toward Ascel.

He lunged in the air as icicles burst around him and landed on the solid ground, tumbling shoulder first, rolling to a complete stop.

"You did it!" Ascel screamed, jumping up and down.

"Ranmau?" Destrou shot up, looking around. "Where are you?"

Explosions hit their ears as Ranmau leapt in the air toward De-strou. His body twisted and flipped, landing in front of Destrou.

"You don't have to worry about me," he smirked. "I'm protect-ing you, remember?"

"No," Destrou laughed, playfully shoving Ranmau's chest, "I'm protecting you now, remember!"

Ranmau wrapped his arm over Destrou's shoulder, patting his head, and pulled him closer to his chest.

"What's this?" Destrou said, noticing blood drip down Ran-mau's good arm. "You're hurt!"

"I'm fine," he said, pulling his arm back. Sizzling underneath the large hole in his shirt there was a deep, bubbling gash on his bicep.

"Oh no," Destrou gasped, reaching out for Ranmau's arm. "This isn't good at all. That's your only arm."

"I'm telling you,"—Ranmau shoved his arm away—"I'm fine." He reached down to pick up a stray rock. He winced as if a pain shocked through his arm, dropping the rock immediately.

"I'm sorry," Destrou said. "It's my fault. I moved too slowly. If I moved faster you wouldn't have been hit. You wouldn't have—"

"It's not your fault. I'm the one who came up with the plan."

"And you did your part well... I'm the one who messed up. I can't make mistakes anymore. You didn't make mistakes when I needed you—I can't make them when you need me. I made a promise that—"

"Well... I think this might be the end of the challenge for us. I-I don't think I'll be able to win. Not like this." Ranmau's eyes glazed as he glanced at his arms. "And you know what I need you to do, right? You need to—"

"No!" Destrou shouted, feeling a sting behind his eyes. "I won't lose this on purpose for you. No! You need the food more now than ever. You need to be healed and it will heal you, I know it can! We can still do this. The Guardian said—"

"I DON'T CARE WHAT THE GUARDIAN SAID!" Ranmau yelled. "And I don't care about the stupid food!" His voice carried so much power that the echo was followed by a distant scream for help. "Right now, we have two more to help. I trust you. We can still save them. We can do this."

"Why do you care about them, huh? Tell me!"

Ranmau said nothing.

"Tell me what's more important than your freedom! Why do I want it more than you?"

Their eyes met. Destrou choked up when he saw tears flow from Ranmau's eyes.

"Just please... trust me when I say that there are more important things. But right now, we have two more to help. We can still save them. We can do this."

"O-okay," Destrou said, feeling a lump in his throat. "I won't let you down, again."

The second boy was recovered much easier. Coughing and queasy, Destrou looked up to find Ranmau in the same condition. The constant running, jumping and diving with their lives on the line was exhausting. The two bodies were placed next to another. Ascel attended to them, wrapping a piece of his cloth around the patches of open, swollen flesh.

Why is he risking his life to save them? I still don't get it... He changed so much since the Box. What was he thinking about in there?

After a battle with endurance, the third and final boy was saved. The whole thing, from running in circles and diving around, couldn't have taken more than a minute or two. The twins sat there panting, rubbing the ends of their mouths. But Destrou winced again as he glanced at Ranmau's arm.

"It looks like it's getting worse," Destrou said.

Ranmau covered his arm, noticing Destrou's look of concern. "I said I'm fine. Stop looking at me like that. I don't need that kinda look, I'm Ranmau, remember?"

Destrou looked away, rubbing his eyes. *He didn't change too much. He still has his pride.*

"But it looks like we are good to go now," Ranmau smirked, patting Destrou on the shoulder. "We did better than I thought. If you really want to try for it then we need to hurry up if we want any chance to win. Just be careful about the stray pieces of ice and we will be fine."

"Of course we can still win this... we've never lost one. Win or lose this will be our last challenge together, we can't end it with a loss, right?" Destrou held back a knot that swelled up in his throat. The thought created small pockets of tears at the corners of his eyes. No matter what... this was their last one together. It suddenly hit Destrou out of nowhere. This was their last challenge together. That was it. Brothers no more after this. This was more reason to win.

The way Ranmau's eyes rested flat, it seemed like he didn't need to be reminded; he knew that whether they won or lost, this challenge would be their last together. Destrou noticed him shiver as if the thought made him uncomfortable. Ranmau twisted his body away from Destrou.

A faint gasp, like a suppressed sob, was heard.

Ascel's mouth dropped, as if he saw something completely unexpected from Ranmau. What did he see? Unfortunately, Destrou wasn't able to witness it. But then another realization hit Destrou: Ranmau was the strong, unbreakable brother not because he wanted to be but because he needed to be. He couldn't reveal the softer, vulnerable side to Destrou. Not then, not ever.

"Thank you," a soft sound struggled to escape from one of the boys' mouths.

"You're welcome," the brothers said in unison.

"Yeah," Ascel said, shaking off what he had just seen, attending to the third injured boy. "Thank you. You didn't need to do this... especially after everything we've done to the two of you."

"You mean what the Leader has done to us," Ranmau replied. "If I were to take it out on the rest of you boys, I'd only be punishing the punished. I'd be worse than the Leader. We all have already gone through too much... Just make sure they are okay." He glared directly into Ascel's eyes. "Can I trust you with them?"

"Yes, of course," Ascel said worriedly. He stood upright as if Ranmau's gaze caught him off guard, making him feel uneasy.

"Let's do this," Destrou said, shaking Ranmau, calming the tension.

It was clear that Ranmau still had his doubts about Ascel, but maybe it was because he didn't know him like Destrou did.

Maybe I should let him know why I know Ascel is a good one...

but then I know he'd ask too many questions—questions that I'm not ready to answer. Not yet, at least. There's no way I'll be able to lie to him. I don't want him to find out about the secrets... about us... and especially Elu's cave. No one can know. That's our place. That's her place.

The Tree was Elu's place for solace and she treated it as a shrine. It was a sanctuary meant for secrecy—even from his own brother. He wanted to keep it pure... for her. That was what she had always wanted.

"After you," Ranmau said to Destrou. "Lead the way, protector."

"Okay," Destrou smirked.

Destrou didn't wait. He dropped his hands and sprinted into the darkness, twisting to get a glimpse of the shimmering sharp shards soaring past his skin. He slid to the ground as multiple projectiles penetrated into the path behind him. In the instant that it took for Destrou to recover onto his feet, Ranmau launched over him, twisting and twirling, causing Destrou to dive to the side, evading more icicles.

Rolling thunder erupted behind Destrou as he sprung forward, flipping over his hands, in full pursuit. The brothers split up, running in a wide arch away from one another. The bursting noises behind them confirmed that there was nowhere to go except forward. Everything was clear from this point. The emblems were getting closer. The next stage was moments away.

Suddenly the ground jerked beneath Destrou's feet, and he flung onto his side, hitting the ice. Panic erupted and time froze as his elevated heart rate slowed to a stop. He heard the shard release from its captivity, making its way down toward his head. He felt a wave of air press onto his face as the force of the projectile traveled downward. The fear for his life caused his vision to blur. The world felt like it was spinning fast, really fast and he could see the emblem just ahead of him split into a series of images like a kaleidoscope. This couldn't be the end—not like this. He dug his hands into the ice, trying to get traction, but they slipped from beneath him, his chin crashed to the ground, splattering blood onto his face. Between the feeling of helplessness and death nearing his head, he had to squeeze his eyes shut. There was nothing that he could do except wish that he wasn't the death that the Guardian expected.

But he knew death was here for him. The way his gut churned as if it had been stabbed by a thousand knives, he knew. The ink had dried and there were no more pages left to his story. This was the end.

23

DESTROU OPENED HIS EYES. His stomach contracted at the idea of what to do next. At the corner of his eye he saw dark objects descending toward him—one was much larger than the others. A sharp pain struck his side, lunging him forward as he crashed into the podiums.

Ranmau screamed as blood sprayed into the air.

Destrou jolted to Ranmau, avoiding the bloodstained ice that spread out from the open wounds across his body. Destrou was able to see what the shards did when they made contact. They pierced into the flesh, turning into a clear liquid that oozed out of the wound, melting into the skin around it. The skin dripped down onto the ice as if it were no longer attached to his body. He clenched his mouth, holding back the feeling of throwing up. Ranmau's body had many holes in it that bled this light red, thick substance as if his blood had fused with skin. The unfamiliar scent of burning flesh tickled Destrou's nostrils.

"I'm so sorry," Destrou screamed. "I'm so so so sorry!" He kept screaming those same words, grabbing onto Ranmau's hand, pulling him onto solid ground.

Ranmau screamed as some of his flesh peeled off the ice with a sizzle. The tearing sound made Destrou's stomach churn.

Destrou's eyes swelled with liquid. His heart raced and his mind raged with fears that he wanted to keep locked away. His darkest fear of losing his brother was on the forefront of his mind. Again. And being the reason made his heart sink with guilt.

"This hurts." Ranmau gasped, clenching his teeth so hard that they chattered. "This hurts a lot. I wish... Ascel could feel this." His short laughter was interrupted by bursts of breathing that sounded like hisses.

"You better be okay," Destrou said, puffing his chest. He was unable to chuckle, though his body had really wanted to. He pressed his face against the top of Ranmau's head. "I keep failing you... but I promise you that I won't be the one that stops you anymore. I will win the food for you. You need it."

"No," Ranmau said, grabbing Destrou's neck with an unsteady touch. "I'm proud of you. We have made it this far. Let it go. We did better than any one of them expected us to. The whole Village wanted us to lose and look how far we made it. We did it."

"No," Destrou said, wiping the tears from his face. "We didn't do it until I've won! I don't care what they expected from us. It's about what I expect from us—from myself. And it's not ending like this. We are not losing like this. This is not how our story ends."

"It needs to. Promise me that it's over."

"It's not over until I go into the NoGo to claim my prize."

"No... please—" Ranmau's eyes widened and glazed over. He may have said more, but he gasped and held onto his chest.

Destrou's teary eyes winced at the sight of the open wounds. "The food will save you... I'm sorry. I need to go. I can't see you like this... because of me. This is all my fault. I will fix it. I have to fix it."

Destrou grabbed Ranmau's hand, prying it off his neck.

"No. Please... don't." Ranmau's eyes glazed. "The food... is not that important."

"But your life is," Destrou said, standing up and pulling the emblem off of the podium. "When I win… I will come back for you."

"Promise me!" Ranmau screamed, tears were now flowing from his eyes.

Destrou said nothing.

He had his reasons for needing to win the tournament. Ranmau was more than just a friend. He was his brother, his protector, the one person that he could rely on when the world crumbled before his eyes.

I don't know why I'm fighting so hard to save you. I don't know why I'd risk my life to save someone who I feel like I should hate. A part of me thought that I would have loved to see you just melt away… but I didn't. I don't know how to explain it. The feeling of losing you wasn't a good one, not at all. It actually made me feel empty, very empty… like when Elu was gone. I guess I just know that you deserve freedom more than any of us. The Sensu will help, I know it will. Your dream is to become a Crystal Soldier. To meet the Supreme General. You gave up your dream of freedom for me, I won't ruin this one. I don't know exactly how I feel about you. I don't know if this is hate or love. I don't even know what love is anymore. But when I'm gone, I want you to remember me as the one who never gave up. The one who risked his life to give you your freedom.

Destrou walked away from Ranmau, each stepped sent a chill up his spine. This challenge was the most dangerous one yet, but it was also the first time that he advanced without Ranmau. There was a great trial facing him with the chances of winning looking as grim as ever. He wasn't challenging his body to win for himself. This was much bigger than that. It was to help his other half that made him whole. Placing the well-being of someone else above his own gave him power that he never knew existed. He couldn't fail. He didn't allow it to become an option.

With the emblem pressed tightly in his hands, he wandered

deeper into the unknown. The tunnel was dark and mysterious. He no longer felt fear. There was nothing ahead lurking in the shadows that would scare him more than the thought of his brother dying. He knew what he needed to do—even against his brother's wishes.

This is all my fault. I will fix it. I'd like to see the Leader try to get in the way, It'd take more than a Village to stop me.

He held the emblem tighter. His eyes burned with rage. He forgot where he was or what lay ahead, he only knew that he needed to reach the end, and save him. He ran wildly into the darkness, unmindful of danger, ripping through icicles and branches, through anything that kept him from reaching the end. In his mind, nothing—not even Ranmau—could stop him from his goal.

I will save you.

As far as Destrou could tell, the third stage of the challenge involved running down a dark tunnel with many small obstacles to dodge. There was a putrid smell that made his eyes water, reminding him of the Guardian's breath. His feet moved so fast through the icicles and branches that he struggled to skid to a complete stop, and happened to slide through a transparent wall, made of something he couldn't describe, that rippled as he entered. It felt like liquid ice had poured around his body but he was completely dry. His body felt weightless for a moment as if he were falling, yet his feet remained planted to the bricks of ice. He was too focused to even attempt to make sense out of what happened.

Up ahead there was a dead end with only two options to choose between: left or right. Destrou's eyes narrowed with confusion. Ice was all around him and blue pulsating lights resonated behind the walls.

He heard commotion, like boys barking commands at one another, but he couldn't tell where it came from. The air was still, but a cool chill grazed across the right side of his body. An opening. He quickly chose the path to the right and maintained a fast pace.

There were no more sounds and the air was neither hot nor cold.

His confused face crumpled with despair as he ran into another crossroads. To his surprise, this path looked identical to the last one. He didn't have much time to think so he quickly chose to go left.

A few moments later, he stumbled upon the same intersection—at least it looked exactly like the last two. Everything was the same from the three large circles carved into the wall to the intricate designs around them. The circles were spaced evenly apart and with the level of detail involved, the way the lines contoured and the ice sculpted, it seemed impossible to replicate. The artwork was hauntingly majestic. It was beautiful—too beautiful for a place designed for death. It reminded him of the masterpieces that he had seen inside of Elu's cave: the Tree.

"This is impossible," he screamed in frustration. Unknowing what to do next, he threw his hands in the air and took a right.

Then a left. Right. Left. Right. No matter which direction he took, there was a crossroad after a crossroad. Either his mind was playing tricks on him or it seemed like he had passed the same engravings each time.

He slowed down to catch his breath. He pressed his face closer to the wall, analyzing every detail on the carvings. He pulled out his emblems, twisting and turning them around in his hand. The markings were similar to the ones on the wall. Inside of the three circles there were slots. The two outer circles' slots were semicircles; the middle one was a circle.

He shuffled the two emblems in his hands, looking at which one would fit where. They both were semicircles but the patterns on them didn't line up with the ones on the walls. The pattern consisted of three shapes: two triangles with a diamond wedged in between them. The emblem's shapes made a clear design while the wall's looked disorganized.

"This is really impossible," he sighed. "It looks like they're supposed to go in there, but how am I supposed to fit these stupid things inside?"

Out of frustration, he threw one of the medallions toward the right entrance.

There was silence. He was surprised to not hear a sound, expecting at least a faint thud.

He then heard fluttering behind him, like a large gust of wind blasting through, but there was no wind.

"Ow," he screamed, turning around, furiously rubbing the back of his head.

The emblem had bounced off his head, ricocheting onto the icy floor.

What the? How did that... how is any of this possible? I don't get it. None of this makes sense, at all.

He struggled to make a complete thought.

What is this place—and who could make a thing like this? This is definitely nothing a Villager could do.

Suddenly, a faint noise scraped behind him that sounded like ice grinding on ice. When he turned around, he saw the patterns on the wall shift slightly.

"This is really weird," he said to himself, scratching his head. "Now I really wish you were here, Elu. You'd actually be able to figure this out. You *always* had an answer."

He analyzed his emblems again, noticing they were a closer match to the designs on the wall.

As weird as this seems... I think I kinda get it now.

After a few minutes of trial and error, running left, right, and back from where he came from, he realized quite a few things. The markings shifted in a counterclockwise direction whenever he ran to the left and they would shift clockwise when he ran to the right. And they would reset back to normal whenever he went through the entrance that he came from.

"No matter what I do these things aren't lining up. It's impossible to get out of this... Wait, no! If those krillens can do it, then of course I can. There has to be a way—something that I'm not seeing."

He pushed his palms against the cold wall, pressing his forehead into the center circle. A freezing sensation shot through his body as he tried to calm himself down.

"Breathe," he said to himself.

He looked up, peering his eyes so close to the wall that he could feel the waves of frost on them. He analyzed with an acute attention to detail that the angles shifted slightly more than they normally did. *I need to find out this secret.*

After what felt like an hour more of trial and error, he uncovered an intricate detail to the patterns. He found out that the maze worked in a way where if he went left twice then right twice the left triangle would move more to the right, but if he went right twice then left twice it'd move slightly to the left and shift the right triangle slightly to the right. He found out that there were an infinite amount of combinations to shift the shapes differently and he was forced to remember them all.

"Okay, I went left twice, then right twice, then left, right, right, left... right, left, left, right... left, right, left, left, left, right..." He paused, realizing that he was going crazy, talking to himself for a few minutes. *Or was it... left, left, right, left, left?* He scratched his chin and scrunched his nose. *I'm sorry but that's way too much to remember, Destrou. Am I talking to myself? Yupp, I guess that's how my thinking voice sounds. Oh, wow. I feel bad for people who hear my voice if it sounds the way I think. I'll have to apologize to Ranmau after. At least my name sounds kinda cool. I like how my name sounds. Destrou. Destrouu. Destrouuu. Like Des-tro. And Ran-muh. But anyways, even I know you're not that smart. Or is it I'm not that smart? I don't know but there has to be a better way to remember this stuff.*

It was clear that mental fatigue began to wither his mind away. He didn't realize there was a problem until he started biting his fingernails to the point of eating some of the flesh around them. Not because he was nervous, but his mind thought of them as food. He needed sleep but he became obsessed with figuring out the maze. It bothered him that the others were able to solve it yet he couldn't.

He went back through the original entrance, resetting it all over again then decided to name each combination.

An Elu would be named after going right four consecutive times because she was always right. Left three times then a right was called a Ranmau because he was left behind for the right reason. No matter how corny it was, he needed something to help him remember the combinations and shorten the amount of things that he needed to memorize. There was a name for each combination: Elu, Ranmau, Ascel, Destrou, Forest, Wall, Guardian, Archon, and the list went on.

He lost track of time and had no idea how long he had been inside there. It could have been a half hour... an hour... maybe even three or four. After a few more minutes passed, he sprinted through the tunnels, shouting out a long list of names, catching his breath in between each exhale. "Archon, Ascel, Ranmau and... Elu."

He paused, stopping in front of the wall as the shifting ice slowly made its way into perfect alignment. His face mustered up the strength to form a smile. The shapes looked exactly like the markings on his emblems.

"Wow! I did it! I actually did it!" he cackled so loud that the bursting echoes scared him. "Ew... wait. I hope that's not how I sound when I laugh. Yuck, I don't like that either. I need to change that."

He closed his eyes, pressing the medallion into the slot.

He heard a *click* then a hum that vibrated from behind the wall.

"What?" An excited burst of energy rejuvenated his face. Immediately after, his nose tingled with the familiar scent of burning flesh. The pulsating blue lights turned into a dark purple. He then heard a roaring sound followed by constant splashes. When he turned around, he saw a puddle of the liquid that gave him tremors, thinking about it oozing off of Ranmau's skin, peeling his flesh.

"Oh no!" His eyes widened.

He reached his left hand out to press the other medallion into the slot but his reach was too short. The wave was crashing in faster, he could hear the rush bouncing off the walls. He pressed onto his toes, stretching his body to its limits. His fingers pricked the end of the medallion, extending it out farther. The putrid smell was closer. It was all around him, seeping into his clothes. The wave crashed around the corner, he could see it clearly now.

He heard another click, the hum grew louder. The second medallion absorbed into the wall. The two semicircles slid into the middle, illuminating the center circle with a blinding glow. A breeze of cool air whisked around Destrou as a slight crack appeared underneath the wall. It was a door.

He pushed with all of the strength that he had but the door didn't budge. It felt as immovable as the Guardian's door. This stage wasn't just one for intelligence... but brawn as well. His muscles felt like they were tearing open as veins bulged out of his skin. He knew that he couldn't fail now, he was too close.

Visions of Elu and Ranmau shot through his head. He needed to find the strength to continue—the strength to push through the pain.

"You're special," floated through his mind in Elu's soft tone. He felt something within him that he had only felt twice before. His body felt warmer—too warm. His mind was relaxed—too relaxed. He took a deep breath then exhaled a roaring scream. The door pushed open just enough for him to dive through the side, tumbling hands first onto the cold stone floor as the wave splashed against the door.

The door sealed shut but remnants of the liquid found its way under the crack.

Sitting on his rear, he walked backward with his hands, making sure that the liquid didn't touch his body. It slowed to a sizzling stop, melting a hole into the glossy floor.

"This is a deathtrap," he said with widened eyes, taking deep breaths. Yet a smile broke through. He was ecstatic that he could finally take a break.

Or so he thought.

"Hey... how'd he get here?" a loud voice erupted from behind him.

"No way he got out!"

"Not without knowing the code. The Guardian said it'd be impossible without it!"

"Yeah, what's the deal? Only people who knew it could get out! Who gave him the code to get out?"

"Why you lookin' at me?"

"The Leader's going to kill us if we don't find out who helped him!"

"Well it wasn't me, I know that for sure!"

"The code?" Destrou said to himself softly. It immediately made sense to him once it left his lips. They knew something that he didn't.

Destrou looked ahead beyond the boys and saw what he needed. The next emblem was illuminated on a separate island off in the distance. There were supposed to be five but three remained. An erupting roar momentarily diverted his attention toward the mob of charging boys.

The Leader and the Giant aren't here, it looks like they are the only two who have moved on. Why haven't these boys went across? How do you get across, anyways? Destrou thought, paying no mind to the sprinting boys.

Destrou charged forward into the horde of angry boys, looking through them at the void of darkness that wrapped around every inch of the area.

There are five boys here but none of them went for it? This can't be good.

The remaining ones were the oldest and toughest of the Village. They not only had a few years on Destrou but they were also almost two feet taller. They wore the same white fur clothes as the rest of the Village, except they each had large cloaks that had a beast's head as their hood. The heads had large fangs and pointed ears. They were called the Bruisers because they once led the Village with brute force, winning every challenge, until the Leader and the Giant received their growth spurts. After the shift of power, they then became the large boys with broken minds and sunken faces.

Destrou was reminded of the times they disfigured his face, punching him until he was unconscious. He remembered waking up a few hours later with a marred face. He'd never forget. They were as mean as they were tough. Although he was tiny compared to them, he wouldn't let that stop him this time. He made a promise that he intended to keep. No more mistakes.

He leapt over the first boy, kicking him in the back of the head, and flipped over the next. When he landed, he evaded a few strikes that would have been deadly if they landed. He slammed his fist against a boy's jaw, ignoring the pain that sent through him as if he had punched a wall. Fueled by not wanting to disappoint Ranmau, the one punch became a flurry. The great effort momentarily weakened each of the boys, but within seconds they recouped. They knew that Destrou was too small for them, their bodies were too big and for years they had endured much greater acts of pain. Destrou needed more power behind his punches to cause any damage.

As one, the boys charged toward him.

They did their best to combat their unexpected foe. Destrou was too quick. Fists were thrown at his body to cripple him, but Destrou dodged them. He retaliated with strikes of his own from high above, barely bruising their thick skin.

He rubbed the stinging sensation off his knuckles. *Ranmau was right... nothing works against the Bruisers.* They were the infamous Bruiser boys, after all. They were known for their chiseled jaws that must have been created from stone slabs. They were as hard as rock and able to withstand a lot of damage—more damage than Destrou could create.

"I get it," Destrou said, catching his breath. "The Leader must have had the Bruisers stay behind to slow me down."

"Hah," the largest one with long dark hair said, "more like none of us want to die trying to get that stupid medallion."

"Yeah," another one said, cracking his knuckles, "but the Leader will reward us if we do stop you."

This one must be bad if the Bruisers didn't even try to get it. Destrou had never seen them scared of anything.

"Why... what's out there?" Destrou asked aloud, hoping to get as much information as possible.

"Like we gon' help you," the dark-haired boy laughed. His laugh quickly multiplied and seconds later, the blare of a horn filled the air.

"Heh," a Bruiser said, "looks like the challenge is almost done."

At that moment, Destrou noticed one of the boys beginning to fidget. He trembled. Why?

Destrou heard a faint sizzle in the darkness. The sound that engraved a dark memory in his mind—one of burning flesh that he would never forget. He saw long, thin strips connecting their island to the other side where the emblems were. The strip was smaller than the width of his foot.

"We have to get across on that?" Destrou gulped down a difficult breath.

It made sense to Destrou why they were too afraid to advance. Their feet were too big to balance themselves on the beam and it seemed that somewhere at the bottom of the darkness there was a pool of the acidic liquid awaiting their demise.

He knew that it was useless to stay and fight. The Bruisers would never fall and it would only waste valuable time and energy. Two things that he was running out of.

"Bruisers don't fall. They never have and never will," Destrou said to himself as if it were something that the Villagers recited numerous times. Overcoming his gut feeling telling him not to, he decided to go with a foolish, brash plan. "They'll never beat us. I won't fail you, Ranmau."

With a swift motion, Destrou ran toward the Bruisers, jumping over them, using their shoulders for support, and continued his pace toward the emblems. He wanted to hesitate, but the nearby shouts urged him forward. There was no more room for mistakes. His feet were small enough to cover the entire platform. As he ran over the darkness, he heard the crackling of liquid beneath him. He could feel the bursting of bubbles scar the soles of his feet.

Destrou knew that what the Bruisers felt was fear stopping them, but fear was not real. It was the product of the thoughts that they created. The danger was very real, but fear was a choice. And Destrou chose to overcome it.

The Bruisers watched on with envy as Destrou did what they could not. They didn't hesitate to stop their pursuit. He was on his own now.

Destrou jumped onto the island. Steam formed around his feet as his heels melted the snow upon impact.

He did not have to question where the next destination could be found, for when he grabbed the emblem, a glowing pattern in the shape of a rune appeared on the base of the podium. It absorbed into the ground, and a gaping black hole opened in the snowy mounds at his feet.

Slowly Destrou approached the edge of it and peered inside. A set of stone steps led down into the hole, their edges tattered rough by years of neglect.

As he drew closer to the doorway, he felt a warm wind rush up the stairs, coming from deep inside the darkness and escaping through the hole above. The wind brought not only the sound of droplets of liquid ice, but the unmistakable scent of humidity and sludge.

He jumped down into the darkness. The impact stunned his bare feet, but something absorbed most of the fall. He lifted his foot. A gooey texture created resistance, clinging him to the ground.

"What is this," he said, struggling to walk toward a distant light. A sharp scent rushed into his mouth as his palms clenched his lips, gagging. The thick scent made the Commander's feet smell like a bed of roses. He held his nose tightly, limiting his breath to a whimper.

He trekked ahead as his feet made contact with ice. It was thin and cracking under his feet. The ice walls to either side were smooth and glazed. There were stone figures carved into the wall—at least they appeared to be stone.

Destrou grazed his fingers along them, feeling a rough texture that resembled aged cloth. It took him a moment to realize that they were bodies. A chill jolted up his spine. Why were there bodies down here? Were they the ones that the Guardian was talking about—the ones who died? Were they buried alive? Were they killed? Did they fail?

He had forgotten to look where he was going. When he tripped over something hard, he pressed his hands forward, falling onto a series of solid objects. They came in different shapes and sizes. They were long, thin, round and small. He couldn't make out what they were, but there were too many of them. He struggled to find a spot to place his hands to push himself to his feet. The clutter kept scattering around whenever he tried to stand up. What was all of this stuff?

Destrou barely set his foot up when he felt his hand stuck inside of a cold object. He looked up in astonishment, pulling his hand to his face. It felt like his hand pressed into a solid block of ice but it looked like a head absent of flesh and skin—a type of head that he had never seen before. It wasn't human, at least not the human that he was used to seeing. Its forehead was much larger and the eye sockets were tiny and too close together.

"What is this?" he said examining it calmly—too calmly as if he was used to seeing corpses.

He was terrified but more curious than scared. His heart pounded against his ribs as he turned the glazed skull around. It had a pure reflection to it as if it were a mirror. It trembled in his hands as he saw a shaky reflection of himself—his deep sockets, worn, dark eyes, and messy hair.

"Oh," Destrou said, disappointed, "I was actually hoping that I didn't look like this."

His eyes blackened with fear, fixating on a moving object lurking behind his reflection. The dark figure grew larger. He could feel its presence over his shoulders. There was cold air that pressed against his neck in long, sharp pulses. The breezes stopped. Destrou didn't know how to respond.

A loud, high-pitched scream boomed directly behind him. Destrou ducked his head as a blade swung over his head, slicing the skull in half, causing fibers of hair to float across his face. It was in that moment when he realized that he will be the next corpse stuck in this challenge.

24

DESTROU'S HEART RACED AS HE JUMPED and rolled forward. He landed on solid ground and still wasn't used to the thin ice crunching underfoot. Regaining traction, he moved noisily from the pit and headed into the tunnel ahead. After a moment, the beast roared, then smashed the walls with forceful swings from one of its extremities.

"What is that!" Destrou screamed as the beast chased after him.

Destrou ran quickly but needed to increase his pace—the walls were collapsing around him at an alarming rate.

"This can't be human," he shouted, hearing guttural growls with each crushing blow.

Destrou's first sight out of the tunnel was an open area with tall stone arches that rose overhead, disappearing into the fog in the distance. The stone had the same qualities as the ones he saw in the beginning—they were fused with ice, pure, aged white, and polished. It looked like a massive cave that was converted into a cathedral.

As Destrou ran deeper into the space, he saw the columns crumble to a rubble. The rubble dispersed like dark marbles thrown onto the ground. The specs of debris must have had a purpose though, they followed Destrou, gaining speed.

Destrou turned around, finally getting a look at the beast. It was a tall, shrouded figure that ran on its hands and feet, despite looking like a deformed human. Extending out of its elbows were long, curved blades that were almost the size of its body. Out of its head were similar blades that looked like twisting horns. Maybe the purpose of this stage was to stay and fight, but then again, that could have explained the collection of bones—the ones who tried to fight. Running, and running fast, was his only plan.

Just as Destrou thought this challenge couldn't get any worse, he glanced at the rubble that had fallen. They cracked open like eggs, revealing thousands of tiny insects.

While appearing harmless at first, the insects multiplied by the second, covering the entire area behind him with a chattering blanket that swarmed over the monster. The beast shrieked in pain as the insects disposed of its existence in a matter of seconds, devouring it as if it was never there.

As much as he tried to fight it, fear overwhelmed every emotion in his body. Survival motivated each stride, pumping adrenaline into his veins. Looking ahead, he saw a stone wall blocking the entire area except for a small opening underneath it.

Without losing momentum, he slid, feet first, underneath the obstacle. Immediately after, he climbed over a wall that was slightly taller than he was. His feet stung when he fell down and made contact with the stone floor, rolling into a crouching position. He pressed his palms against his knees, scoffing for whatever air his lungs could find.

"I needed this," he sighed. "I need a break—I can't keep going like this." Inhale. Exhale. Breathe. A few deep breaths later, he shot his head back with a smile. He had never been so happy to hear silence... until the silence was interrupted by a clacking rumble behind the wall. He glanced up and saw the first of many tiny creatures, climbing over the wall, falling to the ground at different speeds.

"What the?" Destrou sighed. He didn't know how much more he could endure. He didn't have enough time to recover. His lungs burned, legs cramped, and heart tried to pound its way through his ribs. His body was not prepared for this level of torture. He tried to fathom how people went through this to prove themselves worthy enough for the Crystal Soldiers, but none of it made sense. This wasn't a challenge, it was an elimination.

Fatigue weighed him down, but the thought of keeping his promise allowed him to tap into energy he didn't know he had.

The more he ran, the openings became tighter to fit in and wider to slide through. They required more speed to get across. The torture: when he wanted to give up and slow down was when he needed to speed up and keep climbing.

He knew that if he was just a step slower then he wouldn't make it through. The walls became taller, requiring a greater jump to climb over. To say that it couldn't get any worse was an understatement.

He dragged his body across the stone floor and couldn't tell if he was getting slower or if the creatures were getting faster, maybe it was a combination of the two.

"When does this thing end?" Destrou wondered, rubbing his sweaty palms on his legs. He observed the seemingly infinite depth of the tunnel. None of this challenge made sense to him. How did anyone create this deathtrap? How did anyone survive this? But more importantly, why would the Kingdom make people go through it? All of the pain just to be a Crystal Soldier? It didn't seem worth it.

The creatures were so close that they started to leap at Destrou. He frantically brushed his shoulders and back as some managed to jump onto his clothes. He felt them eat away the fibers instantly as if he was never wearing clothes. There were numerous sharp pains eating into his back that felt like he landed on a floor filled with broken glass. His eyes sealed shut as he screamed with agony. He peeled an eye open just in time, before he ran into another blockade.

With no regard to injury, he slammed his back to the ground, sliding a few feet underneath the stone structure. There was no severe amount of pain that he wouldn't endure to relieve himself of the torture of his flesh being eaten away.

Fortunately, the slide managed to peel the majority of them off of his back. He jumped, reaching his hands up to grab the top of the wall, pulling off his insect-filled shirt during the fall.

The drop was much higher than he expected. When he landed, the impact made his knees buckle, hitting his head on the floor. The room spun around. He saw patches of blood scattered throughout the floor. He pressed his hand on the ground, attempting to stabilize and reorient himself. He felt blood seep out from the open pores on his back. His hair had a red dye to it as blood dripped down his face. There was a red filter, obscuring his vision, noticing a red light at the end of the tunnel. He knew he needed to reach it.

Destrou turned around to the sounds of thuds. Insects fell from the wall, some landed on their backs before turning themselves over.

"Get up," he said to himself through his chattering teeth. "No more mistakes."

He could hear their pincers moving wildly, wanting to feast onto more of his flesh.

"Get up!" he screamed. "No more mistakes!"

With the last of his strength, he hobbled to his feet, limping toward the light. His limp turned into a stroll then a jog. By the time he regained partial consciousness, his pace evolved into a full-fledged sprint for his life.

He noticed that the light wasn't a light, at all. It was a hole that appeared just large enough to fit his torso, any smaller and he would have been trapped. He needed to jump perfectly through the hole but his vision was still fuzzy. He saw three different holes to jump into. Knowing that there was only one, he had just one chance to choose the right hole.

"No more mistakes," he screamed, placing his hands above his head and dove into the wall.

He winced, hearing the tearing sounds from the hole scratching his bare body, striping his skin with thin red lines.

A horn blared as he made it through.

A stinging sensation jolted through his body, like knives digging into his open wounds, as he splashed into a large mass of liquid ice. Swirls of red bubbles streamed by his face, mixed in with floating insects. Although they were no bigger than his thumbnail, he could see their many legs and sharp claws. Apparently the liquid ice instantly killed the remaining ones inside of his body; the feeling of drowning had never felt so good, he thought.

Before he could enjoy the moment, he heard two more splashes overhead. Two shadowy figures dove into the liquid ice, heading straight toward him.

The Leader and the Giant? he thought in a craze. His body was weak, wishing to give up at any moment but he knew that if they grabbed ahold of him, his life would be over.

Since they were above him, the only direction was to go deeper into the liquid ice. It was a death wish, but he had no other option.

He felt a stream of pressure pass by his face as his hands blindly flailed about. When he looked over his shoulder, he saw that his guess was correct: the Leader and the Giant were within an arm's reach away.

Were they waiting for me the whole time? Why haven't they moved on yet?

He believed to have answered his question when he saw two faint shimmers of light at the very bottom of the liquid ice. The two emblems. They looked like they were hundreds of feet away. How could anyone get there in one breath?

His lungs burned for air. His arms couldn't push any more. Luckily, the Leader and the Giant both gave up, floating back to the surface. He knew that he couldn't go back up, they'd be waiting. The options were grim: either die down there or at the surface. His eyes bulged out, desperately looking for an answer to the puzzle. There must be something that he wasn't seeing. If he knew one thing it was that this challenge was designed to be winnable; difficult, but winnable.

Even though swimming deeper into the liquid ice was foolish, he accepted the risk to win at any cost.

The deeper he swam, the more his vision blurred. His lungs cried for help as his mind floated in and out of consciousness. He remembered a time when the Giant pressed his weight around his neck and chest, squeezing every wisp of air from his lungs, and he was helpless, struggling to inhale, exhale, to do anything. In the past, he could rely on Ranmau to save him; but this time he was on his own.

Bubbles engulfed his face. He dug his broken fingernails into his neck as if panic wrapped around his throat, restricting any air from entering. He lost his calm, twisting and turning with no sense of direction.

Thud! The bubbles stopped as his feet ricocheted off of what appeared to be a large bubble submerged in liquid ice. How was it solid? What was it doing there? He realized that he couldn't question things anymore; he just needed to accept that his world was much different than he expected.

Destrou's hands pressed against the cold, slippery barrier, frantically searching for an opening of some kind.

Here! He saw his hand appear inside the clear enclosure. His hand rippled but felt dry and warm. With his last ounce of air, he dug his head into the opening, releasing a long inhale.

Air! His head jolted crazily, as if he was being stabbed, though filling his lungs with life.

He let out a frustrated scream. He wanted all of this to end already. He was alone, trapped deep inside of liquid ice, feeling a hook of regret tug at his heart. But he needed to shake it off; he chose this path. He chose to advance, to fight, to save Ranmau. He couldn't stop now, he made it too far.

Then he heard another set of muffled splashes overhead, as if the Leader and the Giant grew impatient and stormed toward Destrou.

He had figured out this stage. It was now a race to the bottom and he had a head start.

He knew that before he submerged himself again, he needed to find the next pocket of air. His gaze fixated on random ripples, looking for any type of clear imperfection.

There! He swam deeper to the bottom to the next air pocket about fifty feet away.

He had another moment of panic and found himself wishing to stop again. His negative thoughts were influenced by the constant, stinging sensations in his ears the deeper he swam. It felt like the insects made their way into his head, eating away at him from the inside.

About halfway down, the pain intensified. His ears throbbed so forcefully that he couldn't help screaming bubbles into his face. The ringing felt more like a hammer crushing his brain. He needed both of his hands to swim deeper, but he couldn't help pressing them against the sides of his head.

The next pocket was shallow and wide. There was just enough room to tilt his head to fit his nose and mouth. With winced eyes, he took a moment to observe the different architecture.

It's beautiful down here, he thought, trying to distract his mind.

There were spiraling columns along the walls that were dark and green as if they hadn't seen the light of day in centuries. It was cold and dank, with floating fluorescent globules lighting up the bottom of the ground. They created a beautiful starry night in the midst of nothingness.

He took a breath and saw the emblem underneath him. It was

about a hundred feet away. No matter how hard he looked, he was unable to find another pocket to travel to. Something in him burst then deflated like a popped bubble. He ignored it. He needed to try for the emblem.

This looks like the last one. It's now or never, he thought, looking up at The Leader and the Giant making their way toward him. *I can do this. I can actually make it to the finals.* He shook himself in a way that reminded him of his antics with Ranmau.

Sharp, icy chills bit his exposed skin as he dove one last time toward the emblems. The two of them appeared as large half moons, glowing in a starry night's sky. He held his breath the best way he knew how, repeatedly telling himself that he could do it. He closed his eyes and heard Ranmau's words in his head, urging him to never give up. "Don't stop!" It were these words that helped him achieve the impossible. "Don't stop! Keep going!" Those were the words that pushed him to climb the revolving pole and get the Eye of Eve. He did it. He did what no other villager had done. "Don't stop! Keep going!" He wasn't the krillen, he was Destrou, the boy who could do the impossible, just like his brother, Ranmau. *"Don't stop! Keep going!"*

Fighting the burn in his lungs, he stretched his arm out as far as he could.

Then it happened. He felt something warm in his hands. When he opened his eyes, he gasped. *I did it?* His hand wrapped around the slippery medallion. He attempted to pull it out but it wouldn't budge. He could barely grab it without losing traction.

Are you serious? he thought, feeling his heart race faster. *I don't know why I thought this would be easy.*

The emblem seemed to be fused into the podium—a part of the ground just as his head was a part of his body.

Now what am I supposed to do? Time was of the essence. There was nowhere to go except forward. Even if he did have the lung capacity to swim back up to the pocket, *they* would be waiting for him.

He tried twisting, pulling, pushing, and jerking. Nothing worked. He was running out of time. His lungs could only handle so much pain. *Everything has a purpose in these challenges, what's the purpose in this stage?*

One of the fluorescent orbs, that could only be described as an underwater snowflake, floated past his face. He felt a warm glow hover near his body as if it were made out of the acid.

He knew that it didn't make sense to grab it, but that was the exact reason why he did.

His hand wrapped around it, sizzling his palm. He felt layers of his skin disintegrate with a burn. He forced his glowing palm onto the emblem as his surrounding darkness was eradicated with a piercing white glow. Bubbles streamed out of his mouth, eyes, and ears as he pulled with all the strength that he had.

The emblem broke off with a *pop*, and Destrou immediately felt a force pull him deeper into the ground. He tried to fight it at first, but failed as waves of pressure wrapped around his ankles, making its way up to his torso, as if he was trapped in a tornado. His feet clamped together as his body helplessly flushed down the hole that appeared.

Darkness consumed him.

The hole turned into a twisting slide, twirling him around, accelerating him down in a dizzying rush. He had no control over his body as it toppled around, crashing into the sides of the tunnel at an alarming rate. He tried to catch a breath, but gushes of liquid ice splashed in his face.

After a few moments passed, his body came to a complete stop. Heart pounding and adrenaline burning through him, the challenge was almost over. He did it. He actually did it. He did what was thought to be impossible: he made it to the finals... without Ranmau.

Surrounded by darkness, he tried to move to take advantage of the head start, but nothing happened, not even a budge.

"I can't move, " he screamed as his breath bounced back into his face. He gritted his teeth, wiggling to move his arms, legs, hands, anything. He was stuck. He only had enough room to move his fingers around. Anxiety rushed through his mind as he felt himself enclosed in a cylinder barely large enough to fit his body. The space was so tight that his heavy breathing was restricted. His chest and stomach were unable to rise or fall without hitting the cold wall. His hands and feet were clamped together like he was being devoured by a snake.

"Help!" he screamed at the top of his lungs. "Okay... okay. Relax, Destrou. I need to relax." He paused for a moment before screaming again.

He slowed his breaths down, breathing in his own air.

"Make sense of this, Destrou. How can I get out?" he said, shrugging his shoulders.

Again, there was nothing.

"I can't move!" he screamed as frustration transformed his voice into a high-pitched squeal. "There's absolutely nothing that I can do," he sighed, closing his eyes. *Make sense of this, Destrou. What should I do. What can I do? There's always something, right?*

After a few moments passed, his eyes widened as he found the answer. He remembered the Guardian's words. "This whole challenge is about having the final two compete against one another. I guess it's made so that the last two would challenge one another."

From the very first horn, this challenge was designed for the final two to battle it out in the end. This entrapment made sure that the challenge performed as it was designed to.

Destrou thought this would be his chance to catch his breath, but if anything breathing was restrictive making it more exhausting than comforting. Standing on his feet for so long made his legs cramp. There was no break. No chance for relaxation.

At least he had plenty of time to think, the one thing that he was certain they could never take away. Questions formed, making him wonder why a challenge like this would ever exist.

"No matter what happens... this will be our last challenge, brother. Heh, I can't even call this a challenge. I can't believe real people died trying to win this. For what? If this was what someone had to go through to become a Crystal Soldier, then I don't even want to know what to expect. What could they be training for anyways? What was out there that made people think this was a smart idea? To go through all of this? I don't get it——what were they preparing for? Does Ranmau even know what he'd be getting himself into?"

He paused for a moment, as the reality settled on his mind, weighing him down. "The Archons?" He shivered. "They must have been real. Why else would there be beasts in here as practice? If that was their practice... what was the real thing? How tough could Archons have been where even after all of this training, it still took dozens of Crystal Soldiers just to try to take one of them down. The stories are just that, though: stories. There's no way... they can't be real. Archons can't actually be that powerful, can they?"

Fluttering noises interrupted his concentration as liquid ice poured into the cylinder next to his. His barrier was transparent enough to allow him to see the Leader slide into the container.

The Leader's body was a snug fit—immovable. The look on his face was nothing short of fear. Even the Leader didn't possess the mental capacity to handle the entire challenge. And the moment he was fully sealed, the blocks of ice started to rise above their heads, freeing their limbs.

"They said that I was too small, too weak, too dumb and too useless. They said that I'd be nothing if it weren't for my brother always saving me. Well, guess what? I made it this far. Even though my body wants to stop, my mind won't let me. I may not be the strongest, the smartest or the greatest, but I'm closer than I was yesterday. I'm as ready as I could ever be... I just hope it's enough."

There was no time to second-guess anything. Ready yet terrified, he felt the barrier rise over his torso. His cramped fingers moved, making sure that he still had feeling in them. A warm breeze rushed around his body. He lifted his head, absorbing its freshness into his nostrils. His vision was obscured. A blinding light forced his eyes to seal shut as the ice rose over his head. Slowly he peeled open his eyelids, fighting the urge to keep them closed.

You will get your freedom, brother.

I promise.

A horn blared.

The final challenge had begun.

25

THE SOUND OF A HORN BLARING hammered Destrou's ears. He was already off to a terrible start. The ringing in his ears didn't seem to stop and his eyes still hadn't been able to focus. Everything was blurry. And time and space had lost meaning as the dizzying lights pulsated through his brain, disturbing his senses even more. Everything felt surreal.

The entire stage was ice from the two lanes projecting into the horizon, to the forest of icicles hanging far above their heads. There was an eerie red glow that flashed within the ice, as if creating a sense of terrifying urgency.

Destrou felt that terror shake through his knees.

Parts of him were gone, or nearly gone. He was famished. His legs no longer wanted to move. His lungs had no desire to endure the burning pain of each breath. Despite it all, a glimmer of relief shocked through his body as he looked at the Leader who appeared to be just as distraught.

I think I'm faster than him, I can do this, Destrou thought, peering ahead at the straight path with a five-foot-tall ice wall separating their lanes.

A warm breeze had sprung up again. And with it came a sudden feeling of remorse. He had sympathy for the other boys who had almost died; they were just Villagers. They weren't kind, but they didn't deserve torture. No one deserved this. Despite his years of abuse, to him, no one in the Village should suffer in such a way. But it was him who needed to clench his teeth and tough it out until the end. He crouched his knees and pulled his arms to his side, focusing on the trail before him. He was ready.

He breathed slowly and closed his eyes. When he heard a horn blare again, he felt the shackles around his ankles break away, his eyes jolted open and the stage became a blur.

He dashed, gaining a slight advantage ahead of the Leader.

A rumble vibrated his body, causing him to crash into the barrier.

That smell. He turned around, immediately sending the message to his body to run—faster. A tidal wave carrying that toxic scent surged its way toward them.

He sprinted as fast as he could, hearing the booming splash reverberate around the room.

As they passed a gateway, the ground disappeared, except for dozens of columns spaced a few feet apart. A deadly free fall with no clear bottom separated the columns. Destrou felt the rush of the waves from behind.

He couldn't stop.

Just do it.

They both hopped perfectly from one platform to the next as the gaps became longer after each one.

The last leap was about twelve feet away. *This is way too far.* It took him about five seconds to realize he'd die if he didn't jump. The waves roared behind him. He crouched to prepare for the jump.

But nothing happened. One second, two, three seconds passed, and his legs refused to lift, his knees rattling. He couldn't stop imagining the fall to his death. What was down there? How far of a drop was it? It had to end eventually. He knew the limits to his weakened body and he didn't want to find out what awaited him at the bottom.

The more anxious he was to jump, the more it eluded him. Finally, he found the courage just as remnants of the flood splashed onto his heels. He jumped, feeling as if his body was on fire, and soared through the air.

The breaking wave descended over him.

The distance was too far.

He wasn't going to make it, even when he reached his hand out.

He'd thought that maybe if he grabbed onto the ledge then he'd be able to hoist himself up, but even that seemed impossible. His legs didn't have enough power. His body dropped before reaching the platform. His eyes widened with fear, thinking about what type of torturous death awaited him below.

He closed his eyes, accepting his fate.

I knew I couldn't make it. I wasn't supposed to make anymore mistakes. I failed y—

His thought was interrupted by a jerking pull, swaying his momentum like a pendulum. He catapulted upwards, evading the breaking wave as something let go of his wrist. His body twisted and turned before landing shoulder first onto the stone floor.

A *thud* shocked through his body, wondering if he had died or if it was just a dream.

He looked up, watching feet move soundlessly across the stone tiles.

"The Leader?" he said to himself, rubbing his eyes. "Did he just save me?"

The question relived a moment in his mind that he had almost completely forgotten about. He was too young then so the details remained blurred, but he remembered the Leader having an older brother named Massa. Much like Ranmau, he was the best of the best in the Village; he protected the Leader when he was too small to defend himself from the bullying of the Bruisers. Yes, even the

Leader couldn't escape its wrath. Massa was so great that every boy in the Village was convinced that if anyone had the ability to climb the Wall, he did. The seed was planted and they all encouraged him to make the climb. All but one: the Leader. He stayed up all night, desperately trying to sway Massa from the decision. He failed. And the next morning he witnessed Massa's body fall hundreds of feet, turning into a puddle of skin and minced bones upon impact. He mourned for days. And on the seventh day, he gave Massa's leftover food from the challenges to every boy in the Village. While most of the memory was cloudy, Destrou vividly remembered when he placed the food inside of his starved palms. "It was something that Massa would have wished for me to do. I have a promise to keep," he said, recalling the Leader's words.

Maybe there was still some good in him. Why else would he save me, Destrou thought.

Destrou then saw the Leader get swallowed up by the darkness.

Destrou followed and ran into a large opening with two large statues on both ends. They were humans made of stone and ice that stood twenty feet high. They held large swords in their hands with elaborate armor decorating their bodies. He didn't know what Crystal Soldiers looked like but whatever visual he had before was instantly replaced by these. Destrou recovered from the awe and brushed the debris off of his knees.

"This doesn't change anything," he said, straightening his back. "I'm still here to win."

Behind the opening, he could see nothing. He ran into it, unknowing if there was a steep slope or even a cliff. His bare feet stung, landing on rocks both jagged and smooth. There was a slippery, slimy texture to them, forcing him to focus on balance as he ran down the rocky strip. He heard the soft whispers of liquid ice flowing over the rocks. To his left and right, the rocks were covered with a bright green grime.

Since it was a bold color unfamiliar to him, he kept his distance from it. Curiosity wasn't worth the risk. He was close enough to see its hairy texture sway with the soft waves of liquid ice, but he didn't have the luxury to soak in the experience.

A part of me wishes that I could stay here. Something about this place feels so peaceful. So right.

The soft sounds, vibrant colors, and calming presence stilled his fear and gave him a feeling that he was home.

All of a sudden, he was overwhelmed by the thought of Ranmau. Home. He didn't know what happened to him. Was Ranmau dead, alive, injured, fine? How would he escape? Would he be trapped in here forever like the skeletons he saw? The last vision that he could create was Ranmau wincing with glazed eyes and a body filled with newly formed holes.

I promise I will win this for you. Somehow. Someway.

He was frozen with shock. Up ahead, he saw the Leader rubbing his hands against a wall of ice with nowhere else to go. Was he trapped?

"Now why hasn't he moved on? There is always something stopping us," he said to himself, looking around. "Maybe this is another climbing stage? But there's nowhere else to go... or maybe we have to—"

He was interrupted by a rumble beneath his feet. The Leader turned around, staring directly at him. Destrou grunted, knowing that he was no longer hidden in secrecy. The look on the Leader's face was unexpected, his eyes widened as his brows lifted.

Why does he look scared of me? Maybe I'm more powerful than I thought.

Another rumble caused him to fall onto all four, stabilizing himself as the ground shook from underneath him.

Within a moment, he was elevated five feet in the air as the rocks extracted from the ground with a thundering roar. Five feet turned to ten. Ten turned to twenty. Before he had the chance to understand what had happened, he realized that he was mounted on the head of a thirty foot monster made of stone, sludge, and slime. Saying that the beautiful, peaceful moment was ruined would be an understatement.

With a bellowing roar that spewed out grime from the hollowed crevices between its limbs, the beast shook the entire area.

Destrou fell backwards, rolling down its jagged spine. Gashes on his body reopened upon impact. He attempted to latch onto one of its extremities, but the slimy texture was too slippery. He crashed to the ground, diving out of the way, avoiding a stomp.

The BANG turned the stone floor into rubble.

"What the?" The Leader's screamed echoed a dozen times. "What is that thing!?"

"How am I supposed to know?" Destrou screamed back, jumping out of the way, avoiding another stomp.

They had seen many things during their lives in the Village, but nothing comparable to the enormity of this beast. Its body resembled a giant but it had no face, just a large, rounded boulder that dripped with slime and rubble. The rocky path turned into its spine and tail, jagged and sharp. Digging into the depths of the liquid ice, it pulled out a large stone slab that looked more like a tower than a spiked mace.

Destrou ran a slippery path toward the Leader, sliding to a halt.

"There is nowhere to go!" Destrou said, observing the room. In front of him was a dome of solid ice. Behind him was the only way out that was now filled with the monstrous beast.

"Duh! I would've found it already. What are we supposed to do?" the Leader screamed, diving out of the way as the mace smashed into the ground, shaking the room.

This BANG was the loudest one yet.

"Why do you keep asking me? How am I supposed to know?"

"Well, figure it out!" the Leader screamed as the monster pulled the weapon out of the ground, revealing a deep crater.

What Destrou wanted most, at the moment, was rest. He wished that he could let his body recover from the punishment and fall asleep and pretend that the challenge was just a nightmare; one that he'd wake up from at any moment. But that wasn't the case. The reality was that he was trapped in a dome with a beast who could obliterate the Guardian's lair with one swing. *With one swing? With one swing!*

"That's it," Destrou screamed as he looked around at the dome. He dove to the side, avoiding a thundering attack that sprayed shattered ice into the air as it struck the wall.

"What's it?" the Leader replied, ducking under a slash that embedded deep into the wall. When it pulled the weapon out, a piece of the dome crumbled with it. "What's the plan, you krillen? Tell me!"

"His swing," Destrou said, ducking underneath the mace that swung backward.

"What about it, krillen?" the Leader screamed, inching backwards until his back pressed against the cold wall.

"Dodge it!"

"Dodge it?" the Leader screamed, glaring at Destrou with a curled lip. He dove to avoid another strike. "Wow! What a smart idea! Why didn't I think of that? That's all that you have to say? Do you take me for a fool? What do you think I've been doing!? Dancing around for no reason!?"

The beast's wide frame trapped the Leader from moving any direction.

"No, try to dodge like this," Destrou said, grabbing a block of ice and throwing it at the monster's head.

The beast turned around with a roar that rumbled from its core. Despite the risk Destrou took in getting its attention, he knew it was the right choice. The monster, the mace, the dome, the trap. There was always an answer to the challenge based on its surroundings. He understood the concept of this challenge; he was sure of his plan. If only he wasn't so sleep deprived and starved...

The time had come when he heard the rumble before the strike. Through the gap between its legs, he could see the relief on the Leader's face. The growl faded out and the air went black for a moment. The mace was held high, its shadow casting over Destrou. A year ago, Destrou would have trembled, calling out for Ranmau. Instead, he was as confident as ever, awaiting the strike that could crush his life into a million pieces. He walked backwards until his back pressed against the cold ice. It was a familiar feeling. He had been surrounded by different for so many hours that he missed the common things. He took a deep breath as the spikes on the mace enlarged and curled one by one.

Destrou jumped just as the sweeping strike ripped through the bottom half of the dome, revealing a stone wall of some sort behind it. Destrou noticed random engravings carved onto it, like the ones he had seen on the Wall.

Destrou then twisted in between the curling spikes that seemed as sharp as swords. He ran up the weapon and jumped onto the goliath's head.

The beast stomped and shook its body as Destrou flipped off of its shoulder, landing on the ground for a moment before evading another sweeping strike.

The Leader watched on as Destrou evaded each attack, destroying the dome's foundation with each one.

Finally, what looked like the bottom half of a large stone door was revealed. An escape. Destrou's plan had worked. The Leader made his way toward the door and Destrou followed. The monster lifted its mace above his head, preparing for another strike. The two had the same plan in mind. As the monster lunged its weapon forward, they dove toward opposite sides.

BANG! The door obliterated open. The rubble was instantly sucked deeper into the void.

Their hair and clothes were pulled into the darkness like a vacuum. The shattered door revealed a tunnel into a dark room. They wasted no time running toward the opening. Once inside, they found two pieces of rope dangling from an unknown source. There were separate tunnels for each seemingly infinite piece of rope. Arching his head back, Destrou wasn't able to see when the tunnel ended.

"Only one way to go," Destrou said, jumping up and grabbing the rope. "I don't want to see that ugly thing ever again."

The Leader did the same.

It was now a race to the top. Destrou knew that they both battled exhaustion and starvation, but he also knew that their teamwork ended back there. If he stopped moving, the Leader would pass him and be gone in a second. He knew that the Leader wasn't the type to give up and his body was physically made for this type of challenge.

The climbing ate away at Destrou's fatigue. Cold seeped into his bloodied body as the walls of the cylinder grazed his skin. Destrou wrapped his legs around the rope, trying to not rely on what little upper body strength he had left. He had always lacked arm strength, but now it was even worse. He needed to get up their first, but for a moment he stayed there, digesting the whole challenge. The stages, the boys, the torture, the liquid ice, the monsters, the design, the enormity, the adversity. The challenge made him realize that Elu was indeed right all along: there was a world beyond the Wall that had the answers she longed for.

He didn't know how much time had passed. Ten, twenty, maybe thirty minutes of climbing. Suddenly, the rope ended. His hand touched solid ground, barely possessing the strength to pull himself up. He was shocked to see that he made it up first. It was an empty room that reminded him of an enlarged version of the Box. It wasn't the best reminder to have.

What's the purpose of this stage? he thought, observing the room. There was nothing special about it. It was an ice box with four walls and two holes. Simple... except for a circle that was engraved into one of the walls. He approached it, searching for a clue.

The circle looked horrifyingly familiar, making his jaw drop. His eyes widened.

He understood the reason. *Of course.* He sighed, shaking his head. *I shouldn't have expected anything else.*

His heart then dropped to his stomach as he heard deep breathing from behind. He was right. He wished he wasn't.

"So, this is where we finish, huh?" the Leader groaned, stretching his arms and legs. He only stretched like that when he was preparing for one thing: combat.

The final challenge would be a duel.

The circle on the wall was two half circles. Destrou lifted his hand, analyzing the half circle emblem burned onto his palm. *And this is what he needs to advance.*

Out of everything that he hoped wouldn't happen in the challenge, combat with the Leader was on the top of the list. He would have rather bathed in the odors of the Guardian than resort to fighting the Leader.

Slowly, Destrou arched his back and cracked his neck. There was no running. He needed to stay and fight. He had to.

"Now that we don't have some monster trying to kill us, I need to know something," the Leader said, circling around Destrou like a lion sizing up its prey.

"What's that?" Destrou replied, steadily backtracking.

"Loyalty is very, very important to me," he growled. "So, I'll go easy on you and make this less painful if you just tell me who helped you."

"Helped me?" Destrou narrowed his eyes.

"You heard me, krillen!" he snarled. "I was being nice, don't make me mad. Who helped you?"

"Helped me with what?" Destrou said. "I don't know what you're talking about."

"Don't lie to me! Lying is a reason to kill you right now!"

"I'm not lying," Destrou said, feeling his heart pump faster.

"Krillen, I do not like being lied to; so, I'm going to give you one... last... chance to tell me who the traitor is," the Leader said, pounding his fists together.

Destrou said nothing.

"Tell me!" the Leader screamed, belting saliva from his mouth.

Destrou didn't know how to answer the question. If he continued to say nothing the Leader would be angry, but if he asked another question then he would be furious. "Why'd you help me?" he whispered to himself.

"What!?"

"Why'd you save me... back there?"

"I didn't save you back there."

"You... did though."

"No, Elu saved you back there. If it were up to me, you would have been dead and I'd be the winner by now."

"Elu... saved me?" Destrou's eyes welled up.

"Yes!" he groaned. "Elu made me promise to give you one chance to live. Elu made me promise to pardon your life just once if your life was ever in danger and I am a man of my word. I gave him my word. MY word! As much as I hated saving you, what would I be if my word meant nothing? Our word is all that we have here; which is why I need to know who defied me. I spent a long time making this Village work the way that it does. It works. And order makes it work. Loyalty makes it work. When krillens sneak behind my back and give you the code to the challenge, then I need to know who did it because they will be punished. Because now... there is nothing left to save you. No more word. No more pardon. So, you better start speaking."

Destrou felt something within him find a peace that he had been searching for. Elu saved his life despite no longer physically being a part of the world. Destrou's heart smiled for a moment, thankful to call her a friend—a guardian angel of some sort. But he couldn't remain distracted. He had a challenge to win.

"Code?" Destrou said, shaking off his thoughts, and remembered what the boys had said earlier in the challenge.

"Don't play dumb! Don't play dumb with me! Don't do it!" the Leader said, slamming his fists against the wall until they bled. His eyes told the story of the Village's affliction to wither away one's mind to the brink of insanity. It was the author to every painful story told. "The Guardian said that it'd be impossible—IMPOSSIBLE—for anyone to move on unless they had the code. He said no one, not even a Crystal Soldier was able to solve the maze without the code, so don't lie to me. WHO. HELPED. YOU!?"

"I didn't have a code," Destrou said. Many questions rushed through his mind. "Why would the challenge be designed that way?"

"Hah," the Leader cackled. "Don't you get it? Only people they want to become Crystal Soldiers become one. That's the way the system always worked. It's smart if you ask me. You know, to make it seem fair and all. But unless they were given the code, they were left to die in the maze. It was their way to make sure that krillens like you didn't become one and ruin their name. What don't you get about that? They don't want krillens like you to become one of us, they never have and never will. Look at you!" He pointed his finger at Destrou. "You're too small and weak. It's for people like me! I deserve it! That's why I was chosen! I will win this and then I will win the tournament—just as they planned. They said I will able to see my father again. I will make it happen! And you and your brother will not even be alive to witness it."

Death began to settle on him. His world was spinning. *How could they do that to people? So not everyone can become a Crystal Soldier, only people they want? You mean it didn't even matter if you were the strongest or the best, it only mattered if they liked you? This world is a terrible place.*

The fatigue that weighed him down wasn't the usual tiredness that he felt after a challenge. Mentally, he was exhausted. Physically, he was starved and bruised. Even the simple act of thinking made Destrou want to groan. Or sit down. Or at least ease his aches with relaxation on a comfy skin of fur. But neither was happening. In the moment, he had death looming over his shoulder, wishing to introduce himself. *What was the point of going through all of this if they already had the winner set in their mind?* The answer that formed in his head sent a chill through his spine, blackening his eyes.

"So, tell me. Who is the traitor?" the Leader said.

Destrou glared at the Leader, tightening his fists and sliding his feet into position, tiny shavings of ice crunched at his soles. "You are," he growled.

"So this is how you want it to end?" he cackled, cracking his knuckles. "This will be fun."

* * *

Vayp dropped the book with a loud thud. He scurried away from the pages as if they were venomous snakes.

"Who is the traitor?" Vayp repeated the Leader's words and stared up at Han'sael. Vayp dropped his voice and proceeded in a sort of low rumble. "Admit it, Hanny… you won't be my friend once you find out who the traitor is."

And although the thought of a broken friendship with Han'sael made his heart sink, suddenly a buried thought made his chest collapse. "You *will* make it… won't you?" Vayp wanted to say more but something was stuck in his throat. After gazing at Han'sael for what felt like years, he continued: "I don't know what I'll do… if you… if you don't." Vayp looked away. "It'll all be my fault… because… I am the traitor."

Do not worry about the boy, a cold thought appeared in his mind. *Worrying will not increase his chances in surviving. If it is not in his stars, there is nothing any of us can do about it.*

When Vayp turned around, he was shocked to see that it wasn't the usual shadow. Where had this one been all this time?

I have been thinking.

"About what?" Vayp said.

Nothing... yet everything. I have been reflecting on my time here... and how much I may miss this. It will all be but a memory soon enough.

"What do you mean?"

I will be going home soon. The shadow then walked to Han'sael. *I hope he does survive. We all are doing our part. The world will be ending soon. But appreciate the time you have with your friend while you have it. It can all be gone within the blink of an eye. And then all you will have are memories; but memories will never take away the pain of what you lost. They will just be haunting reminders of what once was.*

Vayp looked at the shadow, who now gazed up at the sky. He understood what the shadow meant, it was the reason he avoided thinking about Ah'nyx.

I have seen how you can spend a lifetime alongside someone, yet feel as if you were never there. I have seen how a connection with someone is not determined by how close or often you stand by them... but how many times you look at one another... and feel nothing. I hope this does not happen to you.

Vayp didn't know what to say. He looked up at Han'sael and prayed to the Divines that Han'sael will survive this.

The Divines will not answer your prayers... you are one of us now.

One of us, Vayp thought. Was that really how the world will remember him...

You know, he was not always like this. And neither was I. He has more pain in his heart than love, but love is there. I feel it in his silence. You may hate him now, but one day, when you wish for a second chance at life, you will appreciate all the sacrifices he made. He may have lost much of him, but he has never lost his word. He said he will take me home, and I trust him. Just as you should when he said you will get your Sol back. But I am afraid for him. For when I go home, he will have no one.

I will have my master. The shadow emerged in front of Vayp, black smoke billowing from his shoulders. *Do not get soft now, we still have a plan to execute.*

We do.

"Who is your master?" Vayp said.

He is the one person who took me in and let me know of my destiny. The one who let me know I am not alone, that there are others like me.

"What about your family?" Vayp said.

Family? At once, Vayp collapsed to his hands and knees as a great force pulled him to the ground. It felt as if he was at the complete mercy of a gravity so powerful it could make the planet implode. *Family is the disease of the planet. The love for family is the most selfish love of all. It is what creates wars. My family. My father. My mother. It is always my my my. And it is this selfish love that manifests the disregard for others. Because it starts as defending my family, then my people, my Kingdom, my race, and my element. This selfish My is what makes the others the enemy. And it all stems from the disease of family love and its sheepish selfishness. This is why I love watching entire family trees disintegrate to ash.*

There was a time when you did not.

We all are naive at one point.

Then the ground rumbled with such a force, it felt like the planet had broken orbit.

Well, it seems the Ma'sahk is finally ready.

Vayp arched his back and saw a shadowy beast so large Vayp was unable to see its head. He felt his lungs sink to his stomach.

And I will be going home soon?

Yes.

They stared at one another for long moments, not saying a single word.

And is that all?

Yes.

"What will happen to Han'sael?" Vayp said, pressure building up behind his eyes.

I do not make promises I cannot keep. You will get Ah'nyx back when you kill S'rae. And he will go home when he is ready. The shadow pointed at Han'sael.

"What does Han'sael have to do with his home?" Vayp said.

You will see soon enough. So get back to reading. The end… is here.

26

FUJAK

IT WAS ONE OF THOSE NIGHTS SO VIVID in nightmares, yet something Fujak had never thought would actually become a reality. The room was cold and dry. On both sides of him the silence from their rooms let him know that he was not alone. That they felt for him. That they understood what he had endured. The silence was complicated. On one hand he wished for it to end, for someone to speak. To say a word. To attempt to comfort him. But on the other hand, he wanted nothing more than to forget any of this happened, and talking about it would only relive the memory. And for that… he was thankful for the silence. He was thankful for them.

Fujak touched the right side of his face. He felt the smooth skin despite his chapped fingers. He gripped his chin, then slowly touched his lips, then pressed a finger to his nose, but his hand trembled as he made his way to the side he hadn't dared touch since leaving that room. The room where the Warden had brought him, bound him to a chair, and dipped a dagger into an incurable, flesh-eating substance known as Archon's Blood. A part of him was thankful for the darkness, he had no way in seeing the disfigurement, but now his curiosity finally wanted to feel the damage that was done.

He grabbed his wrist and took a deep breath. And when he went to touch the left side of his face, the first tear was shed. His sense of touch gave him vision in the darkness... and what he saw... was a face he'd never want to see the light of day ever again.

He felt a deep crevice as if a jagged shovel had dug flesh from his face.

He then heard Reyna sob as if she had seen it for herself.

"I am so... so sorry." Fujak heard from the sobbing in the other room. "I shouldn't have let it happen."

Fujak wanted to say something, anything, but all he could do was rub the side of his face and imagine what it had looked like before; he wanted to hold on to a single image of who he was before this scar, if that was what he could call it.

His hand trembled harder as he touched his eye and realized the scar had extended beyond it, to his forehead. It then occurred to him that he could be blind from that eye and have no way in knowing.

That thought alone made Fujak collapse inside. He made sure that his mind was tough, that he did not scream, but now he felt it breaking down. As if he had just understood what Reyna had said since the beginning: *There is no leaving Alsi'jin, only dying.*

He was innocent... yet he was going to die here as a murderer? And there would be no tears from the public, only celebration. But sad as that was, it wasn't what bothered Fujak the most. No, what made his heart ache was that he would not be the first innocent to suffer such a fate.

And when he fell to his knees and cried into his arms for what felt like days, he finally found the strength to say a word: "Can you... sing to me?"

He needed an escape, anything. And much like the memory he had of a mother he could barely remember, who would sing him to sleep with a voice from the heavens, he felt like that same child who needed someone to tell him that his nightmares were not real, that there was good in life, and it was waiting for him.

He heard shuffling behind the door and a loud thud as if Reyna's head had hit the wall.

"What would you like me to sing?" came Reyna's voice with a hiccup.

"Anything… anything good."

Fujak closed his eyes as Reyna's notes took him to a different place. He felt her words sweep him from his feet, then float him down the metal hallways, through the gates, and lift him into the sky. And much like her song, the view was breathtaking. Beautiful. And most of all, it was exactly what he needed.

> "When the crops no longer came, and the birds no
> longer sang…
> The sun, oh the sun it still rose.
> When the dragons could not be tamed, and the
> thrones could not be claimed…
> The sun, oh the sun it still rose.
> Sometimes you can miss something that has never gone,
> But you realize it is different and in this difference you mourn.
> And when life fades like a season, and you wish
> for something to believe in…
> Just wait child and you will find your reason.
> Because life comes and goes.
> With strife, fun, and woes.
> And death finds his part, filling your heart with
> sorrow and pain.
> But it will not remain.
> Because the sun, oh the sun it still rose, and tomorrow is still yours to change."

And when Reyna stopped singing, Fujak felt his spirit fall from the heavenly clouds and the bright blue sky and land back into this dark, cold room. But he felt no sadness upon his return, because that trip was indeed exactly what he needed.

"Thank you for that," Fujak said, letting his hand fall from his face. "That was beautiful." He stood up to his feet and sifted through Reyna's melodies, focusing now on the words. "*When the dragons could not be tamed...*" Fujak closed his eyes. "What is the song referring to?"

Fujak heard movement behind the wall, then came her voice: "It was just a song my village elders would sing."

Fujak heard the hesitation in her voice. "It is *never* just a song. Not one like that. That is an allegory."

"You *are* a smart one. Well, they did say that the *sun* was not a sun at all, but a person."

Then Fujak heard a soft thud from the opposite room. "Most interesting."

And judging by the gasp Fujak heard from Reyna, she too was caught off guard.

"And where have you been all this time?" Reyna said excitedly, as if happy to hear that their friend was still alive.

"Oh me?" the voice said. "I'm much older, I need many more hours of sleep."

"More like many more days," Reyna said in a somewhat joking manner, because there were times when they had thought he had died.

But still they remained, yet the wonder of *how long* was the unasked question that made the air colder whenever they said their "Good night." They all understood the truth: that it was unknown if their last night would be their last night.

"Good to have you back," Fujak said.

"Good to see you are still alive," the voice replied.

And then it hit Fujak. "What is your name, friend?"

"How kind of you to ask," the man said. "You can call me Terese."

The three of them then talked for hours and hours about anything and everything. From the Great Wars to politics of the Kingdoms to the Circle of Time and the special elements. It was this topic of the elements that was most foreign to Fujak that received most of his attention.

"So, Reyna, you mean to tell me that there are myths of Elementials exceeding their own element's limit?"

"Well, I wouldn't say they are myths," Reyna said. "Like look at Va'han,"—which made Terese gasp—"it was said that he exceeded his element so divinely that he practically became the God of Time."

Fujak scratched his head. "And which element was that exactly."

"Water," Terese chimed in.

"Well," Fujak said, "if this was truth, not a myth, why wouldn't anyone else know about this?"

"Because you do not know it, it does not mean *they* do not," Terese said. "It simply means it is another thing they wish to be forgotten, not learned."

"Why would that be?" Fujak said.

"Because those in power fear that what is more powerful than them," Terese said, a slow tapping was heard as if he had rolled his fingers against the wall. "Have you ever paid attention to the Kingdoms' marks? The secret is hidden inside them. Ever notice the hourglass inside Sereni? Or the energy of Harahn'de or the—"

"What about Fujita?" Fujak said, his eyes wandering about as if his world was spinning.

"It is said that when one exceeds Wind... they will be able to break the speed of sound and control it in the process."

Fujak said nothing. Though everything was black, he stared down at what he knew to be a cold metal floor. "And what about Earth?"

"Only the most powerful of them all," Reyna said.

And Fujak did not need to think much of who that would be. "Eve." Fujak felt his stomach imploding. What else had they been hiding for him, the heir of Fujita herself. "What of the dualities? Does Metal, Lightning, Ice, or Shadow have such a God?"

"It is said that there are only two of them who achieved such a status. The all-powerful Vy'ken is one... and..." Terese said, and Fujak could hear sorrow in his voice. "And the other happens to be the most powerful person of them all."

"Even more powerful than Eve?"

Terese laughed then apologized immediately after. "This person is far, far more powerful than Va'han and Eve. This God is so powerful... they say even the Divine One is no match for him."

"How could that be possible?" Fujak heard his voice break with worry.

"How could the Circle of Time be possible? This is why it is important that the final Geddon is not reborn."

Fujak felt the hairs on his arms stand on end at that name. Then moments flashed before his eyes. He was suddenly reminded of his purpose, of his destiny, that he was a Chosen One. He heard Gabrael speak of the Shadow Army and of Geddon being reborn. And without thinking, a deep voice, stronger than any he had ever heard from him before, leapt from his throat. "I need to leave this place."

"There is no leaving, Fujak," Reyna said. "There is only—"

"Oh... but there IS a way out," Terese said.

"No..." Fujak heard Reyna's voice shake. "No, there is not!"

"You of all people know that there is," Terese said, and Reyna went silent.

"It is *not* a way out. It is death."

"It *is* a way out... if one believes it is. And I believe Fujak may have what it takes."

"You do not understand the Warden," Reyna's voice shook so much, Fujak heard the tears that followed. "This would be exactly what he would want."

Fujak's head kept twisting from left to right as he heard the two of them argue. His curiosity finally peaked. "What is this way out?"

"It is—" Before Terese could speak, Reyna had screamed at the top of her lungs.

"LA LA LA LA LA!"

"What was that?" Fujak said.

And when Terese repeated it once more, it was drowned out by more of Reyna's screaming.

"I couldn't hear you," Fujak screamed.

Then finally with a BOOM that rattled the room, Terese shouted: "THE ALTA'JRIBA!"

And at once Reyna went silent and Fujak heard a loud thud followed by even louder sobs. "Please, Fujak, I beg you… please… don't!"

"What is the Alta'jriba?"

"Just don't," Reyna cried. "Please… don't!"

"It is your way out," Terese said. "And if you are as innocent as you say you are, that means the killer is still out there. Your friend may need your help."

"S'rae…" Fujak's voice choked out into a gasp.

"That's her name," Reyna said. "She sounds beautiful."

"And more," Fujak said.

"Would you be willing to risk your life to save hers?" Terese asked.

Fujak didn't hesitate to answer. "I would."

"You are a great friend, Fujak," Terese said. "It pains me to see you stuck inside here. This is your way out. Take it."

Reyna's voice went cold. "Do you… love her?"

Fujak said nothing.

"Sometimes no answer… is the answer," Reyna said.

"Don't worry," Fujak said, "when I leave here… I will come back for you, both of you. I will free you… and I will right the wrongs of the flawed system. I promise you."

"Do not worry about me," Reyna said. "I am a dumb, stupid Earthie who failed at everything in life, my life is worthless."

"Reyna... I have learned more from you than I have in my years of education at Fujita, the School of Wind and *Wisdom*. You are far brighter than you would ever know. Maybe... the issue was never that you were not smart enough... maybe the issue was that you were not taught the element you were truly meant for."

And Fujak's words must have hit a chord inside Reyna, because she sobbed even louder.

Then Fujak touched his face and the reality set in. He was no longer who he used to be. "Can a monster be loved?" Fujak felt tears flow over his hand as he rubbed his scar.

Reyna stopped sobbing at once. "Your heart and your mind are what's most important. And they are the greatest I've ever seen. If one does not love you because of your scar, then she does not deserve your heart."

Fujak took a deep breath. "That was the nicest thing anyone has ever said to me."

"I do not lie... either."

"Thank you—" Then Fujak was interrupted by the sound of banging as if a stampede rushed toward them.

"No..." Reyna gasped, as if she knew what that sound meant: the Warden was arriving.

Then a silence swept through the hall. It weighed him down in ways he wasn't prepared for. It was the type of silence that was like the calm before the storm. The type that let him know he was fine, for now, but once the silence finally broke, his world would never be the same.

And so the silence was bittersweet, broken only by the occasional sob from Reyna.

And then the door opened, and the storm arrived. It came as rolling thunder as footsteps roared down the hall. It came as lightning that shocked life into him as his cell door blasted open. And finally, it came as rain… as tears fell from his eyes just before he said the words: "I request Alta'jriba."

A faint thud was heard as if Reyna had fallen to her knees.

Then came the low growl of the Warden's voice. "Oh how perfect the day is! How the Divine must be smiling down upon on me! Justice will indeed be served. This is just the revenge I have been waiting for."

Fujak winced as a tight grip wrapped around his neck and flung him out his cell.

"Have faith," Reyna said, "and faith will have you. We are here for you."

"I will miss you two," Fujak said. "No matter what happens, I am glad that our paths have crossed. And when I am free, I will set the two of you free."

"Hah!" the Warden cackled madly. "You truly have gone mad. Who else are you talking to? There are only the two of you here."

"Two?" Fujak and Reyna said at once.

"What about Terese?" Fujak said.

"Terese?" The Warden squeezed Fujak's neck tighter, feeling as if it would break under any more pressure, and he shouted with laughter. "Oh, Terese, you there? Terese. Oh, Terese! Where are you?" And when nothing was heard, the Warden pulled Fujak's head closer to his mouth, so close, he had smelled the stench of his breath. "You fool, I made sure there are only the two of you scum here. You truly have gone mad. I suppose you chose the perfect time… to die."

And if it were not for the confusion in Reyna's voice as well, Fujak may have thought he had gone completely mad. But as the Warden dragged him away and he blocked out Reyna's sobs, he thought to himself: *who was Terese?*

27

"⟨⟨OH YES, YOU'RE ABSOLUTELY RIGHT, this looks *just* as beautiful as I imagined," S'rae said, turning to grin at Bele who hung onto a branch beside her. He helped her up onto the branch, and his hand rested politely on her waist, just above her vine belt.

Bele then lifted her into the air as she grabbed onto another branch that glistened white, the same ivory color of all the leafless trees that surrounded them.

"You know, if I wasn't a genius," Bele said, "I would think you were being sarcastic."

S'rae smiled back at Bele. Her hands now clamped around a branch as they climbed higher up this pure white oak tree.

"Well, you said I'd be seeing one of the most beautiful things Gaia has ever created, but all I see are empty trees."

"You just wait, S'rae, we haven't even gotten to the best part yet!" Bele smiled up at S'rae, dozens of branches striping her vision of him.

"Oh I'm waiting alright. Waiting for the biggest disappointment ever." Though she said what she said, she certainly didn't mean it. She felt her face flush at the idea of a handsome man showing her a surprise. A part of her still did not want him to see just how easily he could make her smile; she didn't want him to view her as a vulnerable little girl.

"Here we are." Bele leapt up and landed as the tree rattled. They stood atop the highest point in the White Forest and S'rae began to appreciate what Bele was talking about. A group of squirrels were found carrying nuts into holes inside a tree. And woodpeckers added a delightful *tap tap tap* as birds accompanied them with beautiful songs of their own. It felt like she was suddenly at an orchestra created by nature. None of the sounds were random, they were all perfectly timed as if the music was somehow planned.

Bele turned to S'rae, a smile glowed from his lips and she felt her heart flutter. Was this his plan?

Bele leaned in to S'rae's ear, his soft whisper smelled like citrus and tickled her skin, sending pleasant shivers through her body. "I want you to whistle this tune."

Bele stood behind her and placed his hands on her waist. And then the most pleasant sounds came from his mouth as she felt all the hairs on her body stand up. He whistled a tune so beautiful and pure it must have come from the Divine One himself.

And when he finished, S'rae let out a soft moan and unclenched her fists. She shook her head, wondering what sorcery had just happened to her. It felt like her soul had left her body in a state of ecstacy.

"Now you do it," Bele said, "but louder. Here—" Bele pressed his thumb to her temple. "—this will help."

And suddenly she began whistling the harmony so flawlessly that her eyes widened. And the longer she whistled, the more the other animals joined in with music of their own. Birds chirped to her melody, woodpeckers added the percussion, even the squirrels and rodents joined in with rhythms of their own.

Then the ground rumbled, feeling as if the tree would collapse underfoot. A one-hundred-foot fall was not the surprise she was looking forward to. But before anxiety had the chance to surge through her, birds of every different color rushed by them from the ground to the sky. Dozens flew up pass her, then hundreds; they kept swooping by at an alarming rate until they filled the sky, creating a rainbow murmuration that waved and danced to the rhythm of their song. It was their song, hers and nature's. And Bele was right, the way the rainbow colors flowed in the sky, switching direction at random as if all the birds were one, it truly was one of the most beautiful things S'rae had ever seen.

"Now, whistle this," Bele whispered into her ear.

And when S'rae did, birds broke away from the murmuration and swept them from their feet, drifting them into the sky, as if they were now riding on a rainbow-sparkling carpet through the clouds.

And then it began, a magical tour of GroundStone. They swooped by great pyramids, the mile-high statues of Sols, the temples and their golden towers. They burst by giraffes and elephants picking fruits from the trees. They watched Wave Riders and Runners sprint atop waves of sand, and they even stopped to eat Chocolate Gold from the hut where bees and chimps fused their honey and cocoa, which tasted even better than it sounded. And as the hours went on, S'rae felt herself unfolding slowly out of her shy behaviour around Bele. She no longer tried her hardest to hide her smile, and because of that, her face hurt after smiling wide for what felt like forever. She even found herself laughing. And she had Bele to thank for it.

Worries? There were none.

"This was amazing! Truly the most beautiful thing Gaia ever created," S'rae exclaimed. And when to her surprise, Bele shook his head, she said, "Well, at least I thought so."

Bele, whose skin reflected the blues, purples, and pinks from the birds, turned to her and said, "I've saved that for last."

She felt her stomach lift to her lungs as they descended down into an open courtyard filled with statues. Before they landed, the birds halted immediately as a swirl of dust burst around them, and they were gently placed on their feet.

"Bye, amazing birds!" S'rae waved wildly as they flew off. "I think they're my new best friends! I was honestly trying to think of a name for each one, but there were so many!" S'rae turned around and realized she was talking to herself. No one was around but dozens of statues of a beautiful Goddess, most likely Eve. "Bele?" S'rae turned around. The smile that she had worn for the past few hours wavered slightly. She prayed this wasn't a trap.

"You know what is most fascinating about you?" The voice from behind her made her jump. She turned and saw Bele, who for some strange reason looked even more attractive than before, though nothing about him changed physically. To her, he glowed with some unexplainable energy that she could not put her finger on.

"What's that?" S'rae said, covering her cheeks.

"You should be much like me… one of the most confident people around. You are an excellent student, yet you consider yourself a failure more than a success. You have a mind as sharp as a talon, yet at times you question yourself. But… most of all… and the reason we are here… you, S'rae—" His hands wrapped around her waist as their eyes locked. "You are the most beautiful thing, person, gift that Gaia has ever created, yet you would never believe it. And it is important for you to know that. Why? Because once you start to understand the truths about you that you try to deny, then you'll be able to see just how special you are."

"I am *not*—" S'rae giggled and blushed before she could finish the sentence. "I am *not* anywhere close to being the most *anything* of Gaia."

"Well, I would argue that you would be the most oblivious then," Bele smiled.

S'rae was shocked, not by his comment, because she expected something like that from him by now, but by her reaction. She did not want to punch his punchable smirk. No. She wanted to do something else completely. She didn't know exactly what that was… but it felt like the exact opposite of punching.

"You know, I did a little research about you," Bele said, tossing a berry into his mouth.

"Oh yeah? And what did you find?" S'rae felt sweat seeping into her shoes without really knowing why she was nervous. What could he possibly find out about her?

"Yes. You see… you told me a few days ago that you were fifteen point nine years old. So that made me question, when were you born? I then thought to myself, with the attitude you have, you must have been born on a full moon. So I checked back to the dates of full moons, and it turns out… that sixteen years ago on this date was a full moon. And so this—" Bele tossed another berry into his mouth. "—this day was my surprise birthday present to you. Happy sixteenth birthday, S'rae."

S'rae said nothing, but her eyes were already watering. It then occurred to her that she had been focused on absolutely everything else that has been going on that *she* forgot today was her birthday… but *he* knew. No one had ever planned an event for her birthday before. No one at Fujita even knew when it was her birthday… but him… Bele… he went through the extra effort to make sure she didn't miss it.

"The sixteenth is an important birthday, I figured it should be a memorable one."

Without thinking, S'rae had wrapped her arms around Bele and cried into his chest. "Thank you so much for this! No one has ever done something like this for me—" Then immediately her breath was cut short. A memory flashed before her eyes without notice.

She was back at Opella, playing with Ah'nyx and Vayp in the sand field. She then saw herself crying inside their hut, most likely sad about still not having a Sol. She saw herself tucked in her bed as Vayp snuck out in the middle of the night. She had wondered where he went and she had stayed up all night to make sure he came back home safely. What she thought would have been only an hour or so ended up being the whole night until sunrise when Vayp snuck back into his bed, pretending that he had been asleep the whole night.

And when she walked into the village courtyard, she saw dozens of foreign animals waiting for her. Vayp had acted like they arrived by accident because it was her birthday, but she had cried into his arms, because she knew he had traveled dozens of miles to bring them to her. And what made her cry harder was how after none of the animals were her Sol, Vayp had done that night after night, putting in hours of work each night, just to round up as many animals as he could to surprise S'rae with her potential Sol.

S'rae was snapped back into the moment as Bele caressed her head. Her tears kept pouring. She rubbed her eyes into the soft fabric of his robe. She was thankful for Bele because now her greatest birthday moment was no longer held by the traitor. But still she wept, thinking about their childhood together and how everything once felt so perfect.

"What's wrong?" Bele said, pulling her away so their eyes met.

"I bet you don't think I'm the most beautiful person now," S'rae chuckled as she wiped her eyes, knowing she must have looked like a mess.

"What do you think?"

"I think the berries got you drunk again," she smiled, and Bele chuckled.

"What do you think about these statues?" Bele said, pointing at each one.

"I think I wish I could be half as beautiful as her." S'rae rubbed her eyes to get a better look.

"What if I told you that you do not think you're beautiful because the only times you view yourself in the mirror are when you are sad. But if you were to see yourself as I do, as we do, you'd be convinced of how breathtaking you really are." Bele walked up to a statue of a girl smiling wide, with her palms pressed to her cheeks.

"She's absolutely beautiful," S'rae exclaimed.

"I know," Bele smiled. "That was you when you first met Mysol." Bele walked over to a different statue, the girl's eyes were majestically wide, as if they were the happiest eyes could look. "This was you when you first transformed into the squirrel."

And S'rae thought he was lying because the girl in the statues, the ones she was looking at, was exactly what she pictured when she thought of what a happy, beautiful girl would look like.

"These... can't be me." S'rae shook her head. "They look... so beautiful."

"And now you're beginning to understand... why you are the most beautiful girl Gaia has ever created." Bele grabbed her hand.

"Why are you being so nice to me?" S'rae's eyes began to water. "Nothing good happens to people who are nice. My best friend was found guilty of attempted murder... and my brother—"

"You have a great destiny ahead of you, S'rae. I believe you are one of the Protectors of Eve and Gaia. I believe you are ready for your dragon. And I believe you need to be confident in yourself to be able to handle the powers that come with having one."

This night could not have gone any better, S'rae thought as the purply blue sky faded to black.

And as Bele and S'rae stared into one another's eyes, not saying a word, commotion was heard beyond the walls of the courtyard.

Bele snapped his fingers and all the statues absorbed into the ground. He glanced at S'rae and, as if noticing her eyes droop, he said, "Don't worry, those statues are in the most important place of all." He pointed at his head. "They are gone, but not forgotten."

They walked toward the commotion into a square garden surrounded by sand walls with lit torches and statues of beasts. People dressed up in all types of costumes were walking around the edges of it, murmuring in low voices as if they were sharing secrets. None of them noticed S'rae and Bele as they approached a table where kids were slamming cards onto the table and screaming loudly.

"The Card Duels tournament will be Sol rules!" a boy with black and white face paint said, yanking the hat off of his head and throwing it by S'rae. "You know what this means, don't ya? Huh? Do you know what this means? It means you ALL will crumble by the force of my master deck!" The boy cackled maniacally before meeting S'rae's eyes. He then jumped down from the table and stomped his way toward her. "Excuse me, S'rae, I understand you are the GroundStone Champion and all, but, you're looking at the next Card Duels Champion. So I know what you're thinking... does the GroundStone Champion have a chance with the Card Duels Champ, and the answer is, I'm not interested in grandmas, but because you don't have a chance, it doesn't mean I don't want you here. If you promise to keep this meeting between us, I will allow you to be in my presence while I train."

Bele laughed out loud and S'rae elbowed his stomach.

"And who are you?" the boy Yash said to Bele. "Are you trying to sneak in and steal my strategies as well?"

Bele looked at S'rae, who shrugged and shook her head, then said with a chuckle, "I was planning to walk the grandma home. She gets forgetful with her old age."

S'rae grimaced at Bele, who wore the widest smirk she'd seen from him.

"Very well, then," Yash said. "But if any of you dare try to tip my secret, I swear—"

"HEY!" A loud voice from the table interrupted Yash, who grabbed his hair and pulled.

"Do *not* interrupt the future Card Duels Champion!" Yash screamed. "I was—"

"But... the Card Duels tournament is SOL RULES! You can't use Gabrael!" the boy said.

Yash turned to S'rae and placed his arm on her shoulder. "You see what happens when you try to play with peasants?" He then stomped to the table. "Listen, I too was a peon like you at Card Duels, many years ago, but I've grown. You see, Gabrael can be used because—"

"Not uh!" the boy, who was dressed up as panther, interrupted. "Only Champions who have Sols are allowed to be used in this Card Arena!"

"If you interrupt me one more time, peon, I will not allow you to be graced by the presence of the future Card Duel champion, do we understand ourselves?" And when low voices mumbled in agreement, he continued proudly. "You see, I have in my possession, within my almighty deck, one of only TWO cards like it in all of Gaia! For inside my Binder of Legends, I have the defeater of tournaments, the claimer of champions, the winner of duels, the key to the greatest deck in all of Gaia, I have the Sol of Gabrael!"

S'rae looked over at Bele with widened eyes, but to her surprise, his expression remained the same as if this came to no shock to him. *Gabrael has a Sol?*

"Gabrael don't have no Sol!" a boy said, who was dressed as a dragon. "Prove it!"

"Normally I would not fall to the pressures of mere mortals, but since we have a fellow champion in our presence." Yash lifted his arms and pointed at S'rae. "The cards were created by the great Olkisi, who made sure that all details were historically accurate! If Olsiki says Gabrael has a Sol, then it is fact that Gabrael has a Sol!" Yash breathed heavily through his mouth for a few long moments before continuing. "I suppose I shall show you peons my greatness." He swept his arms across the table as stone statues and cards fell to the ground. He pulled out a fiery card that blazed in his hand and slammed it onto the table. "Behold! Gabrael, the God of Fire!" And the moment the card had touched the table, a fire ignited and a stone clone of Gabrael, no bigger than a foot tall, stood in the center of the table. It held a small sword that blazed a bright red.

"Yeah, so what?" a boy who was dressed up as a pink gorilla

said. "I have a shiny Gabrael too!"

"Heh!" Yash scoffed. "You mere mortals are not ready to witness the almighty Sol of Gabrael—" Yash pushed his hand into his binder while biting his tongue until his eyes lit up. He then slowly pulled his hand out. A fiery card blazed in his hands, its glow fading from purple to red. "And here… is the card that will crown me the champion tomorrow!" He lifted his hand up before slamming it down on the table so hard the clone of Gabrael fell over. "I present you, Harahn'de!" And at once, a purple and red flame erupted from the table, scorching several feet high, and after a few seconds a three-foot-tall dragheonix was floating above Gabrael's clone.

The entire crowd was stunned, including S'rae. The draghoenix was so elegant—its wings were webbed, yet they had molten feathers that scorched purple and red. Its talons and tail were made of flames so bright, S'rae couldn't stare at them for long.

"Harahn'de… is… Gabrael's… Sol?" S'rae said, turning to Bele.

Still Bele said nothing for a few moments, then he grabbed S'rae's arm and escorted her out of the garden.

All S'rae heard was Yash screaming maniacally. "Good luck tomorrow, you peasants! The tournament is mine! Harahn'de will bury you mortals with fire and ash!"

They approached a set of double bamboo doors set into a wall. Bele, after glancing around, took an emblem from his pocket and tapped it against the wall. The door changed from bamboo to— S'rae pulled back with shock—the door was no longer made of bamboo, but instead it looked like a window staring out at a beautiful panoramic of GroundStone, like the hill where S'rae and Retro'ku would train.

Bele led the way as they walked through, and when S'rae turned around, she noticed that she was exactly where it looked like she'd be… but how? They were now standing on the hill where she'd train.

"How… Wh— what are we doing here?"

"Tomorrow is an important day for you, S'rae," Bele said, looking up at the night and its twinkling stars. "I don't want you to get sidetracked. You need to be focused. You need to be ready."

S'rae walked up to Bele and leaned her cheek against his back. "So… tomorrow I find my dragon?"

Bele remained staring up at the stars. "Yes."

"And you really think I'm ready?"

"I wouldn't risk it if you weren't."

And that word *risk* made S'rae jump back slightly. "What do you mean?"

"I mean… it is dangerous." Bele took a deep breath. "Bad things could happen."

"Like what?"

Bele took another deep breath before talking. "Like death."

S'rae clutched her robes to stop her hands from shaking. "I can… die trying to get a dragon?"

Bele said nothing.

"Bele… talk to me, please," S'rae gently pulled at the back of his shirt. Then suddenly a dark thought appeared in her mind. "Is this… is this why you did all of this for me? Is this why you planned a great birthday… why you're taking me to the Ball? Because… just in case I die… I—" S'rae froze and when Bele said nothing it was like he was not willing to argue. "So… all of this was some kind of pity treatment?" S'rae felt an anger boil inside. "Like I'm some kind of a pig before a slaughter? You wanted me to have a happy life before I… I die?"

"You may die… but you may not," Bele said. "But… you deserve a good life."

S'rae felt her eyes water up. "Why is everything about me… about death? Why… why can't I just live? Why can't I just… be me?"

Bele turned around and held her in his arms. She ran her hands over his arms. They felt hard, like iron, chiseled with hard muscles. She felt his chest, solid like stone. Then her hands found their way to his back, cupping the back of his neck. She didn't know why her hands were exploring his body, but even when she told them to stop, still they wandered. Maybe it was her body telling her that the end was near and to just live in the moment. Maybe…

She tore away from him, just now realizing the damage her hands had done. What was she thinking? Was she even thinking at all? Bele was beautiful, but he was a Professor, what was she doing here, spending all this time with him? She didn't know the answer, but as she wrapped her arms back around Bele, she realized that in his arms was exactly where she wanted to be right now. She felt safe, comfortable, and warm. A type of warmth that seeped through her skin and soothed her heart.

"Bele…" S'rae whispered. "Why are you doing all of this? Why are you being nice to me?"

"You remind me of myself," Bele said, his fingers caressing her scalp in a way that made her eyes roll and her body shiver. "But I want you to see life and all its wonders, like me. I've seen the Sereni waterfalls, the way they'd brighten even the darkest of nights. I've seen the Great Fujita Wall and all its wonder. I've seen triple rainbows and walked the clouds with them. I've seen all the beauties this world has to offer… yet still—" Bele's cheek rested atop S'rae's head. "—Still, I stand by what I said… that you are the most beautiful wonder that Gaia has created."

S'rae felt her fingers squeeze into the muscles of Bele's back. "I don't want this night to end. I don't want it to. Tell me more. Tell me your secrets. Tell me your adventures. I just want to know you. I want to learn what you know. I just… want to hear you speak."

So Bele went on and on for hours and hours. They spoke of life of love of family and adventure. They spoke of school of wisdom of kingdoms and prophecies. S'rae absorbed it all… and it was then when she realized the truth… she was helplessly falling… and she just wished that he'd be there to catch her.

It wasn't his muscles or his hypnotic eyes or his humor, not even confidence. His mind was truly what captivated her. The way one topic can jump to two then three, all keeping her yearning to find out more. He felt like a library and she was an eager student searching for the next book to read.

"So..." S'rae said, her head on his lap, his fingers grazing through her hair as they watched the dark night slowly fade to blue, "does that mean you believe that there is life out there?" S'rae pointed to the stars.

"Your favorite professor, Professor Ki, should have that answer for you," Bele said, looking up at the stars. "Do you know how old Gaianium is?"

"No."

"It is over ten billion years old. Do you know how old Gaia is?"

"Six billion?"

"Correct."

S'rae's head turned to the side as she made eye contact with Bele. He looked down at her and nodded.

"The very metal that the Mechas are created from are older than our planet itself. It is said that Mechas came here billions of years ago, before humans even populated the planet."

"But... how is that possible?"

"That's what Professor Ki has been researching. They've been working on vehicles that can travel through space."

"Why would they do that?"

Bele said nothing.

"Hey, Bele... why would they do that?"

Bele still said nothing.

"Hey, Bel—"

"I can see why you were accepted into Fujita," Bele smiled.

"Why, because I'm super smart?"

"Because you ask a lot of questions."

S'rae laughed and punched Bele lightly in the stomach.

"You know, I had a choice to go to Fujita," Bele said.

"Really? You mean we could have been at the same school to-gether?"

"For a year, yes."

"Why didn't you go?"

"I have my reasons." And just then, S'rae noticed a glimpse of sorrow behind his eyes.

"And what reasons are those? Fujita is Fujita, it's every smart person's dream to get accepted there."

"Well, I didn't just get accepted. If I remember correctly, the letter said *Congratulations, you have received our highest score in over a century.*" And there it was again, Bele's not-so-punchable smirk.

"Oh how humble you are!"

"I try."

"So… about those spaceships… don't think I'd forget about it because you changed the subject!"

Bele chuckled. "Well, let's just say the enemy isn't always who you think it is."

"What's that supposed to mean?"

"The issues of Gaia are trivial compared to what's going on out there. Gaia is a planet. Within a galaxy. Within a universe. And the greatest issues we have on this planet… are nothing compared to what's waiting out there."

"Mechas?"

Bele nodded. "Professor Ki believes they'll be coming back. And he is afraid we will not be ready for them when they do."

"But what about the Gods? Surely they can fight them off."

"If only that were true." Bele shook his head. "Speaking of Gods, do you have any idea how powerful Vy'ken is?"

S'rae was taken aback by such a random question. "No, why?"

"He fascinates me the most. He is the only God that no one

knows where he actually came from."

"What do you mean?"

"The myths say that one moment he was just there, when the previous second he was not. His powers fascinate me. He would be our greatest chance against Mechas." Bele nodded several times. "But… he also lost his mind, so there's that."

"Wasn't he Gabrael's brother?" S'rae said.

"He is Gabrael's brother as much as any God is his brother or sister. It is the language of Gods."

"And what was Yash talking about with the whole Gabrael having a Sol?"

"That is what the myths say."

"And what happened to Harahn'de?"

"That's not a topic I can speak of."

"Why?"

"Because there are only three people alive who know what happened to Harahn'de."

S'rae closed her eyes for a moment and thought about who they could be. "Gabrael, Raaz'a… and Retro'ku?"

Bele nodded his head.

"How come I never heard about Gabrael having a Sol? How did this person Olkisi know?"

"Olkisi isn't a person. It is a group of the greatest minds in Gaia, who wished to create a game that could spread information that they refuse to teach."

"Well who are they then?"

Bele froze for a second. He looked down at S'rae and smiled. "You truly are a Fujita with your questions." S'rae returned the smile and dug her head deeper into his lap to get comfortable. "Well, Olkisi. Ol… is for Olivia of GroundStone. Ki… is for Ki of Fujita. And Si… is for Silas of Sereni."

It was then when Sianu's visions flashed before S'rae's eyes and she felt her heart beat out of control. Anxiety rushed through her body as she felt her skin sizzle.

"What's wrong?" Bele said.

S'rae did not want to ruin the moment. She did not want to talk about what she had seen and what she knew about Olivia, who she really was. S'rae had a feeling that if she asked about Olivia and the Sol'adari, this perfect night would be ruined. She had already learned that lesson.

"Nothing," S'rae said, she pressed her arms to her chest to control her shakes. "This night… it was perfect. Thank you for this."

"You are welcome, S'rae. Tomorrow is the most important day of your life."

"I know, I get my dragon."

"Well… I was talking about how you're going to the Solermony Ball with me, but I guess getting a dragon ranks as a close second."

S'rae hated that she chuckled at that.

"I'm looking forward to it." S'rae paused for a moment, a troubling question eating away at her. "Do you really think I'm ready?"

"I would not have done all of this if I didn't think you were. You are ready, S'rae. The next wave is coming."

28

THE SUN WAS SHINING BRIGHT by the following morning, illuminating the once golden terrain of GroundStone, but now it was filled with vibrant flowers and vines and veils hanging from just about every crevice. S'rae could still see some of the monkeys and rodents working tirelessly as they swung down from vines and placed flowers on untouched ledges. Today was the big day!

The animals looked so lively as they cleaned the streets and decorated the towers. S'rae, on the other hand, her eyes were still tired, and from the looks of all the Earthies dancing and playing in the streets, she was the only one. Well, maybe Bele was as well.

Just one thought of him and their magical night together made her press her hands to her mouth and smile wide.

"And what are you smiling about over there?" S'rae heard Lynn's energized voice.

"Oh…" S'rae let out a faint sigh and clutched her robe, "nothing."

"Well, that sounds like something alright!" Lynn jumped on S'rae's back, smiling wickedly. "I'm going to need ALL the details!"

S'rae filled Lynn in on the events of her surprise birthday with

Bele as Lynn brought them to the GroundStone trio's underground hall. The green torches that illuminated their Great Chamber were flickering bright. They were all gathered around one of the long stone tables, Brick at its head, Milla and Lynn at S'rae's left. Kaul sat farther down with a quill in his hand, scribbling madly onto a piece of parchment.

"What's he working on over there?" S'rae asked as she stuffed her mouth with honey nuts.

"We are *not* talking about Kaul," Lynn said, her arms wrapped around Milla. "Not after the night you had!"

"And what night was that?" Milla raised an eyebrow so perfectly sharp it looked like it was drawn by the hand of a Divine.

"With that fine new professor," Lynn grinned.

"Oh really?" This time Milla raised both eyebrows. "I'm impressed, many girls have tried, none have succeeded." Milla then twisted her head and nodded with puckered lips. "I'm thoroughly impressed. But you have to watch out with him, he's a damaged one."

"What do you mean, *damaged*?" S'rae said.

"He has been through a lot."

"Like what?"

"Like a traumatic event I am not allowed to speak about, so I will not."

S'rae looked curiously at Milla for a few long moments. "Okay… well, that's good to know, I guess."

"Just guard your heart, that's all." Then Milla turned to Kaul, who was still scribbling madly. "Hey, loser, no matter how many plans you come up with, you're still going to lose! It's in your blood!"

"WE ARE RELATED!" Kaul shouted, then kept writing.

"I still think I'm adopted." Milla laughed. S'rae quickly looked away, putting her head down. Lynn elbowed Milla in the ribs and whispered something to her. "Oh, I'm sorry, I didn't know."

"It's okay," S'rae said. Although she didn't hear what Lynn had said, she was able to draw her own conclusion.

"OKAY! I got it!" Kaul stomped toward them and slammed the parchment on the table as plates rattled. "Oh, hi!" Kaul said, finally noticing S'rae. "I'm glad you're here! I was actually just working on some things for you! So, Leonna told me many great things about you, and I think that's great and all that you can ride waves, but it's a completely different skill to ride them in an actual match; so... because of that, I have you as a Healer instead."

"A HEALER!" Milla and S'rae shouted at once. Milla then snapped her finger and threw a blob of mud at Kaul's face, splattering over his hair and clothes. "You're doing that just because she's a GIRL, huh?"

"No! No!" Kaul said, wiping the mud off his face. "It's not like that at all, it's just that I really want to get my first win and Leonna trusted me to—"

"Leonna trusted someone who has never won before to try to break the First Years Curse?" Brick laughed at the head of the table.

"Well, it took a lot for me to convince her—"

"That," Milla said, "and he forgot to mention the detail about no one else wanting to coach this year."

"Well, that detail's not important!" Kaul said. "What is... is *this* master plan! So, S'rae is a healer because Leonna said she's one of the top healing students in class." Though S'rae was annoyed to be given the task of being a healer, being called one of the top students brought a smile to her face. "And with her keeping the Defenders healthy and... and... look here—" Kaul opened up the roll of parchment some more. "See! S'rae scored highly in fatigue restoration! So, if she can keep the Wave Runners running longer than the other team's, then I think that's how we can win! With her as healing! We can do this!"

And as Milla and Kaul fought over assigning a girl to be a Healer in the Boulder Dash game, S'rae couldn't help but think about what Milla had said about Bele. What could he be hiding from her?

S'rae thanked them for breakfast and headed out to her first class. Today being the day of the Sol Fest and Solermony Ball must have definitely had a positive effect on the professors, because each class that she went to was the best class all year. Fa'laz was smiling, though a part of her thought that could have been because Gabrael had put him in his place, and the animals they practiced against were cute and fluffy and she wanted to take each one home with her. If anything, the only classes that seemed a little awkward were Di'Tukia and Leonna's. Half the class was spent talking about channeling earth spells, creating tunnels with an arm, and finding medicinal herbs by licking the ground, and the other half of the class was all about Boulder Dash. Di'Tukia would mention being undefeated and how great the parties were after the victory, while Leonna would talk about finally ending the First Years' Curse almost every other sentence.

S'rae couldn't help but chuckle at their friendship. They were more like sisters in a budding sibling rivalry than peers.

But it wasn't until her final class of the day did she realize why she was so happy to wake up with a smile this morning. She arrived at her Sol class, her finger twirling her hair the entire time. And she appreciated how remarkable of an actor Bele was. If she didn't know what she had known about them, she wouldn't have the slightest clue that there was anything going on between them. As if the night they just had didn't even happen. That she was just a regular student. But she knew she was much more, and Bele had a way of making each eye contact worth it—whether it was the subtle smirk or holding their gaze just a second longer, enough to make her heart flutter.

But what made this class even better was how he brought them to the Valley of Dreams, where all the students had their Sols standing beside them, and told the first years about the process of their Sols evolving today.

"Without even knowing," Bele said, waving his hands, "today may very well be the first day of your new life. When your Sol changes... something inside you does as well. But it is a good change, it is an evolution, a better version of who you were yesterday. So embrace the new you and understand that although you are good enough right now, it does not mean you cannot seek to improve yourself later. So I am most excited to see the transformations your Sols will go through today. And I will love the chance to help them master their new abilities."

The students clapped and cheered and the Sols roared, chirped, and stomped.

After the Valley, Bele brought the class to the Forest of Life, and S'rae couldn't believe her eyes.

"These," Bele said, lifting his arms at a gorgeous forest, where each tree had their unique colored leaves that shone bright with a fluorescent glow, "... these are your new homes after today! They have spent the school year blooming and they will be ready for you to live in!" Bele then pointed as his waist. "Your belts, whether they are Stone, Ground, or Sand, will guide you to your new home! May you feel one with nature even when you are sleeping!"

Only when she gripped her aching jaw did S'rae realize she had been smiling wide at Bele throughout the entire class. She had wanted nothing more than to run up to him and wrap her arms around him, but she knew better. It took everything in her to not approach him when he dismissed the class, but she thought of him the entire way back to the hill, where she would train with Retro'ku and Lynn before the Sol Fest.

But once she arrived, it was completely empty. She waited a few more minutes before heading back to the city to see where they could have been. There was only one place that came to mind: the Golden Palace. It was where Gabrael had been staying, after all.

When she arrived at the large golden doors with carvings of different animals embedded into them, she didn't know if hands were even allowed to touch something so pristine and flawless.

She pulled her sleeves over her hands and pushed on the door, making sure to not leave even the slightest fingerprint. Though they were two entirely different schools, kingdoms, and cultures, she treated this building the same way she did the chambers at Fujita.

The doors opened.

S'rae's mouth fell open; she closed it quickly, but not before a gorilla strolled by, shaking its head at her. This room was one of the biggest she had ever seen, a huge domed space; the ceiling, some hundreds of feet high, seemed out of place, however. It was made of brick, despite the gold that surrounded her, and seemed to be put together by a blind man, with each brick painted a random color and no clear design or order to it. Odd, very odd. Why would such a design be so unreachable?

She then circled her fingers as she walked the halls, channeling soundwaves to search for any sounds that could lead her in the right direction.

And after a few minutes, her eyes widened as familiar voices reached her ears in the form of whispers. She found them!

"I am sorry, father, but I do not agree. I do not think she will be ready in time."

"And I disagree. She is ready, she simply needs to find what is stopping her."

"But time, Master, time is not something we have the luxury of. I sense the Shadow Army is nearly ready."

"Well, Raaz'a, what do you suggest then?"

"What I have already suggested."

"Surely you are not considering the very thing I told you not to consider, no?"

"But, Gabrael, Vy'ken's power could give us a chance."

"Yes, but as I have already said, if Vy'ken gets controlled again, we will have far greater worries than a Shadow Army."

"Is Vy'ken that powerful, father?"

"He is."

"Master, then how about this, for the sake of all of us here, for the well-being of families who wish to see their loved ones another day, if all hope seems lost, then... can you summon Vy'ken?"

S'rae heard nothing for nearly a minute, only the soft sounds of feet hitting stone.

"Only then, Raaz'a... only then. I just pray it does not get to that point."

"Haz'tu ro'mah!"

"*Haz'tu ro'mah!*"

"Should we warn the people, father?"

"That will only cause chaos."

"Can I... Can I—"

"Go on, son."

"Can I... let the *others* know?"

"Unfortunately... I do not believe now is the right time. Lynn and S'rae are protected because they are with me and a part of a destiny greater than any of the laws of Gaia. But *they* are not protected in the same way. If you let them know who they really are... about the blood that travels through their veins—"

"Then they will know they are descendants of a King, and not peasants of a world."

"This is true, son. When the time is right, they will know, and the School of Fire will be reborn. We will find the Children of Fire once more, I just do not want to see our people suffer a terrible fate again... Once was enough."

And again, silence swept over, no one said a word for what felt like an eternity, as if they had taken this moment to pray to a Divine.

Then finally, Retro'ku's voice was heard. "I understand, father. I understand."

The sound of a door opening then closing caused S'rae to jump. She heard footsteps coming toward her and she needed to think of something quickly.

She ran silently behind a statue as the footsteps got louder and louder. And right when the person was about to see her crouching behind a statue, the noise turned the corner and headed down a different hallway.

"And what are you doing sneaking around?" S'rae heard a dark voice behind her that made her heart skip a beat.

When she turned around it was Raaz'a, grinning.

"I see you have not given up your spying days yet," Raaz'a said. "Come with me."

When S'rae followed, she found herself in a long downward-sloping golden hallway. The walls, floors, and ceiling all became darker the deeper they went, and S'rae couldn't help but feel her heartbeat escalate. Where was he taking her? Every few feet a torch was lit as they passed, fading from red to blue.

A door opened with just the wave of Raaz'a's hand as they approached it. It then slammed shut behind them.

"Why—why are we here?" S'rae said.

"Because... I am not sure how much of the conversation you may have heard, but it is important for you to know the truth." Raaz'a's eyes became softer, as if he was almost ready to cry.

"The truth about what?"

"Everything..." Raaz'a's eyes then became dark.

S'rae grabbed her pants as her legs shook against one another. "Why are you telling me this?"

"Because... the end may be near... and we do not know who will survive. But if something happens to us... the truth will die with us."

Suddenly, S'rae had an inkling as to what Raaz'a may have been hinting at. "What happened... at Harahn'de? Why does everyone here hate Gabrael?" Her heart hammered against her chest excitedly, she had been dying for the truth ever since she had first arrived at Harahn'de. Were all the terrible rumors about Gabrael true?

And as if Raaz'a had read her mind, he placed his hand to his face and grabbed the bridge of his nose. "You are not the only one who uses a smile as a disguise… to hide the pain." Raaz'a lifted his head and S'rae saw tears leaking from his eyes, yet still he smiled. "It hurts." Raaz'a then grabbed a vial from his robe and quickly took a sip from it.

S'rae's head lurched back as the familiar scent reached her nose. "Archon's blood?"

"It is. A little bit a day… keeps the nightmares away."

"What… happened?" S'rae's mind raced through everything she had learned about Gabrael over the last five years, but the one thing that popped up in her head was… "Kiya'shin?"

At once, the torches in the room erupted into a fiery blaze, scorching the ceiling.

"How… where did you hear that from?"

S'rae stuttered before getting a chance to say a word.

"That spell is the most powerful in all of Gaia… but with power… must come control. And as we saw at Harahn'de—" Raaz'a wiped his eyes as more tears fell, "—even a God cannot control it."

"Gabrael?"

Raaz'a nodded. "You see, three thousand years ago… there was a Great War, but you will never see the truth in any of the books in any of the Kingdoms. What they want you to believe is that the war was against the Shadows… but in reality… it was against a threat far greater."

S'rae swallowed a difficult breath. "M-mechas?"

Raaz'a shook his head. "Mechas would assume there was an army of them… but I am afraid not. We were lucky there was only one."

S'rae's eyes lit up. "A war was against only one Mecha?"

"It was far more powerful than anything our planet could create. Eve fled right before the fighting started. Allies were made. The

Shadows actually joined us to defeat it."

"Joined?"

Raaz'a nodded. "An agreement was made. That we needed to side with them in order to defeat the true enemy."

"Then what happened?"

"The… *Kiya'shin* happened." Raaz'a's eyes went black. "We were not enough for it. It was far too powerful. But we still had a fighting chance. The greatest minds were coming up with a strategy, but Gabrael had already made up his mind. He said that this way would result in the least amount of deaths. And he may have been right, but we will never know."

"So what is the *Kiya'shin*?"

"Do you know why there are only three of us left?"

"Three of the Fire?"

Raaz'a nodded.

"Because they sealed up the walls three thousand years ago?"

Raaz'a let out a depressed chuckle. "Oh, S'rae… that was after all of them were already killed… by the *Kiya'shin*."

And just then… S'rae's heart dropped to her stomach.

"You see, the Kiya'shin takes the energy and fire from the body and soul until they are left as a frozen statue of who they once were. Gabrael needed to channel this spell, sacrificing the energy of all his students so he could create a blast strong enough to destroy the Mecha."

"And did it work?"

"It did… but it cost us everything. Not only did he destroy every pupil of Fire during that spell, but he also made sure to eliminate his allies… the Shadows. They feared that without students of Fire, the Shadows would rule over Gaia. It was blind fear that killed them—no different than a human killing a harmless bee for the fear that it would be stung, though it had no intention of doing so. It is fear that we must overcome. And that is why I brought you here." Raaz'a placed his palm on S'rae's shoulders. "Gabrael believes in you… and as do I. We will need you, S'rae… we are not enough. The Shadow Army will destroy GroundStone. Lives will end when they arrive. But, the fear you are feeling right now—" S'rae's arms and legs trembled. "—yes… that fear… you *need* to overcome it. And I hope this meeting has helped."

"Well…" S'rae took a moment to catch her breath, her voice shaking. "Well… I am definitely scared, yes. But… why were you so curious about Fa'laz? How can they help?"

"Ah… the Metal Man… well, much like Vy'ken, those who are able to control the duality of an element… become far more powerful than they could ever imagine. If I could find the person who did that to him, it will only help our chances in winning."

"You would fight alongside a Metal person?"

"I would. It is not Metal that we should fear, it is what they do with the Metal that should concern us. If on our side, it can be a wonderful alliance. If not… then we are in trouble."

"So they can be Metal and still be good? Does that mean they can control both elements?"

"If they are powerful enough, yes, they may be able to harness both within them. But even Gods would perish if they tried to use both at the same time. The Universe has its laws that no God can break. That is one of them." Raaz'a stood up and brushed off his robe then smiled wide. "Use your smile as a disguise, S'r—" He then stopped what he was saying and looked at S'rae most curiously. "Hmm… I just had another moment of déjà vu with you… but it was different… I cannot explain it. But anyways, you have quite an important day today, I hope you are ready. Haz'tu ro'mah."

By the time S'rae made it back to her home, she had no time to reflect on everything that Raaz'a had said because Lynn and the GroundStone trio swarmed her at the door.

"We've been looking everywhere for you!" Kaul shouted. "Where have you been? You haven't practiced with us or anything, the Sol Fest is starting soon!" Kaul ran around in a circle, breathing heavily, talking to himself, and slamming a roll of parchment against his head.

"Don't mind him," Milla said, "he *really* wants to win."

"It's not just me!" Kaul shouted. "Leonna will kill me if we don't win... or worse! Nutmeg will!"

S'rae followed them to the colosseum, which was now lavishly decorated with flowers of every kind, lining the rows, seats, and columns with red, blues, pinks, and purples. When she made it past the golden gate and into the arena, she gasped.

"WOW!" S'rae suddenly felt nervous once she saw the enormity of the playing field.

"Beautiful, huh?" Kaul said. "So here's the plan! I want—"

"Hi!" a familiar girl walked up to Kaul, poking his back. "What do you want me to do?"

"Oh hi... err... well... you see," Kaul said, grabbing the back of his head. "S'rae is still alive so we won't be needing a starting Healer, BUT!" Kaul put his finger up. "But... we can use you as a backup, just in case anything happens to S'rae!"

"Sound great to me." The girl smiled and turned to S'rae, sticking her hand out. "Hi! My name is Plumita, I'm a huge fan!"

"Err... thank you!" S'rae still hadn't gotten used to the whole concept of having fans, she at times forgot that she even had the title of the GroundStone Champion; she had tried to forget that day, not remember it. "So... we're on the same team?"

"Yupp!" Plumita nodded excitedly. "Have you ever played before?"

"My first time."

"*Oooff.*" Plumita shook her head. "It may be a little rough for you then. But don't worry, healing is simple, you have three spells to focus on: *Su'rea*, this one gives the runners a speed boost. *Ta'qa*, this one helps people when they get tired. And *Shi'fa*, this one heals people when they're injured."

"*Su'rea, ta'qa,* and *shi'fa*?" S'rae repeated.

"Correct! Exactly! You're good at this already!"

"And uh… what do I do when no one needs to get healed? Do I just stand around?"

Plumita laughed out loud. "Oh no… see the Defenders' jobs are not just to block goals… but they are there to protect you, because Runners' jobs are not just to score goals… but they are there to destroy you." Plumita smiled wide as if what she said wasn't the least bit alarming.

"D-destroy me?" S'rae gulped.

"Yupp! But don't worry, you'll be fine! Just make sure to watch your back when you're channeling spells and I'm sure you'll make it out with only a few injuries."

"Only a few?" This game started to sound less and less fun.

"Alright, alright, we ready, Earthies?" Kaul approached them waving down the other members of the team to huddle up. "Here are our team colors!" Kaul threw a blob of mud at each player's chest. It splattered then absorbed into their robes, turning into a bright green. "I didn't choose the color, so don't look at me! Look at her!" Kaul pointed to the audience, where a bouncing Leonna was, throwing her Nutmeg in the air and catching her. "Her team, her colors. Any complaints? No? Great! So here's the plan. I want yo—"

"CAN WE HAVE THE *FIRST YEARS' CURSE DESTROYERS* STEP INTO THE CENTER OF THE ARENA PLEASE!" A loud, rumbling voice resonated from the colosseum's walls.

Kaul looked at the team and shrugged. "Her team… her name!"

S'rae felt a rush of panic surge through her body as if she had just been thrown into a lion's den. Because that was exactly what it felt like. She hadn't found the time to read up on the rules or strategies or even how a team wins. And since Boulder Dash was GroundStone's greatest sport, it seemed like they just assumed that every Earthie should know what to do. But she did not.

And as they made their way to the center, she saw thousands

of Earthies pile into the seats, all wearing either green, for S'rae's team, *The First Years Curse Destroyers*, or gold for Di'Tukia's team, *We Are The Champions*—though most of the crowd was dressed in gold.

At either end of the arena were two goal rings: one was a gaping hole in the ground and the other was just above it, with a net made of vines, hoisted up by two stone columns. Flying high above them were large eagles holding a banner with the teams' colors that had swirling pockets of sand that would keep track of the score and time.

Sand would swirl on the banner and take the shape of names. She noticed that her name followed by *GroundStone Champion* had popped up, which made the whole colosseum rumble so hard, she thought it'd collapse. They clapped and cheered and roared for their GroundStone Champion.

Kaul gave S'rae a nudge with his elbow, which she took as a sign to acknowledge the crowd. She simply waved her hand and twirled around to face all sides, the arena erupting louder wherever she faced.

S'rae tore her eyes away from the crowd and looked over her shoulder to see who else was on her team. There was a large boy wearing a mask, who may have been their har'is (the one who defended the goal posts). Then there were three boys with fur pauldrons on, making them look a hundred pounds heavier, they were the Defenders. And then there were the two boys who made S'rae's eyes narrow because they had rollerballs at the bottom of their feet—they were Wave Runners, what she was supposed to be.

And then drums boomed across the arena as elephants trumpeted and stomped their way into the center. They wore gold banners with a beautiful sabertooth tiger as its logo.

"WELCOME BOULDER DASH'S FINEST... WE ARE THE CHAMPIONS!"

The crowd clapped and stomped their feet as waves of sand

filled the arena. Much like S'rae's team, this team was all boys, except for one girl, who was most likely their Healer. That thought alone made her lip curl.

"You know, they weren't always called that," Kaul said to S'rae. "Their name used to be The Tigers, but apparently their rivalry got a little more hostile this year."

The music stopped. S'rae stood there, watching the elephants stomp their way out. She then looked to the crowd and saw dozens of chimps walking the aisles, throwing bags of food into the crowd, most likely their famous honey nuts.

And before S'rae could ask Kaul a question, a horn blared and boulders big and small launched from the ground, high into the air. S'rae quickly dove away and watched their descent just to make sure they didn't flatten her.

She then saw waves of sand shoot into the air after the boulders.

Everything was happening too quickly for S'rae. One moment the boulders were in the air, and the next they were being launched by her, aiming for their goal rings. The speed was amazing. A part of her was suddenly happy that she was just a Healer.

She watched as their goalie stomped on the ground and slammed his palms to his knees as a massive stone hand appeared from the sand, swatting a boulder away. But as he focused on the aerial boulder, he missed the Runner who slid by and dropped a boulder into the hole on the ground.

"TWENTY POINTS FOR THE CHAMPIONS!"

The crowd erupted.

"GO AND DO SOMETHING, S'RAE!" She heard Kaul yell over the crowd.

But what was there for her to do? And when she looked at her team, she realized she was already failing. Her two Runners were flattened underneath a boulder and the three Defenders seemed to be gassed as they were sprinting at Runners who were ten times faster than them. This was completely hopeless.

"FORTY POINTS FOR THE CHAMPIONS!"

"SIXTY POINTS FOR THE CHAMPIONS!"

"GO AND HEAL THEM! THEY WIN ONCE THEY HIT 100!" Kaul shouted.

And when S'rae dashed toward the first Runner, she performed a flip as she dodged three boulders that shot by her.

"The GroundStone Champion isn't so good now, is she?" one of the Runners laughed as he blazed by her on wave that spiraled overhead and lunged a boulder through the ring.

"SEVENTY POINTS FOR THE CHAMPIONS!"

S'rae curled her lip. She surveyed the arena and based on the math from the score, she saw that a team received twenty points when a boulder went through the hole in the ground and ten when through the air. She quickly counted the boulders and there were only two remaining. But then the ground rumbled as three more boulders were launched into the air.

"GO HEAL THEM! WHAT ARE YOU DOING?" Kaul shouted again.

But S'rae had other plans. She saw that healing them would do no good. The other Runners were already planning on scoring the remaining thirty points with the two boulders they had left; and it was then when the crowd went silent as her eyes went white.

The ground quaked in a way that made her whole body vibrate. And as the Runners launched their boulders, she stomped her foot into the sand.

A wave boomed from the ground, grabbing the two boulders before they entered the rings, then soared high into the air, scooping the other three boulders. S'rae then ran up the wave, looking down at the shocked crowd. Even the commentator, who couldn't shut up, had stopped talking. S'rae ran across the sky with five large boulders atop her wave. She saw her only chance to win... and it was right there, a hundred feet below her. The wave crashed down. She dug her hands into the sand as her hair danced wildly in front of her face. She just about to land. She closed her eyes, bracing for the impact. It was now or never.

And with a BANG that rattled the arena, the five boulders broke through the hole and she fell deeper into a dark abyss. Though the boulders had turned into sand and cushioned her fall, she still landed hard on her hands, feeling them break under the pressure.

She winced in pain as she looked up at the light striping down on her, streams of sand disrupting it.

She grabbed her arm and it hurt immediately. It must have been broken. And as she thought about how she'd escape this mess, she heard a low, rumbling growl somewhere in the darkness.

"Hello?" S'rae's voice trembled. "Anyone there?" She groaned as she tried to stand up to her feet, but it proved to be impossible. "Who's there? Show yourself."

The growl intensified, followed by a hiss, that sounded like— S'rae's eye's widened—she had heard that sound too many times while at Opella. That was the sound of a very hungry... very large feline, ready to feast.

S'rae squirmed a bit more as a paw came into the light. It was practically the size of her head. S'rae then screamed, but it was cut off into a gasp as she clutched her ribs. Were they broken too?

Then the feline roared and S'rae froze in place, though her entire body shook. The feline prowled its way closer to S'rae, baring its sharp fangs curling up at the corners of its mouth. A saber toothed tiger? It came so close that their noses practically touched. And it was then when S'rae noticed something that made her heart pump so fast, she thought it'd explode. The marking on the tiger's head, between its two horns that glowed orange, she had seen it before... it was the same one... that was on... her killer's mask.

And as the tiger roared again, it vanished just as a blazing light crashed down on the spot where it once was.

"Are you okay?" S'rae heard a voice through the blinding light. She placed her hands over her eyes. And once they regained focus, she saw that Bele was there holding his hand out. "S'rae... are you okay?"

"I am now." She tried to jump up and hug him, but pain immobilized her.

"You stay put, I'll get you healed in no time."

"How'd I do?" S'rae coughed.

"You were the worst healer the world has EVER seen." Bele laughed.

"Oh, great. Looks like no more Boulder Dash for me."

"What are you talking about?" Bele said, lifting her up with ease. S'rae took a moment to appreciate the way his muscles wrapped around her body. "You are the Great S'rae who finally broke the First Years' Curse."

"Well, I don't feel so great."

"You should."

S'rae didn't know how she should tell Bele what she had just seen down here. There was still so much she needed to know about the Sol'adari. All she knew was that Olivia was a part of them... and Bele was close to Olivia. "Can I trust you?" S'rae asked Bele as she pressed her face into his chest.

"Of course you can."

"The killer... he just tried to kill me again. I would have been dead if you came a second later."

Bele said nothing for a few moments. And then finally he looked down at S'rae and said with the deepest voice she had heard from him. "I am *never* losing sight of you again." Then his lip curled with anger. "And when you get your dragon... they will be praying to all their Divines, because they will regret ever trying. I promise you."

S'rae couldn't explain what she felt, but a burning heat radiated from Bele's body, so hot it felt as if she were lying by a campfire.

But all that she could explain was the feeling she had whenever she was in his arms. It was something that told her she was exactly where she was supposed to be.

"Bele... you *are* my next wave."

29

DESPITE ALMOST BEING KILLED AGAIN and having the bones in her arms and chest broken, S'rae found herself in a good mood. That was because Bele's lotioned hands were massaging her back and arms as he applied 'Leonna's Healing Ointment for the Injured' to her skin. She laid atop warm rocks that felt more like pillows and the cool air was perfumed with the scent of cinnamon and roses from the candles that surrounded her. S'rae was feeling at peace with life as Bele's fingers and knuckles rolled into her muscles and cracked her back, making her feel as if she was drifting into the sky, with absolutely no desire in coming back down to the real world.

Until the door slammed open and Leonna barged in.

"Well, well, well," Leonna said, twisting her head, "what's going on here?"

S'rae crashed back down to reality as she mumbled a bunch of words.

"You are supposed to apply it like *this*." Leonna smacked a slab of her cream on S'rae's back and practically leapt into the air and dropped all of her weight onto S'rae with a thundering elbow.

S'rae had expected to be paralyzed after that maneuver, but instead, she stood up feeling better than ever.

"See!" Leonna swiped her hands swiftly. "It's the magic touch! Much like what our GroundStone Champion here has! The First Years' Curse is no more! See you at the Solermony Ball, and oh yeah, don't forget, the Evsolution is happening soon!" Leonna then looked at S'rae. "Sorry, although you'll be going to the Solermony Ball, unfortunately you will not be able to witness the Evsolutions. That is strictly for Sols and their owners only."

"I am most sorry, Leonna," Bele said, wiping his hands clean before shooting Leonna a serious look. "But I am not allowing S'rae to leave my side."

Leonna stared directly into Bele's eyes for a few long moments. S'rae couldn't tell if there was tension between their gaze.

"Aren't those eyes so dreamy?" Leonna said to S'rae. "You know, my man is *very* lucky I'm a *very* faithful lady, or you'd be my date to the Ball!" Leonna shimmied her shoulders. "But yes, since she's the GroundStone Champion and the First Years Curse Destroyer, I guess if you want her there, she can be there! BUT, you owe me a dance tonight!"

"Thank you. I look forward to it." Bele bowed as Leonna left.

After S'rae was healed back completely, Bele had brought her to the Valley of Dreams, where many Sols and animals were found playing, grazing, and sleeping.

S'rae looked carefully at each one to see if she could remember any of them. She recognized a black panther, an elephant, a snake, a pink gorilla, and a raven, of course she'd remember the raven, that was Yash's. But there was one that caught S'rae's attention: a lone, large naked mole rat, that seemed to have been repulsive to the other animals who stayed away from it.

And as S'rae went to approach it, Bele had already slid across the dirt and tackled it. They rolled around several times before Bele had landed on his back, lifting the rat into the air. "Aren't you so beautiful! Look at you!" Bele smiled wide. "I'm so glad Mother

Nature created you just the way you are! You know that!"

The mole rat squeaked and jiggled as it tossed around in Bele's hands.

S'rae couldn't help but smile at how Bele handled himself around these animals. Not only did he make the outcast feel welcomed as the mole rat now joined in with the rest, but the way he played with them, rolling in the dirt and jumping on their backs, made her appreciate Bele even more. He wasn't the cocky, stuck-up person around the animals. Around them, he looked like a child, free of worries, and just living life with nature and friends.

"You better come join us before the students get here!" Bele said as a panther mounted him and slobbered over his face. "This is the best time! Right before they mature!"

S'rae couldn't say no to that. So she and Bele spent the next half hour playing with dozens of different animals. They rode on their backs, they wrestled, but most importantly, they laughed... every single second of it.

Bele and S'rae were then laying on the ground side-by-side surrounded by dozens of equally-winded Sols.

"You have a great way with animals, you know that?" S'rae said, staring up at the beautiful blue sky.

"You have to treat animals the same way you'd treat family."

"Why's that?"

"Because... they may very well be your family." S'rae heard Bele's voice crack before he finished the sentence. She knew there was something buried deep inside that comment. And after a few moments of silence, Bele continued. "Sometimes... I like to think that one of these animals is my sister finding her way back to me in another life."

S'rae tilted her head to Bele and noticed how his eyes were glazed.

"I'm sorry."

"It's okay... the next wave is coming." He then turned to S'rae as their eyes met. "The next wave came."

S'rae giggled and pushed her hands to her cheeks. Everything about this moment was going perfectly until an elephant farted so loud the ground rumbled. Its tail swished a few times before it got up and walked away.

The two looked at one another with bloated cheeks as if they were holding their breath, until finally they belted out with laughter, curling up into one another.

"Well," Bele continued to laugh as he covered his mouth with his shirt, "at least he likes you!"

"How do you know?"

"He told me."

S'rae laughed and pushed Bele's shoulders. "Yeah, sure he did!"

"Would I lie to you?" His gaze met S'rae's... and suddenly it seemed like he may not have been joking.

"Prove it!"

"Go... whisper something to my friend, Nyx, there, the graceful black panther."

S'rae turned her head and was shocked to see a black panther lying down just above her head. "Don't cheat!" Bele then covered his ears with his palms. S'rae eyed him most suspiciously as she whispered into Nyx's ears. "You know... I wish... he wasn't so perfect. I wish... I wasn't falling for him. And I hate that I like his punchable smirk now."

S'rae turned to Bele and nodded, as if to let him know she finished.

"Okay, great!" Bele stood up with a wide smile and stretched his arms. He seemed to be the happiest she had ever seen him, even more than when he was playing with the animals. "It's time to get ready for the festivities! It's starting... well... it's starting now."

"Wait!" S'rae said, standing up quickly. "Well, aren't you going to guess what I said?"

"I don't need to guess." Bele shrugged. "She already told me."

He winked and then there it was again, the punchable smirk.

S'rae was taken aback. "Oh yeah? Well… what'd I say then?"

"Nothing important." Bele smiled.

"Mmhmm, just as I thought." S'rae and Bele began walking to the waterfall, where the ceremony will take place. "I knew you couldn't."

"I guess you're right." Bele kept walking. They came upon a downward slope of a rock-lined pathway, leading straight to a gorgeous waterfall, where dozens of students were. And before they parted ways and Bele walked up to the podium, he turned to S'rae and said: "Oh yeah, one more thing! I had a feeling you liked my punchable smirk."

And there it was again. The smirk.

Except this time her mind couldn't even call it punchable. Her cheeks went red as the word kissable came to mind.

The ceremony began and it truly was one of the most beautiful events S'rae had ever seen. A student would walk up to the podium as Bele painted a symbol on their forehead and then they'd turn to face their Sol, who now had the same mark painted on theirs. The two of them would step into the water, but the student would remain at the front, water barely at their ankles. The Sol would keep walking until the waterfall consumed them. Bright lights would then stripe out from the mist and a few moments later a new Sol would emerge from the waterfall.

S'rae saw a garden snake evolve into a python with flower petals at its end; a pink gorilla tripled in size; a wolf came out with fur made of leaves; and her favorite, a small bug transformed into a beautiful three-foot tall butterfly.

S'rae recognized the little girl as the butterfly flew toward her, its wings releasing dust that sparkled.

"She is… so beautiful!" the girl cried as she hugged her butterfly.

"I remember Olivia's words to you," Bele said. "She would be very proud of you right now. Much like you, your Sol went through many transformations. And now you will understand why Olivia said: *who you were then will not define who you will grow to become. And that is something greater than you could ever imagine."*

"I miss her so much!" the girl continued to cry.

"I miss her too," Bele said, puffing his chest as if to hold back tears. "So much."

And suddenly S'rae just wanted to get Sianu's vision off her chest. To tell Bele what she saw, but a part of her was afraid of what he would say. Afraid that it'd change what they had become. But she needed to know if Bele knew the truth about Olivia... and with that... she needed to know the truth about Bele, and who he really was.

When the ceremony ended and the new Sols stood by their owners, who were all smiling wide, Bele announced: "Congratulations on this wonderful achievement! Your Sols, like yourselves, have reached a new level. Your bond is stronger and now more will be expected from you. But each and every one of you will live up to such expectations. Because here at GroundStone, by the end, you all will become the best you Gaia will ever see. And with that being said, you will have a *Jamal* waiting for you when you get back. They can alter one's appearance so much that you would be unrecognizable even to your own mother, but that is not their purpose here. Their purpose is to search your soul and design you to your best outfit, your best hairstyle, and ultimately your best you. Because students... the Solermony Ball has arrived!"

When S'rae made it back to her room, Lynn was already there with a blindfold over her eyes, sitting on a chair made of vines. A lady dressed in white hunched over her as she mumbled words and waved her hands around.

S'rae saw how the vines leeched off the stool and began attaching themselves onto Lynn's clothes. They traveled up her back and began braiding Lynn's hair before twisting it around into a flawless bun.

As the lady chanted louder, the seat began to spin so quickly that it lifted Lynn to her feet. Then spiders—S'rae's jaw dropped—yes, *spiders*... dozens of them... began dropping from the ceiling, practically covering Lynn's entire body.

S'rae suddenly understood why Lynn was blindfolded... a part of her felt like she wasn't even supposed to see this, because there was no way she wouldn't freak and jump out the window if she knew spiders were crawling all over body.

But to S'rae's surprise, Lynn's smile glowed brighter as the seconds passed. And once they returned back to the ceiling, S'rae let out an accidental: "OH. MY. DIVINE!" She then cupped her mouth.

"S'rae?" Lynn said, tilting her head. "Is that you?"

S'rae squeaked. "Yes, sorry!"

"How do I look?"

The lady, who was covered in white from head-to-toe, pressed her finger to her mouth as if to silence S'rae, then shook her head.

"I guess... I'm not supposed to say." S'rae took a step back.

The lady nodded and waved her hand as a mirror formed from the sand. She then snipped the blindfold with her inchlong fingernail. And as it fell to the ground, Lynn screamed and cried in the mirror.

"I LOOK SO DAMN BEAUTIFUL!" Lynn shrieked. "HOW! HOW DID YOU DO THIS? Can I take you home with me? I could make you like SUPER RICH at Sereni! Do you have ANY idea how many girls would kill for this?!"

Lynn turned to S'rae and S'rae's jaw dropped again. "You are easily the most beautiful girl in all of Gaia!" A part of her did not want Bele to even see Lynn like this, he'd probably rather go with her instead. The last thing she wanted was for Bele to feel like he was settling with the ugly duckling. There was no way he'd still think she was the most beautiful girl in Gaia with HER standing here.

S'rae shook her head. She hated the fact that she knew she was getting jealous. She had been the victim of it when Lynn was jealous of her; so she tried her hardest not to be, but it was oh so tough!

And as Lynn walked toward S'rae, wearing her elegant, floaty, cerulean-blue silk gown, S'rae caught the scent of a perfume made of fresh seawater. S'rae's nostrils followed Lynn as she passed.

And when S'rae turned back to the lady in white, she was staring at S'rae with her finger pointed to her chest.

"Me?" S'rae said, looking around. "Is it... my turn?"

The lady simply nodded. She lifted her arm as a chair of vines sprouted from the ground. And when she lifted her other arm, a dozen spiders instantly created a silk blindfold.

S'rae felt her nerves already getting the best of her. *Don't worry... they won't kill you... they are... good spiders?*

And the moment she sat down on the seat, all her worries faded away instantly. She couldn't explain it but it felt like she was connected to nature... to Gaia... to all its lifeforce. Each breath she inhaled felt like it was her first time breathing. Energy pulsed into her as everything, including the contents from outside the window, came into a crystal clear focus. She saw the most minute details like bugs crawling on a building... until the blindfold wrapped around her eyes.

Darkness.

She felt tiny sensations sprinkle all across her body, like soft raindrops, that made her feel as though she was getting her second massage of the day. Then what she knew were probably the spiders crawling all over her body actually felt like soft feathers caressing her skin, sending pleasant shivers throughout her body.

And when the blindfold fell and she opened her eyes, tears began to fall.

"I... I... love it!" S'rae turned to the lady and hugged her. "This really is the best me!" S'rae turned to the mirror again and saw how flowers and vines were braided into her hair, though only half of her head was. The other half of her hair felt flat, with small sparkling roses poking out from underneath the brunette sheet. It was different... but it was her... she was different, and that was what she loved about it.

S'rae then looked down and saw her green silk dress that looked as if it were made of transparent leaves.

Though the lady's mouth was covered with a white scarf, S'rae noticed her smile. S'rae hugged her again before quickly running downstairs to show Lynn.

The moment she turned the corner, Lynn had her arms wrapped around Milla and their heads were practically fused together.

Once Milla opened her eyes, she quickly pulled away and said, "Hi... err... sorry... she looked way too good to wait."

Lynn wiped her lips. "There is absolutely nothing to apologize about!" Lynn then turned to S'rae and her smile flinched a little.

S'rae hesitated a bit before asking what they thought, they definitely didn't seem too thrilled and that made her feet and hands begin to sweat. After nothing was said for a bit, S'rae bit her lip and finally found the courage. "So... what do you think?" She shrugged her shoulders and gave a half smile that wavered as the seconds passed.

"I..." Lynn said, turning to Milla. "I... I don't know... what do you think, Milla?"

"I... I think... I think it looks... you know... it looks good. Yeah, yeah... I'd say it looks good."

"Yeah," Lynn agreed, nodding her head. "Yeah, it looks good."

S'rae felt her heart collapse without really knowing why. Maybe it had to do with this supposedly being the best version of her... yet it didn't seem enough to them. S'rae's eyes began to water, and the girls took notice.

"Hey, listen, S'rae," Lynn said, "it's not that we don't like it... it's just... you know, it's made for you, not us. And I think it's great for you."

"For me, yeah," S'rae said blankly, sniffling. "When will my best ever be good enough."

"Aw, don't say that!" Milla said. "Listen… all that matters is what *you* think!"

"But… what if I want others to like me too?" S'rae said, turning away as she felt more tears beginning to fall. "You know what… I'm just going to ask her to change it. Yeah… just going to see if maybe there is another better me."

"You look like nature's finest." S'rae heard a soft voice say as she had turned around. When she turned back, she saw Retro'ku wearing a black sleeveless shirt with loose black pants and a golden belt. He looked even more handsome than ever before. And in his hands were purply-blue lilacs.

S'rae then felt her heartbeat escalate as she suddenly realized why he may have been here. "Umm… hi… hi, Retro'ku."

"Hello, S'rae." His charming smile glowed bright. "These are for you… they are your favorite, no?" He looked down at the flowers, then back up again at S'rae and his jaw dropped. "I would not change a single thing about you. You look perfect. I am excited for our day."

S'rae blushed as she turned to look at Lynn, whose eyes were the widest S'rae had ever seen.

"Umm…" Lynn stuttered, grabbing Milla, "yeah… I'm like… definitely going to go right now! Bye! Good luck!" And before she made it out, she collided into a dazzling man wearing a white silk suit with a gold trim. "Er… S'rae… I think… we have a problem here."

"What is the problem?" Retro'ku smiled as he turned to the entrance, and at once, the candles in the room faded from red to blue as a chilling cold swept through the room. S'rae saw her breath dance around. "What is he doing here?"

"*HE* is *her* date," Bele said, stepping up to Retro'ku. There was an unexplainable, unseen force that took over the room at that moment. It felt as if S'rae was sinking into the ground and the planet was spinning faster. Even the candlelight angled inward towards them.

Retro'ku turned to S'rae. He clenched his fist as the lilacs burst into flames, its ashes falling to the ground. "I knew this was a mistake. I do not have time for fun, anyways. I should only be training." S'rae saw the pain in Retro'ku's eyes and she wanted to say something, but as sharp as her brain may have been, it was not prepared for this situation.

"Retro'ku!" S'rae said, reaching out for him. "I'm sorry! I didn't know you were still wanting to—"

"You did not know... or you did not care? Or did you not remember?" Retro'ku shook his head. And before S'rae could say another word, an explosion rattled the room and a stream of red and black smoke blasted to the horizon.

"He makes quite the exit, I'll give him that." Bele smirked.

But S're was not in the mood for laughing, she shook her head, disappointed in herself. *Why do you always have to ruin everything! WHY! WHY! WHY!*

Bele, as if reading her thoughts, walked up to her and said: "S'rae... accidents will always happen in life. Mistakes will always happen. Bad moments are only seconds of your day. Do not let seconds affect what will be the best day of your life." Bele grabbed S'rae and held her close to his chest. "I am sorry that this happened. But remember today... remember tonight... remember, the next wave is coming."

The colosseum looked majestic today as the blue sky faded to a dark purple. Rather than the golden columns, everything was pure white. And rather than an open top, there was a white cloth draped over the opening.

The entrance felt strange, filled with people wearing different colors instead of the usual brown robes. Bele held S'rae's hand with a firm grip as they made their way to the front of the entrance. S'rae barely recognized some of the students, until one of them, who was talking up a storm around a crowd, broke away and bee-lined straight to S'rae.

"Hello there, GroundStone Champion," Yash said with his chin held up high.

"Hello, Yash," S'rae said.

Yash coughed loudly and gently nudged the medallion that was pressed onto his white shirt. "Ahem." He pointed at it again once S'rae said nothing.

"Oh." S'rae squinted her eyes to see that it had a symbol of a dragon and read Card Duels Champion. "Well, congratulations, Card Duels Champion."

He bowed, then said, "That was all I wanted to hear. The Card Duels Champ has other matters to attend to. Do not feel bad that I do not have the time to give, I will eventually make some for a fellow champ. Carry on!"

Bele couldn't help but chuckle as this small boy walked away with the most confident steps. "I aspire to be like him one day."

"So I can cut your tongue off?"

"Oh believe me," Bele's whisper tickled her ears. "You would *not* want to cut it off once you find out the things it can... do." And S'rae could not explain what happened, but she felt a shiver travel from the center of her body to her head then down to her toes. She let out a soft moan as she closed her eyes and took a deep breath.

"What did you just do to me?" S'rae said with a gasp.

His mouth leaned in closer to her ear. "Oh S'rae... that was nothing."

S'rae felt anxious without really knowing why.

"Why hello there, beauties!" Leonna said, who was looking quite pretty in robes of bright turquoise, to match her hair. She didn't look enthusiastic about having her man with her, though.

And when S'rae glanced at him, she was shocked at what she saw. He was a very handsome man dressed in blue. "Your two left feet better keep up with me tonight, I'm not playing around! I will replace you like I did my socks this morning, okay? Okay. Great. I love you!"

"And look who we have here!" Professor Di'tukia approached them.

"Oh... we're not really that important." Leonna grinned wickedly. "We're only the Boulder Dash Champions."

"Well... congratulations on a great victory!" Di'tukia smiled, she then turned to S'rae. "And I would like to thank you, S'rae."

"Me?" S'rae was taken aback. "Why?"

"Because of you—" Di'tukia turned around and poked a girl on the back, who was wearing a beautiful red dress. "Here, meet J'Sea. She is a very gifted Wave Runner, like yourself, but she was always made the healer. But because you put on a wonderful show, you helped pave the way for aspiring girls."

"Thank you," J'sea said. "I'm officially a starting Wave Runner now!"

"WAIT! HOLD UP!" A little girl barged into the conversation. It was Emi, her olive skin glowed against her fluffy purple dress. "Did you just say you're a WAVE RUNNER!" Her eyes went wide.

"I did," J'sea smiled.

"So... you mean to tell me that I CAN become a Wave Runner... as a girl?"

"Of course!" Di'tukia, Leonna, J'sea, and S'rae said at once.

"THIS IS THE BEST DAY EVER! I promise I will become one of the greatest Wave Runners ever! And I'll send you a thank you message!" Emi then skipped away happily.

Just then, the doors opened and white doves flowed overhead, dropping their feathers, making it appear as a beautiful winter's snowfall.

And as Bele led the way into the colosseum, S'rae was shocked to see that it looked absolutely nothing like the arena she had battled in. Instead of sand covering the ground, there was a pristine marble floor with a thin layer of dove feathers, making it look like a winter wonderland. The walls were covered with a sparkling white frost, with crystal silver vines and ivy creating beautiful designs. The tables were marble and ivory, the ceiling was pure white, with the illusion that there were snow clouds overhead. The doves helped with the majesty of the setting as they continuously flew overhead, giving the effect of a light snowfall.

It suddenly occurred to S'rae that it never snowed down here in the GroundStone district, so it made sense why they would make the Solermony Ball so special with this theme. And since she wasn't the biggest fan of cold weather... she found herself loving this more than an actual snowy setting.

S'rae concentrated on not tripping over her dress, she was not used to walking in shoes this high. Bele seemed to be enjoying himself; he was alert yet beaming at S'rae the entire time, as if ready to laugh the moment she fell, or maybe ready to catch her when she did.

And as Bele guided S'rae to their table, where the other professors were, the music began playing. When she scanned the area for the source, she saw a band of animals with their instruments. But what shocked her the most was this divinely elegant white parrot with a long spindly tail that had a singing voice from the heavens. Its beautiful vocals blended perfectly with the sweet string and wind instruments.

S'rae felt a hand press against her lower back. "Shall we?" Bele whispered.

"I would love to!" S'rae smiled wide.

S'rae thought back to what her mother had said: "You can tell you found the one when you create an effortless triangle between you, your partner, and music. You become a unit. You become one. There is no thinking or talking because it is your bodies that are communicating with one another. And that is when you know."

And S'rae finally understood what she meant. When they danced, it was effortless. They were twisting and turning and pushing and pulling as if they had choreographed this a thousand times. And it wasn't until the music had stopped did she realize that all eyes were on them. S'rae felt her face go red.

"Splendid!" Di'tukia shouted from her table.

"That was a'right, I guess." Coars said, dressed in black. He would be, S'rae thought.

"Why can't you dance with me like that!" Leonna said to her husband. "That's it, I'm getting my promised dance!" Leonna came straight towards them and said: "The dance you promised me, Bele."

"Why yes, of course." Bele bowed and grabbed Leonna's hand. Her shoulder pushed up to her cheek and she smiled wide.

And as S'rae watched Bele and Leonna dance throughout the floor, S'rae felt a hand grab her hip and turn her around.

"Do not scream… and no one else will have to die," the voice said. And when S'rae looked up, she saw a man wearing a white mask. "Let's dance."

30

S'RAE HAD NO IDEA HOW SHE COULD ESCAPE this situation. Bele was dancing with Leonna, Fa'laz looked as if he was getting drunk with Coars, and everyone else seemed preoccupied with their partners.

"Tell me, S'rae," the man said, "why won't you just die already?"

"I suppose I'm having a good time being alive."

"Ah, a somewhat good sense of humor."

"Why don't you just kill me already?"

"I've tried. Twice. The first... was due to underestimating your speed. But the second... the second should have worked."

"Well, why don't you kill me right now?"

"I would if I could... but we have rules."

"Oh, sounds like a nice place to work."

Nothing was said for a few moments.

"You have quite the personality... at first I couldn't understand why they'd want you dead... but now it makes sense."

"What is the Sol'adari... and why do they want me dead?"

"That's what I've been trying to figure myself. You know, usually deaths are the easy part."

"Sorry for making your job difficult."

"They always said the one hundredth would be the most difficult."

S'rae immediately thought about Sianu's vision... and how Olivia was on her one hundredth kill.

"So... I take it you'll never find out why they'd want me dead?" S'rae said.

"There is always a good reason for a death. It's just every other time... it was clear. But with you... besides your annoying personality, I see no reason why you should die. But... since I want my freedom, unfortunately... your time is up."

S'rae then thought about Sianu, how his approach was with his killer. "So... tell me about yourself. Have any friends or family?"

"I do not have time for small talk."

"Is that a *no* to family?"

"My family is the Sol'adari."

"So, I'll take that as a *no* to family then."

"Well, that makes both of us then... judging by the research I've done. And what about you... your friends. How many of them need to die before you do?" S'rae then felt something get stuck in her throat. "Your friend... Fujak... they say he may be dying soon... you could change that, you know. Your death could set him free."

S'rae's heart collapsed as she thought about Fujak dying inside Alsi'jin—the prison claiming the life of an innocent person... "I'll free him."

"You may not have much time to. The song is done. So is our time here. Don't be selfish. Save your friend. Just remember: *The true enemy you should watch for is the one closest to you.*"

"You can have your little partner back, S'rae." Leonna's voice erupted from behind. "He couldn't keep up with me, anyways!" S'rae turned around and noticed Bele hunching over as Leonna went straight to her table.

When she turned back around, no one was there. Gone, as if he was a ghost.

"Phew!" Bele grabbed S'rae's shoulders, making her leap back. "You know... that lady has some grooves in her moves, I'd have never known."

S'rae remained still, staring blankly, unsure what she should say to Bele.

But before she could speak on it, Bele had already sensed something was wrong. His eyes scanned the crowd. "Where'd he go?"

"How'd you know?"

"Your eyes... I've seen them twice already... they're the same eyes you give each time you see him." Bele grabbed S'rae's arms as they walked quickly by dozens of dancing couples, none seeming to notice them even as they exited the colosseum.

When S'rae thought they'd stop walking to talk about what had happened, still Bele kept moving. They walked and walked until they reached the Golden Palace.

Bele, after glancing around, took an emblem from his pocket and tapped it against the massive golden doors. A section of the door turned white for a moment before becoming completely transparent.

Bele grabbed S'rae's hand as they walked through the opening that faded away the moment they entered the palace, as if the door had always been solidly gold.

"What... what are we doing here?" S'rae whispered.

"This is the best time to come here, while everyone is busy at the Ball."

"So you never wanted to actually stay at the Ball?" S'rae felt a little disappointed that her dress and hair were going to waste.

"I'll explain later," Bele said, grabbing S'rae's hands and placing them on the wall. "Stay put, just like that. Don't move."

He muttered a few words and suddenly S'rae felt light-headed, but more confused than anything else. Because it seemed like she was leaning up against a wall, but it felt like she was doing a push-up.

And suddenly everything clicked once she saw Bele start to walk up the wall.

"That Di'Tukia spell?" S'rae said as Bele reached his hand from the wall to help her... up?

And just like that, they were walking on the wall and it made her head spin.

A noise was heard somewhere, and they set off. As they went, the wall started to look more and more like a floor, as if this was its intended purpose from the beginning. Her mind couldn't wrap around the idea of how it felt like she was walking down a long hallway with torches burning on either side and a mural overhead that depicted Gods and Goddesses at peace. The torches burned with a bright-red glow, illuminating carvings in the walls—the same design, repeated over and over, of a dragon bursting through flames and a phoenix rising from the ashes. This looked strikingly familiar.

And after walking for what felt like an hour, they had finally reached the ceiling, a multi-colored brick wall that seemed chaotically put together.

Bele then took his emblem out once more, mumbled a few words, then tapped it against a brick.

Nothing happened for a few moments and S'rae began to wonder what the plan was.

Then a rumble was heard from beyond the ceiling. Then movement was seen as the bricks rattled in place. And after a few seconds, the first brick launched from its spot, hovering in midair for a few seconds before replacing the spot of another brick that shot off the wall. This juggling of bricks going in and out and swapping locations went on dozens of times until finally they settled... and S'rae's jaw dropped.

Before her eyes... was a building that she had seen before. "But... that's impossible."

"You will soon find out... that nothing is impossible," Bele said.

The once multi-colored, disorganized ceiling, now looked like a perfect mural of... the Spire at Harahn'de.

Bele grabbed S'rae's hand as they walked through the wall, feeling water cover her entire body, yet she remained dry. And when she looked around... she saw hundreds of destroyed Mechas, looking like a metallic graveyard. "How... how are we here right now?"

"I think the better question would be... why are we here right now."

S'rae's mouth was still dropped. "Is this... this to get... my dragon?"

Bele nodded as he examined one of the Mechas. "Do you know what destroyed them?"

"I don't know... one moment I thought we were all dead... and the next moment... lightning covered the entire area."

Bele's eyes widened. "Lightning... fascinating. This was definitely Vy'ken's work! You were actually in the presence of *Vy'ken*!" Bele jumped atop one of the Mechas and walked across its body. "This one still seems operational."

"Let's hope not."

"Why? Are you scared of a Mecha?"

"Shouldn't you be?" S'rae raised an eyebrow.

"Not at all." He gave his kissable smirk again. "Now *this* one is a different story." Bele leapt high into the air and landed on a massive black Mecha with a solid red on its head. "This is a PriMecha. It's said that this could challenge even a God."

"So only a God can beat it?"

"Pretty much."

"Well... how about we go then," S'rae said as she heard some type of ticking noise from inside its core. "I don't think this one is... dead. Is that right? Dead? Can Mechas die?"

"Well, whatever it is, I don't want to be here if it does wake up," Bele said as he led the way into one of the many openings that led underground.

The heat became so humid that S'rae felt her hair and clothes stick to her skin. That familiar stench of mold hit her nostrils.

They reached a metal door with no handles, and Bele tapped his knuckles against it twice before hearing a *pop* and a *crack*. The door sparked with a brief gold light and swung open. Bele stepped inside and S'rae followed behind. The door was hefty, and closed with a tremendous BANG behind S'rae, nearly destroying her eardrums; she threw her arms out into the pitch-darkness, waving her hands around, trying to find Bele. "Where are you? Come on… don't play around like this."

"Shh…" S'rae heard a soft voice breeze by the back of her ear. She then felt a warm finger press against her lips. "Listen… do you hear it?"

S'rae remained completely still, hoping to hear whatever it was that was in this darkness.

Then finally she heard it, there was a high, screeching sound followed by a low grumble.

"Is-is that… breathing?" S'rae's voice wavered.

"It is," Bele whispered.

S'rae rubbed her sweaty palms against her dress. "Well… what am I supposed to do right now?"

"You wait… you remain calm… you do *not* move quickly. We only have a few seconds to know if he is the one."

"A few seconds!" S'rae breathed out her loudest whisper.

"Don't worry, have faith." S'rae felt Bele's firm hands wrap around her arms from behind. This comforted her, but she still couldn't shake off the terror of how scary this situation was. Not only was the soft breathing incredibly loud, but now she felt it press against her face, whipping her hair back with each exhale. "H-how big is this thing?"

"You see that Mecha up there?"

"Yes." S'rae gulped.

"Well… that's a baby compared to this."

At once, S'rae's knees shook furiously.

"Don't get nervous. It won't help."

"Yeah… well neither does saying *don't get nervous*." S'rae's heart hammered against her chest.

She then heard a flicker and a sizzle as a light resonated in front of her. "Remember…" Bele said softly, "only a few seconds."

The gold light grew brighter, highlighting the floor of the room. S'rae saw bones and thick chains scattered about. And as the light floated higher into the air, S'rae suddenly realized just how massive this room must have been. There was no ceiling in sight, just an endless blanket of darkness. Until… she saw puffs of steam billow out. Then she saw scales the size of her that surrounded two black voids that must have been nostrils.

The nose slowly lowered itself down to S'rae. Her skin felt like it was being roasted as if she was out in the desert on a blistering hot day.

It took one sniff and S'rae's dress and hair was practically sucked into its nose.

She tried her hardest not to scream, she was terrified… or was she?

What she thought at first was fear… may not have been. Yes, her heart was pounding against her chest like a drumroll, but it did that when she was excited as well.

S'rae slowly reached her hand up, wavering slightly only when the nose flinched. And once she touched the scale, she felt an unexplainable warmth surge through her body.

"What do you feel?" Bele's whispers reached her ears.

"I feel warm." She gently rubbed the scale. "I feel…"

Just then, a flame burst out from its nostrils.

"S'rae… we only have a few seconds… I need to know if you feel complete."

"I… I don't know."

"Does it feel like you two are connected?"

"I… I don't know."

Then another set of flames shot out. "We need to go!" Bele grabbed S'rae's arms, the worry in his voice broke her out of her trance. The light faded away as Bele pulled S'rae into the darkness.

Then a screeching roar shook the room so hard that S'rae fell on top of Bele. A series of flames were seen dancing in the air until a resounding BANG erupted from its mouth.

A blue flaming wave that must have been the size of Mecha had burst through the darkness and exploded a wall.

S'rae's mouth dropped as she saw the night's sky through the rubble. The dragon was merely a giant silhouette cast against the moon's light, but it ran, leapt, and dove out of sight. S'rae heard screeching get softer and softer as blue smoke filled the air.

"What happened," Bele said, wrapping her arms around S'rae, squeezing her tightly. "I thought I was going to lose you." He pressed his face to her neck.

S'rae wished she could say something… anything, but she still felt the wave of her shock ripple through her, so strong that for a second, she didn't even know where she was, never mind that Bele had been shaking her and screaming into her ear.

"S'rae!" Bele shouted. "Are you okay! Speak to me!"

"So…" S'rae finally spoke. "So… a dragon… isn't my Sol." And then the reality of it crushed her. She was not special… she was just a girl who would never receive a Sol, and she felt like this was the awakening that she needed. And as Bele squeezed her tighter, she said, "Maybe… maybe I'm just… maybe… I'm just not meant to be a chosen one. I'm not meant for this destiny. I'm just me… I'm just S'rae."

Bele then lifted S'rae in his arms and carried her to the court-yard above. He stopped at once. "This isn't good."

But S'rae still said nothing, just staring at nothing at all. A part of her wished they hadn't ever tried to make her feel special… because now it hurt more than ever before. Beyond hurt… to the point that her body had gone numb as if to protect itself.

"Wait here," Bele said, placing S'rae down gently. "Our way back was destroyed from that blast. I'll be right back! Don't move! Please!"

But S'rae had no intentions on moving, she lay there expecting to cry, but no tears arrived... and that troubled her even more. She felt broken. "I thought... I thought it was mine. I thought... I was special. I thought... I was loved."

And as the seconds passed, a soft ticking sound was heard, but it may have just been in her head. But as she thought more about being a failure, the ticking sound only became louder. It wasn't until the ground shook, when she finally snapped out of her daze.

She sat up and looked around. All she saw was a valley filled with chaos, destroyed buildings, statues, and Mechas.

But then *it* moved.

S'rae stood up at once, adrenaline now coursing through her veins. "Uh... Bele..."

The black PriMecha's fingers slowly began to curl.

"Bele..." S'rae said softly.

Then the red light on its head began to flicker.

"Bele!" S'rae screamed. "Bele! The PriMecha! It's moving! Bele!"

And as *zaps* and *clangs* filled Harahn'de, Bele finally ran from the Spire with a book in his hand, steam radiating from his fingers. "What's wrong? I heard you screaming."

And just then, a shadow eclipsed over them. Bele looked up and his mouth dropped.

"Do you trust me?" Bele screamed at S'rae as wave of energy began to swirl around the Mecha's chest. A droning hum reverberated through the area. She had seen this before, it was the attack that consumed Gabrael.

"I do!" S'rae screamed.

As the Mecha shot a wide beam at Bele and S'rae, Bele had

slammed his palm into the dirt, creating a hole that shot miles through the ground.

S'rae grabbed onto Bele's chest as an explosion erupted overhead. But that wasn't the worst of their problems, because S'rae had now just realized they were free-falling through the sky.

S'rae kept her face against Bele's chest as the floating island of Harahn'de began to fall away behind them. And as they fell through clouds, S'rae noticed that the island and the infinitely long pole that connected it to the planet were becoming more and more transparent the farther they fell.

Soon Harahn'de's island was invisible, as if it was never there, and they were soaring weightlessly down to the planet below.

S'rae would be lying if death wasn't on her mind, but for some reason, being wrapped around Bele's arms made her feel safe... as if everything would be okay. As if she trusted him with her life.

But a brief vision crossed her mind. That if ever there was a way she'd want to die, it would be like this, in his arms. And for once, death no longer scared her, she was at peace with whatever outcome that would happen from this freefall.

But Bele had other plans.

His voice sang a beautiful song that made her close her eyes against the pressures of the wind. She felt his words lift her higher into the sky, feeling them move around in her stomach. His song felt like feathers caressing her skin. Like warm bodies, making her feel warm and loved.

And once his beautiful voice stopped whistling, he said, "You can open your eyes now."

And when she did she saw that she was flying atop dozens of birds that had morphed into a large one, carrying them through the sky. Her eyes watered as she appreciated how majestic Gaia looked from this perspective.

"I am sorry the dragon wasn't your Sol," Bele said, looking back at S'rae as his hands clamped onto the bird's neck.

Then something hit her, like a sword through her heart. She was no longer special to him. She was no longer the one who he would help to get a dragon. S'rae sniffled and wiped her eyes. "Well... at least now I won't be holding you back. You don't have to be nice to me anymore. I'm not special... anymore."

Bele looked over his shoulder, his eyes drooped as their eyes met. "S'rae... do you want to know how I know you're special?"

S'rae shook her head, then turned away from him. She didn't want him to see her tears that fell.

"S'rae..." Bele pressed his forehead to her shoulder. "I've never felt this way for anyone else. That is how I know."

S'rae felt a sliver of a smile appear, but still, this could have been Bele trying to be nice. "When we get back to GroundStone... I'll probably never see you again."

"Well... who says we're going back to GroundStone so soon?" Bele smiled.

"Where are we going?"

"I want to show you that there is much more to life. And there is no better time to explore the world with you... than now. Hold on tight."

S'rae hugged Bele as the bird blazed through the night's sky.

Bele knew exactly how to make S'rae smile. Once again, when she felt most inadequate, questioning if her life mattered, he was always there to let her know of the version of herself that she wished she could see in herself.

They flew north to the Fujita mountains with their snow-tipped peaks illuminating under the moon's light. Like a bullet through water, they burst through the air with a ripple, and when they halted, S'rae's mouth fell open.

"Beautiful, huh?" Bele said.

"Is... that... Sereni?" S'rae said, her eyes wide.

"It is."

And as they swooped down pass the floating waterfalls that

glowed a fluorescent blue, S'rae noticed how Serenicea, the City of Water, looked flawless in design. Its canals were perfectly symmetrical, creating gorgeous shapes and figures that made the district look more like a floating masterpiece than a group of cities.

They swooped down and grazed the water as soft splashes hit S'rae's skin. Everything she had ever thought about the beauty of Sereni had been wrong... the pictures did it no justice.

"I wish I could go to school there!" S'rae said as dolphins were found leaping from the water underneath them. "They would be my best friends!" S'rae screamed as she extended her arm down as far as she could to try to pet one.

A smile glowed from her face. She lifted her arms up as they flew above an incoming wave and said, "Let's explore the world together!"

It was true what they said: that the smile after your darkest point was the brightest of them all. S'rae radiated as she squeezed her arms around Bele. "You truly are my next wave. I don't know what I'd do without you. I don't even know if I'd be alive."

"You'd live your life without me, S'rae," Bele said. "YOUR life. Forget about a Sol. About this destiny. About being a Chosen One. I want you to live YOUR life, S'rae. What is it that YOU want to do."

"I want..." S'rae didn't need to put much thought into the answer, it came out as naturally as breathing. "I just want to be with you." Then something caught S'rae's eye as she noticed golden towers, mile high statues, and great pyramids fade away from her. "Hey, we just passed GroundStone! Where are we going?"

"There was something that has been troubling me." Bele lifted his head. "During the first Sol event, at the Valley of Dreams... there were many more animals there than ever before. They wouldn't tell me why, because they couldn't explain what they felt. And that made me most curious. And it turns out that all the animals came from the same location. All east of GroundStone. Just a funny feeling—"

S'rae's gasp had cut Bele short.

"What's wrong?" he said.

"This…" S'rae looked down at the familiar backdrop. She saw the valley, the hills, the range, she saw the plateaus, and the Abyssal Forest. "This… was my home. This is Opell—"

BANG! Without warning, they had collided into an invisible wall that broke upon contact. They found themselves crashing down into a foreign area where light was forbidden.

The birds screeched and broke apart as a thick black substance, like tar, had covered them. They were falling at an alarming rate.

And before they landed, Bele had leapt into the air and slammed his palms together. A wave of sand arched, forming a hammock that coddled the birds and S'rae before gently placing them onto the ground.

"I think they're dying!" S'rae screamed as the birds squirmed about. The dark substance had a mind of its own as if it was devouring them. "We need to help them!"

But Bele said nothing. He stood up and looked around before falling to his knees.

"S'rae…" he said softly, but S'rae was still wildly freaking out, trying to attend to the birds.

"S'rae…" This time louder, and when S'rae didn't respond, he shouted once more. "S'RAE!"

S'rae let go of the black birds and turned to Bele, who was staring at the sky. When her eyes followed his, she too fell to her knees. "What… what… is that?"

"That… is the end of the world."

And as S'rae and Bele were gazing at a shadow monster that was as tall as the sky, the birds behind them began to take shape. First jagged pincers popped from their heads, then legs, then a spiked tail. Within a few moments, they had been surrounded by dozens of shadowy beasts without ever noticing.

"We need to warn everyone, S'rae." Bele said.

But S'rae was frozen in shock as she stared at the beasts prowling toward her. She told her body to do something… anything, but she remained a statue of herself. With much effort, she finally managed to blurt out a soft. "Bele…"

And when he turned around, S'rae had seen a side of him that she had never seen before. His eyes turned gold as a droning hum shook the ground. Even the beasts took a step back. He turned to S'rae, his voice deep and life-threatening. "Warn everyone!"

And before she could stop whatever he planned to do. He had slammed his palm to the ground as green lines illuminated the dirt, creating an ancient relic where she stood. And as the shadow beasts jumped on top of Bele, the relic sucked her into the dirt and the next moment she opened her eyes, she was laying inside a cold, stone room, alone.

"BELE!" S'rae screamed, slamming her fists! "BELE! WHERE ARE YOU?"

31

“PLEASE!” S'RAE SCREAMED LOUDLY AS SHE SLAMMED her bruised hands onto the stone floor again. They may have been broken by now, but she didn't care. The pain helped numb the reality… that Bele was gone. “PLEASE! DON'T LEAVE ME! I NEED YOU! I NEED YOU IN MY STORY!”

S'rae had cried and cried. Though Bele had told her to warn everyone, she couldn't shake off what she had seen—the shadow beasts that had jumped onto Bele, latching their claws into him.

“You are my next wave.” S'rae cried into her arms.

“And you are mine.” She felt warm hands press against her back.

At once, she jumped to her feet and practically tackled Bele.

“Please don't do that! Please never do that again!” S'rae cried into his chest. “I saw life without you… and… I never… I never… I just don't want a life without you.”

Bele held her tightly then wiped the tears from her eyes. “I promise, S'rae. I promise I will protect you at all costs.”

“But not if it means you die. Please don't do that again.”

“I cannot promise that, S'rae.” Bele shook his head. “Your life is more important.”

"Don't say that!" She slammed her palms onto his chest. "I never thought it'd hurt that much. But... the moment... the moment I thought you were no longer in my life." S'rae looked up and gazed into his eyes. "All I thought about was regret. All I thought about was missing out on the things I wanted to do with you. I want us to explore the world. I want—"

"S'rae..." Bele said, grabbing her hands, which were still on his chest. He couldn't peel his eyes away from hers, as if there was a fire inside them that he had never seen. He then caressed her head. "A danger is coming... the world may—"

S'rae pressed her finger to his lips. "If the world is ending... then..." *What are you doing, S'rae. You take your hands off his chiseled chest. Oh no, chiseled. Don't use that word right now.* But as S'rae's hands wandered Bele's body, a different voice appeared in her head, with a tone that she had never heard. *I'm doing what I want now.*

And without thinking, her face lunged forward; her lips met his, and his hands lightly clamped around her throat as he pulled her closer into him.

S'rae couldn't explain what she felt or happened. She had never kissed a boy before, never felt a boy's lips on her own, never mind her neck, shoulder, chest, and stomach, which shuddered under his touch. She was not herself... this was some other S'rae that she had only dreamed about, but this was real. She felt it as Bele's tongue rolled from neck to her ear as he whispered: "You won't want to cut my tongue off after this."

And everything happened so quickly after those words made her bite her lip. One moment she was high up, legs wrapped around him, as he kissed her neck, their sweat becoming one as their hair stuck to their heads in waves. And the next moment she was lying down as his fingers grazed every part of her body, making her gasp in places she didn't even know were sensitive. He touched her as if she was his berry, soft and with care, which left her breathless.

And much like the berry that he would caress with his tongue… his tongue followed the same path that his hands made, and that was when everything became a… blur.

Minutes? Hours? Days? She didn't know how much time had passed. All she knew was that her legs were still shaking and her body would shiver with the slightest touch. A part of her didn't even know if she was awake. It all felt like a dream she didn't want to wake up from—a state of ecstasy she never wanted to go away. And after she took a few breaths, she realized Bele had been trying to talk to her.

"Huh?" S'rae let out a soft moan, not even knowing where it came from. "What did you do to me?" Her eyes rolled to the back of her head as she bit her lip and shifted her hips.

Bele's mouth moved and she couldn't help but stare at how soft and red his lips were. He must have been talking, but still she lay there, her toes curling and fingers clenching onto the soft fur blanket.

Bele had walked away and she heard the soft whispers of water bouncing off skin. It then occurred to her that he may have told her that he was going to take a shower, but what would she know, she was still too busy drifting through the clouds.

She wanted to know how something as small as a tongue could make her feel so helpless and alive at the same time. She found herself sighing only to close her eyes and try to reminisce on the experience she had.

She clutched her chest and rolled over, her hand fell off the side of the bed, and knocked contents off the side table. There was a sound of a crash. A sudden fruity scent, as of citrus, filled the room.

S'rae bent over the bed to pick up what had fallen and noticed it was his phoenix emblem, the same one Olivia had given her. And as her head nearly hit the ground, she noticed the phoenix symbol on a brick underneath his bed. Though she was still in a state of bliss, with her eyes half-opened, she swore she wasn't seeing things. She picked up the emblem and pressed it against the brick, and the ground rumbled.

She shook her head, trying to snap some life into her as the ground swirled downward. A spiraling staircase appeared that led her deeper into the hole. The stone steps felt warm on her bare feet. She was still convinced that this may have been a dream. But the moment she reached the bottom, her dream-like state vanished instantly. Her eyes widened as she pressed her shaking hands to her face.

"No..." S'rae fell to her knees and whimpered. In front of her, hung up on the wall, was the mask of the killer and a bow and arrow.

Suddenly she heard a crack overhead. "I'm sorry you had to find this."

"All this time... it was you?" S'rae wiped her eyes as tears fell. She felt ashamed, mad, a fool... all at once. Why couldn't she have just listened to herself, why did she have to fall for his charm?
"I trusted you..."

"Let me explain," Bele said as he waved his arm to chest. At once, the hole S'rae was in was no more and she stood on solid ground.

She turned away from him. "What happens now?"

"You listen to what I have to tell you," Bele said.

"I knew about Olivia," S'rae blurted out.

Bele's eyebrows rose.

"I know she's one of you... the Sol'adari."

"Indeed she was... that was hers down there. Locked away for thousands of years."

S'rae turned around, catching Bele's eyes, which seemed convincingly sad. *Don't fall for his tricks again. Don't trust him!*

"I think it is time I tell you something only one other person knows... and she is gone now."

S'rae remained silent with her arms crossed.

"I was a boy when my family died. I came home and my parents were dead... but my sister... her body was nowhere to be found. I searched everywhere, everyday, from morning til night... and I found no trace of her, as if she never existed. But she was my everything, I would not just forget about her."

Bele paced around the room and picked up the book that he took from Harahn'de. Steam sizzled from his fingers as if the book was melting his hand, but Bele didn't even so much as flinch. "I spent the rest of my life trying to search for my parents' killers. A part of me wanted to believe that my sister was still alive. I researched the entry points... they were arrows of some sort, but there was no trace or evidence of them. This made me believe that they were arrows of wind. I read every book regarding such a thing... I had decided to attend Fujita for that reason. But then... I met Olivia. She took a special interest in me. And she told me that if I come here and help her... she would help me. I didn't think I'd ever be able to see one... but then you came."

S'rae's shoulders locked up.

"You brought the Sol'adari to me... to GroundStone... and I couldn't shake how Olivia told me there was no such thing as coincidence. I've been spending the past few years questioning if this quest was even worth it, if she is even still alive, if I just wasted all of this time searching for something that I will never find. But then you came. And all of it became worth it... because it led me to you. I can't explain what draws me to you. I can't explain why it feels like I've seen you before—but that couldn't possibly be the case—you would be dead. But then... I realized, some things are not meant to be understood, they are meant to be appreciated. With you, I no longer cared about tracking down the Sol'adari. I cared about something more, for the first time in my life. I cared about fulfilling Olivia's quest... and I cared about you."

S'rae choked up. She wanted to believe what he was saying, but she couldn't... she just couldn't.

"This..." Bele said, lifting the book, "... this may help us both understand what brought us together, and what we wish to take down: the Sol'adari."

He placed the book on the bed: *The Sol'adari Pact*.

"That's the book I told you about—" S'rae would have said more, but one look into Bele's eyes and she looked away.

"It says here." Bele flipped the pages. "That no one sees a Sol'adari and lives. They either die... or become one. I think this was exactly what I needed. That all my years—" Bele wiped his eyes. "—that they weren't all a waste. I think my sister may actually be alive." Bele's voice cracked as tears fell from his eyes.

And S'rae couldn't help but shed tears of her own. "So... all this time... you knew Fujak was innocent?" S'rae couldn't fight the anger that boiled in her gut.

"I am sorry," Bele said. "I knew from the first arrow that it was not him."

"And you let him suffer in that damn place... knowing he was innocent." S'rae wiped the tears that fell from his eyes. "My friend may die in there and YOU'VE DONE NOTHING!"

"You do not understand the Warden." Bele looked away. "He... he was not always a terrible man. Bad, yes, but not terrible. And there was a time when he was even a beacon of good."

"What happened?"

"I happened."

S'rae was taken aback. She pulled her chin to her neck and took a step back.

"The Warden had a daughter... who loved me."

S'rae didn't know why, but a wave of jealousy surged through her. "Did you love her?"

"I did not... and he did not like that."

"Why would that make him terrible?"

"Because of the Trial of Gods."

"What's that?"

THE LEGENDS OF EVE

"It's when someone fights to the death to prove their innocence. A girl was imprisoned for life. She chose the Trial to gain freedom." Bele choked up as he looked at the ground.

"What happened?"

"The Warden chose me to fight her." Tears flowed from his eyes. "And I couldn't kill the little girl... not when she reminded me so much of my sister. I just couldn't do it." He wiped his eyes. And S'rae was shocked to see so much emotion come from him. "I couldn't kill her. But someone has to die." And when S'rae replied only with wide eyes, Bele continued. "I was going to let her kill me. I felt like this was karma for not protecting my family. But before she took my life... Arelia... the Warden's daughter intervened."

"But..." S'rae said, eyes wide. "But... you said someone has to die."

Bele nodded with pursed lips. "You are not allowed to interfere with a Trial of God. She sacrificed her life to save mine... and ever since then... the Warden wants to see every one and thing die a terrible death."

"So you didn't save Fujak... because you're afraid of the Warden?"

The candlelight in the room all angled toward the center as S'rae felt her stomach start to implode. Bele's eyes looked fierce. "I am not afraid of anything."

The room then normalized as the candles flickered per usual.

"So... why do you think the Sol'adari wants to kill me?"

"I did not know... until I found this book."

S'rae's heart wrenched. Was she about to find out why?

"Right here." Bele flipped the pages, "it tells the story of how the Sol'adari began..."

* * *

Long, long ago, before the Valley of Gaia sealed its walls, there was a pact created between the Monks of Fujita and GroundStone. They both shared similar beliefs, one of which was the belief that the

Tree of Va'han held the answers to knowledge, wisdom, life, and time. They prayed to it daily and lived peacefully among one another. It was a sacred life not meant for the faint of heart, but the true.

That was until… the first fruit fell. None knew what to make of it. Though there were no laws yet made, they all believed it to be forbidden to eat from such a sacred tree.

After much debate, they held a tournament. The winner would be given the fruit as the ultimate prize. Once the victor had won, he decided to eat it without hesitation. If he were to die, it was in his stars. But on that day, the universe had other plans for him.

Instead of death… he saw the opposite. He saw life. He saw lives. Dozens of them… hundreds… thousands… millions all flashing before his eyes, from the past, present, and future.

But of all the lives he had seen as glimpses… there was only one that he took a journey with. He saw life through this person's eyes. He saw his birth, his parents, his adventures, his first love, his life. It was a splendid, humble one, filled with joy and promise, but then the vision ended abruptly, and he was left with only this one person on his mind. It was as if he was destined to meet him. He had just lived his life in a matter of seconds. He could recognize him in a crowd of thousands as if it was his own reflection.

He then had the crazy idea that not only was the person alive, right now… but it was in their stars, by way of the Prophet Va'han, that they were to meet.

So he sought out to find him. He packed his life in a bag and began his journey. It quickly became an obsession. He thought more about where this person could be than he did of food or water. And it was then, when he had decided to give up… it was then when he noticed a building that he had seen in the person's vision. This was the sign he needed. This was Va'han showing him the way.

This was the person's home. The monk was exactly where he was destined to be. And then it happened. The man walked by him as if they had never met, yet he knew everything about him. It was a bizarre feeling indeed, to be a part of someone's life who one viewed as an old friend... only to be a complete stranger.

It was then when the monk pondered his fate. Why would Va'han lead him down this path? Why was he meant to meet this person? There had to be a reason. He wanted the answer, so he studied the man. He watched the man perform the same routine every day. During the day he would put on a show for the village, using puppets to act out hilarious scenes; then at night, he'd enter his hut, light candles, create a casting circle, and chant until he fell asleep.

It was therapeutic how robotic he was. Wake up, puppet show, light candles, casting circle, chant, then sleep. Never a skip... never a hesitation.

And each day that passed, the crowd that he would entertain would get bigger; and each night that passed, the casting circle would as well.

It seemed as if he was committed to mastering only this one spell, and this intrigued the monk even more. The monk was ready to ask him about his routine.

And it was on this day when he decided to ask... it was then when the man decided to draw the casting circle in the center of the village, where he would perform his puppet act. It was wide, spanning almost the entire courtyard.

The village became increasingly excited, this time drawing every last one of them in to enjoy the spectacle.

What entertainment did he have planned now?

But minutes passed... and the village waited in great anticipation... yet the man was nowhere to be seen.

The monk surveyed the crowd. The entire village was in attendance, but not the most important one of all. He went into the man's hut. Nothing was there. It was as if he had just left and started a new life.

The monk then left the village in hopes of finding the man; but again, he was nowhere to be found.

Giving up, the monk then decided to head back to the village… and on his journey back, that was when… he saw it. A great meteor, thrice the size of the village, was falling from the sky.

Before the monk could react, or scream, or breathe, or think… the meteor crashed into the village, instantly eradicating thousands. Its blastwave alone was almost enough to kill the monk. He barely survived, with near-fatal injuries.

The monk limped all the way back home, to the Tree of Va'han, and thought of what this journey meant. And it suddenly occurred to him. The Tree of Va'han had showed him this man's life for one reason… to stop him from committing the atrocity that killed thousands of innocent lives. He had the power to stop it. *He* did. That was the destiny Va'han had given him. To stop it. And he failed.

He was too focused on the good life that this man had lived that he didn't realize the evil he was preparing to unleash.

And it was on that day when the monk arrived back from his journey, when the Sol'adari Pact was born. It was the pact between the Monks of Fujita and GroundStone, to assassinate the person the Tree of Va'han assigns to them, stopping them before the evil occurs.

This was the first kill. There would never be a kill as important or as difficult as the first… unless… it was the assassin's one hundredth.

* * *

"So… what are you saying?" S'rae said, her hands shaking.

"That… if the Sol'adari is after you… it is not what about what you have done… but because of what you will do."

S'rae fell to her knees and cried into her arms. "Why can't I just live my life?"

Bele ran to her and held her in his arms. S'rae had expected to shove him away, but instead, she wrapped her arms around him, nuzzling her head into his neck. "I'm so sorry I didn't trust you."

"It's okay, S'rae," Bele said, rubbing her shoulders. "It's okay.

The next wave is coming."

"The next wave is here!" A sinister voice growled from the doorway.

When S'rae and Bele looked up, they saw the Warden with two Guardians in full metal armor on either side of him.

"You have been summoned." The Warden grinned, showing his nasty teeth.

"For what?" Bele said, standing up, puffing his chest.

"Well, for the Alta'jriba, of course," the Warden snarled.

And at once the Warden's smirk faded away as he held onto the Guardians. The ground shook with such a force that S'rae was sure the planet would split in half.

"Impressive." The Warden braced himself as the rocking stopped. "I see you will make quick work of your opponent."

"Wait…" S'rae said. "What's the Alta'jriba?"

"I suppose the normal folk will know it as the Trial of Gods," the Warden said.

And S'rae's heart collapsed right then. Bele would have to fight to the death… again? She was not ready to picture a life without him. Not after what she had just went through.

"And who will my opponent be?" Bele said.

"Fujak."

32

DESTROU PROTECTED HIS FACE WITH HIS FISTS as he stared down the Leader. Tough for him to understand how he had reached this point, but he was no longer afraid of what could happen. There was no more fear of death; he couldn't produce a single emotion to save his life. *What's wrong with me?* Despite his anger and hatred that he built up throughout the challenge, the realization came to his mind as a whisper.

"I am turning into *him*," it said.

"Ranmau?" he whispered to himself. Pain changes people. Maybe there was something that Ranmau had been trying to tell him. A message beyond the silence. Beyond the expressionless eyes. *I never know when something's wrong... What have you been trying to tell me? I guess it doesn't matter. No one will stop me—not even you, Ranmau. And especially not you, Eli'jah.* He pressed his weight onto his back foot. *He always attacks first. Get rea—*

The Leader roared, lunging all of his weight forward, just as Destrou expected.

He missed.

Destrou countered, lifting his fist toward the Leader's chin.

He missed.

The Leader spun his foot toward his chest.

He missed.

Again and again. Strike after strike. Miss after miss.

The series of strikes and misses were exchanged back and forth, depleting what was left of their energy.

Normally, Destrou could track a pattern to the attacker's method, but the Leader's punches, knees, elbows, and kicks came from every angle. He even had to block three of his kicks in one jump. It was clear to him why the Giant could never beat the Leader: he was too smart of a fighter. Fighting him became more about solving a puzzle than using physical strength.

There was not a single opening. Destrou jumped in the air, spinning his legs twice in the air. There! He lunged his fist at the Leader's jaw.

And again, he missed.

The Leader had moved his face just enough for Destrou's fist to feel the cold of his chin.

It's impossible. How'd Ranmau do it? What did Ranmau do so differently? He made it look too easy.

The Leader kept a grin on his face.

Duck. Dodge. Move. Lunge, Destrou thought.

A burning sensation made breathing difficult. Destrou's heart pounded faster. His hands were no longer able to fight gravity as they dropped below his face.

BANG. The first punch landed across his chin, dizzying his senses.

"Don't make mistakes. Keep your hands up. You know better than this," Destrou said to himself.

The Leader tricked Destrou into defending one side then quickly struck the other.

He landed the same move again. Destrou saw it coming but couldn't stop it. That was when doubt first shown its face.

Wait for it. Don't be a krillen. Look at his feet. Notice the way it's angled in? Like that? No. Right there? Yes, just like that. one... two... three... now. Go!

Destrou jumped immediately before the Leader did. The moment the Leader extended his leg out, Destrou's foot had slid across his face, splattering blood across the room.

The Leader crashed to the ground. He held his face for a moment before spitting blood. "You're going to wish you never did that," he snarled.

"I got more of that for you... don't worry," Destrou said, struggling to lift his hands to his face.

His mind reached a point where thoughts were discussed as if he had a team of coaches in his head, directing him on all of his movements.

The Leader jumped up, shuffling his feet so quickly they looked like a blur.

You see that one? His left? No, the right. That one? Yes. That's what I said. Oh, well, wait for it. What? That? I see it. I think. Last time it looked differently, though. Trust me. Okay? Okay. Wait, that one? Yes! Okay, relax! Right... now. Go!

The Leader's feet moved so rapidly they created marks, digging into the ice. He planted his feet, twisting into a kick. The moment he turned around, his eyes made contact with Destrou's heel, crushing his nose. Blood poured from his nostrils.

The Leader fell backward, clenching his face with his palms. He was on the ground, defenseless. The perfect opportunity to strike presented itself but Destrou never believed in hitting someone while they were down. It was something that Ranmau had always taught him. Still, even when he wasn't around, he didn't want to let him down. No exceptions.

Destrou's greatest weakness had just revealed itself to Eli'jah: his kindness. The challenge was designed to strip someone of that flaw, but he refused to let it change him more than it already had.

"Mer..." the Leader mumbled, wiping blood from the corners of his mouth. "This isn't fun anymore. Time to not go easy on you."

"Heh, you're lucky I want to finish you off the right way." Destrou smirked.

"Tsk. The right way?" he cackled. "The right way is overrated. I was hoping to save this for Ranmau, but let's get this over with quickly. I'm tired of you, krillen."

The Leader pulled a small orb out from his pocket and slammed it onto the ground.

The orb fizzled and sizzled, releasing a cloudy gas.

He took more out of his pocket, throwing them around separate parts of the room. He then lifted his shirt over his head and wrapped it around his face.

"It's not about the right way. It's about winninnnggg," the Leader's words muddled in Destrou's mind.

The room began to spin around.

"The Guardian gave me these in case Ranmau made it to the finnnnnallllllsssss," the Leader said. His voice registered much deeper and slower. "But this wasn'ttttttttttttttttttt goin' anywhereeeeeeeeeeeeeee."

A smoky haze blocked Destrou's vision. He was barely able to see one of the three boys in front of him. The other two were swallowed up by the gas.

"Wait... three?" he said to himself, his voice sluggish. "Why are there... three?"

"Youuuuuu... didn'tttttt... thinkkkkkkk youuuuu coulddddd winnnnn," the Leader said. Each word burning slowly into his brain. "Didddddddd youuuuuuuuuuu—"

"This isn't... fair," Destrou screamed—or at least tried to. His scream sounded like laughter. Everything seemed to be a blur. He heard Elu. He saw Ranmau.

"You failed me," Ranmau laughed at him. "I can't believe you thought that you were anything better than a krillen. I'm glad the Leader taught you a lesson."

"No... I haven't failed you."

"Look at you, you krillen. Of course you did," Ranmau said.

"No... No I haven—"

"And I hope he kills you... just like how I killed Elu."

BANG! Destrou pressed his palm over his mouth as his head shot back randomly. Of course he would recognize this bitter taste that filled his mouth.

"Bluudoooouuod?" Destrou said, trying to remember how to say the word.

He heard cackles and screams as his head slammed backwards again. There was a constant ringing noise, muffling all sounds that tried to enter.

BANG! It felt like the back of his head was being crushed, but he didn't know if he was standing or lying on his back.

"I knewwwww... y-y-y-you... f-f-f-failed," Ranmau said, grabbing Destrou's hand.

Destrou heard laughter erupt from his own body as his palm burned with an agonizing pain. He felt a layer of his skin rip off and pressure build on his ribs as if his heart pumped out of his chest. The whole thing was unearthly and he lost his understanding on what was real.

"You... lost," Ranmau said. "Just... gi-gi-vi-vi-give-give up, krillen."

Destrou's eyes glossed with a red filter. Ranmau stepped away, walking up one of the walls, disappearing into the red mist.

"I won't fail... you," Destrou screamed but it came out as a silent thought. His head rocked back and forth, trying to reorient himself. The world started to bend in surreal ways. He saw Elu fly above him, exploding into the wall as a spray of blood splattered over his face. The blood was real. It tasted like his own.

Then it felt like gravity slammed him against the ceiling, not allowing him to fall down. His eyes spiraled in and out of consciousness, hearing a piercing scream that sounded like the exact one that he had shouted a minute ago.

He saw the ground... or ceiling... or whatever it was glow with a bright circle. Immediately after, he felt wind wrap around his torso, pulling his hair and body toward the light. It rushed by him as if he were in a wind tunnel. He pressed his body against the ceiling... or wall... or whatever he was on, lowering his center of gravity. The room spun around in circles until the wall thrust open, revealing an open area. It was vast and infinite as if he was staring out at the Forest of Ness.

The air was sucked out of his lungs as the rush pulled the gas out of the room.

He slowly regained consciousness, seeing Ranmau transform into the Leader.

The Leader stood over the ledge and looked down.

Destrou finally heard sounds again. He heard the soft whispers of liquid ice splashing against rocks. A refreshing, salty scent tickled his nostrils, it was heavy and thick. He couldn't see any ground, just a large cylinder of light shining down from the center.

"The final emblem," he said to himself. "That must be it."

"Pathetic, really," the Leader said, "that a krillen like you actually thought that you could beat someone like me. In what world would a krillen ever be able to beat a leader. You lose."

Eli'jah placed his hands to the ground, sitting himself over the edge. And with one push, he vanished. Destrou heard a booming scream that softened until it was just a faint whisper.

"I... promised... you," Destrou said, gritting his teeth and pulling himself to his feet. "Who am I if my word means nothing? I'd be worse than the Leader." His body seemed to have tripled in weight. He had a broken face, scarred body, and cramped muscles. His legs buckled when he stood up. He felt like a newborn whose body was ready to crumble and topple over, but he refused to stop. He refused to fall. If he fell, his body didn't have the energy to get back up again. That would be accepting defeat.

"I... will... win..." he said, stumbling to the edge.

When he looked down, he saw a crescent shaped slide that shot straight down into the darkness. Based on the light shining on top of the plateau in the middle of the area, the drop looked like it was at least a couple hundred feet. He looked at the center column once more. It didn't look like a plateau... it looked more like a massive forearm, and at the very top was a hand that was pressed open, the light overhead shone through the cracks of its fingers. But what he saw couldn't have been real... how could an arm be that big... and even more alarming, how was it made out of metal?

Without wanting to get sidetracked anymore than he had been, Destrou shoved aside his fear of the unknown. Instead he looked down and saw that the drop was the scariest thing he had ever seen, and that said a lot since he was the one who climbed the pole and retrieved the Eye of Eve. *Don't think... just do!* Not allowing his fear of heights to deter him, he sat on the slide and just pushed.

And just like that... he fell hundreds of feet down into the unknown.

He felt his stomach push up into his lungs. His heart raced as wind wrapped around his body. And his mouth fluttered while he belted out a scream that echoed for seconds. The descent felt like it lasted for a minute but it was more like ten seconds until he felt the cold wall press against his back, arching into a slope.

In a flash, his body was on a thin layer of liquid ice, gliding horizontally like a bullet. He slowed to a stop as a large wave of liquid ice broke over him.

"I still have time," he said, observing the stage.

He saw the Leader running along the edges of the expansive, circular area. There was a large body of liquid ice separating the spiraling rings from the massive metallic hand in the middle. The light that shone above looked like a hole draining out direct sunlight. Where in the Village could that glow be coming from, he thought.

Destrou felt weak but his *why* was greater than his pain. He had little strength left to run, but this was the final stage, this was the final emblem; he needed to find the strength to continue. He couldn't give up now.

"Even Ascel could beat me right now," he chuckled, trying to make light of his situation. His thoughts then turned to Ranmau. *He, more than anyone in the Village deserves his freedom. To be a Crystal Soldier. Not some... krillen who needs to cheat to win.* He felt something within him spark, giving him life. *You will get your freedom. I will keep saying it until it becomes real!*

He jumped down into the spiraling lane and ran as fast as he could. The half an hour of running was agony, but he did it.

As he turned the corner for the final stretch, he saw the Leader in the distance. He knew that he needed to keep moving but he was trembling, feeling weightless with each step.

"Don't stop." He reminded his body. "Don't stop until you have the emblem in your hand."

He was so focused on his exhaustion that he didn't realize his surroundings. The metallic hand, at least three hundred feet high, with chunks of rock and stone molding into it, looked more like the hand of a God ripping out of the planet from where he stood; the light directly above it made it seem like a Divine One reaching for the sun. At the surface, there were sizable rocks all around him, larger than he had ever seen. He hoped that none of them transformed into that rock beast he had fought earlier, but he never ruled out the possibility. His eyes remained wide open.

BANG! The boulders ahead toppled over, smashing and rolling toward him. His body trembled as if the ground was moving. Was it moving? He looked ahead, beyond the deadly boulders, and saw large stone slabs eject out of the liquid ice. There were dozens of them, launching toward the roof at least a hundred feet in the air. They moved around the center plateau in different paths before submerging into the liquid ice again.

The ground was moist and his feet dug deep into the dirt with each step. He needed to dodge the tumbling boulders, but he barely had any mobility. And to make it worse, there was a slight incline, forcing him to lean most of his body weight forward.

In between the cracks of the rolling rocks, he saw the Leader leap onto one of the columns, lifting him high into the air. By the time Destrou dove around more of the rocks, he saw the Leader leap off that column and land onto another while on its descent.

There is a design to this. The columns aren't moving around randomly, it must be another puzzle.

He hadn't passed the boulders but he was already planning on what to do next. He needed to rush but he knew that going in with a plan was more crucial. Focused on the columns, he made quick work of the boulders, ducking under some and diving away from others.

When he made it to the ledge, he saw what prevented the Leader from swimming across; there was a massive whirlpool surrounding this stonish, metal hand.

The world had transformed to chaos. Shifting, mountainous pillars of rock that ascended and descended roared by with whirling winds that made it difficult to keep his feet planted. All he could do was follow the patterns, the curves and angles, when they went up and down, and when to jump to the next one. But the challenge wasn't designed for patience. The boulders that burst into the wall below dispersed like marbles thrown on the floor. A carpet of insects covered the ground and charged toward him.

His feet froze as one of the columns whizzed by him.

"I need to get the next one," he said, looking over his shoulder at the terrifying insects. "They are even faster than before."

Another pillar flashed by too quickly. The speed was paralyzing, but worse than the speed was the wind, which threatened to push him off the ledge if he wasn't going to jump. Jump, drown, or get devoured, his options weren't the best. And with the sound of the pincers chomping getting louder, he leapt into nothingness, timing it perfectly as a stone column found its way underneath his feet.

"I did it," he screamed, kneeling down, gripping the sides of the columns as wind wrapped around his body. The stone felt smooth and slippery. The air was salty.

In a matter of seconds, his next move needed to be made. He remembered which column went where.

This one! He jumped onto the next pillar just as their heights matched. It was much tougher than the Leader made it seem. Not only did he have to time the jump at the right height but he also battled the momentum while fighting against the powerful winds. "One wrong move and I'm gone," he said to himself, heart racing and adrenaline pumping.

Destrou and the Leader soon became familiar with how to navigate through the stage. The two of them jumped from column to column, giving it their all, understanding that they were only moments away from victory.

The Leader was ahead of Destrou, but Destrou gradually closed the gap.

Destrou tried to win the psychological war by showing the Leader he was fine. But, inside, he was dying for all of it to be over. In a matter of minutes, his chest and throat burned. The discomfort of each breath sent a throbbing pain through his chest. Despite his body breaking down, he saw the light and he had come too far to just give up. He had to keep reminding himself of that, it was the only thing that kept his legs moving.

The pain. The cramping. The wind. This jumping stage was a lot to handle but there was still more after. It looked like he had to run or climb to the open palm on top of the plateau. He was too far away to make out the details, but he knew that he needed energy to make that final push. The dichotomy dawned on Destrou. He had to slow down his pace to better his chances, but he had to speed up if he wanted a chance.

The Leader turned around, furious that Destrou was only a few columns away. And that distraction cost him. A strong gust of wind pushed his back in a way that made him lose balance and slip on liquid ice. The momentum shifted and his body ejected off of the column.

"HELP!" he belted with a high-pitched scream that never broke. His body collided into a different column, wrapping his arms around as much of it as he could. He dug his broken fingernails into the stone, trying to climb back up. But between the forces of inertia, wind, and acceleration, it was an impossible feat. "Please! Help me!"

"I did it!" Destrou screamed inside. "I actually did it." His body broke into tears. Emotions overwhelmed him. He jumped to the next platform while trying to soak in the moment. All he needed to do was make it to the plateau and he won.

"Help me! Help!" He could hear the bellowing screams even over the roaring winds and rushing tides.

When Destrou finally came to his senses, he stood still, waiting for the next message to be sent to his body.

Nothing.

"What do I do?" he said to himself. "Why am I thinking twice? I won. I can end this already. Just go!" His body froze and he wondered where the feeling of guilt came from. "He did save me once already... but that was because of Elu." He jumped to the next platform. "But what if Elu would have wanted me to do the same? This is her brother. Do I owe him? Do I owe her? What would she want me to do?"

The Leader's screams echoed about a dozen times. They were momentarily drowned out by a suffocating cough, then continued again as if he reappeared out of the liquid ice. His shrieking pitch made it clear that he was hanging on for his life.

The challenge was made to break people and turn them into monsters. Was he one of them? Did it change him? Destrou made his decision and hopped onto the next column.

Unlike the Leader, he didn't need a binding promise to do the right thing. He leapt from column to column, derailing from his set path.

The Leader's cries mixed in with the other noises created a cacophony of white noise. Destrou saw Eli'jah's body being ripped away from the column as his scream was muffled again by the liquid ice gushing over his body. The only thing that kept him from being swept away was his grip that seemed to loosen more by the second. Unknowing how long much longer he could hold on, Destrou dashed, bouncing off the stone pillars shooting toward him.

He landed on top of the Leader's column and reached his hand out.

"Grab on!" Destrou screamed as the wind wrapped his dreads across his face.

"I can't!" the Leader screamed, unable to lift one of his arms up.

Destrou placed his stomach on top of the pillar, grabbing the Leader's hand. He kneeled, arching his back, pulling with all the strength he had.

"Hold on! I got you!" Destrou screamed.

"Thank you!" the Leader screamed as one of his legs curled over the top.

Destrou no longer struggled to pull the Leader up—instead... instead, he struggled to break his hand free. The Leader's fingers tightened around his wrist, cutting off all circulation.

"Ow," Destrou said, looking at his wrist with discomfort. It was then when he looked up at the Leader and saw his eyes. They were blackened and evil.

This was a mistake.

"Thank you," the Leader growled with a deep, cold tone.

In one moment, Destrou felt an immense force almost rip his arm out of its socket. He catapulted over the Leader's head, plunging into the disastrous whirl. He immediately became helpless and was at the complete mercy of nature and its wrath.

And as Destrou thought about the error in his ways, a huge wave lifted him up with such massive power that his skin would have been torn and bones broken if he hadn't pressed both of his hands forward and grabbed onto the stone. He clung onto it, groaning, until another massive wave passed by. This time he felt an unexplainable amount of force push him in two different directions. A pressure pulled him from the top and pushed him from the bottom. He was powerless. He hadn't felt strength like nature. Its power was incomparable.

His lungs filled up with liquid ice, choking on his regrets. He couldn't push in any direction, there was no hope to reach the surface.

"No... more... mistak—" His body went limp, sucked out of all of its life. It was lost in the rushing liquid ice.

The Leader had what looked like a moment of remorse, eyes drooped and mouth frowned. But after a few moments passed, it morphed into a grin. "You never stood a chance anyway!" He hopped from column to column until he performed one last leap, landing onto the base of the plateau.

The moment the Leader's feet landed on solid ground, the entire area started to collapse. The massive, moving pillars stopped to a halt before tumbling down in all directions.

The Leader dove every which way, avoiding the columns and its shattering rubble.

The whirling liquid ice also slowed to a stop.

Destrou's body was caught in full force in its backward rush and it carried him with it, colliding into the jagged rocks of the plateau.

He was too weak to avoid the turmoil that exploded all around him.

Liquid ice coughed out of his mouth as he squirmed to his side.

His knees gave way and his hands shook, he had nothing left.

This challenge took absolutely everything out of him. A part of him still didn't know how he hadn't given up hours ago. He laid there breathless, speechless, with swollen flesh and bursts of liquid ice still gushing out of his mouth and nostrils. He was unable to move a muscle and overwhelmed by a terrible exhaustion. When he became partially revived and a slither of life returned, he looked up and saw the Leader jump onto the stone slabs, large and small, that spiraled around the metallic forearm. He looked overhead and squinted at the sourceless light beaming down.

"I've come this far, I can't give up now. I won't fail you any-more. I made a promise." He struggled to stand to his feet. "And I will keep it."

With no energy left he decided to push his body to the limit. His feet pressed forward, jumping from one stone slab to the next. His legs, chest and arms were numb, like moving objects that were no longer a part of his body. It was horrifying yet calming. Despite feeling detached from his body, he was happy to see that his limbs hadn't given up on him yet. Long before he could even fathom the thought of giving up, he thought of every reason why he held on for so long.

"My word!" his voice escaped in a whisper.

The Leader and Destrou took separate paths that looped around the plateau without ever intertwining. The metal forearm was even wider and taller than it looked from the ground. The constant splashes of liquid ice circling above him told the story of where the Leader was.

"I'm getting close but he's still too far ahead," Destrou said, looking up at the top of the plateau, watching the long metal fingers come into focus. He had to quickly look away. His eyes were used to darkness for so long that it pained him to look directly into the light. "I can get there if I move just a little bit faster. If only I could feel my body, I don't even know how to tell it what to do right now. Move. Go. Come on!"

Without knowing, he had learned an invaluable lesson that many would live their entire lives without ever discovering: that when the mind tells someone they're done, they're only halfway there. The mind was just a barrier. And in that moment, he broke through its wall.

"Must... keep... going..." he shouted to himself, almost losing consciousness as his body propelled itself forward.

He wrapped around the final corner and saw the Leader across the platform already making a run for it. The emblem was glowing in the center, trapped inside the light.

Destrou screamed at the top of his lungs as his legs stomped rapidly into the cold metal.

The Leader was close to grabbing it.

Destrou was too far.

The Leader reached his hand out.

Destrou lowered his body to a crouch, putting every last strength that he had into a lunging leap.

BANG! Their bodies collided into one another, bouncing off of the podium, rolling toward different ends of the palm.

They both laid there lifelessly. Every last ounce of energy they had was depleted in that final run. They no longer had the strength to even open their eyes.

A rumble was heard somewhere underneath him.

The platform creaked and shook. Slowly, it extracted itself from the ground, elevating toward the light. There were *hisses* beneath him that sounded like the releasing of gas. While the light grew larger as they reached the ceiling, the entire area moved around, reforming itself back to new again, as if a challenge had never occurred.

The platform pressed through a transparent wall that rippled as they passed it just like the one before the puzzle—the feeling of diving into liquid ice yet remaining dry.

When the platform screeched to a stop, they were in the middle of the Village in front of the Guardian's lair, and surrounded by every boy in the Village. It was solid ground with no way to look down into the challenge.

The boys looked on in awe as they watched the Leader and Destrou struggle to move a muscle.

Ranmau was in the crowd, breathing deeply. His body was wrapped in cloth. He, like the others, didn't know how to respond.

"Who won?"

"I don't get it."

"What happened?"

"They weren't even gone for that long... it was only what... like a minute long?"

"It's already over?"

"That was quick."

"Must've been easier than we thought!"

"Weird... I thought the final challenge would be longer and better than that!"

After what seemed like a few minutes had passed, the Leader and Destrou rolled onto their stomachs. It took everything in them just to turn over. Slowly, they pressed onto their knees, inhaling and exhaling with large, steady breaths.

They both stumbled to their feet at the same time. The Leader dragged his head upward. Destrou followed. They looked at one another with no life in their eyes. Their eyes told the tale of confusion and exhaustion.

The Leader brushed his hands around his body, which then enraged into furious strikes, ripping parts of his clothes off.

"What? Where?" the Leader mumbled, almost drooling over himself.

Destrou looked confused, sidestepping, almost falling to his hands. He pressed his hands on his pants and felt a solid object.

"What?" Destrou muttered.

The crowd of boys turned to him.

The Leader lifted his head, glaring at him with half awake, seething eyes.

Destrou reached inside his pocket and pulled out an object.

The crowd was filled with gasps.

The Leader's jaw dropped.

Destrou looked at it as if it was foreign—because it was. His face was expressionless. "What is this? Where'd it come from?"

After a few moments passed, his eyes shot open.

"Wait," he choked on something in his throat, "is this... the... no... wait. Is this... the final emblem?"

Destrou scanned the crowd, looking for the most important set of eyes.

There. There Ranmau was with widened eyes that told a story of panic and worry. They were of fear more than jealousy; of sorrow more than envy.

"I did it?" Destrou whispered to himself. "I did it. I did it! I did it!" he shouted in the form of a whimper that barely escaped his throat. He couldn't hold back the empty tears that shed from his eyes. His body tried to sob but it appeared as inaudible yells.

He looked down again, clenching the emblem tightly in his palm. "Anything is possible. I kept my promise. I won. I actually did it."

Immediately, Ranmau's eyes dawned on him. The sorrow. The fear. It made him think of the Village, the Kingdom, the Guardians. The Crystal Soldiers. The Supreme General. The torture. The maze. Their plan. The pain. The world was unkind. Was there something that he was trying to tell him? Was it not just about pride? *When did Ranmau ever lead me into danger?*

Thoughts ran through his mind so quickly that he had forgotten about how important their word meant in the Village.

"His word," Destrou said to himself. "My word."

His eyes closed, and he thought of a world where hate triumphed over love and promises succumbed to deceit. To the Village, their word was priceless. To him and Ranmau, promises meant everything, but after they were broken, a simple sorry could never mend them back together.

Without thinking, his hand lifted in the air, releasing the emblem.

"You need it more than I do," Destrou said as the emblem embedded itself in the snow just in front of the Leader's feet.

Destrou hobbled toward Ranmau with a shackled step.

"I kept... both," he struggled to say, crashing into Ranmau's chest, "of our promises."

His body went limp. All life was sucked out of him as his bloodied body slouched against Ranmau's.

The Leader erupted with a coughing cackle. "You're going to die! You two are going to die! I won! I won! I'm going to be a Crystal Soldier! You two are going down! The brothers will die!"

The deadly chants were shouted the entire way back to their igloo.

Ranmau dragged Destrou onto his bed. He laid there peacefully, finally getting the sleep that his mind and body had been craving.

A smile shown on Ranmau's face, as if he was glad that Destrou kept his promise; but then it faded away almost instantly. His neck snapped upright as if a worry shot through his spine. As if he knew with certainty that their greatest danger lurked ahead. That their end was near.

33

DESTROU

W ITH THE AID OF BANDAGES WRAPPED AROUND
him, Destrou lay watching the small drops of his blood seep
through the cloth and splatter onto the floor. They were constant
and rhythmically soothing. Several times throughout his slumber,
he drifted off briefly and then snapped awake, filled with anger and
guilt. After a few hours later, his eyes shot open again, trying to
wiggle his toes or move his hands. Nothing. He was still too weak.
And after what felt like just the blink of his eye, he saw the night
turn to day again. There was still no Ranmau in sight. His room felt
as empty as his body. And with one last blink of his eye, he saw day
turn to night.

"I need to wake up already... ugh—" Destrou said, squirming to
get life back into his body, "—how long have I been asleep?"

"About two days," Ranmau said, hobbling into the room. "Two
long days."

"What's wrong with you?" Destrou said, wincing his eyes as a
pain jolted through his body. He saw bruises and scars all over Ranmau's face and body that oozed with freshness. "What happened?"

"Classic Destrou," Ranmau replied, "there you are all banged
up, sleeping for days, and worrying about *me*." He laughed, then

immediately choked on a cough.

"What'd he do to you?" Destrou said, knowing that this was the Leader's doing.

"Relax, I said you never have to worry about me, okay? It was nothing that I didn't plan for," he said reaching into his shirt. "I paid him a visit while you were sleeping and let's say that I got what I wanted... and beat up during the process. Badly. Very badly. But that was expected."

"W-why would you do that?" Destrou coughed.

"For this." Ranmau pulled out a tiny portion of Sensu food. "There's no more left, but it's what I could take without him noticing. It's not a lot, but you were right: it's amazing. My body felt better and I only had a small piece. I can't imagine how strong the Crystal Soldiers were if they ate it all of the time, because the Leader's strength is... His strength is—"

"W-what?" Destrou trembled, trying to understand each word.

"I've never felt anything like it before. It was... wow. He lifted me with one hand like I was a slab of meat. I couldn't do anything to fight it. He's massive now, even the Giant couldn't spar against him. With one hit, his body went limp, flying probably about twenty feet. But enough about him. Here, eat up," he said, reaching his hand out toward Destrou.

"W-what about the tournament then?" Destrou replied, ignoring the food.

Ranmau said nothing, staring at the ground.

"Y-you still have... a chance, right?"

"I don't know, Destrou," he said calmly. "I don't think there is a chance. His strength is stronger than ever, stronger than I ever was. Maybe if I had both arms, but with only one... I really don't know."

"No... I refuse... Then why did you want me to lose?" Destrou screamed, holding his chest.

"I didn't think that—"

"Why did you want me to lose, huh? I went through all of that...

for you. I wanted to die knowing that you'd get your dream. That you'd become a Crystal Soldier. And I threw it away, because of you."

"I'd rather have it be this way."

"Rather have both of us dying in the tournament? Why? I just don't get it! Our lives will mean nothing. Our story will mean nothing."

"You don't understand."

"Of course I don't! You always shove me away when I try to understand anything! What'd I do to you? Why do you always push me away?" Destrou coughed, holding his chest in pain.

"Because I NEVER want you to go through what happens after.... I never want you to see or feel what happens behind those doors. You don't want to know. I never want you to even know what I have to go through each and every time. And I would rather die than see you go through it. I would have failed as your brother. Is that better?"

"No! That's the choice that I should make!"

"No! No, it's not!" Ranmau's eyes glazed over.

"Well, now everything is ruined! Now none of us will get the freedom. I went through all of that... for you, Ranmau, not for me. And it was all for nothing."

"I'm sorry."

"Sorry..." Destrou chuckled, pulling his hair. "Sorry for killing my *only* friend... sorry for ruining your *only* dream. Your sorry means nothing anymore."

Ranmau paused for a moment before heading for the door. He turned around with a deep sigh. "I admit that I didn't think the Sensu would make him this strong. That was my fault. I just didn't know."

"I tried to—" Destrou said.

"But even after knowing," Ranmau said, gazing out at the Wall. "I'm still glad that you didn't have to go through what he did to get it… Eat up. You're going to need your energy back, if we want to survive another day." He threw the Sensu food at Destrou. "And I'm sorry… I'm sorry that I never told you this, but… I… I… n-nevermind. If... if only life was… If only…" His voice trailed off and within a moment, he was gone.

Destrou cringed for a few seconds. He knew that he shouldn't have let his anger boil to that point, but guilt troubled him.

"Maybe I shouldn't have gave up the emblem," he said gritting his teeth. "I knew it! I knew it! I knew it!" Destrou kept slamming his fist into the igloo's wall. "I knew I shouldn't have! Why does it feel like *everything* is always my fault? It feels like life would have been so much different… and better... if I was just never born."

At once, he felt the monster reappear. *Not you again!* Rage filled his heart, but he couldn't blame Ranmau for the decision. A part of him willingly gave away the emblem because he didn't want to go against his brother's wishes. He didn't want there to be any resentment. He didn't want to be remembered as the brother who disappointed him, letting him down any more than he had already. Despite his best efforts, he felt tears starting to fill his eyes and bitterness wrench his heart. All of the times that he tried to do the right thing he failed and made things worse, he thought. The understanding only upset him even more. He placed the Sensu meat in his mouth. His lips salivated, absorbing its gooey texture.

"We always found a way to win… When I wake up… I'll fix all of this. This is all my fault. I will fix this. It's not over…" he promised as he drifted off.

* * *

A few hours later, Destrou performed his classic maneuver, flipping off his bed.

"The food worked," he grinned, clenching his fists with slow and steady movements.

He glanced over at Ranmau, sleeping in his bed. He softly lifted his hand to Ranmau's head and caressed his hair. The simple movement left him shaky and dizzy.

"I know that we aren't the same anymore. I know it doesn't feel like we're brothers anymore, but I refuse to let the world ruin what we had... or may still have," he whispered softly, stumbling to his bed. "I need to make sure that I'm ready before I start training tonight. There's no more time to waste."

He felt alone and needed a place where he could recover in solitude. A place where he could free his mind and escape the pain of guilt. There was only one place in mind: the Tree.

* * *

Destrou entered through the tunnel, pressing against the cold walls as he descended. The air was frigid. The frost felt familiar, forming a faux smile on his face. The peace he sought had already began to seep into his body. He felt the warming presence of memories with Elu fill his thoughts.

"Elu," he said softly, landing onto solid ground. "If only you were still here. I really need you. I just really want to remember what happiness felt like. I want to laugh again. I want to smile. I want you to tell me what to do. You always have an answer."

When he peered around the corner, his eyes widened with horror.

"What happened?" he shouted, examining the ravaged walls and chunks of ice scattered along the floor. It was chaotic as if a tornado swept through, uprooting the Tree with its wrath. "Who did this!?"

He slammed onto all four, picking up pieces of the rubble, trying to find where they belonged on the walls. There were streaks of red everywhere his hand touched.

"This was Elu's work... she worked so hard. Who did this? This can't be real. This is a bad dream. I know it. It must be!" Destrou's scream echoed a dozen times. "WHO DID THIS?"

Destrou felt himself going crazy as he frantically tried to pick up the pieces and ran around looking at more of the havoc. His heart broke just thinking about it. This was their place. This was *her* place.

The beautiful scenery became a bloodshed cave as if artwork had never graced its walls before. The feeling of peace was replaced with pain. There was nothing that resembled handcrafted perfection, only destruction. The air was drained of its freshness, leaving behind a trail that smelled like uncleansed feet.

Destrou jumped back several feet as a body appeared from behind the Tree. Was he watching the whole time? Was he the one who ruined its peace? Destrou's eyes blackened as the thoughts ran through his mind.

The body was covered in ripped clothing with red slashes in every direction. The clothes looked familiar had they been in one piece.

It was Ascel.

"W-what... who... don't tell me you. Don't tell me you, Ascel," Destrou said, clenching his fists. "Don't— just don't tell me. . ."

"N-no," Ascel said, stepping out into the light, revealing a face more disfigured than Ranmau's. "It wasn't me."

"No!" Destrou screamed, slamming his fists on the ground. "He needs to be stopped."

"I don't know what to do. He's out of control now... he's become a monster."

"I will stop him."

"You can't."

"I will... watch me."

"You don't understand, it's not just the Sensu that changed him. That made him powerful, but it was a thought that pushed him."

"A thought?" Destrou's eyes narrowed.

"He's convinced that someone betrayed him. That's what made him crazy... like really crazy."

"No one betrayed him!"

"Tell that to him. He punished everyone since no one told him who it was. But then..."

Destrou walked up to Ascel, placing his arm over his shoulder, comforting him.

"A lot of the boys told him that it was... me," Ascel said, soaking Destrou's chest with his tears. "I thought I was alone... but... he followed me here and... brought the Bruisers with him. I just remember a lot of pain... before waking up not too long ago... to this. I'm just glad the pain ended."

"I'm so sorry," Destrou said, hugging Ascel tighter.

"It's not your fault."

"It is. If I never finished that maze or puzzle or whatever that was... none of this would have happened. If I never gave him the emblem, none of this would have happened. If I was never alive—I am the problem. I made this one, and I will fix it."

Ascel dug his face deeper into Destrou's chest. His shirt absorbed the moisture.

"What?" Destrou said alertly. His ability to read bodies appeared to rival Ranmau's. Every bone in his body said that bad news were ready to follow.

"T-tomorrow... will... be the... end." Ascel sobbed, struggling to get out each word.

"What do you mean?"

"The Leader... he really doesn't like change."

"What changed?"

"The Village... we don't look at him the same way now. And he blames you and Ranmau."

"Why would he do that?" Destrou paused. "Ascel... what'd you do?"

"I'm so sorry," Ascel cried.

"What happened?"

"I told some boys about what Ranmau did for us in there. How he wanted to save us. You two risked your lives for us and the Leader didn't even care about us. Well, the boys didn't like that."

"And what does that have to do with tomorrow?"

"The plan," Ascel hesitated.

"Plan?"

"Ranmau." Ascel tossed Destrou a sorrowed glance. His words froze behind his heaving chest. "It will be your last day together. He's going to kill him."

Destrou's body went cold. His head sank to the ground. "No," he whimpered between his palms. "I'm not ready yet. I don't know what to do. This can't be happening."

"Well, it's happening," Ascel said, rubbing his eyes. "Promise me something."

"Not another promise. I can't handle another promise. I just can't..."

"Just promise me that you won't trust anyone. Don't... trust... *anyone*, Destrou, I mean it. And no matter how much you hated Ranmau... he needs you."

"I know," Destrou said, wrapping his arms around Ascel. "Thank you."

"Tomorrow is going to be very dangerous. I wish I could tell you what's going to happen, but I don't even know—just be careful out there. It *will* happen... you can either watch it happen or do something about it. But before you make your decision—ask yourself: what would Ranmau do in your place? What has Ranmau done when he was in your situation?"

"Well, I need to go then," Destrou said, pressing Ascel's shoulders away from him.

"Go where?" Ascel replied. His eyes were glazed and bruised.

Destrou felt his stomach contract and his breath drew suddenly short. "I need to train," he said, struggling to keep his voice calm. "I have a plan to stop. No matter how impossible it looks... I created this mess... I will end it."

* * *

The Leader's plan to kill Ranmau before the tournament was one that Destrou couldn't have prepared for. But at least it compelled Destrou to train harder than he had ever trained before.

That night, a visual of the Leader hurting Ranmau kept replaying in his mind while he trained. The visual morphed into a horrifying one of him being killed.

With bruised knuckles, he furiously punched through the solid ice, shattering it until there was nothing left. With calloused palms, he lifted a boulder that was twice his size above his head and, with one, giant roar, he catapulted it deep into the Forest of Ness.

He stared down into the Forest, expecting to hear a disruption, but there was nothing. Only darkness.

This cannot be the way that our lives were supposed to be lived. If there is a way to change it, I will. You taught me that anything is possible; even the impossible. And tomorrow, all of this ends. It all ends. Life will never be the same. No matter what, something will end tomorrow. You will either get your freedom, or I will die trying. I've grown used to the fear of death staring at me, but this one feels more real. It feels like it's waiting for me—it's waiting to bring me back to Elu. Elu, I may be seeing you soon. And Ranmau... if only life was kinder, we could have been the greatest brothers to have ever lived. And if tomorrow is my last day here, then there is one last thing I need to do. One last thing that I need to prove: that I can protect you, or I will die trying.

* * *

Vayp took a deep breath and looked up at Han'sael, bubbles streaming from the mask that covered his face. "I want to protect you... and I believe... I'm willing to die trying."

It was then, while gazing at Han'sael, when the *other* shadow emerged from behind the container. "Oh, Vayp... and if you *were* to die tonight, is that how you would like to be remembered? As the hero, the protector?" The shadow looked down at Vayp. "Is that how you would like for your story to be told? What does life mean if it is not the culmination of every second leading up to the last?

The truth is… that since the first breath that you take you are already dying. You are already one step, one breath, and one moment closer to the end. You are given a finite amount of time to complete as much as you can and with only a finite amount of seconds left in your life, what would you do differently if tonight were to hold your last remaining ones?"

"Err—" Vayp squirmed. He couldn't help but feel uncomfortable at that question.

"You see, just as there is beauty in your first breath, there *is* beauty in your last. The beauty in death is that if you accept that it exists and that it will occur, then once you accept it, you will live your life trying to prolong it. You will appreciate every moment of it. You will not take the simple things for granted. The laughter. The love. The life. And much like anything in life, if we have an infinite supply of something, we tend to take it for granted. It is when we realize how precious time is… and how limited it is… that is when we fight to preserve it. To protect it. To prize it… as a present that shouldn't be a luxury for a few, but a right for all… even us *Shadows*. So, I ask: what would you do if tonight was your last night and you could do anything that you wished?"

Vayp said nothing, he remained in silence, looking at Han'sael, as if waiting for him to say something first. Then after a few moments, he spoke: "It's too late to do what I would have done," Vayp said coldly, now staring at the ground. "I would… have said goodbye to my family one last time. I would have told my brothers that I did it. I finished my training. I mastered the arenas. I did it even though they didn't think I could. I'd tell them that I can change the world now…. I *can* change the way that it's shaped and the way that it looks. But all of my power means nothing since I can't bring them back. I would have told my parents that I listened to them even though it may have seemed like I ignored them. I would have told them that I will avenge their deaths…"—Vayp stared the shadow directly in the eye, unafraid of the consequences of what he said—". . . and that their son did turn out to be as great as they hoped for. I made sure of it. I-I—" His voice cracked and eyes swelled. "I would want to let them know that I didn't mean to become a bad person. And that I will not end up as the villain in this story... I *will* be the hero... and I just hope that they'd forgive me for... what I'm going to do."

"You mean what you are going to do to your sister?" the shadow said.

Vayp nodded.

"I understand. I too once had a Sol and a sibling. As much as I loved my Sol, I do not know which I would choose." Vayp lifted his head to catch eyes with the shadow, staring into the blackened dots that appeared as bottomless pits. "But the truth about your family... is you had no way of knowing. You see, they were all a part of the bigger plan. Everything has happened for a reason. Because of them, Gaia now has one of the most powerful pupils of Earth that time has ever created. For that, we must thank them. Their destiny was fulfilled and their purpose was paramount. For now, your role in the Circle of Time is crucial. Important beyond words. Because of you, you will be able to live life with them all over again. Your last time you've seen them was not the last time that you will see them."

"Is that why you're doing this?"

"I have my own reasons," the shadow said as he stared longingly at the Book of Eve on Vayp's lap. "I will be going home soon. But yes, if I could get my old life back, I would. If all of this promises that I could be given another chance, then I will not hesitate."

"If I see one of those Mechas... I swear..." Vayp said, clenching his fists. The ground trembled and quaked as large boulders burst from the ground.

The shadow remained still as rocks large and small lifted into the air.

Though darkness surrounded him, Vayp's eyes had a white,

wavy glow emitting from them. Tears floated up his face and past his short, now flowing hair.

Pillars of stone appeared and burst into hundreds of shattered rocks. The debris orbited around them like the rings of a planet.

Despite the chaos, the shadow looked on with a smile. In a moment, the warm smile faded into a cold gaze.

"It looks like you will get your Sol back sooner than I thought," he said alertly, staring into Vayp's eyes.

The boulders and rubble halted, free-falling to the ground. The quakes stopped immediately.

It was then when *the* shadow emerged from the shadows.

"The Shadow Army is now ready... and so is the Mas'ahk." the shadow said, black steam billowing from his body. At once, Han'sael's container floated into the air as the metal contorted and shifted around before transforming into a device with wheels. "I cannot promise he will survive. But as long as you do what you are told, he may have a chance. Now read."

Then a tremendous BANG reverberated throughout the valley, sounding like a trainwreck of noises all at once.

"It is time," the shadow said, lifting the Eye of Eve to the air, its light fading from black to white then back again. "GroundStone *will* fall. Eve will be ours."

34

SNOW BEGAN FALLING ABOUT HALFWAY through the night. The storm clouds approached abruptly, obscuring even the light of the moon. Destrou and Ranmau slept peacefully until a group of shouting boys stormed into their igloo.

"Get up!" a dark-haired Bruiser yelled, tearing the fur off of Destrou and Ranmau. Other Bruisers grabbed them, yanking them off of their beds.

"What's going on?" Destrou said, waking up in a frenzy, still believing it to be a dream.

"Let go of me, krillen," Ranmau said, shoving the Bruiser off of him.

"We need to get the Snake ready before the storm destroys our chances. The Guardian will not be happy. The Leader's orders," he said, snarling at the two.

"Ranmau," Destrou whispered to him, "we need to be careful."

"I know," Ranmau replied. His eyes were flat as if the thought of danger didn't faze him.

"You know... what?" Destrou said, narrowing his eyes.

"Everything," Ranmau said.

"I don't think we're thinking of the sam—"

"Get up. Now!" the long haired Bruiser said, yanking Destrou's arm. "We don't have much time. We're all waiting for ya krillens."

"But—" Destrou struggled as they pushed him out of the room.

"But nothing." The Brusier grabbed Ranmau arm.

Ranmau shrugged the Bruiser off of him. "I can walk by myself. Don't touch me again if you want to keep that hand."

The Bruiser grinned at him, then walked away as if he weighed the chances in his mind.

* * *

Within moments, the storm had worsened. The boys shielded their faces from the wind sending shards into their faces that felt more like ice than snow. The howling wind obscured any vision of what was even a foot in front of them.

Finally, they approached the mound of snow that had already grown significantly in size.

"To the end!" the Leader's deep voice resonated over the storm's howl.

Destrou's jaw dropped when he saw the Leader appear out of the storm. *Are you serious? They weren't lying!* The Leader no longer had a neck. It looked like a block of muscle. His arms, legs and body were twice in size. Beneath his large fur cloak, Destrou could see his clothes were unable to contain its growth, ripping in some spots more than others. *All of that from Sensu food? How strong can he be?*

"You krillens get the rear, as always." Even his voice changed. It was deeper, carrying a throaty rasp.

Through the flurry of snow, Destrou was able to scan the faces of the boys. They were blemished with deep sockets, bruises, and torn flesh. They seemed troubled, all wearing the same cold, emotionless face.

"Something isn't right about any of this," Destrou said to himself. "How could he do this to everyone? Now that he's certain to be a Crystal Soldier... does he not care how he treats them? But still...

I can't trust any of them, though."

"It's not going to lift itself," the Leader said, digging his fingers into Destrou's shoulder.

A pain shot through his spine. He felt every bone in his body cringe in pain. The shock was overwhelming, immobilizing his limbs.

The moment he released Destrou, his body crashed to the ground, falling to his knees. He had never felt anything like that, he thought his bones were going to break. Ranmau was right.

Ranmau aided Destrou to his feet. "Don't do anything foolish, Destrou," he whispered. "He's too strong right now. Believe me."

Despite Ranmau only having one arm, they were able to hoist the Snake out of the snow.

"This feels too heavy," one of the boys groaned. He walked for a few more steps before toppling over, causing the Snake to crash to the ground.

"What happened!" the Leader screamed, running to the fallen boy.

"I'm sorry," the boy squirmed, "it was too heavy."

"This is what happens to krillens," the Leader said, kicking him squarely in the stomach. His foot disappeared momentarily in the clothes around the boy's midsection. The boy instantly jerked over to his side, rolling in pain.

Destrou made a move to attend to him, but Ranmau shot him a look. A few of the boys around him noticed Destrou's attempt.

"What are you going to do about it?" the Leader yelled at Destrou. "I don't have time for you krillens. The Guardian said we need to get this Snake going before the storm gets worse. He would do much worse than me if we don't."

The boy squirmed to his feet, grabbing the Snake.

"Now no more stopping, *right*?" the Leader shouted.

Murmurs and sluggish responses scattered throughout the wind.

"*RIGHT?*" the Leader screamed again, louder.

"Right," the boys said in partial unison.

"*Good*, now let's go!"

Once they made it to the Edge, the boys began to lift the body up with the ropes. The wind howled as the Snake wobbled, swaying side-to-side. The boys struggled to keep it still.

"Help!" one boy screamed.

"I need more help on this side!" said another boy. "It's about to fall."

"Well, what are you doing?" the Leader said to Destrou. "Help them out!"

Destrou grabbed the slippery rope, wrapping it around his fists. Three other boys joined in but they were no match for nature. The rope snapped and the Snake crashed down toward the boys. They dove out of the way as its claws dug deep into the ice.

"What are you krillens doing?!" the Leader roared. "Whose fault was this?"

A loud argument diverted the attention from the Snake. The Bruisers and the boys had a difference of opinion over who made the mistake. Ascel's name was brought up, a notion that Destrou quickly rejected. They all turned around, glaring at him.

At first the Leader suggested that they fight it out. Even in his rage, however, it occurred to him that it might create more harm than good. To settle it, he ultimately decided that Destrou needed to walk back toward the Village and get more rope.

The boys cleared a path, revealing Destrou at the other end.

Destrou hesitated for a moment. "Why me?"

"Because I said so... do you have a problem?" the Leader growled.

"Only if Ranmau comes with me," he replied back.

"Are you trying to tell the Leader what to do?" he said, cracking his knuckles. He waited a few moments, looking around the Edge. "Fine... but I don't trust you two together. One of you krillens go with them."

Silence.

"I SAID one of you krillens go with them!"

After a few moments, Ascel shakingly replied. "O-okay, I w-will."

"Great! You know where the rope is... you're the master at them anyways, right? Go get us some more and hurry! We don't have much time."

Ascel stepped forward. "Remember what I told you, Destrou. Don't trust anyone," he whispered into his ear.

"Yeah, I'm glad that you decided to come. Thank you."

Ascel placed his torn hood over his head, pressing down on it with one of his hands, blocking the wind from hurling the snow into his face.

The three of them trekked back toward the Village. They were surprised at the intensity of the storm. The usually light snowflakes had exaggerated into a full-blown blizzard, swirling winds driving heavy snow. Eleven inches or more had accumulated, deeper where drifts had formed. They didn't expect the walk to be this far—the discomfort made it feel longer than it may have been. Despite the pain, they let out a little cheer, focusing entirely on the large block of ice that appeared.

"There it is!" Ascel shouted. "Phew! Finally there!"

Ranmau grabbed Destrou's arm and pulled him closer. "What did I tell you about trusting people," he whispered to Destrou.

"He's a good one," Destrou said. "The only one that I could trust out of them. It could have been worse."

"Okay!" Ascel shouted, turning around, shielding his face from the wind. "Help me push it open." He nudged his rear to the door, squatting into it.

Destrou and Ranmau assisted Ascel, digging their frostbitten fingernails into the ice, pulling with all the strength they had. The pressure of the roaring wind didn't make the task any easier.

The ice door budged, slowly creaking open. The room was

512

pitch black inside.

"You first," Ranmau said to Ascel.

"Sure." Ascel hesitated. "It's dark in here."

"Relax, no wonder you never made friends," Destrou whispered to Ranmau. He stared into the darkness. "Where is this rope anyway?"

"Over here." Ascel's voice echoed. Sounds of grunting and struggling filled Destrou's ears. "I need a hand... this is heavier than I thought."

Destrou felt a little uneasy yet relieved that they were shielded from the chilling winds. He gladly walked into the darkness while Ranmau kept his distance at the entrance.

"Where are you?" Destrou said, feeling around.

"Right here," Ascel said underneath him.

"Okay, try to put it in my hands. I can't see anything."

Silence.

"Hey, Ascel... where are you? I can't see anything?" Destrou whispered. When he tried to turn around, he felt resistance at his feet.

"Ascel?"

Silence.

"Ascel?"

"I told you not to trust *anyone*." Destrou heard a voice in the darkness.

"I know." Destrou turned around, trying to search for where the voice came from. "I heard you the first ten times. Where'd you go?"

"No you didn't," Ascel said, his voice softer. "I told you not to trust *anyone*."

Clang! "What's this?" Destrou's chest felt heavy as he kicked into a solid rope of some kind. His feet were unable to move beyond that point. "Ascel... what'd you do?" He moved frantically, struggling to get his feet loose. "Ascel... where are you!? I can't move my feet! Hey, Ascel!" Worry deepened his tone.

"I'm sorry." Destrou heard a whisper coming from the entrance.

"Sorry?" Destrou replied, shuffling his feet abruptly, creating a clanging sound, like metal on metal. "Sorry? No... Ascel. Not you! Sorry for what? Ascel!?" His eyes teared up and voice cracked. "Ascel!" The thought suddenly weighed down on him, restricting his breaths, crushing his chest. *Ranmau was right, he always is.*

"I told you, Destrou, to not trust *anyone*." A soft sob was heard. Destrou heard the sound of struggle outside.

"What's going on?" came a cry from the entrance, along with an onslaught of cackles and mocking laughter.

When Destrou turned around he saw the Bruisers smash Ranmau across the face with a large slab of ice, continuously hitting him until his body went limp. They dragged his body along the snow, leaving a red streak the entire way.

"No!" Destrou screamed. "What's going on Ascel!? I thought I could trust you!"

"I'm sorry, Destrou... I thought you would have listened to me. I tried my best to help."

"You coward!" Destrou shrieked, tears poured down his face. "You krillen! What'd you do!? Get me out of here!"

"I'm sorry, he would have killed the only brother I have left. I hope you'll forgive me in the afterlife."

"Ascel!" Destrou's voice cracked as they sealed the door shut. He was trapped in the darkness.

"Get the Crystal Sword." Destrou heard one of the Bruisers say from outside.

"The Crystal Sword?" Destrou's eyes widened with fear. The Crystal Sword was the Guardian's weapon back when he was a Crystal Soldier. It was the sharpest blade in Gaia, made from the strongest material. Elu said it came from the same unbreakable type of ice used to create the Wall. But Destrou knew that asking for the Crystal Sword meant only one thing. "No! Ranmau! Please, no! Not like this! Ascel, help me get out of here! I can't let this happen.

I can't! Please get me out of here!"

"The rest of you watch him... just in case." A voice outside snickered. "It ends now."

Destrou screamed at the top of his lungs, moving around crazily. He had gone mad, slamming his fists into the ground, yanking whatever it was that was tied around his feet. He was helpless. It was too tight around his ankles and too sturdy to budge. He pulled his legs until he felt it dig deep into his flesh. He screamed, tugging on the metallic rope.

"I will NOT let you die. NOT LIKE THIS!" his scream turned into a high-pitched shriek. "You saved me every time. You gave up everything to save me. RANMAAUUUU!"

With one final scream, he felt the skin rip off his feet as they freed themselves in a bloody mess.

He then lost control of his body. Everything went numb. There was a warm sensation that was strikingly familiar. It was the feeling that made him realize just how cold his body had been.

Despite the thickness of the wall, Destrou let his fists fly. He fought against a growing sense of panic, a vicious circle of revolving fears. He kept punching the solid ice until his hands became wet with a mixture of liquid ice and his own blood. His feet rippled through puddles of liquid ice with each thrust. He didn't know how much time he had. His mind blacked out until he heard an unfamiliar scream. He recognized the voice.

"*Ranmau*!!" Destrou screamed. His punches became faster, harder, and stronger.

The puddle grew as the hole widened. With one final thrust, his hand burst through the wall. He pulled his face closer to the hole, witnessing boys huddling around the structure.

"What happened?" one of the voices said.

"I think he's trying to get out," said another boy.

"Impossible! It's too thick!"

"Well, look at that!" a boy said, placing his eye against the hole.

The wall crumbled as Destrou's bloodied feet burst through the wall and connected into the boy's face.

When Destrou looked up, it arrived, a vengeance more perfect than even his imagination could create. He turned his body toward the growing crowd of boys and felt his body prepared for the task.

He looked down at the Bruiser and something unexpected began to happen. The perfection of the moment began to evolve. The other boys huddled around him, and in their eyes, Destrou saw fear, not malice; doubt, not conviction. *I'm ready, krillens.* He waited for one wrong movement from the entire group of boys to justify the fight.

He was surrounded by the entire Village, except for the Leader and the Giant, and he couldn't find Ascel either. He was probably hiding like the krillen he was, he thought. Despite being outnumbered, Destrou looked like the one who was ready.

The Bruiser's first strike aimed for his face. Destrou moved out of its way, retaliating with a strike of his own. At once, the remaining boys charged in.

Destrou saw the next punch coming, but did not even wince. He turned his weight into the punch. He could feel the cartilage snap in the Bruiser's nose, saw the tunnel of blood run free. He had imagined the moment a thousand times, and it had finally arrived. He remembered seeing Ranmau take on the entire Village when he was helplessly bound to the spike, and a part of him was always jealous of that feat. He always hoped that he could match Ranmau's dominance. His chance had finally arrived.

More boys and Bruisers ran in. Destrou caught one under the chin, knocking him backwards into a pile of snow. His body vanished.

Destrou charged into the boys, erupting in a rage of punches and kicks. When the blood started to spread over his hands and feet, he decided to target his attacks to their stomachs, immobilizing them just as effectively. One by one and blow by blow, the boys fell.

He stopped, noticing a sparkle glow amidst the fog of the storm. *The Crystal Sword,* he thought. Nothing else could sparkle that bright. *I need to get there now.*

Destrou accelerated the process by grabbing one of the staffs from a fallen boy's hands. He twirled it around his body, connecting into the boys' faces. Strike after strike, they fell. They dropped at an alarming rate until he was the only one left standing. He stood above the fallen Village of boys, holding their faces and bodies in pain. His whole life... all he had known was the perspective of defeat from the ground looking up—this moment made his victory all the more satisfying.

Unable to soak in the moment, he pulled the hood over his head and ran into the storm, chasing after the light.

Destrou crashed to the ground after hitting a wall. At least he thought it was one. When he looked up, he stared at the Giant. His face was swollen and bruised. They glared into one another's eyes for a few moments until the Giant lunged his hand down.

Destrou flinched, defensively pressing the staff across his chest. The Giant hadn't attacked. His outstretched hand was with an open palm. *Is he helping me up?*

Destrou hesitated for a moment, slowly reaching his hand up. The Giant yanked him to his feet.

"Go," the Giant grunted.

Destrou was silent.

"Go!" he grunted louder. "Ram need yuh."

"T-thank you," Destrou said, glancing at him with narrowed eyes. *I'm not supposed to trust anyone.*

Destrou's breathing began to slow down as the heavy snow obscured any sign of the light. He looked around, as if suddenly aware of the ring of boys surrounding him. He stared for a long time at the staff in his hand, then clenched it tighter.

Danger was here. He sensed it shiver through his bones.

How did they get here before I did? The Bruisers really don't stay down for long. Where can you be, Ranmau?

"Ranmau! Where are you?" Destrou screamed. His voice was barely heard over the rushes of wind. "Where did you bring him?" he shouted to the boys surrounding him.

"He's right here," a deep voice boomed through the storm.

The circle opened up as the Crystal Sword brightened the area.

He was at the Edge. He saw the Snake, the Crystal Sword, and the Leader, but he couldn't find Ranmau. He saw what at first looked like a mound of snow buried underneath the Leader's foot, but as the snow cleared up, he recognized Ranmau's cloak.

"Get off of him!" Destrou screamed. "What's the purpose of this? What are you trying to prove?"

"I'm trying to prove that I'm the Leader and any time someone tries to disrupt the order that I created, they will pay the ultimate price," he said, raising the sword above his head.

"We don't have to do this. If this is life... if this is how we are forced to live, then we need to make the most out of it. We need to stick together."

"Shut up, krillen!" the Leader screamed. "Do you think I care about any single one of you? I'm going to be a Crystal Soldier and the rest of the Village is going to starve, rot, and die here. Why am I going to care about you krillens?"

"This is what they want us to do," Destrou said, his voice more relaxed than he expected. "They want to see us tear each other apart. They are the ones who don't care about us. We are all that we have—we need to stick together."

"I said shut up! I say what goes. I am the Leader!"

"Well maybe that's what needs to change then."

"What did you say?" the Leader groaned softly.

Despite the roaring noises from the wind, gasps were heard.

"You heard what I said. Since you are the Leader, I challenge you to a duel."

"Hah, this krillen has lost his mind," the Leader cackled.

"Hah, this krillen is too scared," Destrou mocked. "If you win, you get your wish: the brothers are gone. But if I win, then you won't enter the tournament. You will not become a Crystal Soldier. You *will* let it be just between me and Ranmau."

"Hah!" he cackled louder. "Why would I ever listen to you?"

"Because your word means more to you than any of us here. And it was your word that said that you would accept any challenge as long as it wasn't Ranmau. Well, I'm not Ranmau. So, I'll ask: what are you so afraid of, krillen?"

"Yeah, what so afraid of?" the Giant said, stepping next to Destrou.

"Yeah, that was your word," said another boy, walking to them.

"Yeah."

"Yeah."

"Yeah!"

In a matter of moments, Destrou was surrounded by a village of boys. The pain in their sunken eyes told the tale of why they'd support the duel for a new leader. Someone finally had the courage.

"If this is what you krillens want... then okay. I can't wait to kill the both of you," the Leader screamed. "Starting with Ranmau!"

The Leader raised the Crystal Sword above his head, preparing for a strike. Destrou performed a spin, launching the staff toward him.

BANG! The staff hit the Leader's arms right before he impaled Ranmau, sending the Crystal Sword over the Edge.

"How dare you!" the Leader growled, kicking Ranmau's body a few feet into the air, crashing at Destrou's feet.

"I will get him for you, brother," Destrou said, kneeling down. "And if I don't make it... I want you to know that I don't hate you. I couldn't hate you even when I tried. Thank you for always being my brother and my protector. It's time for me to protect you. I forgive you, and I love you."

"Don't," Ranmau whimpered.

"There's no turning back now," Destrou said, lifting his head. "It ends now."

Destrou's eyes blackened. He peered at the Leader with a seething glare. The Leader smirked.

He always strikes first... not this time. Destrou ran against the wind, leading with a jumping kick.

The Leader saw it coming, and he did not move.

Destrou soared through the air, wind and snow wrapped around his torso.

Destrou connected into the Leader's jaw, but he stood motionless.

With a swift motion, he grabbed Destrou's calf and slammed him into the ground.

The Leader delivered a brutal kick. Though he tried to contain it, Destrou groaned at the impact of the blow. He felt the life and air exhale out of his crammed throat. The Leader stood above Destrou's crumpled body at his feet.

Destrou was panting and choking for a breath.

"This will be easier than I thought," the Leader smiled. "That was nothing compared to what I have for you."

He grabbed Destrou's squirming body, lifting it easily over his head and threw him toward the end of the Edge.

Destrou landed shoulders first, rolling until his feet hung over the Edge. He struggled to roll his body back onto solid ground. He felt his heart pound at his temple, and each breath burned on its way to his lungs.

He's way too strong. That hurt a lot more than I thought it would. I don't even know what to do. Think, Destrou. He pressed his palm against his chest.

The Leader reached down again, grabbing Destrou by the neck.

Destrou squirmed as his eyes began to pop out of his head. He felt the back of his neck begin to crack as the Leader tightened his grip. Destrou saw veins that he had never seen before bulge out of muscles that he never knew existed. His vision started to blur. He gasped but even that was cut short. In a last effort, he lunged his knee into the Leader's chin, knocking his face back.

The Leader effortlessly pushed his face back into place, as if unharmed, then slammed Destrou onto the ice.

BANG! Destrou didn't know if he heard his back break or the ice shatter, but there was a crunching sound that made the boys gasp and look away for a moment.

The Leader kept slamming Destrou's back onto the solid ice until blood drained from his eyes, ears, mouth and nose.

"Is this what you all wanted to see?" the Leader said as saliva spat into Destrou's bloodied face. "Again, in what world would a krillen like you ever have a chance against a leader like me?"

Destrou eye's shot open as he heard the sound of cracking underfoot.

"Kuhh..." He tried to speak but the Leader had his windpipe sealed shut.

"What do you have to say?" the Leader mocked him. "What's wrong? Can't talk anymore? You had such a great speech just a minute ago. Hah!"

"Kuhh..."

"Kuh? Kuhh what?" he leaned his ear closer to Destrou's face.

"Kuh... rillen..." Destrou forced his best smile.

The Leader roared, slamming Destrou to the ground.

BANG! The ice spiderwebbed. One creak turned to two, then three, then ten, then a cacophony of them. Then in that instant, the ground burst, separating from the Edge.

They tumbled down the avalanche of snow and ice into the Forest of Ness.

"Oh no!" the Giant groaned. "Get the rope! Get lots o' ropes! Get them out! Not good!"

Ranmau struggled to get to his feet. His eyes stricken with worry. "We need to try and get them!" No one had ever went over the

Edge and lived to tell about it. "I shouldn't have let this happen!"

Destrou and the Leader's bodies rolled helplessly, blending into the snow and ice.

Two *cracks* sounded after one another as they landed onto solid ground. A thick freshness entered Destrou's nostrils as he struggled to his feet. There was no sign of the Leader, only a shattered mess.

The Leader roared as he broke through the boulders of ice that were wedged on top of him.

"I feel unstoppable!" he screamed. "Not even the Forest can stop me!"

Destrou limped trying to get into a fighting position.

"Right now they are trying to find a way to get ME out of here. Your dead carcass won't even have a burial. You'll never see Ranmau again. Don't worry... I may kill him much faster than I'll kill you. *May*. Only if he begs."

"I won't let it... happen," Destrou struggled to say, almost toppling over.

"Don't you get it? I was born to be a Crystal Soldier. You were born to be a krillen. You and your brother may have thought you were special, winning the challenges, but they don't mean anything. In the end, I win! And that's what matters."

The Leader lunged in, putting all of his power into a punch. Destrou dodged it, landing a kick across his jaw.

"That was it?" the Leader laughed. "Don't you get it? I didn't even feel a thing."

Doubt began to settle in Destrou's mind. *Not only is he stronger, but I can't even hurt him. I don't know how I'm going to do this.*

Destrou used his speed to his advantage, dodging numerous attacks and connecting counters of his own. The Leader still seemed unfazed. While Destrou's energy was running out, the Leader remained as ready as ever.

I let you down. Destrou was unable to protect his face anymore. His legs could barely move. His heart was working harder than ever, yet he couldn't move a muscle.

The Leader wrapped his arms around Destrou's body.

Destrou felt the bones in his body crack the tighter he squeezed.

The Leader slammed Destrou's back onto the ice and wrapped his palms around his neck.

The Snake dropped down, thundering into the side of the wall. The mound of shattered ice cleared a path up to it.

"It looks like I'll be rescued. I'll tell them how you died. Screaming like a krillen." He pressed his weight onto Destrou's neck as saliva mixed with blood shot into the air. "Ranmau will be next!"

Destrou felt himself losing consciousness, his last breath trying to find a way to escape the Leader's grips.

Destrou heard a ghastly scream. He saw a light, blinding his vision. His life had flashed before his eyes. It looked like the Eye of Eve. Inside the light, he heard laughter with Ranmau. He saw all of the moments when Ranmau saved him. The countless visions replayed in his mind. He then saw Elu. Her face was smiling and bright.

"You're special," she whispered to him. "You're destined for great things. I don't want to see you yet. It's not your time."

The light faded away and the Leader was no longer on top of him.

What happened? Am I dead? Is this what happens? Did Elu save me again? His mind began to reorient itself.

He felt a warming sensation emit from his body as footsteps stomped around him. There was a shrieking sound of ice scraping ice, circling around him. When he moved his eyes to the side, he saw the luminous blade of the Crystal Sword drag along the ground.

"You know... I never wanted to become the Leader, it was supposed to be my brother, Massa," the Leader said as he picked up the Crystal Sword. "But when he died... I knew I couldn't protect Elu'nex anymore. It was my promise to him. *Protect our sister,* he said. And I promised him that I would. That I would keep my word. That if I became this monster, people would fear me... and that fear would keep Elu safe. It worked, though. Oh yes, it worked." The Leader slid the sword through the rubble. Its hilt, with its shiny blue jewels, glistened in the night. "I became a monster because it'd keep her safe. But now... now she's gone... and I'm still a monster, but there is no turning back from it now. She was the only one I cared about; I don't care what happens to the rest of them."

"She wouldn't want you to do this." Destrou coughed.

"I already gave you a pass in the challenge, you're out of luck now. And this is how it ends for you," the Leader said, standing over Destrou's body. He gripped the sword with two hands and lunged it into Destrou's chest.

Destrou accepted his fate. He knew what was coming and closed his eyes. It was then when he heard a high-pitched "DESTROU!" come from within the Forest of Ness.

Before he could think about if what he heard was real or not, he opened his eyes and gasped; his vision blurred.

The Leader was above him, grunting, pushing more of his body weight down, unmoving.

Destrou realized that he was surrounded by a puddle of liquid ice. The ice underneath him had melted into a crater. And when his eyes finally focused, the Crystal Sword was wedged inside his palms, almost touching his heart. His eyes emitted a white glow, with traces of red, that flowed like steam.

Drip. Drip. Drip. Liquid ice splashed onto his chest as the Crystal Sword began to creak. The Crystal Sword, the indestructible weapon of the Crystal Soldiers, created a spider web of cracks.

"This. Is. Impossible," the Leader screamed, pressing more of his weight down. "I. Will. Kill. You!"

"You're special," floated through Destrou's mind in Elu's soft voice. Was that the voice he heard in the Forest of Ness?

"It ends now," Destrou said in a deep, cold voice. A voice he had never heard before.

In one scream, Destrou's palms crashed together, breaking the blade in two. Before the Leader could react, Destrou spun to his feet. Steam radiated off his body, whirling around him, melting the flurry of snow that surrounded them into liquid ice. He planted his feet, crouched his knees, and launched his fist into the air. A red aura burst around him as he jumped, connecting his punch into the Leader's jaw, spinning around during the process. He felt the Leader's jawbone break upon contact as his limp body flew high into the air. Destrou saw the life get sucked out of his eyes as he collided into the Snake.

Destrou landed on his feet, looking at the lifeless leader. An aura of steam rippled from his body, turning everything from the snowflakes to the ice around him into liquid ice. A few moments later, his eyes normalized. His body felt cold again. He glanced at his hands. *What happened? Was Elu right? Am I special?*

Ropes fell down as the boys shouted instructions to tie them around their bodies. Destrou grabbed the rope and wrapped them around the Leader's arms and legs.

Destrou tugged on the rope, to let the boys overhead know it was secure, then looked up and saw the Leader colliding against the wall while being hoisted up.

It was in that moment when Destrou heard a deep growl from somewhere behind him. He didn't know how to respond. Suddenly... the reality weighed down on him, slowing his breaths to a stop—he was inside of the Forest of Ness... The forsaken land. The home of... Archons.

Slowly, he turned around. His heart stopped. His eyes widened. He saw a silhouette against the backdrop of trees. The more he squinted to get a better look... the more it looked like... "Elu?" Destrou shouted. "Elu?" Tears started to stream down Destrou's face. "Is that you? I've missed you so much." The silhouette disappeared, then off in the distance a larger one emerged. This one made

Destrou's chest tighten as if he was staring at Death. The figure made the Guardian look like a small toy and there was a shadowy glow emitting from its body. Piercing red dots where eyes would be contrasted against the darkness.

"I-is... that... an... A-Archon?" He refused to believe his eyes. "That can't be one ... it's too big. How could anything fight that?"

The Leader's body collided into the wall again before being pulled over the Edge, which caused Destrou to flinch and look over his shoulder.

When he turned around to face the Forest, without even a sound, that shadowy being was within inches from him. They were breathing the same air. He looked up, expecting his heart to tremble, but he couldn't tell his mind to react. It was as large as the rock beast from the challenge and infinitely more scary. Destrou never knew what true fear was until he realized it had the ability to shut down his entire body.

Destrou was frozen, unable to even breathe, just staring directly into its hazy, red eyes. Something within them moved as if there were people trapped, wishing to escape. Destrou was calm, too calm. He accepted that there was nothing he could do even if he tried.

There were hardly any definite features to notice. The shadowy glow rippled from its body, obscuring details. A gust of air exhaled from its blackened face, traveling down toward Destrou. But before it reached him, it dispersed, flowing to the left and right of him as if it hit an invisible wall. The breath traveled up and down and side to side in perfectly straight lines before dissipating into nothingness.

"Bound by the four elements?" he slowly said to himself, remembering Elu's words. He swallowed a deep breath. "The Archons are ba—"

BANG! Destrou's senses were so alert, that without wanting to, he flinched and turned toward the Snake, watching the ropes dangle off the Edge. And when he turned back around, it was no longer there.

What was that? What just happened? I must be seeing things. Am I losing my mind? Is this what happens to people after the Box? Was that my imagination. That's it, yeah, my imagination. It had to be my imagination... because if it wasn't... then that'd mean—he gulped—*the Archons are back.*

When Destrou climbed over the Edge, the Giant grabbed Destrou with all his force, throwing him onto his shoulders. He didn't know if he should attack or defend himself.

At once, the boys cheered on in unison.

What's going on? He had just went through the most traumatic, paralyzing moment that it took a moment to realize what was actually happening. His dream had come true. Not only did he accomplish Ranmau's dream to become a Crystal Soldier, but he was finally surrounded by a Village of boys cheering him on. *I never thought this day would ever happen.*

"Our new Leader!" the Giant smiled.

"Go Destrou!"

"Yay!"

Then Destrou felt a tug on his pants. When he looked down, he saw Ascel with a face filled with tears. "I am so sorry... please... please forgive me!"

Destrou did not even have to think twice. "You were protecting your brother, just as Ranmau does for me... and what I would do for him. You were Elu's best friend... Elu would want me to forgive you. Elu would tell me that you aren't the enemy, they are." Destrou's head turned to the Wall. "I forgive you, Ascel."

"Thank you!" Ascel fell to the ground, digging his face and hands into the snow. "Thank you so much, our Leader!"

This can't be real... None of this can be real. But please... please let this be real. I don't want to wake up. Please let this not be a dream. Destrou's eyes watered, looking for Ranmau through his blurred lens. When he made contact with Ranmau, he saw something that he hadn't seen in years: a glowing smile from his face. Destrou couldn't handle all the emotions at once. Tears poured from his mouth and nostrils.

"I DID IT!" Destrou screamed. "I DID THE IMPOSSIBLE!"

* * *

That night, Destrou went to bed with a smile on his face. Ranmau was getting his freedom, after all. There was no greater day in his lifetime. He was surrounded by friends, but more importantly, his brother, whom he had loved more than life itself. He had almost forgotten what his smile looked like. Seeing that made him more happy than making friends. Though the tournament was just a few days away, Destrou had made up his mind. He would rather die than kill Ranmau. After everything Ranmau had been through, no boy in the Village deserved freedom more than him. Yes, he was sad about Elu. Yes, he never thought he'd be able to forgive him for what he did, but the way Ascel spoke about Ranmau... Destrou knew that it must have been an accident.

I forgive you, brother.

As Destrou laid in bed, staring at the night's sky. Ranmau walked in with a smile, approaching his bed.

"I know that I've never said this to you before, but I'm proud of you. You did it," Ranmau said, placing his palm on Destrou's forehead. "You proved to everyone just how great you are. The Village will always remember that. They will always remember you as the one who did the impossible. You beat them when the world said it wasn't possible. If these are our final moments together, I want you to know how proud I am that I watched you become greater than great. I'm proud that you were my brother. We will always be remembered as the ones who never gave up without a fight... and we always found a way to win. I love you, brother."

Destrou's cheeks pushed up in a way that seemed physically impossible. He had never heard Ranmau say those words before. "I love you too!" He couldn't stop the tears from flowing.

There was no greater way to fall asleep than knowing that he loved and was loved, but he couldn't help but wonder why it sounded like a farewell.

That night, Destrou's eyes sealed shut like never before, it was as if he had finally found that peace that he had been searching for.

* * *

"You are ready now. They won't be able to hurt you anymore. Goodbye, my brother. I love you."

Those words disturbed Destrou's dreams as he woke up in the middle of the night. His eyes scanned the room, wondering if he was still dreaming. His forehead felt moist as if it had just been kissed. He remembered that feeling, he woke up to that once before. He glanced over at Ranmau's bed. It was as empty as the night's sky. And in that moment, the realization hit him. *You couldn't leave me... not like this.*

Not like this. Destrou laughed. "You couldn't leave me... not like this!" He laughed even louder. "You were... waiting for me to be ready... this whole time? All of this? All of this was to make sure that I was ready? And... once you knew that I was... ready. Once you knew I could be alone—" His laughter burst even louder. He didn't know how to react right now. It was as if his whole world had come into focus and he realized that his life was a lie. "You... you... were finally ready to leave? It all makes sense now." His laughter transformed into tears. "I can't believe that I was so mean to you... and this whole time... this whole time... was like a test? Were you waiting for the right moment to leave? Could you have left all along, but you suffered just to make sure I was ready? So... we could both be free... just like you promised?" Destrou choked up. "I... I am going to miss you so so so much. I'm going to miss you more than anything. I won't be holding you back anymore. Enjoy your freedom, Ranmau. I love you, too, brother."

And just like that, Ranmau was gone; with a smile, Destrou peered at the Wall, knowing that this time he was not coming back.

And then suddenly everything weighed him down as if the world pressed against his mind, revealing a dark, hidden truth. He thought of Ranmau's freedom... and of his own, as a potential Crystal Soldier. He thought of finally being able to meet the great Supreme General, the Master of the Kingdom and Crystal Soldiers. They both could receive their freedom now. They both will get what they had dreamed of ... yet he shook with sorrow and grief. Why?

He thought of leaving the Village and abandoning his new friends. His friends, who were just laughing and smiling, would remain trapped behind the Wall. The same wall that made them enemies to begin with. The Village wouldn't get their freedom, they'd still live in a terrible world filled with hunger and slavery. They would never be free—they would remain trapped until they die a horrible death, which would be inevitable here.

His body broke down with a shock that forced his knees to collapse to the ground. "What is freedom?"

And in the end, they were all just boys, torn on the idea that freedom, and only freedom, could heal their brokenness. What they hadn't known was that through the lens of shattered glass everything would appear to be broken. Destrou trembled because his epiphany showed him that gaining freedom would never fix the glass—it would only force him to forget that the glass was ever there... as it had already done.

* * *

"Wait..." Vayp screamed. "Wait... where did the words go?" Vayp's hands quickly moved across the pages as the next sets of words slowly vanished, as if they were written with invisible ink. Vayp flipped the book over and saw that the flaming orb was flickering low as if its fire was dying. And after a few slow pulses, like the last pumps of a dying heart, the fire doused.

The fire emblem became black like burned coal.

Vayp jumped back as a cold hand touched his shoulder.

"It is time," the shadow said. He then lifted his head and repeated it louder. "It is time!"

It was only then when Vayp realized that he had been so consumed with reading the book that he hadn't realized the great distance they traveled. They had migrated miles and miles while shrouded by this blanket of darkness.

The main shadow then emerged in front of Vayp, and without a second's hesitation, a shadowy sword materialized in his hand and slashed through Han'sael's container.

Vayp felt his heart collapse. "What are you doing?" he screamed.

"Fulfilling my promise," the shadow said. The container sliced cleanly in half as water burst through the opening; but Han'sael's body didn't move, it remained in place, held up by the tubes attached to his body. "Give me the book," the shadow said, turning his head to Vayp.

Vayp hesitated for a moment before lifting it up to him. "What do you need it for?"

"Because... he is going home now."

The shadow mumbled words as Han'sael's eyes shot open. They were bright white yet lifeless as if there was no longer a soul inside.

And then Han'sael began screaming words in a language Vayp had never heard before. His voice was muffled and deep, as if he was submerged in water.

Before Vayp could make sense of what was happening, the entire planet of Gaia began to shake. The sun appeared and revolved clockwise around them a dozen times before slowing down and revolving a dozen more times counter-clockwise.

And while Vayp was trying to understand how he had just seen day turn to night multiple times within a second, the book burst open and its pages fluttered madly.

As Han'sael's chanting became louder, a tear appeared in the air above the book. Vayp's eyes widened as Han'sael somehow cut the air open in a way that resembled a knife tearing through flesh. The tear opened up more, revealing a snowy terrain. It felt like Vayp was gazing at a picture of a tundra that was floating in the sky.

"Dynas," the shadow said, and Vayp was shocked to finally hear a name.

But Vayp wasn't the only one who was surprised. "I haven't heard you call me by my name in millennia," Dynas said.

"I want you to have this." The shadow held a fabric in his hand that looked like a headband of some sort.

"But... this was *his*," Dynas said.

"I have no more use for it." The shadow paused for a second, and Vayp didn't know if he was hearing things, but it sounded like the shadow's voice may have cracked. "Consider it... a gift, old friend."

And even more to Vayp's surprise, the two shadows hugged.

"Farewell, friend," Dynas said. "And if it all works out... I will be seeing you again. This is not goodbye. We will have our adventures once again."

"I will..." the shadow looked away. "I will... miss you. I have faith that you will accomplish what you are destined to do. It is in your stars, Dynas."

Dynas bowed his head, then turned to Vayp. "I hope you choose wisely."

Before Vayp could say a word, Dynas walked into the tear just before it had sealed up.

The book then slammed shut with a resounding BANG, and Vayp looked around, as if hoping he'd be provided an answer.

"He is back home, Vayp."

"Where is home?"

The shadow pointed at the book, which was now pitch black as dark steam billowed from it.

At once, Vayp jumped to catch Han'sael just as his body fell to the ground. The tubes had detached themselves and Han'sael was now free from the contraption. But the moment Han'sael's skin touched Vayp's he was immediately reminded of Ah'nyx when he was found dead. Han'sael was frozen, with no pulse. Vayp's eyes watered. "What... what happens to him?"

"I suppose... it was not in his stars to survive." The shadow shrugged and turned away.

"No! Please no!" Vayp cried onto Han'sael's chest. He felt the cold waves from his body freeze his tears. "I can't lose you, Hanny! I can't! Please... please live! Please! I need you to! Don't die, I was supposed to protect you!"

"A part of me thought he would be strong enough," the shadow said, "but... what is done is done... the longer you cry over him, the more S'rae gets away. You do... want Ah'nyx back, right?"

Vayp had stopped crying for a moment, his tears freezing to his skin. "You promise... I'll get Ah'nyx back—"

"That is a promise I can keep. I made no promises for Han'sael. We must go." The shadow then walked ahead. "Take the book with you... we are almost there."

Though his knees were weak, Vayp wiped his eyes, picked up the book and sniffled as he walked backwards, staring at Han'sael the entire time. "I am so sorry... I am so so sorry." And the moment he took his eyes off of Han'sael, he saw the thousands of shadowy people prowling toward them. Vayp looked up at the sky and saw the Mas'ahk... and he knew that the world was over.

Vayp couldn't function. His heart ached for Han'sael, and he longed for any type of an escape to take him away from this pain. He opened the book, hoping for something, anything, but to his surprise, each and every page was now as dark as the night. *What happened? What did Dynas do to this book?* In a craze, Vayp flipped through dozens and dozens of pages, each one was blank—as if the paper were made from shadows—until... he landed on a black page with white letters that said:

* * *

"Help me!" a girl's voice screamed in the darkness.

"Where are you?" Destrou screamed.

"I'm over here. Come find me!"

"Where?"

"Here! OH NO! Watch out! It's behind you! It's going to kill you! Run! NOOO!"

A gut-ripping slash was heard as a roar reverberated throughout the darkness.

Seven years later...

An older, well-built Destrou lunged out his bed in a sweat-soaked daze. Another horrible dream, somehow this one felt more real than the last. That said a lot. He laid on the floor in his unchanged igloo room. While the room remained the same, Destrou seemed much different. For starters, he actually had muscles, they fit his mismatched, patchy clothing quite well. He also had much longer hair, dreads that were tied back into a ponytail, with a few strands left dangling on his cheeks. But most strange of all was the dark cloth wrapped around his eyes and the tiny remnants of damaged scar tissue around the fabric, where his eyes would be.

Despite being blindfolded, he stood up and navigated around the room. His hands wandered about, grabbing a scepter that leaned against the wall of the igloo. He paused, grazing his fingers along an empty bed that was once Ranmau's. A soft sigh escaped. He tilted his head to the side, hearing a distant noise approach the door.

"Wake up! Did you forget that today is the day the Supreme General arrives?" the Guardian stated in a jubilant tone. "The Master of the Kingdom! The Leader of the Crystal Soldiers!"

"Wow! He's actually coming, right now?" Destrou replied.

"He is not just coming, he is already here!" the Guardian replied. There was an eerie, peaceful presence about him. He left the room with a smile on his face.

Destrou placed the scepter ahead of him, guiding his way toward the exit. He ran out with haste to his step.

Before he made it out, he collided into an immovable object standing at the entrance.

It was a tall figure who wore a crystallized armor covering his entire body. It shimmered brightly any time light touched it.

"Who's there?" Destrou stared from the ground, feeling around for his stick.

Silence.

After a few more moments, he asked: "Hello? I know someone's there? I'm blind, not dumb."

"So, you are the one who survived an Archon attack?" a deep voice resonated within the armor, making Destrou's shoulders lock up.

"Yes, I believe so," Destrou said, slowly feeling for his scepter. "That's what they say."

"What do you remember of the incident?"

"Not a thing."

"You do know how rare it is to see an Archon and live to tell about it, right?"

"That's what everyone tells me. I didn't even know they were real."

"They are very real." The voice trailed as he wandered around the room. The clangs from the armor echoed about. Each step that he took left a deep white layer of frost that dispersed on the ground. "What do you remember?"

"I'm sorry, but I remember nothing. I don't even remember what it looks like."

"Do you remember meeting a girl?"

"A girl? No, I've never met a girl before."

"Hmm... Really... never? Does a girl named Elu ring a bell?"

"Elu... hmmm... I do remember a boy named Elu, I don't know where he went though. He was a nice one."

"Interesting... something or someone doesn't want you to remember what happened."

"What do you mean?"

"Do you know what this is?" A vial materialized from the armor on his hand. It had a peculiar scent to it, that Destrou couldn't pinpoint. "We believe the Guardian used this on the entire Village to hide the identity of a girl. A girl that they hid from the Kingdom. Does anyone else here know of a girl."

"If there were ever a girl here, I'm sure we would all know about her. Well... maybe there's one person who would know. He knew everything."

"Who?"

"Eli'jah."

"Interesting. And where is Eli'jah?"

"Well, he should be in the Kingdom by now. A Crystal Soldier."

The man hesitated. "I see... so he must have won the tournament that I requested."

"That you..." Destrou gulped. He was speaking to the Supreme General? He assumed this was his aide at the very least, but the actual Supreme General? The leader of the Crystal Soldiers. The most powerful man in the entire Kingdom was right here in front of him... in their village... talking to *him* of all people. Destrou could hardly contain the excitement or the confusion.

"You see, there is also another girl that we are searching for... and prophet Va'han told us that you may have been in contact with her."

"Really? Two girls? Well, I'm sorry that I won't be able to help you."

"Oh but you may. We have very gifted people who are able to do very gifted things. Your thoughts are not your own, she will be able to see what you've forgotten."

"Forgotten?"

"Yes, we would like to know what had happened to you for the past seven years. Where you've gone. Who you've met. And how you became... the way that you are now."

"I'm sorry, but I've just been here in the Village."

"Then what would explain what happened to your eyes?"

"An accident, I believe. I wish I could remember, but the Village would be able to tell you."

"Ah yes, I am sure they could. Well, do you remember, at least, what happened seven years ago?"

"Of course!" Destrou said with the utmost confidence in his voice. "That's something that I'll never be able to forget. How could I?"

"What happened with him? Is it true that someone left you like this—trapped behind the Wall to suffer? The Wall was designed to be inescapable. How did he do it?"

"Why are you—" Destrou paused. *Don't ask questions.* "I don't know how he did it, but if anyone could, it would be him. He was the greatest person I knew. I don't know what happened, but I know that I no longer held him back. He finally got the freedom that he deserved."

"Freedom," the Supreme General paused. "That is such an interesting word. Was it freedom that he wanted?"

"Yes, and he deserved it," Destrou replied.

"What if I told you that freedom wasn't what he dreamed of."

Destrou said nothing. His head tilted to the side, hearing the crisp crackles that the Supreme General's frosted footsteps made.

"What if I told you that he wanted more than freedom. Freedom that was... not just for himself."

Destrou's head tilted again. Something was stuck in his throat.

"What if I told you that he came back seven years later to make sure that he kept a promise that he made. His intention was never to leave you, but to free you. What if I told you that he came back seven years later as the Supreme General to prove that anything is possible and that we can change our destiny." The Supreme General bent over, grabbing Destrou's hand. A chilling frost calmed

Destrou's anxiety. "What if this is him keeping his promise? The world out there is unlike anything we could have ever imagined. I'm here to take you back to the Kingdom. . . brother."

"It can't... it can't be you..." The cloth around Destrou's eyes became darker, absorbing moisture. His breaths were difficult to swallow. "Ranmau?"

"I am glad that you are alive, I have too much to tell you. The last seven years—"

"What happened?" Destrou choked up. "I've missed you so—"

"You wouldn't believe me if I told you. I know so many secrets about this world. It is bigger than we could have imagined."

"I want to know everything. I want to know it all! Tell me all your stories, tell me your secrets... anything... please!" Destrou was overwhelmed with too much emotion right now. The only person for the past seven years who had been lodged in his memory was Ranmau, his brother. It all felt surreal. He prayed to all the Divines that this wasn't a dream. That his brother, Ranmau, was back. And that he was... the Supreme General of all things.

"Okay, just one secret, for now," Ranmau said.

"What's the name of the girl?"

"The one who Prophet Va'han believes you could help us find?" Ranmau paused, and when Destrou replied with an excited nod, he hunched in close so no one else could hear. "Her name is... S'rae."

* * *

"S'rae!?" Vayp screamed as he slammed his palms on the book. His breathing was heavy and his eyes wide.

"What about her?" the shadow said aloud.

"No-nothing," Vayp lied. He didn't know what to say, none of it made sense.

"Hm... interesting," the shadow said. "Well, speaking of S'rae... it looks like your chance has finally come."

And as Vayp lifted his head, anxiety surged through his body. It was actually happening. Just ahead, he saw the massive golden gates of GroundStone surrounded by its great wall. They were here. Vayp's heart ached as he thought about how none of them inside knew of the death that awaited them. But of all the deaths that were about to happen… one stood out over the rest. S'rae.

"THE END—" The shadow screamed, as the Shadow Army screeched and roared and stormed the walls by the thousands. "—IS NOW!"

Vayp clutched his chest, trying to sooth his hammering heart. He thought about Destrou and Ranmau… how even after everything they went through, Destrou still forgave Ranmau. Destrou still loved him. But Destrou didn't have a choice to make, he didn't have to choose between Ranmau or Elu. Vayp did. The time had finally come. He had to choose… S'rae or Ah'nyx. Only one will be alive after today. And he had seen what was in his stars. *Tonight… S'rae dies.*

35

FUJAK SLOUCHED AGAINST THE COLD METAL of the wall, thinking. Feeling around the empty, dark room, he sighed and pressed his ear against the door, hearing the pounding of drums that hadn't stopped for the past ten minutes. At times, there was a burst of cheers and clapping that joined the drums, which made him realize just how much he appreciated the silence from before.

Fujak gave another sigh as he pressed his hand to his face, feeling the permanent mark that the Warden had given him, letting him know that his life would never be the same—if he even had a life to be lived once this gate opened.

The Warden said that Fujak's opponent was powerful beyond words. That if Fujak did not manage to kill him, then at least Fujak's death would weigh his opponent down with guilt. Fujak was nothing more than a puppet in the Warden's game. But Fujak had other plans. And that was why he slouched against the cold metal, thinking.

It was tough to formulate his plan with the constant interruptions just outside, but it became most difficult when he heard what sounded like thick liquid metal swirling down a drain. It was accompanied by the sound of metal creaking, groaning and bending as the scent of rust filled the room.

What's that? Fujak crawled to a wall and tried to visualize what was making the noises. It was getting louder until he heard a *pop* and a voice say, "This may be the last time I see you, I don't want you to be alone, like I was."

"Reyna?" Fujak shouted, but a finger quickly pressed against his lips.

"Shhh," Reyna whispered in Fujak's ear. "The gate may be opening any second now."

"But... but how'd you get here... these walls are made of—" Fujak gasped. "—they're made of... metal."

"Yes." Fujak heard the sorrow in her voice. "Do you hate me now... now that you know what I am? Am I evil, like the laws say? Does this mean my life doesn't matter?"

Had these questions been asked just a few months ago, Fujak would have answered immediately with a "yes." But tonight, right now, all he could think about was how no Shinshei Law could ever convince him that Reyna was not worthy of life.

"Your life matters," Fujak said. "No... you are not evil."

Fujak heard Reyna sniffle, as if she was teary-eyed.

"Thank you..." Reyna said. "That means a lot coming from you. I wanted to tell you the truth... but I was scared of ruining what we had."

Fujak felt her arms wrap around his torso, and he returned the hug with one of his own.

"It's okay, I was scared to let you know I was a Fujita... and you embraced me," Fujak said. "But, you've been here before... in this room?"

Fujak felt Reyna nod into his shoulder a few times.

"You've done this before... the Alta'jriba?"

She nodded again.

"And you lived? How?"

"Because... the Divine One must have been in a good mood

that day." Reyna paused for a second. "It was luck that saved me."

"I do not believe it was luck," Fujak said, squeezing Reyna tighter. "I do not believe in coincidences. I believe you survived because you have a greater purpose."

"So I can die here in Alsi'jin like the Sol-less loser that I am?"

"That will not happen, because I will come back for you."

"I hope… but your opponent… he is—"

"Strong beyond words… yes, I've heard."

"And… how do you plan to beat him?"

"I have a plan."

"What is it?"

"It's a plan. I have faith in it… so I can only hope faith has me."

"And what about this?" Reyna touched Fujak's face, and she suddenly gasped. "Fujak… you are—" Fujak was already expecting the worst. He was a monster, and now she finally saw it. Her fingers gently went from the scar to his chin to his ears to nose. "Fujak… you are beautiful! Like… very beautiful."

Fujak's eyes widened at that comment. "I wish you could have seen me before."

"I consider what I see right now a masterpiece… and anyone would be a fool to think otherwise," Reyna said, gently rubbing his face again as if she couldn't resist soaking in his details.

"I… Thank you… I… I just… I just don't think I'm ready to have people view me as a monster again." Fujak briefly thought back to when he was ridiculed for looking different, and it made him shiver.

"You don't want… her to see you like this… huh?"

Fujak said nothing.

"I understand. Consider this my gift to you," Reyna said as Fujak heard the same swirling liquid metal sounds he had heard earlier. Then he felt a cold substance press against his face.

"What is this?" Fujak gasped as the cold chilled his skin.

"It's a mask… I'll make sure it's perfect for you."

Fujak felt a pressure behind his eyes. "But... won't they know you helped me?"

"I don't care about my fate right now... I care about yours."

Fujak was taken aback. "I am so glad that I came here," Fujak said softly. "And I never thought I would ever say that. But you let me know what true friendship is like. You didn't know what I looked like, and I still don't know what you look like, but none of that mattered. You didn't care about the family I was born into. It was what was inside that brought us together, and for that, I will never forget this. I'll never forget you."

Fujak felt the cold metal wrap around his eyes and down his cheeks, stopping just short of his mouth.

"Your face was never your best quality, Fujak... I never knew why I stayed alive... until you came. You gave me hope in life. You are beautiful... beyond words, before I even knew you were beautiful." And just then... Fujak felt something soft on his lips. It remained on his lips for a few more seconds... until Fujak finally understood what had just happened. And without thinking, he kissed her back. It couldn't have lasted more than a few seconds, but his heart raced as if it lasted a lifetime. "My gift to you," Reyna said softly. "I don't want them to see you as a damaged person. I want them to see you as I do... the strongest, most brave person I know."

The cold liquid metal then sealed over the rest of his face.

"Please..." Reyna wrapped her arms around Fujak, her voice choking off into a sob. "Please win this."

"If she is my friend... I have faith in my plan."

Then the drums sounded louder. Movement was heard behind the entrance as the door groaned open. A small light at the end of the tunnel showed him where he needed to go. This was it. The battle was about to begin. Someone's death awaited the moment he entered the arena. It could not be him. He had a new purpose. He had lives other than his own that he needed to save... and that gave him the courage to walk toward the light. To walk toward the sounds of the beating drums and the crowd cheering. To walk toward his unknown fate. Though it had finally settled on him that this could very well be his last night on Gaia, he refused to let Reyna know his confidence wavered. He had finally found who he wanted to become... who he was meant to be. His life could not end right when he found his purpose. Not right now.

"This is not goodbye, friend," Fujak said as the door slammed shut behind him.

* * *

S'rae grabbed the hood of her brown robe and stretched it down over her face. Looking around the grand colosseum for an empty seat, she squeezed in between two men who were jumping to the beats of the drums, slamming their bottles that sloshed about. By the strong stench of Grizzly Beer that oozed off them, she knew they were drunk.

"Bele is... Bele is... f-for sures gonna c-crush that wee' little boy!" one man said, toppling over the other.

"Serves 'im righ'!" another man said, whose belly was practically the size of S'rae.

But S'rae remained silent and hidden. Bele had made her promise to stay discreet, but for a different purpose. She was supposed to secretly make it back to the Golden Palace and warn the others of the dangers they had seen: the Shadow Army. But she couldn't. She couldn't just... let whatever was about to happen... just happen. A part of her did not want to witness it, but a different part of her knew that no matter who died, they deserved someone who cared about them to be there. To show they were not alone during their final moments.

Then the crowd erupted into an uproar as an emaciated boy, wearing a shimmering silver mask, appeared from a tunnel.

"Is that..."—S'rae leaned her head forward to get a better look—"That can't be him... he would never cover his face." S'rae then pressed her hands to her face, horrified. What did they do to

544

him? His face was too handsome not to show; everything inside her knew it was very unlike Fujak to do something like this.

Before she could think more of it, the crowd roared once more as Bele emerged, rising from the sand in the center of the arena. S'rae's heart jumped as she stared at him, looking confident with his head held high and fists clenched. He wore brown robes that seemed designed for peasants, not a professor. Most likely the work of the Warden.

But then S'rea's heart dropped immediately as she watched Fujak limp toward Bele. He seemed unhealthy and unfit to fight in any battle, never mind a Trial of Gods against someone as powerful as Bele.

S'rae did not know how to feel, she could not choose who she wanted to win. They were both special to her in their own way. Bele was the one who had her heart, but Fujak… he was a true friend. He was only trying to protect her, yet she was afraid and thought of him as the killer when he needed her most. What friend would she be to allow an innocent to die for the wrong reason?

Then a horn blared and the crowd erupted into a frenzy of stomps and cheers. She saw sand get thrown into the air, as if this was some type of tradition for the spectators.

But to her, this was nothing to celebrate, only mourn.

Without hesitation, a stone staff had formed in Bele's hands, while Fujak appeared to be desperately searching for a weapon of his own. It hurt to see someone she looked up to as a beacon of confidence appear so defenseless and weak.

Bele quickly swept the staff under Fujak's legs, but before Fujak fell to the ground, he flipped in the air, landed on his hands and propelled a kick at Bele's face. But Bele simply blocked it with his finger as the crowd gasped.

"If you're going to win, please don't toy with him," S'rae thought forward to Bele. "He doesn't deserve this." Her eyes watered just thinking about what she said.

Although it was an exciting battle to watch, Fujak displaying some of his speed and agility with kicks and punches, he appeared much too slow for Bele, who dodged each attack almost effortlessly and landed a few punches and kicks of his own.

Each time Fujak fell to the ground, S'rae cringed as her stomach tightened. But no matter how many times he fell, he kept rising. S'rae could tell by the way Bele would shake his head, that even he wished Fujak would not drag this out.

But S'rae knew Fujak was not one to give up so easily. And what troubled S'rae the most was how Fujak had yet to use any Wind abilities. It was as if his time in Alsi'jin had completely drained him of his power. That thought alone made S'rae feel even more terrible. He never even had a chance.

After a well-placed strike into Fujak's chest, Fujak fell to a bended knee. That was when S'rae's heart pumped the fastest... because Bele's staff had now morphed into a giant axe. Only one thought passed through her mind: decapitation was the most humane, quick death to give a person.

Tears began to flow from S'rae's eyes as she finally accepted that Fujak would no longer be a part of her life. And it was then... when his life flashed before her eyes.

She saw herself atop the Fujita's terrace, overlooking the sky, appreciating the way it would sometimes ripple as if the sky was their lake they could toss rocks across.

Fujak had a glowing smile on his chubby face. He was so adorable with his bowl-shaped haircut and the way he would stutter when he got nervous.

"S-so, S'rae... does this mean... we're best friends?" Fujak's round cheeks flushed red. "Because... it'd be cool to finally tell my family I have one!"

S'rae smiled back at him. "Of course we're best friends! Thank you for making me feel welcome here! Without you, I don't know... I'd probably just be in my room all day."

"Well, I'll help you get more friends then!" Fujak stood up and gazed at the sky below.

"What are you a miracle worker?" S'rae chuckled.

"I'm m-more like a planner. I know how these kids think. None of them actually really like me. They just like that I'm a Fuj... and that my family has a lot of cool things. If I wasn't a Fuj... I'd be a complete loser."

"That's not true!" S'rae said, patting Fujak's shoulder. "I'd still be friends with you!"

"Do you really mean that? Because that's what they all say."

"I do!"

"Well, they say fake friends are only there when they need you... but your true friends, they'll be there when you need them the most."

And after that night, Fujak was right. Children, boys and girls, all swarmed after S'rae to find out how the night went at the Fujita terrace. Only members of his elite family were allowed to go there, so this made her an important topic of discussion.

"Like... is it actually everything they say that it is?"

"Is it super beautiful?"

"Can you walk really walk on the sky?"

"Can you dance on it? I hear they have dance balls on the sky over there!"

Finally S'rae was given the chance to speak. "It was definitely as amazing as they said it'd be."

"Isn't the Fuj family so amazing!"

"Yeah, Fujak is so lucky! I wish I was him!"

"Yeah, imagine if I was Fujak how cool I'd be?"

"Much cooler than him! How can you be a Fuj and be a loser at the same time. That means he's probably the biggest loser in the world."

"Yeah! Imagine if he wasn't a Fuj!"

All the students laughed as they pushed one another around, but

S'rae didn't… she couldn't… it didn't feel right; but she felt so out of place. This was her chance to make friends.

"Yeah, S'rae, and didn't he try to kiss you?"

S'rae's eyes went wide.

"Oh! Fujak tried to kiss you! Obviously you didn't, right!"

"No, I didn't, but that's because we're frien—" S'rae was interrupted.

"Ew, you aren't *actually* friends with him, are you?"

S'rae didn't know what to say. They were all looking at her as if there was only one thing she could say to ever have a chance at being friends with them. She hesitated a few moments longer, feeling guilty even before saying a word. "Of course we aren't *actually* friends! Yeah! Like… he actually thinks he can make a best friend. I feel sorry for the boy." S'rae felt her stomach tighten with disgust after saying that. She felt so sick that she asked to leave, but they kept her around.

All they did was make fun of Fujak the rest of the night, until finally S'rae screamed. "ENOUGH! Fujak is a great boy, greater than any of you will ever be! He doesn't deserve this. He never said anything about any of you… other than the fact that you guys make fun of him. It's wrong! This is wrong! And if this means he's my only friend I have… then I'm okay with it!"

But when S'rae left and met up with Fujak… apparently the damage was already done. She remembered the way his eyes were watery… the way he refused to talk to her or see her.

And as S'rae was thinking about the memory and staring at the boy on his knees ready to die… she began crying uncontrollably. Here he thought he was dying alone… with no friends around… but she was here. She wished she could just let him know what he means to her. She closed her eyes and a million thoughts ran through her head. She didn't know what to do. She heard the crowd gasp and could almost visualize Bele lifting the axe above his head, ready to slam it through Fujak's neck. More tears flowed from her eyes.

What was she supposed to do? Either Bele died, her love. Or Fujak died, her best friend. Or… neither of them.

S'rae then heard a tremendous BANG overhead that rattled her eardrums. The entire crowd gasped once again. Still she kept her eyes closed, tears seeping through the cracks of her eyelids.

Then a quivering voice reached her ears. "S'rae…" Still she kept her eyes closed. "Why, S'rae… why?"

And when she opened her eyes, she was down in the arena, her entire body had hardened into stone as a great axe pressed into her outstretched forearm.

"Because," S'rae said as tears and snot poured from her eyes and nose. "Because fake friends are there when they need you… but true friends are there when you need them the most."

"But," Bele said, his voice cracking as he shook his head in disbelief, "but… they're going to kill you. I can't save you."

"But I can." S'rae heard Fujak finally speak from behind her, with a tone of confidence she had never heard from him before… as if… he had been saving all of his strength for this one moment.

And then it happened, a distinct *SWOOSH* that made her ears perk up as she saw an arrow head straight for her heart. This time, she could barely move. She was practically a statue with an axe keeping her in place. This was the end of her. The end of her story. This was a trap.

But then a BANG rippled the arena. One moment she saw the arrow about to rip through her chest, and the next moment she felt her insides vibrate as she saw a ghost of Fujak pass straight through her body, as if he had somehow broken himself down into molecules, into… sound?

She couldn't explain what she felt… only what she saw, which was a transparent Fujak dematerialize, pass through her body, then reemerge back into a physical form just in time to catch the arrow with a resounding BOOM. A sonic boom?

The blast wave rumpled the arena, the crowd screamed in horror as columns and sections collapsed under this force.

But then S'rae's eyes widened as she saw a person in the audience suspended in air, wrapped up in swirling tentacles of wind. The twister slowly levitated down into the arena.

Fujak was breathing heavily as if this one move took everything out of him. As if this was his plan all along. She thought back to what Fujak had always said: "If you show your strongest hand too soon, you become the target. The trick is to appear weak, and save your strongest hand when the enemy thinks you have nothing left."

"You... you saved me," S'rae said, still in shock. "You knew? How?"

Fujak was breathing so heavily it took him a few moments to finally be able to speak. "This... this is your killer," Fujak said, staring up at the subdued crowd. "Terese."

36

S 'RAE'S BODY HAD MORPHED BACK TO NORMAL as the additional stone from her armor fell to the ground in waves of sand. She struggled for a moment, opening her mouth, then closing it with a confused look, then repeating the process.

But before she could ask what was troubling her, the killer spoke with a low growl. "How did you know, Fujak?"

Fujak ran a hand along the side of his mask. "I was left to think for too long." Fujak glanced back at the tunnel where he entered from. "I remembered how shocked Reyna was to hear you were there. The subtle way you'd bring up S'rae. How the Warden said you were not real. But the question was never if you were real… it was why you were there."

Terese's head tilted slightly as he squirmed a bit.

"You wanted information," Fujak said. "To know that we were friends. That I'd do anything to save her." And hearing that made something in S'rae's stomach wiggle. "And that was when you planted the seed. You wanted me to do the Trial of God to lure her here, knowing she would come."

"You forgot the most important part," Terese said.

"And what was that?"

"There were going to be two arrows. One through her heart, and the other so close to yours that they'd think you were dead. And when you survived, they would know you were innocent. You would get the freedom you deserve."

Fujak's hand clenched a little. "You're a killer, why would you expect me to believe that you cared about my freedom?"

"My only mission was to kill S'rae. I have no desire to kill anyone else. I already had one wrongful death on my conscience... I did not want another."

The ground rumbled, and S'rae looked to the side. The Warden stormed toward her and grabbed her wrist.

"The price will be paid," the Warden growled as he yanked S'rae.

But Bele stopped the Warden with a hand to his chest. "We found who the killer is, this won't be necessary." Bele pointed to Terese, who was still squirming inside the chains of wind.

The Warden glared at Bele. "There was no sympathy when I plead my case about my daughter!" S'rae noticed the pain and anger in his eyes as they blackened. "I refuse to allow my daughter's death to be justified and let this one go!" He pulled on S'rae's arm tighter, feeling as if it'd dislocate from her shoulder.

But before the Warden had moved another muscle, Fujak stuck his hand out and lifted his palm. It angled directly at the Warden's chest. Despite wearing a mask, S'rae saw bright white lights glow where his eyes would be. "I promised... that I would hear you scream."

As the Warden opened his mouth, an aura burst around Fujak's body, looking like silver flames. And with one BANG, a twister wrapped around Fujak's torso, down his arm, and then exploded through his hand, sending a gust of wind that launched the Warden toward the wall of the arena. The Warden screamed the entire time until his body crashed through the base. The colosseum rattled as debris fell from the opening.

A wave of gasps shot through the crowd.

Bele walked up to Terese and said, "I've been waiting my whole life for this. You will take me to the Sol'adari."

"Hah," Terese laughed, "you wish."

Then a gold glow flickered behind Bele's eyes as the ground rumbled. "That was not a question." S'rae noticed how even the killer's body went stiff. She then turned her focus to Fujak.

Fujak did all of this... for her. Without thinking, she wrapped her arms around Fujak and dug her face into his chest. "I missed you so much! I am glad you're okay."

She then pulled away and looked carefully at his mask. When she reached out to touch it, Fujak turned away.

Before S'rae could ask about it, she let out a horrific scream and fell to her knees.

"What's wrong?" Fujak and Bele said at once. Bele attended to her.

S'rae's eyes widened as she felt negative energy course through her veins like barbed wire. "I feel him." Her voice was shaky.

"Feel who?" Bele said.

"Our link... wasn't broken."

"What link? Talk to me!"

"The tracking spell... he's here... Vayp is here!"

At once, drums and horns roared throughout the area. They were so loud that her insides and the colosseum rattled with each BOOM. Then the entire audience erupted into a frenzy of shrieks and screams. Stone peaks formed everywhere S'rae looked as they most likely were transporting themselves to the safe location.

"They're here!" S'rae screamed, looking up. And that was when they saw it. It looked like a comet made of ink, so black that it cast a silhouette against the backdrop of the night's sky. It flew through the air and obliterated the Golden Palace. S'rae saw shadowy beasts drop from the wreckage.

Then the loudest horn yet blared.

"We need to go!" Bele screamed over the roar, and for the first time, she had seen complete fear in his eyes. "Cast the spell and meet with the others underground!" Bele instructed S'rae. "Go! Now—"

But Di'Tukia, Coars, Fa'laz, and Leonna emerged from the ground. They all spoke at the same time, blurting out orders that S'rae couldn't understand.

"Coars, seal up all the tunnels you know of. And find as many hidden ones as you can!" Fa'laz shouted. "We cannot risk any entry! Bele, release all the Sols, we will need all ready for battle." Bele nodded. "And we need to seal GroundStone!" Fal'az looked up and pointed at the open air as dozens more of those shadowy comets were flying over GroundStone's walls.

"I will take the Sol'adari with me," Bele said grabbing onto the chains that surrounded Terese.

But when a comet crashed into the colosseum, dozens of shadowy beasts came running at them.

"Samaniel!" Di'Tukia shouted.

"Nutmeg!" Leonna shouted.

At once, green relics glowed in the sand as Nutmeg, the tiny dog, and Samaniel, a giant saber toothed tiger, hopped out from the ground.

Di'Tukia and Leonna grinned at one another, then at their Sols. "Get them!"

Samaniel ran full speed at the charging shadows as Nutmeg had jumped onto his back. And the moment they slid to a stop, a giant wave blasted from the ground, sending the shadows so far and high into the air, S'rae thought they would land somewhere on the moon.

Nutmeg wagged her tail joyfully as Samaniel drenched her with saliva after one big lick.

"Aren't they the best!" Di'Tukia smiled.

"This Shadow Army is going to learn the hard way," Leonna said. "To not mess with little Nutty and big Sammy."

The two professors bumped their butts together, but their celebration was short lived. Two more comets crashed into the colosseum, but instead of small beasts, the wreckage morphed into—S'rae's eyes widened—they looked like…

"Canavars!" Fa'laz screamed. "RUN!"

But there was nowhere to run, they were surrounded by four fifty-foot-tall shadowy bears, with claws the size of Samaniel.

And as the canavars stormed at them, a fireball shot straight through one's chest as it disintegrated into ash. A girl covered in flames rose from the ashes.

"Lynn!" S'rae screamed.

Then another fireball swooped through the arena, impaling the other three Canavars as they burst into black smoke.

"Retro'ku!" S'rae screamed. A part of her didn't know if she should approach him or not, especially with Bele there. But this was the middle of war, all drama they did have should be squashed, right? And the other part of her was upset that she was useless, wishing she was able to control fire to help out. She shook off the pang of doubt that tightened her chest and made her feel worthless, and she stared longingly at Retro'ku, at the fiery lines burning into his body like hot embers, wishing she could help. Fighting off this Army was too much to ask for them.

Retro'ku did not even acknowledge any of them, his eyes were blazing red and focused.

"More are coming," Retro'ku screamed, but at no one in particular. His gaze remained fixed at the sky, watching more of these shadowy boulders get launched over the wall. "Lynn, stay with the others!" Retro'ku pressed his palms into the sand as the fiery lines that burned on his back slowly traveled down his body into his arms, then onto the sand. The ground glowed with a fiery ancient relic burned into it. And when Retro'ku slammed his fists together, a phoenix as large as a canavar burst from the ground. Its wings, talons, and tail were ablaze with a fire so bright S'rae had to turn away.

And when S'rae turned back around, all she saw was a streak of red smoke and ash blast through the sky, slicing through another comet before it landed.

"We need to seal up GroundStone, they'll destroy us from above!" Fa'laz screamed. Then he turned to Coars, who quickly drew a relic into the sand before Fa'laz yelled at him again. "I SAID GET THE TUNNELS! NOW!"

Bele approached Terese and the moment he grabbed him, Terese's body crumbled into sand. Bele's eyes once again burned gold with rage. "NO!!" He clenched his fists.

Great, the killer was gone, once again, now S'rae needed to watch her back for shadows and the Sol'adari.

She grabbed Bele's arm and said, "I need to go somewhere."

"I'm not leaving you to go by yourself."

"I was hoping you'd say that." And when S'rae turned to Fujak, he quickly looked away. "Fujak… will you come too?"

Fujak said nothing for a few moments, then he replied. "I can't." He turned back to S'rae. "I have a promise to keep." And with a burst of wind, Fujak had dashed back into the entrance where he had come from.

"BE SAFE!" S'rae screamed, feeling pressure build up behind her eyes. And then she ran off with Bele.

"Where are we going?" Bele said, running with his head up. They were in a complete warzone. Dozens of boulders kept launching over the wall, obliterating buildings upon contact. The screams from women and children joined the crumbling of rubble, and S'rae couldn't help but feel guilty for this.

"I should have warned everyone," S'rae said, "like you told me. I ruin everything!"

"DO NOT blame yourself for this! Don't do it!" Bele grabbed S'rae's arms. "This is NOT your fault. You are not a part of the problem, but you will be a part of the solution. Now, where are we going?"

"There!" S'rae pointed at the now destroyed Golden Palace that may as well have been renamed the Dark Palace. That dark inky substance had covered almost all of it, and when S'rae stared at the base of it, she saw too many of the shadow beasts.

On top of the cacophony of destruction, a new noise made the area rumble. When S'rae looked up, she saw the valley that surrounded them slowly lengthen as if they were looking to encapsulate GroundStone within a stone dome. But her heart raced as she saw what was looking down at them.

"Bele...." S'rae pointed a shaking finger to the sky, beyond the shadowy comets that were falling. "We're all dead."

When Bele followed her finger, he too saw what made S'rae's knees buckle. A beast as tall as the sky had its mouth wide open as purply black shadows spiraled around, as if it was a PriMecha loading up a deadly blast. But even S'rae knew that the damage this thing was capable of was far more deadly than a PriMecha.

She saw Earthies transform trees' branches into spikes, spears, and arrows that launched flaming projectiles over the wall and into the Shadow Army on the other side. Though the sky was lit with possibly hundreds of them, S'rae knew that GroundStone's defense still would not be enough. Their wall will fall.

"S'rae... we need to think about leaving," Bele said. "Everyone who stays will die!"

"But not everyone can leave," S'rae said, thinking about the thousands of nomads who came here to GroundStone because they did not have a home. They cannot easily transport themselves like Earthies could.

"This is war, S'rae... deaths are unavoidable."

"But we can at least TRY to stop them!"

Bele looked at the fire inside S'rae's eyes for a moment and reluctantly agreed. "What's at the Golden Palace?"

"A tunnel that I don't think they know about."

"Do you know how to seal it?"

"Di'tukia taught us. But what about them?" S'rae pointed at the shadow beasts that surrounded the Palace.

"Don't worry about them." Bele's eyes turned gold. "Just do what you need to do." And within the blink of an eye, a gold light jolted ahead, blasting the beasts into the sky.

That cleared the way as S'rae ran to where the phoenix emblem would be. She rubbed her palms together and chanted: *"Ma'ne na'faq—"*

But before S'rae finished channeling the spell, a creak was heard, and she looked up. An arrow was pointed directly at S'rae's face.

"I could have killed fifty in the time it has taken me to kill you," Terese said.

"I don't have time for this. If you're going to kill me, just do it now!" S'rae was shocked to hear the conviction in her voice.

The arrow was hesitating a bit. "I have a lot of respect for Fujak…" Terese said, "and it bothers me that someone like him would risk his life to save you. And I cannot help but question why I'm meant to kill you."

"There will be no killing." A voice was heard as a gold light zapped by S'rae. When her eyes finally regained focus from the blinding light, she saw Bele standing over Terese, who was now lying on the ground as if gravity had bound him. A gold aura glowed off Bele and Terese's body, and S'rae couldn't help but question where Bele's power came from.

"If we make it out of this alive," Bele said to Terese, "you're taking me to the Sol'adari, I have something I—" At once, Bele stuck his hand out as a tiger leapt at him. It froze in mid air, a gold glow surrounding it, before it was slammed to the ground. "Your tricks will never work on me."

Bele's eyes, despite being gold, seemed angry and life-threatening, but it all changed once he glanced at the tiger crunched into the ground.

"Z-Zola?" Bele said, his voice now soft. "Zola… is that… you?" Bele crouched down and observed the tiger's features, its horns and stripes that glowed orange. "How… how can this be?" S'rae noticed Bele's eyes fade back to brown as tears welled up inside of them. "If… you are Zola…" Bele turned around and walked to Terese. His steps were staggered as if he was injured. He stomped on the ground as Terese shot upright, bound by rocks that covered his entire body. But his mask was free. Bele slowly reached out, his hand shaking, and grabbed the mask. And after a deep breath, he pulled it off and immediately fell to his knees and cried.

S'rae was taken aback, until he looked at Terese's face. He was not a he… he was a she with short hair and looked like a splitting image of Bele… as if they were twins… as if they were… brother and sister.

"Chesta…" Bele stood up, his knees shaking. "Chesta… it is you."

"I do not know who Chesta is," Terese said.

"It's you!" Emotions caught Bele in the throat as he struggled to say the next set of words. "Y-y-you… you're actually alive. I always believed you were. I never stopped believing."

"You got the wrong person," Terese said.

"You are my sister," Bele said.

"I have no family. My family is the Sol'adari."

As if hearing her say that hurt the most, Bele sobbed into his arm… until a cold voice appeared from the rubble where S'rae stood.

"I absolutely *hate* family reunions." A shadow emerged in front of S'rae. And S'rae felt the air get so cold, her body shivered uncontrollably, her breath danced in the wind. The power was unlike anything she had felt before.

The shadow lifted his head and stared into S'rae's eyes. "Oh… what a lovely coincidence this is. It is you, S'rae." And hearing this *thing* say her name sent a chill through her body so severe, she almost fell into shock. "I happen to have a friend who will be killing you tonight… to get something he has been waiting many years for."

S'rae did not need to think long about who he was referring to. *The traitor.* But what was the *something* he was talking about? Her eyes suddenly went wide. Ah'nyx?

And as if the shadow could read her mind, he nodded his head.

Bele stepped forward. "There will be no such killing here."

The shadow laughed. "Is that… so? Well, it looks like you are already late for that surprise. Many have died already… and the fun…" The shadow looked up at the Mas'ahk in the sky. "… the fun has yet to begin. Once the Mas'ask's blast lands, say goodbye to GroundStone."

S'rae looked up at the Mas'ahk, the purple glow inside its mouth had now multiplied in size, and she saw rocks, debris and leaves slowly float to the sky as if it was made out of a gravity stronger than Gaia's pull. And when she took her focus away, S'rae was surprised to see Bele walk directly to the shadow, almost to the point where their noses could touch.

"You must be a fool… or someone who is ready to die," the shadow said.

"I am not afraid of you," Bele said.

"Oh… but you should be."

"A wise man's quote: never be afraid of something that you could so easily destroy."

S'rae's chest tightened. She knew Bele was confident, but now he was getting in over his head.

Bele tilted his head. "I know many things. But one of the things I *know*… is that you are not the enemy."

"How noble of you to say, while all of your friends are dying."

"You are a mere speck in the universe. A dot in the galaxy. You and I both know… there is a greater danger ahead."

"And how do you know this?" S'rae noticed the shadow's voice was curious, not accusatory.

"Because… we have risen."

"We have risen… and what is that supposed to mean?"

"Why do you think I'm not afraid of you?"

Suddenly the shadow took a step back. And Bele took a step forward. "Impossible. It cannot be!" S'rae heard fear in the shadow's voice. He then whipped a sword out that blazed like a black fire, with dark steam billowing from it. "Prove it!" He then stabbed the sword into the ground as shadows bubbled up to the surface.

S'rae felt her heart collapse as she saw large shadows take the shapes of elephants, rhinos, bears, lions, and every type of animal she could imagine. It then occurred to her… he was resurrecting dead Sols.

But Bele remained unfazed as a hundred or more beasts surrounded them.

"You should have stopped me," the shadow said, "now you are dead."

The beasts screeched as they jumped at Bele, and S'rae felt her heart hammer into her chest… until… a golden BANG erupted from Bele's body.

Golden, fiery wings extracted off Bele's back as his eyes burned a bright gold. S'rae was frozen, unable to process her thoughts, never mind speak. What… just happened?

And it was when Bele roared, a distinct screech so loud and trembling that S'rae felt scared for her life. But then her eyes darted from side-to-side as she tried to recall where she heard that sound before.

She saw Bele with a gold aura and golden wings blazing the night's sky, and she couldn't help but feel like she had seen him before. But where? How? Where did she hear that screech from? She closed her eyes and saw herself at the Valley of Gaia as a shadow leapt at her. This thought still made her stomach churn as the panther dug its claws into her. The poison ran through her veins. Death was inevitable. She was helpless as the poison nearly paralyzed her and the panther lunged in for the killing blow… until… something collided into her and destroyed the panther. There was… a gold glow… and a distinct roar that she had never heard before… or again… until now.

"Bele…" S'rae said, her mouth dropped. "Was that you… who saved me at the Valley?"

Bele turned to her. "It is you… I didn't believe it when I first saw you here. You resembled that girl… but the poison in her veins would have surely killed her… killed you."

"You… you… were the one who saved me?"

"I do not believe in coincidences. S'rae… you are my light."

"Oh spare me this, please!" the shadow said, looking up at the Mas'hak. "So it seems… the dragons have risen. The Legendary Flames are back." To S'rae's surprise, she heard the shadow's voice shake in fear. But then her eyes widened as she soaked in the shadow's words and looked at Bele. *The dragons have risen? Bele… is a… dragon?*

The shadow raised his sword into the air. "I am glad the Mas'ahk is about to remove GroundStone from the map, and you two along with it. THE END IS NOW!"

S'rae looked around and saw that the shadowy Sols were all immobilized by a gold glow, she then looked up at the Mas'ahk, whose mouth was the brightest star in the sky. It resonated a purple glow that pulsated as if it had a mind of its own; and it was so large, it seemed as if it could destroy all of Gaia and the moon.

"Bele…" S'rae hated that she heard her voice shake. She wanted to be brave, but right now… all she knew was that they were all about to die.

The purple ball was getting so powerful that S'rae's hair and clothes were floating into the sky as if it was ready to suck Ground-Stone inside before destroying it. She watched as towers crumbled and floated into the sky.

"Bele!" S'rae screamed. "What do we do?"

Bele still said nothing. He simply stared up at the Mas'ahk for a few long moments as if he was battling with a tough decision. "S'rae…" Bele said, "I have a plan. Do you trust me?"

"Of course I do!" S'rae exclaimed. And she meant it. Around him, she felt safe and secure and unbreakable. And that was before she found out he had a dragon inside of him. Whatever anxiety she had, it would always vanish whenever he said those words: *Do you trust me?*

And with those words, everything around her went white. A glow so strong that even when she closed her eyes and put her face to the ground, she still saw white. And finally when it subsided, and she lifted her head, and opened her eyes, she saw the nose of a golden dragon touching her own. Its glow resonated as if it held the power of the sun and it flowed endlessly throughout the sky, seeming as if it was a winged serpent able to wrap around the planet of Gaia itself.

S'rae kissed the scales on its nose, and pressed her cheek onto it, hugging it as if she never wanted to let go. And she wouldn't have if it weren't for the purple blast that was now on its way down to the planet, ready to destroy GroundStone. The dragon roared as it flew high into the air and wrapped itself completely around the top of GroundStone.

S'rae watched in awe at how majestic and powerful Bele looked, the way he tangled his body in between itself so that there were no cracks for the blast to seep through.

"I trust you," S'rae said, ignoring the rising panic in her chest, the dread she had been fighting since she had first seen the Mas'ahk. But if there was anyone who could stop this beast, it was him. It was Bele.

She trusted him when he said he'd surprise her, and it ended up being the greatest experience she ever had. She even trusted him when a PriMecha was staring her down, ready to end their stories in one blast. And that led to the other greatest experience of her life, when she traveled the world through the sky.

Bele had a way of making the impossible seem possible and this was exactly why she trusted him more than anyone else.

"I have faith," S'rae whispered, squeezing her eyes shut, "and faith will have me."

And then it happened. A resounding BANG overhead followed by the most heart-wrenching screech that rattled the planet of Gaia. And although the noise made her heart collapse, she was happy to see that Bele's plan was actually working. She felt butterflies toss around in her stomach. Some of the purple blast striped through little cracks that fell onto GroundStone, but other than that, S'rae felt her heart swell up with excitement as she saw Bele shielding off the entire attack.

"I knew you could do it!" S'rae screamed. "I had faith and faith had me!"

And after what felt like a year of screeching. The purple glow faded. Bele's plan had worked, GroundStone actually survived. S'rae jumped in the air and waited excitedly for Bele to return back. Any second now, she thought, as the dragon remained exactly where it was, shining a bright gold... that seemed to flicker slightly.

"Bele! You did it!" S'rae screamed, but still the dragon did not move, its golden glow seemed to fade like the purple blast... until it completely vanished, leaving the sky blacker than she had ever seen, much like how her heart felt as she watched the long dragon slowly fade back into a human form that fell lifelessly down to the planet.

She couldn't stop the tears that poured if she tried. She needed to think of something, but pain paralyzed her, freezing her in place. She looked over and saw the shadow, who was grinning as if that was the greatest spectacle he had ever seen.

S'rae thought of Bele... thought of everything he meant to her.

How he was the one who brought about the brightest smile during the darkest times. How he was able to make a girl who felt like nothing, feel like the center of the universe. She thought of how thankful she was that such a person existed during her gash in time. She thought of his beauty, his soul, and his songs. And it was in thinking of his song when an idea came.

She sang and sang, and whistled to the best of her memory. She tried her hardest, but the tears made her voice break. Finally, the first bird appeared, then the next, then the next. Soon after, dozens had flown into the air to catch Bele and bring him down softly to the ground next to S'rae.

A smile slowly began to reveal itself... that was until she watched him struggle to say a word.

"Bele!" S'rae cried. "Bele! Wake up! You did it! You saved us! I knew I could trust you!"

Bele, whose face and body was now charred black, moved his head and his mouth as if to say a word, but nothing came out.

S'rae buried her face into his chest. "Please... please stay with me!" Her tears soaked into his shirt.

And as she sobbed into his burned shirt, she finally heard him speak. "S'rae... pro-promise... m-me... y-you... w-will... l-li-li-live... your life. P-promise me..."

"Not without you," S'rae cried, her hands squeezing what was left of Bele's shirt. "Not without you!"

"Y-yo-your... ne-nex-next... wa-wav-wave... i-is... c-co-co-com-com..."

"Bele!" S'rae screamed as his eyes closed. "BELE! BELE!! NO!!" Her arms wrapped his body that felt as cold as ice. She squeezed onto him, praying to all the Divines that this wasn't happening. But worst of all... this was not the first time she felt like this. This was not the first time she felt the cold body of someone she loved die in her arms. And as she closed her eyes and tears leaked through, a dark memory flashed before her eyes. So dark, she kept it hidden even from herself.

"No! NO! NOT AGAIN! PLEASE!! NOT AGAIN!!!" She kept screaming those words as she saw a little girl playing in the dirt with a wolf pup. She kept screaming those words as the wolf pup bent down to eat an apple. She kept screaming as the wolf pup ate it and began choking furiously. And she screamed as she held it in her arms, his body was deathly cold. And all she thought about was how she NEVER wanted to relive this moment again. It was her greatest fear that she had locked away since that day. And now she was forced to relive it as the love of her life was dying in her arms… yet again. She screamed and screamed and screamed and screamed as it felt like the entire world of Gaia was ripping open.

She screamed so loud that she was unsure if the explosions she heard were from her or not. But all she knew was that she did not want to open her eyes, just as she did not want to when Ah'nyx died in her arms. She knew… the moment she saw him… it would be real, but she just wanted to hang onto the idea that Bele was some-how still alive in her arms, not a shell of who he used to be.

And with one final scream. "NO!!!! NOT AGAIN!!!" She opened her eyes and the entire world of Gaia was on fire, as if it was a hellfire inferno. She saw everything through a red tint as steam flowed from her eyes, tears evaporating before they could touch her skin. And when she looked down, inside her hand was a flaming sword. The brightest she had ever seen.

37

"IT ENDS NOW," S'RAE SAID AS A FLAME BURST from her body and scorched the sky. She was not like herself; she felt nothing, no sadness, no anger, no doubt, nor pain, all she felt was a burning desire to kill this shadow. To end this war. She felt like she had ruined everything, that if only she did things differently, GroundStone wouldn't be destroyed, Ah'nyx would be alive, and Bele would still be here. And as her flaming sword ignited, she said it once more with narrowed eyes that bled flames. "It ends now!"

S'rae dashed ahead and the whole world felt like a blur. The flames that were dancing all around her had suddenly went still as if time had frozen. They remained still as she lunged her sword at the shadow's chest. They remained still as he dodged and leapt high into the air. And they remained still as she blasted through the air, their swords creating sparks as they blocked each attack. It was then when S'rae noticed that the walls that were once slowly meeting at the center overhead, to encapsulate GroundStone within a dome, had suddenly stopped as well.

S'rae couldn't understand how nothing was moving, though she and the shadow had been fighting throughout the entire warzone.

One moment, she struck him and they were in the colosseum as Nutmeg and Samaniel were seen frozen, growling at several Canavars. The next moment, they were exchanging strikes in the Valley of Dreams as hundreds of Sols were lined up in formation, peering down at hundreds of shadowy beasts that seemed to be charging toward them, had they been moving. And then, as S'rae slammed her fist across the shadow's jaw and watched him blaze through the sky like a shooting star, a fire ignited from her soles as she burst toward him, only to realize the next second she was fighting him over the blue waters of Sereni that glowed like stars in the night's sky.

S'rae didn't have time to process what was happening, all she thought about was finding the right moment to kill this shadow, whose speed was unlike anything she had seen. Then he poofed away, and S'rae growled as she followed the stream of smoke, which lead her above the snowy mountain peaks of Fujita. They fought in the beautiful white sky as the severe snowfall appeared as crystals suspended in the sky, like a still painting.

They appeared as red and black flames shooting throughout the sky, until finally S'rae stabbed her sword into the shadow's chest, flames exploding from her feet as she darted through the sky and plowed through the soil of GroundStone like a bulldozer through gravel.

S'rae growled as she watched the shadow struggle to breathe. She was mounted on top of him, with her sword blazing inside its chest. And when she finally spoke the words "I told you the end is now," that was when everything finally came back into motion. The fires blazed, the smell of sulfur hit her nose, the walls slowly closed in, the screams and roars overwhelmed her eardrums, and she stared at the shadow who now coughed up an inky black substance. She did it. She ended the war.

The shadow coughed once more before grinning. "Do you know what happens to a fire that blazes bright?" S'rae dug her sword deeper into his chest as he screamed in pain. And after a stuttered breath, he said: "It fades away just as quickly as it appears."

And it happened all too soon, the fires that scorched all of GroundStone had suddenly vanished. And she felt the fire in her soul douse as well, and saw her sword disappear along with it. GroundStone was in complete darkness, and that was when she felt a tentacle wrap around her neck, so cold it burned around her throat as if she had swallowed magma. It then lifted her into the air. She was suffocating, her entire body wringing in pain, twitching around as she felt her life fading away. She saw white spots appear, knowing that she would pass out at any second… and that this would be the end of her story. And all she thought about was how she had the opportunity to end this… if only she had just went for the kill when she had the chance.

I ruin everything, she thought as the life was sucked out from her. And the moment she squirmed about, feeling the last seconds of her life ebb away, that was when she saw the shadow lift his arm and strike at her chest. She closed her eyes, and knew this was the end. It felt like an icicle had stabbed through her, but yet… somehow… she was still alive, and the shadow loosened his grip around her neck.

When she opened her eyes, she gasped and saw that he had the amulet in his hands. The Eye of Va'han.

"*Where*… did you get this?" the shadow said, twisting it around in his hands with the most peculiar interest.

S'rae's voice was choked off into a gasp. She tried to scream, but it came out as a whisper. "Give that back! That's mine!" It was so soft, she barely heard her own voice. "Give that back!" She whispered again.

"Where… did you get this?" He stared at the way the blue waves spiraled about inside of it.

"It belonged… to the greatest person I knew. You don't deserve it."

At once, the shadow released his grip and S'rae crashed to the ground, holding her throat as she struggled and gasped for breath. "Give that back!" S'rae's eyes watered. She had already lost Bele, and now, all she thought about was how the other greatest person she met was Sianu, and he trusted her with this. It made her feel connected to him, and she did not want to lose him either. She heard his words, to trust that the world was good and with good anything was possible, but where was the good in any of this?

"Give it ba—" S'rae choked. "You don't deserve it! It belonged to the greatest person I know, better than you... you will ever be."

"I don't deserve it?" The shadow twisted it once more in his hand, then tilted his head at S'rae. "And why would I not deserve something that I created?" S'rae's eyes widened as the next few words might as well have stabbed an icicle through her. "I am... Sianu."

And without expecting to, S'rae fell to her knees and slammed her fists into the dirt and burst into tears. She couldn't handle this, not at all. First Bele... now Sianu. There was no way that sweet, innocent boy could be the devil in front of her. She refused to believe that life could turn even the most good of people into... this.

"Oh... but it did," Sianu said, as if he had read S'rae's thoughts. She then saw something like ink drip from his eye. Was he... crying?

"I'm so sorry!" S'rae screamed, her heart feeling like it couldn't take any more of life. A part of her just wanted it all to end already. "I'm so sorry for whatever happened to you!" She cried harder into the dirt. There was no good in life. This was proof of it. Sianu was wrong, and she cried because she believed him. And now, it felt like all hope was lost. There was no having faith. There was no believing in good. There was only the realization that the world was a terrible place, filled with terrible people who will kill the good in life... or turn them evil with enough time.

The shadow took a few steps toward S'rae and she felt his cold presence freeze her tears to her face. His voice, even colder, then reached her ears like a frigid winter's breeze. "I will not kill you, little girl."

S'rae looked up, blinking and wiping the icicles off her eyelashes. Maybe there was still some sliver of good left him in after all.

"Oh no, no, no, little girl," Sianu said, shaking his head. "I did not say you will not die... I only said I will not kill you." S'rae then heard footsteps crunch into the destroyed soil behind her. "*He will.*"

And when the footsteps stopped, S'rae turned around and saw a boy wrapped in black from head-to-toe. She saw him. The traitor.

"Vayp," she growled as she clenched her fists and the ground rumbled.

"I look forward to bringing you Ah'nyx back," the shadow said as he squeezed the Eye of Va'han tighter, then vanished like black sand thrown into the wind.

S'rae's fists clenched tighter as the ground rumbled harder. Slowly pebbles began to lift off into the air, then rocks, then boulders.

A green aura glowed around Vayp and S'rae as sections of GroundStone began breaking off and drifting into the air, until their section did the same. S'rae felt her stomach move about weightlessly as she found herself on a massive island that slowly lifted higher into the sky, which was now fully enclosed by a magical barrier.

Nothing was said between the two of them, but words were not needed. The way the world was crumbling before them, let one another know that they were not going to go easy on each other, not this time. They were fighting for much more than becoming the Champion of Opella or the GroundStone Champion. And it showed. S'rae wanted to prove once and for all... who was truly the strongest between them. There was no more holding back.

And the moment their platform split in half, that was when the first moves were made. They both leapt into the air, stone staffs forming in their hands right before they made contact.

And when their weapons collided, a BOOM rippled the air that launched them backward several feet. They each landed on a boulder and leapt from floating rock to floating rock before finally jumping at one another again.

This time, Vayp's eyes turned green as his staff absorbed many of the rocks that surrounded him, turning it into a massive hammer, the size of a hut, and slammed it down onto S'rae. She quickly hardened her body into stone as the hammer shattered into dozens of pieces, but before the debris fell to the ground, they had morphed into different versions of S'rae, who were now jumping at Vayp and striking him down with kicks and punches.

Vayp dodged each S'rae as he twisted and turned and ducked and jumped to a separate boulder. It was then when he slammed his palms together as one of the rocks formed into a sharp disc. He threw his hand toward the clones as the disc sliced through them as they burst into clouds of dust; Vayp's glowing green eyes darted from side to side, as if he was controlling the disc's routes with his mind.

S'rae jumped off her platform just as the disc sliced through it. She flipped and spiraled in the air, avoiding it two more times before landing on top of it and morphing it into another clone of hers. S'rae then pushed the clone toward Vayp as she tackled him, sending him down to the ground with a devastating crash that made dust billow into the air.

S'rae fell to the ground and landed softly as the ground molded into a pillow-like substance. Her clones landed soon after, sounding like the pitter-patter of rain. They all crouched into a fighting stance, awaiting Vayp, knowing that the fight was only just now getting started.

Green light striped out through the rubble before an explosion sent rocks bulleting toward S'rae. Some of her clones got struck, instantly bursting into sand, while others flipped and dove away.

And when the dust finally settled, Vayp stood there, fists clenched, hood over his eyes, as rocks slowly levitated in the air. With one scream, they shot at S'rae like a machine gun. The clones never stood a chance, but S'rae performed twisting aerials and cartwheels as she evaded the bullets that destroyed everything in sight. The moment she dove behind a tree, it'd collapse; behind a boulder, it'd crumble. There was no place left to hide, and that was when she turned her body into rock and ran directly at Vayp, the bullets deflecting off her body as she accelerated toward him.

S'rae threw her hand back as her fist enlarged into a massive boulder and punched Vayp, watching him smash through countless trees before crashing into a boulder. But before she could smile, Vayp had appeared underfoot and uppercutted her into the air.

She felt her jaw shatter as if his hand was made of stone.

Before S'rae landed, Vayp stomped his feet as two stone hands slapped together, sandwiching S'rae in between them. Then Vayp jumped into the air and lifted his hands as the debris spiraled overhead, creating the largest boulder she had seen, before throwing it down onto her. The boulder was more like an asteroid that cratered deep into the ground.

By the time S'rae had crawled to the top of the wreckage, her once thick layer of rock skin had practically crumbled, leaving her defenseless.

Vayp wiped the blood from his lips, then spat.

S'rae held her shoulder, wincing as if she may have broken it.

The two looked at one another, clearly exhausted and drained of their energy, but neither were ready to give up.

S'rae knew Vayp was here to kill, and it was that thought alone that kept her pushing. Too many deaths had already happened tonight, hers would not be one of them. She stomped her foot into the ground as two rocks lifted into the air, transforming into a shield and scimitar just as she caught them.

And when Vayp tried to do the same, S'rae noticed that he

failed. His shield had turned to mud as it fell to the ground with a splat. It was then when S'rae noticed a glint of silver on Vayp's hand. And suddenly she understood why. Each element had a core value, and that value was where the power was harvested. For Fujita, it was focus and intelligence. For Harahn'de, it was fear and courage. For Sereni, it was clarity and peace. And for GroundStone, it was solely about protection. S'rae had been channeling her spells with the purpose of protecting her life from someone who wished to kill her. But Vayp... Vayp was using Earth for the wrong reasons, going against the balance. The elements did not lie, his agenda was clear, he only wanted to kill, and now the element was rejecting him. He was... converting.

Vayp was becoming... Metal.

And this was her chance to win, she thought, though panic was causing her chest to constrict, and she felt as though she could barely breathe. Regardless, she kicked her feet into the dirt as a wave shot her toward Vayp. Just before it made contact she flipped off and kicked at his head. He ducked and returned with a kick of his own. She blocked it with her shield, and returned it with a strike from her sword. A *clang* echoed about as it struck Vayp's metal arm, and for that short moment, she saw Vayp's sunken eyes glint through the hood; and she gave a gasp of horror. He was no longer the Vayp she remembered.

S'rae's mind was racing. This was the end of *them*. The Vay'rae duo.

Before she could think much of it, Vayp's metal fist shot past her face as she twisted her neck. And so began an exciting battle where they each struck and countered and evaded one another's attacks as the ground rumbled and broke apart at their feet. Their fate was unknown, but one thing was certain, the two greatest pupils of GroundStone were giving the show that every Earthie would have dreamed to witness.

They fought and fought, even when their bodies were bruised

and faces swelled. They fought and fought, even as their chest rose and fell rapidly. Until finally, S'rae's stone fist had collided into Vayp's jaw, just as his metal fist crashed into hers.

They both fell to the ground, and lay there for several moments. The knot in S'rae's stomach tightened. She didn't know what she was thinking about as she gazed at the dome overhead, and that troubled her the most. Her mind was just blank as if everything that had just happened had turned her into a ghost incapable of emotions. A part of her didn't even understand why she was fighting. Why did her life even matter anymore? The world was ending. The Mas'ahk was loading up yet another blast to destroy the barrier. After that the Shadow Army would swarm and overwhelm Ground-Stone, then Gaia… and none of this would matter. It was over. Why still fight?

She heard movement to her side as if Vayp had suddenly decided to get to his feet, so she reluctantly followed suit. Every part of her body hurt as she pushed herself up to kneel, then took several deep breaths before lifting to her feet.

S'rae didn't have the energy to initiate the fight, and by the looks of the way Vayp's chest was pounding out of his robe, he didn't either.

What were they supposed to do now? Someone had to win. Someone had to die.

And it was then when Vayp winced and clutched his metal hand. His head then looked around frantically as he sniffed the air. S'rae noticed his eyes blacken, but what was he up to?

Then a peculiar stench of rust and oil reached her nose. She had smelled this before… it was the smell of a—just then, electrical snaps, crackles, and sizzles were heard as the air around them rippled like static before turning into solid metal.

S'rae looked up and saw a black PriMecha, without question the same one that she had seen at Harahn'de, and it must have been watching their entire fight while being invisible.

PriMechas were the ultimate killing machine that took in data before upgrading itself. And by watching two of the greatest GroundStone pupils fight it out, it now had the information to create even stronger Mechas. And this realization made S'rae's chest tighten harder.

But before she could dwell on the situation, it had lifted its foot, ready to squash S'rae. She didn't have the energy to move, but apparently Vayp did. Before the foot landed, the ground moved quickly, launching S'rae to Vayp's feet.

He… saved me? S'rae thought, looking up at Vayp's blackened eyes as he clenched his metal fist. *Why?*

S'rae didn't have time to answer the question. The PriMecha stuck his palm out and shot a laser that melted the ground just before they dove away. Vayp and S'rae then looked at one another, and though no words were spoken… it felt like they were suddenly ten again, creating a plan with just one glance. S'rae knew what those eyes meant. For right now, this moment, their feud did not matter. The PriMecha was now their enemy. And… the Vay'rae duo was back.

S'rae jumped and kicked the ground twice as two waves spiraled through the air around the PriMecha. They each took their own wave as they jabbed their weapons into the PriMechas frame, to no avail. The wave carried them so high that they towered over the one-hundred-foot tall PriMecha. And though Vayp could only use one hand, the waves then spiraled around them as they created a giant spike. They grabbed hold of it and screamed as they threw it down through the PriMecha's eye, completely impaling it as sparks crackled from the exposed wires.

When Vayp and S'rae flipped to the ground, they nodded at one another, pushed their palms together and chanted, "AL'LAH" as the ground cracked open like ocean waves during a storm. Then they screamed even louder: "HA!!!!" The ground cratered beneath their feet as dozens of spikes shot into the PriMecha. Some were ten feet long, others were twenty, but the longer they screamed, the larger the boulders and spikes became. They screamed and screamed, joining the raucous of rocks exploding against metal, as their hair danced across their faces and their robes whipped out. Smoke and dust filled the air as they finally went silent.

Their chests swelled up with each breath as they looked at one another with the same shocked face they had when they had beaten the Canavar. It was the look that told the story of how this would be another secret of theirs that no one would believe.

Despite not having the energy to even think, a smile briefly showed itself on S'rae's face. That was until a red light glowed bright amidst the cloud of smoke.

"WATCH OUT!" S'rae screamed. With that last of her energy, she twisted her fingers and created a twister that blew them away from the blast radius in opposite directions. S'rae felt her back smash into a boulder, feeling like she was now paralyzed, and Vayp crashed into an uprooted tree.

And when S'rae looked up, she saw that her life was over. Though the PriMecha had a spike through its body, nearly splitting it in half, it still had enough function to lift its foot and end S'rae's life.

She felt the wind wrap around her as the massive foot was stomping down on her. She closed her eyes and braced for the death that awaited. Her entire body trembled as her arms were wrapped across her face. But what happened? Why... wasn't she dead yet? When she slowly unfolded her arms and opened her eyes, she saw the metal sole of the PriMecha's foot an inch away from her face. It was shaking as if there was resistance stopping it from stomping her. And when she twisted her head, her mouth dropped. She saw a dark gray glow radiate from Vayp's silver body. His body, from head-to-toe, was completely metal. Even his eyes looked like a swirling tempest of liquid metal, his hair like strings of exposed wires. His hands were pressed forward, trembling as if it was taking everything he had to channel this ability.

And with one horrific scream, Vayp slammed his palms together as the PriMecha exploded, bursting into thousands of pieces that fell all around them.

S'rae shuffled back on her hands, observing the chaos around her. Did... they actually... beat a PriMecha? A killing machine designed to kill Gods? S'rae then looked at Vayp, who remained still, appearing as a metal statue of himself.

And the moment she opened her mouth to say a word, a silver spear shot straight through her chest.

38

I JUST KILLED S'RAE AND I WILL NOW GET AH'NYX BACK. Vayp kept repeating those words in his mind to stop him from feeling guilty. But he wished he could pinpoint how he felt about her death. He certainly didn't feel happy, but he wasn't sad either.

To the left and right he paced, consumed with anger and frustration, grinding his teeth and clenching his fists, casting angry looks at the corpse of S'rae with the metal spear still inside her chest.

Why was he angry? This was a good thing, right? He was getting what he had always wanted. Ah'nyx would be back in his life; but no matter how many times he told himself that, he still couldn't shake off whatever it was that he was feeling.

He then looked at his hands, arms, and legs, seeing the metal glisten in the night. Was all of this worth it? Sadly, he didn't know the answer.

He walked past the wreckage of metal from the exploded Mecha and glanced down at S'rae's corpse. There she was, lifeless. And though his mind didn't feel a thing, apparently his body did, because liquid metal began pouring from his eyes. He wiped them then observed S'rae's body. His eyes narrowed, shocked to see that there was no trace of blood.

"So it's true." A voice appeared from the shadows as S'rae's body faded away like sand blown in the wind. "You actually are trying to kill me."

It was then when he realized she must have swapped with a clone. She was still crafty, he thought.

And before Vayp could react, a fireball burned into his back. When he turned around, another ball of fire burned his chest, making breathing difficult. He choked on the smoke as two arrows shot at him, ricocheting off his metal body with *clangs*.

S'rae then leapt into the air and spun around like a tornado drifting through the air; she landed five kicks across Vayp's face before he had the chance to defend himself. She was quick, too quick. She then blurred around Vayp, running so fast that he saw dozens of her, until S'rae lunged in, kneed him in the face, then thrust her foot deep into the stomach. He collapsed to the ground, surprised she was able to hurt him through the metal.

S'rae flipped away, and when she landed, she clapped her hands as stone hands grabbed onto Vayp's arms and legs before hardening into rock. He was stuck, finding himself helplessly unable to control the Earth that bound him.

A distinct *SWOOSH* forced him to look up as two arrows bounced off his metal face, feeling like punches from a gorilla.

S'rae huffed and puffed, seeming unsatisfied with her attempts. She then looked to the sky as dark clouds now crackled with lightning. Vayp couldn't help but think if Vy'ken had arrived to fight off the Shadow Army.

S'rae then pointed the bow to the sky and narrowed her eyes as she tried to pull an arrow down. Her hand shook and the ground quaked as if this one move was taking all she had.

Vayp's heart shot upward into his throat, letting out a sudden gasp. He remained motionless, staring at the sky and the dark clouds as they were funneling down into S'rae's bow. Vayp's heart now thumped uncontrollably as the arrow in S'rae's hand began to spark and crackle with electricity, glowing a bright white as if it was Vy'ken's lightning bolt.

Lightning spiderwebbed through the sky as thunder boomed. And after a few moments of silence, Vayp heard the pitter-patter of rain and the fresh scent that followed. Without warning, they were stuck in a downpour. And now... S'rae had the arrow pointed directly at Vayp's head. And he knew his metal would not be able to defend against the power of this arrow. This one was going to be the death of him. And there was nothing he could do about it, no matter how hard he tried to manipulate the ground. Even when he tried to focus on the metal, nothing happened, it was as if him destroying the PriMecha was a moment of pure luck. He wished he knew how to control that power again, it made him feel invincible, but now he was beyond vulnerable, he was the prey, stuck in the trap, waiting for the hunter to kill him.

And she was the hunter. He stared at the arrow in her hands, wondering why she hadn't released it yet.

Lightning crackled. Thunder boomed. The rain fell harder.

Vayp couldn't tell with all the rain, but it seemed like S'rae may have been crying. The arrow quivered in her hands for a few moments, until lightning surged from its tip, creating a fountain of sparks that illuminated the darkness.

The moment finally dawned on Vayp. Here they were, two students destined to be the greatest Earthies at GroundStone... and now one of them was hardened into Metal, while the other had lightning surging from her arrow. But despite the thunder that boomed and the rain that now roared, nothing was said. In fact, since meeting S'rae, the only word Vayp had said was for the incantation they used against the PriMecha. And a part of him knew why. He knew he was unable to say a word to S'rae without tears being involved. There were too many emotions attached to the words directed at her, so silent he remained.

It was then when lightning crackled once more and thunder

boomed, when S'rae finally spoke. "Why..." S'rae said softly before looking away for a moment. She then repeated herself, this time louder. "Why... why did you do it? Tell me. Why?"

The rain poured harder.

And the more Vayp thought about the question, the more he felt his body return to normal. His once silvery hair was now black and plastered against his tan face in waves.

"Tell me, Vayp!" S'rae screamed louder, he could hear the emotion in her voice, the way it would crack. "WHY—"

"You..." Vayp spoke finally, and S'rae went silent. "You... of all people... are asking me... why *I* did it?"

The lightning that consumed the arrow faded away at once. The bow and arrow soon disappeared as well.

"*You...*" Vayp paused, trying his best to fight back the tears. "You did it... *you* did it and you have the audacity to ask me why *I* did it?" Despite his best efforts to stop them, tears began to fall from his eyes. "I cried for weeks. And you said... *nothing*. I needed you... I needed you there for me... and you said nothing. And now I know why." Vayp sniffled as something got stuck in his throat. "Because it was you. You killed Ah'nyx... And you left me when I needed you the most. I had no one left. I had nothing. I needed you. And it hurt." Vayp looked away, feeling his eyes burn from the pressure. "It hurt so much."

At once, the stone that trapped Vayp's arms and legs had absorbed back into the dirt.

And after a few moments of listening to the booms of thunder and the roars of rain, S'rae finally spoke. "I... I ruin everything." S'rae wiped her eyes. "Everything is always my fault." She took a few deep breaths then placed her arms to her side and puffed her chest. "If killing me gets Ah'nyx back, then come on! DO IT! KILL ME! Get Ah'nyx back! But when you finally get everything you wanted..." S'rae paused as her voice had cracked. "I had everything I ever wanted. I had it all here at GroundStone. I had the life that I always dreamed of. But when I had it all... something felt missing." S'rae's voice cracked once more as she took a few deep breaths. "Something was missing... and it was you." This time there was no guessing, it was obvious that S'rae was crying, and something inside Vayp seemed to tug at his heart. "It was you. You were missing. I just wanted you there with me. So... when you finally get everything you thought you wanted, something may feel missing, if I meant anything to you, like you meant to me."

Vayp refused to say a word, he knew the next word he said would be followed with tears. And all he wanted to think about was getting Ah'nyx back.

"SO DO IT!" S'rae screamed as the thunder boomed. "My life is worthless anyways! It doesn't matter anymore!" S'rae then created a dagger in her hand and sliced her arm as blood dripped from the wound. "This is the real me this time! DO IT!"

Vayp picked up the metal spear. And suddenly his stomach became weightless as he received a flash of déjà vu. This... this was the moment he had seen. This was his future. He was surrounded by metal, the spear was in his hand. And there S'rae was, soaking wet with her hands to her sides, ready to be killed. He knew what he needed to do.

He tossed the spear then caught it and charged ahead. He pulled the spear back and then with all his force, he lunged it straight into S'rae's chest. And the moment it broke her skin, a streamline of visions flashed before his eyes. But they were not just any visions, they were hers. Her thoughts, her memories, it was the tracking spell, still linking their minds together.

He saw S'rae in a forest, trying to stop Ah'nyx from eating an apple. Saw her cry as he was choking in her arms. He saw her watching Vayp through a crack in the wall, then run away to a corner where she'd pull her hair and scratch herself. He saw her in a Fujita airship, fighting with them to give her a chance to say goodbye to Vayp. He saw her cry herself to sleep nearly every single night at Fujita. He saw how excited she was when she met Vayp at the Valley, and how wide her smile became when they had be-friended Han'sael. He saw their greatest moments and her most heart-wrenching, but then the one that became most clear in Vayp's mind was when he saw them playing as kids, lying down on a cliff, gazing at the stars. He heard the promises they made: "Vay'rae duo… always and forever."

Then Vayp was brought back to the present with a BANG that rattled the world. And when he opened his eyes, he saw S'rae with her eyes squeezed shut, trembling as tears leaked through the sides. On her chest was a red dot, from the puncture wound, and to her sides was a wall made of metal, stretching to the sky.

"This… was for Opella," Vayp said softly, "because you are family. And you *are* my sister." Though her eyes remained closed, those words made her sniffle. "But the next time… it *will* be for Ah'nyx. I *never* want to see you again."

S'rae's lips trembled.

And when Vayp turned around and walked away, S'rae blurted out, "What about Han'sael?"

Vayp's lips flinched as a tear fell. "He is… gone."

Though Vayp kept walking toward GroundStone, he heard the *splash* of S'rae falling to her knees and then the sobs that followed.

39

FUJAK

THE DRUMS AND HORNS kept rattling the halls as Fujak had ran back into Alsi'jin. The rooms were dark and silent, save for the sound of dust sprinkling to the ground after each boom. He let his hands guide him through each room and hall. If his memory served him well, their room would be right around... here.

"Reyna..." Fujak screamed, "Reyna... are you here?"

"What are you doing here?" Fujak had never thought hearing a voice could bring such a smile to face, but he felt it widen into the cold metal of his mask. "What happened?"

"You're not going to believe it," Fujak said as an explosion roared overhead and the ground shook furiously. "But how do I get you out of this?" Fujak's hands waved madly across the metal, looking for a handle of some sort. "We don't have much time."

"What are you doing? Stop! You're going to get in more trouble."

"I took care of the Warden, we have bigger problems now."

Fujak then heard creaks and groans as if metal was bending and breaking, then he heard Reyna's voice just under his chin. "Took care of the Warden?" Reyna pressed her hands to Fujak's chest. "That sounded sexy coming from you... but... you did it, you came back for me."

"Like I promised." He wrapped his arms around her. "You deserve your freedom." Fujak then paused, feeling his heart throb against his chest, understanding that time was not in their favor right now; but still, he had something else eating away at him that he needed to do. "Reyna... can you open up all of these doors?"

"Yes," Reyna said, with a curious tone, "why?"

"I... want to free everyone here."

"Everyone? Are you sure? There are some bad, *bad* people here."

"Well, let's consider this their second chance."

Reyna paused for a moment. "That was sexy too. I like this new Fujak." Fujak could almost hear the grin on her face.

And as they ran through the halls, Reyna stuck her hand out and grazed the walls as they passed. Fujak would scream out to the prisoners that they were free as the smell of iron filled the halls. It was as if she was melting the doors with just one touch.

On top of the cheers and roars from the freed prisoners, Fujak then heard distinct screeches followed by screams and slashing sounds.

"We need to go!" Fujak screamed, feeling around for Reyna's hand. "They're here!"

"Who's here?" Reyna shouted back just as she grabbed hold of Fujak's hand.

"The Shadow Army."

"The WHAT!?" Reyna shrieked. "Don't you think you should have told me this BEFORE we ran the other way?"

"Then you may not have wanted to save the others."

"And you are most definitely correct! Of course I wouldn't have! What good is freedom if we all die here?"

Fujak wished he had an answer. There was nothing but darkness and painful screams surrounding them, and Fujak had the hunch that these creatures could see in the dark. They were as good as dead.

"You know," Reyna said, "usually the girl is supposed to wait for the guy to save the day, but I don't hear anything coming from you, Fujak. Follow me!" Reyna pulled Fujak as she ran into a room. Fujak then heard a *clang* as if she smacked the metal wall, he then heard more groaning as if she was bending it open.

"You need to hurry up!" Fujak said as he heard more movement outside, like the sound of marbles being thrown on the ground. "They're coming!"

"You saved me," Reyna said as a *pop* was heard. "And now it's my turn to save you. Let's go!" Reyna grabbed Fujak and charged into the wall.

With a tremendous BANG, they smashed through and fell into a large tunnel.

"I know exactly where we are!" Reyna shouted. "COARS! WHERE ARE YOU? COARS!" Reyna paused for a moment, hearing her own echo. "COARS!"

"OH WOULD YER SHUT YER TRAP, I HAVE TUNNELS TER SEAL UP!" Fujak heard a miserable, scratchy voice somewhere down the tunnel.

Fujak was thankful that he was now at least able to have some sight in here. Yes, it was dark, but there was enough light to see that he was running through a massive tunnel. But just when he felt his body calm down, he heard a BANG from where they had just came from, followed by thuds, like bodies hitting the floor.

"Reyna!" Fujak screamed. "They're coming!" But this time, it was his turn to step up. He slammed his palms together as a white glow emitted from his eyes. A roar, like the sound of a turbine, began to hum around them as his hair and clothes danced about. "Hold on tight!" Fujak shouted to Reyna as he placed his palms forward and a serious gust of wind burst down the tunnel. He heard the sounds of bodies crashing against the walls get softer and softer as the gale carried the shadows far away. "This gave us a little more time. Who are you looking for?"

"Our way out," Reyna said as a silhouette of a small man emerged. "And there he is!" They ran ahead; Reyna grabbed him by the shoulders. "Coars, the shadows are behind us, we need to get out of here! NOW!"

"Tayna?" Coars grumbled, and Fujak noticed Reyna quickly glance at Fujak before turning away again. It then suddenly occurred to him, this was Reyna… he was actually now able to see what she looked like. And he was shocked to see that she was… gorgeous, well, at least her brown eyes were. The rest of her head was covered by a black scarf wrapped around her hair, nose, and mouth. "Tayna?" Coars said once more. "What… what are yeh doin' out? Yeh free? Does Fa'laz know?"

"No… I just got out, but we need to go now!" Fujak heard the anxiety in her voice. "Forget these other tunnels, we are DEAD if we don't go NOW!"

Coars' face crumpled as a thin line formed between his eyebrows. "Well, I 'spose won't do no good if I'm dead." Coars took a deep breath as his chest inflated, then screamed as loud as a little person could. "GET OVER HERE YER LITTLE OL' ROCK BABY! I NEED YER!"

Fujak held on to Reyna for balance as the tunnel quaked, then to his surprise, he saw the exact opposite of what he had expected. Instead of a little ol' rock baby, a gigantic snake made of boulders rumbled from the ground, scooping them up, and quickly slithering its way out of the tunnel.

Fujak had no time to celebrate when they escaped the tunnel. The moment the moon's light shone down onto them and the vast Valley, he saw hundreds of silhouettes, some massive, some small, cast on the horizon. The sight of the Shadow Army made Coars gasp. Fortunately, they were not alone.

"Hope we gots 'nuff Sols for this battle here, or we mighta well stayed in der tunnel," Coars said, petting one of the hundred or so animals lined up in formation, their owners standing nervously next to them. Fujak could see their bodies shaking underneath their brown robes. And it suddenly dawned on Fujak just how slim their chance of survival was. Shadows were coming from the north, but he knew it was only a matter of time until they came in through the tunnel as well. And he looked up at the slightly transparent dome that sealed them inside, knowing that a defensive strategy only prolonged the inevitable defeat. To win a war, they needed offense.

Fujak stood at the entrance of the tunnel, practically shaking with adrenaline. When he spotted the approaching figures, he clapped his hands as his gusts swirled around his wrists and his silver mask glowed white. "Get ready! We have company!"

He wanted to remain confident, but inside he felt his lungs collapse. Just when he had found a friend in Reyna... they had to meet under these conditions. But at least if this was how he would die, it wouldn't be alone... and it wouldn't be without a fight.

Fujak clenched his fists as dark clouds swirled overhead, lightning crackling. Soon after, little pockets of tornadoes slowly began to funnel their way down.

And right when Fujak was about to send a tornado into the tunnel, three large Sols with riders came leaping out from it. One jumped off his stone rhino and slammed his foot on the ground as the entrance crumbled.

"This will buy us some time," the boy said as he removed his hood.

"Kaul?" Fujak said.

"That's my name." Kaul looked at Fujak cluelessly. "And how do you know me?" He glanced blankly at Fujak's mask then observed his torn clothes and emaciated body. "I could be drunk and I'd still know who those yummy abs belonged to. Nice to have you back, Fujak."

"Things got a little brighter, at least," Milla said, removing her hood. "We need all the help we can get to protect the northern front."

"Thin is in, don't worry, scrawny." Brick pat Fujak on the back so hard he took a step forward.

"Tayna?" Fujak heard a deep voice from over his shoulder. A large man approached her, wearing a professor's brown robes. "It is you." Fujak heard the man's voice shake with a hint of pain. "I am so sorry you had to suffer."

"It's okay," Reyna said, her hand reaching for his face. "I'm sorry for what I did to you." Her hand slid down into his, and Fujak's mouth dropped as he noticed his hand was glistening with metal. He must have been the professor that she was accused of turning into metal. "I hope your family accepts you one day… you don't deserve this, Fa'laz."

"Thank you," Fa'laz said, a new energy to his voice. "AL-RIGHT! Assume formation!" He shouted as everyone squatted down and grunted. The GroundStone trio's Sols then glowed before transforming. The rhino's stone body doubled in size, thick horns of granite now curled off its body. The rainbow-colored bird's wings suddenly glowed red like magma. And the lion simply disappeared, when just the previous second it was right in front of Fujak.

Then the students stomped their feet and slammed their chests. Each stomp was followed with a loud "GROUND!" then they pounded their chest with "STONE!"

And as the GroundStone chants got louder and louder, Fa'laz began talking. "This is the moment we were born for. This is what we have trained every day to do. We are PROTECTORS! This is OUR HOME! Let's show them why our walls are the most unbreakable in all of GAIA! Let's show them why only fools would attack a fortress of protectors. LET'S SHOW THEM THAT WE DEFEND OUR LAND UNTIL OUR LAST BREATH! Some of us will not make it… and your soul will be given to the lifeforce of Gaia, the very lifeforce that WE ARE PROTECTING RIGHT NOW! So just know that even if you leave us here, just know, we still will be fighting for you! We still will be protecting you! Because we are GROUND! STONE!"

They kept chanting and stomping their feet as the Shadow Army closed the gap between them. And just when Fujak felt his heart leap out of his chest, expecting death to arrive at any moment, a flaming comet crashed into the shadow as a phoenix's tail whipped around, like a fifty-foot long ribbon on fire, slicing down half of the shadows with one swoop.

"Retro'ku!" Milla screamed.

Then another flaming comet exploded more of the shadows, and Fujak saw the way Milla bit her lip and her face went red as a girl rose from the ashes. "Oh, Adalia, that's my girl!"

Before Fujak could question if that was the same Adalia he knew, within a blink of an eye, the flaming girl was standing in front of Milla. The fire faded away, and surely enough, it was Lynn. It did not surprise Fujak that Lynn was mastering Fire, what surprised him the most was how he no longer cared to see someone practicing more than one element. If anything, a smile glowed on his face as he saw the confidence in Lynn's. She made him feel safe.

"I have an idea," Fujak said to Lynn as more shadows came storming in from the horizon. "Light a flame."

"On it!" Lynn exclaimed. She flicked her finger and twisted her hand as a flame rested on her palm.

Fujak pressed his hands to his chest, forming a triangle. He took a deep breath in, and then pushed his hands out as he exhaled. The flame shot out hundreds of feet into the air, combining with the small twisters that had formed. He silently thanked S'rae for this idea. And suddenly, it seemed as if they had a chance. Flaming tornadoes wiped out shadows as they came.

"We need to move quickly!" Fa'laz screamed. "We don't have much time til the Mas'ahk takes out our shield."

And as hundreds of more shadows came piling into the valley, a fiery battle unfolded. Retro'ku and Lynn were seen flying around, shooting waves of fire. Sols were creating earthquakes, launching boulders, and enclosing them in walls. And Fa'laz created massive stone goliaths. But unfortunately, Fujak was right, too many shadows kept piling in and they did not have enough fire to take out the existing ones.

Fujak looked at the battlefield, he saw many students' lives already being claimed, and everything slowed down for him. Death was all around, and what was he doing to help? Hardly anything at all. But he could change that. Yes, his family may disown him for what he was about to say, but he no longer cared about the laws of the land. Right now, there were more important things than broken laws. Survival.

"Retro'ku!" Fujak shouted. "Throw me a hilt!"

Retro'ku smiled as he slashed down a Canavar, flicked his finger then launched a hilt toward Fujak.

And the moment he caught it, a blazing fire burned in his hands.

"Hah!" Fujak heard Retro'ku laugh, which he had never heard before. "I knew you would have the fire in your eyes, Fujak!"

"WATCH OUT!" Fa'laz screamed as a purple blast shattered the dome overhead. The shield broke apart and collapsed like flakes. "This is not good! BUT WE MUST FIGHT!"

Fujak looked up and immediately his eyes widened with fear. He was looking at a shadowy beast as tall as the sky. That must have been the Mas'ahk. If it was able to destroy GroundStone's shield with one blast, how could anyone defeat it?

He looked down at the flaming sword in his hand and suddenly felt so insignificant compared to that *thing*.

And now more shadowy boulders were shooting through the air. This truly looked like the end of the world. Within minutes, there were now thousands of shadows approaching them. Retro'ku and Lynn had already seemed overwhelmed. Now it was overkill.

"Where is Gabrael and Raaz'a?" Fujak shouted.

"They are beyond the walls, taking them out before they enter!"

That was the only idea he had to prevent the impending doom. He then glanced at Reyna, who everyone else seemed to know as Tayna, and thought of how special she was. Fujak knew that there was no such thing as a coincidence. She must have been a part of their destiny somehow. That was why she remained alive, though she questioned living. He knew she was destined for much more. There was a reason why she failed at Earth. A reason it rejected her and made her control Metal. And a reason why she hadn't found her Sol or her element. She was not meant for Earth... she was meant for more.

"Retro'ku!" Fujak screamed, then glanced at Reyna. "Throw her a hilt!"

And as the hilt flew through the sky, Fujak's stomach felt weightless, as if he had lived this moment before. It was déjà vu.

And the moment Reyna caught it, Fujak witnessed the most beautiful sight he had ever seen.

An explosion rattled the sky as blue flames scorched so high the clouds overhead evaporated.

Fujak was at a loss for words. Everyone was. Even the shadows had stopped for a moment to watch the blue flame blaze so bright.

Retro'ku was the first to speak. "Can this be—first the golden... now the azure. They are back. They have risen. She is... a Legendary Flame."

"What's a Legendary Flame?" Reyna shouted, a tint of blue glowing on her skin and clothes. "What does any of thi—"

A piercing, loud screech then interrupted her.

Fujak looked up to the sky, searching for where the sound came from. And then flutters were heard, as if an airship was landing... but instead of an airship... it was a—Fujak felt his jaw drop—a dragon.

It screeched as it landed directly in front of Reyna. It was massive with four legs, blue scales and bat-like webbed wings that arched off its back. And to Fujak's surprise, Reyna was not scared, if anything, she stared into the eyes of the dragon as if it was a past lover, a friend, her child... her Sol?

A black smoke poofed in front of Reyna, and Retro'ku emerged. "She is yours," Retro'ku said.

"What do you mean... mine?" Reyna's eyes widened.

"You are a Legendary Flame... a true Protector of Gaia... and she is your dragon."

"I have a... I have a.... DRAGON!" Reyna squealed. "Err... what do I do with it?"

Retro'ku simply nodded at the shadows that barreled in.

Reyna then grinned and pointed at the shadows. "Err... ATTACK!"

And just like that, the tide had turned. The shadows never stood a chance. The dragon flew through the air, shooting waves of blue flames that incinerated them upon contact.

It couldn't have lasted more than a few minutes. And when the dragon landed and nudged its nose again against Reyna's face, Fujak appreciated the way Reyna's eyes smiled so bright. She found her purpose.

"I believe we have a chance now," Retro'ku said to Fujak. "This area will be safe with you all here. I can now help out the others." He then nodded at Fujak with a congratulatory smile. "I believe you may have just saved us."

"AHEM!" Reyna coughed loudly. "Oh sorry, I'm just the girl over here with the DRAGON!"

Retro'ku smiled. "You saved us as well."

"That's right." Reyna grinned at Fujak and curtsied.

Fujak loved how adorable she looked just then. He immediately dashed ahead and hugged her. "I always knew you were special," Fujak said.

"And if we make it out of this alive," Reyna looked up at him and touched his silver mask where his lips would be, "I want another kiss!"

Fujak wished she could see how wide his smile was just then. "I would be a fool to refuse."

But Fujak's content mood faded the moment he saw Retro'ku walk away with clenched fists that blazed a fiery red. "Where are you going?"

Retro'ku stopped and took a deep breath. "We may have won this battle…" Retro'ku looked up at the Mas'ahk as his eyes narrowed. "But I have seen my future, we have yet to win the war."

40

MOONLIGHT POURED INTO THE center of GroundStone. It was a warm, soothing light, despite the chaos of war that surrounded Retro'ku. It glistened past the courtyard as rodents scurried by. It lit the dying flames from the torches that lined the pathways. But most importantly, it glowed down on the monument of a beautiful girl named Olivia.

Retro'ku analyzed the statue made from a special type of stone that became transparent like glass, he noticed the lively glow on her skin, as if she had never died. This design truly kept her body preserved, just as Gabrael requested.

He appreciated the serenity of the scene, of this moment. It helped block out the screams and cries and explosions and allowed him to focus on the true danger that awaited. But he couldn't help but notice two sparks dancing throughout the sky like shooting stars. A part of him wished he could go and help Gabrael and Raaz'a, he knew there were too many shadows beyond the wall, even for a God and his Guardian; but he also knew where he was destined to be. It was here where he had seen himself in his vision, one of the many that showed he was never strong enough; so he trained and trained for this moment, and now he needed to focus on the true danger that awaited.

Retro'ku closed his eyes and relied on his other senses.

It was then when he heard the danger arrive. It came in through the sound of whispers masked as footsteps that chilled the ground. He felt it; the way the warm air had changed its texture, feeling as if a thick sheet of ice had pressed against his back, raising his hairs. And then he smelled it, the scent of rotten corpses that burned his nostrils.

"Brother," Retro'ku said as a chilling cold passed by him, yet still his eyes remained closed.

"It has been three thousand years… and you still know when I arrive," the voice said.

Retro'ku's eyes remained closed, even as he felt the presence approach so close, the cold from his body made Retro'ku's sweat freeze to his skin.

"It has been three thousands years, seven months, and twenty-seven days," Retro'ku said.

"You remember even down to the date, I am impressed."

"It is easy when you think about that day more than you think of the present." Retro'ku's eyes remained closed.

"Nothing has changed… you still find ways to waste your life away. Do you still train more than you sleep and eat?"

Retro'ku simply nodded.

"All this because of the vision I gave you. You cannot change what you saw. The end will happen as it always does. Instead of trying to change what you cannot, maybe you should have tried to… live."

"That was not the only reason I trained," Retro'ku said, disregarding the seed of doubt he tried to plant.

"Is that… so?"

"I trained so I would be ready for the challenge…"—Tears began to leak through Retro'ku's closed eyes—"… so you would not have to."

"LIES!" Frigid air passed through Retro'ku.

And then it happened all too quick. Retro'ku had opened his eyes and instantly wrapped his arms around the shadow before he could react.

"I have missed you, brother," Retro'ku said, hugging the shadow, whose arms were outstretched. "I have missed you so much… Sianu."

"Why?" Sianu said, frozen as if he did not know what to do. "I am a monster."

"Not to me."

"LIES!" Retro'ku felt a wave of cold air chill his insides.

"I will never think of you as a monster. It was not your fault." Retro'ku squeezed the shadow tighter. "Even you knew you were not ready. That was why I trained. So I could take the challenge, not you."

"DO NOT LIE TO ME!" Retro'ku saw dark shadows swirl inside Sianu's eyes, like ink in water.

"I have waited over three thousands years to tell you this, I have no desire to lie."

"But… they told me you were too scared to. That you did not want to die."

Retro'ku pulled back. "Who would tell you such a thing?"

"Gabrael… and Raaz'a—"

Suddenly a blaze of light shot through the sky and landed next to the monument. The fire scorched for a few moments before revealing Gabrael in charred and ripped clothing. He was breathing heavily as if the battle beyond the wall was too much for him.

"That is *not* the truth, son." Gabrael's voice made the ground tremble. And Retro'ku turned to Gabrael with narrowed eyes that blazed.

"Why would he lie about this, father?" And for the first time ever, he had spoken to his father, the King of Gods, with a tone of defiance. "He died because of it…" Retro'ku felt a sting behind his eyes. "Why… would he lie about this?"

"Precisely, brother. I should have listened to Heron'da when she told me NOT to trust anyone, especially you." Sianu pointed his finger at Gabrael. "I should have listened."

Gabrael placed his hand on the monument. "You knew of her… as Heron'da. But she had spent the rest of her life known as Olivia." Gabrael looked up at Olivia's crystalline face, reflecting the moon's light.

And as if just now noticing the statue, Retro'ku saw what little life was left in Sianu's face, completely drain away.

Sianu's face dropped, the shadows that swirled in his eyes went still. He slowly walked toward the statue as the shadows in his eyes now poured down his face like ink. "My… Heron'da… My light." He disregarded Gabrael and reached past him, lifting his hand up to touch her face. "I am doing this… all of this… for you. We will be back together. In our next life."

"It does not have to be this way, son," Gabrael said.

"It is easy for you to say that, you are not the monster of this world," Sianu said, his face now planted against Olivia's stomach.

"Oh… but I am," Gabrael said, and Retro'ku heard the pain in his voice. "I have done far worse things than you."

"Well, none of this matters, Gabrael," Sianu said. "Your destiny is ruined. I have broken your Chosen Ones right from underneath you. Vayp is on our side. And by now… he would have killed S'rae to get his precious Sol back."

"I am sorry to disappoint you, son," Gabrael said, "but he did not kill her."

"IMPOSSIBLE!" Sianu roared as the ground beneath them turned to frost. "He knows what awaits him. Much like Retro'ku, he had seen his future… And there is *nothing* more powerful than the connection one has with their Sol. He would do *anything* for it. He would never spare her life. I made sure of it."

"That is where you are wrong," Gabrael said. "He did spare her.

For... there is only *one* thing more powerful than the connection one has with their Sol. I would know this." Retro'ku clasped onto his hands as Gabrael's eyes drooped with a sadness he had never seen from his father before. "For I had made that choice as well."

"Vayp..." Sianu said so softly that Retro'ku barely heard it, "he... loves her..."

"This is not just love, it takes the strongest kind of love to make a decision like that; a love people could live a lifetime and never once experience its power."

"What do you know of love?" Sianu growled.

"Everything." Gabrael walked up to Sianu so that they were now face-to-face. "See for yourself. See what happened." Gabrael grabbed Sianu's hand as steam sizzled. "I trust you inside my mind, the most dangerous place you could be." Gabrael placed Sianu's hand to his head. "You will see what really happened that day."

* * *

The Valley of Gaia looked elegant and rich, filled with trees that held leaves of vibrants colors, hills of bright green grass, a sky that was crystal blue with fluffy clouds powdered about, and of course the sweet sounds of fun and laughter. Students in their red robes were training against one another, flaming swords in their hands, while others were racing through the sky, fire erupting from their soles as they blasted through large, floating rings made of black smoke. And then there were the brothers: Retro'ku and Sianu, sitting atop a massive statue of their father, as they watched the students train below.

"So when do you leave?" Retro'ku said, kicking his feet out. His dark skin glistening against his red robes. A black headband wrapped around his forehead.

"Mother says soon," Sianu said, who appeared as a slightly younger clone of Retro'ku. "Will we be able to have an adventure today before I leave... or..." Sianu looked away, seeming embarrassed at the idea of asking for attention, "or... will you just be training all day again."

"You know the answer to that," Retro'ku said. "I have seen my—"

"Destiny... yes, I know... a part of me regrets ever showing you it... that's all you wish to do now. You do not wish to live... only train. What good is this life that you are given, if you are only wasting it away?"

"Because... if it means *you* are able to live beyond that moment, it was not a waste at all," Retro'ku said before standing up. "I will see you when you come back, brother. And then we can go on an adventure."

"Promise?" Sianu's smile became wide.

"I always keep my promises." Retro'ku smiled back.

"That is what I have learned from you. As do I."

Retro'ku placed his hand on Sianu's shoulder, then unwrapped the black cloth around his head before placing it into Sianu's hand. "I wish you luck at GroundStone. Why will they be sending you there? Isn't water your greatest element? You do value family and love above all else, after all."

"And trust," Sianu smiled. "But, mother made me promise not to tell anyone about why I will be there."

"I am sure it is for good reason."

"I could only hope." Sianu's smile wavered.

"Will you be sad that you cannot take the Book with you?"

Sianu then grinned for a moment as he glanced at his shadow on the ground, which seemed to place its hands to its mouth as if it was giggling. "I suppose yes."

"Will you be ready for the Challenge?" Retro'ku's eyes then dropped slightly.

"I do not know... but I suppose they will choose whichever student would be best for it." Sianu's smile wavered.

"Which is me," Retro'ku said.

"Not while the Great Sianu is here," Sianu laughed, and Retro'ku hugged him with a laughter of his own.

A horn then blared, vibrating the statue underfoot. "I suppose it is time."

"Farewell, brother!" Sianu said. "And do not take the challenge while I am away, I will be prepared soon enough."

"Farewell."

Then the Valley of Gaia wisped away into dust that swirled around an empty void before creating the scenery once more. But this time there were no lush trees or vivid terrain, it was a battle-field, with many red-robed bodies lying lifelessly on the ground. It was then when a metallic figure, far off in the distance grew so tall its head was as high as the highest peak.

Gabrael was seen creating an orb in his hand, so bright it seemed to hold the power of the sun itself. And as he released the devastating blast, the Valley of Gaia once again dematerialized then drifted away like sand; and the next moment, Gabrael was in a dark, underground hall, where two golden doors were the only source of light.

He was sobbing uncontrollably as he held a lifeless boy in his arms. It was Sianu, a black headband wrapped around his forehead.

Gabrael cried and cried as he lifted him up and brought him into the center of the courtyard.

"What happened!" screamed Retro'ku as he burst into the ground, like a flaming asteroid. "What is wrong with Sianu! Why is he not breathing?"

When nothing was said, Retro'ku dashed to Sianu and held him. "What is wrong with him?" He touched the headband on Sianu's head as tears and snot poured from his face.

"He failed the challenge," Raaz'a said.

"I told you he WAS NOT READY!" Retro'ku screamed. "I TOLD YOU I WOULD TAKE THE CHALLENGE!"

"There was no time," Raaz'a said, attempting to comfort Retro'ku. "And you know how Sianu is... he did not want to risk seeing his brother take it."

"BUT I WAS READY! HE WAS NOT!" Retro'ku screamed as lava spouted through the cracks in the ground. "No! Sianu! PLEASE! NO, I promise... I promise you we will have our adventure!"

"Raaz'a." Gabrael approached him. "Why would he feel he was ready?"

"He had just arrived back from GroundStone... and saw that all of his friends had died... and he said that there was no more time to waste." Raaz'a wiped his eyes before hugging Gabrael. "But... there is a way to bring him back." Raaz'a lifted his head and met Gabrael's eyes.

The lava that had spouted in the air froze into blue waves as if time had stopped. A chilling cold swept through the Valley, turning it into a tundra at a moment's notice.

"Harahn'de..." Gabrael said, looking up at the elegant draghoenix that was screeching and soaring in the sky.

Raaz'a nodded. "You must lose the life of a loved one... in order to bring one back. This is your Sol... a symbol of your connection with Eve, the hybrid of Eve's dragons and the Fire's phoenix. This is no simple sacrifice. The one who controls Harahn'de... controls the world."

Gabrael looked away for a moment, staring at the ground with a burning hatred, despite the snow that circled around him. "There is a connection greater than that one has with its Sol," Gabrael said as Harahn'de screeched and landed in the courtyard. The enormity of its presence caused the ground to break open and for lava to burst through the snow. The way purple and red flames ignited from its talons, feathery-webbed wings, and long tail, showed that he harnessed flames that not even a God could control. Harahn'de truly was the most powerful being in all of Gaia... and here it was, gracefully bowing its head as it knew it was about to be sacrificed.

Gabrael walked to Harahn'de, tears leaking from his eyes as he pet his best and oldest friend. His Sol.

No smiles were seen as the ceremony was performed. As the flames that scorched from Harahn'de turned to ash that darkened the snow, Sianu rose from the ashes.

But there was no celebration, his body now blacker than the night overhead. He was one of them. He was a Shadow.

Sianu erupted into a black flame and vanished without a moment's notice.

"Was it worth it?" Raaz'a said to Gabrael, whose eyes lit up at the question.

* * *

"Was it worth it?" Gabrael heard once more as he was snapped back into the present with a sharp pain inside his stomach.

And when he looked down, he saw a black, fiery blade poking out from his shirt.

Gabrael coughed blood into Sianu's shocked face as he turned around and stared into the blackened eyes of Raaz'a, who was now covered in shadowy flames.

"Geddon *will* be reborn," Raaz'a growled.

* * *

Retro'ku remained still like a statue, frozen in shock, trying to process what he had just seen and why. Within the blink of an eye, Raaz'a had burst into a black flame and stabbed Gabrael. But why? Retro'ku felt the world spinning too fast, feeling as if he was going to throw up. It was already bad enough that the shadows were massacring GroundStone, the Mas'ahk was loading up another blast that had purple waves swirling inside its mouth, and the world seemed to be ending; but then this... a betrayal so deep that it made Retro'ku finally give up all hope.

This truly was the end. And there was nothing he could do about it, no matter how hard he trained, he was not prepared for *this*.

"It was... you," Sianu said in barely whisper, his eyes still wide. "It... was you who mother was afraid of. The reason she fled to GroundStone. It was you who lied to me and made me believe that

I was ready... and that Retro'ku was not. I... trusted... you." Retro'ku saw black flames burst from Sianu's clenched fists.

"You are forgetting the most important piece, young apprentice," Raaz'a growled as he slid the sword out from Gabrael's stomach, who fell to the floor with a loud thud. "It is I who am your Master." And that statement came as much of a shock to Retro'ku as it did Sianu. "I took you under my wing and taught you how to survive as a shadow. I told you how you could get your old life back, with the Circle of Time. How you could get *her* back!" Raaz'a pointed at Olivia's statue. "It is I who planned all of this, even down to *this*." Within a blur, Raaz'a had snatched something deep inside of Sianu, as if he had grabbed his heart. But it was no heart at all, it pulsed with a vivid white glow. It was... the Eye of Eve. "And with this... I will now be able to control Gaia's greatest weapon. Just as I had planned." Raaz'a glanced at Sianu. "Yes... even your death was a part of this plan. This is our destiny. This is your destiny. The Circle of Time will remain."

Gabrael coughed as he squirmed about on the ground.

Raaz'a then leaned closer to Gabrael. "I had to watch and suffer as you killed all of my people. Now, I want you to witness what betrayal feels like. I trusted you. I was the one who convinced them to come and fight alongside you, and you killed all of them out of fear. I *trusted* you when you said peace could exist for all of us. I suppose your saying is true: *Those who are not embraced by the Fire, will burn the world down to feel its warmth.* But I enjoy this one more: *The one who controls Harahn'de... controls the world.*" Raaz'a squeezed the Eye of Eve tighter.

Retro'ku's eyes widened as he suddenly realized Raaz'a's plan. He was planning to resurrect Harahn'de.

Not today! A flaming sword combusted into Retro'ku's hand as he dashed toward Raaz'a.

Raaz'a effortlessly parried his attack with his shadowy sword. Retro'ku struck and struck, following Raaz'a into the air as they rocketed throughout the warzone of GroundStone.

"It is too late, Retro'ku," Raaz'a grinned. "Your prophecy did not lie. You will not win. You must choose… continue to fight me… and watch your friends and GroundStone perish. Or… help them, and watch me leave. Choose wisely."

Though Retro'ku's blade kept sparking as it hit Raaz'a's, the situation dawned on him. A part of his mind was focused on the shadows below, watching them slaughter the lives of many, and the other part was focusing on landing a killing blow on Raaz'a, which seemed to be increasingly impossible the more he thought about the deaths below.

"Then I will try both," Retro'ku screamed. He punched Raaz'a across the face, sending him higher into the sky, then he burst through the battlefield, killing a few canavars before they crushed two of the female professors, who fought alongside their dog and tiger Sols. He then blazed through GroundStone and helped out Lynn and Fujak and Reyna, who seemed overwhelmed by the thousands of shadows surrounding them. And after all of that, and killing a few hundred shadows, he still had enough time to rocket into the sky and continue fighting Raaz'a.

This was why Retro'ku had trained. His father was no longer able to fight, Raaz'a was a traitor, and the only other pupils of fire were just students. He was the only one. It was him and him alone who could stop this. But how? Raaz'a was correct, the more he fought Raaz'a as they blazed through the sky, the more deaths he witnessed when he tried to help the others below. He could not do both… but he could not let Raaz'a flee with the Eye of Eve.

What do I do? Retro'ku wished he had someone nearby who could help him decide. And it was then when he heard a soft voice that made his heart flutter. "… the *Kiya'shin?*" S'rae's voice appeared in his mind. And as much as he had hated it when she had said it… it suddenly occurred to him… that it was the only option.

Yes… that would mean that everyone here would die… but at

least the Shadow Army and the Mas'ahk would as well. The alternative was that everyone else still died, while the Shadow Army lived on.

Raaz'a and Retro'ku then burst through the sky and landed back into the center of GroundStone, where, to Retro'ku and Raaz'a's surprise, Sianu was comforting Gabrael.

"I am sorry," Sianu said to Gabrael. "I just don't want this to be how you remember me. I just want to go back to the old me. I just want my old life back. I don't want to be the monster."

"But you are the monster," Raaz'a said. "None of us chooses how the world views us. There will always be someone *they* wish to cast away, to say they are the villain. Well, we have the chance to change that, with Geddon. Through him, we can control our destiny."

"I am..." Gabrael coughed, "sorry..."

"Do not apologize." Raaz'a shook his head. "Do not. You were my friend. You had me believe that peace could exist between the *normal* ones... and the ones who were different. Do not apologize. You sealed your fate the moment you allowed fear to control your actions." Raaz'a gazed at Sianu, who was still hunched over Gabrael's body. "Now watch your world crumble."

Raaz'a stuck his hand out as black lightning channeled into Sianu, lifting him into the air as he screamed so loud, Retro'ku needed to hold his ears. Shadowy sparks crackled from his body, landing on the ground as black puddles. "You will be mine once again, Sianu! Do not show sympathy for your father, he is the enemy!"

And as lightning surged throughout GroundStone, Sianu slowly floated back to the ground. "I am yours, Master."

"Splendid." Raaz'a smiled. He then looked around at the debris and rocks and uprooted trees that were drifting into the air before glancing up at the Mas'ahk, whose mouth now held a massive purple ball. "Ah, it appears the final attack is ready. Say goodbye to GroundStone. Unfortunately, I will miss out on all the fun, we must go."

And before Retro'ku could take another step, Sianu and Raaz'a disappeared into a black mist.

Retro'ku dashed quickly to Gabrael as the layers of stone and bricks that made the floor broke apart and floated into the sky. "Father... the world is ending."

"Run... flee... live another day," Gabrael spoke in whispers.

"I cannot run... there are too many lives that will be lost."

"But you will be the King when I am gone."

"And if I were to become a King." Retro'ku stood up with a conviction of fire that burned in his eyes. "Then this is how I will lead."

"What are you doing?" Gabrael grabbed onto Retro'ku's pants.

"The only thing that is left to do," Retro'ku said, staring up at the Mas'ahk.

"Don't... you'll become a monster, like me. I don't want you to live in that shadow."

Retro'ku said nothing and took a step toward the Mas'ahk as more trees and boulders were lifted into the sky towards its blast.

"Please... Retro'ku," Gabrael croaked. "The Gods will punish you. It is the most sacred of the Shinshei laws."

Still, Retro'ku said nothing as his eyes and hands caught fire.

"RETRO'KU! PLEASE! YOU CAN DIE FROM THIS!"

Retro'ku looked back at his father as his clothes and hood gravitated toward the sky. "Then let that be my punishment."

With a resounding BANG Retro'ku rocketed into the air, darting past trees, rocks, and broken statues.

He suddenly came to a stop, staring up at the Mas'ahk, feeling the force of its blast pull him in.

"All the training I've done truly meant nothing. I was not strong enough... but maybe... I never needed to do it alone. Maybe..." Retro'ku stuck his hands out as fire swirled around his palms. "... maybe... I needed help from others all along." Retro'ku felt his eyes swell up. "I just hope some of us survive…"

Retro'ku closed his eyes as flames spiraled around his hands, growing in size. It was then when something happened. The screams that he had heard seemed to fade away into silence, as if they were dying and there was no more fighting to be done. The ground then became a deep white frost, spreading throughout GroundStone with a ripple. Within seconds, GroundStone had turned into a tundra covered in white, with the only sign of color coming from these ghastly streams of light that flowed into the air toward Retro'ku, looking like an aurora borealis.

These streams were the lifeforce from every living being down below. The Sols, the animals, the trees, the rocks… the humans. The more Retro'ku channeled the spell, the more light that floated into the sky, and the more white the ground became.

Snow now fell, dancing with the colorful glow of the sky. But as beautiful as this setting looked, one sight of Retro'ku's eyes and the way they blazed with a fiery inferno, would make even a God tremble with fear.

Retro'ku's body shook with an energy he had never felt. He suddenly understood what Gabrael meant when he said he could die. This power was so overwhelming, he felt his heart hammer into chest so hard, he felt his ribs breaking. But still he kept his palms open as the fire within them glowed bright, almost as bright as the purple moon that was bearing down on him.

The same purple moon that had released itself as it now fell toward GroundStone.

Retro'ku clenched his fists. It was now or never. A red aura burst around him, scorching hundreds of feet, practically reaching space. He placed his palms together as the purple blast slowly pulled him in. He felt the world break its axis as buildings now gravitated toward the sky. This truly looked like the end of the world.

"BUT NOT TODAY!" Retro'ku screamed as he felt his veins bubble through his skin. "*KIYA'SHIN!*"

And everything went white. He felt the life completely drain from his body as a ball of fire, the size of a moon, collided into the purple blast. Retro'ku felt his stomach lift as he fell weightlessly through the sky. His eyes barely had enough energy to stay open just enough to witness the *Kiya'shin* overwhelm the Mas'ahk, sending it deep into space as if it was now a shooting star. And as Retro'ku fell, he saw streams of light break off into thousands of fireworks that exploded the sky. The light zipped and blurred by him as they penetrated into the Shadow Army.

It felt like he was dreaming. And all he could think about was the question: "Was it worth it?"

The Shadow Army was dying. The Mas'ahk was finished. GroundStone was destroyed... and all its people along with it. And now... as he fell to his own death, he could not help but think... *Was it worth it?*

He had been alive for over three thousand years... yet he never really lived. And it was this realization that he had right before his head smashed into the ground.

His eyes shut as he felt his skull collide into the earth, but for some reason, it was soft, not hard. The fall surely should have killed him. And instead of breaking through the soil, he felt himself passing through it as if it was a stream of feathers that then bounced him back into the air as if the ground was a pillow.

It was then when he felt cold hands reach around him and lift him up. He didn't have the energy to know what had just happened or how... but all he wanted to do was thank this person... whoever he was.

Retro'ku opened one eye just enough to catch a glimpse of a hooded boy with brown eyes and a scar on his face.

Retro'ku then passed out as he let out his last word: "Vayp..."

41

VAYP

WHEN VAYP LOOKED DOWN INTO HIS ARMS, he saw a shattered prince who had given his life to save a Kingdom. Vayp wished he was half as brave as Retro'ku, but more than that, he wished that he would survive. But judging by how numb his cold body made Vayp's arms feel, Vayp knew that there was not much hope left for him.

This warzone was far from the GroundStone he remembered. It seemed drained of everything that once made it special. Instead of the life pulsing through the streets and the golden towers and peaks, now, it was a barren, wintery graveyard, with cold bodies covered by a thin layer of frost and snow. There seemed to be absolutely no survivors. But still he trudged away to make it to what he thought was the center of GroundStone. There was nothing around that resembled it, all that was left was a statue that somehow remained remarkably untouched.

To his surprise, he recognized the person inside this glass figure. That was Olivia, the Professor of Sols. His heart felt for her; she was one of the good ones here. She was a nice person, who was always concerned about Vayp. Always trying to find a way to help him cope with his loss of a Sol... as if she knew what he went through. As if she was the only one who could understand the pain. And maybe she did.

Then a movement from underneath a patch of snow made Vayp jump and almost let go of Retro'ku.

A survivor? Vayp gently put Retro'ku down and attended to the mound of snow. When he pushed the snow away, his heart dropped as he saw that it was Gabrael.

Vayp felt anxiety surge through his veins, expecting to be killed on the spot. He was the traitor, after all. He was the reason for all this destruction and damage and death.

But instead... Gabrael smiled. "I knew... I had always known you would come back."

"How?" Vayp felt his throat choke up. "Why?"

"Because," Gabrael whispered as if it took every bit of his energy, "I had faith... and faith had me." Gabrael then lifted himself to one knee. "Thank you for saving him." He smiled warmly.

"I hope he's going to make it." Vayp looked away, still ashamed at himself. "It's the least I could do... all of this was my fault."

"No," Gabrael said bluntly. "Do not for a second believe that, Vayp. The blame can be cast on dozens of people before your name could ever be brought up." Vayp felt a smile slowly form. "If I did things differently, none of this would have happened. This is more my fault than it ever would be yours."

Vayp then fell to his knees and cried into Gabrael's chest. Gabrael soothed him with soft touches.

"You are forgiven, child," Gabrael said.

"Here." Vayp reached into his robe and pulled out the Book of Eve.

Gabrael observed it with narrowed, curious eyes. "Wh-what happened to it?" He observed the blackness of it as if it was charred, then flipped the pages to see they were all black.

"One of the shadows... he went inside the book."

"Inside!" Gabrael's voice found a new energy. "This is not

good! We need to retrieve the next orb, now!" Gabrael then shot Vayp a most serious gaze, as if he had asked him a question with just one glance. *Are you ready?* His eyes said.

And all Vayp could say was: "Yes… if it is in my stars."

"And it is in your stars," Gabrael assured Vayp. "You *are* the Chosen One. You are a hero in this story."

Gabrael had a power to lift spirits up with words alone, and it seemed to have worked better than ever.

Vayp felt rejuvenated even as they passed hundreds of unmoving bodies. It was a burial garden of frozen bodies, belonging to animals, Sols, and humans.

He tried to not look at them, because a brief image of Ah'nyx appeared whenever he did. And the last thing he wanted to think about was the regret of not having him in his life right now.

"What happens to them?" Vayp said, looking at a frozen boy covered in snow.

"Their light… is dwindling away. Unfortunately, this will be the end of their stories. But ours will live on. And it will be our goal to make sure their deaths were not in vain. That they had a purpose."

After a few more minutes of crunching through thin layers of snow, they finally reached a pair of golden doors, which must have been GroundStone's Chamber where the next challenge would take place. Gabrael had said that there was a trial hidden inside each school. Retro'ku had completed the first one, and now it was in Vayp's stars to do the same. Or so he hoped.

Vayp gentled placed Retro'ku to the ground as Gabrael handed him the Book of Eve.

Gabrael then nodded at him, as if letting him know that everything was going to be okay. And Vayp hated to admit it, but right now reassurance was everything that he needed.

Vayp then pressed the book against the doors, expecting to be sucked inside; but instead, with a hiss, white smoke poured out through the crack as the ground rumbled so violently the doors rattled and fell off their hinges.

Vayp jumped back as the doors crashed to the ground with a heavy BANG.

And just then… something unexplainable happened.

A blinding white light erupted from the room and traversed GroundStone. It roared as if he was stuck in a tornado. Glowed as if he was on the sun. And smelled like fresh flowers that had just bloomed.

And when the light started to fade, he heard crazy noises outside that sounded like waves breaking at the coast. He immediately ran to the entrance to observe.

What he saw next was easily a moment he would never forget. His jaw dropped as he watched plants bloom before his eyes, trees grew so tall and green that he started to believe he was dreaming. Golden buildings formed from the rubble, now overwhelmed by the greens, pinks, blues, and purples of the plants that flourished throughout GroundStone. In the five years he had spent here, he never once saw it look so alive.

The sandy patches were now green with texture. The brick roads now shone a bright silver. It was as if this was how GroundStone was designed to look. Like an oasis. A heavenly abode filled with the most beautiful plants and animals that existed in nature.

But it was not the lush environment that made Vayp's heart fill up with pure joy. It was the movements from the bodies that did it. The guilt that he had of killing thousands of Earthies and Sols and animals faded the moment he saw them lift to their feet, brush themselves off, and gaze around cluelessly as if they had just been born, their first glimpse at life. And to Vayp, it might as well have been.

But then he heard clapping and cheering as a familiar face came into view.

He saw Lynn, who was looking as if she had been through war, with her hair a mess and her black robe ripped in places.

He then saw the GroundStone trio, who didn't seem to recognize him at all, and a part of him was happy about that.

Then a boy with a silver mask emerged, and behind him was—Vayp's jaw dropped.

"Tayna!" Vayp screamed.

"Why does everyone call you that?" the boy with the silver mask said to Tayna.

"Because… that's my real name." Tayna innocently shrugged. "I don't like to give my name out to strangers, sorry. But now you aren't one! So, hi, my name is Tayna!" She put her hand out for the boy to shake.

The boy chuckled as he shook her hand. "My name is Fujak, very nice to meet you!"

Vayp felt the hairs on his body go up. Fujak? What happened to him?

Before he could ask, professors came piling in. He recognized one of them as the Healing professor and the other as the Sandsportation one. But the one that caught his eye the most was Fa'laz, because he was teary-eyed, staring at his hand.

Didn't he have a metal hand?

"Fa'laz!" Tayna screamed, running to him. "You're healed! You can finally go back home!"

Fa'laz nodded many times as tears poured down his face. The two of them hugged tightly.

Then, as fast as a spark of lightning, a black panther pounced at Fa'laz, wrapping its massive paws around his body. Vayp wished he had spotted it sooner to warn him, until he noticed that they were now play fighting.

"You finally remember me!" Fa'laz cried into the panther's body. "Oh how I've missed you! Today truly is a blessing from the Divine! I have my Sol back!"

But nothing… absolutely NOTHING made Vayp's heart collapse quite like the sound of this next voice. "Where's duh food up in this place? How do yuh 'spect a hungry Chosen One to survive?"

"HAN'SAEL!" Vayp screamed, running over to tackle him to the ground. "You're alive! You're alive!"

"I was alive!" Han'sael laughed as they rolled around on the grass. "But not for long, yuh tryin' to kill me!"

"But for seriously." Han'sael stood up and brushed off his clothes, his belly jiggling. He had long brown hair that waved over his face and wore robes that were once white but now appeared gray and unclean. "What does a kid gotta do to get some food n' water around here?" Han'sael scrunched his nose and pressed a finger to his lips. "Hmm... let me change this!" He pressed a thumb to his head and bit his tongue, as if he was thinking very hard. "Oh! When did I learn this spell?" He shook his head, then placed his palms to the ground and chanted words.

Within seconds, the ground rumbled as water sprouted from trees and statues, appearing as geysers and fountains.

Vayp saw many kids run around, laughing and playing in the water.

"Hmmph... dunno where I learned that from, but no complaints here!" Han'sael snorted.

But Vayp couldn't stop staring at Han'sael with the widest smile on his face. "I missed you so much!"

"Missed me?" Han'sael said. "I was only gone fuh like a second! But... I guess I am kinda irresistible... or is it irreplaceable... or irresponsible? I dunno, but I'm one of those irrs!"

Then Han'sael's jaw dropped as he turned to look at Lynn, who still looked like a complete mess with no make-up and hair all over the place. "Holy Food Gods! How did you get MORE beautiful?"

And Lynn's cheeks flushed red.

Milla then stepped forward. "Hi, the name's Milla, and she's with me."

Han'sael stepped forward too. "Hi, I remembers you from the Valley... and she's with us too! We can share her!" Han'sael smiled wide as he cocked his head back and let the water fall into his wide open mouth. He then wiped his lips—his clothes and hair were now completely drenched—and said, "PHEW! At least that jerk Fujak isn't here! I know what you guys thought! That *I* was the smelly one! But it was him! He was the one fartin' all the time!"

"I'm right here." Han'sael jumped up as Fujak put his hand on his shoulder.

Han'sael's mouth dropped. "Hi! Err... the mask! It's a good look on you, you look much better now. I mean... not that you... I mean you looked good before, but now you just look cooler! Can I get one of those masks too?"

Fujak laughed and patted Han'sael on the back. "Good to have you back. And I'm sorry for being a jerk to you before. I'll make it up to you."

Han'sael grinned. "Oh yeah! Make it up to me, aye? Idunno, I'm a pretty tough boulder to crack."

"Well..." Fujak smirked, "my family has an unlimited supply of food—"

"STOP right there!" Han'sael clutched his chest and took a deep breath. "You had me at food!" Han'sael then looked at Vayp. "Err... you won't get mad if we're best friends, right?"

Both Vayp and Fujak couldn't contain their laughter, and it felt so good to have Han'sael back.

"Ahh!" Han'sael stretched his arms as his shirt lifted over his belly. "The Chosen Ones are back in action! Wait... not all of us." Han'sael quickly turned around, pointing his finger at everyone. "Er... where's S'rae?"

Gabrael glanced at Vayp, who quickly looked away.

"She is on her own journey," Gabrael said, "to find herself. But I have faith that she will be back. I have faith indeed." Gabrael nodded at Vayp with a warm smile.

"So what happens now?" Retro'ku said as he slowly wobbled to his feet

"Welcome back, son." Gabrael smiled, then pointed at the Book of Eve in Vayp's hands. "Now, Vayp must take the challenge. I am confident he is ready."

They then walked toward the room where the light came from, Gabrael leading the way.

That was until he stopped short and Vayp accidentally collided into his back. Before Vayp could ask what was wrong, he noticed the shock in Gabrael's wide eyes as tears began pouring from them. He had seen him cry before, but never like this.

Gabrael stuttered as tears and snot poured from his face. "It… it is… you."

Then Vayp heard a serene, beautiful voice that sounded like it was singing. "I have been waiting… for you."

Vayp looked inside, though there was still a pulsing white light that hurt his eyes. And once they focused more, he was able to see a throne made of bark and vines and leaves and flowers. And sitting on top of it was the most beautiful lady he had ever seen. Everything seemed perfect about her. Flawless. The way her dark skin glistened. The way her veil wrapped around her head, with nature's finest flowers. And her silky green dress that seemed to be made from leaves. She was just… perfectly beautiful.

"I-I h-ha-have…" Vayp was still shocked to see how someone as composed as Gabrael was to find difficulty choosing the right words. "I… have waited… so long… to see you."

"And *I* have waited only seconds." Her smile almost made Vayp faint.

"Seconds?" Gabrael questioned. "But it has been thousands of years. Three, to be exact."

"Well, with our gifted son, he made this room for me. A second inside here could be hundreds of years outside of it."

Retro'ku stepped forward, a slight limp to his step.

Eve's eyes watered as her mouth dropped. "My son… you look as handsome as ever. And where is my other son?"

Retro'ku turned to Gabrael, who said nothing.

"Gabrael... where is *our* son?" Eve's voice was a little louder.

"He is—" Vayp heard the pain in Gabrael's voice. "He is with *them*."

Vayp felt the texture in the air change, for a brief moment it became too difficult to breathe.

"I am sorry," Gabrael said, "I wished to protect him, but I failed. We were betrayed."

"And that was why I left the Valley. Sianu gave me a vision, and the vision ended with my death... inside the Valley. I was no longer safe there. And nature seemed to have warned me. So I had to leave, Gabrael. I had to. We came here. We had a Jamal change Sianu's appearance so he would not be a target of suspicion while he created this room. So I could survive."

"Well, we have found you now. Your plan has worked," Gabrael said.

"My plan?" Eve said, tossing a curious glance at Gabrael. "My plan was never to find me. It was to find Eve. And by now, nature has chosen its new mother."

And suddenly Vayp felt his heart collapse just as everyone's eyes widened at once.

"The sun... the sun it still rose," Fujak whispered softly.

Eve nodded her head at Fujak, and then she took a particular interest in Tayna, staring at her with a subtle smile.

"If my plan worked as you say it did, my Light," Eve said to Gabrael, "then she should be here with us. Who is she?"

Vayp then thought about everything strange that had happened since he was born. He remembered trying to find S'rae a Sol—Vayp's eyes then widened—he remembered the random downpours that would happen shortly after she had failed.

"Eve..." Vayp cleared his throat nervously, "can you... can you... get a Sol?"

"I cannot," Eve said. "For I cannot link with something I am already connected to."

Vayp fell to his knees as he thought about growing up at Opella. He thought of their gift... their princess who would bring about a better harvest for their village. And then he felt something in his pocket. When he pulled it out, he was shocked to see that it was an amulet with a lotus and the letters V.A.S. engraved into it. He gasped. "I know who she is. Her name is... S'rae."

THE END.

We hope you enjoyed your stay at the magical
GroundStone, School of Earth and Rock

Thank you for being a part of this journey.
Which magical school will this journey take you to next?

Only time will tell.